Critical Acclaim for
SUSAN ISAACS and *LILY WHITE*

"Self-deprecating candor is typical of Ms. Isaacs's skill-fully drawn and immensely likable heroines, brave not because they refuse to admit doubt but because they do. They're vulnerable enough to feel it, strong enough to acknowledge it, honest enough to say it aloud and vigor-ous enough to overcome it."

—*The New York Times Book Review*

"Her richest book yet."

—*Newsday*

"Riveting . . . best of all is the character of Lee, smart and sassy . . . self-deluded at the same time. Her good-humored, self-knowing, self-mocking voice is a start treat for the ear."

—*The Boston Globe*

"Fiction done well, and done with a difference . . . a sophisticated storyteller, with a wry view of the world."

—*Washington Post*

"The ingredients for another best-seller."

—*Baltimore Sun*

"Not only an entertaining legal drama, but a chilling account of family scapegoating . . . reading this smart, sassy book on the beach will be the very picture of civilization and its contents."

—NPR's *Fresh Air*

"Susan Isaacs knows the art of dialogue the way J. S. Bach knew the art of the fugue."

—*The Seattle Times*

"Ms. Isaacs is a master of the smart, accessible novel."

—*The Wall Street Journal*

"Lily is a funny, nervy survivor of some major betrayals . . . one house guest you'll wish could stay longer."

—*Glamour*

"A well-written, moving story that will keep the reader engrossed all the way."

—*The Miami Herald*

"On one level Isaacs has created a pitch-perfect social satire. . . . on another . . . she has written a psychological thriller whose portraits of an amoral conman and his mate, of the dehumanizing effects of the prison system and of the state of a criminal investigation are rendered with snappy authenticity."

—*Publishers Weekly*

By Susan Isaacs

Novels

LILY WHITE*

AFTER ALL THESE YEARS*

MAGIC HOUR*

SHINING THROUGH

ALMOST PARADISE

CLOSE RELATIONS*

COMPROMISING POSITIONS

Screenplays

HELLO AGAIN

COMPROMISING POSITIONS

*available from HarperPaperbacks

SUSAN ISAACS

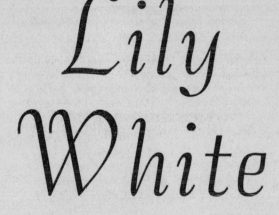

Lily White

HarperPaperbacks
A Division of HarperCollins*Publishers*

![HarperPaperbacks logo] **HarperPaperbacks**
A Division of HarperCollins*Publishers*
10 East 53rd Street, New York, N.Y. 10022-5299

This is a work of fiction. The characters, incidents, and
dialogues are products of the author's imagination and are not to
be construed as real. Any resemblance to actual events or
persons, living or dead, is entirely coincidental.

ISBN 0-06-109309-2

HarperCollins®, ![logo] ®, and HarperPaperbacks™
are trademarks of HarperCollins*Publishers* Inc.

Cover illustration by Neal McPheeters

A hardcover edition of this book was published in 1996 by
HarperCollins*Publishers*.

First HarperPaperbacks printing: April 1997

Printed in the United States of America

Visit HarperPaperbacks on the World Wide Web at
http://www.harpercollins.com/paperbacks

❖ 10 9 8 7 6 5 4 3 2 1

To my daughter-in-law,
Leslie Stern,
with admiration and love

Acknowledgments

In researching *Lily White*, I spent time in the library, in jail and in court. I also sought help and information from the people listed below. Being a novelist and not a reporter, however, I did not hesitate to twist their facts to serve the needs of my fiction. I thank them for their kindness and apologize for my inaccuracies:

Robert Anderson, Frank Argano, Jim Bartell, Brian Bochicchio, Joan Brenner, Thomas DiNapoli, Jonathan Dolger, Janet Franzese, Eric Gould, Cara Nash Iason, Lawrence Iason, Leonard Klein, Edward M. Lane, Judith Lane, Anthony Lepsis, Ellen Markowski, Susie Miller, Henry Putzel III, Ralph Smith, Sheila Riesel, Cynthia Scott, George Stofsky, Andrea Vizcarrando, Paul Vizcarrando, Claire Weinberg, Mina Weiner, John R. Wing, Jay Zises, Justin Zises and Susan Zises.

Additionally, I am especially grateful for the generosity and incredible patience of three fine lawyers: Arnold Abramowitz, Linda Fairstein and Sara Moss. (And thanks for lunch.)

I thank my assistant, AnneMarie Palmer, for her hard work, her good humor and her commendable equanimity.

The interior designer, Susan Lawton, answered every question I had about antiques, furnishings and architecture with her usual authority and awesome wit.

I appreciate the aid of the librarians at the New York and the Port Washington (N.Y.) Public Libraries.

This is the sixth book for me and my editor, Larry Ashmead. For me, it has been a joyous collaboration. I thank him for his guidance, for the mail, the books, the early-morning jokes—and for giving me all the time I needed to finish the novel as I wanted it finished.

My agent, Owen Laster, has been a fount of wisdom, a rock of strength and a wonderful guy.

I thank my wonderful children, Andrew and Elizabeth Abramowitz, and my daughter-in-law, Leslie Stern, for their love, support and fine editorial advice.

Lastly, my eternal love and gratitude to my own in-house counsel, Elkan Abramowitz. He is (and I'm being objective here) the best person in the world.

One

I was never a virgin.

Okay. In the technical sense, of course I was. But even in my dewy days, I never gazed at the world wide-eyed with wonder. If I wasn't born shrewd, at least I grew up too smart to be naive. So how come in the prime of my life, at the height of my powers, I could not foresee what would happen in the Torkelson case? Was I too street smart? Had I been around the block so many times that I finally lost my sense of direction?

A brief digression: Ages ago, soon after I became a criminal defense lawyer, Fat Mikey LoTriglio hailed me across the vast concrete expanse of the courthouse steps. "Hey, girlie!" His tomato of a face wore an expression that seemed (I squinted) amiable, pretty surprising considering he'd just been sprung from Elmira after doing two and a half years on the three counts of aggravated assault I'd prosecuted him for.

"Come over here," he called out. "Hey, I'm not gonna kill you." In Fat Mikey's world, that was not hyperbole but a promise; he got busy straightening his tie to demonstrate he was not concealing a Walther PPK. "I hear you're not working for the D.A. anymore," he boomed. I strolled over, smiling to show I didn't hold any grudges either, and offered my hand, which he shook in the overly vigorous manner of a man trying to show a professional woman that he's comfortable with professional women. Then I handed him my business card. I was not unaware that Fat Mikey was one of three organized crime figures the cops routinely picked up for questioning on matters of Mob-related mayhem. To have Fat Mikey as a client was to have an annuity.

He glanced down at my card to recall my name. "Lee?"

Naturally, I didn't respond "Fat?" And to call him "Mike" after having called him "a vulture feasting on society's entrails" in my summation might seem presumptuous. So I murmured a polite "Mmm?"

"A girl like you from a good family—"

"Are you kidding?" I started to say, but he wouldn't let me.

"I could tell you got class, watching you at the trial," he went on. "You know how? Good posture—and not just in the morning. Plus you say 'whom.' Anyways, you really think you can make a living defending guys like me?" He didn't seem so much sexist as sincerely curious. I nodded encouragingly. "This is what you had in mind when you went to law school?" he inquired.

"No. Back then I was leaning toward Eskimo fishing rights. But this is what I'm good at."

He shook his head at my folly. "When—pardon my French—a guy's ass is in a sling, you think he's gonna hire a girl who says 'whom'?"

"If he's partial to his ass he will."

Fat Mikey's upper lip twitched. For him, that was a smile. Then, almost paternally, he shook a beefy index finger at me. "A girl like you should be more particular about the company she keeps."

Years later, I would learn how wise Fat Mikey was.

Nevertheless, from the beginning I knew there were limits to keeping bad company. I could be sympathetic to my clients without getting emotionally involved: A lot of them had sad childhoods. Many had been victims of grievous social injustice, or of terrible parents (who were themselves victims of terrible parents). Still, I never forgot they were criminals. And while I may have delighted in a bad guy's black humor, or a tough broad's cynicism, I was never one of those attorneys who got naughty thrills socializing with hoods. You'd never catch me inviting a client—let's say Melody Ann Toth, for argument's sake—to go shopping and out for Caesar salads so we could chitchat about old beaux . . . or about what she might expect at her upcoming trial for robbing three branches of the Long Island Savings Bank on what might have been an otherwise boring Thursday.

For their part, most of my clients (including Fat Mikey, who retained me two years after that conversation on the courthouse steps) wouldn't think I was exactly a laugh a minute either. Whatever their personal definition of a good time was, I wasn't it. Unlike me, Fat Mikey simply did not get a bang out of crocheting afghans or listening to National Public Radio. With fists the size of rump roasts, Mikey looked like what he was: a man for whom aggravated assault was not just a profession but a pleasure. As for Melody Ann, with her pink-blonde hair that resembled attic insulation, the only reason she'd go shopping at Saks would be to knock off the Estée Lauder counter when she ran out of lip liner. My clients had no reason or desire to pass for upper middle class.

For that reason alone, Norman Torkelson was different right from the beginning.

Of course, a con man cannot look like a crook and expect to make a living. If Norman Torkelson had resembled the no-good rat he was, he would have been a sawed-off runt with a skinny mustache like a plucked eyebrow. But then the nine hundred or so women he had proposed marriage to would have told him: Get lost, creepo.

However, he was not sawed off; he was six feet five. Lucky for him, since in America everyone knows a man's character increases in excellence in direct proportion to his height. Not that Norman was content with mere tallness; he was clever enough to trip over his own size-thirteen feet every so often, which made him . . . Some of the descriptions in the witnesses' statements taken over the years from victims of his scams were: "sensitive," "tragic, like Abraham Lincoln," and (my personal favorite) "caring." So all those women to whom he proposed said yes—Yes, my love! Yes, Norman! (or Yes, whatever alias he was using)—and got their hearts broken.

I wonder now: What if we hadn't met in the Nassau County Correctional Center? What if he hadn't been wearing the official uniform—pants and shirt in an orange that inevitably leeched the life out of every inmate's face? Would I have wanted to trace with my fingertips the lines of his Mount Rushmore face? No. I would not have.

Still (before I leave the subject of color), even the vicious glow of that orange could not hide the fact that Norman's eyes were such a startling blue they seemed more a Crayola than an eye color: Viking blue, a shade somewhere between royal and turquoise. If not for those eyes, would the hundreds of women thrilled to empty their bank accounts for him have found themselves destitute, suddenly dependent on disgusted relatives or the public dole?

However, let's not go overboard on the blue eyes business. A con man cannot afford to be suspiciously handsome, and Norman Torkelson was not. First of all, he had a too teeny nose. Instead of the cute upward tilt you'd expect from a nose like that, it hooked; in certain lights, you'd swear Norman was half man, half parakeet. So not gorgeous—an asset to a con man because true beauty evokes curiosity. And not slick. At least, he didn't seem slick. Like any professional swindler, he was just convincing enough to persuade a woman who had never met a man from Yale that he had gone to Yale.

Furthermore, a competent con man never overacts. Norman may have listened avidly when a woman spoke, but he never pretended to drown in the depths of her eyes; he didn't shift around in his seat either, crossing his leg to hide an alleged erection. Oh, one more handy imperfection: He had a slight lisp.

I heard his first words as: "I thwear I didn't do it, Mth. White." He lowered his big head and whispered, "Jethuth!"

"It's not me you have to convince, Mr. Torkelson," I told him. "I'm on your side. It's the D.A. who's a problem."

He clutched the top of the white Formica barrier that separates inmates from their visitors. "Please," he begged me, "call me Norman."

Amazing: He threw his entire being behind that request. His forehead furrowed, his shoulders tensed, his Adam's apple bulged, every part of him seemed to yearn: Call me Norman.

A con man's hokey trick? Absolutely. I tried to be cool, glancing around the visitors room, a huge space filled with rows of Formica-topped tables, which resembled a school cafeteria. However, instead of patrolling teachers there were armed guards carrying semiautomatic rifles, and closed-circuit cameras.

Despite the ugly publicness of the place, I felt a private flush of gratification at my client's request: Please, call me Norman. Almost as if he had willed it, I actually eased my attaché case off my lap and set it by my feet, then pushed my chair back so he could get a fuller view: I carried on as if I were OD'ing on estrogen. I actually crossed my legs, movie starlet style, and began to inscribe a sexy O with my foot.

Naturally, all this took place within a microsecond. Then I realized I was being manipulated—which only proved to me what I'd already suspected. Norman Torkelson was not a great con artist. Just a fairly competent one.

"I was not—and I quote—conning Bobette out of her money!" he announced in that very instant.

"Norman," I said, uncrossing my legs, "let's get our priorities straight. The fraud by false pretenses charge is the least of your problems right now."

"Bobette and I were *friends*," he insisted. "She was *lending* me the money. I told her: 'Have your attorney draw up the proper paperwork, with whatever interest you feel is fair. I'll sign it. I won't have it any other way!'"

"Norman." I tried to cut him off.

"This was a legitimate business transaction!"

"It may have been, but right now you're not in business. You're in the slammer, and Bobette Frisch is on ice over at the medical examiner's." A small shudder vibrated his shoulders, a not unusual reaction new clients display when I talk like a defense lawyer—i.e., straight. But I believe straight is better than cute, especially when a guy is looking at fifteen to life. Let me amend that: Straight is better than cute, period, which is not to say a lawyer can't mitigate the effects of brutal directness with an empathetic smile and a mastery of the New York penal code. I peered right into Norman's eyes. "You're facing a murder charge," I reminded him.

"I didn't touch her!" Norman unclasped his hands

and gripped his side of the table. "How can they think I could take a human life?"

I shook my head despondently to show how utterly unthinkable such a notion was to me and then explained in my tranquilizing, consoling, I-know-you-don't-deserve-to-be-in-the-hoosegow voice: "From what I gather, at around two-thirty last Friday, Bobette went into her bank and withdrew forty-eight thousand of the fifty-two thousand dollars she had in her account. After that, no one seems to have seen her—until yesterday."

"Who . . . " He cleared his throat, presumably to show me how choked up he was. "Who found her?" he asked.

"Some local kids. They were selling chocolate bars so their high school band could go to the Hula Bowl. When they knocked on her door, they smelled something. One of their parents called the cops, and the cops found Bobette. There was no sign of the money."

Norman sat back in his molded plastic chair as if amazed: No sign of the money?! The performance over, he leaned forward, his face flushing with outrage. "How did the cops get to me?"

"Fingerprints?" I suggested helpfully.

It is the rare miscreant who comes right out and tells his attorney: I'm a crook. Career criminals are too sophisticated to admit to a specific crime, because they know their lawyer cannot put them on the stand if the lawyer knows they are going to lie through their teeth. Besides, most have an aversion to responsibility (to say nothing of an antipathy to reality). They cry out: "Who, me? I didn't do anything." And it goes double for someone accused of murder. They not only deny guilt; they play victim: Why are you picking on *me*? As their lawyer, my job isn't to get them to confess; it's to give them the best defense possible. To do that, I have to nudge them, gently, until they're facing the facts.

"Fingerprints?" he repeated. I studied him as he mulled that one over, rubbing his big chin with his big-boned hand. For my money, anything over six feet in a man is wasted on height, but a lot of women do delight in leaning against something the size of a Plymouth Voyager. It makes them feel protected, petite—and it probably makes them anticipate a sex organ larger than the average totem pole. Sadly, I thought about the utter joy that would light up some two-hundred-fifty-pound lonelyheart when Norman would beseech her: Lean on me, darling.

"You're wondering how they found you?" I asked. Norman shrugged, which meant he was dying to know. So was I. "You didn't give Bobette your real name?"

"Only because I was afraid her lawyer might want to do a credit check. Need I tell you how long that can take?"

"What name did you give her?"

"Denton Wylie."

"Ever use that name before?" He shook his head, not without a touch of pride. Less industrious con men have a roster of about ten names, or they stick with some variation on their actual initials: Jimmy Dellacroce on one scam, John Doughtery on the next, and so forth. The pros take on a new name each time. It makes life harder for the cops. But my guess is it must make a con man feel clean, as if rising from a pure stream after being baptized by total immersion. "Did you have your phone listed under Denton Wylie?"

"No."

"The place you're living?"

"No."

"What name are you using there?" He hesitated, and before he could make up something new, I added: "I've got to figure out how the cops got to you."

"Robert McNulty," he admitted reluctantly.

"And your address?"

"I gave it to your secretary when I made my call."

"The real one. If I have to send out an investigator, you're going to go broke fast if he winds up checking out the address of a vacant lot." He took one of those shaky deep breaths made up of small, nervous inhalations. "Norman, you've got to give me something to work with."

"Fifty-four Homewood Avenue—in Mineola. It's an apartment." I waited. "Apartment 3-C."

"Do you work alone?"

"Of course," he responded. He sounded so utterly convincing. I figured he was lying through his teeth. He was. "I live with someone," he said after a half minute. (Try sitting in the inmates' visiting room with your lawyer eyeballing you, and you'll see how oppressive thirty seconds of silence can be.) "She's just . . . I love her."

"What's her name?"

"Mary. She's the sweetest, most innocent person in the world."

"Mary what?"

"Mary Dean. We live together. I swear to you, Miss White, by everything I hold holy, I work alone. Mary doesn't even know . . . " He covered his face with his hands and rubbed his forehead with his fingertips, hard, almost brutally, as if applying counter pressure on a terrific headache.

Well, why shouldn't he have a headache? It was too early to know how much evidence the cops really had, but Sam Franklin, the Homicide sergeant in charge of the case, offered me a hint a half hour later, when I suggested it might be possible that the police had acted too fast and that Norman Torkelson, although admittedly having a rap sheet that could circle the globe sixteen times, might not have choked Ms. Frisch to death and a murderer could (at that very moment) be running amok on Long Island. "Whoever did it could kill again!" I said passionately into the phone.

"I don't have time for your act today, Lee," Sam said, which suggested he had already been assured by an assistant D.A. in the Homicide Bureau that this was a good case. Then he hung up the phone disdainfully, not bothering (as he usually did) to slam it down. So I had to revise my estimate. Not a good case: a great case.

But I should begin at the beginning. I should—

Two

❧

In truth, Lee White, B.A., Cornell University, J.D., New York University School of Law, did not have a clue as to where the beginning really was. She might have told you it was the moment J. J. O'Shaughnessy (a retired lawyer devoting his golden years to twirling wisps of hair that grew from his ears while watching Court TV in the Dominican Village retirement home in Amityville, Long Island) referred an old client, Norman Torkelson, to his poker buddy Chuckie Phalen; Chuckie, busy trying a first-degree arson case, passed Norman over to his law partner, Lee.

Or if Lee was in a rare reflective mood—let's say sitting with her gentleman (a lawyer himself) before a roaring fire—she'd muse: It must have begun the summer after my second year in law school, when I was interning in the Manhattan D.A.'s office. Do you know, that was the first time in my life that I ever had an abstract thought! It sneaked right up and bit me on the ass. The gentleman, amused, would chuckle. Lee would go on: All of a sudden—ka-boom!—I comprehended the beauty of the criminal justice system, its balance, and that a person accused of a crime is also entitled to a defense—*must* have one—even if he is utter scum and guilty as hell.

But Lee White, like most people, had no idea where the real beginning really began. So to commence:

Let us start with the White business. Had she been a premature baby, her last name would have been Weiss. Two weeks before her birth day, her father, Leonard, took off from work to go to court and change the family's surname to White so that the son he was anticipating could flash his birth certificate anywhere in America and not be challenged.

Although now White, Leonard and his wife, Sylvia, did not abandon the old-world custom of naming a baby for a dead and inevitably boring relative. Leonard and Sylvia called their surprise daughter Lily Rose, after Sylvia's maternal grandmother, Leah Rivka Mutterperl, a woman who became distraught upon realizing, on her second day aboard the S.S. *Polonia*, bound for Ellis Island, that she had left her false teeth on a washstand in a hovel in a shtetl about sixty miles due south of Cracow three weeks earlier and who never again was able to regain her equanimity.

Before Weiss and White, the family's name had actually been Weissberg until 1948—two years before Lee's birth—when Leonard shortened it to Weiss. When asked, "Weiss?" by a customer who acted as if she had heard something unpleasant, he replied (too quickly): "Weiss means 'white.' It's actually a very common German name . . . like White is here." As the fur trade was in those days an industry of men named Glickstern and Steinberg and Rubin, the knowing smile on his customer's face mortified Leonard and determined him to be White, although it took him two years to get up the courage to actually do it.

In any case, until Lee was born, Leonard and Sylvia

were so confident in the imminence of a son (whom they planned to name Bartholomew, after Leonard's grandfather Baruch Weissberg) that they barely gave a thought to what to name a daughter, much less to how silly Lily White sounded, especially when, after a few months it became obvious that the girl's coloring was going to be decidedly Mediterranean.

Fortunately, their firstborn's childish pronunciation of Lily was Lee-Lee, so in a sense, Lee christened herself . . . although in the case of the Weissberg-Weiss-Whites, christened is obviously not the right word, while "jewed" would be not only a misnomer but might give offense, however unintended—somewhat the way "lily white" began to in 1954, in those months just after *Brown* v. *Board of Education* was handed down.

That Leonard WWW would be sensitive to the feelings of the Negro is not surprising, since he was the incarnation of that old Nixonian saw that Jews live like Episcopalians and vote like Puerto Ricans. His liberalism, however, was not the usual concern for the underdog. He really didn't care about the underdog unless the underdog had managed to get a few bucks together and was in the market for a fur garment for his wife or lady friend. No, Leonard's liberalism was his inescapable inheritance from his card-carrying-Communist father, Nat, a shop steward for the Fur Workers Union, and his big-hearted, big-mouthed mother, Bella.

Leonard received one further legacy: While Nat could not help his son gain admission to Harvard or obtain a seat on the stock exchange, he was able to secure him a position as floor boy in the back room at Frosty Furs in Forest Hills. Thus began his career: in 1942, seventeen-year-old Leonard—safe from the Army's clutches because of a quirky kidney—traveled from Borough Park in Brooklyn to Queens. He swept the floors and scoured from workbenches the reeking grease that dripped off untreated raccoon pelts. He stretched lynx skins on a board for the cutter and marked patterns onto garments. He was a hard worker, and an excellent one too. But nothing he did was good enough for his boss. Whenever there were no customers around, his boss, Isadore Frumkin, would growl, "Move yer whatsis, sonny boy!" He would scrutinize Leonard's every move with the tight-clenched face of the congenitally sadistic.

Was revenge on Mr. Frumkin the spark that made Leonard determine that someday *he* would be the boss of Frosty Furs and when he was, he would treat his floor boy like a human being? Who knows what ignites the entrepreneurial fire in a young man? Rebellion against his Trotskyite father? The ignominy of sweeping up scraps of muskrat and cigarette butts as well as the curlicues of oily lettuce that appeared to molt from the wet-breaded sardine sandwich Milton Kuperschmidt, the cutter, devoured every noon? Was it glancing out the window onto Austin Street and seeing Mr. Frumkin's resplendent 1942 Packard illuminating the February dusk? Or could it have been observing Mr. Frumkin, kneeling on the floor to better gauge the hemline of Mrs. Whitcomb Knoll's broadtail, casually run his hand up Mrs. Knoll's pale and silky and Protestant calf?

In those days, Queens was not yet the vigorous ethnic mishmash it is today. Entire neighborhoods—Douglaston Manor, Forest Hills Gardens—were not merely lily white: even the lightest Jews were prohibited, and, indeed, Catholics—including the fairest, without O's or Mc's or excessive offspring—were encouraged to reside elsewhere. To young Leonard, delivering a lapin muff and bonnet for Mrs. William Warren's little Amanda, or picking up Mrs. Bradley Mercer's nutria jacket (onto which Mr. Bradley had upchucked five Rob Roys and Welsh rarebit on New Year's Eve) for a cleaning, Forest Hills Gardens was paradise. A mere three-block walk from the store put him on a street where flaxen-haired angels tossed balls to airborne blond dogs. Velvet lawns encircled four-bedroom, mullion-windowed houses that Leonard was soon to learn were called (albeit redundantly) English Tudor.

He rarely saw the masters of the house; they were a half world away, fighting Heinies and Japs. Or at least they were in Manhattan, writing advertising copy for stool softeners.

But the women stayed home in those days, and Leonard moved quickly from being merely enamored to falling in love with them all: the debutante daughters, the newlyweds, the young mothers, the matrons, the menopausal. It was, of course, pure prejudice, the viewing of an entire group as the Perfect One: a woman in tennis whites, with shiny hair and a voice as soft and luxe as lynx. (Clearly, this passion for anything female and Episcopalian was an indication that Leonard had a few unresolved odds and ends in the Oedipal department; they would remain problematical even after he undertook psychotherapy a decade later. It should be noted here, however, that his mother, Bella, a good-hearted, effusive woman who claimed a brief career as a character actress in the Yiddish theater, weighed nearly three hundred pounds and had dyed her frizzy hair the color of a rusty steel wool pad. Bella's voice was so lacking in mellifluence that a simple "How are you, *tataleh*?" was, to her son, more agonizing than a thousand pieces of fresh chalk screeching along a blackboard.)

But these women of the Gardens were so removed from Leonard's experience they might as well have belonged to another species. He could only worship them from afar. While he could easily (very easily) picture himself wrapping a golden sable cape around pearly shoulders in the front hall of one of the grander Tudors and hearing a grateful wifely "Thank you, Leonard, my dearest," he could not actually bring himself to smile his wide, engaging smile at one of them, so afraid was he of rejection—or perhaps of acceptance. His only sexual encounters took place in another borough: exchanging chaste kisses with Brooklyn stenographers—and feeling up Flo Feinman, the Slut of Borough Park. Secretly, he was afraid he would never find anyone he would desire enough to marry.

Six years passed. Since this is Lee's story, not Leonard's, suffice it to say that much happened in that time. Although Leonard remained innocent of the wondrous topography of women, in business he was on his way to being a man of the world. He had risen higher than he had ever dreamed—thanks to that louse Isadore Frumkin. Leonard's boss's black market diet of marbled steak and Hershey bars led, inexorably, to a crippling heart attack shortly after V-J Day. Leonard, backed by a loan arranged by an eager-beaver junior vice president of the East New York Savings Bank (a member of Nat's Communist cell), became the owner of Frosty Furs just before Christmas in 1946. A year later, he proved he was a natural capitalist. Business was booming to such an extent that he repaid his bank loan, bought a 1947 Lincoln Continental that made Mr. Frumkin's Packard look like a hunk of junk—and told his father, "Absolutely no contributions to Communist front organizations!" when Nat hit him up for a fifty-dollar contribution to the Soviet-American Folk Dance League.

Leonard was not only putting some distance between himself and his past. He was also hard at work to get the polish he hadn't been born with. He went to the theater and saw Cornelia Otis Skinner in *Lady Windermere's Fan* (which he'd thought might have something to do with the fashion business). He listened to WQXR for culture. He went to the movies for diction lessons (although he did drop his lord-of-the-manor "How teddibly luffly of you" pretty quickly after his mother, Bella, started yukking it up, mistakenly believing that her son was indulging in a rare moment of frivolity and doing an imitation of Ronald Colman in *The Late George Apley*).

But his urbanity wasn't entirely superficial; Leonard went to every Furriers Industry Council meeting and absorbed his tony Manhattan colleagues' wisdom on everything from remodeling Astrakhan coats to what whiskey to drink (Johnnie Walker Black) and precisely how to order it ("on the rocks, splash of soda—no twist, sweetheart"). He overcame his natural shyness by forcing himself to ask his customers leading questions. ("What are your Thanksgiving plans, Mrs. Fiske?" "No, really, I'd love to hear about your Easter centerpiece, Mrs. Guilfoyle.") Thus he gathered an enormous amount of data on the folkways of the preeminent stratum of the upper middle class.

Gradually, the young man gained confidence. His customers began to find him charming: "Mrs. Johnston, that seal would clap his flippers if he could see you in his coat! No, seriously. I mean it. You look"—he'd take a deep breath as if to clear his head so he could find the perfect word—"lovely." At twenty-three, Leonard was almost on top of the world. He had money in his pocket, a firm jaw, a head of lustrous jet-black hair (more than one customer thought of him as a Jewish Robert Taylor), and a developing sense of style. All he needed was a wife.

Early in 1948, Sylvia Bernstein came into Tudor Rose (the fur salon's new name, which Leonard selected after nights in the library poring over everything from Amy Vanderbilt to *Boutell's Heraldry*). Leonard checked out her well-cut gray wool suit with its flared-at-the-hips peplum jacket which only the slimmest women could wear successfully, looked into her blue-gray eyes, took in her prominent cheekbones and her sleek, blond-streaked hair and thought, in essence: Hubba hubba! But he acted all business, assuming she'd been recommended to him by one of his more genteel customers. Wait, she had no wedding ring. So she must be one of his customers' daughters. Ah well, at least she might be good for a red fox chubby. He asked, "May I help you, Miss . . . ?" When she answered, in the most euphonious tones possible: "Sylvia Bernstein," he would have fainted, if he hadn't found himself falling in love.

It wasn't just her looks. Sylvia had class, Leonard was relieved to discover. All right, people hearing her speak would realize she wasn't a Vassar girl. But she never, even on the hottest summer day, left the house without wearing gloves. Her apartment building was classy too (Tudor style, no less), with leaded windows in the lobby and a lion stantant on the pediment over the elevator. Not only that: Her mother, at age forty-five, was still a natural blond.

And her father was a judge!

The first time Leonard met the Bernsteins, he could

scarcely breathe. That was how emotional he became, wishing that he could have had such parents. They were perfect.

Take Sylvia's mother. Not only did she cook and clean. If sock-darning were a competitive sport, Eva Bernstein would have had a mantel full of trophies. What a housewife! But there were holes too big for even Eva to repair, and when one of these occurred, she would adopt the sock as her own, wearing it and its non-holey brother over her stocking feet so she could glide through the apartment without running her nylons or disturbing her husband, Judge Bernstein. "Shhh!" she'd warn Sylvia and Sylvia's younger brother, Victor. "The Judge is taking a nap!" "The Judge is reading!" "The Judge is on the phone!"

Judge Arthur Bernstein was more than a pillar of rectitude; he was a five-foot-nine-inch pillar of quietude. In the Queens Domestic Relations Court, where he presided, court stenographers griped that they deserved battle pay, they had to strain so hard to hear his feathery voice. But other than that, there were no complaints. His reputation was neither sterling nor tarnished; he was not unduly harsh with the litigants who appeared before him (although he did seem a little too eager to rule an ex-wife's petition for support out of order if her ex-husband was represented by a lawyer with links to the Ronald Goldberger Kew Gardens Democratic Club). However, to colleagues, neighbors, friends, and certainly to Leonard, Arthur Bernstein was nothing but a gentleman. He removed his hat in the presence of a lady. He wore an alpaca coat, used a small but genuine tortoiseshell holder for his Philip Morrises. When expressing gratitude to anyone, he simply nodded—but in such a gracious and dignified way that he made those who vocalized their "thank you"s seem almost vulgar.

And compared to Leonard's parents! Nat the Commie had an articulated opinion on everything, from dialectical materialism to how to grow string beans on the fire escape: "Hey, Lenny, you don't drown 'em, you schmendrick. You water 'em every other day!" And Bella, with her demands that he loosen up! Each day as he left for work she made a game of blocking the door. "What d'ya got, an ice cube up your *tuchis*, Lenny? Smile! It don't cost nothin'." He'd try to sidestep her and grab for the doorknob, but despite her bulk, she was more agile than he. "Come on, pretend I'm a lady buying a fur. 'Excuse me, my good man,'" she'd twitter, giving what was actually a pretty fair imitation of a Vanderbilt voice. " 'I'm looking for something smart in a mouton, fingertiplength.'" Eventually, Bella would start to guffaw at her own performance, doubling over with laughter; that's when Leonard would make his break for freedom.

In those days, young men did not get their own apartments, so Leonard was doubly grateful to Sylvia: for getting him out of his personal hell in Brooklyn and for giving him a judge and a natural blonde for in-laws. And of course, Sylvia was grateful to him, because at age twenty-two, she had no prospects. The loss of Selwyn Youdelman, a Brooklyn Law School graduate with offices in Kew Gardens, had devastated her parents a year earlier. That the loss was due to his choosing another girl over Sylvia made it more painful to the Bernsteins than if he had merely died. Sylvia knew that they blamed her for his leaving, that she'd shown off her artistic nature too much, that she'd kept pushing him to go to operas and museums, while all a normal fellow wanted to do was go see *The Bells of St. Mary's*, for God's sake, or go for a malted. "I *didn't* push him!" Sylvia explained tearfully.

"Shhh!" her mother responded. "The Judge is in the

bathroom." Both women took a moment to compose themselves and whisper more quietly.

"He asked *me* what did I want to do," Sylvia tried to explain, "so I said I read how they had a Turner exhibition at the Metropolitan Museum. He's this English guy. And Selwyn was the one who said how he loves good pictures and never gets enough of them."

"That doesn't mean he actually wants to go into the city on a weekday night! The man is an attorney!" Sour acid rose from Sylvia's gut and burned the back of her throat. She wanted to throw up. But the Judge was in the bathroom, and even if he finished right away, it would have to air out or she'd never stop vomiting for the rest of her life. She rushed away from her mother, into the bedroom she shared with her brother, flung herself facedown on her bed, and wept—silently.

Unfair! Unfair! She'd bring a date into the apartment, and right away he'd hook his finger over his tie to loosen it, as if he were suffocating. Well, why not? The place was gloomy, airless. The windows were never open, the blinds were always drawn tight, and there was barely enough light—just enough to see the dust sparkles dancing in the living room air. Even before her mother could breathe, "Shhh! The Judge," the date would get that Lemme-outta-here look, like he was inside Boris Karloff's tomb.

But Leonard actually liked her parents! She knew part of it was that they had wall-to-wall carpeting and his parents were, as he explained, working-class people. But even guys who'd been all hepped up because her father was a judge—like Selwyn—were somehow repelled by the silence in that apartment, by the radio that hadn't been turned on since FDR died. There was something about the Judge, she realized, that was . . . not right. And her mother, too, was . . . not right.

Not right? Wacko was probably closer to the truth, but that would have been too revolutionary a notion for Sylvia. And while Leonard (had he been cross-examined under oath) might have admitted something was not quite right about the Bernsteins, the cryptlike quiet made him feel they were, at the very least, a classy family.

In fact, the first time Sylvia let him put his hand under her skirt, he was thinking: I'm bringing Sleeping Beauty to life. He was thrilled with her. Sitting on her living room couch, her parents inside, sleeping, he wanted to whisper, "Your thighs are as soft as chinchilla." But he stopped himself because he didn't want her to get the wrong idea and think he was low class, comparing her to a rodent, or worse, that he thought her thighs were furry, although they did feel a little . . . fuzzy. So he kept mum, always a good idea in the Bernstein apartment.

Three months later, when Leonard asked for Sylvia's hand, an idea suddenly popped into his head. He decided that in addition to an engagement ring, he would give his Beauty a silver fox stole that would set off her pale prettiness. Which was too bad, because Beauty *and* her mother had been thinking more in terms of a Breath of Spring mink jacket, if not a full-length coat. Still, a fox stole is better than nothing: Even though he was not a professional man, not even a college graduate, not even a guy with a couple of years at CCNY, Sylvia knew Leonard was the best she could hope for. At least he was nice looking, and he owned a decent business, which was nothing to be ashamed about—even though she was.

Well! Three years later, when Lee was born, things had certainly changed! But more about that when the time comes.

Three

Bobette Frisch stood apart from my client's usual victims. Most of Norman Torkelson's women lay somewhere between vulnerable and defenseless. Not Bobette. Starting out in Brooklyn, a venue not known for fragile females, she moved due east to Queens in the early sixties when she was about twenty. She worked as a waitress at a tavern in Flushing called the Dew Drop Inn. A couple of years later, when the crowd got meaner and the barkeeper took to tucking a hammer behind the Wild Turkey for protection, she moved east again, this time into Nassau County.

Like me, Bobette wanted a career. She took a bartending course and found a job at Murray's Shamrock in Williston Park. It took her another ten years, but she finally moved from labor to management, after convincing Murray's frantic creditors that the joint could actually turn a tidy profit if it were run by someone sober enough to use a cash register. She became half-owner— keeping an eagle eye on the goings-on so no bartender could pour free drinks for his pals. She tossed out the roughnecks and was always on the lookout for known queasers: to get them up and out of the place so they wouldn't (as they say with such delicacy here on Long Island) blow their chunks all over the bar.

Bobette watched over her property from a dimly lit table way in the back. This turned out to be a good idea. First of all, she apparently wasn't the talkative type. She greeted patrons with a friendly enough "Hiya," but that was it in the conversation department. If she had an opinion on the Yankees or school taxes or the novels of Danielle Steel, she kept it to herself. After the murder, bar patrons who had no idea what she was like created their own Bobette Frisch for the media, murmuring into the Channel 12 mike: "You could see sweetness in her face. But it was, uh, um, a quiet sweetness. What's happening, that someone like that gets killed?" And: "She was ultra shy. You know? But a wonderful human being." However, an anonymous *Newsday* source referred to her as a "major cheapo who wouldn't let you owe her two bucks," and someone interviewed in the *Post* referred to her as Blobette. The blob business is a little unfair. According to the charts, Bobette was not terribly overweight. Her body, unfortunately, resembled a beer keg, stout and compact. Her oval face, framed by light brown hair, might have been pretty, or at least not unappealing, except that she had fleshy folds that ran from either side of her mouth down either side of her chin. Thus her jaw appeared to be attached in the manner of a marionette's. Patrons of the bar first took to calling her Mrs. Howdy Doody, then inevitably, behind her back, Mrs. Doody.

Bobette was shrewd about money. By the eighties, she owned three bars and two apartment buildings. Starting at four every morning, she made the rounds in her frost-beige Cadillac Eldorado from Williston Park to Franklin Square to Hicksville and personally picked up each night's receipts. She collected her monthly rents in person.

Neither the cops nor my investigator ever found a scintilla of evidence that she was a pushover when it came to guys, or that she might be susceptible to a sweet talker who would con her out of her life savings. On the contrary: She was all business. When queried about her love life, the people who dealt with her drew a total blank. Huh? Wha'? "Bobette" and "sex" did not seem to belong in a single sentence.

This was her life: She managed her holdings—which included her own modest but pretty two-story colonial on a sixty-by-one-hundred-foot plot in Merrick. Each Tuesday she visited the Mane Event salon and got her hair washed and set in a style Patricia Nixon favored in the 1956 campaign; once a month, she had it cut and colored. Every single Saturday afternoon she went to the movies and, afterward, stopped at Mario's for a salad and an order of linguine and clam sauce, which she took home with her. She attended mass at St. Agnes Cathedral in Rockville Centre every Sunday morning at ten-thirty. The local libraries or video rental stores had no record of her.

Her parents were dead. She had one brother, in Cherry Hill, New Jersey, a mechanic at a Honda dealership. She had no enemies. She had no friends.

I cleared my throat and asked the cop: "What makes you think Bobette's dealings with Norman Torkelson were anything other than business?"

Since he had successfully ignored me for the last five minutes, I knew Sergeant Samuel Franklin would not enjoy a reminder that he and I were standing within two feet of each other. Sam sucked in his already sunken cheeks. A second later, he took in a mouthful of air and blew up the lower half of his face. Ergo, he could then make a revolting noise at me as he exhaled and yet, technically, be not guilty of making fart sounds at a lawyer.

Sam was the archetype for all those smug "Think Thin!" pieces that have plagued me since adolescence, the articles that advise you to mimic the behavior of the congenitally lean. "Do natural-born skinnies just lounge around? No, no and no again. They're *always* in action! So get going!"

Sam never stopped moving. So skinny that you could test your recollection of tenth-grade biology by trying to name each protruding bone on his skeletal frame, Sam burned calories as easily as I stored them. Besides keeping his face in constant motion, he was always tapping his feet, cracking his knuckles, twisting his torso, stretching and flexing his arms. This time he added head swiveling, checking out the acoustical ceiling tile, the floor, the doors along the hallway of the D.A.'s Office. It went beyond his usual hyperkinetics; much of this movement was to avoid looking at me.

"Don't the cops investigate homicides anymore?" I asked, using my courtroom voice so he couldn't pretend not to hear me. Sam, my former friend, drummed his twiglike fingers on the file folder he was clutching; his skin had grown so dry that pale cracks crisscrossed his knuckles. "Come on, Sam." He kept trying to ignore me. Unfortunately, he was successful. "What's going on here?" I persisted. "You dust for prints, run them through the computer, come up with some guy who happens to have a criminal record. So you say, 'Oh, goody, let's charge this Norman Torkelson with murder. That way, we can all take the weekend off.'"

"We're supposed to wait for Ms. Nuñez to discuss

this," Sam said to the dangling frosted globe of a municipal lighting fixture, thus managing to respond to my protest without fully acknowledging my presence. The absent Holly Nuñez was the newest assistant district attorney in the Homicide unit.

"We've been waiting for twenty minutes! She made a ten-thirty appointment."

"The secretary said she was in the ladies room," Sam explained to the lighting fixture.

"I'll go find her."

"I wouldn't."

"Why not?"

No answer. The fingers on his left hand were pulling at his pants leg, trying to get it to fall properly over his shoe. It didn't work. In his baggy navy trousers, he looked like a Weight Watchers lecturer modeling his old clothes to display his eighty-pound loss.

"Sam, take a long, hard look at Norman's rap sheet. Do you see anything resembling violent behavior?" His only answer was an I-am-being-incredibly-patient inhalation followed by an exhalation between pursed lips. That pissed me off, which I guess was the point. "Norman Torkelson did *not* kill Bobette Frisch," I told him. "Guys like Norman hate women too much to kill them. They don't want the pain they cause to come to an end."

He was not moved by this dandy insight. But then, there was nothing I could say anymore that would move Sam Franklin. The thing of it was, years before, when I first came to the Nassau County D.A.'s from the Manhattan D.A.'s, we'd been buddies. He had recently joined the force after getting a master's degree in sociology from Adelphi. He'd been handsome back then, with the pulled-tight skin and prominent cheekbones of those Calvin Klein underwear models. He looked absolutely stunning in his blue patrolman's uniform. Sam had been the arresting officer on a robbery case assigned to me. What a cutie-pie! was my first thought. But my second was: He's smart. I was impressed—wowed, actually—by his written report. It was so thorough, so cogent, so downright lively (and actually grammatical), I could hardly believe a cop wrote it. Anyway, we hit it off. We both loathed the D.A., loved jazz, enjoyed each other's humor, and respected each other's political convictions—the last not exactly a challenge, as we were both a step and a half to the left of Democratic center.

Also, we discovered we were united in a secret conviction that although we'd both been born and bred on Long Island, we were too big for this burg. Over biweekly melted cheese sandwiches at Bob and Cathie's Coffee Shop, we could tell each other what we couldn't say to our colleagues: I coulda been a contender.

SAM: I coulda been a contender; a social worker evaluating grant applications for the Ford Foundation, but after our fourth kid, my wife was diagnosed manic-depressive and I needed bigger bucks and a better medical plan.

ME: I coulda been a contender, one of the top litigators in New York. NBC and CNN camera crews would have dropped by my office to hear my analysis every time a celebrity got arrested on a criminal charge. Except my husband let me know, without ever saying a word, that he wanted out of Manhattan—and that our marriage depended on my following him to the suburbs.

Two big fish in a small pond: That's how we saw ourselves. Although to be honest, none of the other fish swimming alongside us ever suggested they felt that Sam Franklin and I were in any way exceptional. Still, we offered each other validation: Hey, you could have been great. You have it in you. However, since both of us were busy puffing ourselves up in the other's company to show how smart we were, how uncomplaining about the hand we'd been dealt, any admission of vulnerability was unthinkable. Thus genuine closeness was impossible. But we put away a lot of melted cheese and white bread together. We probably had crushes on each other. It was a blow when I left the D.A.'s to go into private practice and our friendship died. Abruptly.

I'd noticed small changes in Sam, but his good company and better cheekbones had kept me from seeing the truth: Five years on the force had turned him from that rarity—a do-gooder with a tough mind—into a right-wing lunkhead. To him, I was suddenly disgraceful. No, wicked. I had gone over to the other side. He stopped saying "Hi!" and took to giving me a fast, hard nod that said: *criminal* lawyer. He insinuated that the only reason individuals accused of a crime were permitted legal representation was undue pressure from the Pinko-Fruitcake Lobby. One day, I ran into Sam right before lunch. When I suggested we could agree to disagree yet still go to Bob and Cathie's for number 14s, he stared at me, amazed that I could even dream of such a possibility. So I went back to my office and Xeroxed the Sixth Amendment on my letterhead and mailed it to him. Naturally, he didn't respond. The next time I saw him, at Mr. Big's, a bar where a lot of cops hang out, I said, "Hey, Sam? That little section of the Constitution of the United States? Did you read it?"

Sam said: "It made me want to puke." The words came out lightly, but that's because there were about twenty people standing around us. What made me want to puke was I knew he meant it.

Just before Holly Nuñez herself came into view, her heels came clacking down the hall. I had ten seconds left: I could not appeal to Sam's sense of guilt, since he no longer had one, so I decided to play to his pride. "Fast work doesn't mean good work," I told him. "Twenty bucks I'm going to learn on discovery that your investigation went beyond indifferent—all the way to sloppy."

"Bullshit," Sam began, but he caught himself after the "Bull." Smiling, knowing I'd gotten to him, I gave Holly a warm greeting, even though I could see she'd just spent nearly thirty minutes setting her hair on hot rollers. Her normally stick-straight hair was pumped up and round, like a beach toy. A peach-colored electrical cord dangled from her tote bag. Dead giveaways. Two seconds later, I understood: the hair exhibition was to show me she could afford to be arrogant because the prosecution was holding all the marbles. I hate it when lawyers pull this sort of cheap trick, and double-hate it when that lawyer is female; it reinforces the stereotype about women being so devoted to playing games that they can't be relied on to act as adults.

"Sorry," Holly said, trying to sound breathless, although it is conceivable that the malodorous cloud of hair spray hovering about her head was causing breathing distress.

"No problem," Sam and I responded in an inadvertent duet.

Holly's tiny office was a cube with the lowest ceiling the building code allowed, and with three people in it, you had to work to avoid a panic attack. Plus the place was just plain ugly. Whichever subanthropoidal Republican bureaucrat had chosen the wall color from a paint chip probably thought he was choosing off-white, but the color turned out corpse-yellow. As there were no funds in the county budget to clean the windows, one wall was a rectangular painting of the gray residue of foul weather and pollution. Holly had done her best to liven up the space in predictable Don't-worry-that-I'll-cut-your-balls-off-with-a-pinking-shears-because-as-you-can-see-I-am-not-threatening female litigator tradition. She'd hung a couple of framed museum posters—a Cassatt mother and child and a Renoir ballerina—and set an oxblood vase filled with silk delphiniums and hydrangeas on her desk. But the truth was, the only place less inviting than an assistant D.A.'s office was a men's cell in Building D of the correctional center.

"What have you got, Holly?" I asked. Sam presented his folder to Holly. Like that of a knight handing over his sword to his liege lady, his action made it clear who was in charge. Since this definitely wasn't Sam's modus operandi—he usually held forth as if he were senior partner to any assistant D.A. he was working with—I figured there had been a power struggle. The amazing thing was that Holly had won a fight against Sam Franklin that all the big, hairy-chested, street-smart, politically connected assistants routinely lost.

She opened the folder as if she couldn't wait to read it. Such damn chipperness. Except for her sparkly dark eyes and her name, however, there was nothing about her to indicate she was Hispanic. Still, I knew the Nuñez was legit because my partner, Chuckie Phalen, had gotten into a fight with her for speaking Spanish. She was in the Robbery Unit then and meandered over to the defense table and kept making comments to Chuckie's client in Spanish before court convened. Naturally the client was delighted to have someone speaking his language in this dread, alien place, began talking a blue streak. "Shut your trap!" Chuckie had boomed at him. Then he turned to Holly and threatened her with everything except death. "I was only saying it was a nice day," Holly chirped. "Yeah," the client agreed. "A nice day." The client wound up with five to seven in Sing Sing.

After five minutes with the folder, it was clear that for all her eager-beaverness, Holly was either a slow or a very thorough reader. Sam kept busy moving his feet around as if following diagrams for variations of the cha-cha; his seated dance got faster and faster.

One of the blessings of middle age is that while you do need reading glasses, your long-range vision improves. So I had no trouble making out the papers that covered Holly's desk. (Any criminal lawyer worth his/her salt learns how to read upside down.) A couple of subpoena forms, a fax from the United States Attorney in the Eastern District of New York regarding jurisdiction over a bank robbery/homicide—and the first of the Horchow spring issues. It featured a wicker basket overflowing with pastel gloves. I felt that simultaneous rush of yearning and giddiness mail order catalogs induce, and was actually rubbing the suede of a celadon size seven between my mental fingers when I spotted a couple of Polaroids stuck under a corner of the telephone. The first crime scene photos, made so the investigators have something to work with while the lab develops the actual photos, which have a much clearer resolution. The Polaroids were face-up, but I had a hunch the body was Bobette's. I reached across Holly's desk, and since neither Holly nor Sam slapped my hand, I picked up the pictures and checked out the information on the backs: "Bobette Frances Frisch, DOB Oct 26, 1940."

Bobette was wearing one of those lavender peignoir and nightgown sets meant for new brides. At least I've always assumed that's whom they were for, since who else but a honeymooner has the leisure to manipulate seventeen layers of chiffon in order to urinate? She lay on dark carpet, blue or purple, the kind with wavy lines cut in so it looks as if it had been plowed. The night-clothes were bunched up around her waist. Her heavy hips were pinched inward to accommodate the tight space between the dark wood leg of a coffee table and the couch from which she'd probably fallen. Three tan bank envelopes lay nearby on the carpet, near her thigh, ripped open.

In the cruel light of the camera's flash, Bobette's bare legs and hips were, literally, dead white, except for a slight shadow of pubic hair. I'd been a prosecutor and a defense lawyer for too many years to be horrified by any but the most brutal crime scene photos. (Also, I think we women lawyers train ourselves not to flinch, so our more swinish male colleagues won't think we're weak and, therefore, worthy of the contempt in which they would dearly love to hold us. I have no idea why we're perpetu-ally fighting this stereotype and proving how tough we are. It would be a great pretrial ploy to convince oppos-ing counsel that we are prime wusses before going into court and trouncing them.)

Anyway, back to Bobette. Her peignoir set formed a lavender puddle around the upper part of her body, so if you squinted and ignored the blackened bruises on her neck . . . "Strangled?" I asked.

"Uh-huh," Holly muttered, not looking up from her reading.

"But not raped?" I continued hopefully. They weren't talking. "It looks as if the nightgown worked its way up when she fell off the couch. I don't see any indications of bruises on the lower extremities." Holly read on and Sam remained silent, so I couldn't tell if they were holding back on playing a sexual assault card or if there really hadn't been any sexual attack. Still, with imprints of large fingers on Bobette's neck visible even in the photograph, I couldn't pretend that the injuries which led to her death were self-inflicted.

"I can't cut you any slack on this one, Lee," Holly finally said. She closed the folder. "We've got too much."

"Give me a for instance," I said lightly. She looked dubious, the mark of a novice, because any experienced prosecutor would be glad to show you she's holding all the cards. In order to get you to plead your client guilty, she'll be up front with you about all the damaging information, especially if it's incontestable, like physical evidence. "Are you playing poker with me, Holly?" I asked.

She blinked her big, black and very pretty eyes. "No!" she said. She belonged in Colorado or California, doing something aerobic. She was entirely too cheerful for Long Island. "I wouldn't play poker with an old pro like you," she assured. Instantly, I could see, she regretted saying "old," but it was too late.

"Old," I said, "but not yet senile." Before she could apologize and thus no longer feel she somehow owed me one, I added: "I know you found my client's fingerprints."

"Not just on a door bell or somewhere innocuous. On the tape that was used to tie up all the bank envelopes together. The bank officer did it for her. You can see three of the envelopes in that picture." Then she added, with much fervor, "*Ripped* apart."

"Torn open," I said calmly. "Anyway, my client doesn't deny knowing her. In fact, he was in a business deal with her."

"Lee," Holly said, "he wiped the doorknob and the switch plate of the light near the front door. But he left prints all *over* the house! On the thermostat in the living room! On the toilet flusher in the bathroom off her bedroom!"

"That just puts him there on a day between 1890 and the present."

Holly flashed me a nauseatingly perky smile, as if to say: Aren't you cute! But then she added: "You're forgetting his prints on the Scotch tape. She picked up those envelopes Friday."

"So maybe he was waiting in a car right outside the bank. She handed him the envelope and . . . " Holly's smile turned into that amused prosecutorial smirk that says: Do you really think a jury is going to believe *that*?

"Anything else?" I asked, not allowing myself to show that I would dearly love to wipe that smirk off her face. "Because if this is your case, it's spectacularly unimpressive."

Holly patted her inflated coiffeur. "How about an eyewitness who puts your client at the scene right around the time of the murder?"

I could practice criminal law for the next hundred years and a remark like that would still get me— *whomp!*—right in the gut. But over the years, I'd learned to keep my gut to myself. "Define 'around the time of the murder' for me," I suggested.

Holly leafed through the file, looking for an answer. Sam, I was sure, had the autopsy report memorized. He indicated as much by stopping his cha-cha and leaning forward in his seat. Holly actually glanced up at him, but did not give him permission to speak. Sam and I waited. Finally she announced: "The M.E. says the murder took place between six P.M. Friday and eight A.M. Saturday."

"And your eagle-eyed witness says what?" I asked.

"The witness saw the accused at approximately six-thirty P.M."

I gave her what the man in my life refers to as my Barbara Stanwyck Knowing Smile. "Last *Friday*? Your witness is positive of that?" This is about a third of what I do for a living: smile knowingly as if there is nothing else to do but be amused at the extent of human folly, so the smilee will think: Maybe my case isn't as good as I thought.

"Last Friday," Holly maintained, her eyes bright, her own smile spirited, as if to say, Gee, this litigation stuff is *fun*! For someone with the last name of Nuñez, no matter how assimilated, you'd think she'd have retained a little Spanish *dolor*. But she displayed as much tragic sense of life as a drum majorette.

"And where did the eyewitness see my client?"

"In the company of the deceased—at her house."

Oy. "Was the decedent already deceased at that point in time?" I inquired politely.

At this juncture, almost any other new assistant in the Homicide Bureau would have peered over at the cop in charge of the case, or at least hesitated. Not Holly. "No. She and the accused were seen walking together on the street, then going up into the deceased's house." She paused. "Hand in hand."

"First of all, assuming your witness saw Bobette Frisch with a man who is indeed my client—an assumption I, for one, am not about to make. Does that sound like a tête-à-tête that's going to end up in murder—or dinner? I vote for dinner. Second of all—"

"It was your client. His car was parked in the driveway of Bobette Frisch's house. The witness is her tenant. Ms. Frisch rented out a room, bath, and kitchenette in the basement. Torkelson's car was blocking the tenant's, and he'd rung the upstairs bell. Ms. Frisch was out, so the tenant waited by the driveway, pacing, having a fit. He couldn't get his car out and he works nights, something with computers over at Snapple in Valley Stream. He said this was the second time Torkelson—"

"Or someone else," I interrupted.

"Or someone else six foot five with a little beaky nose and blue eyes," Sam burst out. Holly licked her index finger and began lifting off bits of lint from her desk blotter. A meaningless gesture, yet Sam immediately understood he should not have spoken up. " 'scuse me, Holly," he said, much too fast. Was his voice actually tremulous? At best, it was an octave higher than usual. How the hell did she do that? Twenty-eight, twenty-nine years old, and she was able to make Sam Franklin squeak like a rookie.

"You know," I said, hating to interrupt such rich psychological interplay, "about the tall guy your witness saw: You see someone tall one time, and the next time someone large looms over you, you don't bother looking up. You assume it's the same tall man. But it could have been *anyone* tall."

"It was Norman Torkelson," said Holly, cutting me off. "Our witness not only saw them together but called the local precinct and reported Torkelson's car—and the license plate." She didn't even give me a second to comfort myself by thinking: Norman is far too gifted a con man to ever drive a car registered in his name. "It was listed under Robert McNulty, at 54 Homewood Avenue. Apartment 3-C," she reported. "In Mineola." I couldn't believe it! What a jerk! "We sent a couple of guys over there Sunday," she went on, "and there was your client, Norman Torkelson, a.k.a. Robert McNulty, a.k.a . . . " She opened the file folder again. I really didn't want to hear the upcoming recitation, but I had no choice. " . . . Henry Reuther, a.k.a. Philip Nugent, a.k.a. William Brightman, a.k.a.—"

"Holly, I'm not telling you he's never used an alias or been arrested or convicted of fraud. I'm only saying he is not a killer. If it was Norman at Bobette's, he wouldn't leave her dead. He'd leave her with a smile on her face and a song in her heart. I'm only saying—"

"*I'm* only saying he can plead to second-degree homicide and I'll recommend twenty-five years."

"You know I can't accept that, Holly," I said, moving forward in my seat as if ready to stomp out of her office, which of course I had no intention of doing. I'd spend another twenty minutes dickering and come out with twenty.

Except Holly stared at her watch and an expression of horror passed over her face. She rose. "Take it or leave it," she said, real fast. Then she added: "Sorry, but I have an urgent appointment and I'm fifteen minutes late." She stood and quickly fluttered all ten fingers at me. "New acrylics," she explained. "Do I have to explain? You *know* how long they take. I mean, forever."

"*Acrylics?*" my partner, Chuckie Phalen, demanded. I'd wandered downstairs and into the courtroom where he was trying his arson case and waiting until the judge— who truly believed the governor was, any second, going to nominate him to run for an opening on the Court of Appeals as a reward for having gone to Harvard Law School—declared a recess. As these recesses happened on the average of every fifteen minutes so the judge could call Albany and demand "Any news yet?" I hadn't had to wait long.

"What the hell are acrylics?" Chuckie demanded.

"Fake nails."

Chuckie Phalen, at sixty-eight years old, was one of those second-generation Irish-American males who prefer a night out with the boys to any other human endeavor, so I elaborated: "Artificial fingernails. So she can have long nails that don't break."

"If a guy A.D.A. pulled something like that . . . "

Already I regretted complaining to Chuckie because by nightfall, the quarter of the Nassau County criminal defense bar that hung out at TJ's Taproom would be snickering over "acrylics" and, to an Old Boy, would recount the story for the ten or twenty years whenever someone brought up the notion that a female performing some role in the courtroom beyond stenography might not be a bad idea. That I and a couple of other women attorneys were somehow absolved of the taint of frivolity in the first degree didn't make me feel any better. It just meant that for some reason, the boys at TJ's had declared us members of some neutral, nonthreatening gender that had nothing to do with other girl lawyers.

Chuckie pushed back his chair from the defense table and stretched out his short legs. Even that minor exertion caused him to breathe hard, and with each breath, I could hear the faint whistle of the emphysema that was killing him. And perched on the edge of the table, I could smell the bitter odor of cigarettes that clung to his dark-gray suit; it commingled with the harsher stench of the cigars he and his pals lit up five nights a week at TJ's.

"I hope Holly Nuñez will be a little more flexible," I mused. "I'd hate to have to go to trial with this guy."

"He's guilty," Chuckie said, not even bothering to put a question mark at the end of his question.

"If he's not, then there's a guy with his size-giant fingers who made some nasty marks on one Bobette Frisch's neck. Oh, and that same guy seems to have left his prints everywhere in her house, including on the Scotch tape that was tying together all the bank envelopes with the forty-eight thousand bucks she'd withdrawn earlier that day." I glanced down. A run had formed near the toe of my black panty hose and was working its way past my shoe, over my instep, so I could add to the pleasure of my day by having to run into Bloomingdale's and buy five more pair, one of which I'd leave in my glove compartment, one in my attaché case, and three in my office, and yet the next time I had a run, as if by witchcraft, the panty hose would have vanished and once again I'd be back at the Bloomingdale's hosiery counter, where I know the saleslady by name: Dorothy. "If I could put Norman on the stand, he could probably con a jury into thinking he won the Nobel Prize for goodness. But he has a record."

"A long one," Chuckie wheezed, knowing without being told.

"The longest. And he was pulling the marriage con."

"Aw, no." Chuckie shook his small head with great sadness. I tried to imagine Chuckie sitting beside Norman at a defense table. He was short, and slight to the point of being tiny. If there were a class play for sixty-eight-year-olds, Chuckie Phalen would be cast as a leprechaun. "You can't put a fella like that on the stand." He glanced up at me. His eyes were eclipsed by cataracts. "Did he actually marry them?"

"No. Just proposed, as far as I can tell. I haven't read the whole printout, because there aren't enough hours in a day. But he tells them he came from an upper-class family, went to Yale, the family lost its money, but he made it back in 'investments.' Except then his wife took him to the cleaners, got custody of his kids, and now he's down on his luck. Your heart would break from reading some of the witness reports."

"*My* heart? In Phalen and White, Attorneys-at-Law," he said, just as the bailiff shuffled back into the courtroom, "there's only one heart capable of breakage. It ain't mine, Lee."

And on the subject of hearts, the next morning in the visitor's center, I watched Norman Torkelson react to the news about an eyewitness who not only could place him at the crime scene at an hour when the homicide, according to the medical examiner, might have occurred, but also called the local precinct to complain about his car, thereby giving the cops a record of his license plate number. He pressed his hand against his chest. "But the car wasn't registered in my name!" he declared.

"It was registered to Robert McNulty, the same name you used for your apartment."

"It couldn't have been!" he replied, angry that I would accuse him of such rank amateurism. "I sent Mary over to Motor Vehicles with ID for . . . " He thought for a minute. "Daniel Stevenson. I distinctly remember that. I told her, 'Take the Dan ID and—' "

"Maybe she just grabbed the wrong papers."

Norman's face flushed red, then deepened to a fierce purple. Just as I was about to leap up and call a guard over—Hey! Get this guy to the infirmary, fast!—he regained his composure. The dark cast receded, the hands relaxed as he crossed his arms over his chest. "It's not that she's unintelligent," he said quietly. "People think that, but they're wrong. It's just . . . Mary's an innocent. She doesn't get it." He shrugged. "I guess that's why . . . " His face colored. Pink this time. "I love her," he said softly. "You should see her. Then you'd understand . . . "

"And Bobette?" I asked.

"Business," he said crisply. "Nothing going on there. Strictly dollars and cents."

"You know, I've seen your record, read some of the complaints against you. You might want to consider being more direct with me. I need all the help I can get, and the D.A.'s Office is not in a generous mood when it comes to . . . " I paused for effect. Hokey, but I knew it would work. " . . . homicide."

"How can I impress upon you that this was strictly a business deal? We didn't have sexual relations."

Of course, the problem with most professional criminals is that you never know if they're lying. The smarter ones, however, tend to be straight when it is in their best interests to tell the truth. With con men, this generalization does not always apply. The pleasure of the lie might be headier than the joy of freedom. "If you did have sex," I said, "there may be evidence of it. A person can wipe door handles clean and still leave fingerprints. And he can leave body fluids, if not semen then saliva, or a hair or two with roots on them and—"

"No sex," Norman said. His tone was harsh, as if he were a teacher and I an incorrigible, the worst student. "No sex!" He waved the guard over to take him back to his cell. "No sex!"

four

❧

S-E-X.

It is as good a way as any to return to the marriage of Lee's parents. So let's spell it out. The first letter, S: for svelte. Before Lee's birth, Sylvia had a model's figure—that is, she had a large, finely shaped head that sat atop a long neck, which arose from a body that had as many curves as the average flagpole. Besides being thin, Sylvia was one of those born-chic people who can put on the plainest white shirt, fold back the cuffs, lift the collar, and—voilà—look as though she'd been done by Monsieur Dior. But in the weeks postpartum, it became clear that her outline had softened. Her chemistry had changed, her cell walls losing a bit of their resilience, and even though she'd gained only ten pounds, her pre-pregnancy waist had thickened. Her hips became almost curvy. Not just that: Her bosom swelled from what her mother-in-law, Bella, referred to as "a coupla fried eggs" to two noticeable bumps beneath her cashmere sweater set. Note the cashmere.

Tudor Rose Furs was a gold mine. By the late forties and early fifties, soldiers and sailors, back in civilian jobs, were celebrating the peace and reveling in a booming economy. They wanted to make up for lost time. How better to show the stuff they were made of than to buy a fur coat for the little woman? (Or a fur boa for the little woman's competition?) By 1951, Leonard and Sylvia were able to buy their first house, a luxury, luxury ranch, as the real estate agent solemnly described it.

Just over four miles north and ten miles east of Forest Hills, their house might have inhabited another galaxy. For the son of a Commie and the daughter of a not-dishonest judge, Great Neck was so profoundly luxurious that the Whites kept saying to each other: "I want to pinch myself." Their house, the agent assured them, had all the latest features. Not all: But on its over-half-an-acre plot, it did have a stone fireplace that opened onto both the living room and the den, a finished basement, with built-in cedar storage bins that doubled as seating, and, behind louvered doors right off the kitchen, a laundry center.

"I want to pinch myself," Sylvia admitted to Leonard as she ran her hand over the chilly white porcelain of the dryer. Leonard's hand cupped her buttock and gave it a fast pinch. The male in him loved the feel of her newer, rounder, more ample ass, even as the snob yearned for the prepregnant Sylvia, whose hollow cheeks and fleshless flanks announced: No sloppy lower-middle-class excess here. He couldn't get over his disappointment that she had let herself lose that sucked-in-cheek, snooty look he'd prized. She still looked like Lauren Bacall's twin sister, but a twin who couldn't lay off the halvah.

And another thing. Once they got past the thrill of

home ownership and finished with the business of the marriage—should the master bathroom have gray or peach tiles? could they afford to go to France on vacation? and if so, should they leave Lily with his parents or her parents?—he had nothing to say to Sylvia. Nor did she seem to think she owed him any talk. He could understand her lack of conversational ability because he was aware of her background: Nobody said anything at the Bernsteins' for fear of disturbing the Judge. But he could not forget that article he'd seen in *Collier's* written by a Ph.D. psychologist. "Are You Married to Your Best Friend?" That title was a slap in the face.

Would a best friend just shrug—she'd shrugged!—when he'd taken her out to a French restaurant and ordered wine and confided his dream of opening a store in Manhattan, on the Upper East Side, away from the fur district, and have it so elegant that only the most silk-stocking types would feel comfortable going in? Of course, once they were customers, *everyone* would want to go. Although the rude-crude types would be told they had to make an appointment. Not that he didn't want their business. Frankly, they bought at least double what tightwad rich Christians did, but—see, Sylvia?—he wanted them to feel they were trespassing. They would have more respect for the store that way. Not store. Salon. And wait till those Christian ladies walked in the front door! They would love it, with skinny Frenchmen for salesmen who would say "May I help you?" in French. He'd even looked it up in the Forest Hills branch of the Queens Borough Public Library: "*Puis-je vous aider?*," although he didn't dare to try to say it himself, being smart enough to realize the first word was probably not pronounced "Poo is-gee." But of course Leonard would insist the salesmen switch to English if he saw the customer getting scared. Fear was bad, he explained. Intimidation, on the other hand, was good, because then the customer and her husband would order an even better garment, just to prove they could afford to buy in such classy surroundings.

So he'd poured all this out to his wife for almost an hour and a half, and she'd *shrugged*. "Is that all you can say?" he'd demanded. Finally, she'd said, "I think it sounds wonderful," but he could tell she didn't. She was probably scared. Selling a booming business in Queens and opening up cold in Manhattan. Such a risk. Didn't she realize he woke up at four in the morning with his intestines tied in knots? Such a huge outlay, what with inventory and a showroom with parquet floors and those antique French chairs with arms that cost about two hundred dollars each.

Still, the way her skirt fit over her backside, like the skin on a knockwurst...

"I said pinch *myself*," Sylvia laughed, wriggling out of his grasp, moving into the kitchen to deal with the bags of groceries that filled the room. Stock up, Leonard had commanded her the day before, their first full day as home owners. She had left the baby with her mother, who was helping out till they got settled, and had gone on a shopping spree that had left the assistant manager of the A & P with his jaw hanging open—although he *had* been able to say: Can I have one of the boys put your bags in your car, Mrs. . . . And she'd filled in his blank. White, she'd said. To be perfectly honest, it had been humiliating, going from Weissberg to Weiss to White, but now that they were in a new community, starting out fresh as White, knowing he wouldn't change it again (despite a few days' flirtation with "Whyte"), she was glad Leonard had insisted. Anyway, the A & P assistant manager—he was very broad-shouldered, probably from lifting all those cartons of canned peaches—he said . . .

"How much did you spend?" Leonard inquired.

"What you gave me," Sylvia responded, a little edgy because she *had* gone overboard, sweeping roll upon roll of paper towels into her cart, stocking up on Chicken of the Sea chunk white like the tuna was pheasant under glass or something. And she had pulled jar after jar of preserves off the shelf, until she had strawberry, black-currant, cherry, raspberry, gooseberry, plum, apple butter, and orange marmalade.

But to his credit, Leonard wasn't cheap. Nothing but the best. Well, not *the* best, because the best kind of a house was an English Tudor or something called a Georgian, he'd told her. Except then your furniture had to be antiques or at least come from B. Altman, so it was better to have a modern house. Then it could be spare. Spare. That was his new favorite word; it superseded "classic," which came after "luxuriant," which supplanted "discriminating." He always had some snotty new word. To be honest, he had some nerve acting so snotty, what with Lard Lady, his mother, and his old man, Nathan the Red. "Spare." Well, her clothes were spare, but then, she'd always had terrific taste. It was part of her artistic talent. Like, with her Hardy Amies green wool suit: a green felt hat trimmed with green feathers, but black suede pumps. She didn't want to believe it when the salesgirl had suggested green alligator. No! She knew when enough was enough. Black suede gloves, large gold button earrings, and *that was it.* No bracelet, no necklace, no scarf. Spare.

She loved buying. The dark jewel colors of the jams in the A & P. The sleek Danish-modern coffee table with those skinny blond legs that made it look as though it was tiptoeing over the cocoa-colored carpet. And on top of the table, casual, as if someone had just stopped reading them, not in a neat pile, the half-price artbooks she'd found in a store down the block from the obstetrician's: how the dark red on the Utrillo's cover echoed the scarlets and carmines on the Rembrandt's. She wasn't like some women, buy-buy-buy out of boredom. She loved what she bought, took pleasure in an object every time she saw it in her home. Okay, not a box of Lipton's tea bags. But like that petticoat she'd bought in 1949, in a lilac so pale it was almost gray; it had narrow ribbon shoulder straps and scalloped ribbon trim along the hemline. Every time she opened her lingerie drawer, she'd feel good, just seeing it—and the yellow nightgown with the quilted bed jacket too.

She thought about her things a lot, and about things she saw when she went to the city, things she couldn't afford but remembered as if they belonged to her. She never forgot something once it caught her eye. Like in an antique store window on East Fifty-eighth, a silver tea set with the most delicate leafy pattern etched into it. The lid of the pot and the sugar bowl cover were topped with roses made out of silver. Incredible work. The last time she passed it, the store owner had waved to her from inside the store. Like: I know just how you feel. Wait: more than that. I know you'll be back. He was very good-looking, with white hair and a white mustache, wearing a dark-gray suit that was almost black. Very slim. Neat. Like a well-packed cigarette.

Leonard was clean. There was no man on earth cleaner. He used four Q-Tips every morning on his ears. But he wasn't . . . what was that word he'd liked but not loved? Fastidious. He'd used that for a week or two. But he wasn't fastidious, because he wasn't in complete control over himself, not like the man in the antique store, with his hankie sticking out of his pocket in six perfect points. Nervous, Leonard would run his hand through his hair, and by late afternoon the Brylcreemed ends would no longer lie flat, but would coil like tiny springs at the back of his neck. Or he'd dribble something on his tie, a tiny drop of something, but then a poppy seed would stick to it. And in terms of looks: He wasn't dapper, but he wasn't a man's man either, like the assistant manager at the A & P, with black hair peeking out from under his white undershirt, making little twirlies right below his neck. Or her still-life teacher, Jeffrey, at the Great Neck Center for the Fine Arts, with his black eyes and tight blue jeans. Leonard was just okay-looking. Dark-brown hair, brown eyes. Okay. Skin? Not like he had pockmarks, but you could see pores on his cheeks. Five-feet eight-and-a-half, even though it said five-ten on his driver's license, so not quite tall enough. Not getting fat, but in the last year, in his new, slim English jacket, it looked like he was wearing a fox boa under it instead of a belt.

Let us leave Leonard's love handles and Sylvia's mind and return to S-E-X once again. The E. If the vertical stroke is the institution of marriage, and the two Whites are the horizontal lines on either end, then clearly there is something between them. Remember, this was now 1951. They were neither sophisticates nor libertines, so it was nothing kinky. They *seemed* like a happy couple. They said "I love you" to each other every night just before they went off to sleep. They had sexual intercourse three times a week. At this point in their lives, the mere thought of taking a lover had never crossed either of their minds, so whatever was between them was certainly not another man or another woman.

They had more disposable income than Great Neck neighbors twice their age. True, Leonard's big plans might put them in the poorhouse, but as the Bankers Trust Company was willing to underwrite his grandiose fantasies of a showroom with Louis XV bergères on Lexington Avenue and East Sixty-fifth Street, its sales force taught from birth to inquire "*Puis-je vous aider?*," it was not money that had come between them.

Could it have been that having a child had caused some rift? Highly dubious. If not a great child, our heroine was certainly an awfully nice one. In the late spring of 1951, Lily Rose White, thirteen months old, had three teeth and a sweet smile. Well, sweet when it came to friendly people, a smile in response to a smile: up on the right side, a quiver on the left—before spreading across her face and lighting up her big brown eyes. Definitely not one of those Aren't-I-fabulous smiles the born-confident flash. But engaging enough.

And she got better in the ensuing months. Some ordinary children are, for a short period, overcome by a monomania that lights them up like a holy spirit. Who knows why an ordinary little boy becomes incandescent at the sight of a garbage truck? Or how a plain little girl transcends her commonality and becomes a toddler goddess at the sight of an animal? For Lily Rose White, a blue jay evoked delight, a cat rapture, and a dog . . . bliss beyond all understanding. Sylvia learned that the fastest way to obtain her daughter's cooperation was to threaten to withhold either the blouse with a Scottish terrier appliquéd on the collar or a cup decorated with an owl and pussycat. Leonard was the more positive parent. He discovered that to take this nice enough (but after ten minutes of peekaboo rather boring) female child to the Bronx Zoo was to turn her into the Best Kid in the World. Show her a tapir and she'd howl with jubilation, a giraffe and she'd fall into silent awe.

So it was not the child who came between Mr. and Mrs. Leonard White. What was happening that while allowing them to say "I love you" to each other once every twenty-four hours did not allow them to *feel* love? It is easy to tick off items on a list: Narcissism. Lack of trust. Self-loathing, the belief that anyone worth loving could not love them. Emotional immaturity. But the truth is, some questions have no answer. Suffice it to say that although Mr. and Mrs. White looked as if they had it all, they did not. They were wanting.

Having avoided that issue, let us not avoid concluding S-E-X. Note how the two lines of the X intersect at only one point. Well, two years after their move to Great Neck, Sylvia and Leonard came together. She was two months pregnant with their second child. (A son, Leonard prayed to no one in particular. John Bradley White? Radley Wilson White? Did he dare Dalton Kendall White III?) Having successfully lost the ten pounds she had gained with Lee and not yet put it back on, as she would inevitably and irrevocably do, Sylvia had regained some of that high-cheeked, honey-haired elegance one would anticipate from the wife of a polo player, assuming one knew polo players. On those nights when she would stop by the salon to wait for him before they went out for dinner with other furrier couples or to the Museum of Modern Art, where she had made him—he was grateful—become a Donor so they got invitations to all the openings, Leonard could see his customers' heads turn: Who *is* that woman in the Lanvin evening suit, its jacket lined with leopard-print silk, a leopard coat slung casually over her arm? Sylvia was at her peak.

As was Leonard. He was now the proprietor of Le Fourreur, a Manhattan fur salon so exclusive that it was rumored that Mrs. John Foster Dulles was told in no uncertain terms that she'd have to wait two months if she wanted a full-length tawny brown ranch mink. *That* was how great the demand was for exclusive designs by Jean-Louis, Leonard's couturier. The rumor about Mrs. Dulles was not true. It had been made up and spread by Leonard, who also invented "Jean-Louis" for his designer, who until then had been Bobby Anello, hitherto of Westchester Fancy Furs.

Rumor was only one of Leonard's many marketing strategies. He called the twenty percent break he routinely offered all his good customers a "fashion industry deep discount" when he phoned the editors of *Vogue, Harper's Bazaar,* the *New York Times,* and the *Herald Tribune* to tell them about it. When they dropped by Le Fourreur, he charmed them by serving tea in Haviland cups and by throwing in a black or silver fox stole with whatever garment they bought and paid for as a way of saying Thank you for your patronage. After a spectacular December 1952 season, the Whites were no longer comfortable. They were well-to-do.

Sylvia had charge accounts at Saks Fifth Avenue, Tailored Woman, and Henri Bendel. Leonard went from ready-made English suits off the rack at Moe Ginsburg's to perusing a book of swatches in a suite in the Plaza that M. Thierry Boucault, the noted Parisian haberdasher, occupied on his semiannual trips to New York. They hired a live-in maid. They bought a suite of signed Picasso lithographs for the living room. They donated money to the United Way and the Boy Scouts. They bought a Christmas tree. (However, Leonard could not figure out how to get it to stand up on its own. He forbade Sylvia to ask the maid how to do it, so the tree lay dying on the living room floor until the second of January. They waited until the following year for their first real Christmas: Leonard spent a half hour on an early December Saturday at Colonial Nursery and Garden Supplies, pretending to survey their inventory of snow shovels but actually checking out their Christmas tree. Its secret was finally revealed: underneath a ladylike green velveteen skirt lay a clunky metal brace. To decorate their tree, Sylvia spent an entire day at Bergdorf Goodman—without even stopping for lunch—choosing ornaments: blown-glass orbs within orbs, a galaxy of silver stars.) And they sold their house two weeks before the raspberry bushes Sylvia had planted in the fertile soil of Great Neck bore their first fruit. Once again, the Whites moved eastward and upward.

Getting back to the X for a moment. Sylvia had some bad times right after her first child's birth. There she was, drained, pulled at by episiotomy stitches and dragged down by the blues, and Leonard had sauntered into her hospital room with a huge bouquet of white roses and an I-don't-care-that-it's-not-a-boy grin, and she'd thought: Who is this man? Of course, she knew he was her husband, and the father of her baby, but he had looked so strange. Those big lips, the insides displaying themselves, pink and wet, like some insect-eating tropical flower. He'd come over and sat on the edge of the bed, taking her hand in his. She tried to gaze into his eyes, but those giant lips filled her range of vision and they moved, inexorably, toward her, puckering slightly for a kiss. She wanted to shriek the way that woman did in—what was that horror picture?—*I Walked with a Zombie*. Grotesque! Abominable! Please, please don't get any closer! Don't . . .

Well, he'd kissed her and she lived through it. In the next couple of years, however, those horrible moments recurred, and a couple of times the lips seemed to puff up right before her eyes. How could his customers think he was so attractive, the Christian ones with husbands whose lips were never any wider than zippers?

But things had gotten better. And better. They'd had a good anniversary the past June. Leonard had taken her to the best restaurant in the city, Le Pavillon, where he'd shaken the hand of the man in the front, except she realized he was giving a bribe or a tip or whatever. The man had glanced into his hand and gotten very charming and offered them a nice table. Leonard ordered champagne and then let the wine waiter pick out their wines, and by the end of the evening, Sylvia slipped her foot out of her black peau de soie Chanel sling-back and was using it to rub the inside of Leonard's thigh. And that September, he told her to meet him in the store—salon—right after closing. He asked her to try on the Russian sable Mrs. General Motors had ordered. But then he said: "This is too good for Mrs. General Motors. Why don't you keep it?" When she finally comprehended what he was talking about, she almost fainted from joy, and the salesmen, who were still there and Dolly, the model/bookkeeper, who'd peeked out from the office, had applauded.

Thus the intersecting of the X. Sylvia finally understood what his customers saw in her husband. While no one would call Leonard conventionally handsome, with his made-to-order suits and beautifully cut hair he could look ultra smart—in an Italian kind of way, but upper-class Italian, from Italy. She remembered how once she'd loathed his lips, but now realized that if you looked at him as a whole, he was very appealing. Now and then, even stunning.

And Leonard's heart softened too. He realized that while his wife's diction all but shouted "Born in Brooklyn! Bred in Queens!" throughout her childhood she'd been forced to whisper instead of talk. So who heard the accent? To look at her, she could be an English horsewoman.

But after the legs of the X cross, they again part. So it was with Mr. and Mrs. White. In her third month of pregnancy with her second daughter (who would be named Robin Renée), Sylvia came down with terrible morning sickness. Then it became all-day sickness. Leonard worried about how thin she was getting, how bad it was for the baby because sometimes Sylvia's entire dinner would be a single Ritz cracker. Her face became spotty and her hair lost its shine, but when he got home, he would take her in his arms and say something reassuring, like: "It won't last forever."

But instead of being comforted, she got all weepy and clung to him. Sitting beside him in the movies over the weekend, hugging his arm, stuffing it in the divide between her two swollen breasts. Butting her pillow against his at night, so he could feel her hot breath on the back of his neck. And it wasn't just physical clinging. She called him first thing in the morning: How was the ride in on the Long Island Rail Road? Late morning: Who are you having lunch with? Early afternoon: What did you have for lunch? Was it good? Did you have dessert? Late afternoon: How's it going? Any good customers stop in? Early evening: What train are you taking home? She's pregnant, he told himself. And she loves me.

But that made him realize that she had never before displayed this interest, this passion for him. Did the hormone changes in her make her feel more free? Well, she hadn't been so free when she was pregnant with Lee. In fact, sometimes he knew Sylvia was pretending to get excited, and she was a lousy pretender. Oooo. Oooo. Always Oooo, repeated two times. But now she had a repertoire of noises, and they were for real. She'd become crazy for him. Now that he was well-to-do.

Now she always was ready for him. Not just ready: If he didn't come to her, she'd come to him. Now, no matter what she wore, her nipples always stuck out. He could feel them when she clung to him. Well, he thought, trying hard to be fair, I'm a big shot now. That's very attractive to women. But a voice called up from his subconscious: Hey, Len. Is that the real thing, when the girl has to see sable before she falls in love?

A couple of months after she fell for her husband, Sylvia dropped by the salon on her way to Tailored Woman, to use the bathroom. Leonard introduced her to Mrs. Wriston Brandt, wife of *the* senior partner in *the* biggest Wall Street law firm, a man once referred to as "Mr. Trusts and Estates" by the *Wall Street Journal*. Instead of saying "How do you do," or, if that was too stuffy, "Hello," Sylvia had said "Hi." But the way she said it, all nasally, with that New York intonation. It came out "Hoy." To his credit, Leonard admitted to himself that he was a terrible snob—and that the only decent pedigree in the entire White household belonged to their new collie, Duchess. But still . . . "Hoy."

Mere weeks after the Mrs. Wriston Brandt incident, Leonard was going over accounts payable with Dolly Young (who had come to New York from Bristol, Massachusetts, to be a Conover model but who failed, not for want of oblique facial planes but for lack of length, being only five feet four). The key point here is that in her entire life, Dolly never said

"Hi." Always "Hello." She also said "think yew" for "thank you." In both instances, her speech patterns had to do with regional usage rather than social class. As she and Leonard were looking over the Pincus Notions and Trimmings invoice, Dolly said, "They rob us blind and they don't even say think yew," impulsively, Leonard kissed her.

Thus began an affair that lasted for decades.

five

If I'm right in believing that I'm typical of most American women, then there's got to be millions of bottles of used-but-once hair conditioner abandoned on the floors of showers and the ledges of bathtubs from Maine to Hawaii. Makeup kits must hold so many unfinished mascara wands that each house in the United States could supply a company of Rockettes. And as for the national glut of rejected moisturizers: Better forgotten in medicine cabinets than tossed onto the country's landfills where they could trigger an ecological calamity.

Is this another tirade about how the beauty industry exploits the low self-esteem of American women? Nope, just the opposite. All those social critics: they don't know their ass from a hole in the ground. They carry on about the insecurities of American women and completely ignore the extravagant self-confidence we display. Critics! Listen to the female ego. It's not saying: I loathe myself. No, it's telling you: I am a mere taupe eye shadow away from gorgeousness. Each of us has a breathtaking creature locked inside. And all we need to break through to infinite desirability is a new brand of thigh cream.

Take me, for instance. You'd think, having lived forty-five years, I'd have picked up on God's message: "Lee White, Esq., is not going to be a sex goddess in her lifetime." But no, I don't hear it. Nor do the rest of my sister Americans. Because nothing except death can kill that ravishing dame who walks in beauty inside us. If a normal adult female's just-before-sleep dream is a sweeter, more graceful, poreless version of herself, then what woman does the one-in-a-million true beauty fantasize about? A flatulent, bezitted battle-ax? Right now, you may be tempted to tap me on the shoulder and ask: Hey, what does all this have to do with the Torkelson case? So I'll tell you: All this is a prelude to Mary Dean walking into my office.

It didn't hit me right away that she was the most beautiful creature I'd ever seen in my life. No, keeping pace with my secretary, Sandi, who was ushering her in, she was just a tall young woman, twenty-two or so, with a ton of makeup on, wearing . . . The man in my life once told me there was no one in the world more mean-spirited than a New York clothes snob. So I censored my nasty thoughts about her kelly-green suit with forest-green velveteen lapels. I stood to greet her. "Have a seat, Ms. Dean."

"Thanks," she said, speaking with nervous quickness. Instead of realizing that my right hand was extended in order to shake hers, she thrust a tightly stuffed envelope into it.

"Oh," I said, taken aback by her nervousness. I'd assumed Norman would have himself a cooler cookie. The envelope, no doubt, contained my retainer: fifteen thousand dollars. Cash, and from the heft of it, probably hundreds. A not unusual method of payment, since many of my clients weren't interested in check writing—not if the check was going to diminish their own assets. They liked paying by check only if the assets belonged to somebody else. (Soon after we became partners, Chuckie Phalen told me a precautionary tale: One year out of law school, he'd taken a check from some client. When he went to cash it—after the jury had come back with an acquittal—he happened to glance at the name across the top, the person whose account it was: Charles Michael Phalen, Counselor-at-Law.)

As Mary was still standing, I motioned for her to sit. Then I handed over the envelope to Sandi, who left my office to return to her desk, where she would open it and make sure the retainer was inside—not just a wad of cutup newspaper. You'd think I'd have hated practicing law this way, dealing with such overt sleazeballs. But every time I worked on a nice, clean white-collar criminal matter—sales tax evasion, co-op conversion fraud—a giant yawn arose inside me that the biggest corporate check couldn't stifle.

Mary, still jittery, hadn't taken a seat. She clutched her purse tight against her chest in a pathetically defensive posture, her shoulders and head thrust forward. She stared out the window. It was one of those nasty days in early May, more appropriate to March, rainy, gray, with a low, chill wind that blew down the street and bit at your ankles. I spoke so sweetly I practically cooed: "Please sit down."

"Jeez," she said, alighting on the edge of an armchair in front of my desk. "Sorry. I didn't mean to take up so much of your time." The backs of her hands were red. Her nails were chewed down so low they sliced into the flesh of her fingers. Then she babbled, a long, agitated apology about how the police had impounded Norman's car and how the taxi she'd called hadn't come and how just when she thought she was okay, she discovered the bus she was on was headed to Long Beach. Normally, I would have cut her off as courteously as possible, but suddenly I found myself transfixed by Mary's looks.

First of all, I realized her face was a flawless oval. True, the heavy makeup she was wearing was unflattering, chalky, especially against the peachy glow of her neck. Her cheeks were as bright as geraniums. The lipstick she wore, a neon orange, was applied so thickly that when she formed words beginning with b or p it looked as though her lips would meld. Still, I could see that the makeup was not meant to hide serious imperfections. Her skin appeared flawless.

Mary's too white face was framed by shiny black curls that spilled over her shoulders. The hairdo was neither the elegant three hundred dollar frenzy of a Manhattan cut nor the sculpted perfection of big Texas hair. To me, it looked like a homey attempt to copy the none-of-that-androgyny-shit-for-me style of a Dolly or a Wynonna. Unlike country music stars, however, Mary's hair was not tier upon tier of faultless curlicues. In the sodden weather, the tresses on her shoulders had lost their verve and lay limp, wormlike, on her green suit jacket.

Obviously, she'd chosen the suit color to play up her luminous eyes. Those eyes didn't need any help. On the contrary, the suit was green overkill. In truth, though, nothing could detract from those eyes, not even the opalescent pistachio shadow that covered her lids and orbital rims up to her brows, not the greasy black pencil liner.

Now, as to the rest of Mary Dean: Her nose would have been perfect except it had the tiniest indentation at the tip, as if she'd pressed on it throughout childhood, trying to get it to turn up. And her lips: full, but pretty, not those collagen-injected trout-mouths that had become so trendy. And just before she sat, I finally noticed the figure. High-breasted, tiny-waisted, long-legged. An ambulatory Barbie doll.

Except Mary was human. She was sweating and gave off an odor that was a combination of natural musk, wet wool and cheap perfume—gardenia? jasmine?—that I bet had the word "Jungle" as part of its name. I watched a drop of perspiration slide down her left temple, past her jaw to her chin. It would have dribbled onto her neck, only she wiped it away with the back of her hand. In doing so, she lost control of the black patent-leather envelope-purse she'd been hugging to her chest. It dropped to the floor. Bending to pick it up, she cracked her forehead against the edge of my desk. "Aaah!" she cried, a yelp of pain.

A shudder chattered my teeth and shivered my shoulders, that frisson that comes when you empathize too intensely. For that second, my forehead throbbed in the same spot where she'd hit her head. I buzzed Sandi, requesting a cup of ice, fast. I must have sounded a little desperate because Sandi rushed in with it seconds later. Already a huge red rectangle, like a ledge, was protruding from Mary's brow. I wrapped the ice in a few tissues and pressed it against the bump. Sandi stood by. "How are you feeling?" I asked Mary after a minute.

"A little . . . " Her lovely eyes, floating upward, looked slightly dopey. Tiny black pearls of mascara dotted her lashes.

"You'll be fine in a minute," Sandi assured her, too briskly. Sandi's only other job had been with a malpractice firm. She lived in constant terror of lawsuits. Over the years, I tried to reassure her: No one's going to sue me, but if they do, I can handle it. Nothing I could say could bring her peace. Besides the usual secretarial chores, she stood eternally vigilant, protecting the two oversophisticated rubes—me and Chuckie—from certain ruin at the hands of the shyster lawyers our scum-bucket clients would hire to sue us.

"I can manage now," I told Sandi, who clearly did not believe she should leave me alone with a con man's sweetie who had probably arranged her own subdural hematoma just so she could haul me into court and bring me to utter ruin. "I'm okay, Sandi. Thanks for the ice." Reluctantly, casting a knowing and hostile glance at Mary (whose eyes, fortunately, were still swimming in her head), Sandi left.

After a moment, Mary whispered: "Sorry."

I took off the ice. "Are you all right?"

"I'm fine." Except "fine" came out shakily, in two syllables.

"Are you nauseous?" I asked. "Does your head hurt?"

"No, really, I'm fine," Mary reassured me, offering me a lovely smile. "Just, you know, getting bonked like that. Wowie!" She laughed at her own clumsiness. An instant later, she burst into sobs.

"Does it hurt?" I asked.

"It's not . . . my head," she explained, taking a giant hiccup of air. "It's . . . Norman."

"It must be—" I was going to say something objective and mealy-mouthed, like "difficult," but instead I said: "—awful for you."

"He's in jail for *murder*. And it's all my fault." Her fault? I waited, putting on my Totally Neutral face, an expression of absolute indifference I've cultivated so as to do nothing to either encourage or discourage the person sitting across from me. It's important that I hear it all: the craziness, the bizarre confessions, the monstrous lies that pour forth from that armchair by my desk. Mary took a large, loud gulp of air and went on. "If I hadn't been premenstrual . . . I mean, I get food on the brain. All I was thinking about was stuffing myself. How I was going to stop at BK and shove in a Double Whopper with cheese. And onion rings—they're so salty, I love 'em. I was thinking that I had to remember to buy those teeny Breath Asure things so Norman wouldn't know I'd been to BK, because he gets super PO'd when I eat junk food. And I was thinking about a vanilla shake too. Even french fries. I've never been a big potato person, so you can imagine how bad off I was. So when I left for Motor Vehicle I grabbed the Bob ID instead of the Dan ID. All the names he uses, I get mixed up, even though the last time he tested me I only got one wrong. If I'd've used Dan, they wouldn't have traced the car back to the apartment."

"They would have found him, though. His finger-prints were all over Bobette's place."

"But we could've gotten away once we knew the old lady was dead. The cops would've had to search every house on Long Island. They wouldn't have found us in time. Instead—" She started to cry again. "—they came and knocked on the door. And I opened it! I didn't even say 'Who's there?' If I'd've done that, Norm could've gotten out the back."

"When they're arresting someone on a murder charge, they usually have people staked out in back." But I didn't want to make her feel too comfortable. Since I couldn't get anything much from my client to help in my defense of him, I naturally decided to try Mary. She was feeling horribly guilty. Not for being an accessory before and after the fact to a crime—at best, fraud; at worst, homicide. No, she felt guilty for failing Norman.

"Take it easy," I said, and handed her a couple of tis-sues. (I keep a box in my top desk drawer so I can easily hand a bunch to a weepy client or, more commonly, a nonweepy, sociopathic client's hysterical family.) "Maybe we'll be able to do something for Norman."

"He told me it was hopeless, that the cops think he did it."

"They do. But that's why we have trial by jury. And that's why you've retained me. Maybe among all of us we can figure something out that will convince the jury that Norman is not guilty."

"He is *innocent*," Mary corrected me, and blew her nose. A too ladylike puff, not the HONK! a good-sized, healthy young woman would naturally produce. "He didn't do it!"

"Then help me find something so I can prove it."

"He left that house *one second* after that witness saw him with Bobette, and he came right home to me and we were together from then on. *Every minute* until the cops came."

"What was his relationship with Bobette?" I asked.

She drew up into a prim position, feet and knees together, hands in lap. "He said not to talk about anything."

"Why not?"

"Because . . . you know." I could think of several reasons, the main one being that he did indeed kill Bobette and was worried Mary would unintentionally give it away. If I were Norman, I'd be worried too. I couldn't tell if Mary was simpleminded or merely so new at grown-up life that she hadn't learned to lie without chewing the inside of her cheek and turning red. "Norman said: 'No matter who, keep your lip zipped, and I mean zipped *all the way* up.'"

"Look, I've been a lawyer too long to expect him to break down and confess to me—"

"He didn't do it!"

"Fine. But if I'm going to help him prove that, I need

all the information I can get, good or bad. I'd rather learn it from him than get a big surprise from the prosecutor." Then I added ominously: "She is one scary dame."

"Oh, God," Mary whimpered. She began to nibble her thumbnail. Instead of trying to allay her fear, I narrowed my eyes and flared my nostrils. Suddenly I became one scary dame too, which is what I wanted. I didn't relish going into court with Mary testifying to Norman's alibi. She'd turn to mush after thirty seconds on cross. Plus I sensed that Holly had one of those solid circumstantial cases that make defense lawyers like me pine for the good old days of being prosecutors—when the world was young and the facts were on our side. So I had to scare Mary into opening up. I also figured talking to her would be better than talking to Norman; with Mary, at least, I had a chance of hearing something resembling the truth. But she remained mum.

"Too bad you can't help him," I said, and pushed back my chair, as if I were about to stand to see her out. But she remained where she was, on the edge of her seat. She reached out and grabbed onto the desk, a huge old thing made from a farmhouse table. It looked as though she was trying to drag it toward her.

"If I talk to you," she asked me, "would you have to tell Norman?"

"Well . . ." I stalled. It was one of those questions only a chairman of a bar association ethics committee could love: Is an attorney's ethical obligation of full and complete disclosure of information to a client paramount? Or is counsel duty-bound to cork it if silence is what it costs to buy information that will save said client? "How about this, Mary? Unless it's a matter of life and death, I won't say a word to him. Okay?"

"Okay."

"Tell me about Norman and Bobette's relationship."

"Strictly business," she declared, with finality.

"Then how come she was found dead in a nightgown and negligee?"

"Maybe the murderer changed her clothes after he killed her!" she suggested, pleased with herself. For the first time, she allowed herself to wriggle back into the big armchair, lean back, and cross her legs. Her shoes were designed not for an unseasonably cold May morning but for a gala midsummer bash: Two narrow straps of gold just beyond her toes and another around her ankle were all that held them on. The heels were high gold daggers.

"The murderer didn't change her clothes," I said. "The autopsy would have indicated that Bobette had been moved postmortem. How come she was in her nightgown?" Mary chewed the inside of her cheek a little more, a buying-time mannerism I knew I would never grow to love. She could have said: Norman left before she changed out of her regular stuff. Or: She got into a sexy nightgown because her boyfriend—*the guy who killed her*—was coming over. I explained: "Norman was seen at her place at six-thirty in the evening. You said he left immediately after the man who is the witness saw him. So say that was at six forty-five." Mary inched forward. "From Merrick to your apartment . . . Fifteen, twenty minutes? Sometime around seven—daylight saving time—so it was still light outside, this lifelong spinster puts on a sexy negligee?"

"But he was with me the whole . . . " She sputtered to a halt. She didn't know what to say. Even if I spent weeks preparing her testimony, she'd be a lousy witness. Forget street smarts: She lacked the confidence to utter a simple declarative sentence and leave it alone. "I should say he was with me the whole time, shouldn't I?"

"If that's the truth," I said. "But I'd like to keep you

off the stand. You seem to get a little nervous when you're under the gun."

"You said it!" she agreed.

"So you can see why I need to know more about what was going on. I need something I can use to trip up the D.A."

"Right."

"So let's talk about Norman and Bobette—honestly."

Mary uncrossed her legs, blinked her lashes and opened her eyes wide. "Okay."

"You're telling me what went on between Norman and Bobette was strictly a business deal. If I know that's nonsense, can you imagine what Holly Nuñez, the assistant D.A., knows? She's had a whole squad of homicide cops investigating Norman Torkelson. Now, was he conning Bobette Frisch?" A little-girl shrug, head to the side. Her mannerisms were overly cutesy for such a tall woman. For such a beauty. Either she'd bloomed quite late in adolescence or her mother had been petite and revoltingly winsome. "That's a yes, he was conning her?"

"Uh . . . yes. But he wasn't having sex with her."

Right. "Really?"

"Really. I mean, he told me he *never* had sex with them, even before he met me. He said lonely women . . . " She wasn't so naive that she didn't know what Norman did was reprehensible. But it didn't seem to appall her; at that moment, she was just slightly unsure of how to present it. "Lonely women . . . "

"Say it straight."

"Lonely women . . . I *can't* say it. I can't think of the word. It means 'can't get enough.' "

"Insatiable?"

"That's it!" she squealed. "Hey, you and Norman should play Scrabble!"

" 'Lonely women are insatiable . . . ' " I prompted her.

"So if you start having sex, they'll milk you dry. I mean, if he was doing them, do you think he'd have time for me?"

"So he never goes near them?" I asked.

"He *cuddles* them," she explained serenely, the way Norman must have explained it to her: I know this sounds incredible, Mary, my angel, but it is the truth, and (he'd offer her a sad little shrug here) that's what I'm stuck with. "He holds them and gives them back rubs. Sometimes he'll kiss them, but a cheek kiss or a forehead kiss. Not a kiss kiss."

The drizzle turned to downpour. Raindrops smacked against the windowpane and were driven down diagonal paths by a sharp wind. At the same moment, Mary and I peered down at her feet, naked except for the flimsy gold shoes. They were not just big feet, but spread out, like a hod carrier's—if the hod carrier had given himself a pedicure with coral polish.

"How did Norman meet Bobette?" I asked.

"The usual way."

"You agreed to help me help Norman, Ms. Dean."

"Mary."

"Mary, I want to know everything you know."

"Okay. But I forgot what you just asked me."

"Where did he and Bobette meet?"

"Right! Um, through the personals. In *Newsday*."

"His ad or hers?"

"Oh, his. We use the same ad in every city, except with a different beginning. Like, we used 'Heart of my Heart' in Louisville and 'True Love is Precious Gift' in Scranton."

"On Long Island?"

" 'Looking for Love.' Norm says if any cops or private detectives are tracking him, they're not going to read the whole ad, but . . . You know what his motto is?"

"What?"

"You can't be too careful!" She proclaimed it with pride, throwing back her shoulders, holding her head high, the way a titan of industry's wife would reveal the slogan for a multi-million dollar advertising campaign for her husband's corporation.

"What else did the ad say? The part that was always the same."

" 'DWM'—that's divorced white man . . . Maybe the M is for male. Anyhow, 'DWM, thirty-five, handsome, tall Yale graduate, business executive, wants the real thing.' " Mary burst into a rich laugh. "Norman says: 'They don't know *my* real thing is their money.' Let's see . . . the real thing. Oh, 'You must enjoy Shakespeare's sonnets, beautiful music, travel, and long, romantic walks. Don't want dates. Want a relationship. Please respond with long letter and picture. Help me. I have a hole in my heart.' "

She waited expectantly, so I said: "I bet it worked like a charm."

My acknowledgment of Norman's literary gift seemed to please her. She smiled benevolently. "So then we, like, hang out and wait for the mail."

"Do you get a lot of it?"

"A ton! You wouldn't believe it. Then he makes a pitcher of martinis and I cut up teensy little cheese cubes and we read them and put them into piles."

"Such as."

"Garbage: Too young, living with family, student, low-pay job like waitressing. Or if she has kids or any family she has to take care of—unless it's a total vegetable relative. Then there's Too Pretty. We don't want someone who's using the personals just because she's bored with the guys she already has; she wouldn't be desperate enough. Too Smart: like doctors, lawyers. We watch out for real good vocabulary. Norm says: 'If I have to look up the words she uses in a dictionary, she's too smart for me.' Or a couple of times: women cops! We put the letters from Yale grads on the Too Smart pile too, because Norm could slip up and they'd know it. But you wouldn't believe their letters! They really oughta give a course there: How to Get a Guy. Then there are the Iffys: medium-paying jobs, but there's maybe a pension, or she might have put a lot in the bank. You know, like nurses, teachers. And then"—she paused to run the tip of her tongue across her upper lip; her voice grew husky— "there's Pay Dirt."

I wanted to take a hot bath, scrub off what I was hearing with a loofah and anti-bacterial soap. It wasn't so much the sordidness of what Mary was saying but the sheer pleasure with which she rolled around in the dirt. The mockery, the cruelty, the exultation. I buzzed Sandi and asked for a ginger tea to allay what I knew was incipient nausea. (Sandi and I had a beverage pact. Each time I buzzed her for something to drink, she got a day where she could leave fifteen minutes early. What else could a feminist, knee-jerk-liberal employer do? Naturally, I made the deal knowing that she is an obsessive-compulsive worker; in the six years she'd been with me, she'd left early twice.) "Who gets on the Pay Dirt pile?" I asked.

"Anyone with a fancy address. Norman does his homework and really knows where the rich neighborhoods are in each city we go to. Anyone who has a business. Like Bobette. Anyone who's been to Europe or on one of those cross-country tours. That's why he puts in about loving travel; if they've actually done it, it can spell m-o-n-e-y."

Mary told me that while there was no variation in the ads, Norman's responses to the letters he received were tailored to each woman. A little flattery here ("Fifty-one isn't old!"), a little bridled lust there ("I could not keep my eyes from that exquisite curve where your hand meets your wrist. Excuse me. I don't mean to be over-stepping the bounds. But I hope you'll forgive it if I say you look like you combine elegance and emotion, which is a *very* interesting combination, I must say"). From her wallet, she drew out copies of the photos he sent to them when he wrote them back. There were two. One in a suit and tie, sitting on the edge of a mahogany desk, his arms crossed across his chest, a Mona Lisa smile on his lips—what a *Business Week* centerfold might look like. The other in corduroys and a plaid shirt, a lock of his hair tumbling over his brow, his sleeves rolled up above his elbow, leaning against a tree in the middle of an autumn forest. Norman would decide from the tone of a woman's letter which photo to send.

"And then?" I asked.

Mary clapped her hands together, gleeful. "Well, a half hour before the first date, I go to the cocktail lounge or restaurant—Norman says, if they sound like they don't want to drink, meet them for lunch. It's what's called an expense of doing business. But some of these fatsos, they can order three courses, so no dinners. One of them once—"

"You work with Norman?" I asked, amazed that she had any active role in a confidence game. She struck me as someone who could get flustered inserting her card into an automatic teller machine.

"Sure."

"I didn't realize he had a business partner. You were saying that you show up about a half hour before he gets there. To make sure it isn't a setup?"

"Yes!" she said, delighted with my powers of deduction. "Norman says: 'You've got to cover your *a-s-s* in this business.'" Especially with a rap sheet like his, I thought. Where did he find this girl? Yes, I know: woman. But Mary was barely into her twenties. True, she didn't have it all, but she had a lot. Movie star beautiful—if she'd invest in a chisel and chip away those layers of makeup. A sweetie-pie manner. Well, until she spoke about Norman's crimes. Then something sexual, a throaty intensity I didn't want to hear, crept into her tone.

"On the first date, Norm lets the woman do the talking. I mean, you'd think they'd know they should draw the man out, but he said their talking is the key. They're desperate to talk, and he's such a great listener. You know why?"

She waited, so I asked, "Why?"

"Because he really *does* listen. Never forgets a thing. Never mixes up one with the other, even if he's working two at the same time, which he hardly ever does now. He says he used to do it when he was in his twenties but it knocked him out, the traveling back and forth and having to write double love letters and make double good-night-I-love-you and good-morning-I-love-you phone calls." She paused and cocked her head to the side. "Is this helping you?"

"It may." If I'd been a male lawyer, I probably would have delighted in her sitting across from me in that green suit, with coral toenails shining up at me. My partner, Chuckie, would have told her: You're a bright spot on such a dreary day, dear. But Mary was a blight on my landscape. I love my country lawyer's office, with its blue-and-white toile couch, and framed photos of the Long Island coast—real beauties—that my guy took; they hang on the wall next to my diplomas. True, I'm stuck in one of those awful modern suburban office buildings, white brick and tinted glass, its upper floors occupied by doctors and lawyers, its lower by upscale podiatrists and marginal software companies. But inside I'd made it comforting. With her garish kelly-green suit, Mary was jarring.

Why, you might ask, having comfortably chatted up multiple murderers and wife-batterers sitting in that very same blue-and-white-checked arm chair, did I so object to Mary Dean? I don't know—except to say that her girlish pride in Norman's cruelty to women had a rough sexual side that she didn't bother to hide. Forget hide: she flaunted it. What was with this dame that she was putting on this kind of show? "Tell me about the con," I said.

"Well, nothing on the first date," she said, sitting back in her chair, getting comfortable. "That's just to capture them. That's not the word, is it?"

"Captivate."

"Right!" She massaged the calf of her right leg in a way that, to a man, would be a come-on, but to a premenopausal woman was merely discomforting. Her mind wasn't on me, though. It was on Norman and the titillation of the con, and that made her every move self-aware, sensual. "So the next time, if things go okay, they're giving him dinner at their place. That's 'cause he talked about how down in the dumps he's gotten with TV dinners or eating out, and ninety-nine percent of the time they pick up on that. So he brings French wine and they talk and he tells about his divorce a little."

"Is this a real divorce?" I asked, wishing she'd stop feeling up her leg.

"Of course not!" Mary chuckled, amused, as if I'd made a dreadful faux pas. "He's never been married." Then her amusement faded. "We're supposed to be married, though. June first. A June wedding."

I didn't want to hear about how she was the first woman he had ever loved and how she was banking on me to get him off. "What does he tell his marks about a divorce?" I asked.

"That he'd built up a great little business. An investment advisory newsletter. See, that way they start asking him advice about their stocks and money stuff and he gets a fast idea of what they have and how much they know. But that he'd put his business in his wife's name and she won't give it back to him. The business is useless without him, but his wife let it go bust. He tells them she was from a rich family, so it didn't matter to her. She just wanted to hurt him." She lifted a limp lock of hair from her shoulder and began spooling it between her index fingers, as if rolling a pin curl.

"And he did this with Bobette? She made him dinner?"

"Yes. Yankee pot roast. Norm said it was really yucky pot roast. Then he told her about the business and showed her pictures of his kids. Boy pictures from a wallet he lifted in a mall in Chicago. He's not a pickpocket or anything, but if someone's buying stuff and leaves a wallet on the counter, he'll take it, 'cause he sometimes finds good family pictures. This last one was excellent. It had a few pictures of the same two boys, so he kept one for his wallet and had the others blown up and put in picture frames. They look *so* real."

"He doesn't use the credit cards he takes?"

"No. He says it's too risky. But he uses the ID, just not in the state he lifted it."

"So he showed her the boy pictures." She nodded too hard. I realized that it was a gimmick, to show off her bobbing curls. "Any reason why not girl pictures?" I, mother of a daughter, asked.

"Name one woman in the world who'd want a stepdaughter! A stepson isn't so bad, and these are two cute boys. One's in a Little League uniform. Norman named one Joey and the other Whatever-name-Norman's-using, junior."

"What does he do after that?" I pressed on.

"Nothing till the third date. That's at the Love Nest."

"What's the Love Nest?"

"A little furnished place we take. Not for us. We have our own place. The Love Nest's for him and the mark. See, Norman always used to use one place with his girl-friends and the marks, but then the girlfriends used to have to get out whenever the marks were coming over. And they'd have to hide a big suitcase or a Hefty bag filled with all their stuff in the car trunk, so the mark wouldn't get wise. When I started working with Norm, that's what I had to do." She smiled and blushed like a happy bride. "But then he said he couldn't take me hav-ing to live like that, so the last few times, we got a cheap place for the Love Nest. He tells them it's till he gets back on his feet. He worried it might be too crummy and would turn them off, but . . . Do I have to say it? Nothing turns them off."

"Where is this Love Nest?" I asked.

"In Manhasset. It's not all *that* bad, except the toilet seat has a big chip on the side and it looks like—you know—caked-on poo."

"When does he use the Love Nest?"

"Not too often, but he has to show he has a place. And so I can call about repossessing his car." I waited. "See," she went on, "we have this thing. He goes to the bathroom at exactly nine twenty-five. That's when I call and leave a message on his answering machine, except the volume is way up: 'Mr. Whatever-name, this is Ms. McDonald, calling on behalf of Pinnacle Collections Agency.'" Mary's voice took on a clipped edge that was annoyed, almost angry. "'Listen, unless you can come up with the money for your car, it is going to be forfeited as per your former wife's judgment against you. We've been more than patient, Mr. Whatever-name.' "

Usually I'm pretty good at figuring out scams, but this one took me a minute, and I needed help. "The mark hears the message and . . . "

"Norman acts all embarrassed. But then he pretends to open up to her. He shows her a picture of his car. A Jaguar XJS convertible. Sometimes a Mercedes E320. We go out for test drives, and I take a picture of him with the top down."

Then I had it. "So the mark thinks he is in love with this car."

"Yes. Well, he does love cars. Really and truly. Anyway, he cries when he talks about his car. He tells them it symbolizes the whole divorce, everything he's lost."

"And so to make him happy, she knows she has to ante up thirty or forty thousand to get back his car for him?"

"Oh, they cost more than forty!" She smiled at my ignorance. "Buy them back or help him buy it back. But that doesn't happen that night or anything. I mean, he just keeps seeing them all the time. By the beginning of the third week, he says he wishes he was in a position to get serious with her. By the end of that week, she's ready to go to the bank. But he holds off. He says: 'I absolutely will not allow any such thing.' "

"So how long does it take before he lets himself be convinced?"

"Another two weeks." I must have shown surprise that it took that long, because she explained. "That way, they fall so hopelessly in love that when he gets the money and goes to get the car, they don't—you know—get it. He calls to say he's tied up with the paperwork and then—bingo! We're out of there. Meanwhile . . . " I think she understood that good taste would preclude a delighted grin, but it kept trying to break through. Her eyes sparkled. "They wait for *days* before they figure it out and call the cops."

I said: "I guess you know that with a marriage con, a lot of marks never call the cops at all. They're too humiliated."

"Too in love!" she said brightly. "They can't believe that he'd run off because he's such a great actor. I mean, I tell him I think he half falls for each one of those turkeys, 'cause otherwise he couldn't convince them that it was so real." Her voice softened and grew silky. "I've never met a woman who didn't love him. I mean, even if they meet him for just a second. The lady in the Chinese laundry. The ticket lady at the movies." She eyed me as if she expected me to wave my hand in the air and shout: Me too! When I didn't oblige, she added: "It's like he has a magic wand. I remember something I read, like from a fairy tale. Or maybe from a paperback: 'She was powerless to resist him.' I mean, there's no woman alive who can resist Norman. There are some men like that. With me, I fell in two seconds. He could have just tossed me aside after that night."

"But he didn't."

"He said he never knew what love meant till he met me." The gleam in her eyes turned to moisture. A single tear was detained by a mascara roadblock. Maybe this particular tear wasn't out of adoration, though, but out of fear. Mary's features froze as if she'd been on film and the final credits were meant to roll over that expression. Maybe she realized how brutal the con was, how it showed the depths of Norman's hatred of women. Did she honestly believe her beauty exempted her? Or did she sense that she, too, was Norman's victim? Had she been secretly afraid he would use her and then sneak out on her one night?

"Where were you going to get married?"

"The next city. He said Boston. He hadn't worked Boston for over ten years. I said: '*Boston*? Like maybe Miami Beach for a honeymoon?' He said all those rich old widows down there were too smart about cons. They almost expect it. But he said we'd just get away from Long Island after Bobette was done and figure it out."

"What did he do with Bobette's money?" I asked.

"He never got it! He was still working on her." But I knew that Bobette had taken out forty-eight thousand dollars the afternoon of the day she was murdered. Mary went on: "Norman said Bobette was one tough nut, but once he got through her shell . . . "

"What?"

"He could tell. She was going to be real juicy!"

Six

✕

Catholics say that a child of seven has attained the age of reason. Not being Catholic, there was no reason for Sylvia White to know of this milestone. Still, she was vaguely aware that a seventh birthday had significance. So she redecorated Lee's bedroom.

Down came the wallpaper with the pastel lambs, off came the yellow-and-white gingham bedspread. A shaggy persimmon carpet was laid. A couch covered in a heavy baby-pink cotton with a design of interlocking triangles of raspberry and burnt orange was brought in to serve as a bed.

For the prepubescent daughters of the aggressively upwardly mobile, a pink-and-orange palette was not unheard-of in the annals of 1950s interior decoration, but on the North Shore of Long Island, Lee's room was the first of its coloration. It earned Sylvia kudos from the group of fashionable suburban women who were her friends: "I'm speechless. Gorgeous!" "I couldn't

believe . . . pink and orange! And it works. That Sylvia
. . . gifted." "Beyond gifted: an artist!"

Aesthetics is rarely an issue with a second grader,
but it had to be for Lee. She missed her pastel lambs.
However, since she had, indeed, reached the age of
reason, she understood what really mattered to her
parents: clothes first, furniture second. She was a quick
study. A stylistic faux pas would invariably provoke a
fierce reaction—what she thought of as Mommy's Mad
Breathing, a snort of annoyance amplified by smoker's
phlegm. It didn't take her long to figure out how to
avoid it. When her mother would thrust, say, a swatch
of tangerine polished cotton under her nose and
demand: "What do you think?," she learned first to
check which expression Sylvia was wearing—the "Ick"
or the "I love it"—and then to respond accordingly.

Not that Lee was a submissive child. Far from it. But
having figured out that her mother cared primarily
about appearances, all Lee needed to do to be deemed
a dutiful daughter was to use her nailbrush, say "Thank
you" frequently, smile a lot, and cede to Sylvia all
decisions about clothes and interior design. Silence on
the subject of the day's barrettes seemed not too great
a price to pay for freedom. Then she was on her own.
No clandestine nocturnal cookie retrievals for this kid.
No oxygen deprivation under the covers to hide book
and flashlight. Lee could gorge on Mallomars. No one
would stop her from reading and rereading *The
Bobbsey Twins' Merry Days Indoors and Out* till the
wee hours in the bright circle of light from a one-
hundred-watt bulb beneath a pumpkin-color glass
shade shaped like a coolie hat that hung over her bed.

By age seven, Lee realized (as she sat on Sylvia's
pièce de résistance, a lounge chair shaped like an
amoeba, covered with an apricot-and-shocking-pink

awning-stripe fabric) that deference to her mother's fashion whims was the best way, actually the only way, to have fun with her mother. A trip to the city to buy a new spring coat and Mary Janes could be a laugh-filled lark: a "just us girls" lunch in a restaurant with aqua tablecloths and hot popovers; making fun of Ick dresses, like the one with cherries pinned on the bosom at Best & Company; dropping in on Daddy's fur store, where Mommy tried on all the new styles and Dolly gave her a piece of chinchilla to stroke. She understood that saying "Gosh!" when her mother modeled a three-quarter-length silver fox was politically wise. It showed that Lee knew what was important in life—fur and style—and it made her whiny, I-want-to-go-home little sister look even worse.

At age four, Robin Renée White had traded in the infantile digestive irritability that had kept her awake and screaming twenty hours a day for a permanent colic of the personality. Nothing made her truly happy. She never giggled. The company of other children made her edgy. Playground noise gave her headaches. She could become agitated by a game of Candyland. Of course, there were times—listening to "Bibbidi-Bobbidi-Boo" on her *Cinderella* record, cutting out dresses for paper dolls—that Robin's lovely heart-shaped face took on a touchingly soft expression. Sylvia and Leonard would glance at each other and exhale a sign of relief: Maybe the worst is over. Maybe now we can have the photographer come back and she'll smile and not wail in terror—"Oooo! Wooo!"— when the flashbulb goes off. (In fairness to Robin, it should be noted that on these rare occasions when her taut nerves relaxed and she began to smile, Lee was not beyond sneaking up from behind the moment Sylvia and Leonard's backs were turned and poking

Robin hard and fast in the ribs, causing the little girl to lose the little equanimity she possessed and break into demented screams.)

Still, Robin was competition. No doubt about it. She was far prettier than Lee, if one's definition of pretty is huge eyes in a waiflike face, and a rosebud of a mouth. Her daintiness was memorable. Lee was the sturdy sort: Her body was saved from the inevitable consequences of Mallomars only because she had picked up a stray gene for athleticism. (That particular gene had last turned up in the girls' great-great-grand-father on their father's side, who was the fastest runner in exurban Pinsk—a not unwelcome talent, considering the proclivities of the neighboring peasants.) Otherwise, Lee was generic Girl. Her brown braided hair was neither straight enough to gleam in the sun-light nor curly enough to render her adorable. Her fea-tures were certainly pleasant but not singular enough to be remarked upon.

Robin was also smarter than Lee, if intelligence can be measured by standardized intelligence tests, age of onset of reading readiness, and ability to view long division as an intriguing process rather than an afflic-tion. But that would come later. At four, smart little Robin had a tendency to make derisive tsk-tsk noises whenever her seven-year-old sister expressed an opin-ion—a frequent occurrence. That Lee merely ignored this scorn and kept on talking was an early, conspicu-ous, and of course unheeded sign that she was cut out to be a litigator.

From her lounge chair by the window, Lee could see the downward swoop of the lawn, the kidney-shaped swimming pool in its summer turquoise splendor. (The Whites' house itself, a not ungraceful assemblage of wood, fieldstone, and glass rectangles, designed by an architect who had studied under an architect who had worked for Frank Lloyd Wright in 1937, sat on two acres of velvet green lawn.) Lee could see, beyond the cabana—an overpriced shed with two changing rooms and a wet bar—that her mother was creating art. Or trying to.

Sylvia White was living disproof of the myth of Jewish intellectual superiority. She had scant imagination, hardly any curiosity, and only basic intuitive smarts. What she had was style. She looked smart. She was always a pleasure to behold—even in rolled-up, paint-stained cut off khakis and the old white oxford shirt of Leonard's she used for painting. Her honey-colored hair was tied back in a blue bandanna, so if a stiff breeze came along, it would not blow her hair onto the wet canvas that stood on the easel before her.

The painting! From where Lee was sitting, it looked as if Sylvia was stabbing her picture. But Lee understood that her mother was making leaves on the sycamore she'd been attempting to capture for the last three months, stippling green on naked gray-brown branches with the flat of her brush. Pow, pow, pow, went the brush. Lee was too far away to make out the details of the canvas, although she had already seen enough of her mother's work to know the truth: lousy. Even a seven-year-old child with almost no artistic ability could tell that Sylvia's trees were flat, lifeless things. Ditto with Sylvia's still lifes—orange sections and a hammer, a vase of flowers beside a hatbox . . . to say nothing of her portrait of Duchess, the collie. Sylvia had hung that one over the fireplace in the living room. Lee watched her father sneaking fast, abashed glances at it. A couple of months later, it was taken down and replaced with a picture of black squiggles that she heard her father say, not without pride, cost enough to float a battleship.

Thus, at the age of reason, Lee had already grasped her mother's mediocrity and deduced that she cared deeply only about superficialities. Well, with one exception. Lee recognized that there was a single genuine passion in her mother's life: her father.

As Leonard's coolness toward Sylvia changed to complete detachment (on the way to coldness), as he turned his attention to Le Fourreur and his model/bookkeeper/lover, Dolly Young, his wife's ardor for him grew. It was a perfect inverse proportion. Lee observed her mother's eyes devouring her father as he brushed barbecue sauce on spare ribs—so many brush strokes that it was clear to Lee that his mind was on something other than pork. She observed her mother's coquettishness—her kiss on the back of his neck while he was watching his first *Meet the Press* on the new TV in the den, her curling up on the lounge chair beside him when he was reading the Sunday paper by the pool. All Sylvia's come-ons seemed to arouse was irritation. Still, the woman clearly could not help herself. Watching her mother get ready for her father's return from work, reworking her hairdo, putting on another dot of liquid rouge and spreading it over her cheek, like a caress, fiddling with the neckline of a peasant blouse—taking it off her shoulders, back up, letting it slip off one shoulder, tugging on it to bare a bit of bosom, Lee knew without a doubt that Sylvia was capable of feeling.

So how come she could not spare a little extra? Not that Lee consciously asked that question: Why is a privileged American woman incapable of the same devotion to her young as the average hyena? It was a good question. But at seven (and fourteen and probably even at twenty-one), even the most analytical child cannot answer it satisfactorily. It boils down to this:

Her mother does not love her because she is, indeed, unlovable.

But at least there was some tenderness, a little physical affection in Lee's life. She received it once a month, during visits from her father's parents, Nat the Commie and Big Bella.

To be hugged by three-hundred-pound Grandma Bella ("How are you, my beautiful, vonderful tootsie-pie?") was to risk suffocation between those two monstrous marshmallows that were her grandmother's breasts. To have your hair tousled in gratitude by Grandpa Nat because you snuck upstairs and emptied your piggy bank (so, he explained, you could give your seventeen dollars and forty-four cents to Deserving Negro Children Down South) was to risk baldness.

It was worth the risk. Humans are, after all, warmth-seeking creatures. However, once a month is not enough, and the Weissbergs' visits to the Whites were marred by terrible tension: Leonard's face turning ashen, then livid, almost blue, at the sound of his mother's voice ("You're such a big shot, sveetheart, you can't kiss your mudder anymore?"). Sylvia's appalled expression upon spotting her father-in-law's white, hairless, skinny bowed legs in red Bermuda shorts. Inevitably, being a quick-witted girl, Lee realized she was not getting her birthright—love—from her elegant, well-modulated parents. Why not? Weren't they supposed to offer love without qualification? And how come her grandparents, who *were* willing to give it, made her parents almost sick?

But if the classical psychologists are correct, it is the mother who is the key figure in a child's life. Lee, while no stranger to self-examination as an adult, never had a clue as to how many stratagems she employed throughout her childhood to try and woo this woman who stood, at that moment in 1957, five hundred feet away, before a dreadful painting of a very beautiful tree.

For the sake of fairness and in the interests of feminism, however, let us not make Sylvia Bernstein Weissberg-Weiss-White the villain. First, there are worse people in this story. A lot worse. And second, even if we accept as true the notion that the mother is the star in a child's firmament, Sylvia was one of two parents. If she was dysfunctional, how come the other parent could not step in and function a little? Did Leonard think four trips to the zoo, an occasional excursion to Carvel, and bedtime readings of *Madeline* when Lee had chicken pox made him a good father?

Did he honestly believe that all he had to do to be a good family man was pay for his daughters' ballet lessons and not divorce his wife and marry his mistress? Leonard knew better. He *felt* better, experiencing occasional surges of love for his children that came straight from his heart. But those times, when Lee's prowess at crab-apple tree climbing filled him with great fear and greater elation, or when Robin's exegesis of Jerry Lewis's role in *The Delicate Delinquent* made him proud, and he grabbed her, hugged her and covered her with kisses, he unfailingly sensed a change in Sylvia. He'd look up: No, nothing, just a wide Isn't-that-just-the-sweetest? smile. But (was it his imagination?) the smile seemed a touch too broad, so even her back teeth were on display. So he merely unwrapped the little girl's arms from around his neck, gave her a friendly wink and a pat on the backside, and sent her off for another year or two.

Beyond Sylvia's easel, where the well-fertilized lawn ended, was a hundred-foot-wide strip of trees that, in full leaf, gave the illusion that the Whites' property was baronial, backing up onto a great forest. But from her second-story window, Lee could see it wasn't so. The land rose about forty feet, then leveled off at the beginning of Hart's Hill. Yes, a house with a name. Not that Lee could see it from her window, but she knew it was there. An estate. The estate next door.

Hart's Hill got its name in the late eighteenth century from the deer that roamed the north shore of Long Island. These noble mammals (albeit hopelessly tick-ridden) seemed drawn to that particular promontory. They grazed that very spot where, in 1757, 1820, and 1898, the manor house would be built. (The first house was destroyed by a fire in the hearth that claimed one Mrs. Rebecca Taylor as well as the rum syllabub she was preparing. The second was razed by a Mr. Arthur Taylor and the third erected by same after he made his second million in attorney's fees advising Edward Harriman during Harriman's acquisition of the Union Pacific Railroad.)

But before all this construction and upward mobility put an end to the noble hart, a real deer could wander right to that place. Its coat glowing red in the sunlight, a stag might gaze northward across the stern gray waters of Long Island Sound to look upon the dark-green forests of mainland America.

The Taylors of Hart's Hill themselves weren't much given to gazing, at least by the time their neighbor, young Lee White, became aware of them. They were too busy. Foster Taylor had left the Manhattan law firm of Willoughby, Crane and Buffet to serve on the United States Olympic Committee; he was also a trustee of the Boy Scouts of America, the American Bobsledding Association, the Iron Lung Alliance, and A Mighty Fortress, a traveling Episcopal goodwill choir. Georgina, his wife, was known as Ginger. It was said that if

she hadn't gotten married in her sophomore year at
Hollins and then gotten pregnant (the events actually
occurred in reverse order), she could have been a professional tennis player. In addition to her daily work-
outs on the grass court at Hart's Hill, Ginger raised
and showed basenjis, dogs that are inherently neigh-
bor-pleasing since they do not bark. However, they do
defecate, and entire broods of basenji puppies would
often scamper down the hill and leave odoriferous
brown lumps among the phlox in Sylvia's all-white
garden.

Foster and Ginger were tall and lissome. Each carried two rare recessive genes that suppressed fat on
thighs and upper arms, which they passed down to all
their four children, so the younger Taylors, too, grew up
tall and lean-limbed. And handsome, with their
mother's finely wrought features and their father's high
color. Since Fos and Ginger were an effervescent couple, finding hilarity in everything from bobbing for
apples to knock-knock jokes, they had a real belly
laugh when they realized their initial initials were right
next to each other in the alphabet. F for Foster! Ha-ha-
ha! G for Georgina. Ho-ho-ho! So they named their
children Hope, Irene, Jasper, and Kent. (They might
have gone on to Lawrence, Melanie, and even
Nathaniel, but Kent was born retarded, and Foster
thought that sort of killed the fun, Kent's not getting the
joke.)

Unlike the basenjis, the Taylors did not scamper
down the hill. In fact, while they were vaguely aware
that someone had built a modern house on the property beneath them, they remained happily unconscious
of the Whites' existence.

The same cannot be said for the Whites. There was
not one single day that Leonard did not think of the

Taylors. As with a man haunted by a lost love, the most oblique reference could evoke their presence. Words: *athlete, hill, tennis, old money, lawyer, rich,* and *Olympic* made him dizzy with a mixture of desire and fury. Sights: a sailboat in the background of a Philip Morris ad; a church steeple; a dog (in fact, even Duchess, instead of barking and scaring away the little fuckers, seemed to view the basenjis' excretory activities with an admiration approaching awe). Fos Taylor, himself standing on the platform of the Shorehaven station, holding his *Herald Tribune* at arms' length to compensate for his farsightedness, or giving his train pals (whom Leonard thought of as the Taylor Boys) his idiosyncratic greeting, a stiff military salute, but using only his index finger. One time, he'd given that salute to Leonard—or so Leonard had thought. An explosion of joy went off inside Leonard, so powerful that it knocked him senseless. Somehow he managed a crisp salute in return. He thought: I've been tapped. (Tapped! what a wonderful word!) I'm one of the Boys. A second later, he saw Fos's eyes blink-blink-blink at the wrongness of his, Leonard's, behavior and he knew . . . Turning around, he spotted one of the Taylor Boys right behind him, the fat one, who looked like an overblown Audie Murphy balloon. "Sorry," Leonard began gamely, "I thought you were saying hello to . . . " Yes, he knew all about how crazy they were for acting as if nothing was bothering you even if you were in the middle of an A-bomb detonation, but by that time, Fos and Fat Boy had somehow managed to move off sideways. Not only that: They were saluting Paper Boy, the one who got on the train every day with the *Times,* the *Trib,* the *Journal-American,* and the *Wall Street Journal.* They were grinning too, as if they couldn't wait to tell him something hysterical.

Smells: The odor of dog shit enraged him. Once, he had to restrain himself from grabbing the leash of a toy poodle from a woman on Lexington Avenue, just down from Le Fourreur, and strangling her with it. In his mind, he could picture the skin of her neck reddening, puckering under the leather leash, and it gave him pleasure, as did imagining the squoosh sound as he pushed her dying body into the tiny brown pile her shitty little dog had made.

Sounds: The *thwomp!* of tennis balls from the Taylors' court moved him to melancholy to wrath and back again. The Taylors were a large family, and each member seemed to have a hundred friends who played, so *thwomp!* went on from seven on Saturday mornings to dusk on Sundays. Once, when Sylvia's parents were over for Mother's Day, the Judge had whispered: "Your neighbors play a lot of tennis, don't they?" Leonard became disconsolate. All he could do was nod. Then he excused himself and went into his bedroom, locked the door, and called Dolly, breaking his own No Contact on Weekends rule. They talked dirty for two and a half hours, until Sylvia banged on the door. "Leonard? What are you doing in there? Is anything wrong?" He didn't bother covering the mouthpiece. He never did. He had no secrets from Dolly. "It's Jack Feldman, Syl. You know, from Siberian Sable. They had a warehouse fire. Please, I can't get off the phone now." Sylvia apologized and went back to put on the charcoal herself.

Actually, Leonard did have one secret from Dolly. He knew she was game for anything, but although he was dying to play Mr. and Mrs. Taylor, he didn't have the courage to suggest it. How he wanted to put on that accent from Princeton or wherever and be Fos ("Ginger, dahling, I am not like all those other chaps on crew, am I?"). Dolly would be Ginger, which was not such a stretch, since she was actually slender as a reed. But as powerful as Leonard's desire was, so was his fear that, knowing this about him, Dolly, if she turned against him, could blackmail him for everything he had. And he would give it to her, that's how horrible it would be if anyone found out his secret.

Of course, if he left Sylvia and married Dolly, they could play Fos and Ginger all the time. So how come he didn't? Ah! That was one more secret Leonard kept from Dolly: that he would never marry her. Even if he could get free without Sylvia killing herself, which he doubted, and even though he loved Dolly with all his heart, he knew she wasn't good enough for him. She was trying to be, taking French lessons at Hunter at night and going to matinees on Saturday; she had seen almost every play on Broadway and could discuss them very intelligently. She was taking riding lessons in Central Park. But if something terrible happened and Sylvia died and he was free, he wouldn't marry Dolly. He would want the real thing.

Seven-year-old Lee, of course, knew nothing about her father's affair, although in the intuitive way of smart children, she knew there was something fishy going on with Dolly. Why was Dolly so inexhaustibly wonderful to her? Dolly would practically gasp with delight on those rare occasions when Leonard brought Lee to work with him. "Lee! What a surprise!" she would gush, and then look toward Leonard: "Please, Mr. White, would it be okay if I took Lee out for an ice cream sundae?" And her father would consent. When they'd get to Schrafft's, Dolly would ask Lee what seemed like hundreds of questions about second grade and about Robin and her mother. And no matter what she said, Dolly was thrilled. Even if she said something stupid, like: "Uh, gee, I dunno what my favorite color is." Dolly was very sweet, and always looked beautiful and smelled like flowers, but the child wished she'd just shut up so Lee could concentrate on her sundae. Peach ice cream with hot fudge, whipped cream, and a cherry, although they were a little cheap with the fudge this time. Lee hoped Dolly would notice and ask her if she wanted more, and she'd say: Maybe just a teeny bit. But then the man behind the counter would think she looked like a real nice girl and feel awful she'd gotten so little hot fudge, so he'd give her two— no, three—of those big spoons full. But instead Dolly was waiting for her to say something. Oh. Favorite color. "Uh, yellow. No, red." Dolly would gasp: "Red! I can't believe it! I love red too!"

Actually, even though Lee knew Dolly's delight in her was, well, phony, she liked Dolly. It was wonderful to sit there with someone who felt you were important enough to fake pleasure in your presence. With her mother . . .

It had never been good. True, Lee was clever enough to know that when her mother brought home a box that said Tailored Woman and took out a suit or a dress, she had to say: "Mommy! That's beautiful!" Not only that: Having gone through all that trouble, Sylvia wasn't really satisfied unless her daughter added something original—and cute. But what qualified as cute? One time, as her mother took a yellow chiffon dress from its tissue-paper bed and held it up against her to model it, Lee asked: "Mommy, can I have that dress when you die?" Her parents thought that was very cute, or, her father's new word for cute, "droll." So the next time her mother got something—a Balenciaga coat—she asked if she could have the coat when her mother died. This time, though, her mother snapped:

"Stop it!" So she had to think up something else cute. It was very tiring, or, as her father said, "wearing," to be droll all the time, because her mother bought something new nearly every day.

And if she wasn't cute, her mother wasn't happy with her. Not angry, to be fair. Not mean. Just . . . bored. Her mother found her boring because the things Lee found interesting—the collie, her new bike with training wheels, her *Madeline* book, and thinking about what she was going to get for lunch—her mother had no interest in.

But Lee was determined to win over her mother. Just then, gazing down from her window, she noticed her mother setting down the paintbrush. Why was she doing that? Oh, there: It was Ethel, the latest live-in maid, walking across the lawn, bringing out Robin after her nap. Through the open window, Lee could hear a faint "Mimmy," as Robin cried out for Sylvia. (Lee knew this was a bad sign for Ethel, because by forcing Robin onto Sylvia, Ethel was Not Taking Responsibility, which meant Sylvia would talk to Leonard and Leonard would fire Ethel first thing Saturday morning. Firing maids made him very crabby, so it would be a bad weekend.)

"Mimmy!" Robin's voice wasn't so high that it made you cover your ears, but its pitch worked its way through your semicircular canals and into your head and grated your nerves; a few more "Mimmy"s, and Sylvia's and Ethel's teeth would start grinding. Nonetheless, Lee had to admit Robin's curls were golden. Even more ominous, Lee realized, Robin was showing dangerous signs of Fashion Smartness. Just the other day, sitting on the kitchen floor, she'd pulled on the ribbon of Sylvia's espadrilles and said: "Pretty!" Sylvia's color had gone all rosy, and she'd laughed and said: "Yes. Pretty and *very* expensive." Lee jumped out of the apricot-and-pink lounge chair and raced downstairs.

By the time she got across the backyard, Robin was sitting on the grass and whimpering. "What's wrong?" Sylvia was demanding, her hands on her hips, her brush dripping dark-green paint onto the grass. At the sound of her mother's displeasure, Robin's whimpering changed to whining. While this did not displease Lee, she did understand that the short, sharp spikes of grass on which Ethel had plopped her sister were prickling the little girl's legs. So Lee hauled Robin up, drew her over to the swing set, and sat her on the glider. "Thanks, sweetie," her mother called out, and went back to her painting.

It was a lazy August afternoon. Now and then a bird tweeted or a bee buzzed on its way to Sylvia's rose arbor. Lee sat across from her sister and glided, slowly, so as not to scare Robin. Day camp was over, third grade was two weeks away, her best friend, Dorie, was visiting her grandmother in New Jersey, and she'd torn up her paper dolls and flushed them away because her mother had said: No more toys. You have the nice paper dolls. Lee had come to her and said: I can't find the paper dolls. Unfortunately, her mother had found a paper leg (wearing paper Capri pants) floating in the toilet bowl and Lee was being punished with no Ed Sullivan on Sunday.

"Want to go inside and play with my dollhouse?" Lee asked Robin.

"No."

"Want to put on our bathing suits?" Lee tried to make it sound like the opportunity of a lifetime. "Turn on the sprinkler?" Her voice reached heights of delight. "Run in and—"

"No!"

"Want to color?"

"No."

"In my Peter Pan coloring book, Robin. You can use my crayons."

Robin started to climb off the glider. Quickly, Lee brought it to the fastest, smoothest halt she could. Still, Robin fell onto the ground and went screeching back to Sylvia. "Mimmy!" Sylvia slammed her brush into a can, threw Lee a dirty look, and, grabbing Robin by the wrist, half led, half dragged her to the patio.

The chairs, made of white wire mesh and resembling a cupped hand, were parts of an ensemble of metal outdoor furniture Leonard had ordered from France. They left funny marks on the backs of your legs if you were wearing shorts, Lee knew, but they were comfortable. Her mother lit up a cigarette, closed her eyes, and smoked. When she exhaled, she pursed her lips into a little bird mouth. Robin, seeing her mother's eyes safely shut, brought her foot up to her mouth and started biting her toenails. "Stop it!" Lee mouthed, but Robin ignored her. Lee closed her eyes, leaned back in the wire chair, and smoked an imaginary Pall Mall, breathing out a perfect thin column of smoke.

So neither Lee nor Sylvia noticed when Robin slipped out of her chair and headed toward the swimming pool. The gardener had finally oiled the gate of the white iron fence surrounding the pool (after receiving a nasty note from Leonard on the subject, enclosed with the monthly check), so neither Lee nor Sylvia heard a thing when Robin reached up and, with remarkable dexterity, flipped up the childproof latch. And of course, when Robin walked down the four steps into the pool, there was not a sound, because by the time her feet reached the bottom of the pool, the water was over her head.

Peril ought to be accompanied by the roar of a tidal wave or the screech of metal crushing metal in a car crash. Not by silence. Sylvia smoked on. But Lee opened her eyes. Something was not right. What? Oh, the absence of Robin crying, sniveling, or even shuffling. Lee swiveled her head, checking out the field-stone wall of the house, the swings, the perennial garden, the woods that rose up the hill.... But she couldn't spot the buttercup color of her sister's playsuit. Lee climbed out of the wire chair. "Mommy."

"Shhh."

"Mommy, where's Robin?" Sylvia, sluggish from the heat, listless with boredom occasioned by her own art, shrugged and inhaled deeply. It must be said that she did not comprehend the import of Lee's question. Without malice, it can be said Sylvia was in another world: picturing how to achieve the most drama in an arrangement of pineapples, grapes, and melons for a fruit platter she was planning for a Labor Day pool party. A flash of yellow caught Lee's eye.

In an instant, she flew across the crew-cut lawn to the pool. Before her mother had a clue that anything had gone wrong, Lee White opened the pool gate and took a step into the pool. Robin was in the shallow end, but too far to reach from the steps. Another step down. The water was overheated. It lapped around her calves and felt awful, almost hot. The stench of chlorine was so strong, as if it were masking some other, terrible smell. She should get out, call her mother. "You're not the boss of Robin," her mother was always telling her. "*I* am. Leave her alone." One more step, up to her waist. She could dog-paddle, but then what could she do about Robin? She couldn't grab her and swim with just one hand, could she? Robin was right at the spot where the shallow part got deep, over both their heads, so she'd be stuck out there too.

"Mommy!" Lee called, but Sylvia didn't hear her.

Robin was just floating there. No, not quite floating, because she was a little bit under the water. Not moving, her arms held out, limp, as if she were pretending to be a dead bird. Was this what drowning was? In the cartoons, you always hear "Heeeelp! Save me!" But not a sound, except the *glub-glub* of bubbles from the pool filter. Drowning? Yes!

And what could a seven-year-old child do? Run get her mother? Dial O and say, the way they taught you in school: "This is an emergency. My stupid sister is drowning"? There was nothing to do. Which was when the nascent trial lawyer took over and, nevertheless, *did*. Lee plunged forward into the water, swimming over to her sister. Dog-paddle, dog-paddle, she thought. Uh-oh, I'm in over my head. I could drown. I'm not allowed out this far. Keep going. Dog-paddle.

Like Lassie. So Lee thrust her head forward and, with her teeth, grabbed the yellow playsuit—and, in doing so, dragged her little sister out of the jaws of death.

Sylvia, roused by the splash of the paddling, was there when Lee brought Robin up the stairs. "Oh God!" Sylvia screamed over and over. "My baby! Oh, God." Shut up, Lee thought, as her mother, shrieking, grabbed Robin away from Lee, as if Lee had done something wrong. "Oh, God in heaven!" Sobbing, Sylvia held the limp child so tight that, through sheer luck, she squeezed some of the water out of Robin's esophagus. The child regurgitated up the rest all over her mother, to Lee's satisfaction. "What happened?" Sylvia cried, a question directed toward God more than Lee, planting anguished kisses over the little girl's head and face.

"She went into the pool," Lee explained.

"Why didn't you stop her?"

"I didn't see her."

Now that Robin was coughing and gagging and clearly alive, Sylvia laid her gently on the flagstone pool deck and, weeping, almost silently, crouched over and dipped her forearms into the pool to wash off the vomitus. She rubbed and rubbed, then sniffed her skin and pulled her head back in disgust.

"Mim—" Robin gasped.

"Baby," Sylvia said, taking the child back into her arms, although admittedly averting her nose from the stench.

"Mimmy."

"Baby."

Lee turned and walked back into the house. Neither her mother nor her sister noted her departure or her absence. And that would have been that, except for Ethel, the eighth maid to whom Sylvia had said, upon hiring her: I hope you'll soon be a member of the family. On being fired by Leonard that Saturday, Ethel, twenty-three years old and up from Macon, Georgia, knowing there was more to the world than picking peaches, and not willing to take any guff from a white man who had just told her she was Not Willing to Do Her Fair Share, told him he was a mean ole dog with a ninny for a wife—

"I've heard enough!" Leonard shouted at her.

—and he should tell his girlfriend not to wear so much makeup because it came off on his shirts, even if the ninny didn't see it, and did he know Lee saved her little sister's life when the ninny fell asleep and the baby almost drowneded in the swimming pool. Huh? Did he know that?

"What happened?" Leonard was shouting at Sylvia.

She closed their bedroom door so he wouldn't wake the girls. "Nothing."

"She wasn't drowning?"

"No!"

"Goddamn it to hell, Sylvia. I'm sick and tired of having to deal with these maids, and if you can't make do with the next one, then you're stuck. *Stuck.* Either you train them properly or you make the beds yourself. Do you understand me?" His voice rose even louder, filling every inch of the room. There was no corner safe from his anger. "I will not fire another goddamn one of these stupid girls and have them open up a fat mouth to me and—" The knocking on the bedroom door must have been going on for some time, but Leonard and Sylvia didn't hear it until he paused for breath so he might continue his tirade. Instead he opened the door.

"Mommy? Daddy?" Lee wore a pale pink night-gown with tucking all over the chest. She would have preferred Little Lulu pajamas, but her mother had said no, this is much finer-looking, and besides, the pink is perfect in your room. She squinted to keep out the bright lights of her parents' room. "I heard yelling and I got scared."

"Lee," her father began.

"Stop it, Leonard," said Sylvia, trying to cut him off.

"Lee, did anything happen in the pool with Robin?" Lee was no dope. She knew her mother wanted her to keep quiet. But she had been like Lassie. Brave and keen. And no one had said: "You are a noble-hearted creature, Lily Rose," or even: "Thank you."

"Robin was drowning," she said, cocking her head to the side in order to look pert and putting on (it has to be conceded) an obnoxiously smug smile. "I saved her. Like Lassie."

"Where was Mommy?"

"Mommy was . . . " Too late, Lee realized this was a subject better left alone. She shrugged as if to say: Gee, I forgot what I was gonna say.

"Where was Mommy?" Her father's voice was so loud it shook the mirror over her mother's dresser. "Where?" She could feel the voice in her stomach. "*Where?*"

"On the patio," Lee whispered.

"What was she doing?" Lee looked to her mother. Her mother looked away, as if there was something behind the bathroom door that was demanding her attention. "*WHAT WAS SHE DOING?*"

"Smoking." Lee mouthed the word rather than enunciated it. "Her eyes were closed for a second. That's why she didn't see. Just for a second."

Her father sent her away then, without asking to hear the details. That's what she had wanted to tell him about. The details. They were so wonderful: the too hot water, the dog-paddling, the chlorine taste when she grabbed Robin's soaking playsuit between her teeth, the water down her throat and up her nose, what a load Robin was, so don't think she's so skinny compared to me. And to hear her father say: Lee, you were brave and keen.

What she got instead was Greta Wolff, a thoroughly decent, indefatigable, ever vigilant, utterly humorless martinet from Frankfurt am Main, who served as a perpetual reminder to the entire White family that Sylvia was ineffectual and a liar, that Robin needed constant coddling, that Leonard was master of the house—and a merciless one.

And that Lee was a born troublemaker.

Seven

Believe me, I'm not in favor of coddling criminals. I don't want my purse snatched or my head bashed in any more than the next dame. But there's something more than justice we Americans dish out to people who violate our criminal laws. Take Norman Torkelson (or any one of my clients I can't spring on bail). Once they're locked up, we don't just take away their freedom. Nope. We humiliate them.

You want an example? Take the food. To call it unspeakable is to be kind. Three times a day, the inmates receive mounds and patties and globs of stuff the flat, gray-brown color of those splotches of year-old gum that adhere to city sidewalks.

A prison food digression: Years ago, when I was still prosecuting, I spent a day interviewing an inmate, a guy named Alfred Dunder, six feet two, three hundred pounds, with front teeth so buck they protruded almost perpendicular to his gums. Facing life without parole, Alfred had decided to cooperate in our investigation of a homicide—i.e., rat on his fellow murderers. Naturally, I wanted him to live long enough to testify, so our meeting had to be secret. He, Sam Franklin, and I sat in a room near the medical unit that was not much bigger than a stall shower. Around one o'clock, Sam's stomach grumbled, joining mine for a duet. Just then, one of the laughing boys from the sheriff's office brought in Alfred's lunch. He slammed down a tray on which was a plate with three different varieties of stuff Nassau County was calling food. Not only did it look revolting; I had to breathe through my mouth so as not to smell it. Alfred, despite his eighty-five IQ, his brain damage from twelve years on smack and PCP and his total lack of empathy for his fellow human beings, picked up my disgust in two seconds flat. "Hey, Missus D.A., wanna—" he sneered at me, "—eat my lunch?"

But the food is not the most degrading aspect of prison life. If you really want to test-drive your gag reflex, give a look at the toilets in the adolescent men's cell blocks. Or if you find fear more compelling than nausea, take a peek at the inmates themselves. Well, not at them, since many of them are not at all unattractive; they work out and are well-muscled; some of them have lovely smiles and, despite an occasional missing tooth, appear no more malign than the average gas station attendant. No, the peek should be at their rap sheets. Or at their victims' statements—often made from hospital beds, sometimes from deathbeds. I'm not objecting that we put malefactors away. Why shouldn't we? Don't they deserve incarceration in order to garner the traditional benefits of a prison sentence: rehabilitation and deterrence? (That neither occurs very often is a point that should surprise no one in America.)

But if nobody is rehabilitated or deterred, something does happen in our jails. Just about everyone who stays in longer than a month comes out a career criminal. Less than four weeks, a first-timer may still be so staggered by what he experiences, and as yet unable to adjust to the brutishness, that he vows: Never again.

A hard-assed cop like Sam Franklin would say these bad guys are already past redemption when they go in. I don't buy that. I've seen enough eighteen-year-olds go to jail merely stupid or angry or cocky. Two years later, they emerge irreversibly vicious.

Maybe the food and the toilets and the stink and the total depravity of prison are society's way of getting even, as in: This is all you deserve, you thieving/murdering/check-kiting/dope-dealing bastard. Or the ugliness could be the prison authorities' expression of their own rage, as in: This is payback for me having to spend my life working in a jungle, keeping you animals under control. Of course, what makes a person want to be a prison guard is another story: One guy, with a round, cheery, freckled face, the kind of guy who leads everybody in another chorus of "Toorra-Loorra-Looral" on St. Patrick's Day, told me he used to be a Long Island Rail Road conductor, but being a guard paid two thousand bucks a year more. Two thousand extra bucks per annum to spend forty hours a week in hell? I can't believe it's the money that drives a man or woman to put on that uniform any more than the need for sex drives a rapist.

In any case, what we, as a society, do with our rotten eggs is a topic the man in my life (did I mention he's a lawyer too?) and I kick around every so often—like whenever there's a prison riot, or after some guard's finally prosecuted after sodomizing a hundred or so inmates.

I say our prisons have become our mad scientists' labs, in which we create our own monsters. My guy says that my sensibilities are too exquisite for me to be any judge of how the criminal class reacts to revolting accommodations and bad company, since I'd rather die of a ruptured bladder than go to the ladies' room at Shea Stadium. I say: "See? You said it yourself! Criminal *class*." And he says: "There's always been a criminal class, Lee. It's a criminology cliché—pickpockets working the crowd at public hangings of other pickpockets." And I say: "Name one thing we're doing in America to stop the growth of the violent criminal class we're perpetually hysterical about. We're breeding sociopaths as if we had a Department of Agriculture subsidy." And he pours himself another glass of red and says . . .

Forget what he says, because it only goes to show how perverse we must be: two litigators, people who earn their living by arguing, choosing each other.

But he's right about me and the ladies' room at Shea. That's just the point. If I were thrown into the slammer, I might recoil at the food, retch and heave mightily at the sight of the toilet, but sooner or later, I'd eat. I'd go to the bathroom. And after a time, ingesting and eliminating would simply become another part of my day and I'd have no reaction at all. How come? Well, my guy would say you can get used to anything. Inmates don't notice it, if they ever did. And I'd say back to him: They don't notice because their humanity is being ground down. Their senses get duller. Whatever standards of cleanliness and gentility they once possessed get worn away. Ergo, they lose that individual "you": As you are diminished, you become an undifferentiated member of the herd. You mean less. Human life means less.

Which brings us back, once more, to Norman Torkelson, who walked into the visitors room looking less of a person than he had the day before. Part of it was the uniform, of course: those angry orange pants and the matching shirt that hung loose, like a maternity blouse.

They drained his color and degraded his maleness. As he moved to sit in the molded plastic chair across the barrier from me, he braced his hands on the edges of the seat and, as if infirm or arthritic, slowly lowered himself.

"How are you holding up?" I asked.

"Not bad." His voice came out soft, a little weak, as if he hadn't had the strength to expand his lungs fully. "You saw Mary," he said.

"Yes." Then, seeing that he was waiting for more, I added: "She was very nice." That wasn't quite enough. "And so beautiful!"

Norman's face took on a bit of color. His spine straightened, till his posture was erect but nonchalant, displaying a pride of ownership similar to that of the possessor of a new BMW. "She's as beautiful inside as she is outside," he assured me.

"Then you're a very lucky man."

"She talked to you, didn't she?"

"About what?" I asked, looking him right in the eye.

"About my business." He sighed. "She tried to keep it a secret that she told you everything. That lasted about five seconds."

"Mary wants to help you, or help me help you. The last time you and I talked you told me she had nothing to do with your work. I guess it slipped your mind that what she was doing is something lawyers call aiding and abetting."

Norman offered me a boyish grin, one side of his mouth breaking into a real smile, the other blasé, only mildly amused. I caught myself smiling back as if he'd just said something absolutely delicious.

"You'd be surprised. Mary's a good little actress," he remarked, as I worked on returning my face to its Lee White, Attorney-at-Law, unenchanted expression. "She can put on a whole bunch of different voices. You should hear her. Sweet as sugar in real life, but when she's calling about repossessing my car—it's like an icicle in the heart." He stopped short, made a fist, and started to gnaw on his knuckles. Something was eating at him. "Listen, she doesn't have any exposure on this, does she?"

I gave the knuckle on my index finger a quick, companionable chew. "Well, in your, um, what Mary called the Love Nest . . . Isn't that where she left a message about repossessing the car that Bobette was supposed to overhear?" Norman nodded. "If the cops somehow find out about the Love Nest and get a search warrant, they'll seize the tape from the answering machine. That would implicate her."

"Shit! Listen, do me a favor. They have one lousy pay phone for the whole cell block here. Make a call for me. Just tell Mary to go over—make sure she's not being followed—and get the tape and deep-six it."

I shook my head. "I can't tell anyone to destroy evidence."

I knew he'd be on the phone with her the second he could, saying: Rip it up, stomp on it, burn it. I couldn't stop him, but there's never a percentage in violating the canon of ethics for a criminal client. First of all, the law is a noble institution, if you'll pardon my mush, and lawyers should respect it. I'd much rather think of myself as a cog in the wheel of justice than as a scum bucket for hire. Besides, even if a client were to pay you a fortune to play a little dirty or simply to look the other way, you can't trust him not to turn around and rat on you—big time—the minute it's to his advantage.

"Norman, I understand that part of your business is protecting yourself and the people you work with. But I'm your lawyer. To the extent you keep me in the dark—like not telling me about Mary—you're making yourself vulnerable to attacks by the prosecution. If you're open with me, then I can anticipate their attacks and be prepared to fight back."

"What do you want me to do? Confess to a murder I didn't commit?"

"Of course not. But if you're going to tell me something, don't con me. If you'd rather not talk about it, just say so and I'll move on." I realized that my chances of getting Norman Torkelson to be candid were as great as my ever getting my upper arms firm enough that I'd be able to wear a strapless gown. But a girl's got to try.

"What do you want to know?" he asked.

"Bobette. You said there was no sex the evening of the murder."

"That's the God's honest truth."

"Mary seems to believe you never had sex with your marks." I looked straight at him.

Norman leaned back his chair, crossed his arms over his chest, and laughed. "What else am I supposed to tell her? Why hurt her? It's not fun; it's work: I have to make bells ring for ladies who may never have known that bells exist. Believe me, I don't push it, but I can't do business without it."

"How long were you having sex with Bobette?"

"For nine days. It's nine days with everybody. That's the ideal time: when they're starting to feel sure of you and before any doubts arise. I tried to make it shorter—"

"The time between beginning to have sex and the actual sting?"

"Precisely. Nine is the magic number."

"Do you have any set time you wait before initiating sex?"

"Oh, no," said Norman, a little surprised that I wasn't appreciating the subtleties of his operation. "That depends on the lady. I will say, even if it looks as though she doesn't have that much in the asset department, if

I'm going to bother to take what she has, I wait at least two weeks before sex. You know, so she feels secure that she has a *relationship*."

"Women like that," I observed. "Relationships, I mean."

"Absolutely," said Norman. "They want to be cared about as a human being. That's what I give them. That, and then the sex. But what I said to Mary is a hundred percent true: It doesn't mean anything." He brought his chair back down on all four legs, and by the time he did, he wasn't laughing anymore. "She's had such a rough life."

"Mary?"

"Yeah. I met her, she was nineteen years old. She'd been out of the house from the time she was sixteen. Her parents beat her. Her old lady would bop her over the head with a broomstick until she was unconscious. The man she married—to get away from her family—he wasn't much better, so she ran out on him. Then she married an older man, but he died. His children screwed her out of everything. And she really loved him. When I met her, she was working as a chambermaid in a motel outside Phoenix. You wouldn't believe it! Her hands were bright red—almost purple—and all swollen from an allergy to the cleaning stuff. And in nineteen years, not one single person had ever behaved decently toward her." Norman looked down at the floor for a minute, then back at me, perplexed. "I don't get it," he said, so choked up his voice gurgled on the "get." "How could someone *not* want to do wonderful things for Mary?"

"Did you always have someone working with you?" I asked. "Making the call about the repossession, that sort of thing?"

"Not at the beginning," he murmured, clearly not liking the subject, wishing we could continue the Ode to Mary Dean. "I didn't want anyone getting messed up in this. I did okay working alone. You know, I had to relate the story of the car repossession myself, and that's not as credible"—he hesitated for an instant to check if I'd noted the "credible" and was appropriately impressed by his vocabulary—"as someone else calling up and putting the squeeze on me. But then I became involved with someone about ten years ago. She was the one who pushed me to be a part of it." Paled as he was by his uniform, pasty from prison food, fluorescent light, and recycled air, he didn't look as if he could attract anyone to a life of crime, much less get women to open their hearts and their savings accounts to him. At our first meeting, the dark hair on his forearms had been appealing. No, more than that: erotic. Now he looked like a dying animal, its sickly skin shining through its thinning pelt.

"What happened with her?" I asked.

He shrugged, not wanting to answer. I waited. "Nothing. It didn't work out," he said finally.

"Any others?"

"Any others . . . what?"

"Did you work with any other woman besides this one and Mary?" He shifted in his seat but didn't answer. "Norman, I'm not your mother trying to pry out information about your girlfriends. I have to worry that on the off chance a story about this case goes out on the wire services or on some cable news program, someone will recognize your name or M.O. and be willing to give information. It wouldn't be a plus if the government put a witness on the stand who could recite the details of your business practices."

"I used different names with them."

" 'Them' meaning your lady friends, your accomplices—not just your marks."

"Right."

"So they don't know Norman Torkelson or Denton

Wylie or . . . What name did you use for renting your apartment?"

"Robert McNulty. No, I never use the same name twice." Of course, once caught he was officially stuck with Norman Torkelson, since he had a record with fingerprints attached. Whether Norman was his true name or not I didn't know, but it was the one he was using when he was first booked in 1978 for possession of a forged instrument, having tried to cash a check from a checkbook he'd filched after a night of love with one Lorraine Krumholz, age forty-two, in West Quoddy Head, Maine. He was then eighteen.

"You must have a good memory, with all those names," I said.

"You know the old saying"—he smiled—"that a liar has to have a good memory. I have a *great* memory."

"Then do you remember receiving the forty-eight thousand that Bobette withdrew from her bank?" He didn't answer. "I don't have to tell you about the attorney-client privilege, do I? Whatever you tell me stays with me." I knew this was not exactly a major news item to him, and sure enough, he nodded. "And I'm not trying to find out how much cash you have so I can squeeze more money out of you. Remember, we both signed the retainer agreement."

"Bobette gave me the money."

"And then what?"

"I thanked her for her faith in me. Then I left."

"You never saw her again." Wearily, as if I was becoming stupefyingly boring, Norman shook his head: That's right—I never saw her again. "You know why I ask you that, Norman?"

"No," he muttered.

"Because if for any reason you came back to the apartment and, say, found her dead or dying, there might be some physical evidence of your presence *postmortem* that could link you to the crime. I hate to keep harping on it, but this is a murder charge, and the D.A. doesn't seem inclined to let me bargain this down to, say, manslaughter."

"I didn't kill her!"

"Then all the more reason that we may go to trial, and if we do, I don't want their serologist finding—um—let's say some of your skin cells under her fingernails, on the chance she tried to grab on to you for emotional support as she lay dying . . . if you happened to come upon her after she'd been attacked."

"There's none of my skin under her nails," he said sullenly.

"Good. I need that kind of information. The worst damage you can do to your case is to let me be surprised. I hate surprises. All criminal lawyers do." I tried to look him straight in the eye—in his lovely, limpid blue eyes, to be accurate—but he was staring over at the platform where the guards in charge of the closed-circuit TV monitors are stationed. "Do you have anything more to say on the subject, or should we move on?"

"After she gave me the money," Norman said quietly, "I went out to buy champagne. I always do. See, deep down, the marks are afraid I'll do exactly what I *do:* grab the money and never look back. Subconsciously, they know that my wanting them . . . it's too good to be true." He grinned. "Well, it is. So if I just pick up and leave, some of them might start getting nervous after an hour or two. I can't afford second thoughts. I don't want them calling their bank or a relative or the police. So I go out, buy a bottle of champagne, and bring it back—surprise!—to celebrate. I offer a toast, something like: 'I love you for you. If it was possible to love you more—which I don't believe I can—I'd love you for your faith in me.'" Norman's big head turned up, heavenward, and as he delivered his lines, there was not a single trace of discernible slickness. For that moment, it really did look as if the light of God were shining through Norman Torkelson as well as upon him. "'I was so down-and-out,'" he continued his spiel. "'I thought: All right, I'll just have to live like this forever. Half a life. I can do it. I've got to do it, for my boys' sake. But then'"—together, Norman and I gulped with emotion—"'you gave me back my passion.'"

God's light flicked off. Norman cleaned under the nail of his index finger with the pinkie nail of his other hand. "When I got back with the champagne, she was dead."

"Did you touch her?"

"No," he said, glancing up from his nail grooming. "I could see she'd been murdered. Strangled. Her neck . . . " He leaned forward and, with great feeling, added: "Her face wore the mask of death!" Too loud. One row away, another lawyer—a blight on the profession whom I'd known for years—and his drug-dealer-to-junior-high-school-students client turned to check out Norman's violation of the unwritten etiquette of the lawyers' visiting hour: that all business shall be conducted in a mumble. And it wasn't only that Norman was too loud. His performance was way over the top. His already long face was stretched out by his high seriousness, as if he was playing up the Lincoln resemblance, trying to capture the Gettysburg moment—just after "shall not perish from the earth" and before the applause.

"You're positive you didn't touch her mask of death?" I probed. I might have phrased my question less sarcastically, but I'd been up late over at my guy's house (he had a lousy chest cold) and I was tired—both from lack of sleep and from Norman's relentless lying. I had to know. I did not relish the prospect of suddenly hearing Holly Nuñez introduce an addendum to the medical examiner's report that stated (to give you a for instance) that a half pint of Norman's saliva had collected in Bobette's cleavage as he drooled with delight while strangling her. "You didn't touch *any* part of her after you found her dead?"

Ethically, I felt I was walking a pretty slack tightrope here; it was hard to balance. I needed to gather all the information I could for Norman's defense, yet some of my questions would inevitably suggest to any person with an IQ higher than that of a Chicken McNugget that just in case he left some trace of himself on the body, he'd better say: Oh, yeah! I did touch her *postmortem.*

"Oh, yeah, I did touch her," Norman said. "I know I shouldn't have, but I was really shaken up. I mean, to walk in with a bottle of champagne and see *that.* I wanted to be absolutely sure she was dead. She *looked* dead, but what if she wasn't? I might have been able to do something."

"Do you remember what part of her you touched?"

"God, I'm not sure. I guess . . . her hand or her wrist, maybe, feeling for a pulse. And I guess her face too. You know . . . " He closed his eyes, I assumed to imagine the scene. "I put my face up close to hers, to see if I could hear her breathing."

"Do you think you might have touched her neck?" I asked.

"You mean, where she was . . . " Norman seemed to find swallowing difficult and, with his thumb and index finger, massaged the sides of his Adam's apple. " . . . choked?"

Clearly, this thought was distressing to him. As often happens, the girl in me began to fight the lawyer in me. The girl wanted to tell Norman: Never mind. Don't even think about those big ugly finger marks on Bobette's throat. *So* upsetting. However, he wasn't paying me two hundred fifty bucks an hour for being a girl. "Yes," I said, "where she was choked." Then I added: "You can see the marks left by the killer's fingers in the autopsy photos."

"Why would I touch her there?" Norman demanded, his voice rising, as if I'd asked the stupidest, most impertinent question he'd ever heard.

"I have no idea. But in stressful situations, even the most rational, stiff-upper-lip people can react in strange ways."

"I don't know." Norman exhaled. "I may have reached out and just . . . I think for a second, I may have put my finger on her throat. Kind of out of pity."

"Okay," I said coolly, as if my large intestine wasn't going to contract into a knot that would take three days to untie. "I'm glad you told me."

Right. Ladies and gentlemen of the jury. Those very large thumbprints you saw in the autopsy photos, the ones that make it seem as if some fiend had applied horrific force to the area over the larynx . . . Those prints were left by the defendant after he found Ms. Frisch dead. They were a gesture of pity and—yes, ladies and gentlemen—love. (Why, you may ask, do I do this sort of work when I could be the Queen of Matrimonial Law and get home at five-thirty, in time to finish the ball fringe on an afghan I've been working on for the past eight months, poach a nice sea bass and reread *Great Expectations*? I really don't know.)

"I felt sincerely terrible," Norman was saying. "A terrible, brutal thing to happen to anyone. And I *liked* Bobette."

"What kind of a person was she?"

"Smart. Native smarts. She wasn't educated or anything. But she had a steel-trap mind when it came to money. Knew the rent for every apartment in the buildings she owned, who owed what, and how many more months they had to go on their lease. Never had to write a thing down."

"Would you say that she was a nice person?"

A small smile of embarrassment passed over Norman's lips at having to speak ill of the dead, but as I'd already graded him B-minus as a con man, it didn't surprise me that he was faking it—and poorly. "She wasn't very nice. In fact . . . she wasn't like your typical lady, wanting to be liked. Wanting to be loved, actually. No, she was pretty unusual: going about her business, and if you didn't like her, it was fine with her."

"She sounds tough. How come you were able to touch her?" I inquired.

Naturally, Norman didn't buff his nails against his chest or make any other gesture of smugness, but the fluorescents in the visitors room were too strong not to reveal the flush of pride that colored his forehead. "She was lonely."

"She was fifty-six years old. Presumably, she'd been lonely for years."

"But see"—Norman leaned forward, so his chin looked as if it were glued to the white Formica barrier between us—"the ladies I deal with preselect themselves! The fact that they answer my ad in the personals means they're lonely. Maybe even desperate, because they're not meeting other men."

"So this tough cookie was looking for love?"

"Hey, that's the headline in my ad that she answered! 'Looking for Love.' In her letter she said she just wanted companionship, but then she fell for me."

"Why? I mean, you're a nice-looking man and all that—"

"That's okay," Norman said generously. "Please don't apologize. You see, I play to their desires and their weaknesses. Bobette wanted love: that was her desire. And she was embarrassed about not having a good education: her weakness. So I quoted poetry to her—'Love is not love / Which alters when it alteration finds.' That's Shakespeare.

And from Elizabeth Barrett Browning, a sonnet: 'How do I—' "

"I know it," I told him.

"I showed her a different world. A better, finer world. I took her on nature walks. You know, we'd go to a wooded area and I'd point out plants and stuff and give her the Latin names—"

"You know the scientific names of plants?"

"Are you kidding? I just use a few names I've made up: 'It *is* pretty, but it's a common gorse weed, Bobette, a *Rowinda numonica*.' That's where we were that last day, when that tenant of hers called the cops about my car. On a nature walk."

"Tell me about the tenant."

"I don't know his name," Norman said.

"Did you ever see him?"

"Yeah. He was foreign. Sort of dark. Not like Indian or anything. Probably from one of those countries that was behind the Iron Curtain. The way he said her name: 'Miss Frisch.' As if he had a big gob in his throat. But that's the way they pronounce things. Guttural."

"I know."

"Sorry," he muttered, trying to look boyish and abashed, not totally succeeding. However, I did feel my heart rise a few millimeters and wished I could find something to say to cheer him. That's what con men do, even the lousy ones. They bring out the best in you— your sweetness, your concern, your love, your passion— and then, when you're wafting about on your cloud of goodness, above mere mortal meanness . . . Whammo! They kick you off so you plummet to earth, headfirst.

"Did you ever have any encounters with this tenant before?"

"A couple of times. I pulled my car behind his crappy Hyundai and he had a fit."

"What kind of a fit? Yelling? Carrying on?" I was thinking: Ladies and gentlemen of the jury, you've seen Mr. Whosis on the witness stand. You've seen his hair-trigger temper. You've seen his clear bias against my client. No, strike that. His *hatred* of Norman Torkelson. His is the *only* testimony linking my client to that house on the day of the murder. But as His Honor will charge you, a witness's demeanor must be taken into account . . .

"No carrying on. Just had on a pissed-off expression. He kept saying: 'Damn it!' over and over. 'Dommit!'" Norman mimicked. "'Dommit! Dommit! Dommit!'"

Later, back in my office, I repeated "'Dommit! Dommit! Dommit!'" when I called my guy and told him about the morning's events and checked up on how he was feeling. "Any relief yet?"

"Well," he said, "my fever's gone down, but I'm still feeling pretty crummy. But you know us guys. Lousy patients."

"Want me to come over for lunch? Bring you something?"

"No. I'll be okay. So what do you think?"

"About what?"

"About your client, Norman."

"What do *you* think?" I asked, having revered his gut reactions in criminal cases for . . . God, nearly twenty years. "Is he guilty?"

"Lee, what do *you* think?" I got that low feeling, when first your stomach drops, then everything else seems to give in to the pull of gravity and falls as low as it can go.

"You tell me. What do *you* think?"

And my main man said: "Guilty as hell."

Eight

✦

Greta Wolff, the housekeeper, clanged pots together and hummed a little ditty from *Der fliegende Holländer*. Not a hummer by nature, and far too deliberate to be a pot clanger, she was trying to drown out the sounds of Leonard and Sylvia's warfare upstairs so that Robin would eat her dinner. Ten-year-old Lee sat at the kitchen table also, but Greta did not concern herself about her. Lee would abandon a meal only if the house blew up and the ceiling collapsed onto her plate.

"I ask you just one thing, goddamn it to hell!" Leonard was raging. Some combination of materials in the house—stone and wood and the wool of their bedroom rug—had synergized and created a trumpet effect, so despite Leonard's deep-voiced fury, his tone descended to the kitchen as a nasal *whaa-whaa*. Greta stirred something vigorously. Lee suspected it was water. But the metal spoon clanging against the stockpot was merely an annoyance, not a distraction. "Be a mother to those kids. Is that too much to demand?"

"I was under so much pressure. I had too much to do—"

But he wouldn't let her finish. "I get a call from the school—"

"Sweetheart, Leonard, please, *please* keep it down," Sylvia shrieked.

Without realizing it, Lee brought her finger to her lips. "Shhh," she hushed.

"The goddamn door is closed," Leonard was hollering. "Now listen: I get a call from the school—"

"I know! I admit it. I made a mistake."

"Shut up and listen when I talk to you! 'Mr. White, we hate to bother you at your place of business, but Mrs. White was supposed to pick up Robin. Her temperature's over one hundred.' *Over one hundred!* 'And she's complaining of a sore throat and earache.'"

"Don't be mad," Sylvia pleaded. She's going to cry, Lee thought.

She glanced over to her sister. Robin, now seven, was repeatedly plunging the tines of her fork into the liver and onions Greta had made for dinner. Apparently Robin hoped that by making enough holes, she would render the meat so porous it would lose its materiality and become invisible.

But on second glance, Lee observed Robin's head pulled, turtlelike, between her knobby shoulders, as if the confrontation upstairs was an attack on her, each word a bashing. The girl's white skin had turned ashen, her breathing rapid and shallow. Sensitive: That was the word for Robin, with family friends and Leonard's employees courteously omitting the "hyper-." If Lee's little sister had been a fictional character, she would have been the pretty princess who detected the pea while lying atop fifty mattresses—notwithstanding that before any consciousness of the legume, she probably would have been weeping and wheezing from an acrophobic attack.

"I apologize. What more can I say?" Sylvia asked. But of course she thought of more. "*Lists.* You say I have nothing to do, but—"

"You don't cook!" It galled him. Last Memorial Day, they'd gone to the annual Shorehaven Estates Beach Blast and he'd overheard Ginger Taylor telling two women that after she and Fos saw that foreign film at the Manhasset Cinema, *La Dolce Vita*, she had bought an Italian cookbook. Ginger had them doubled over with laughter: You can't believe the things I can do to spaghetti! The three of them were like Blonde, Blonder, and Blondest. All of them with beautiful, throaty laughs. And so perfectly got up for the Beach Blast. Dungarees cut off like Bermuda shorts, and sleeveless blouses. Sylvia had on a green linen trouser suit and an enormous straw hat and was pathetically overdressed. And all their neighbors had known exactly what they weren't, probably because of the way Sylvia looked. Shoes with a grosgrain bow and little heels, for Christ sake, for a party where you *know* you're going to stand in the sand! Makeup! None of them wore makeup—except red lipstick. Oh, God, the red lipstick with the streaky blonde hair! True, most of the neighbors had nodded or waved or even said Hi, but the Whites wound up at a big round table for ten—except the only people sitting with them were a couple in their sixties named Turtletaub, and Frank and Louise Petullo from Harbor Road, the same Petullo the *New York Times* had informed him was Frankie "Salami" Petullo, the reputed brains behind the underworld's takeover of the sand and cement industry. Leonard had wanted to run, flee the horror, but he had to sit there making conversation with Beaky Turtletaub, who kept pushing for an offer of a silver fox wholesale.

"Tell me what you do!" Leonard yelled at the top of his lungs. "You don't clean! You don't—"

"How can I? You're always giving me lists. Get new garbage cans. Get a pegboard for the garage for your tools. *Why?* You never use tools. You bought that power drill set for fifty-four dollars and never once—"

"Shut the hell up!"

"Did someone tell you Foster Taylor has a pegboard and a power drill in *his* garage—"

"I'm warning you." Anger grabbed Leonard by the throat, squeezing his voice higher and higher until it was such a terrible, shrill cry that Robin had to cover her ears. "No more, Sylvia!"

"Leonard, just listen—"

"Shut up, or I'm leaving and not coming back!"

Lee's gut went into a sudden, agonizing spasm. She would always endure this pain in times of severe stress. However, unlike her more high-strung sister (hands over ears, chin aquiver, eyes swimming in unshed tears), Lee could take it on the chin—or in the gut— without falling apart. It was not that her suffering was any less intense than Robin's. The awful contraction just above and to the right of her navel hurt so that she could not catch her breath. However—except for once in her life—Lee had the strength to endure pain. While this may not have been the style of heroines in books— victimized beauties, or stouthearts who are allowed only moral courage, not physical valor or derring-do— this was Lee White. A hearty girl. A stand-up dame.

"They'll get over it, Robin," she said. Robin's hands, clapped over her ears, shook so badly her head bobbed up and down. Lee then tried a diversion. "Hey, Rob, you know next-door's new puppies?" Lee was referring, of course, to Ginger Taylor's latest brood of basenjis, but everyone in the house, even Woofer, the new weimaraner they had gotten after Duchess died, seemed to pick up on the waspishness that the name Taylor roused in Leonard, so they avoided mentioning it.

"So listen," Lee went on "Guess who got one of the puppies?"

"Who?" Robin hiccuped.

"Cathy Foti, in sixth grade. Her parents bought one from Mrs. Whatsis!" Robin blinked, and tears began to spill. Lee tried harder. "Those puppies! *So* adorable— okay, not when they're pooping. They got into Mommy's herb garden yesterday. Mommy had to pull out all her parsley. Anyway, Cathy's mother picked her up at school, and the puppy was in the car. You should have seen it!" Lee massaged Woofer's belly with the toe of her saddle shoe to soften the pain of her betrayal. "Teeny-weeny wrinkles in its little doggy fore-head. Oh, and the itty-bitty curly tail."

The experts, having embraced the concept of sibling rivalry, are too quick to dismiss the force of sibling love. Lee, nuzzler of puppies, cuddler of kittens, could not fail to be moved by the fragility of seven-year-old Robin's frame, by the almost cartoonishly-big gray-green eyes that dominated the younger girl's dainty face, by the angelic softness of her pale hair. When not exasperated by Robin's excessive response to people and noises and smells, Lee wanted to protect her from reality.

"You made me take back Grape-Nuts Flakes," Sylvia was squawking.

"Don't make it sound like I held a gun to your head. I asked for Grape-*Nuts* and you bought *Flakes*. You know I hate them. Jesus H. Christ, is it such a big deal to return something to the A & P? What the hell else do you have to do all day?"

"*What else?* Pick up the black wing tips that were get-ting new heels. Take your gray tweed sports jacket to the

cleaners for one-day service." She was probably enumer-
ating, Lee thought, holding down each graceful, tapering
finger, its nail perfectly polished—Cherries Jubilee this
week—with the index finger of the other hand. "Pick up
a baby gift for your accountant's sister—"

"How could you neglect your own child?" Leonard
boomed. "How could you leave her in the nurse's
office, in pain?"

Lee thought that if she were her mother, she would
demand: How come *you* left her in the nurse's office in
pain? You didn't exactly run to grab the next train back
to Shorehaven. Her mother, Lee noted—with a clarity
of thought that coexisted with the ripping pain in her
gut—was a lousy arguer, never coming up with a good
enough answer. And after these fights, her mother,
shaken, ashamed, would take to bed for days, shutting
the louvers of the blinds, refusing to come down for
meals, not combing her hair or brushing her teeth. Her
father, on the other hand, having blown off steam,
invariably seemed lighter-hearted than usual, although
that may have been because Sylvia was so despondent
as to be mute and, thus, incapable of making any emotional demands of him.

But for the moment, Sylvia had not yet given up trying to win over the unwinnable. "Leonard, hon, Robin
wasn't dying, for God's sake. It was just a sore throat.
She gets sore throats all the time." She added vaguely:
"I really should talk to Dr. Gould about her tonsils."

At last, Robin's tears fell. Lee was full of the envy
and admiration she always felt. What dazzling crying!
First, Robin's huge eyes would glisten. Then perfect, fat
teardrops would meander down each cheek. No sobbing, though, although her reed of a body would jerk
as if someone were screaming "Boo!" at her again and
again. Miraculously, Robin's silent suffering brought

her double—no, triple—the attention the average cat-
erwauling child could get.

It wasn't only their parents' fighting that brought
tears to Robin's eyes, however. Lee watched the little
girl blanch as she took another peek at the liver. Any
external event could cause an inner storm. Right that
second, it had switched from her parents' fight to dinner. Robin was probably thinking: Doomed. There they
were, sitting in the breakfast nook, with Greta just
yards away alternately clanging pots and picking over
the apples she was going to turn into applesauce. No
way could Robin escape the dread liver. True, Greta's
powerful back was turned toward them, but that meant
nothing. A scrape of the chair leg at a decibel level so
low that not even Woofer could hear it would make
Greta spin around and blare: Ha! In any other house in
Shorehaven Estates, children could flip food to the
family dog, but Woofer was as awed by Greta's authority as Leonard and Sylvia were, so even though he lay
right there under the table, he could not be relied upon
to be the consummate disposal unit dogs by nature are.

Another thing about Robin's genius for crying, Lee
mused. You'd think a kid who was such a bundle of
nerves would always be grabbing wads of tissues, or
wiping off her cheeks with her fingers, or blotting her
nose with the back of her hand. But no, Robin never
wiped away her tears; they accumulated around her
nose or left shining trails until they dripped off her
chin. They were mesmerizing, beautiful.

Robin's crying made Lee want to weep with jealousy. At the same time, it also forced Lee to come to
her sister's aid—instantly. "Give me your plate," Lee
commanded, but softly.

"What?"

"Pick it up quietly and hand it to me. Don't slide it.

She'll hear. You take my plate. Don't be *too* quiet or she'll turn around."

"Why should I give you my plate?" asked Robin.

"You're too upset to eat your dinner. I'll eat it for you."

"You're kidding!" Robin's face reflected incredulity, then wonder.

"I'm serious."

"Oh, Lee-lee," Robin cried in her tiny high voice. Although not too loud. (Even as an adult, she would tend to sound like Tweety Bird.) "Thank you!"

"Welcome." Lee, naturally, played the liver for all it was worth, cringing at the taste, shuddering with revulsion at the texture. However, the truth was, she was crazy about liver and onions. In fact, after years of Sylvia's medium-rare meatballs and Chinese Jell-O—an ill-starred combination of lemon-flavored gelatin and julienned water chestnuts with a dash of soy sauce— there was nothing Greta cooked that Lee did not love. Although in later years Lee would refine her palate, her lifetime food preferences remained those of a Hessian day laborer.

"I'm done, Greta," Robin sang out.

At the exact same moment Leonard roared: "You went to Garden City, to a shoe sale at Saks, when your child was sick as a dog in the nurse's office!"

"I said I was sorry." Sylvia was screaming now. "What more do you want me to say?"

"I want you to say: 'I have no other responsibilities except to be a mother to my goddamn kids!'"

Greta set aside her apples and wheeled around for inspection of Robin's plate. "See?" Robin said. Her eyes were still wet. "All finished!" Her heart of a face was suffused with the light of grace under pressure: I have done my best under terribly trying circumstances.

Shrewd Greta turned her pale eyes to Lee's slick

lips and shiny chin. "You think I was born yesterday, Miss Lee White? You think I don't know?"

Even way back then, in 1960, Lee would never cop a plea. "Know what?" she inquired, projecting genuine curiosity, even though she was beginning to feel a little nauseous from eating nearly a pound of liver—although not so distressed as to make her willing to forgo dessert.

"Know that you ate your sister's supper. Shame on you!"

"I didn't do anything!"

"No dessert tonight."

"Come on, Greta!" Lee protested. "That's not fair!"

"*I* decide what is fair!" Greta banged her fist down on the dish drainer; a colander rattled, and Robin shook.

Don't be too harsh on Greta here. True, she was a dreadful stiff, but her steel-rod spine grounded the White family. Because of her, floors were washed, dinner was served, Woofer got his rabies shot and the girls their polio boosters—all of which left Sylvia free to pursue her God-given talents: eyebrow-plucking, smoking, and creating bad art. And Greta never once complained, although working in other people's houses was a sad and wearying job.

(Greta had come to the United States in 1937 with her husband, who had determined that being a half-Jewish labor union organizer was perhaps not the ticket to a happy life in Nazi Germany. Although it was still the Depression, he managed to find a job operating a machine that sliced pumpernickel at a wholesale bakery in the Yorkville section of Manhattan. While he did not thrive, he did well, except for his high blood pressure, which he didn't know about. In any case, he dropped dead of a stroke a few days short of his first anniversary in America. Greta took the bit of money they had managed to save and enrolled in a secretarial course. But during the late thirties and early forties, her heavy German accent was an insurmountable obstacle to office employment. However, the same business big shots who would not let her take their dictation did not mind her scouring their bathtubs. In fact, the upper-middle-class families who employed her in the years before the Whites, as well as Sylvia and Leonard themselves, viewed her Teutonic style with approbation. They saw in her inflexible bearing and clipped consonants a benign personification of the efficient German war machine. Therefore, although she was a thoroughly decent person, her employers treated Greta as if she were more apparatus than human—that is, with all the warmth that would be accorded a well-oiled panzer.)

"The little one is all skin and bones!" Greta chided Lee. "How could you take the food from her mouth? *No fresh answers, Miss Lee White!*"

Just as a big grin began to spread across Lee's face, her mother screamed at her father: "Drop dead!"

"Ladies first!"

Lee's grin disappeared, but Robin, no fool, knowing she was off the hook in the dinner department, offered Greta her captivating waif smile. Then she climbed down from her chair and, purposefully, headed to her room. Lee realized: She's going to do it: Until Greta makes her go to bed, Robin will draw, color, and cut out yet another new wardrobe of paper doll furs, mink coats, Persian lamb ski jackets, and sable boas. And the second Mommy and Daddy's fight is over, Robin will be squeaking: "Ooh, Daddy, look!" And Leonard would cry "Fabulous, Robbie-my-baby!" Even Sylvia, in bed, would find enough energy to kiss the top of Robin's head and sigh: "Lovely, sweetheart."

It was going to be a lousy, lonesome night. For less than a second, Lee weighed the advantages of joining

Robin and her paper fashions. But to watch Robin sharpen a crayon so the fur hairs wouldn't look too thick, then painstakingly cut out those stupid tiny paper coats in teeny-weeny nips with her mother's old manicure scissors, was too enraging to be borne. Robin's patience for detail was . . . shitty. And her love of style . . . Daddy, I like the way the sleeves go tight on the coat in your window. Is that sheared mink or mouton, Daddy? He lapped it up like a cat with a bowl of milk. He couldn't get enough. And, Mommy, doesn't it look prettier if I button the top button? Mommy would be in heaven, and they would talk about the vital importance of top-button shittiness for a half hour! Shitty! Lee loved that word: *Shitty!*

She had learned it two years earlier at the school bus stop and had yet to say it out loud, but in her head she'd said it a thousand times. Shitty, Lee brooded. Lately, all Robin did was go to her mother's magazines and copy pictures of furs or clothes, and her parents kept having heart attacks of joy. "You have so much flair!" her father would cry. "If it was real sable, I could sell it to Mrs. Continental Can. Split the profits with you, Robbie-baby." Sylvia would sound reverent: "It almost looks like a Norell! I'm absolutely serious!" Lee thought: She's going to spend three damn hours drawing shitty little fur hairs one at a time, and if one doesn't look right she'll erase it! Shitty little brown-nose.

If Lee had been asked about it, she'd have sworn that word would never ever pass her lips. But the very next day, she actually shouted the word—and in defense of Robin. "Get your shitty lacrosse stick away from my sister's lunch box or I'll punch your fat nose in."

"Yeah?" snickered Jasper Taylor, the boy from the

house next door. The really tall boy. Jasper, at age ten, the third of Fos and Ginger Taylor's four children, was already well over five feet tall and growing fast. Although slender, he had the powerful legs of a natural athlete and the presence of an all-star. Lee's mass was nowhere near as imposing as his, but at age ten, she had an inch on him. "You and who else?" Jasper demanded.

"I don't need anyone else," Lee growled, making a tight fist and holding it up in front of Jasper's face. "I can punch in your nose all by myself."

To which Jasper gave a raucous, derisive laugh. It made Robin wail with terror, a squeal so maddening that it mobilized both the armies that camped on opposite sides of the corner of North Road and Taylor Farm Lane. As Lee glared into Jasper's eyes—an uninteresting hazel, but quite thickly lashed—fist aloft, and Jasper glared back, two fellow fifth graders from the Shorehaven elementary school grabbed Lee and yanked her away. At the same time, three strapping boys, the entire midfield of the Wheatley Country Day lacrosse team, hauled Jasper back to their bus stop across the street—not without much ostentatious grunting as he fought being brought under control.

Normally, there were no hostilities. The two armies, the private day school students and the public school kids, pretty much ignored each other. Oh, except for periodic spit fights. The origin of this particular form of belligerence is lost in time, but each new generation of schoolchildren on that particular street corner in America came to that place with seemingly innate knowledge of the rules of engagement of class warfare: The spitter has to cross the street and run the gauntlet among the spittee's schoolmates, who are free to try to trip or shove the spitter out of the way, although they may not grab onto the spitter's limbs or clothing and attempt to drag the spitter away. However, once the aggressor gets to his or her quarry, he or she is free to deliver the best shot as soon as the spittee's face is no more than a foot away.

Not that Jasper Taylor had targeted little Robin White for a gob of saliva. Far from it. His intended prey was Todd Lomax, a Shorehaven fourth grader, who had the gaunt, haunted look of a future poet. (In truth, Todd was coarse to the core and looked wretched simply because he had discovered the properties of airplane glue years before his contemporaries.) However, in Jasper's rush to expectorate, he forgot to lay down his lacrosse stick before charging; it accidentally banged Robin's lunch-box—*clunk!*—putting a slight dent in the picture of the Fairy Godmother, beaming as Cinderella stares down at herself, amazed to see the ball gown just transmogrified from her rags by a touch of a wand. That was when Lee jumped forward in defense.

"Up your nose with a rubber hose," Lee yelled to him.

"Shut the fuck up," Jasper called back. He sounded bored.

Lee didn't follow him with her eyes. She didn't feel her heart beating faster. In fact, Jasper was out of her thoughts moments after he was back across the street. Unlike her father, she had almost no interest in the Taylors. True, she admired their puppies immensely, but Fos and Ginger's children left her cold. Any curiosity she had was aroused solely by her father's inexplicable response to anything Taylor.

Like last summer. When the sounds of "Sail Along, Silv'ry Moon" poured across the patio at Hart's Hill and down over the Whites' lawn, indicating that the Taylors were throwing still another party, Leonard did not react visibly. He did not stiffen in anger in his lounge chair or cover his face with his hands and weep in grief at once again going unnoticed and uninvited. No, he lay motionless so as not to display to his wife his most sensitive area. Still, Sylvia had picked something up.

"Leonard? Want some lemonade, Leonard?"

"No."

"It's not too sweet."

"No."

"Greta made it."

"No."

"Anything wrong, Leonard?"

"*No.*"

Lee had sensed her father's turmoil as well. How? A slight movement, perhaps, a hollowing of his chest as if he had just received a knife in his heart as the music wafted over him. Or a change in his aura—if successful furriers reading the business section of the Sunday *Times* do indeed have auras—from a self-satisfied peachy beige to a thunderous gray. That the Taylors had the power, simply by playing a Billy Vaughn record, to drive her father to near insanity, even for an instant, made them an object of concern for his eldest child. But not dread. She had seen the Taylors: They were simply not scary.

Lee had seen Mr. Taylor only a couple of times. A creep, in her estimation. His chin was attached to his neck by a large, flappy patch of flesh, like a pelican's. His eyes were bulgy. He looked like a slow reader. Mrs. Taylor was blonde and pretty, except if you saw her walking down Main Street and she passed you up real close: You could see wrinkles crisscrossing every part of her face, hundreds of tiny tick-tack-toe patterns. And the kids: The two big girls now were away at boarding school. They were okay, except the one whose freckles were so close together it looked as though she had a brown butterfly tattooed on her face. She was always giggling. The other girl never smiled. Jasper, admittedly, may have been a jerk, but no worse than any of the Wheatley jerks in their stupid ties and jackets, like they were on their way to an office instead of fifth grade. There was a little Taylor brother, too young to go to school, who always waved at whoever he saw, flapping his hand back and forth in a floppy-wristed frenzy. "Hiya! Hiya! Hiya!" he'd call.

"How's your father, the goy?" her grandmother Bella inquired. The question could have been asked the following weekend, since it was one Bella invariably posed, but it was now two years later.

Lee was not perched on the brink of adolescence, as are many twelve-year-olds; she had gone over the edge. Her breasts were now larger than her biceps, and she had forsaken her tree climbing, her racing, and her roughhousing with the neighborhood boys for the lesser pleasures of the junior high school girls' tennis team. Coming of age as she had in 1962, at the height of the Jacqueline Kennedy mystique, and being Sylvia's daughter, Lee bore herself rather elegantly. She sat with her legs crossed only at the ankle, no matter how her body yearned to slump and tie itself into its comfy prepubescent knot. Lee's figure was fine, even noble, with the lovely shoulders and strong thighs of Winged Victory—although in a family of the small-boned and wasp-waisted, she felt too large, which she interpreted as being fat. She was beginning a lifetime crusade against an ever evolving list of wicked carbohydrates and satanic fats. Her face had lost its round girlish good looks and had yet to come into its bright-eyed, clear-skinned adult prettiness; every day at least one pimple popped up on one feature; her nose had bloomed faster than her cheekbones, forehead, or chin and would have totally dominated her face if not for the competition from her stick-out ears. Her hair had become her crowning glory, turning from plain brown into a thick chestnut mix—the warm gold of the nut mingled with the intense red-brown of the shell.

"Daddy? He's fine, Grandma," Lee replied absently, all her energies focused on a single loop of pink wool.

"Who's he fooling—*White*—with a schnozz like a knockwurst?"

Lee was tempted to ask what "schnozz" meant but, fearing it was yet another Yiddish word for "penis," kept silent. She was spending the weekend at her grandparents' apartment in Brooklyn and, as she always did, had taken over Bella's crocheting. This current project was an afghan comprising of squares with a tricky rose design in the middle that required all her concentration.

"They fight?" Bella inquired, with a casualness that immediately caught Lee's attention. Bella always described herself as having retired from acting, but truth is, even in the Yiddish theater, where extravagant gestures were anticipated and overacting was applauded, Bella had been deemed lacking in subtlety. The truth was she had not jumped off the stage; she had been pushed. But as Bella did not find the truth appealing, she ignored it and created her own Biography of a Star (she had been too great to be a mere ingenue) who had left audiences weeping and critics gnashing their teeth in despair at her departure. And she did it all for the love of—as Bella always told it when relating the details—"a regular Joe named Nat."

"Fight? Who? My parents?"

"No, not your parents. Debbie and Eddie." Bella patted her hair, pleased with her show business allusion. She had a new hairdo, Lee noted, a bun of dyed red hair, a swollen thing, that looked like a bite from a huge and vicious insect, but her grandmother seemed quite pleased with her appearance. Then again, Bella believed herself to be a ringer for Rita Hayworth, demonstrating an exuberant ego not often found in three-hundred-pound, fifty-six-year-old working-class women in the outer boroughs of New York City. Satisfied with her hair, Bella let her left hand drift over to the coffee table, where it discovered a bowl of M&M's, and scooped up just three fewer than the critical mass of sugar-coated chocolate that would induce diabetic shock. "Of course I mean your parents. Hey, you're stretching the wool too tight, Miss Lily Weissberg."

"That's not my name."

"It's what your name oughta be. Now it's too slack; tighten up the littlest bit. Good. And you know it and I know it and your father, Mr. White, knows it. White! Like he's from Ohio, with a cow. 'Howdy, Farmer White. How's your alfalfa this year?' 'Not bad, if I say so myself.'"

Lee smiled and, abandoning what her mother called "proper carriage," wriggled deep into a corner of the couch: Ah, a perfect meeting of buttocks and cushion. The furniture in her grandparents' living room had been sold to them at a going-out-of-business sale by a salesman who swore the entire suite—couch, two club chairs, a side table, and a coffee table—would last forever, little knowing that for once he was telling the truth. Besides being rugged it was comfortable. And unusually hideous, a Brooklyn restatement of French Provincial style that might have been better left unsaid: painted white wood with flecks of gold, skinny legs, upholstered in royal blue. An odd choice, perhaps, for a card-carrying Communist and his apolitical (but nominally fellow-traveling) wife, but the Weissbergs were blind to its pretensions and saw only its brightness. "Livens up the whole apartment!" Bella had decreed. Lee, whose aesthetic judgment had been honed by Sylvia, grasped that the suite was in the worst possible taste. Nevertheless, side by side with her certitude of its hideousness lay the contrary belief that her grandparents' furniture was the most regal anywhere. Besides, with its fat pillows filled with cheap, chopped-up foam-rubber, it was vastly more comfortable than the icy spareness of the Whites' Bauhaus furnishings.

"So?" Bella demanded.

"What?"

"Do they fight?"

"Once in a while."

"What about?"

"I don't know. They go upstairs and shut the door. I just . . . Their voices get louder, but I can't hear what they're saying."

"You think I was born yesterday?" Bella demanded. Her voice, easily capable of projecting from the Flatbush section of Brooklyn to an audience on the Lower East Side of Manhattan, resounded in Lee's ears. A second later, she softened her statement, smiling in kindly fashion, her mouth a tiny upturned crescent in her round moon of a face. "You don't gotta tell me nothing if you don't want to, toots."

"There's nothing much to tell, Grandma."

"Fine by me."

Two silent stitches, then: "There's nothing Mommy does that makes him happy. Even when she tries."

"So give me a for instance," Bella said, sitting back,

crossing her arms and resting them on her shelf of a bosom.

"Like dinner parties. You know? Like they had twelve people over, and I helped her set the table. It looked beautiful, with the Georg Jensen silver—"

"Who?"

"Their good flatware."

"Flatware," Bella breathed. "God in heaven."

"Anyway, she made a centerpiece with a bunch of twigs and dead leaves and white roses." Catching her grandmother's about-to-curl lip, Lee added: "I know it sounds icky, but it was really beautiful. Very . . . What Mommy and Daddy call 'stark.' That means plain but in a very good way." Lee took a deep breath, hesitating to give her grandmother ammunition in her campaign against her son's life. "He came in, around six-thirty on a Saturday. He'd been at the store all day. Mommy took him into the dining room, you know, to kind of show it off. And he said: 'Oh.' Just 'Oh.' And right away Mommy started acting too happy, the way she always gets when she's …"

"When she's what?"

"Afraid of him. No. I don't know. When she's . . . She wants him to love what she does, but the second he saw the centerpiece, he just stared at it. And she started acting even happier—laughing too much—ha-ha-ha!— telling about how she'd walked in the woods in back of the house to find the twigs and stuff and how she copied the idea from the dinner dance at the Museum of Modern Art . . . just blabbing away a mile a minute."

"And what did he say?"

"Nothing. No, wait. He said, 'They did those arrangements *two years ago.*' Then he said he had to go up and shower and change, but she kept hanging on to his arm and asking over and over 'Is anything wrong, Leonard?' So finally, he said: 'No. Everything's fine and dandy.' And then he just yanked his arm away and went up. Mommy sat down on one of the chairs and started crying, the way she always does."

"What way?"

"Putting her head all the way back. So her mascara on her bottom eyelashes doesn't run."

Bella took the crocheting out of Lee's hands and put her arm around the girl, pulling Lee into the shelter of her warm, fat body. "Is he like this with you, tootsie?"

"No."

"Is he okay with you kids?"

"I always kid around with him. He says I've got a big mouth, but he doesn't mean it in a bad way. He likes when I'm . . . what's the word? Spunky. And he likes that I'm good at tennis and get mostly A's at school. Robin gets A-pluses. She's a big cry-baby and can't do any sports. Daddy says learning sportsman-ship is key."

"Key for what?"

"For life. But he doesn't play any sports."

"So how does it come to be a key?"

"I don't know. So I tell him about all our games and what Coach says about my backhand—a killer back-hand—and it makes him happy." Lee put the wool rose on her lap. "Happy in a kind of phony, excited way. He says: 'Super-duper!' I think he's happier when Robin draws designs for him." Lee's normally golden skin took on a yellowish hue, as if all the bitterness deep within had risen to the surface. "He's using one of her designs at his store. He's actually having it made up. A raccoon coat with a hood that zips on and off." Lee's mouth tightened until her lips disappeared. "I can't draw."

"Big damn deal. You got a killer backside, right?"

"Backhand."

"Whatever. And you know I love your sister, but if a tennis ball came flying at her, she'd piss in her pants."

"More than piss."

"Right. So you're very, very unique. Never forget that. You can play tennis and get A's and crochet like you was born with a hook in your hand. And you're a good girl too, nice through and through. *And* you're nobody's fool. Smart as a whip. Smart enough to know that nothing is ever going to make your father happy."

"Why not?" Lee asked.

"Because what he wants is to be whatever he's not. Mr. Joe College."

"How come he couldn't get a scholarship? He was smart, wasn't he?"

"It wasn't smartness. It was"—Bella touched an area around her solar plexus—"heart. I kept telling him: 'Lenny, you can be anything you want, Lenny. You're a brilliant kid, and you got a chance at the brass ring good as anybody's.' But he never believed that. He saw the deck stacked against him, with the plutocrats—you know, the haves—raking it in and the working-class getting *dreck*. That's always true, and don't you forget it. But now and then a person can make himself an exception. Something inside Lenny went bad, though. Like a disease that ate out the meat from his heart. Still and all, he did make a good business. Right? But he never got his true dreams. To be a big-shot lawyer in a three-piece suit. To be a sport. To be a goy. He got trapped in his own skin."

"And he didn't have the heart to fight his way out?" Lee asked softly.

"You got it in a nutshell."

"So why is he mad at my mother?"

"Because . . . Maybe you're too young for me to be talking to you like this, but you know what I always say? 'What the hell!' So here's what I think and I told your grandfather and he for once in his life didn't say, 'Bella, you're nuts.' Lenny is mad at Sylvia because the girl of his dreams don't want a furrier."

"But she keeps trying so hard to make him happy. It'll never work, will it?"

"I don't think so, toots."

"So I have one question."

"Shoot."

"If he doesn't like himself, and he doesn't like her, and they'll never be—you know—a fun couple . . . There's a fun couple next door, in that big house, up on the hill. But not my mother and father. They'll always be a pair of losers my father can't stand."

"Go on."

"Don't losers have loser kids?"

"No! Not on your life, toots."

"It's not what I think, Grandma. It's what Daddy thinks. He's got me and Robin. But if he had a son like . . ." The name Jasper Taylor choked her. She couldn't say it. She had watched her father standing transfixed, adoring, gawking up at Jasper racing along the perimeter of Hart's Hill's grounds with a huge kite shaped like a sailboat streaming behind him. Leonard had been so taken up with Jasper that he was oblivious that he had turned the pool backwash lever and that water was gushing out over his kidskin loafers.

And so Lee changed the subject and asked for a vanilla Coke. Thus, she never got to say Jasper's name to her beloved Grandma Bella, who died of a hot fudge sundae three months later.

Jasper disappeared from Lee's life the following September, when he went away to prep school, the same school Foster had attended, a prestigious, pedagogically third-rate institution named for an Anglican saint so obscure the Archbishop of Canterbury would not have recognized his name. The next time she saw him was three years later, the summer of 1965, when they were both fifteen. She did not recognize him.

"Jazz!" one of his friends called from the counter of Dante's Pizza, and Jasper-now-Jazz slid out of his booth and ambled over, barefoot, to help his buddy carry the sodas.

It was his feet that drew Lee's attention away from the half-plain, half-sausage-mushroom-meatball pie that lay between her and Robin. Naked feet. "Ick!" Lee said. Going sockless was one thing: In Sylvia's book even that was tolerable only if accompanied by white duck yachting trousers, a striped boat-neck sweater, and a net income of over one hundred thousand dollars per annum. But a kid who went barefoot, even in his own house, was inviting society's condemnation and opportunistic infectious disease.

"Ooky-pukey," Robin agreed. Despite this comment, she was a much-improved child. The onset of menarche, which signals a period of tribulation for so many young women and their families, had actually calmed her. Some biochemical magic soothed her overstimulated dendrites, and while she was certainly still high-strung, she was no longer an identifiable basket case. "Barefoot!"

Jazz's feet were big, Lee noticed as he passed her table, with some light brown hair on the tops and the toes and black filth on the soles. His calves were hairy, although he was tan and the brown hair had turned gold. Muscular calves. She looked up. Blue-and-green madras Bermuda shorts and a blue golf shirt with an alligator on the breast. An alligator! *Mon dieu*, Lee actually said to herself. (She was at that time traveling with the Shorehaven High School intellectual set, and she let out a fast exhalation, a cross between a snort and a sneer.) His biceps looked predictably strong, but what aroused her interest, to say nothing of her libido, were his forearms. Clear muscular definition. Powerfully developed brachioradialis bulging under the tanned skin. And those curly golden hairs; she sensed she could lift one with the very tips of her fingers and it would spring back. Lee glanced up, but he was standing at the counter, beside his friend, a tall drink of water, kibitzing with Dante, Junior.

"I'm full," Robin announced.

"No shit, Ajax," Lee mumbled, her eyes on the forearms.

"I'm going to tell Mommy you said 'shit,'" Robin said, with less malice than a realization that her sister's attention was elsewhere and she wanted it back. Greta had taken one of her rare days off, and her parents had gone to a charity party in a tent somewhere far out on Long Island, at the "cottage" of one of Leonard's customers—which Lee knew was rich-talk for an estate on the ocean (unless the rich person happened to be referring to the hovel in the woods where his groundskeeper lived in degradation and squalor). Bred as Lee was by Sylvia and Leonard and molded by Galsworthy's novels (*The Silver Spoon* had fallen off the shelf at the library and hit Lee on the shoulder as she was browsing—at a time when she should have been studying for her plane geometry regents), her knowledge of upper-middle-class white Anglo-Saxon Protestant mores was near-encyclopedic, albeit wildly outdated and next to useless, unless an awareness of the proper livery for footmen is considered a good thing to know.

"I don't care what you tell Mommy," Lee told Robin. "Tell her I say 'shit.' Tell her I say 'fuck.'"

At this second, Jazz, passing her on his way back to the table with four paper cups filled with ice and a large bottle of Nedick's, startled. Then he looked at her and smiled. A lovely smile (although his teeth were slightly crooked from overcrowded conditions and a belief by Ginger that nice families do not send their children to orthodontists). He had a pleasing face too. Its contours had sharpened in a fine, masculine fashion, changing from rounded to rectangular. His strong jaw now joined his face at right angles.

Lee looked up at him. His smile, she could see, was neither a snotty smile nor a lascivious one, the kind a boy gives to the sort of girl who would say "fuck" in Dante's. It was …

"He heard you say it!" Robin whispered, aghast. "The F curse!"

Lee didn't deny it, but then, her attention was now focused on his receding back: more specifically, at the angle made by the bulges of muscle that were his buttocks as they tapered into the columnar solidity of his thighs. When he sat in the booth, he chose the seat that faced her. Thank you, she said to the God in Whom she already did not believe. But the boy wasn't smiling at her anymore, not even looking at her. That was good, though, because it gave her a chance to study him. His friends were rich dipshits, probably private school kids, as was he. But he was different. They made loud, stupid sports talk about someone being traded to Detroit and pulled long strings of mozzarella cheese from the pizza up into their mouths and made gross sucking noises. He just sat blowing on the slice he'd taken and looking pensive. No, serene. No, sensitive. That was it! He was so far above the morons he was with it wasn't funny.

"Lee!" Robin whined, demanding her attention. Lee hated this: being stuck with her sister on a weekend.

"Lee!" It was an error, staring at the boy, because Robin turned and followed her gaze. "Why are you staring at him?"

And a bigger error to deny it so vehemently. "I am *not* staring at anyone, you infantile ass."

"You are too!"

"Shut up!" Lee snarled.

Robin fell into shocked silence, not comprehending the intensity of her sister's response. A second later, she did. "You have a crush on him," Robin taunted. "I can tell!"

"I do not!" Lee insisted, feeling her face, her neck, turning red, then purple, with mortification. Lee's throat felt constricted. Her chest tightened. She could barely get out the words because of the terrible feeling she was choking. "If you don't shut up, I'll kill you!"

"Ooh, I'm so scared!"

Lee flared her nostrils, which usually caused Robin to at least squirm in her seat, but this time it was a futile gesture. So she narrowed her eyes and glowered at Robin. "I'll tell Mommy where her three bars of Je Reviens soap went."

"Yeah?" Robin challenged her, although Lee picked up a quaver behind the resolution. "Where?"

"Over to Erica Johanson's for a slumber party, that's where. And if Mommy finds out …"

"You tell her that and I'll tell her you're madly in love with Jasper Taylor!"

"What?" Lee demanded, confused.

"With Jasper Taylor."

"Next-door's kid? Are you kidding? That's who he is?"

"That's him. Pizza boy."

Lee stared at the boy two booths down. "That's . . . ?" Even before Robin nodded triumphantly, she knew it was true. Well, he had been away at school someplace. She hadn't seen him since . . . God, it must have been elementary school. He'd changed so much.

His long leg was stretched out from the booth. His bare, dirty foot—Did rich kids get some guarantee public school kids didn't, that germs wouldn't crawl into minuscule cuts and turn gangrenous, leaving them four-toed, unable to wear thongs for the rest of their lives?—extended into the aisle that led to the counter. This boy was Jasper Taylor? He wasn't that conceited idiot . . . although his eyes and the shiny brown hair . . . Yes! Someone had called him Jazz!

"You love Jasper Taylor!" Robin jeered. Too loud. He didn't hear her words, not consciously anyhow, but his name registered subliminally, and Lee saw his toes stop wiggling for one harrowing second. "You love—"

Lee grabbed her sister's bony wrist. "Shut up," she ordered. "Shut up or—" She was so agitated that for once she was at a loss for words. She couldn't think of any threat dreadful enough to stop Robin.

But Robin stopped herself. The look on her older sister's face: teeth clenched, mouth twisted downward into an anguished grimace, her brows coming together into a terrified V . . . "Okay," Robin soothed Lee. "I won't say it." Lee nodded, unable to speak—and also, Robin noticed, unable to withdraw her eyes from the Taylor boy's face. Lee's shoulders relaxed slightly, but she was still in the grip of some passion that would not release her, to return to being Lee, regular Lee, the big sister with the easy smile and the wise mouth. "Lee?"

"What?" Lee's eyes were on the boy as he licked a drop of tomato-tinged olive oil from his chin.

"Is he *that* good?"

"Yes," Lee told Robin, when she finally found her voice. "He's that good."

Nine

❧

My private investigator, Terry Salazar, had a sweet, raspy tenor, the sort of voice heroin-addicted male blues singers with cult followings have: every word slow, provocative. His is the sound that makes every woman— semi-literate teen punks, Indiana Republicans—fantasize about writhing on rumpled sheets.

"Hello," I said into the speakerphone.

"Hey, Lee!" I didn't have to ask: Who is it? "You are fucked," he gloated.

"Badly?"

"No. Bad." Terry was a real American man. He guarded against any behavior that might remotely be considered feminine, like saying "please" or using the proper adverbial form. "You're fucked up the ass bad." I pushed the button to mute the speaker, lifted the receiver, and listened. "They got Bobette's tenant, his name is . . ." Terry paused, and I heard him riffling the pages of the small spiral notebook he kept on each of his cases. " . . . Eugene Pohl. Eugene got treated to a lineup yesterday afternoon. All five guys were six-three and over—just so you can't bitch about how long, tall Normie stood out."

"Was Pohl able to ID Norman?" I asked.

"It wasn't easy. It took him—Jesus—at least a tenth of a second."

Attorneys like me hire ex-Nassau County cops like Terry to do background on a case because of who they know—law enforcement types who never talk to a defense lawyer. But it's more than contacts: Smart cops know how to conduct an inquiry into a murder case. Terry had been a detective sergeant in Homicide and was a first-class investigator. He did more than just ask questions. Radiating rough charm when he felt it was necessary, he could get an enormous amount of information out of all but the most reticent of witnesses. Women would open up to Terry because they couldn't bear for him to leave. It wasn't that he was objectively handsome, but he was unequivocally masculine: A woman can sense when she is in the presence of erectile tissue. Men reacted to his gruff warmth. Although he didn't brag, they sensed his mastery of traditional male talents: hot-wiring a car, shooting a gun, deceiving his wife. They wanted Terry to approve of them, so they, too, kept talking.

Eugene Pohl, apparently, was one of the few exceptions. "He wouldn't say a word," Terry informed me. "What a pussy! You know, the kind who tucks his napkin in his collar so he won't get soup on his tie."

"Is he prissy, or is he what people imagine when they hear 'computer nerd'?"

"Computer nerd."

"Truly bizarre or just a little nerdy?"

"A big nerdy. Puny, and he's got a shiny bald dickhead. But, Lee, don't get your hopes up. He's definitely not someone you could make the jury believe is more of a killer than your pal Norman Torkelson."

"You have no idea what I can get a jury to believe," I snapped back.

I was angry at Terry for having doubts, for expressing them, but, most of all, angry at myself for going along with his questioning my abilities. Even if only for a second, I'd let myself think: This case is too big for me. In all the years I'd known him, Terry had never given me a boost: Hey, you're going to *destroy* this guy on the stand! No, he was always negative. And my gut reaction always was: You must be right.

"Terry."

"What?"

"You really are a mean-spirited jerk. I'd call you misogynistic too, except you're too ignorant to know what that means."

"Lee, trust me on this. At most, he'll sweat a little. But you think he's going to start twitching on the stand and act real deranged in front of the jury once Holly Nuñez gets done preparing him? What the hell gives with her, anyway? Always so happy. 'Hi! You must be Terry! Grrreat to meet you, Terry!' "

"She's a little on the perky side."

"Doing her must be like fucking a white bread."

Which meant Terry was powerfully attracted to Holly and would make her his pet project over the next six months. I sighed, regretting the wisdom that comes with age, and switched the phone to the other ear. "Find out what you can about Eugene Pohl," I said, weary. "At Snapple—and ask around the neighborhood. Maybe someone knows something. Maybe he was trying to make time with Bobette himself, move up from the basement and become master of the house."

While I doubted this would be my defense strategy, I did not need to hear Terry's rollicking laugh. "Yeah, right, Lee. They'll come back with a 'not guilty' before the bailiff has time to take the lunch order. What are you going to say? Eugene Pohl was jealous of Norman's success with Bobette, so he set it up to make it look like Norman—"

As this was an accurate assessment of a strategy that had been flitting around the back of my mind, I slammed down the phone. I was regretting my childishness, when Terry called back to inform me Holly had told him that the discovery material on Torkelson was ready anytime I wanted it. Then he hooted: "Eugene Pohl and Bobette Frisch!" So I banged down the phone again.

The rest of that morning and afternoon, I got bogged down with a couple of other cases, including an unlawful use of scientific material and transportation of stolen property in interstate commerce, a crime I'd never tried before. My client, a secretary, had been fired from a small company in Lynbrook that did pharmaceutical testing. She admitted to me that she had stayed late one night, copied all their results on a new drug for treating hepatitis A, and mailed the secret data to the CEO of Upjohn— just so the Lynbrook people would "realize their systems weren't secure." The CEO, no lunkhead, called the FBI. My client was, frankly, nuts, so I spent half the day trying to arrange an appointment for me and her therapist (who concurred with my diagnosis) to try and talk the chief of the Criminal Division of the U.S. Attorney's Office in the Eastern District out of prosecuting.

By the time I came up for air it was after five, so I left a message on Holly's voice mail that I was walking over. It was gorgeous out! I couldn't believe I'd missed it, holed up in an office building, the tenderest of spring days, with air that smelled so sweet you regretted the time it took to exhale. The grass around the courthouse was so new, so velvety, you wished you could forget you were an adult and simply roll around for a while on its softness, then lie on your back and let the late-afternoon sun warm your face.

"It's beautiful out there," I told Holly. "Makes me want to gambol in the grass."

In response, she handed me a file that had an ominous heft to it. Without being invited, I sat and started going through the material. At first glance, there was nothing to send me back outside with a song in my heart.

"Uh, Lee," Holly said, with regret so phony they'd be able to smell it twenty-four miles west, at the Fulton Fish Market, "I hate to bounce you, but I have *tons* of stuff I've got to do. Could you read it tonight or tomorrow? Then I'll clear the boards for you whenever you want to talk about it."

"In a second," I muttered, looking for something to get outraged about so I could accuse her of bad faith, put her on the defensive, and, with any luck, give her a bad night. Then, I actually found something! Another set of fingerprints—an unknown person's—all around the first floor of Bobette's house, including on the coffee table in the living room, right where her body had been found. "These prints!" I gasped. Really gasped. Luckily, the walk over to Holly's office with balmy May breezes wafting about had triggered my allergies, so my words came out in a giant wheeze, as though the finding had knocked the breath out of me. "There's somebody else's prints *inches* from where the body was found and *without any further investigation* you still arrest Norman and throw him right in the slammer."

"You know he would have run if we didn't," she said. But I could see the notion of the other prints were causing her a mite of concern, although, God knows, no discernible anguish.

"Why would he run? He didn't kill her."

"Oh, Lee!" she said, giving me one of those peppy-people smiles that display thirty-two teeth. "Give me a break."

"Why should I give you a break? Are you giving my client a break and trying to track down those prints?"

"He killed her. He doesn't deserve a break."

"How hard did you try?" I demanded, knowing the limited resources of the D.A.'s office. "You're holding what looks to me a lot like exculpatory evidence, and you let it lie here in the file?" Before she could arrange her face into still another sprightly expression, I said: "I want a copy of those prints."

"They could be anyone's," Holly objected.

"Like whose?"

"I don't know. The maid's."

"Holly, do you know for a fact that she had a maid?" Holly tried to look thoughtfully at her new acrylic nails, but I knew the answer was no. "Maybe they're the butler's prints," I suggested. She started buffing the shell-pink nail of her ring finger with her right thumb. "Did you check Eugene Pohl's prints, by any chance?"

"They're not his."

"I need those prints, Holly."

"I'll get them for you."

"I need them now."

"Lee, it's . . . " She made a big deal of looking at her watch and letting her mouth drop open. "I can't believe it! I really have to—"

"I'll wait," I told her.

Right before lunch the next day, I met Terry at the Love Nest and handed him a copy of the prints. He had pals everywhere, and I was hoping the one he had in the state police could run a thorough computer check.

We stood on the sidewalk. Terry gazed at the exceedingly unlovely Love Nest, Norman's place of business, with amazement and respect. "He rented this place to take rich women to fuck?" To be a successful seducer in a depressing place like this was no small triumph.

"He must have done his romancing in their places first. After that, who knows? I guess love is blind."

"'Love?'" he demanded, full of pity at my stupidity. "The guy must have had a schlong that went from here to Cleveland."

Though Norman's practice was to tell his marks the place was only temporary, till he could get back on his feet, I was still astounded any woman in her right mind would be willing to go inside. The apartment building, a cube of sand-colored brick, wasn't so bad in itself. Neither was the neighborhood, which appeared largely black and working class. But the site of the building: a mini-slum. Instead of a lawn, there was a packed-down dirt patch that sustained only a few pale-green sickly weeds. The dirt and the front walk were littered with cigarette wrappers that seemed to have blown in from all of Long Island. But that was just small-time litter. There was also a bicycle wheel from which the tire had been removed, a bouquet of pitted aluminum tubes from what once had been a folding chair, old beer cans crushed in the middle.

"Anything else besides the prints?" Terry inquired as he crouched to get a look at the make of the front-door lock. I reached past his shoulder and opened the door. Terry gave me a sour look, but the next second we were in a small hallway, an apartment on either side. On the door to the right, a business card was taped directly under the buzzer: Denton Wylie—the alias Norman had used with Bobette. Centered right beneath the name was printed: *INVESTMENT*, and under that: "The Newsletter for the Venture Capitalist." In the lower-right-hand corner was an understated, lowercase "publisher and editor in chief." Terry eyed the lock on the apartment door. I motioned for him to go ahead; his key ring was so full it would put me on tilt, and sure enough, he got us inside in less than a minute.

The apartment was not as hideous as I'd expected, but that isn't saying a lot. Terry got busy in the kitchenette peering inside cabinets, looking for whatever it is private investigators hope to find: additional corpses or, more likely, unopened bags of Doritos.

I found a tissue in the pocket of my attaché case and used it to lift the lid of the answering machine that stood on a counter that separated the living room from the kitchenette. As I'd suspected, Norman had ordered Mary to get rid of the incoming message tape, which had her Repo Lady impersonation; it was gone. Terry followed me into the bedroom. "Wow!" I said. We stood silently and gazed at the bed: round and so huge that in order to get to what I assumed was the bathroom, you had to inch sideways, your back pressed against the wall. The bed was covered in a too shiny polyester throw that looked more like a tablecloth than a spread. Not that you'd want to eat off it; from its almost imperceptible odor, you knew it had not been laundered, or even vacuumed, for years. Plus it had a couple of pudendum-shaped stains near the circumference. Still, I understood why Norman had rented the apartment. The bed was as effective as a flashing neon sign advertising: HOT SEX! HOT SEX! THE SEX YOU DREAM ABOUT! HOT SEX!

Terry sidled along between bed and wall to go and check the bathroom. When he came back, unedified, he plopped down and patted the mattress beside him. "Have a seat."

"And get gonorrhea from that bedspread?" I leaned against the wall, slightly off to the side so that our knees wouldn't touch in the confined space. "Let me brief you on the discovery material." Terry reached into his inside jacket pocket and pulled out his notebook and a pen. I continued: "Their witness list has the usual cops, scientific experts. No DNA guy. That sounds as though they didn't find any of his skin cells under her nails or anything during the autopsy."

"Let me see the autopsy report," Terry said. Sandi, my secretary, had made copies of almost the entire discovery material for him. I took a fat manila folder from my attaché case and handed it to him. He'd been in Homicide for nine years and knew what to look for better than I did. "It says he didn't fuck her," he said after a few minutes' reading. "Poor bitch's last day on earth, and she didn't get laid."

"She ate a chocolate bar. She still had chocolate all over her mouth."

"I know you think that's as good as getting laid, but it's not."

He went back to the report. I watched him read. Terry looked like a cop, with a too flat hairstyle, slightly too tight blue suit—half an inch too much sock showing—and the kind of mustache that went out of fashion in 1973. He had quit the force three years earlier when he turned forty-one, the day his pension vested, and gone to work as head of security at a fairly upscale shopping center in Greenvale. But despite the big paycheck, the thrill of dealing with stolen Volvos and teenagers walking out of the Gap wearing three pairs of jeans palled after a few weeks. He stuck it out for a year, then opened his own agency, with himself as sole employee. My partner, Chuckie, and I threw what business we could his way, and within six months, Terry was thriving. He hired two other ex-cops to work for him. They were pretty good. Terry was terrific.

"Amazing," he said. "She gives him forty-eight thousand bucks. He gives her no sex."

"Nice work if you can get it."

"Listen, you got a block of cement like Bobette around, who can blame the guy? So listen, Lee, I don't see anything in the discovery material that'll hurt your little Normie any more than he's already hurt, except for the strangling itself: the size of the hands and the strength of the perpetrator." Terry was right. I couldn't stop the medical examiner from saying "very big hands" and "powerful," and the jury would look over at six-foot-five-inch, two-hundred-pound Norman Torkelson sitting at the defense table, his hands folded in his lap, and think: That's our boy. "Anything else in here I should worry about?" Terry asked. "Any nasty surprises?"

"Bobette's wallet appears to be missing."

"Maybe she left it in one of her bars or someplace," Terry said, for once not insisting on the worst-case scenario. But then I glanced over at him and saw he was not really paying attention. He was stroking the bedspread with his thumb, clearly thinking of all that was possible on a round bed. When you looked at his face in repose—past his bad tie, his mustache, and especially past his misogyny—you could understand how appealing he could be. Part Portuguese, part Irish, and part Italian, he had the long, lean, rugged face of an Iberian peasant farmer, soft blue Irish eyes, and a helmet of dark gladiator curls that he blew-dry into submission every day. However, although he was, on these rare occasions, a treat to look at, I wasn't paying him seventy-five dollars an hour and thirty-five cents a mile to contemplate the possibilities of a round bed and look dreamy.

"Terry, write this down." He peered up, slightly dazed at being summoned back to reality. "Check with your pals at MasterCard, Visa, and Amex. See if there were any Bobette Frisch charges starting with the Friday of the murder. Can you do that today?" He nodded and then, seeing that I was waiting for something, jotted a word or two in his notebook. "With any luck," I said, "somebody in San Antonio charged a thousand dollars' worth of chewing tobacco the day after Norman was arrested."

"And the Department will send a couple of detectives to Texas and they'll track the guy down and arrest him for Bobette's murder. Right?" He had a wolfish smile with very large white teeth. "You're dreaming."

The Love Nest offered up nothing more, so we headed down to Bobette's house to meet Sam Franklin. Holly had said he'd show us whatever we wanted to see, but I knew Sam would make it a miserable and difficult procedure. I followed Terry to Merrick in my own car. He would be destroyed psychologically if he had to ride as a passenger with a woman driving; and I would not drive with him: He fit the stereotype for cop slobs, and the car was a four-wheel garbage dump of unfolded, coffee-stained maps, oily Roy Rogers napkins, discarded straws and paper-wrapped, petrified gum globs. A vomitous air freshener in the shape of a banana hanging from his rearview mirror only made matters worse.

Sam Franklin's contempt for me was small potatoes compared to his loathing of Terry Salazar, an ex-cop who now worked for criminals. But Terry and Sam had never liked each other, even in the years when they had shared a desk in Homicide. They were different in every way: Gaunt / husky; introspective / superficial; puritan / libertine; devout evangelical Protestant / aggressively lapsed Catholic.

"Hey, Sammy, how're they hanging?" Terry inquired.

He automatically gave all other men a diminutive ending just to show precisely who was the alpha dog in the pack.

"I have to be out of here in ten minutes," Sam responded. "You'd better get a move on."

Sam stood back and let us walk inside. His eyes didn't leave us for a minute. He was on the verge of protesting as I walked down the two steps from the front hall to the sunken living room over to check out the area between the couch and the coffee table, where Bobette's body had been found. However, Sam knew that I knew he had no grounds to stop me, so he clamped his jaw shut and refrained from grinding his teeth, aware that the sight of him all riled up not merely would delight Terry but could form the basis for a wicked imitation at old boy cop gatherings: Sam Franklin Thrown into a Tizzy by Female Lawyer.

The crime scene photos, with their cruel light illuminating Bobette's body, had given her couch and coffee table the impersonality of furniture in a chain of economy hotels, so I'd expected a house that was as businesslike as Bobette. But it was so sweet that if the two men hadn't been there, I might have gotten all teary over the girl-at-heart who'd had the life choked out of her right where I was standing. Instead I swallowed the lump in my throat and perched on the arm of the couch, letting my leg swing back and forth to show them I was just as casual about this house of death as they were.

The couch wasn't beige, as it had appeared in the photos, but butter yellow, with a profusion of needlepoint pillows, the faultlessly stitched, innocuous ones offered in upscale catalogs: butterflies on a magnolia branch, a white Persian cat, a nosegay of violets, and the fourth, blue letters on a lemon background, which read: "Living well is the best revenge."

The room was so extravagantly girlish that it could have been conceived by a gay set designer as an *hommage* to old-fashioned femininity. A peach carpet, with a garland of blue and yellow flowers as a border. Yellow-and-pink-checked fabric on two armchairs, ruffled on the edges, so it looked as if Bobette had dressed them in pinafores. A collection of glass and ceramic cats on a side table, none taller than three inches.

"Did she have any cats?" I asked Sam.

"What?" I repeated the question, resisting the temptation to say it slowly, as if he were slow-witted. "We didn't find any."

"Are you sure? No litter box? No cat food dish?"

"No."

"A cat?" Terry asked. "Why would she have a cat?"

I turned back to him. "Why *wouldn't* she have a cat or two?"

"Because they're animals. They eat and they shit," he answered.

"So do you."

Unfazed, he took out a tape measure to determine the distance between the coffee table and a large picture book lying on the floor: *Fluff Balls: The Wonderful World of Angora Cats.* I wondered if Bobette's dream of romance had been so intensely cerebral that anything that would demand care—or even minimal attention—would have been a distraction. Just then an antimacassar in the shape of a valentine on a yellow wing chair caught my eye. Norman must have known, the second he stepped through the front door and saw that lacy heart, that her bank account was his for the asking.

We did a walk-through, Sam leading. Whenever we stopped, Sam stood legs apart, hands open and resting lightly on hips, as if any second he'd have to reach for his service revolver to prevent us from committing some felonious act. His eyes flitted from me to Terry and back to me, vigilant, as we looked around. What was there to see? Pot holders in the kitchen: one covered with daisies; another, a mitt, in the shape of a tabby cat. In the downstairs bathroom, a matching turquoise rug and toilet seat cover, each with an embroidered fleur-de-lis in the center; and a satin wrapper for an extra roll of toilet paper, in the shape of Victorian bonnet.

Oh, and her bedroom! Entirely lavender: carpet, walls, bed linens. The floor-length curtains were tied back with a braided tassel of pale lavender and deep purple. On the wall were lavender-matted botanical prints of purple flowers: lilacs, irises, and lavender. The room was romantic—and erotic. Many women would shy away from such a baring of their soul's desire. Not Bobette, although maybe that was because she lived such a solitary life that she felt certain no one could ever discern, by a mere glance around her room, her sexual nature. At last, when Norman came along, she was thrilled to show him, because he was precisely what she'd been praying for all her life.

Sam, Terry, and I stood by the bed, a four-poster with a lace canopy, perfectly made. No sign of lovemaking. Terry checked the drawers of the nightstands. "Zilch," he reported.

"Did you take anything from the drawers?" I asked Sam.

"It should all be in your discovery material," he spat out, as if the question were so outrageous, so disgusting, that it nauseated him to answer.

"There is nothing in the material that refers to items taken from her nightstands," I said. "Therefore, I am assuming your answer is no, you did not take anything you did not record in the report. Naturally, I will ask Holly Nuñez to check up on this, since I cannot get an answer from you." Sam contemplated actually giving me a response—"no"—for a second, but decided against such humiliation. He crossed his arms and beat out a slow, jazzy rhythm on his elbows, as if he were all alone, listening to Coltrane. "You got a positive ID from the tenant, Eugene Pohl?" There was no sign Sam was hearing anything other than "Trane's Blues." "Answer me, Sam, or I'm going after your ass!"

"Yes." The word was almost a hiss.

"And from the guy at the bank?"

"Which guy at the bank?" Sam asked innocently.

I thought fast. A teller doesn't simply hand over forty-eight thousand dollars. "The bank officer Bobette dealt with. And the guard near the door. They didn't see my client with her, did they?"

"No," he exhaled, telling me more about the status of Holly's case than I thought I would ever get.

"Your case is a fairy tale," I told him. "Right from the beginning, it was easier to sit back in your chair and tell yourself stories than it was to get out and investigate." I banged my fist against one of the bed's posts for emphasis, as if there were an invisible jury just off to my left. "No one else claims to have seen Norman Torkelson with Bobette except the tenant, and you know and I know—and the jury sure as hell is going to know—that Eugene Pohl is one very strange bird."

Then, before Terry could mouth off and thus once again antagonize Sam and thus dissipate the tiny cloud of uncertainty I'd managed to float, I grabbed him by the sleeve and yanked him out of Bobette Frisch's girlish dream of love.

Later that day, while Terry was around and about, checking the set of mystery prints that had appeared all over Bobette's house and trying to discover if anyone had charged anything to Bobette's missing credit cards, I went to court for the arraignment of a new client, a guy accused of selling counterfeit Donna Karan everything— shoes, suits, belts, sweaters, nightgowns. I was hoping he'd have an overpowering obsession, so I could at least play around with pleading insanity, but he was annoyingly sane and wanted to barter down part of his legal fee by trading my time for a new wardrobe: "I swear to Christ, Mrs. White. Would I stick you of all people with the fake Donnas? These are *real*, the ones I knocked off from. I'm talking six-ply cashmere." After the arraignment, I dropped in to watch a few minutes of Chuckie's arson trial, then, overcome by an irresistible impulse, spent my lunch hour in Bloomingdale's and wound up with a white cashmere shawl.

And a pair of sling-backs. Also, I bought a lip gloss and with it, for an extra $16.95, got one of those giant, useless makeup kits with circlets of cosmetics in colors designed for cheap hookers—not cheap hookers' legal counsel: hues like Papaya Sunset and Teal Twilight. So by the time I was in the elevator going back to my office, I was, naturally, giving myself a hard time, thinking that if I'd been a man I would have spent the hour and a half at the Bar Association library, looking up arcane case law. Or I would have invited some big-firm lawyer out to lunch so the next time one of his firm's hotshot corporate clients got picked up for statutory rape or vehicular homicide, "Lee White!" would leap to mind. Of course, being a lawyer, I sprang to my own defense, and as I was opening my office door, I was already arguing: So if I were a male lawyer, instead of Bloomingdale's I'd wind up at the Wiz, looking for a longer telephone cord, but instead I'd walk out with a Pentium computer with speakers the size of Mount McKinley and a quad-speed

CD-ROM player, and therefore, wasn't my foray into cashmere relatively innocuous? Of course, a still, small voice inside began a siren song of a new computer, but I didn't hear it because as I walked inside, there in the reception area was Mary Dean.

"Hi!" she said brightly. She wore a red dress with polka dots the size of silver dollars. Its material was of some cheap synthetic so stiff it made crinkly noises when she moved. Her country-music hair was piled on top of her head and held by a big red plastic barrette in the shape of a bow. She was no less beautiful than she had been on her last visit. "Hope you don't mind that I dropped in."

"I'd prefer it if you'd call first," I said, demonstrating that the assertiveness-awareness seminar at the Women's Bar Association had not been a complete waste of time. Then I cast what I hoped was a withering glance at the receptionist who had allowed Mary to stay. She was the granddaughter of a guy in one of my partner Chuckie's poker games, a young woman with the spiritless serenity of a cloistered nun in a washed-up order.

"The reason I came back," Mary explained, after I closed my office door and we were both seated, "is that I remember something else."

"I see."

"You said it's *all* important, to help Norman."

"Anything you remember," I said. "You never know what will be helpful."

"I want to help!" She made a terrible gurgling noise. For a second, I thought she was choking, then I realized it was a sob. I felt for the box of tissues, pulled out a couple, and held them out to her across the desk. But her hands were covering her face so I put them back until she could see them. "I miss him so much," she wept, although it was difficult to hear through the tears and her hands. "It's like . . . without him . . . Oh, please! Get him out of that place!"

"I'm trying. And anything you can tell me . . . . Sometimes the smallest detail can mean a lot."

She composed herself, wiping away her tears with her knuckles. She noticed the streaks of mascara on them, and I handed her the tissues. She wiped her fingers, then blotted the black smudges under her eyes, making tiny, dainty dabs, so as not to pull at the delicate skin. "You know how I told you I called up when Norman had a mark at the Love Nest, saying I was from the Pinnacle Collections Agency? You know, about repossessing his car."

"Right," I said briskly. Mary's voice was shaky, and I didn't want her to start bawling again. To be perfectly truthful, it was less out of compassion than from a desire to get rid of her; I sensed that she was about to tell me everything she knew about Norman, an encyclopedia's worth, and that would put a healthy bite into what was the not overly large retainer I'd charged him. "What else do you have to tell me?"

"I do other things too."

"What do you mean?"

"Like, if he thinks the mark isn't feeling sorry enough for him, I call up and"—she smiled at some memory—"pretend I'm the ex-wife."

"Do you put that message on his answering machine as well?"

"No. Norman says more than one message on the machine would be, like, too obvious. No, I call up and scream my bloody head off: 'Norman, you fucking bastard!'" Mary squawked, clearly taking pleasure in her own performance. This voice, unlike the low-pitched, tough Repo Lady voice, was high, but not an ineffectual squeak. It was rough, mean, like an emery board abrading skin. " 'I'm gonna make sure you're ruined. I'm gonna make sure you're so goddamn, pathetic broke you'll *never* get back on your feet again.' " Her pale skin took on an exhilarated flush from the tantrum. "Anyhow, I just keep screaming like the worst bitch in the world!"

"And you're so loud he holds the phone away from his ear, and the mark hears it."

"Yes! You know, you make me think, like, there's hope," Mary said. "You're so smart. As smart as Norman! I feel like, gee, you can handle this."

"Do you play any other roles?"

She laughed. "Doesn't roles always make you think of *rolls*? Like hamburger rolls—or those little curvy ones? They're in the dairy case, and they're triangles, and you roll them up and—"

"Right. But let's talk about acting roles."

"Well, I play his divorce lawyer's secretary. Like, 'Mr. Powers's office calling for Mr. Whatever-name-Norman's-using.' We arrange a time, and when the phone rings, he's busy someplace and asks the mark to get it and take a message."

"Did you play the ex-wife or the secretary with Bobette Frisch?" I asked.

"No," Mary said. A little tight-lipped, I thought.

"How come?"

"She was so crazy about him, I didn't have to."

I tried to sound casual. "Too crazy about him?"

"A clingy vine," Mary said, pushing out her over-glossed lips into a pout. Not a cutesy pout: the real thing.

"In what way did she cling?"

"Like always begging him: 'Stay over. Don't go home, Norman. I can't stand it when you're not with me, Norman.' "

"Just the way you feel," I observed. Okay, not tactful, but it had been a long day.

"I have a right to him!" She was still wearing that pistachio-green eye shadow, and, with the red dress and lipstick, looked unseasonably Yulish.

"Of course you do."

"Who the hell does she think she is? I mean, I know it's Norman's job to make them feel he loves them, but she was acting like . . . " Mary shook her head; it was almost a shudder. "Like she really thought *he* couldn't stand being away from her. Like she was doing him a favor, letting him stay overnight in that stupid house."

"Did he spend the night there often?"

"Once or twice," she said, resuming her pout.

"Once or twice?"

"I don't know," she said, her volume control going out of whack, until she was almost shouting again. "Maybe three or four times. Okay? Like he would really get into that stupid purple bed of hers and do it to her. Fucking cow!"

"How did he avoid doing it?" I asked.

"Told her he wanted to wait till they were married. I mean, she was so old! Did she really think he could make himself do it without, like, puking?"

"Where did he stay when he spent the night there?" I asked.

"There's another bedroom right next to it. It's more an office, but it has a Hide-A-Bed." Mary was cooling down enough to give me a small smile. "At least it wasn't purple. I couldn't believe it!"

"I went there today. Even the botanical prints on the wall were all purple flowers."

"And did you see her dresser? That whole collection of purple perfume bottles?"

"Right," I said. We sat in silence for a few seconds. I buzzed Sandi and asked her for two glasses of water, hold the ice. "You seem really upset about Bobette."

"Why shouldn't I be?" Mary stopped, a theatrical pause, as if she were on a talk show, waiting for audience approval: Yeah! and Right! "Norman's in jail and—"

"I didn't mean about her murder. I meant about her relationship with Norman."

"No. I mean, I hated it when he slept over, but like he said: 'Unless you put in the man-hours, you don't get the profits.' He says a lot of business things like that. He has a great head for business." She got busy tugging at the hem of her polka-dot dress in order to get rid of the wrinkles around her lap, putting her weight first on one hip, then on the other. The dress was too short and much too tight, at least in terms of wrinkle-prevention. But with her long legs, it did look spectacular, and the dozen or so wrinkles didn't detract from it in the least. However, I felt she was avoiding my question and using the only means of obfuscation she had at her disposal: her sexuality.

"Mary," I said, "I don't buy it."

"Don't buy what?"

"Don't buy your act that you weren't upset about Bobette and Norman."

"What do you mean? Do you think, like, he fell in love with her or something?"

"No. But you tell me. Woman to woman. Something was bothering you."

Mary clasped her hands in her wrinkled lap. Finally, she said: "Swear to God you won't tell him?"

I nodded. That wasn't enough. I put up my right hand and said: "I swear."

"To God."

"I swear to God," I exhaled, thinking that I should double my hourly rates for dealings with my clients' sweet patooties.

"It's like, I've been so worried about him," Mary said.

"He's tired. I mean, you have no idea how much his job takes out of him. The last few cities, when we have mail call—that's what we call it—it used to be so much fun getting all the answers to his ad in the personals. We'd drink our martinis and read them out loud to each other and laugh and laugh." She must have read something on my face, because she quickly added, "Of course, we didn't laugh *all* the time. Some of them were kind of pitiful. But now, when he brings in the mail, it's like it weighs a ton."

"It's weighing him down," I suggested.

"Yes! He says he doesn't have the energy anymore to do the dance. Not a real dance. He means the con. He says it's draining him."

Sandi came in carrying a small tray with two glasses of water. Mary declined hers. "It's bottled water," I reassured her.

"I'm not thirsty."

I waited for Sandi to go out and close the door. Then I prompted Mary: "You were saying how tired Norman is."

"He says: 'I'm bone-weary.' You know how tired *that* is. He says he wishes we had enough money to retire. Buy a condo in Florida or the Virgin Islands or someplace and just, like, spend the rest of our lives together."

Suddenly I asked: "You like being on the water?"

"I love looking at it. Being on the beach. Except it's not as much fun since sunblock." I walked over to the wall facing my desk and took one of the framed photographs off the wall, a shot of a house and dock that the man in my life had taken from a small boat in a canal: his house in Oceanside. I handed it to Mary. "Ooh! Isn't it adorable!" she exclaimed. "A little dream house."

"My boyfriend took the picture," I said, hanging it back in its place on the wall among his other work. He was a terrific photographer. "You know, you've spoken about all the pressures of Norman's job and how wiped out he was, but you still haven't made me understand why you felt Bobette was such a threat."

Mary's eyes were still on the picture. "I was afraid he would leave me for her," she said quietly.

"*What*?"

She seemed gratified by my incredulity. "Not 'cause he doesn't love me. But he's so exhausted. When you're tired of the con, what else is there? Like, on *Montel* or *Leeza*, there was this show: Men Who Get Depressed so They Run Off with Older Women Because It's Like Their Mothers, or something. I remember thinking: Oh my God! Norman!"

"Did he ever indicate that he was thinking of leaving you and going with Bobette?"

"Of course not! But I could see sometimes how much it took out of him just to get up and go *meet* one of these old maids. I think there may have been a teeny-weeny part of him that was saying: 'Finally, here's one who's got more than money in the bank. Here's one that's got an *income*, who could support me.'"

I met up with Terry Salazar again a little before Happy Hour at Plumpie's, a bar that catered to the fringes of the criminal justice system: ex-cops, court reporters, bail bondsmen, an occasional disbarred lawyer. Its jolly name was misleading: Plumpie's was one of those dank, dark-wooded places in which you're grateful for the dismal lighting, because if they put in 150-watt bulbs, you'd see thirty years of unspeakable crud and a cross section of insect life that would haunt your dreams. Terry was drinking straight gin, which never did much for his disposition but mellowed his irresistible voice so it was even more compelling.

"Are you still coherent?" I asked.

Aggrieved, he answered: "It's my second."

I ordered one of the more esoteric light beers, one that Herman Oberndorfer, a.k.a. Plumpie, would not have on tap, so I wouldn't have to drink from one of his never-washed-properly steins. I lifted the bottle and took a swig. "Anything on Bobette's credit cards?" I asked.

"You're going to love this. Over six thousand dollars worth of stuff charged on the date of the murder."

"Maybe Bobette went on a shopping spree early in the day." I tried to sound confident, but I would have to work on it.

"I'm having my pal call a couple of the stores. They're all in that Americana Shopping Center. Like Louis Vuitton." He pronounced it perfectly, which led me to think that his wife had probably given up meditation once again and was shopping (once again) and I'd better make sure Terry wasn't padding his disbursements (once again). "Barney's," he went on. "Someone ran up three thousand bucks there."

"Probably bought two pairs of pantyhose. All right, try to get the information as soon as you can. Not just to time of day. Find out what they bought. My guess is, most of the men's stuff in an upscale place like that wouldn't fit Norman; he's way too tall."

"Maybe he bought something for someone."

"Right," I said, thinking of Mary. "Anything on the prints yet?"

"I had to pass my pal a hundred."

"Put it on your bill," I said, sure that what he passed was probably a couple of twenties. "Were they able to get a make on them?"

"No. Not yet. He can check with the Feebies, but that'll cost you more."

"Do you have a copy of the card I gave you, the one with those prints?"

"I gave it to my pal. I just have a Xerox."

"With you?" He patted all his pockets until he found it. "Do you still keep a fingerprint kit in your car?" I asked.

"Sure."

"Let's go."

Irked at having to pass up the thimbleful of gin still remaining in his glass, Terry followed me out to the street and got his print kit from a tackle box he kept in his trunk. We walked a half block more to my car. I handed him the framed photograph of my man's house that I'd taken down from the wall in my office. "Try for thumb prints on the two vertical sides of the glass," I told him.

Ten minutes later, he told me. "The thumb prints are from the same person who left the latents all over Bobette's place. How the hell did those prints get onto your picture? Who the hell is this guy?"

"Mary Dean."

Ten

❧

The summer before her senior year of high school, Lee White contracted a vicious case of poison ivy when she ran up the hill behind her house to spy on Jazz Taylor playing tennis with his mother.

It wasn't as if she had planned such a mad act. No, she had just been lying on a chaise near the pool trying to catch her breath after swimming laps for forty-five minutes. Her eyes were closed. The sounds of the long, dull summer bubbled through the water in her ears: her own labored inhalation; the outrage of blue jays; the aggressive drone of the central air-conditioning unit; the interminable, cheery tinkle of her mother's Hawaiian wind chimes; the far-off *thunk! thunk!* of balls smacking against rackets on the Taylors' tennis court. Suddenly, out of this chorus of boring sounds, one youthful baritone descended from Hart's Hill: "Lucky shot, Mom!"

Lee was seized by a lunatic passion. Throwing off her towel, leaping from her chaise, clad only in a bathing suit, she charged up the steep rise that separated the Whites' from the Taylors'. Clearing a path, she pushed aside branches and tore away clinging vines with the fierce strength of a battle-crazed warrior. She had known for years that the entire incline was choked with nettles and poison ivy, but in that insane instant, she flung that knowledge out of her mind. Two whole years had passed since she had seen Jazz at Dante's Pizza. Not a single day had gone by that she hadn't thought about him.

When Lee reached the summit, she crouched low, darting in the serpentine fashion Charles Bronson had employed in *The Dirty Dozen* to dodge Nazi fire. She hunkered down behind one of the junipers that screened the Taylors' tennis court. It was only then that she came to her senses. Well, somewhat. To be perfectly frank, Lee looked slightly moronic, glancing behind her as if to ask: What means of transportation got me here? But then the game took over.

Ginger was by far the better player. As much as Lee wished Jazz Taylor would be a god of tennis, wielding a Tad Davis Deluxe Imperial instead of a lightning bolt to strike his mother dead, she was too savvy about the game not to recognize which of the two was just a social player—and which might have once aspired to greatness. To Jazz, it really was a game; he relaxed between points, changing his grip on the racket, wiping his palm on his shorts, shaking out a crick in his leg, combing back his hair with his fingers, squinting into the sun, smiling across the net. But his mother played with an intensity that was almost scary. Ginger's tan, muscular arms and legs were bright with sweat. She was primed for every ball. Without taking her eyes off Jazz, she moved into position so she could cover the court no matter where her son hit the ball.

For God's sake, Lee thought, he's not Billie Jean King! This is your son. Still, she was wowed by Ginger, and a little frightened. She had never seen a woman so intent on winning.

It was a half hour later, as the two Taylors were strolling off the court, when it suddenly occurred to Lee they might catch sight of her behind the juniper. Still, even then, when Jazz actually turned and looked back in her direction, as though homing in on the rays of desire beaming out from her, she stayed calm; her heart didn't pound, her mouth didn't go dry. No, all that was in her head was how extravagantly defined his thigh muscles were, like in those Da Vinci drawings in one of her mother's art books on the coffee table. Such thighs! Then a stray thought popped into her mind and grew and grew: If she were across the net from Jazz and slammed one with her backhand, he would say, "Holy . . . !" And Ginger, from the sidelines, would call out to her: "Nice shot!"

That was when it hit her, how alien these Taylors were from her own family. Not just that they had more money, what her father called old money, and were a different religion and sent their kids to private schools. No, they were alive. They had pep. A nauseating word, Lee conceded, but that was what they had. Plain and simple vigor. Well, Ginger had pep squared. Okay, she was a killer who had no qualms about cutting out her own son's heart. But God, they were both so strong!

Whereas her family: Leonard, who hardly knew a tennis ball from a silver fox pom-pom, was a knob-kneed embarrassment in shorts. Winded by a stroll to the end of the driveway to pick up the Sunday papers, he could only gaze up the hill with his heart corroding with envy, pierced by desire. If her mother were here beside her, behind the spreading juniper, she would eye Ginger's grass-stained shorts and baggy, sweaty Lacoste shirt, sigh, then summon up barely enough energy to pat a stray platinum-on-gold-frosted hair into place, and decree: "Ick!" And Robin: At the first overhead smash, she would drop her racquet and shield her head. But from behind her bush, Lee now knew: *She could play their game.*

That night, Lee's shapely legs swelled until they looked like bowling pins. The tiny red dots that covered them, signaling her immune system's outrage, were so numerous that from the soles of her feet all the way up to her thighs she was a solid blaze of crimson. Her legs were so sensitive that it was agony when she covered them, even with a sheet. Greta had gone off to Frankfurt for a rare week's vacation, her mother was in one of her moods where she never got out of her bathrobe, so there was no one to look in on Lee. For forty-eight hours she lay shivering in the arctic air-conditioning, too sapped from antihistamines to get up and open a window.

But her espionage had been worth it. What memories! What treasures! Jazz's powerful forearms. His brawny wrists. And his shorts! He must have outgrown them, because when he lunged for a net ball she could see his hamstrings as they thickened into the pale crescents of his buttocks. Oh, and she didn't want to forget the bandanna he'd tied around his head as a sweatband. And more! When he and his mother changed over, and he was facing Lee; he looked so . . . Okay, not handsome. But he had such a genuinely *nice* face, and when his mother aced a serve so hard he didn't even see the ball, he hadn't gotten defensive or temperamental. On the contrary! His wonderful face, his absolutely, totally good-natured face lit up with an appreciative grin.

It had been worth it! Jazz, she said to herself. Jasper. Jazz. If she ever met him, what would she call him? Of course, he might say: "Hi, I'm Jazz Taylor." Or: "How do you do? My name is Jasper Taylor. I believe we are neighbors," hopefully oblivious that in fifth grade she'd almost punched him in the suck.

Does all this sound like an obsession on Lee's part? It was. Not a dangerous fixation, the sort you hear of nowadays, where monomaniacs stalk their prey without rest or mercy. Actually, until her sortie up the hill, the extent of Lee's preoccupation with Jazz consisted of calling his prep school (from a pay phone so the call would not show up on her parents' bill) to ascertain when his spring break would be. She then spent an inordinate amount of time walking Woofer back and forth past the Taylors' driveway, hoping (in vain, it turned out) to get a glimpse of Jazz.

She kept hoping throughout her senior year of high school. Aware that they were both in the same grade, she fantasized every night about running into him at college interviews. ("Jasper, isn't that the girl who lives in that modern thing down the hill?" "I think it may be, Dad." Then, Jazz would turn to her: "Excuse me, are you from Shorehaven?") When Jazz didn't show up for the guided tours at Cornell or Brown, she felt cheated, as though she'd just missed him by seconds. She had even gone so far as to arrange interviews at Smith and Mount Holyoke, for the sole reason that, having studied an atlas, she'd calculated that the two colleges were a mere sixty miles from his prep school. In her mind's eye, she could see him waiting at a bus stop just outside snow-covered, Christmas-card Amherst on a frosty New England afternoon, anxious about getting back to be on time for afternoon tea or chapel or whatever. She'd spot him and turn to her mother: "Stop the car!" Then she'd lower the window and say: "Aren't you from Shorehaven?" They'd give him a lift back to school. With the cooperative illogic of fantasy, she was magically transported to the back seat beside him, while Sylvia chauffeured up front; by the time they got to his school, Jazz was slipping his class ring onto her finger. Of course it was much too big, but she knew exactly how to tape it so it would fit.

But the question remains: Was this obsession anything more than the standard teenage crush? Yes, it was.

Lee White clung to the image of Jazz Taylor's sliver of ass, to the remembrance of his vigorous baritone, far longer than might be considered healthy because she was a lonely girl. True, she had a lot going for her. She was a gifted (if not brilliant) student, a key member of the girls' tennis team, and managing editor of the Shorehaven High School *Beacon,* where she was a pillar of strength and fount of common sense for the temperamental reporters and the wild, impetuous photographers. She had a smart and lively best friend, Dorie Adler, three devoted pals, and at least ten acquaintances who thought of her in the warmest possible terms. But she had never had a boyfriend.

Of course, a seventeen-year-old girl who has never had a beau is not exactly a rarity. Still, almost every girl, even the most obnoxious adolescent, stands on the brink of womanhood with the reassuring knowledge that her family's love has always been (and will ever be) there for her. So it is no great loss if she does not yet have a pair of manly eighteen-year-old arms around her, because she knows—from her mother, father, sisters and brothers—that she is intrinsically lovable. In time, Mr. or Dr. Right will embrace her and whisper in her ear precisely what her family has been telling her all along: You are *wonderful.* I love you.

But Lee never got that from her parents. Not just those three little words: the feeling behind them. By the time she was finishing high school, Leonard was hardly home except on weekends. In 1967, there was no business like fur business. Well-off women wanted more than just their full-length minks. They wanted "fun furs" ski jackets of dyed rabbit, trench coats lined in sheared beaver—plus serious furs to show that they were worthy of more than mere mink; they seized fox coats, sable cloaks, shearling tunics, off the racks at Le Fourreur as if they had been sentenced to decades of hard labor in Siberia. Leonard was becoming rich beyond even his wildest dreams.

So it was no problem for him to pay the rent on a one-bedroom apartment on East Seventy-eighth Street so he could have a place to stay weeknights. Obviously, Sylvia could not be there with him. The girls needed her. But he urged her: "Use it whenever you come in during the day. It's a great place to put your feet up for an hour or two before dinner if you've been shopping." (What Sylvia did not know, naturally, is that when she called the East Seventy-eighth Street apartment, the phone also rang in Dolly Young's somewhat larger, more lavishly furnished co-op apartment on Central Park South which Leonard had also paid for and where he actually spent most Monday through Thursday nights.)

So Lee saw relatively little of her father. On school holidays, like Columbus Day or Veterans Day, he would often take her out to lunch, but their conversations were limited to safe subjects: school, polite inquiries about her friends and—the only area of her life that aroused his interest—the triumphs and travails of the Shorehaven tennis team.

"What's your won–loss record?" he inquired one day during Easter vacation of her senior year.

"You had to ask?" Lee laughed as she reached across the table at Miss Pansy's, a tearoom around the corner from her father's store. "We're one–five."

"Even with your backhand?"

"If it weren't for my backhand, we'd probably be five–one." Father and daughter exchanged smiles, each comfortable that this was not the case. Lee picked up a crustless triangle of her sandwich. "What's this gook inside?"

"Pecan cream cheese," Leonard answered, a little nervously. He never knew what Lee would say next. "A specialty of the house."

"Is it a big *goyishe* thing or something?"

"Shhh!"

"They're all *goyim* here. They don't know what I'm saying." Leonard glanced around nervously. "Dad, relax. We're in New York City. It's not against the law to say *goyim*."

"Where did you hear that word?"

"It's not *f-u-c-k* or anything," she said, smiling at his attempt to remain unperturbed. "Grandma used to say *goyishe* all the time." Leonard tried to appear as if this was a surprise to him; Lee made no effort to hide her amusement at his behavior. "And I heard it at Dorie Adler's."

"Oh." Leonard pretended to be absorbed in removing the gluey cream cheese coating from his teeth, following the dictates of good breeding—an impossible task.

" 'Oh,' " Lee mimicked. "Okay, I'll put a help-wanted ad in the paper: Friend Wanted: Only Protestants need apply."

"I didn't mean—"

"Sure you did!" Lee retorted, but she smiled when she said it, and she had such a generous smile that it softened the censure.

"You know what's great about you?" her father demanded.

"No. What's great about me?"

"Your spunk. Men like that."

Lee put down her sandwich. "I don't think so."

"Sure they do," he insisted. "You don't think there are a lot of boys up at Cornell who want a girl with brains and . . . " He searched for a word. Lee waited for him to say "beauty" or at least "good looks." Finally he said: " . . . gumption. Listen, Lee, the most fashionable, beautiful—and wealthy—women in New York come into the salon. And you know what?"

"They don't have gumption."

"Right!"

"But I bet they had dates for their senior proms."

"Maybe. But they can't keep a man's interest. Their husbands—uh—stray, if you understand me. Because when a man comes home from a day's work, he doesn't want a bubblehead. He wants someone he can talk to." Loud silence: Leonard suddenly slammed on the conversational brakes, realizing that his uncommon honesty had almost brought them careening into the very walls of their home. Before it could last too long, he added: "You've got the brains to be someone special. You want to be a doctor? I'll pay for medical school." Considering that the worldview espoused in *The Feminine Mystique* had not yet made an impact on the psyches of male furriers, this was a remarkably decent offer. "A lawyer? A college professor? I'll be behind you a hundred percent." Then he patted her hand, and it was not a mere offhand caress; it was a pat replete with heartfelt warmth, the closest gesture to a genuine declaration of love she would receive from him in her life. "Lee, sweetheart, come on. You'll get your MRS degree too. Iron those wrinkles out of your forehead. Stop worrying. I guarantee it: You'll hook some guy."

Then Leonard waved to Olive, their waitress, a sourpuss he'd been trying to charm for a decade, and told her to bring his almost straight-A daughter who would be going to Cornell—that's one of the Ivy League colleges, Olive—next September a slice of Miss Pansy's famous Nesselrode pie.

The only guy Lee got that year was her prom date, Nestor "Baby" Langley, who weighed two hundred ninety-seven pounds. If his ironic moniker makes it sound as if Baby was a future tackle for the San Francisco 49ers, than it is doubly misleading. Baby got his nickname simply because he called everyone "Baby," believing it made him appear cosmopolitan. An amiable boy whose reputation for wit was based on his total recall of the epigrams of Oscar Wilde, he was as soft as the Ring Dings he was unable to resist. Baby, the editor in chief and movie critic of the *Beacon*, was the only boy in Lee's crowd who still could not find a prom date the week after Memorial Day—not even among the pathetically eager ninth graders in the fast crowd at Shorehaven Junior High. At the urging of a half score of their journalistic colleagues ("How can you *not* go to your senior prom? Even if it's with a friend. It's *better* with a friend, because you *know* how superficial high school relationships are and friendships last forever"), and after Dorie Adler drove over to Baby's house and stood beside him, holding his perspiring hand, as he phoned Lee and formally invited her, Lee and Baby became, ad hoc, an item.

Sylvia was elated. Not about Baby, of course (although Leonard was not displeased, somehow aware that Baby's father, Thaddeus Langley, was a member of Rolling Hills, the golf club to which Foster Taylor belonged). Sylvia was enraptured at the thought of shopping for a gown. "You need something very unique," Sylvia declared as she sat on the edge of Lee's bed.

"Not 'very unique.' 'Unique' means one of a kind." But Sylvia had become distracted. She scanned the room—now white and yellow, with a daisy-chain stencil painted high on the walls and around the edges of the oak floor. Hmm, she seemed to be saying to herself. Apparently, she had forgotten that she'd redecorated it a year earlier. Placing a Bougainvillea Pink–enameled index fingertip on her one-shade-darker Appassionata Pink lower lip, Sylvia appeared lost in thought—although not so lost that Lee could not see where she was headed.

"Mom."

"What?"

"We're not doing my room now. We're doing me."

Sylvia offered an apologetic smile and even touched her daughter's cheek for an instant. "I made a list of places to look for prom dresses."

"Mom, I just want a plain, peasant-style—"

"Why? Are you a peasant?"

"We're not exactly descended from the Hapsburgs."

"Who are they?"

"They live on Driftwood Drive. He's an accountant."

"I don't think we know any Hapsburgs."

"I was just kidding. They were an aristocratic family."

"Well, your father is an aristocrat in the fur industry." Lee knew what was coming next. "How many furriers got mentioned in last August's *Vogue* and *Bazaar*?" Sylvia demanded. "We all have to keep up a fashion image . . . me, Daddy, Robin and *you*."

"The editors of *Vogue* aren't covering the Shorehaven High School prom. It's safe for me to wear a peasant dress."

"Do you want to wear work boots and carry a sack of potatoes out onto the dance floor?" Sylvia, no fool, quickly saw that the notion of work boots was not without its appeal, so she talked fast. "We won't look on the Island, because then you'll see yourself coming and going. But you want something classic. You're not Henri Bendel. I crossed that off my list. Too severe for you. You're Bonwit's. Saks. Bergdorf's too, but their stuff is so matronly this year you could throw up. Don't get me wrong: I'm not talking about anything sweetie-pie pastelly for you. You've got high coloring."

"I'm sallow." Lee didn't close her eyes, because she knew what she'd see in her mind's eye: Jazz Taylor at his prom, twirling a wisp of a girl, an ethereal violet-eyed gamin who had waist-length blonde hair, a letter of acceptance to Radcliffe, and a complexion somewhere between peaches-and-cream and porcelain.

"You are not sallow. You've got what they call a slight Oriental undertone to your skin—and you're the one who won't wear foundation, or even a little dab of rouge, so what do you expect?" It was not lack of rouge that made Lee a plain Jane, although this was one of the rare occasions when her mother was right: a little strategically-placed color would not have hurt. It was Lee's lack of sexual confidence that made her appear drab. Put her in front of an eligible boy, and the spark that fired her during a tennis game or in Honors English class flickered and died. She became mousy. But to defend herself against her mother's onslaughts, she had espoused a staunch No Makeup position. In her mind, the equation read: makeup=my mother=falseness. Too bad, because she had one of those fine, strong faces that cause readers of women's magazines to gush "*Un*believable!" when they compare a ravishing "after" photo to the ungainly, large-featured "before." It was not until two days before law school, when getting her hair cut at Bloomingdale's, she allowed the hairdresser—whose uncle was a judge in Minnesota and who claimed to have memorized every episode of *Perry Mason*—to talk her into an eyebrow tweezing, a facial, and a consultation with Miss Judi, who specialized in the Natural Look, that Lee began to allow herself to see that she was a damned good-looking dame.

"We have our work cut out for us," Sylvia said. "Can I safely assume Baby is going to wear black tie?"

"What else would he wear?"

"I don't know. Something beatnik."

"He's not a beatnik. No one's a beatnik anymore."

"What do you call your friend Dorie, with those black tights?"

"I call her my best friend. And Baby is wearing black tie." Lee leaned back. Her white wicker headboard whined in protest. The truth was Baby could not find a tuxedo to fit him anywhere on Long Island. He and Dorie finally made a desperate, secret trip to a king-size store in southwest Brooklyn, but all that the salesman at Big Barry's Formal Wear + Apparel could offer was an oxford-gray morning suit or a baby-blue tux that he swore had once been rented by Neil Sedaka's piano player.

Lee and Sylvia's shopping forays, while more upscale than Big Barry's, were certainly a lot less fun. Although mother and daughter, they were so different that to differentiate between them was not like comparing apples and oranges; it was comparing apples and catchers' mitts. In a dressing room in Bergdorf's (Bonwit's and Saks having failed them), Lee looked in the mirror and watched her mother watching her model in a navy-blue strapless silk sheath that brought the saleslady and Sylvia to the brink of ecstasy.

"Is it fabulous or fabulous?" the saleslady called from outside the cubicle. Sylvia withheld comment. She was staring at Lee's midsection. By any objective standard, it was not a ballooning midsection. Lee was in prime shape, it being tennis season, and her all-over muscle tone was quite fine. Still, there was a slight natural convexity to her tummy. "Mrs. White?" the saleslady called out again; her voice was tense, as if Sylvia's answer could hurt her. Lee fought down rage as her mother, ignoring the saleslady (and Lee as well), rested her tight, recently-operated-upon chin on the back of her hand so she could concentrate on studying Lee's flawed middle.

Stop it! Lee wanted to shriek. *Stop it!* Such noise as she would make had never been heard in Bergdorf Goodman since they drilled into solid bedrock to lay the foundation! Leave me the hell alone, you scrawny bitch! I hate this fucking dress!

But Lee also knew she was a disappointment to her mother. What more did the woman want, after all, than to have a pleasant mother-daughter day and buy her a gown that cost five times as much as anything her friends would be wearing?

So why can't she buy me . . . Okay, nothing peasant. Then a nice gown with a tulle skirt? Or something in chiffon, like that one in Bonwit's that was such a pale blue it was almost white? But Sylvia had grilled her: "You *like* that? You don't think it says 'Pittsburgh'? You like the way your bust looks with all that"—her voice curdled with contempt—tucking?"

It was late afternoon. Lee was worn down. She sucked in her midsection. "Nice," Sylvia called out to the saleslady. Then she glanced up at Lee. "Do you love it?"

"It's fine."

"Because if you don't love it, we can come in again next Thursday and look in some nice little places on the Upper East Side."

"No. I love it," Lee said. She turned from the mirror and looked at her mother's flawlessly made-up face. It was still tense, unsatisfied. "Thanks for coming with me, Mom."

"You don't have to thank me!"

"I know," she said, "but you're an absolute saint for putting up with me. So patient."

Her mother's expression softened until it was almost benevolent. "Lee," Sylvia said, "don't forget. We have a lot of work ahead of us. Do I have to say the word? 'Accessorize.'"

Three months later, Lee arrived at Cornell University with a glorious wardrobe of pleated tartan skirts, coordinating knee socks, cashmere cardigans, Shetland crewnecks, flannel slacks, a camel-hair Chesterfield, a dark-green loden coat, and not one, not two, but three perfect-for-fraternity-parties little black dresses that of course looked marvelous with the gold Omega watch and double strand of seven-millimeter pearls that were part of her high school graduation gift.

By mid-October of her freshman year, when the leaves were turning such vivid reds and yellows that they looked like a kindergartner's painting of autumn, Lee had barely unpacked. In fact, during her four years of college, the stunningly expensive wardrobe remained just as Sylvia had left it, in its cocoon of flowered tissue paper in a trunk scented with lavender sachets. With the two hundred dollars she had realized from the sale of her eight-hundred-dollar watch, she bought a pair of jeans, a tie-dyed T-shirt, a denim shirt of the sort worn by sharecroppers, and a pair of ankle-high shoes that might be issued to a marine on his first day on Parris Island. Of course, these purchases did not consume Lee's entire two-hundred-dollar profit; she donated ten bucks to Students for a Democratic Society and purchased six joints of excellent marijuana, which she shared with her boyfriend, Philip Mullen, or Flip, as he was called. Flip was a junior who had come all the way to Cornell from Denver, Colorado, to study physics, although in four years of college he probably learned less about quantum theory than Schrödinger's cat.

Flip learned a lot about women, though. He was a true believer in the antiwar slogan: "Make love, not war." And making love was easy, what with the sexual revolution of the late sixties dispelling both the Eisenhower era's peppy prudery and the Kennedy generation's insistence on a certain grace. A young man didn't even need clean fingernails, much less looks or personality or intelligence, to get laid. All he had to say was: "Wanna?"

Of course, Flip was pretty bright. And almost handsome. He looked like a sane Rasputin. His shoulder-length hair was the color of top-grade mahogany, and he had an impressive beard, smoldering black eyes, and a large and lively penis. Flip was a late sixties version of the Big Man on Campus. If he was not the leader of Cornell's antiwar movement (that role being taken by a senior far more organized and much less sexually animated than Flip), he was at least its preeminent follower. The first time Lee saw him, her second day of classes, he was cutting Elementary Real Analysis and working for peace, handing out signs that pledged: "No more men! No more money! No more killing!"

It had been a long day for Lee. Overwhelmed by the vast greenness of the campus, by the disdain of her roommate—a girl who had gone to boarding school in Switzerland and had actually laughed in Lee's face when Lee said: "*Ça me rend heureuse de vous voir*"—and by the difficulty of her chemistry class, Lee only noticed the first exclamation on the sign. "No more men"? She thought: What did that mean? She felt that light-headedness that precedes nausea. *No more men.* Her worst fear: During the darkest part of the night, she terrified herself by thinking about how the world was not precisely half male, half female, but rather, forty-nine percent male to fifty-one percent female. What if she was in that two percent damned to eternal spinster-hood, to birthdays celebrated in her parents' kitchen with Greta's carrot cake and its inch-thick cream cheese frosting? Sylvia and Leonard would be there, dressed for the evening, on their way to the city for dinner, Sylvia in Guy Laroche, perfuming the whole first floor with Mitsouko, Leonard in a navy-blue suit made (he'd inform her for the fourteenth time, while ostensibly picking a thread off the lapel—but in fact mesmerized by the near-invisible hand stitching) by the bespoke tailor who made suits for *the president of the Bank of New York and John Hay Whitney.* Robin would be sneaking looks at the clock, letting Lee know how she was dying to get out and meet her boyfriend, not wanting to ask him to the birthday celebration because that would be cruel, his presence emphasizing Lee's unremitting manlessness. Then one day Greta would die, and the cakes would come from Loaves and Kisses, three blocks from her father's store, because Long Island bakeries made sickeningly sweet ick-look-

ing cakes, so now the cakes would be in chic
Manhattan flavors, like pistachio-cognac. And then
Robin wouldn't be able to come, because she and her
husband and their three stunning children would be
vacationing on the French Riviera. And then her parents
would die and she'd be all alone, because the teachers
in Shorehaven Junior High—that's where she'd wind
up, teaching social studies and coaching girls' softball
because someone else was already coaching tennis—
wouldn't want to call attention to the fact that Lee was
forty-three or fifty-seven and living alone, her only companions a declawed, neutered cat and the seven fur
coats that hadn't been sold after Leonard's lawyers
arranged for a going-out-of-business-due-to-death sale.
"No more men!" the sign said. She did not even notice
Flip. Of course, her apparent indifference fascinated
him.

"Hi," Flip said meaningfully.

"Hi," Lee said apathetically, wanting to get away
from this bearded person whom she thought must be
either a hermit or a Hasid.

"Are you a freshman?"

"Yes," she said, realizing by his persistence and his
clear, western accent that he was probably neither of
the above. However, her mother's influence still
exerted its pull from the north shore of Long Island all
the way up to Ithaca; thus an involuntary "Yuck,
beard" response kicked in. "Excuse me," she said, trying to get around him and his signs. "I have to get to
the library."

"Isn't there something that's more important than
the library?" he asked, trying to burn her with his hot
eyes.

The right answer, naturally, was: The war in Vietnam
is more important than the library. For Lee, who was

smart as a whip but (to be totally truthful) no great shakes as an intellectual, the issue of "Are We Fighting in a Really Stupid War?" genuinely was more interesting than "What Were the Philosophical Underpinnings of the Council of Trent?" To her pragmatic mind, the Domino Theory as a justification for intervention in Vietnam made no sense. "Domino" was not the operative word: "Theory" was. In Lee's short life, she had never found a theory that could explain or serve as a guide to all human behavior. And if Marx and Freud couldn't satisfy her, a couple of guys in wire-rimmed glasses in the Pentagon certainly were not likely to either. Besides, propping up a corrupt government headed by a debauched playboy did not appear to Lee to be an effective way to halt the spread of totalitarianism.

However, there was an alternate answer to Flip's question, "Isn't there something that's more important than the library?"—for which equal credit would be given. That answer was: Yes. You and your incredible broad shoulders under that tight, faded T-shirt are more important than the library. Thus, aflame from moral outrage and from Flip Mullen's smoldering-ember eyes, she reached for a sign and began her real college education. Good for her.

And too bad. While Lee and thousands like her changed the course of American history, she missed out on the historic joys of undergraduate life. No shy glances as she and Flip stood on line in the cafeteria. No stolen kisses in the stacks at Uris: On the second night of their acquaintance, they were engaged in exuberant sexual intercourse on a stained mattress beneath a poster of Che Guevera. She missed out, too, on the intimacy of campus life, heady discussions with professors, close friendships with other girls, thrilling late night disputes as to whether essence precedes existence or vice versa.

Within a week, Lee moved into Flip's off-campus apartment, a down-at-the-heels place he had transformed into a slum. Not merely her lover, he became her professor, her friend, her political mentor, her atheist priest.

So she got a lousy education. Although Flip was not stupid, he lacked the two qualities that most appealed to Lee: curiosity and humor. While he knew the degree of ineffectiveness of Operation Phoenix in neutralizing the Vietcong infrastructure better than the assistant secretary of state for Southeast Asian Affairs, he never took her to a concert. They never discussed a book. Lee spent the first two years of college doing pretty much what she had done in second grade: drawing jumbo letters with Magic Markers—STOP THE WAR! BOMB SAIGON! The rest of the time, she cooked vats of spaghetti so she could feed Flip and his friends when they sat around the kitchen table planning protests. (While the feminist movement was surging, it had not yet raised many consciousnesses among the antiwar set at Cornell University.) On occasion she read one of the books required for her courses; now and then she handed in a research paper. But since exams were periodically canceled in the face of student strikes and many beleaguered professors were willing to negotiate final grades, Lee achieved a stellar grade point average for only a C-minus effort. By the end of her sophomore year, she knew a great deal about making marinara sauce and a bit about the subjects on which she had written papers: "The Roots of Anarchist Thought in Eighteenth Century England," "Mao Tsetung and the Peasant Movement in Hunan Province," and "Weather Imagery in *Bleak House*." She read a lot of Shakespeare and all of Austen. She read the assigned books of the Old Testament for a Bible as Literature course, but all she came away with was that God was not very nice and that her Hebrew name, Leah, belonged to a zero, a born loser, a woman whose husband was disappointed in her from the moment he lifted her bridal veil and who only wanted her sister.

"I'm going," Flip murmured late one night in April 1970. Although May was just a week away, it was still damp and nasty cold in the apartment. A stiff wind rattled the windows and insinuated itself through the cracks in the splintered wood sash. "To Canada."

"Mmm," Lee said in response. It was not that she was uncaring, but Flip had wakened her. She was exhausted. The Cadre of Eight, the leaders of the various antiwar groups on campus, had been eating and drinking and debating whether to take over the student union building until two in the morning, and she had not gotten to bed until after three. She had been busy cleaning up after them, discarding cigarette butts and marijuana roaches, picking up the balled-up papers from the floor, washing dishes and, for half an hour, scouring a black crust of burned tomatoes off the bottom of her sauce pot after one of them, inexplicably, had turned up the burner as high as it would go. Also, Lee did not see Canada as an immediate threat. The night before, Flip had announced that he fully expected to go to jail rather than concede the legitimacy of the draft. Two nights prior to that, he had been musing about joining up with some old movement friends in Sweden.

"I'm leaving right after graduation." She pulled up the blanket—one of her Grandma Bella's afghans which she had brought up to college—so it covered her cold shoulder. He'd change his plans a thousand times more. She was rolling over onto her right side, her most comfortable position, when Flip added: "I got a job in Saskatoon."

Lee froze on her right side, her back toward him. This

sounded serious: a real plan. "Doing what?" she asked, doing her best to sound interested but not anxious.

"Teaching math." She felt his heated breath on the back of her head.

She tried to swallow, but her mouth was too dry. "Saskatoon?" she managed to say. "Up in Canada somewhere?"

"Saskatchewan," he said.

"Where is that?" She was dying to turn around and see his expression, but she was positive she had morning breath.

"I don't know. Up there. Above North Dakota or something."

Knowing Flip, any question she asked would be interpreted as grilling, and she was fearful of offending him further when he was under so much pressure. "Is it definite?"

He exhaled a badgered breath at even this. "Is *what* definite?"

"The job."

"Yes."

"Do you want to tell me about it?"

"Not particularly. Do you think I'm happy about it? Did I go to Cornell so I could teach trigonometry to a bunch of idiot teenagers whose fathers work in a fucking meat-packing plant?" He lapsed into an angry silence. She heard the rapid, dry sound of his rubbing his beard between his fingers.

She knew a really devoted girlfriend would just join him in silence at this moment. But the words spilled out of her mouth. "How long have you been planning this?"

"Jesus!"

"Flip, why couldn't you just have—"

"Wonderful. Let's have a discussion about the relationship."

"No, please, I'm sorry. It's just that . . . I understand this must have been too painful to discuss with me." He didn't put his arm around her and pull her close, but at least he stopped playing with his beard. She slid down the mattress a couple of inches so that when she turned over, her breath would be on his breastbone, not in his nose. "Flip," she said softly when she was facing him.

"What?"

"I love you." He said nothing, but she could feel his exasperation. She had vowed only three days earlier not to bring that subject up again, and here she was, once again, breaking her promise. "I know I'm not sup-posed to say it."

"Then why do you?" He turned on his back and reached for his Marlboros.

"I don't know. I swear, I don't mean to put pressure on you. I just . . . " She took the matches from him and lit his cigarette. He smoked and stared at the dark ceil-ing. (Three years later, Lee would announce in her consciousness-raising group that this had been a masochistic relationship and that she cringed every time she thought of how she had walked down College Avenue carrying a Santa-sized sack of Flip's dirty clothes to the laundromat, where she waited so when they came out of the dryer she could fold them before they got wrinkled. But at that moment, all she felt was ennobled by her love of this martyr for peace.) "I love you so much. You have no idea. You're my life. I'd do anything for you."

"Then leave me alone!"

Lee tried to console herself with the thought that at least there was no anger in his words, only weariness. But the words themselves hurt, and she began to cry. Flip crushed out his cigarette in the saucer he'd taken from the cafeteria to use as an ashtray, but it smoldered and filled the room with a bitter stench. "Please, Flip."

"Please *what*?"

"Let me come with you."

"I knew you'd say something like that."

"Please."

"No."

"Why not?"

"You know why not."

"I don't."

"There's nothing for you up there."

"*You're* there. That's all—"

"You know what you're doing, Lee, don't you?"

"What?" she asked in a small voice, wanting more than anything not to hear his answer.

"Trying to get me to marry you."

"I swear . . ."

He grabbed the Malboros and, snatching the matches out of her hand, lit another. "You are bourgeois to your core. There isn't an inch of you that isn't your mother's daughter. I'll go to Canada and rot and you'll finish school and get a mink coat for graduation and you'll marry some guy with golf clubs. And you'll live happily ever after."

"No I won't!"

"You will," Flip said, with the blasé certainty of an omniscient god. He blew an imperfect smoke ring.

Lee rested her head on his shoulder, relishing the warmth of his body on her cheek. "Never," she insisted. "I'll love you for the rest of my life."

Not quite. By the time he got around to calling her from his rooming house three and a half weeks later to ask her to join him in Saskatoon, she had moved in with a ¡Puerto Rico Ahora! insurgent named Jorge.

Eleven

Pinstripes rubbed up against pinstripes in the Nassau County Correctional Center. If you took a deep breath (never really advisable in the visitors room), you got blasted by the expensive musk of lawyers' aftershave fusing with the raw stink of locked-up men. There were too damn many suits that day. It felt as if every attorney ever admitted to the bar in New York State was conferring with a client under the brutal fluorescence.

Down the row from Norman, a kid with the oily ears of someone who hadn't seen the inside of a shower for too long was asking counsel about the significance of his third conviction for first-degree robbery. In the row ahead of ours, a blond-haired, blue-eyed Christmas-tree angel of a teenager turned out to be awaiting trial for shooting a nun point-blank in the head. The crimes perpetrated by these young felons were always a double whammy, not only devastating their victims' lives but diminishing their own souls. Even if they managed not to get in the way of a bullet, even if they avoided heroin and crack and eluded AIDS, even if they lived another fifty or sixty years, most of them were, already, dead men.

There were a few older, white-collar white men in the slammer that day too. Since they could buy justice that the poor couldn't afford, these guys were stuck in the clink for a reason: Their deeds were so appalling—first-degree assaults with nauseating consequences, like bitten-off ear lobes, or aggravated sexual abuse on a minor—that no magistrate could let them loose on bail. Or they had grown so rich on economic crimes that they were adjudged likely, when their trial date came up, to be sailing off the coast of a tropical paradise that did not enjoy the benefits of an extradition treaty with the U.S. Since the correctional center was, as I have mentioned, the stuff from which nightmares are made, these upper-middle-class malefactors were desperate to buy protection from the horror—or at least distraction from it. Guys like these were always requesting conferences with counsel, and they usually found the sound of "my attorneys" far more bracing than "my attorney."

One of them, directly to my left, had actually been my client. "Call Me King of the Sea!" was the owner of a small chain of unhygienic seafood restaurants. He deserved the death penalty solely on the basis of his cable TV commercials, on which he wore a crown, carried a scepter in one of the lobster-claw gloves he wore, and screeched: "Eat me for just $12.95!" But it wasn't his unmitigated coarseness that got him into trouble; it was his viciousness. I had talked the D.A.'s office into dropping the assault charges against King of the Sea on two occasions but had passed on representing him the third time around. Now, for what must have been the tenth time, he was accused of battering one of his employees, this time a woman who now had a flattened disk of cartilage where her nose had been.

Unlike most of the other times, he could not buy his victim's silence. The beating had been near-fatal—with the dishwasher as an eyewitness—and *Newsday* was on his case. So despite King of the Sea's largesse to the Republican party, not even Woodleigh Huber, our county's utterly conscienceless district attorney, could let him pass the time before trial playing billiards in his estate in Upper Brookville.

The room was so congested with legal talent that Terry had to yank two chairs out from under a team of Manhattan lawyers. They grumbled a lot—impressive, four-hundred-dollar-an-hour grumbles—but they didn't try to stop him. They all had magnificent haircuts, and they all wore worried Park Avenue forehead wrinkles as they huddled across from an abortion-mill owner accused of massive Medicaid fraud.

Having won two seats, we were finally able to inquire of Norman how come his girlfriend Mary's fingerprints happened to turn up all over Bobette Frisch's house when he had stated unequivocally that Mary had never been at Bobette's. "Mary's never been arrested," Norman assured me.

"What does that have to do with the price of tomatoes?" I asked.

Norman looked as if he were trying to gauge the depth of my stupidity. "I'm sure she's never been arrested," he explained patiently. "The cops couldn't have her fingerprints on file. Whosever fingerprints they are, they aren't hers. It must be a mistake."

"It's no mistake," Terry chimed in, ominously drawing out each word. Having intimidated the Manhattan lawyers, he was on a roll.

"As of now, the police don't realize those fingerprints are Mary's," I explained. "They don't know whose they are, and so far they don't care."

Norman swallowed hard. "But it's only a matter of time?"

"It may be."

He blanched. Each time I visited, he looked less imposing. Not in size of course. In luminosity. He had lost his glow; his magic was dying. A thick blue vein pulsed nervously on his left temple. Just below it, a rash shaped like Florida dotted his cheek, its redness clashing with his orange prison uniform. In addition, Terry, glowering beside me, was spooking Norman more than I would have believed possible; that diminished him even more. Of course, when I thought about it, I realized why someone as blatantly, crudely masculine as Terry was so disturbing. Norman's entire world revolved around women: He charmed them, he conquered them, he destroyed them. He was not used to dealing with men. Or maybe he was afraid of them and had carefully crafted a universe in which he was the only male.

"Listen," I said. "If the police decide to investigate Bobette's murder any further, it *will* be only a matter of time before they ask Mary if she'd mind coming with them to headquarters for a little chat. But the way things stand now, there's not going to be any chat. As far as they're concerned, you're it. The D.A. is completely satisfied that Holly Nuñez has a strong circumstantial case against you and can get a guilty verdict."

Norman rested his head against his open palm. Not weary, I thought. The man had made a meticulous study of how he appeared to others. He knew how that pulsing vein on the side of his head could give him away: Over and over again, it throbbed a message: Nervous! Nervous! "Do *you* think they've got a strong case?" he asked.

"I think I've indicated before that it may not be strong, but it is . . . I'd call it solid. If I were the prosecutor, I wouldn't hesitate to go to trial."

"Oh," was all Norman could say.

"I've been straight with you right from the beginning. The way things stand, I can't get you a very good deal. The assistant D.A. says she won't plea-bargain now—although she probably will eventually. But the deal she'll offer will be so lousy that I don't see any choice but to go to trial. Either way, you're looking at a minimum of twenty years."

"I see," Norman replied. I don't know if he actually said it; the visitors room had become very loud. No shouts, but a deep, angry hum, the most ominous male sound, the noise that might rise from a band of wild creatures just before a rampage.

"Do you see that from our point of view," I said, louder, "finding someone else's fingerprints at the crime scene is the first break we've had in the case?"

"But you say they're *Mary's* prints," Norman said. "She's not the murderer. There's got to be an innocent explanation. She couldn't hurt a fly."

"Are you sure she couldn't have hurt Bobette? "

"Positive! The whole idea is ridiculous!" He shook his head sadly. The fleeting half smile of someone faced with monumental idiocy curled his lips. "More than ridiculous. It's insane. *Mary?*"

Yes, I knew Norman was a con man, but I could also see he could not believe that Mary could have had anything to do with homicide. Of course, it was easy for him to have that sort of confidence if he knew himself to be the killer. "Well," I said patiently, "an eyewitness puts you there that day, right around the time of Bobette's murder. You say you did not kill her. Okay. So how did she die? She didn't put her own hands around her neck and strangle herself. Someone else was there. And now Mary's fingerprints put her in that house."

"Listen . . . ," Norman began. But he didn't know what to say.

"Are you a hundred percent sure you didn't know she'd been at Bobette's?" Terry demanded, his slow, husky voice so controlled he was starting to sound maniacal. I gave his shoe a tap with mine, signaling him to ease off a little. He was going over the top with the intimidation business and, instead of being scary, was beginning to sound like Boris Karloff. Norman would laugh in his face.

But Norman answered fast, as if desperate to mollify Terry. "No, I swear I didn't know. Mary never told me she was there. But there *had* to have been a reason."

"Come on," Terry demanded. "Like what?"

"I don't know," Norman said, directing his answer to me, as if I'd posed the question. "Like maybe Mary got insecure about me. I mean, it's crazy, but . . . I stayed over at Bobette's a couple of times. Bobette really wanted it, *expected* it, wouldn't take no for an answer, and I didn't want to queer the deal. It was too close to the big finish. Maybe Mary thought . . . " His voice trailed off.

"What did she think?" I asked. Norman shrugged, so I repeated the question.

"Maybe she thought I might actually go through with it this time. You know."

"Know what?"

"That I would marry Bobette."

"Did you give Mary any indication you were going to?" I asked.

He laughed. "Are you kidding? Of course not!"

"Because you weren't going to marry Bobette? Or because you didn't want Mary to know what you were thinking?" Norman looked down at his big hands, noticing them as if for the first time. His nails had grown long. Their unkempt length was highlighted by arcs of greenish dirt beneath them. He folded his fingers to hide the nails but continued to stare down at them in something approaching horror, as if the first two joints had suddenly been lopped off. "Norman, try and answer my question."

He crossed his arms over his chest, hiding his fingers under his armpits. Looking above the crowd, he stared up into the glassy eye of the guards' closed-circuit camera. He didn't speak for almost a minute. Finally, he said: "Look, you know what I do, what I am. So my word probably doesn't mean anything to you. But I swear to God, I would never have left Mary for anyone." He took a deep, agonized breath. "I admit"—another breath—"I thought of it. Bobette had around fifty thou stashed in the bank. Over two hundred in a brokerage account. And she netted around a hundred twenty-five a year from the bars and a couple of buildings she owned. I could have managed her holdings for her. She was dying to give up all that responsibility and just stay home, be taken care of. But I only considered it for . . . seconds, just seconds. You know why?"

"Why?" I asked.

"I didn't *like* her." His eyes drifted toward Terry, but he pulled them back to me. "I know that may sound funny to you, but I honestly like some of my marks. Some of them are really sweet. But Bobette was a pain in the butt most of the time. And when she wasn't"—a shiver of disgust went through him—"she would act cute. 'Am I your bunny, Denton?'" he mimicked. "Marry that loser? Not for all the money in the world! Not when I have someone like Mary!"

"So what was Mary doing at Bobette's?" Terry asked.

"Have you met her?" Norman inquired, his chest puffing with anticipatory pride.

"Mary? Not yet." Terry bunched his features together, angry with Norman's attempt at male camaraderie. Not truly angry: Whenever Terry wanted to move things along, he'd frighten someone. On a busy day, he could put on his scary face ten or twenty times. He leaned forward as if ready to spring. On the other side of the barrier, Norman pressed his spine as hard as he could against the back of his chair. "You didn't answer my question," Terry persisted. "I want an answer now. *Why are Mary Dean's fingerprints all over that house?*"

"Maybe she was looking for . . . " But Norman Torkelson couldn't think of a thing.

A half hour later, Mary stood in her living room, held up her left hand, and swore: "Honest to God, I wasn't in her house!" I watched as Terry Salazar's hard features softened into that squishy, low-IQ expression of the sexually besotted male.

"If you weren't there," I snapped, "then someone borrowed your fingers and put your prints all over Bobette Frisch's house."

The furnished apartment Mary shared with Norman wasn't as bad as the Love Nest, although all the furniture was grim, covered in variations of institutional-strength nubby beige and brown. In her kelly green silk bathrobe, Mary was far too dazzling for such a dreary place. "Well . . . ," she said, trying to buy time.

But I wasn't selling it. "When were you at Bobette's?"

She glanced over at Terry, hoping to be rescued, but he was still wearing that moronic smile and was useless. So she turned back to me: "*Please.* Don't tell Norman."

"When were you at Bobette's?"

"Oh, God," she squeaked. I waited. "It was . . . It turns out . . . " Mary flashed an apologetic smile to Terry. I was hoping he had come to his senses enough to flash back his hard-boiled private-eye piercing stare, but not only did he beam back at her, but the beam—goofy-grinned, glazed-eyed—was proof that the sight of her had transformed his brain to butterscotch custard. Mary went on: "The day I was there . . . It turned out to be the day she got killed."

"It turned out?" I asked.

"Yes."

"What a coincidence."

"I know."

"What time were you there?"

"Not *when* she got killed."

"What time, Mary?"

"Like, um, most of the afternoon."

"You were in her house?"

"No! Outside."

"What were you doing outside?"

"Watching." She pretended to adjust the cuff of her robe. "I was, like, jealous. Okay? I watched the house. They were inside the whole day."

"Where were you when you were doing your watching?"

"Just hanging out. Walking around the block. I couldn't just stand out in front and look. And I don't drive, so I couldn't rent a car or anything and sit and wait there. But around three o'clock, my feet hurt. I was scared if they came out, you know, that Norman would spot me and have, like, a total shit fit. So I went and I sat . . . " She hung her head and mumbled the rest: "I sat on her back stoop."

"Did you look inside?"

"Every once in a while."

"From the rear of the house?"

"Yes. And from the sides too. But I was scared her neighbor would see me. Her neighbor on one side. On the other side there's big bushes. Then, when I stopped looking, I went back to the back stoop." She sighed. "I shouldn't have worn heels."

I told Terry to find out if the cops had checked for footprints and if there was any indication of high-heel marks. Then I turned back to Mary: "Weren't you afraid Bobette would come out and spot you?"

"No. It was super-cloudy. Very chilly too. She wouldn't want to sit out in back."

"What if she'd left something outside? What if she wanted to empty her garbage?" Mary clearly had not thought of that. "What if her tenant saw you?"

"I didn't remember about him. He came out, though, and I heard him on the other side of the house, giving Norman a lot of grief. You know, about his car blocking the driveway."

"What time was this?"

"Late. I was starved. I kept thinking about fajitas. It was after they got back from their nature walk. Must have been after six. Then the tenant drove away and Norman and Bobette went back in. Chicken fajitas. The beef ones are too greasy."

"So how did you get inside?" I asked her.

"I heard the front door open and someone come out. So I kind of snuck around and peeked. It was Norman. Then he drove off, and then I heard the shower. So with him being gone, I went around to the front. He always presses that teeny little button on the lock of the door of our apartment because he always forgets his key. Sure enough, the door was open! He must have done it. Or maybe Fatso unlocked it for him to get back in. Or maybe she forgot about it. Anyway, I walked right in."

"What did you plan to do?"

"I don't know. I didn't have any plan."

"Come on, Mary," I said, my patience running out. Also, I was experiencing a near-irresistible urge for chicken fajitas. "You must have had something on your mind, going into Bobette's."

"Well, you can imagine what I was thinking."

Out of the corner of my eye, I noticed Terry nodding like a lunatic. "I'm sorry," I replied, not at all snidely. "I can't imagine what you were thinking."

"I wanted to see . . . Like maybe Bobette bought plane tickets 'cause they were going to go away for a honeymoon. Or something. I just wanted to *know*." She hugged her green robe tighter against her. "I can't help it. I get jealous."

"Did you search the house?"

"I went upstairs first, to her bedroom. I figured it would be safe with her in the shower." I waited. "I went through her drawers. Nothing. Just her stupid, ugly fatbras. Then the shower went off. I almost had a heart attack, I was so scared." She put her hand over her left breast and gave it a series of rapid pats. I deliberately avoided looking at Terry looking at Mary. "I didn't have time for her closet. I ran back down."

"And?"

"Oh, God, my heart was pounding! Boom! Boom! I could hear her footsteps upstairs! Clomp! Clomp! Clomp! And then I got even scareder, because I thought: Oh God, what if Norman comes back and finds me?"

"So what did you do next?"

"I just ran out."

"You didn't look around anymore?"

"Maybe for, like, a second, before I got totally petrified. But I didn't find anything."

"Did you take anything?"

"No!"

"You didn't, for example, take Bobette's wallet?" Mary's tongue darted back and forth over her lower lip. "You didn't then take a local cab or a bus and go up to the Americana Shopping Center? Maybe buy a bag at Louis Vuitton?"

Mary's eyes filled up. "How did you find out?" she managed to ask. Then she started to weep.

"You want to help Norman, don't you?"

Mary was sobbing too hard to answer. Terry eyed me as if I'd committed a major human rights violation. Finally, I heard a hiccupy "Of *course* I want to help him. I love him."

"Do you want him to go to prison for a crime he didn't commit?" She shook her head. "So, Mary, we have to get at the truth."

She lifted her tear-drenched face. Terry looked as if his heart would explode. "I bought a shoulder bag," Mary admitted, wiping away a mascara-blackened tear. "The big one. And a cocktail dress at another store." Suddenly she tore away from us. She seemed to be rushing headlong toward the bedroom. I realized that if she could climb out the window, she'd disappear along with Norman's small shot at freedom. I followed her. Terry started to follow me, probably to protect her, but suddenly Mary was hurrying back to us—carrying a shirred white cocktail dress with spaghetti straps, a minuscule thing about the size of a hand towel. "Isn't it, like, *the* best dress ever?" she demanded. "Feel it. It's the silkiest silk." I kept my hands at my sides. But I watched her hands as her fingers caressed the fabric.

"Mary . . . "

"I know I shouldn't have. But it was sooo silky. I mean, how should I know she'd go and get murdered? I thought: Well, Norman's going to score, and why shouldn't I get something nice for myself from her? Not what Norman would give me: something straight from her. I mean, look what she has! Her own house. She can buy all kinds of clothes, that fatso pig, and she has *two* VCRs. So big deal: Why can't I have a little shopping spree before we leave town?"

"But I thought you were afraid that he might stay and actually marry Bobette."

"Not deep, deep down."

"Deep down enough to sneak into her house when she was there and risk getting caught."

"I was just . . . you know. Wanting to reassure myself. And the wallet just happened to be there. You know, that old blobbo had an American Express *and* a Visa *and* a MasterCard! I've been dying for one of those Vuitton bags for, you know, about a hundred years. And when I saw that dress, it had, like, my name on it! It said: Mary, this is yours. Your dream dress for when you go to some really, really expensive club to celebrate after you and Norman get married."

Little Chuckie Phalen was attached to a big tan machine by a clear plastic hose. The machine extracted oxygen from the air and pumped it straight up his nose. He kept the thing right beside his desk; that way, he could, with a quick flip of his scuffed cordovan shoe, turn off the flow of oxygen so he could light up a Camel.

My partner, Chuckie, had always been an affable man. Despite his diminutive size, he was the rare sort who could break off a bar fight with a few good-humored words. He was a great storyteller, too, and was always being asked to emcee some judge's retirement party, or to say a few words on behalf of So-and-so, who was being honored by the Nassau County Guild for Something Legal and/or Catholic. Being so outgoing, Chuckie had naturally chosen the most sociable means of suicide, and I had no doubt there were bets among the boys at TJ's Taproom as to what would get him first: his smoked-out lungs or his Scotch-saturated liver.

He used oxygen only in the office, convinced that

whatever compassion points he could score with a jury by being hooked up to a portable tank would be offset by their annoyance at having to feel sympathy for a sick man. "It's not a good handicap, like being blind. Or having a leg off and being able to roll right up to them in a wheelchair," he'd informed me. We tried to meet at the end of every day for a drink, a Sam Adams for me, a J&B for him, and to shoot the breeze about our cases and office matters before I went home to meet the man in my life and he to the boys at TJ's.

"My heart is in smithereens," Chuckie commented, after I'd told him about my day on the Torkelson case. "You don't think it *really* could have been the beauti-full girl who killed the old maid, do you? I hate the thought of beauty behind bars."

"What if she were ugly?"

"Throw 'er in the clink!"

"Her killing Bobette does sound pretty improbable," I mused, "at least when you first think about it. But Mary has very big hands. Like the hands that left those marks on Bobette's throat. And she certainly has the size and strength to strangle someone."

"She's a *big*, beauti-full girl?" The glimmer in his eye suggested he was recalling something specific: In Chuckie's case, it was probably a porn film he'd seen in 1947.

"She's tall, not big. But she looks pretty strong to me."

"Happen to notice any marks on her forearms? I mean, if she strangled the old maid—"

"Bobette."

"Right. Bobette. If she strangled her, and if the old maid was no weakling—"

"The autopsy report puts her at five-four, a hundred and sixty-one pounds. She was what you could call solid."

"—then Beauti-full would likely have had scratches

or bruises on her hands or arms, where the old maid would've tried to pull her off."

"Possibly. But then again, Norman didn't, either, right after he was arrested."

"So what are you saying: Someone else did it?"

I sipped my Sam Adams from a blue plastic beer stein, a grotesque thing with football helmets embossed on it. Sandi, my secretary, had bought it for me at a flea market. For all its hideousness, it was a great find, with a freezy liquid trapped in its innards that kept the beer at ice-cold perfection. "No, it would really be pushing it to say someone else did it. I mean, there's a tenant, but from what Terry could find out, he's just a creep, not a psycho. But what about Mary Dean? She had motive in her mind, anyway. She was terrified Norman would stay with Bobette, marry her. Maybe she felt she *had* to get rid of her. And she knew the layout of Bobette's house amazingly well. My guess is Mary had been stalking them for some time, not just the day of the murder. And I bet you anything it wasn't the first time she'd broken into Bobette's house. She wanted the threat of marriage to Bobette eliminated. *There's* your motive. Now think about this: Norman had no motive."

"Lee, you're talking to me, Charles Michael Phalen, your partner," Chuckie wheezed. "Or do you think I've lost all sense?"

"Listen, what could have motivated Norman to commit murder? He has an absolutely predictable M.O. He gets their money, goes out to buy champagne, brings it back, and toasts the mark—so the mark feels confident he's not running off with her life savings. At which point he runs off with her life savings. He doesn't have a violent nature."

"Then why were you so sure up to now that he did it?" Chuckie asked.

I was dying for another beer, but I allow myself only one, and a glass of wine at dinner. For that pleasure, I have to run three miles a day, forgo dessert eternally, and eat more fish than is necessary for human happiness. If I had even a single extra sip, I would gain so much weight so fast that I would make Bobette look like Audrey Hepburn. "This is what I thought happened," I said slowly, "when I still was convinced Norman did it: He was at Bobette's. She'd taken the money out of the bank, but maybe she wouldn't let him have it. She wasn't a born patsy. She was a shrewd businesswoman; she might have had second thoughts. Or maybe . . . I don't know why I think this, but maybe she expected fireworks along with the champagne and Norman wasn't able to perform. He was really turned off by her. I know he found her very demanding, insisting he sleep over."

"But why would he kill her?"

"I just had a gut feeling she may have taunted or condescended to him and she did it at the wrong moment. He's a worn-out man. Tired of the game. Wants desperately to be a big shot to this beautiful young woman he's in love with and senses she suspects he's getting weary. So he has this—what do you call it?—performance anxiety. And so if Bobette ridiculed him, he might have snapped."

"Are you defending him? It sounds like you're prosecuting him."

"I'm ruminating, Chuckie."

"Ruminate away, dearie."

"My guess is, Norman was afraid that if he showed Mary how exhausted he really was, she'd run. He was also afraid that Bobette would figure out he was just going through the motions."

"Why? Wasn't he good at the con?"

"Sure, but no one's at his best when he's tired, and

Norman was so exhausted he might not have had the energy to be a great lover. I'm not just talking about the sex part; I'm talking about the stamina it takes to be charming to someone you're either indifferent to or you can't stand. But the irony of it is, that's all he's equipped to do. He couldn't hold down a real job. And he sure as hell can't live off his investments. He's in his mid-thirties. He's been doing the con since he was a teenager. Want to bet that he's never saved any money?"

"Those guys never do. They piss it away. That way, they have a perfect excuse to pull the con again."

"Exactly. So all Norman wanted was to make a quick score and move on. But he's not the man he was."

"Maybe it's because he's actually in love with Beauti-full. I mean, real love."

"I think he is. On the other hand, he does admit he considered actually marrying Bobette. The guy is desperate to stop."

"So, Lee," Chuckie said, swirling the scotch around his glass, "you're not prosecuting him now? You're back to defending him?"

"Right."

"So it was Beauti-full who done it, because she was afraid Norman would marry the old maid."

"Right."

"But are you *sure* Norman didn't do it? The old maid may have laughed at him and he snapped. Remember? Or she figured out it was a con and he snapped. Or she held the money back in some way and he snapped."

"Maybe Bobette wasn't onto him. Maybe she was just kidding around. Like, 'I'm not going to give you the money until you kiss my . . . whatever.'"

Chuckie shuddered. "Dreadful notion."

"It's not a dreadful notion, Chuckie. You're ante-diluvian."

"I'm not antediluvian. I'm Irish, and it's dreadful. Anyone can see that's why the poor fella snapped." I shook my head, but I started picturing Norman's powerful hands around Bobette's throat. Then the next second, in my mind's eye those hands tapered and grew soft and it was Mary who was strangling Bobette. "I can see that the sixty-four-dollar question remains unanswered in your mind," Chuckie said.

"Who done it?"

"Pre-cisely!" Chuckie slammed his glass down on the desk for emphasis. A few drops of liquid sprinkled his hand. "Who done it?" He brought his hand to his mouth and licked off the drops.

I replied: "I still don't know."

As I rose to go back to my office, pack up my attaché case, and go home, Chuckie huffed: "One more sixty-four-dollar question, partner."

"What's that?"

"If she did do it—which strains what little is left of an old man's credulity—is it conceivable that a fella with Norman's character would actually take the rap for her?"

The next morning, I was the first lawyer at the correctional center. But not the first caller. I was chatting up one of the guards outside the visitors room, asking about her son, a kid I'd once represented for carrying a concealed weapon; I'd gotten him off and he was now studying to be an X-ray technician. Suddenly I smelled a familiar gardenia fragrance. At that same instant, a flash of canary yellow registered at the edge of my peripheral vision. I looked in the direction of the odor and color. Sure enough, it was Mary Dean, in a minidress that looked as if someone had taken a bolt of yellow polyester, wrapped it tight around her body, and then, on a whim, added sleeves the size of volley balls. The odd thing was, no one looking at her too-made-up face and trashy dress would say: Boy, does she look cheap. No, there was something about Mary that engendered goodwill. People would think: Aw, isn't it sad that glorious-looking woman can't afford expensive clothes?

"Hi!" she said, too cheerfully.

"How are you, Mary?"

She teetered on her high heels, not because she couldn't balance in them, but because her weight was on the balls of her feet; she looked ready to run—and I got the feeling it was from me. "Me?" she said. "I'm fine!"

"Good."

She teetered some more. "I hate to, like, insult you or anything, but I've got an appointment and I'm already late."

"What kind of appointment?" I asked.

Naturally, she didn't have an answer and it took so long for her to come up with one that even she knew she shouldn't have bothered. "A–uh–a, you know. Doctor."

"Did you just see Norman?"

"Yes," she said, unconsciously slipping her hand under her hair and tossing it lightly. Norman must have just complimented her on it.

"How does he seem to you?"

"Um . . . Listen, I really have to get going. Give him a kiss for me." I must have looked unnerved, because as she hurried off to retrieve her handbag from the lockers and get away from me, she called out: "I mean, tell him Mary sent him a big, juicy kiss."

Norman was not in the mood to receive a kiss. The second the guard who brought him over to me left, Norman snapped: "Leave Mary the hell alone!"

"Norman, I know you're very protective of her. I admire that. But she was in Bobette's house the day of the murder. She stole Bobette's wallet."

"No she didn't!" His brows drew so close together they became one.

"She admitted it to me," I said.

"She lied."

"No, she didn't lie," I replied calmly. "She stole it."

"Listen," Norman hissed, "she did not take the goddamn wallet. She wasn't even in the house the day of the murder. It was another day that she was there. She's confused. Maybe she's covering up for me."

"I'm sorry, but I don't buy that. I think she—"

"*I* stole the wallet. I gave it to her. I said: 'Go ahead. Buy out a store or two.'"

"When did you have time to give her the wallet? She made those purchases late afternoon or early evening the day of the murder, when you say you were still with Bobette, or going out to buy the champagne."

"There was time. And she did not kill Bobette! Okay? Get off that!"

"Then who did? You?" Norman didn't answer. He scowled, and although it looked like an adolescent's sullen expression at first, it was clear his compressed lips were a grown man's attempt to keep from screaming words of rage. "I know this is a terrible situation for you," I went on. "You want to take care of Mary. The last thing you want is to implicate her in a murder. I admire that. But her presence at Bobette's is your only hope."

"Let me tell you something," Norman said. He spoke so softly that I had to move close to the barrier between us. His face was just inches away from mine. I could see bunches of red capillaries in the inside corners of his eyes. "You leave her out of this. She is a sweet, innocent girl."

"Then you're saying she had nothing to do with the murder of Bobette Frisch?"

"I'm saying if you don't leave her alone, you're fucking fired."

Twelve

✤

Graduation day did not start out all *that* badly. A single powder puff of a cloud was all that marred the sky's blue perfection. True, Robin had promised—sworn, in fact—that she would meet the family at nine-thirty on the dot in front of Barton Hall, where Cornell's commencement exercises would take place. By ten o'clock, she still had not shown. Also true, Sylvia's first act upon seeing her elder daughter in cap and gown was to lift a handful of Lee's long, lank hair in her open palm, examine it, and inquire, after a tsk loud enough to be heard at UCLA: "I *know* it's the style, but couldn't you have pulled it back into a ponytail, so it's off your face?"

Lee, who had spent three-quarters of an hour ironing her hair so it would meet her mother's rigid Hair Sleekness Criterion yet still conform to proper student radical standards, snapped: "No. I could not have pulled it back in a ponytail."

"Fine." Wearily, Sylvia upended her palm; Lee's

hair dropped from her hand. "You're the one who's going to have to look at your graduation pictures ten years from now."

Lee had taken Psych 1. While not introspective, she was hardly a bubblehead. She had to have known there was nothing she could do, short of marrying Yves Saint Laurent, that would make her mother happy with her. In fact, in her heart of hearts, Lee probably knew that even Yves would not please Sylvia, for when it came to Lee, her mother was unpleasable. Yet for all her pot-smoking, revolution-fomenting rebellion, Lee could not stop trying. Intent on giving peace a chance this day, she even smiled at her mother. But Sylvia, concentrating on the untweezed inch between Lee's brows, did not notice.

"Girls." Leonard cut into the silence. "Let's make it a happy day."

He was not taking his own advice. To begin with, he was stewing over Robin's failure to appear, although this should not have surprised him. Failure had become Robin's vocation. She had dropped out of the University of Pennsylvania, having failed every course she took her first semester. She then failed to complete applications to any of the other, more tolerant institutions of higher learning that a pricey college adviser had suggested. Following that, Robin failed to show up for work at the Revillon showroom at Saks Fifth Avenue, where Leonard, after much obsequious pleading and pledging of future favors, had succeeded in landing her a trainee's job. The man was at his wits' end. During spring break, he had even confided to Lee that Sylvia suspected Robin might be smoking pot. Lee, subduing an urge to whoop with mean-spirited laughter, merely mumbled: "She never talked to me about pot." Technically, that was no lie. As far as Lee could see, Robin was not much interested in such a namby-pamby hallucinogen as marijuana, preferring lysergic acid diethylamide.

A happy day? Not for Leonard. It wasn't only Robin. In fact, for him, Robin was mere irritation. No, his misery was on a grander scale. He knew now: He was doomed to be forever locked out of the world he yearned to enter. His elder daughter could feel at home in the Ivy League. He could only pay the bills. For some reason, it had taken him forty-seven years to finally comprehend this simple fact of American life: He would never be one of them! Now, as he trudged up the seemingly endless hill that was the Cornell campus, his legs ached. His knees felt as if someone had bisected them with a hatchet. The hammering in his chest made him feel that his heart was trying to crash through his rib cage and roll on the grass in shame. Also, he could not get his wind and had to clamp his mouth shut and concentrate on breathing through his nose in order that all the Old Boys and Old Girls so at home at this place wouldn't think the Ivy League was too much for him.

Now he pulled out his handkerchief and dabbed his forehead: gentlemanly dabs. "I'm a bit overheated," he remarked.

Lee observed her father. He wasn't a bit overheated at all. He was sweating like a pig. Perspiration streamed from Leonard's clipped sideburns down his shaven-to-raw cheeks. It splashed off his jaw onto his starched shirt collar. It dribbled from his chin onto the camera.

"Stand closer together!" he commanded his wife and daughter, trying to pretend he was a man in charge, the family photographer, and that his face was dry and his shirt wasn't soaked. But his order came out harsh and loud. "Closer, goddamn it!"

Suddenly, Leonard saw a passerby, a snooty-looking horse-face in a slub-linen suit, turn and give him a slit-eyed glance. He felt she had peered into his soul—and learned it had been born in Brooklyn. Actually, the woman, an assistant manager of a Big Boy hamburger drive-in in Cincinnati, had noticed neither him nor his disagreeableness, as all her attention was focused in her myopic search for her soon-to-be-graduating grandson. But her glance made Leonard change his tone. His words became cultured pearls:

"Let me see some smiles! Syl, dear." Sylvia, however, didn't realize the voice she was hearing was her husband's. "Syl, over here, sweetheart! Give me a smile."

Clearly, money had been no object when it came to presenting himself and his wife to the Eastern Establishment. And—looking through the hideously expensive Hasselblad camera he had bought for the occasion—he couldn't believe he could have been so blind: He had been so positive that he knew exactly how that presentation should go. For one thing, he had ruled out Sylvia's customary darkly chic French or Italian ensembles. Instead she was decked out the way he'd told her he wanted her decked out: "A tweed suit. English. Don't worry if it itches. It's supposed to itch. That means it's good quality. And stout walking shoes. Remember, tell them 'stout.'" Her fashionable frosted hair, customarily an amalgam of bronzes, coppers, and platinums, had overnight, at his directive, lightened into ash blond. She had drawn it back, the way he urged, post-post-debutante fashion, and tied it with a folded Hermès scarf. (Had Sylvia been the devoted Taylor-watcher her husband was, she would have known instantly that her hair was now the exact hue and style of Ginger Taylor's.)

This is what Leonard saw; irony of ironies, that while Sylvia could pass, he could not. He looked so *wrong*. Inadvertently, his hand smoothed his lapels, stroked his tie. *Wrong*. Oh, God, he had tried. His navy blazer was exquisitely tailored. Gray flannel slacks. Egyptian-cotton button-down-collar shirt. Silk rep tie. Loafers burnished until they gleamed the consummate loafer tone between mahogany and umber. *He* gleamed. In full East Coast Establishment regalia, he could almost have passed for an alum—"Hello, there, '47." Almost. Unlike Leonard, none of the genuine alumni gleamed. Their blazers and slacks and loafers looked as if they had been making the rounds of garden weddings and restricted clubs since the end of the first half of the century. Leonard's own flagrant newness made him a marked man. He bowed his head in shame. In grief. He tried to fake total immersion in focusing the camera, but his face was too wet. And some of the wet stuff was tears at his own gauche sheen.

Lee glanced around, longing for a friend, or even an acquaintance, to dilute her parents' presence. But the few graduating seniors still lingering outside Barton Hall were engaged in agonizing psychodramas with their own families and were thus too exhausted to come to her aid.

Lee looked back at her parents. Oh, God—her father! His hands holding the camera were trembling. And her mother: "Do you think Robin might be waiting someplace else?" Sylvia's voice barely rose above a whisper, but the "else" careened out of control, rising to a high note of incipient hysteria.

"How the hell should I know," Leonard muttered, trying to appear nonchalant, a difficult look to achieve when one is purple-faced and sweating bullets.

So Lee was graduated from Cornell University with absolutely no one paying attention to her. Her father, in his eight-hundred-dollar lightweight wool blazer, was beside himself. Actually, it was Sylvia who was beside him, but she was beside herself too, swiveling her head, trying to cover all the entrances to the cavernous building so she could wave Robin over the instant Robin came through the door. But Robin never appeared in Barton Hall.

However, there she was, waiting outside, when they emerged. Robin's fair, heart-shaped face was clear as fine bone china, her features were small and delicate, her slender body was forever poised between youthful androgyny and womanhood. She squinted into the sunlight and offered her family a feeble wave, more a flick of the wrist than a real salute. An outsider, noticing her pale frailness, might have thought her ill. Her mouth, however, tight with the rage endemic to adolescent offspring of the haute bourgeoisie in the early years of the 1970s, gave her away.

"Hi," Robin said to Lee, her tone sarcastic, as if Lee had done something that merited bitter derision.

"Hi," Lee replied. She did not expect her sister to offer an apology for being late, which was wise, since she did not get one.

"Is it over?" Robin inquired.

"You missed it." Lee had known Robin would pull something on graduation day. Without consciously rehearsing, she had prepared herself to react with aggressive neutrality. Still, she knew that Robin knew she was seething inside. Well, why shouldn't she fucking seethe? Here she was, finally getting her goddamn degree. Headed for law school, for God's sake! She had taken her law boards only as a lark, but they had been so stellar that she felt compelled to apply. True, her average was barely over a B+. She had no extracurricular activities, excluding indiscriminate sex and helping set fires in three ROTC file cabinets. Yet with those spectacular LSATs, she had been offered admission to every school to which she had applied: NYU, the University of Virginia, Georgetown, the University of Michigan.

But this day was not turning out to be a celebration of Lee's achievement. Like every other occasion when the Whites got together, it had become Robin's Day, a time for forced smiles and spastic colons.

"Where *were* you, for God's sake?" Sylvia's voice, usually barely audible, was much too loud. Leonard made a hysterical "Shhh!" sound that lasted until he ran out of breath. But Sylvia wouldn't shush. "You *swore* you'd be here!" she yelled at Robin.

"So? I'm here," Robin replied, and waved to someone in the throng.

Sylvia stared at her then. They all did. But only Sylvia cracked. Why? It wasn't so much that Robin had not washed her face, or that she was wearing tattered—in actual shreds!—polyester bell bottoms in a hideous rust-colored floral print, and a short top that exposed half her stomach and midriff, and a cheap, fake-pewter peace symbol on a leather thong, that made Sylvia start to sob. It wasn't her dilated pupils that caused Leonard to gnash his teeth in rage and humiliation. No, it was that Robin had summoned over a man. Not a boy: He was in his early thirties. At least. Now she clung to his arm.

The man had a matted black beard; what looked like a strand of albumen from a soft-boiled egg bisected its width. His dark eyes were hooded. His nose was hooked. His blemished skin managed to be swarthy and pasty at the same time. If he had been wearing a long black coat instead of a torn T-shirt and what appeared to be bathing trunks, he would have looked like an anti-Semitic caricature.

"Aren't you going to say something?" Sylvia shrieked at Robin.

"Shhhhh!" Leonard hissed.

"What do you want me to say?" Robin sounded like the sound track of a movie being played in slow motion.

"Like 'congratulations' to your sister!" Sylvia's voice seemed to echo through the hills and across Lake Cayuga and come back, louder and brassier, for everyone to hear.

"Shhhhhhh!" Leonard was nearly crazed with embarrassment.

"Don't bother," Lee said to Robin.

Robin gave a coy smile. "How about 'congratulations' to me?"

The Whites stood together in the comfort of not-knowing for a moment. Then Leonard, the head of the family, was forced to speak. "Congratulations"—his deep breath was almost a gasp—"for what?"

Robin rubbed up against the dirty elbow of the man by her side. "Congratulations on my *marriage*," she said, her voice sluggish and coquettish at the same time. "Mom, Daddy . . . oh, and Lee. This is my *husband*." She lifted the man's arm and put it around her shoulder. Then, leaning forward, she grabbed his other hand in hers. The man slid it out of her grip and placed his hand—his hirsute yet disturbingly delicate hand—in proprietary fashion on Robin's naked stomach. Sylvia clapped her own hand over her mouth to stifle a scream. But the scream did not come because she started to faint. Leonard might have keeled over, too, but he leaned against his wife to keep her from flopping sideways onto the grass, which would, of course, have underscored their utter humiliation in front of hundreds of Protestants. The Whites, tilting against each other like two tent poles, were unable to move without humiliating themselves.

Maybe it was the glaring midday sun, but Lee's eyes were drawn to the man's arm that was wrapped around her sister. In the crook, on the pallid, vulnerable skin, she could see a scattering of dark dots. Birthmarks? she wondered. No. Blackheads. Blackheads on the inner arm? she had to ask herself. With this slobbo, why not? Still, she knew, even as she tried other, hopefully better explanations—spattered paint, bites from a small but spiteful insect—that the dots were the tiny scabs of intravenous injections.

Robin laughed an insolent barbiturate laugh. "Isn't he cute?" Her parents remained tipped and dumbstruck. Lee felt the man's eyes upon her. She gazed back into his face; it had absolutely no expression. Her fury at Robin was momentarily replaced by a shiver of dread. Despite his counterculture getup, this man was no aging hippie. He was . . . Lee's heart began to flutter erratically under her gown. He was bad. She knew if she averted her glance he would discern her fear, so she kept staring into his empty eyes. "We're Mr. and Mrs. Ira Kleinberg. Ira, say something." Ira said nothing but at last turned his gaze from Lee to Sylvia. Robin laughed again. Then, with a seductive roll of her hips, she sauntered over to her father. "Daddy," she said. Leonard did not move or speak. "*Daddy.*"

Leonard's mouth formed "What?"

Robin whispered loud enough for all of them to hear: "We need money for a honeymoon."

*   *   *

In later years, Lee would laughingly refer to it as the Summer from Hell. Too bad: She had been counting on that summer between college and law school. First of all, she was going to defeat Richard Nixon. Then, in her spare time, she would read *The Magic Mountain*, listen to Corelli's concerti grossi, visit every museum in Manhattan, and, in short, get the liberal education she would have gotten at Cornell had she not been protesting the war, challenging racism, and cooking pasta for radicals. Admittedly, in the back of her mind, she also knew that she would drive by Jazz Taylor's house a few times a day. Not that she was obsessed anymore, but the memory of him—his well-muscled thighs, the sunlight on his hair, his niceness—remained, her valentine, her most romantic memory.

But by the time Lee said goodbye to her friends after graduation, loaded her clothes and books and stereo in her car, and drove back to Long Island, she discovered that Robin and Ira were already there, having moved into Robin's room. Not that they had asked if Sylvia and Leonard minded. They had simply bumped upstairs the two plastic garbage bags that contained Ira's worldly possessions, pushed together the twin beds with their wicker headboards, and locked the door.

Then the summer began.

"Ask Robin what the hell happened to the thousand dollars I gave them for their honeymoon," Leonard ordered Lee.

"Go tell Robin they have to get out of the room so Greta can change the linens," Sylvia instructed her.

"Please inform your sister that I am doing a white wash today," Greta commanded, "and that if she wants clean underwear, to leave a pile outside her door."

No one mentioned Ira, but they all knew he was

there. They all seemed to fear him. Leonard and Sylvia would rush past Robin's room on tiptoes, as if trying not to disturb the fiend within, who, if angered, would come crashing through the door and rip their limbs from their bodies. Even Greta's equanimity deserted her. She began making three or four desserts at night, offerings to placate the demon Ira, who appeared to feed only between the hours of midnight and dawn, leaving crumbs and crusts on the floor and dirty dishes on the kitchen table.

"Lee, ask Robin if she needs to renew the prescription for her asthma inhaler."

"Find out if it's okay if Jerry from Gold Coast Carpets comes in to clean her rug."

"Would you *please* remind Robin that we have a septic tank system here and she *cannot* run the shower for a half hour."

"I want you to tell her that playing that music at three in the morning is unacceptable! Do you hear me? *Un-ac-ceptable!*"

The Summer from Hell. Sylvia could no longer be relied upon to take to her bed for weeks on end and stay out of the way. Her usual melancholia gave way to agitation. She sat all day and into the night at the kitchen table, sucking on Parliaments, drinking endless cups of black coffee and hyperventilating, her exhalations coming out as mewling sounds.

Leonard was drawn back to his house with the reluctant fascination of a driver passing a bloody crash on the highway. Some workweeks, he came home every single night. None of Dolly Young's considerable tricks could keep him in the city. "Anything happen today?" he would demand of Sylvia, his voice croaking, choking with emotion. Sylvia would shake her head back and forth very fast and fill her lungs with

more smoke. "Nothing," she would rasp, clutching her
bathrobe tighter against her chest. Her hand was a
claw, her neck bones made a pitiful V. She was getting
thinner and thinner but could only bring herself to eat
a bite of the carrot muffins Greta baked fresh every
morning to tempt her. "They didn't come down at all."

"They never come down until we're asleep."

"What are they *doing* up there?"

Lee would get home from her summer job, working
on the petitions drive at McGovern headquarters in
Manhattan, and find her parents standing by the door,
awaiting her, as she came into the kitchen from the
garage.

"Is Robin taking drugs? What do you think?"

"Go upstairs, knock on her door, and see if she
wants to talk to somebody. You know, a doctor."

"Speak to your sister!" they ordered Lee. Tell her: The
third overdue notice for *Steppenwolf*; a funny smell, like
bad cheese, coming through the door of her bedroom;
that girl who's in that *Last Tango* movie with Marlon
Brando is on *Johnny Carson* tonight and she might want
to see her; Grandma Eva is in the hospital; Grandma Eva
is in a coma; does she know where my bone Ferragamo
flats are; Grandma Eva died and the funeral is tomorrow
at eleven o'clock at Schwartz Brothers.

During June, Lee, dutifully, would knock on Robin's
door. Her sister would open it a crack. The room was
always dark and stank of pot and body odor; Ira was
never in sight. "Yeah?" Robin would demand. Lee
would deliver the message. Robin would invariably
respond with "Fuck you, fuck them," and shut the door.

Then, for the first two weeks of July, Lee simply jotted down her parents' entreaties and slipped pieces of
paper under Robin's door.

After that she began a lackadaisical affair with one

of McGovern's advisers on fiscal reform, a forty-eight-year-old corporate lawyer from the second-biggest Wall Street law firm, who had a wife and four children in New Canaan, Connecticut, and a pied-à-terre facing Gramercy Park.

Lee did not return home for the rest of the summer.

You would think, since at least a quarter of the fibers of Lee's being were dedicated solely to Jazz Taylor, that she might have found something familiar about the finely built young man with the square jaw and cascading brown hair—gorgeous, sun-kissed hair—who sat, in New York University Law School's alphabetic tradition, five seats before her. At least, his smile—broad, his high cheeks pushing up his eyes into twin crescents—might have reminded her of someone she had spied upon while hiding behind a spreading juniper. Barring that, you would think, surely, that in the second week of classes, when that mad genius of torts, Professor Myron Blumenthal, actually bellowed "Jasper Taylor!" she would gasp in recognition, or that her heart would leap or her head would spin. But no: nothing, zero, no reaction at all.

Lee was too frightened to notice. The summer had drained her: not being able to go home for fear of either being grabbed by her frenzied parents or, if she could steal upstairs unhassled, having to listen to the bumping of a headboard against the wall as Robin and Ira engaged in one seemingly endless honeymoon hump; the doomed McGovern campaign; the dreary love affair of convenience, made even more burdensome when the corporate lawyer proposed to leave his wife and children and begin life anew with Lee in what he referred to as "a Village pad."

And law school! Could there have been some terrible mistake when they mailed out the scores of the LSATs? Could she have been given some legal genius's number, while some other White—the legal genius—got hers and gave up hopes of a seat on the Supreme Court and was now a junior buyer in the notions and trimmings department at Ohrbach's? The more Lee studied, the more she did not know. She was awed by the penetrating intelligence of her teachers, frightened by the aggressive cleverness of her classmates. No matter how much work she did that first terrible week, she could not make sense of anything that had to do with the law. She searched the faces of the students in her section, hoping to discover fear in their eyes, but more disquieting still, she saw none.

She noticed the young man only because of the manner in which he failed to answer Professor Blumenthal's question: "Can the same act be both a tort and a crime?"

"I really don't know," the young man said. What made her look down the row at him was his air of casual regret. It said: Gee, that's an awfully good question. I wish I knew the answer. He was sitting back comfortably in his seat, looking Blumenthal straight in the eye. He displayed neither the white-lipped, dry-mouthed fear nor the bogus sangfroid that never hid a student's mortification at being caught not knowing.

"You don't know?" Blumenthal boomed. He was a massive man, with a bald head so huge he looked like a monstrous, hydrocephalic baby. "*You do not know?*"

The young man shook his head, and his shoulder-length hair moved with soft grace. "No, I don't." Now everyone was looking at the young man. They were riveted. Lee could see why: He was simply not terrified. What was wrong with him? Did he lack a nervous system?

"May I ask why you do not know?"

"I guess I didn't comprehend the reading."

"You did read it?" Blumenthal snorted a cruel laugh that implied doubt and derision.

"Yes, I did." Not even a hint of panic. Mild regret, and perhaps the onset of the most trifling irritation that Blumenthal was carrying on so.

Blumenthal, poised at the bottom of the amphitheater of a lecture hall, began to vibrate like a tuning fork, unable to decide whether to attack or merely to dismiss the young man disdainfully. To do the latter might be construed as retreat, even cowardice. Blumenthal filled his large chest with air. Lee felt sick for the young man. But then Blumenthal did not strike. Instead he was lowering his enormous head. He was scrutinizing his seating chart. Now he was looking up, ready to attack anew. His voice rang out: "Mr. White!" She looked around, hoping. No Mr. White. "Lee White!" Her guts liquefied.

"What?" was all she could say, because she could not for the life of her remember the question.

"Answer, please, *Miss* White."

She stared at Blumenthal, but there was not a hint on his mask of a face. Torts, she told herself. This is my Torts class, so the question has to be . . . "The same act can be both a tort and a crime," she heard herself saying.

The professor began to shake his head, as if in utter weariness with the human condition. But her answer was right! She remembered reading . . . Oh, right. He wanted the details. "Take the case of an assault," she went on. "It's a tort because it is an offense against an individual." She swallowed. Her throat hurt so much she didn't know if she could go on. And she felt feverish. And her stomach! Any second, she could get diarrhea standing there, and no matter what she did with the rest of her life, anyone at NYU Law School would remember her as the Girl Who Had Diarrhea in Blumenthal's Section. "But it's a crime too, because it's an offense against society."

Blumenthal nodded, but his expression was bitter, as if what she'd said was not merely inadequate but vile. "Can a tort arise out of contractual relations?" he asked, as if not expecting an answer.

"Yes."

"Yes?"

"Like if a person is induced by fraudulent representations to purchase stuff."

"*Stuff?*"

"Merchandise," Lee clarified. Then she saw Blumenthal had begun to breathe another weary sigh. Her words shot out like bullets. "An act can actually be three things: a breach of contract, a tort, and a crime. For instance, the misappropriation of funds by a trustee is a breach of the contract of trust, the tort of conversion, and the crime of embezzlement."

Blumenthal looked away from her, back at the man with the glorious brown hair. "Did you hear that, Mr. . . . ." He consulted his seating chart. "Taylor?"

"Yes," the young man said. He leaned forward and looked down the row at Lee. "Thanks," he said, and gave her a grin that was not merely genuine, not merely good-natured, but heartfelt. It filled her with warmth. She smiled back, more girlishly than in all the years since she had become a student revolutionary and stopped shaving under her arms. And in that second, when at last she was able to avert her eyes from his, his name rang out in her head: Taylor. Taylor? Trembling inside, wishing she were numb, she turned back. Taylor! He was still smiling at her.

*   *   *

"Jazz Taylor," he said, after class.

"Lee White." Shit! she chided herself. She should have said "Jazz?" Why hadn't she sounded at least mildly curious about such a singular name? "Jazz? Are you a musician?" she could have asked. No, too contrived. How about: "Is Jazz short for something?" Now, of course, he'd figure out that somehow she knew him. Not just knew him: He'd put two and two together and realize that she was the girl in the Dodge Dart who kept obsessively driving by Hart's Hill throughout his senior year and even during college vacations. Very likely he knew exactly who she was! She was probably the laughingstock of his whole family. Jazz's girlfriend in that dreadful Dart, ho-ho-ho.

"God, you were cool in there," he said. Up close, his skin was fair but weathered, with the sandy texture and rich red undertone of a born outdoorsman.

"Cool?" she asked. She heard her own voice coming out cold, snotty: like her mother talking to a salesgirl who was wearing cheap shoes. But the words kept coming, and she was powerless to stop them. "Cool like 'Hey, that's cool'? Or cool as in unruffled?"

And now what was she doing? Flirting with him! Shit-ass-rat-fuck! If she were a bystander, watching herself, she would puke. Looking up at him with a starlet's you-great-big-hunk-of-man gaze. Surely in half a second he'd check out his watch and make some pathetic excuse and rush off. Or maybe he was too polite to cut and run, but he definitely had to want to scream with laughter at the sight of her combing back her hair slowly, erotically, with her fingers. Quickly, she stuffed her hand deep into the pocket of her bell-bottom jeans.

"Cool as in unruffled," he replied. "I was so damned ruffled I couldn't remember whether I read that part and forgot it—or just didn't read it."

"You had to have read it," Lee said. "It was assigned—" She stopped because now he was laughing— at her earnestness. Maybe he was one of those Learned Hand–type prodigies who merely had to sit in a classroom in which a few legal notions were bandied about and—Bingo!—all matters juristical became clearer than crystal. She was annoyed at not being able to repress the fast, follow-up realization that if Torts had been clearer than crystal, then Jazz Taylor would not have been caught short by Myron Blumenthal. "Doesn't it scare you *not* to read it?" she asked him. "I mean, every night when I start getting tired, I think: What if Blumenthal calls on me?"

"And so you keep studying?"

"Till I drop," Lee said, now laughing with him. She realized they had walked through the halls of the law school and out the front door only when a gust of hot-dog-scented wind from Washington Square Park hit her in the face. "There's so much intellectual rigor here," she told him. "I'm not just afraid of not doing well. I'm afraid of not . . . " She paused. He was waiting, and doing what no one else in law school had the time to do: listen.

"Afraid of not what?" he urged.

"I'm afraid of not *getting* it. I mean, even if I could memorize each individual case, I may not comprehend what the cases mean in relation to each other, in relation to the law."

"In relation to God too?" He was smiling, but not in fun. In compassion. "For someone in her first month of law school, you're aiming kind of high. Do you really think you have to comprehend the entire history and meaning of jurisprudence? Couldn't you settle for a B in Torts?"

"But it could be an F!" she exclaimed.

"Come on," Jazz said, shaking his head. "You're incapable of getting an F in anything."

She was about to demand: How do you know? But as she strolled alongside him across the park on this bracing gray day—somehow he had led her across the street without her even knowing it—he seemed so certain. For the first time since she began law school, her jaw unclenched. She would pass Torts. In fact, as she stood beside Jazz Taylor on line at the hot dog cart, she suddenly knew she would get at least a B from the bully Blumenthal.

"Mustard?" the man at the cart was asking. Higher than a B if she kept working the way she had been.

"Lee?" Jazz asked.

"Umm . . . " Jazz was going to think she was an idiot. A person either likes mustard or doesn't. She doesn't stand there with a stupid, apologetic grin on her face, assessing the pros and cons of mustardhood.

But the September air felt cool on her face. The people in the park—undergraduates, mothers and toddlers, junkies—all looked radiant. The first fallen leaves, the litter, even the dog shit, appeared to be the perfect examples of their kind. Isn't this the most gorgeous day ever? she wanted to ask him. Red stems brought out the vivid beauty of yellow leaves on the pavement; a Yoo-Hoo bottle resting against the crumpled sports page of the *Daily News* might have been arranged by Renoir; a Newfoundland puppy left a proud, steaming heap of feces. Lee felt something rising inside her. Exhilaration. She was not going to fail. She was going to be a lawyer! Jazz Taylor had made her see that.

"Lee?" And he was saying her name! This wasn't any exceptionally cute-looking guy, slender (but with powerful arms bulging out of his army-green T-shirt). This was literally the man of her dreams, saying her name! "Lee." Jazz Taylor!

"Mustard," she told the hot dog man. "And tons of sauerkraut."

Life is rarely as thrilling as fantasy, or as well scripted, so it was a double pleasure that two days after Halloween, after they had already sipped seven cups of coffee together and enjoyed two dinners in each other's company, Jazz finally got around to asking: "Where are you from?"

"Long Island," Lee responded casually.

"No! You're kidding! Me too. What part?"

The revelation was precisely as she had imagined it. Well, not precisely. They were friends, not lovers. And the sad fact about the pressures of law school was that Jazz was still the only close friend she had made. She didn't yet know any woman in her class with whom she could share the do-you-think-it's-that-he's-secretly-shy-or-that-he's-only-interested-in-me-as-a-friend? conversation and get reassured that he was indeed secretly shy. So unlike in her dreams, Jazz wasn't kissing her fingertips at the very moment he found out where she lived. He was sitting across from her, sipping his usual half-coffee, half-cream concoction—cream of coffee soup, he called it. She said, offhandedly, as if he probably never heard of the place: "Shorehaven."

"No kidding! Me too!" His enthusiasm, as always, was boundless. It seemed that no matter what the circumstance, Jazz was filled with a happy energy. Streaks of exhilaration shot out of him and zapped whoever was in his presence. Lee had watched him outside of class, in the hall in the dorm; anyplace Jazz was became a party. What was remarkable, she decided, was that unlike many individuals with gregarious natures, he was not Class Clown. In fact, he was more Most Popular Boy, which in the fall of 1972 meant that he managed to maintain an air of Jack Nicholson—like perpetual irony. His conviviality was always in perfect balance with his cool.

"Right," Lee said, with the tolerant look of amusement she had practiced so often in fantasy. "You live in Shorehaven too."

"I do! I swear I do!"

She shook her head. "I went to elementary school, junior high, high school and I never saw—"

Jazz put down his mug and leaned toward her. "I went to private school! *That's* why you never saw me. Now tell me where you live."

"No. You'll tell me you live right next door."

"Okay," Jazz said, clearly delighted that he was about to convince her of the validity of his Shorehaven credentials. "I live on Taylor Farm Lane." Lee had practiced so often she knew not to gape; a mouth wide open into an O! would have been too theatrical. But she let her eyes open wide. She puckered her brow, as if she were trying to resolve a most perplexing dilemma. "Do you know where that is?" he asked, although he could tell she did.

"There's only one house on Taylor Farm Lane," she said slowly.

"Right! Mine."

"You're . . . "

"Come on, Lee. What's so funny?"

"Your house . . . what do they call it?"

"Hart's Hill."

"Down the street from there, right near North Road, there's a modern house. Fieldstone front." He nodded. He knew the place. Lee was relieved he had not pretended to retch in revulsion. "That's *my* house."

"No."

"Yes."

"No."

"I swear."

"You're making it up."

"Jazz, how would I make up something that specific? I mean, I know the street name, what the house looks like."

"If you're kidding me . . . "

"Why would I kid about being your neighbor, neighbor?"

And just like in her fantasy, Jazz Taylor finally comprehended that he was the boy next door, and he beamed with unadulterated delight.

Lee and Jazz became the best of friends, a delightful relationship but one Lee hoped was remediable. It was also a friendship with certain limits. They had not yet met each other's families.

In Jazz's case, this was because the Taylors, after the requisite exhausting one-day celebrations of Christmas and Easter, would board the basenjis and fly away to their vacation house just south of St. Petersburg, a stucco-and-Spanish-tile affair they called (with the lack of originality that often goes hand in hand with inherited wealth) Casa Mildew.

For Lee's part, she told Jazz quite openly that she did not want him at her house. Her sister and brother-in-law had remained ensconced in Robin's bedroom in a hostile fog of sex and drugs, thus causing Sylvia to have a nervous breakdown—the ambulatory variety, where she could still, on a good day, go for her manicure. The situation was so excruciating that the stalwart Greta began to suffer what she designated tummyaches but which were, in fact, the pains of peptic ulcers.

Furthermore, Lee could not tell Jazz that she couldn't bring herself to invite him home, because she feared her father would suffer a major coronary, or at least a paralyzing stroke, from the sheer excitement of having a Taylor in the house. Or, worse, that Leonard might make an ass of himself, saying "cahn't" for "can't." "Cahn't" first emerged the summer between her junior and senior years at Cornell: Upon any annoyance, her father would say, "I cahn't abide it," as if he were a character in a bedroom farce. A shiver of dread went through her at each "cahn't."

However, by the end of her first year of law school, as she was packing to go to Washington for the summer, her father came into her room and, in his alluding to what he now called the "Situation"—the seizure and occupation of the house by Robin and Ira—Lee noticed another change in his diction. "I can't take it anymore," he was saying. Lee noticed not just the loss of "cahn't" but the acquisition of a new, cosmopolitan manner of speech: still a little world-weary, yet, despite the solemn words, not upper class. Snappy. He sounded like any successful Manhattan man: a tabloid reporter, a urologist, a (and this surprised her) prosperous furrier.

"So tell them to get out," Lee replied, a little absentmindedly, since she was engaged in a furious internal debate as to whether she should bring a pair of heels to Washington. She was now, after all, an editor of the *Law Review.* And she was going to be an intern at the

Kroll Institute for Justice, a prestigious left-wing think tank where great ideas were mulled over by people in denim and where no one wasted a neuron of brainpower on a subject as frivolous as patent-leather heels.

"It's easy for you to say, 'Tell them to get out,'" Leonard said, in his snappy new manner. "I happen to be her father. I'm the one who would have to deal with the consequences."

"What consequences?" Lee asked. If she took the heels, she'd have to buy panty hose. She sighed, went to her closet, and brought a pair of never-worn heels over to her suitcase. But even if there was a place she could go to where heels were required, would she *want* to be in such a place?

"Consequences like . . . Who knows what can happen to Robin with that putz?" Lee, who had never before heard a word of Yiddish coming from her father's lips, turned to scrutinize him. Despite his anguish over the Situation, he looked good. Well, except for the trendy wide tie with an Op Art black bull's-eye on a white background and his new long, fluffy sideburns. "We've got to get *him* out."

"How are you going to do that? He'd be crazy to get out. Free meals. Clean laundry—not that it matters to him. All the money he can steal. All the silver he can pawn."

"We don't know for sure . . . ," her father began, but then gave up, knowing that the Frank Lloyd Wright silver tea service had been taken not by a burglar with splendid taste, but by their very own in-house junkie. "Listen, I have a plan to get rid of him."

Lee, who was about to take her heels back to her closet, stopped in her tracks. Her father's dark eyes were sparkling, moist with almost lunatic anticipation. Her first thought was: Oh, God, he's hired a hit man to rub out Ira. "How are you going to do that?" she asked, keeping her voice steady so as not to agitate him.

"Move."

"Move?"

"Sell the house," he explained. "Look, I've had it with commuting. All these years." He did not mention that he'd also had it with staying with Dolly four nights a week. What had begun as wild sexual revelry on an antique iron bed they had bought together had ended up as three obligatory screws a week, and he looked forward to the one night with her—usually Wednesdays—when he could just sit in front of the TV with his Chinese food takeout dinner on a tray and watch Merv Griffin. If he had Sylvia in the city, he'd be able to cut Dolly down to one or two nights a week, plus have the perfect excuse not to sleep over at all. "It'll do your mother a world of good, being in the city." Seeing Lee's dubious expression, he added: "You have no idea how many things would open up to us if we were there. Socialwise, living on Long Island is the K.O.D."

"What's K.O.D.?"

"Kiss of death," he replied, in the casual manner of the true insider. "We can't throw a dinner party out here, because no one would come. No one who matters. No one from Manhattan. We could buy a co-op on Park or Fifth with a big entrance gallery and a formal dining room and have people over and get invited"—his eyes grew even more luminous; his chest puffed up—"everywhere!" Leonard, catching his daughter's wary expression, took pains to dampen his fervor. "Look, I'm not talking about being social butterflies. You know I wouldn't go for that shallow kind of life. But why shouldn't I have some fun? I've made a modest success." He paused until Lee smiled at his understatement. "And your mother was born with a great sense of style. She'd be fine, once she got a little self-confidence." He tried an insouciant wink, but all that happened was that his cheek twitched and his upper lip curled, exposing his newly capped canine tooth. "Can you imagine what your mother could do for the gross national product, shopping for a really full social life?"

"Dad," Lee said, "I don't know if she's in any shape for a really full anything."

"That's because she's stuck here, with *them*, with this . . . this unbearable Situation. If we lived in the city, had dinner parties to go to, believe me, she'd be high as a kite."

"She'd be high as a kite if someone told Robin and her husband to get out."

"Where would they go? What would they live on?"

"Whatever they could earn."

He shook his head hard, angry to be yanked away from the dinner party in his head. "You're being simple." Simplistic, Lee wanted to correct him. "You're the one who's going to be the lawyer," he went on. "She'd go out and sell drugs. Do you know how long she could wind up in jail for?"

"That's how she's keeping you under her thumb! Keeping you in fear of all the terrible things that can happen unless she gets her way. Do you honestly think that you can get rid of the problem by selling the house out from under her?"

"That's not the only reason I'm selling it."

"Don't you think she'd move into the apartment?"

"We wouldn't have a room for her!" Leonard said triumphantly. He walked to the window and pulled aside the curtain. In the twilight, all he could see was the backyard and the land rising up toward Hart's Hill. "I've had it with the suburbs, with boring *goyim*. This isn't for me. I spend my business life dealing with the most successful people in the city. They *like* me. And I'm not just talking about the fur business, or even fashion. I could be going to parties with the most fascinating people! Journalists. With movers and shakers in big business. Wall Street. With people in show business, for crissakes. Did you know that your mother and I could have been at a dinner party last Thursday with the producer of *Pippin*?"

Without thinking, Lee shoved the high heels into her suitcase. The next morning, she left for the nation's capital.

She did not wear the shoes all summer. As her Constitutional Law professor had promised, the Kroll Institute was a place for profound thought, so Lee spent June, July, and August in a pair of handmade sandals she had bought at a crafts fair in Ithaca in 1969, and not a single Kroll fellow even glanced at her feet. They were interested—to the degree that they were interested in any of the legal interns—only in her mind. So for fourteen hours a day, six days a week, she researched defective grand jury proceedings in Jackson County, Missouri, for one of the resident thinkers, a man who could not remember her name but instead called her Rita. She countered with "Lee," eleven or twelve times, then gave up for a day or two. But working in the belligerent stillness of the institute and living with a roommate who worked for the Federal Mediation and Conciliation Service, an agency that apparently required a vow of silence, she had a great deal of time to think.

So she thought: If I give up and let him call me Rita, all that will happen is that I'll show myself that I back down easily. Not from direct confrontation. I'm okay at that. But I have a tendency to get wounded by oblique hits: a raised eyebrow by an intern from Harvard at the way I footnote; an invitation to have lunch in the park that I almost said yes to until I realized it was meant for the guy across from me at my table in the law library; not making enough of an impact to have my name remembered. So if I'm going to be a lawyer, I've got to watch out for the indirect thrusts. That's where I'm vulnerable. If I let myself go to pieces when someone mocks my case citations or doesn't ask me to join him for a reading of the Magna Carta at George Washington University, I can't fall apart. Well, I can't let them see me fall apart.

So every time the great thinker called her "Rita," she responded with "My name is Lee White." That made her feel better. But not much.

She missed Jazz so much that thinking of him brought her to the verge of tears. Since she thought about him almost constantly—defective grand jury proceedings in Jackson County not being as fascinating to her as perhaps they should have been—she spent a great deal of time swallowing the lump in her throat and opening her eyes wide, so that even if she blinked she would not cry.

He missed her, Jazz told her when they spoke, usually once or twice a week. Of course, he said it in a friendly way, as in: I miss my great pal. Clearly, Jazz was having a wonderful summer. Through his uncle, the senior corporate partner, he had gotten a summer job at Matthison, Appleby on Wall Street, a plum usually reserved for second-year students with averages a point higher than his. The work, he informed her, was the dullest in the world, and the partner for whom he was working was a drag, a man whose sole passion in

life was his role as peacekeeper in the unending
internecine war at International-Hudson Machine
Tools. But he was sharing an apartment on the Upper
East Side with three of his college fraternity brothers,
and they were having a blast. "And don't think I'm not
getting culture," he told her. "I saw *Two Gentlemen of
Verona* and a play about an English soccer team where
the guys come onstage naked. What a pathetic collection of peckers! And I went to a couple of rock concerts in the East Village. So what have you been
doing?"

"This week?" Making sure not to crinkle the pages,
she leafed through the *Washington Post* until she came
upon the calendar of events and reported having seen
Six Characters in Search of an Author and gone on a
picnic.

"Sounds great!" Jazz said.

"Well . . . "

"It isn't?" His voice was so filled with solicitude that
he seemed to Lee not only to understand her loneliness
but even to know the details of it: the bologna-lettuce-
and-tomato sandwiches on the park bench at lunch,
the solitary nights trying to read *Dubliners* so she
wouldn't be too limited as a human being but instead
falling asleep.

"No. The work . . . I'm okay at it. Not good, though.
And I have a sneaking suspicion that I'm not an intellectual." She laughed, trying to sound lighthearted.

But there was no echoing laughter. Jazz could tell
how miserable she was. "You don't like the work
you're doing?"

"No."

"Why not?"

"I keep telling myself every case I'm reading is a
human life, but it doesn't feel that way. It just feels . . .

like words. And the words are ideas; and ideas *qua* ideas . . . to tell you the truth, I don't give a flying fuck about ideas. I never did. Even in college, all my anti-war stuff stemmed from seeing pictures of people burned by napalm, not from any serious intellectual objection to warfare."

"Okay, so what *do* you give a flying fuck about?" Jazz asked.

A small smile played across Lee's lips: Could I tell you a thing or two about flying fucks! she thought. "People. I care about people."

"See? You've learned something this summer."

"Right. I should have been a social worker."

"No. You learned you're not an academic type. You don't belong in a think tank. And you probably shouldn't think about a big law firm, because let me tell you, all you do for the first twenty years is research one tiny aspect of one big and boring case."

"So? Where does that leave me?"

"It leaves you as a practicing lawyer who represents *people.*"

"Ah," said Lee. "I'm going to law school to be a lawyer." She felt as if Jazz had removed a great weight. Her shoulders relaxed. She rotated her head from side to side and had to marvel at the sudden easing of the muscles in her neck. But with that burden gone, she was able to feel something else: desolation. Alone not only in Washington but in life.

She had no man, and—just as bad, she thought, or maybe worse—no purpose. Sure, she would graduate law school in the top ten percent of her class, but then what? Join a law firm and get the job women lawyers always got: trusts and estates, or matrimonial work? Do something meaningful for society, like researching amicus curiae briefs for redwoods? She could, but those prospects shriveled her soul. With nothing she cared to do, she would probably wind up on the legal staff of some dreadful person who called himself the Ralph Nader of Brooklyn and who picked at his ingrown beard hairs. And she would read in the *Cornell Magazine* about all her friends' wonderful lives: "Philip 'Flip' Mullen and his wife, Astor 'Pooky' Gibson, '71, are thrilled that their twins, Albert and Max, will be freshmen at Cornell next September. Flip, who admits to being a former 'peacenik,' is a fellow in physics at the Institute for Advanced Science in Princeton and is renowned for his work in fluid dynamics. Besides being a judge on the United States Court of Appeals for the Third Circuit, Pooky assists emerging nations in drafting their constitutions."

"Jazz," Lee said.

"Hey, you sound gruesome. I thought I cheered you up."

"I miss . . . " She imagined him slung over a chair in his apartment, his jacket off, his tie loosened, sipping some Wall Street law firm beverage: a martini, a Dewar's straight up. Then she changed him into a pair of shorts and a T-shirt and stuck a joint between his thumb and index finger.

"What do you miss?" Jazz asked.

"I miss" Lee's voice broke "New York."

By the end of the third month of the second year of law school, Lee decided she was not cut out to be a victim of love. She longed to be like the other women in her class, waking up to thoughts of Property, jogging around the park while musing about the impact of the Warren Court on criminal procedure, sleeping with dreams of Clifford Trusts swirling about her head. Jazz

Taylor was a perpetual presence and a constant intrusion and she resolved, sitting in Tax, to get him out of her life, or at least out of her heart. If a thought of him entered her mind, she was going to heed the advice she had read in *Glamour* or *Mademoiselle* years earlier. Tell yourself "Stop it!" and *immediately* think of something else. Just as the article had suggested, she lined up her replacement topics: school, of course; getting a wok and a cookbook and learning to cook Chinese food on the illegal hot plate she had in her dorm room; recollecting her grandmother Bella; calling Dorie Adler and asking her high school friend to arrange a blind date with one of her brother's friends at Columbia Medical School.

So the Wednesday before Thanksgiving, Lee sat on the Long Island Rail Road with something approaching relief. Not that she was anticipating any pleasure in the holiday. Greta would make her traditional twenty-pound turkey, but this year, Leonard had told Sylvia not to pad the guest list. Forget your cousins from Rockland County, he told her. And no lonely new neighbors. Just us. And Sylvia agreed. God only knew in what state Robin and Ira would come to the table, and now they had their friends Bonnie and Nikki with them, sharing the bedroom, eating the Whites out of house and home, and showing no signs of leaving. Company might ask: What are those girls with dirty hair doing there? Who are they?

But Lee felt good, because she had not thought about Jazz in three or four days . . . Stop it! Lee made herself think about a guy in Tax class, Rob Reynolds. Short, which was okay. But awfully small-boned. A mini-man. Would she look like a balloon in the Macy's parade beside him? Was he interested in her? Well, he kept finding a reason to come up after class and—

At which point, Jazz Taylor took the seat beside hers, squeezed her nose, and made a loud honking sound. "Hi."

"Hi," Lee said, not quite knowing how to behave. Part of her resolve to evict Jazz from her consciousness was to let the friendship cool. Having breakfast, lunch, and dinner with him, even in the company of their growing circle of friends, was not the way to get rid of him. Sitting carrel-to-carrel in the library was not a help either, nor was sharing a Coke and a popcorn every Sunday night at the Waverly.

"Where have you been?" Jazz inquired.

Lee pulled out her exclusionary, elitist card. "Hanging at the *Law Review* office," she said, heaving her book bag onto her lap and rummaging through it, as if driven to find a particular book crucial to her legal education. Her hands raced through notebooks and casebooks, pushed aside a small bottle of aspirin, a plastic case for tampons, a Chap Stick, a disintegrating recipe for Mongolian lamb she'd torn out from a magazine in the dentist's office months before.

"What's wrong with you?" Jazz asked.

"Nothing."

"Bullshit." She shook her head, denying anything was amiss, and pulled out a monograph on Crummey Trusts that her Tax professor had suggested she would find scintillating. "Did I do something?" he persisted.

"Of course not."

"Then . . . ?"

"Then nothing," Lee said, realizing that instead of the proper playful inflection she wanted, her intonation was funereal. She had to sound cheerier. Jazz's greatest gift was his understanding. Already he knew she was avoiding company—specifically, his. If she did not start sounding blithe right away, he would figure out exactly what was bothering her; he was that empathetic. "Listen," she said, her voice almost manic with ersatz merriment. "I'm being driven mad by *Law Review*. I mean, I'm barely managing all my course work and then this article on executive clemency in capital cases. It's so. . . . vast! And then on top of that, having to go home and face what passes in our house for family life . . . "

Lee stopped only because he put his hand on hers as if to say: Cut it out. That's not the cause of your ignoring me. She tried to go on but could not think of a thing to say. She wasn't used to Jazz's touch. Sure, he would routinely give her a preadolescent greeting: honking her nose, poking her arm. Once, when they were standing on line for *Soylent Green* and it had been bitter cold, he had hugged her, but it was a jock's bear hug, insulated by the six layers of wool between them. Now, though, it was skin to skin, and the rough warmth of his palm heated the back of her hand. Oh, God, she had to come up with something to say, fast, and she couldn't. A lawyer is supposed to be able to think on her feet, but all she could think of was how hot his hand was. Should she pull her hand away? Give him a fast, chummy poke with her elbow? And what was wrong with him, anyway? Why didn't he take his goddamn hand away?

In truth, Jazz was considering doing precisely that, but at that very instant, the train's electrical system went through a routine malfunction just as the train was accelerating into the tunnel under the East River, and their car was plunged into blackness. Before either of them had another thought, his hand began to caress hers and somehow, despite the absolute lack of light, their lips managed to find each other and Jazz said: "I love you, Lee."

And the lights blazed back on as Lee was saying: "I love you too."

Thirteen

"I'm letting Norman Torkelson stew in his own juices," I announced to the man in my life.

"Not a bad idea."

Since he was the best litigator on Long Island, and probably in the world, I was more than pleased with his concurrence. "Thanks," I replied, debating whether to simply pat myself on the back or open a bottle from the case of Dom Perignon I'd received as a bonus after getting a mob guy off on a charge of criminal possession of a machine gun with intent to use same unlawfully against the person of another. "In fact, thanks a lot."

"Except you seem to have jumped into the same pot."

"What pot?"

"The one Norman's in. You're really stewing." As usual, he was right.

As a criminal defense lawyer, life was simple: Most of my clients were guilty. Especially, and obviously, Norman Torkelson. But suddenly I was not only having doubts but experiencing every clichéd symptom of twentieth-century *angst*—clenched teeth, roiling stomach, lower back pain (with sciatica, naturally), and aching head. Those symptoms then set off my first hot flash. So I figured if I was miserable, why should Norman get a free ride? Since he had threatened to fire me for doing my job—trying to find a way to beat the murder rap that was facing him—I decided to let him stew in stir for three days.

However, considering my aptitude for anxiety, this current distress could not be called one of my major stews. During those three days I managed to work on my transportation-of-stolen-property-in-interstate-commerce case. I also pushed around some papers for a sentencing memo, interviewed witnesses for a vehicular homicide trial I had coming up, edited a court of appeals brief Chuckie had written, met with a new client—a college kid who had knocked down a security guard and torn out of Tower Records with twenty-two CDs shoved under her denim skirt—and bought a seven-hundred-pound cast-iron birdbath at an antique store's going-out-of-garden-ornaments-and-into-art-moderne-furniture sale.

If you're going to defend people on criminal charges, you're going to stew. Period. You make your living dealing with people who commit dreadful crimes, or at least wreak havoc for very cheap thrills. As their lawyer, you learn to put your own morality in a bag and stick it on a high shelf. Yes, the suffering that the person you represent causes to their victims, their own families, and themselves ought to break your heart. But after the first twenty or thirty sleepless nights, you begin to realize how little you can do. You comprehend that many of your clients *need* their problems. They live mainly to bring chaos out of order. And you, their lawyer, cannot change their lives. Also, you can't repair the damage they do and you cannot obtain Justice, at least not the highfalutin kind with a

capital J. All you can do is work your ass off to see that
they get the best deal the system will allow.

So I kept myself busy, which was easy. Since Chuckie
was a god-awful writer, I got so involved with editing his
brief that I decided to give Norman still another day to
stew. But then Norman called the office, pleading with
Sandi to have me come to see him. He told her he was
"conscious stricken" and "full of remorse" over his
"shoddy behavior." So I left Chuckie's "Defendant-
Appellant seeks this Court's review of his uncon-
scionable conviction for illegal and unlawful possession
(with intent to sell) of a certain quantity of a controlled
substance" and drove over to the Nassau County
Correctional Center.

"How can I tell you how sorry I am?" Norman said
from his side of the partition.

"Forget it. This place is a hellhole. It gets to people."

"That it does. Let me explain about Mary. Please. You
may view her as a tough little cookie"—I started to make
a pro forma objection but Norman cut me off—"but get
past her facade. She's terribly fragile."

"I understand."

"I know by your standards I'm no bargain," Norman
went on, "but it so happens I'm the best thing that ever
happened to Mary." With its calculated lack of expression, a poker face would have given me away even more
than the guffaw I felt coming on. So I just nodded stiffly
and concentrated on studying the crumbs on the side of
his mouth. There were also a few trapped in the chest
hair that peeked out of the V of his prison uniform.
Yellow-brown crumbs, which meant the correctional
center had served its culinary masterpiece for dessert:
chocolate-chip cookies—without the chips, as mandated
by the latest round of Republican budget cuts. "She's a
magnificent creature," he went on. "I know: You might

be thinking that thousands of men would want her. And you'd be right. But they would want her merely as an ornament."

Now that he'd gone and apologized, I couldn't be rude and cut him off. But it was like sitting in a lecture hall for some awful required course: Mary Dean 201: The Postpubescent Years. As he kept on, I felt I was coming close to telling him to stuff it.

"In practical terms, Mary cannot sustain a relationship with any of these men. You may ask why. It is because they need her only in a libidinous way. They do not *need* her, so to speak, as a human being or as a conventional wife. Mary has little utilitarian value."

"What does that mean?" I asked before I could stop myself, thereby dooming myself to another hit of Norman's verbiage.

"It means she cannot cook. She is too flighty to be able to care for children. She cannot be trusted to take a simple phone message. She cannot do anything, really. *Except* be a good person."

"A good person," I echoed, thinking about the almost sexual pleasure she'd taken in aiding and abetting Norman in the con, playing the Repo Lady, his matrimonial lawyer, and his ex-wife and thus helping destroy the lives of all the women he preyed on.

"I know I'm *not* good," Norman conceded. "I know that I've lured Mary—very skillfully, I might add—into being complicitous in my work . . . in my crimes. But at least I care about her goodness, which other men don't. And I sincerely want to make her happy—if only for the egocentric reason that she makes me happy. I mean, I don't need someone to cook me dinner. Any one of the marks would have been delighted to be, as it were, my willing slave, but Mary—"

If I waited for him to finish talking about her,

Norman and I would be celebrating my Diamond Jubilee together in the visitors room. So I asked: "How come you got so upset when I suggested Mary might have had something to do with Bobette's death?"

"Because she didn't do it!" Norman spit out. He was losing it again, leaning toward me, his eyes bulging with rage.

I looked straight at him till he abandoned his hostile posture and, after another few seconds, averted his eyes. Then I let him have a minute to get back to himself. Meanwhile, I checked out the visitors room. A colleague, Louie Pacheco, a guy I'd been in the D.A.'s Office with, was strolling my way in the row ahead, getting ready to meet with a client. I noticed Louie was sporting a fancy new suit, with gargantuan shoulder pads tailored to fool the eye into thinking his middle-age pear shape was a young, athletic inverted triangle. Louie, normally the color of boiled chicken, now had a tan one shade darker than a Brown & Serve sausage. A new hairstyle too: a ponytail. Clearly, he had a new, young girlfriend. From the look of him, she had taken charge. From the completeness of his transformation, it looked as if she would be his second wife—although from the fact of his wedding band I concluded that Louie hadn't informed his first about his change of plans. And he probably hadn't mentioned it to any of his four children—none of whom could be over twelve years old.

"Take it easy," I said, turning back to Norman. "I understand you love Mary. I understand your wanting to protect her. But you seem to be overprotective, and that leads me to believe you're fearful for her. As your lawyer, it would help me to know why." He clasped his hands together and rested his chin on the tops of his knuckles. His eyes closed. I understood this was a Meditative Moment, so I looked back at Louie and regarded his ponytail. Gray, limp, it hung dejectedly down the broad back of his dark-blue suit. I offered what might have been—had I been the praying type—a little prayer that the second wife would give him a major myocardial infarction on their honeymoon. "Norman, when I told you about the fingerprints at the crime scene being Mary's: That seemed to scare you."

"I suppose," he said, addressing the ceiling.

"Let's forget for a minute what she did or did not do at Bobette Frisch's house. Does Mary have a record? Is that why you were afraid?" He seemed to be taking a count of the acoustical tile overhead. "The truth would be of interest, Norman."

Norman looked back at me. "A couple of arrests for shoplifting. One conviction. Suspended sentence. No big deal. She likes pretty things and sometimes . . . You know, when someone like Mary is raised in an environment devoid of nurturance, she needs . . . objects. Talismans, if you will, to ward off privation. But if the police were to find out, they'd be all over her in a minute. They'd trump up some charge and arrest her. And let me tell you, one night in a place like this . . . It would destroy her. I can't let that happen! I love her. But even more, I'm . . . " He swallowed hard. Just when I was thinking he was a lousy actor, his eyes squeezed shut. Tears began to leak out of the corners. "I'm a flawed human being," he managed to whisper. I waited the moment it took him to begin speaking again. "I need Mary to make me whole, or as close to whole as someone like me can get. Dear God, I'm so terrified of life without her. *That's* why I have to protect her. No matter what the cost."

In the movies, private detectives always have offices with linoleum floors (on which click the spike heels of sexy clients), milky glass partitions, and overflowing ashtrays. Terry Salazar's had ivory wall-to-wall carpeting, an ivory sectional sofa, and two ivory pull-up chairs beside an ivory Art Deco–style desk. He had taken over the lease of a skin-care products company that had sunk all its assets into a slickly expensive infomercial featuring a porcelain-skinned soap-opera star who was supposed to appear genteel; instead she came across as so snooty that almost all the calls to the 800 number were not orders but denunciations of the bitch. For an additional five thousand bucks, Terry had purchased the furniture, a Packard Bell computer and, it turned out, a closetful of SatinSkin Exfoliating Granules.

In Terry's mind, he was simply buying a white office. It was not until one of his cop buddies started ribbing him about how he must know an interior decorator that he realized his office was—what a nightmare!—*feminine*. For a time, he tried to nullify the place's atmosphere by rolling up his sleeves to display his arm hair and puffing offensive cigars, but in the end he did most of his business in Plumpie's or another extravagantly dirty bar, Big Nick's, and kept clients away from his office.

But he made an exception for me, largely because I'd once sworn never to make a snide remark about his lady-like furnishings or let on to anyone else in the entire criminal justice system about them. I kept my word. Other than the stink of cigars, living and dead, and the dark ink smears from fingerprint kits, it was an appealing place, and I often dropped by. As comfortable as my own office was, I hated being stuck in one place. If a day went by without a court appearance, I'd find an excuse to go to Terry's or the library at the Bar Association or even drop by police headquarters on ostensible business and shoot the breeze for a half hour.

At Terry's, I always took the same spot on the sectional,

kicking off my shoes and putting my feet up on the white marble coffee table, a practice he encouraged because it was so distinctly uncouth. "If Mary has a record," I asked, "how come the cops didn't ID her when they checked those prints in Bobette's living room?"

Terry, leaning back in his ivory leather chair, *his* feet up on his desk, puffed his cigar and said: "Two possibilities." He took his cigar out of his mouth and examined its length, not without satisfaction.

"I'm paying you seventy-five bucks an hour to be a detective, not to look at your surrogate penis in thoughtful silence."

"What the fuck are you talking about, Lee?"

"Two possibilities," I snapped. "What are they? Come on. I don't have all day."

He shook his head sadly at my lack of civility. "One: If Mary had just one arrest, something could have happened with the paperwork and the prints never made it to the computer."

"Does that happen often?"

"More than anyone wants to admit."

"Or . . . ?" I encouraged him.

" 'Or' what?"

"You said two possibilities."

"Cute little Holly forgot to run the prints."

I sat up and put my feet on the floor. "*Forgot?*"

"Why should she?" Terry asked, still sitting back comfortably, licking the tip of his cigar in the usual way guys lick cigars—i.e., the way a dog licks its genitals. He did not seem in the least perturbed about Holly's laxity. "If she checks the prints, then she has to go out and find whoever they belong to, haul him in for questioning. It would only cloud up her case."

"It's her professional responsibility . . . " I began. But instead of offering a speech on ethics, I told him to call his friend and see if the FBI check had come up with anything.

"I can't hurry him," Terry protested.

"Yes you can. I'm paying you and you're paying him and I want an answer."

"You know, when you talk like that, you're so fucking masculine. It's a real turnoff, Lee."

"Good," I said, and sat back while he made the phone call. Naturally, he gave away nothing as he was talking. A few manly chuckles, inquiries about each other's wives, and then a lot of uh-huhs and hmms. He reached over, picked up a pad and pen, and made a few notes.

"So?" I said, the second he hung up. "Come on. You're suppressing a self-satisfied grin. You're thrilled with yourself."

"I'm always thrilled with myself."

"Come on, Terry!"

"Mary Dean has a record."

"For what?"

"Not shoplifting."

"So?"

"A long—and I mean long—record for prostitution."

The record didn't surprise me. The "long" did.

"How long?"

"Twenty-seven arrests."

"Gee," I said. "She's a real pro."

"I bet she is." Terry wore his reflexive lascivious leer, but it was clear he was disappointed in Mary. Hurt, even.

"Do you think Norman knows?" I asked him.

"How could he not?" He furrowed his brow, the way bad actors do on movies of the week, when they want to show they are cogitating. In Terry's case, however, his brain actually was working. "I bet Norman goes out of his way *not* to remind her that she was a hooker. You know, treats her like a princess. I guarantee you, that would make her a hundred times more loyal. I mean, I'll bet he's set it up so she sees only two choices. Being worshiped and taken care of—or getting twenty bucks a blow job for a bunch of guys in the back of a Dodge Ram." Every time I start getting completely disgusted with Terry, he comes up with insights like that.

"Where were the arrests?" I asked.

He peered at his notes. "California, Nevada, Arizona, New Mexico."

"Did she serve any time?" I asked.

Terry smiled. "Five suspended sentences. She sure in hell never got a woman judge. What guy would have the heart to put her in jail?" Just as I was starting to step back into my shoes, Terry announced: "One more arrest."

"What for?"

"Assault."

"Assault?" My foot remained poised over my shoe. "What? Tell me about it."

"Eight months ago. In Annapolis, Maryland. Her alias was Marissa Shaw. She beat the hell out of a sixty-year-old woman. A widow. Facial contusions, concussion, two cracked ribs."

"You're kidding!"

"Mary claimed the woman attacked her. The judge allowed bail, and guess what?"

"Mary ran."

"Of course." Terry leaned back his head and blew a smug stream of smoke toward his ivory ceiling. "She ran."

It took only a few minutes more to find out the sixty-year-old woman's name: Carolyn Knowles. I didn't need a detective to find her; a quick call to 410 Information got me her number. As soon as I heard the click of connection, I signaled Terry to pick up his extension and take notes. She answered my call on the second ring, as if she'd been circling the phone, waiting for someone to call. I explained I had heard about her case from Maryland authorities.

"Are you a policewoman?" she asked. Her voice was overly cultured, her "Are" coming out as "Ah," and every syllable carefully enunciated. Just for the diction alone, I could see why someone would want to give her a contusion or two.

"No, but I've been hired to investigate . . . Well, to tell you the truth, Ms. Knowles, the woman who assaulted you, the woman who was using the alias . . . " I paused, hoping she'd think I was looking at my notes and oblige by giving me the name.

And she did. "Marissa Shaw," she said, her pearly tones making it sound as if Marissa Shaw were someone who'd stopped by for a watercress sandwich and a cup of Darjeeling instead of someone who beat the shit out of her.

"Marissa Shaw is only a collateral part of my investigation. The person I'm really trying to get information on is"—I heard her quick intake of breath—"is known to change his name frequently. However, I can describe him to you. He is six feet, five inches tall—"

"Have you found him?" she gasped.

"I have a pretty good idea of where he is, Ms. Knowles, although right now I'm not at liberty to discuss the matter. Now, as far as you know, was there any connection between . . . Under what name did you know him?"

"Arthur Berringer," she said, tenderly, slowly, as if the name still held magic.

"And did he ever give you any indication that he knew this Marissa Shaw?"

"No." A definite no. "In fact . . . " She hesitated.

"Anything you can tell me would be deeply appreciated, Ms. Knowles," I said, as Terry mimicked the male auto-erotic gesture that signaled a major jerk-off was in progress.

"He definitely did *not* know her," Carolyn Knowles replied. "When it happened, he tried to pull her off and kept saying: 'Who are you? Stop!'" Her voice rose. "'Stop!'"

"Where did the attack occur?" I asked.

"In my car. We drove up to my house in my car. I have a LeBaron convertible and the top was down. We just sat there for a moment. Arthur—my fiancé—took my hand." Then, almost shyly, she added: "We had just come from getting our marriage license." As she paused to compose her thoughts, and probably to keep from crying, I paused too: to reflect that Carolyn Knowles was born to be a mark. Here she was, giving me her entire story—without ever having asked my name. "All of a sudden, from out of nowhere, this woman came and pulled open the door."

"Driver's or passenger's?"

"Passenger. Arthur was driving."

"And then what happened?" I asked, as delicately as I could.

"She must have unlatched my seat belt. Before I knew what was happening, she pulled me out of the car. I literally was dragged onto the sidewalk."

It sounded like a series of sniffles, but I knew she was crying silently. "What a horrible thing," I said.

"Horrible, horrible."

"But Arthur tried to stop her?"

"Yes, but she was amazingly strong. He came around and tried to hold back her arms or pull her off. He was yelling 'Stop it!' and she kept yelling 'Stop it!' back to him—that he should stop trying to stop her."

"Did she give you any indication what the attack was about?"

A huge sob came across the phone. A moment later,

she said "No. She didn't say a word. Just kept punching me. With her fists, like a man. Then she took my head and"—the cultured voice broke, only to be replaced by a high, confused inflection that sounded like an injured child's—"banged it against the pavement."

"Do you remember anything else, Ms. Knowles?"

"No, I passed out. Not for too long, I think, but when I came to, the girl was gone. Arthur was holding me in his arms. When he saw I was . . . well, not all right, but at least conscious, he said: 'I'll run in and call the police and an ambulance.'"

"And did he?"

"Yes."

I knew the answer to my question, but I had to ask it anyway: "Was he there when the police arrived?" I asked.

"No."

"Did you ever see him again?"

"No."

"But you saw her?"

"In a lineup. The police found her an hour later near a shopping center about three miles from my house. A fluke, really. They broadcast the description I'd given—the hair, the heavy, heavy makeup, the cheap sundress, turquoise— and a passing patrol car spotted her. The next day, they brought me from the hospital to the building where the jail is, and I identified her. They thanked me and said the state attorney's office would contact me before the trial. And then, two days later, a judge let her go on bail!"

"And she took off?" I asked.

"She did indeed."

"And you never heard from Arthur again?"

"No. I filed a missing persons report. But in my heart of hearts I knew . . . Arthur must have had some trouble earlier in his life. Things hadn't gone well. His marriage had failed, his wife was a monster, tormenting him. But there must have been trouble with the police as well, because he could not face them. His last words, just before he went into my house to call them, were: 'Carolyn. I love you with all my heart. Never doubt that.'"

"And you didn't?"

"I did not!"

"One final question, Ms. Knowles."

"What's your name?" she demanded.

"Lily," I said quickly. "Did you find anything missing?"

"Missing?"

"Yes."

"Some jewelry."

"Such as?"

"Everything I had."

"And you reported it to the police?"

"Of course. And to the insurance company as well."

"And did they investigate?"

"What was there to investigate?" she asked. "Marissa Shaw—what do they call that—oh, jumped bail. Even if they find her, do you think she will still have the pearl choker and the diamond-and-ruby brooch and the diamond ring and the platinum-and-diamond watch and the—"

"The jewelry wasn't on Marissa Shaw when the police picked her up?"

"No."

"Did the police think that Arthur Berringer may have had something to do with the disappearance of the jewelry?"

"No!" she boomed. "It was perfectly clear that Marissa Shaw had been in my house. They found her fingerprints in there." I glanced over at Terry: So Bobette was not the first mark Mary had spied on. "And I *knew* Arthur as I knew myself. Know, as I know myself. And he would never take what is not his."

"And so you never mentioned him to the police?"

Just as Terry was shaking his head, as in "You've gone too far," Carolyn Knowles slammed down the phone.

"Lee," Terry said, taking his feet off his desk, "if you were a guy I'd call you a schmuck. How could you ask her that?"

"I'll tell you how, schmuck. I wanted to find out for sure if Holly had the cops check out the mystery prints—Mary's prints—near the body. Clearly, they didn't, or they would have found out the prints were associated with a middle-aged woman who had been viciously assaulted. And I'll bet in that file down in Annapolis are all the other latents they found when they dusted Carolyn Knowles's house—the plumber's, the pizza delivery boy's, and Norman Torkelson's. Ergo, schmuck, if I can convince Norman to cooperate, we have priors on Mary Dean that ought to be very convincing to the D.A. And if not to the D.A., then the jury."

"You don't have a chance in hell of getting Norman to cooperate," Terry said. "He's going to protect that girl."

"But she's a known batterer! And it's the same pattern! She thinks he's getting too close to marrying one of his marks, and whomp! She attacks. And not girl stuff—hair pulling and a smack or two. She goes out of control."

"There are no other marks on Bobette except the ones around her neck."

"What other marks were necessary? The ones around the neck did the trick. This time, Mary cut out the preliminaries."

"You just can't stand to lose, Lee."

"Not this one. Because Norman Torkelson did not commit this murder."

Terry Salazar shook his head sadly and, not without warmth, said: "Schmuck."

Fourteen

❧

It was certainly not that browbeater Professor Blumenthal and his torts that finally captured Lee's imagination. Nor was it the charismatic Nestor P. Von Hassel, who unraveled the tangles of corporate law not only for the secretary of commerce but for the hosts of the *Today* show and, thus, for all America. It was not even Kevin McTeague, the Errol Flynn of evidence, with his flowing ebony hair and his swashbuckling presentation of the Excited Utterance exception to the Hearsay Rule. No, in the first semester of her second year at NYU Law School, the one who really made Lee a lawyer was Professor Lucille Poole.

She was a sallow-skinned woman with hair dyed shoe-polish black. Her nose was so long and pointy that, had it been orange, people would have thought she'd snatched it off a snowman. If Sylvia had ever seen the professor, she would have been too sickened to mock her; Professor Poole's wardrobe consisted solely of cheap, shapeless black dresses, as if her clothes were hand-me-downs from working-class Italian widows.

Upon seeing her, people thought: Ah, with those looks, she must be a charmer. Hardly. Each semester, Professor Poole brought nearly every student in her Criminal Law classes to the brink of nervous collapse by lecturing in a double-time monotone. In fact, there was nothing she did not say too flat and too fast: "Swiss on my burger, please," in the cafeteria came out like Swzzbr, plis. Her introductory "Since my time is limited, I assume Your Honors are familiar with the facts and the prior proceedings in this case," to the entire bench of the Supreme Court of the United States of America, became a mere whir of sound. And if you said hello to her in the corridors of the law school, you were never certain if the reply you heard was her reciprocal greeting or simply a rush of air passing over a crack in the wall.

However, despite Professor Poole's next-to-unintelligible speech and her lack of anything that might be construed as a personality, she routinely won the appeals she argued on the issue of police coercion of prisoners. Some of her colleagues muttered that her success was due to her briefs; her writing was so simple a third grader could understand it. Others claimed she won so often because she was a woman in a man's field, or because she was so ugly the appellate judges pitied her. A few asserted it was because she was a manipulator, forcing judges to strain to understand her jabber, thereby capturing their complete attention. What these carpers seemed unable to acknowledge was that while all the above was true, Lucille Poole, that black crow, stood before the bench with the fire of legal brilliance burning within her.

"MsWhi," Professor Poole called out as she entered

the suite, the words hurtling past lips that were puckered like a long-forgotten prune. "Good point you made about the statute of limitations in noncapital offenses."

Lee, working at a table in the Regina and Stanley Farbman International Center for Criminal Justice—a two-room suite in a fleabag hotel on West Twenty-second Street—did not hear the entire sentence. What came through was "G' point" and "statute of." So, with a reasonable degree of confidence, Lee replied: "Thank you," and suppressed the shiver of pleasure that passed through her. This was the work Lee loved best, so much better than the dry, dead stuff at law school. Here she was, exposing the system's stupidity, duplicity, and cruelty where it really counted: in matters of crime and punishment. The real thing, where a person's life or liberty was at stake. To hell with trusts and estates. Screw copyrights. Fuck corporations. *This* is what was important. And how she loved it! "Thank you very much."

"Welc."

The suite resembled Professor Poole: unattractive and cheerless. What had been a living room was now crammed with four collapsible bridge tables, bowing under the weight of books and papers, and dark-brown filing cabinets that resembled upright coffins. In the adjoining room, a plywood bed board resting upon the mattress of a double bed formed the giant desk where the professor, hunched over, did her writing and ate what she ate every single lunch and dinner (and, for all anyone knew, breakfast as well)—ground beef. The rich, fatty scent of hamburger or meat loaf sandwich or meatball hero was always in the air at the Regina and Stanley Farbman International Center for Criminal Justice.

To Lee's surprise, Lucille Poole took a folding chair from another bridge table and sat beside her. "Wha' doing?" she inquired. Lee lifted the yellow legal pad she had been scribbling on, but before she could launch on a spiel about the exercise of reasonable prosecutorial diligence in *New York* v. *Wu*, the professor added: "Not Wu. Summer."

Lee's heart fluttered, then throbbed. A summer job offer? The chance to be Lucille Poole's research assistant! To help draft the reply brief for the Quinones case, which would be argued—Lee swallowed hard—before the Supreme Court of the United States of America in the fall. For just an instant, she could hear Chief Justice Burger saying "Interesting point," and Professor Poole, for once, speaking slowly enough for all to hear: "Credit where credit is due. My student assistant, Lee White, came up with that." Her name in the Court record *before she was even out of law school*. And Jazz would probably do something wonderful, like putting that page of the transcript in a silver frame as her Christmas gift. Although, in truth, she'd rather have an engagement ring, but that appeared too much to hope for. He loved her. He had told her that. But he had said not one single word about the future beyond suggesting they get tickets to *The Ritz* for sometime in the spring. Could it be possible that he would just love her forever without ever asking her to marry him? She could be seventy-two, still without a ring on her ropy-veined left hand. No, worse: On her thirtieth or fortieth birthday—whenever she'd finally get up the courage—she would confront Jazz and ask him if he was ever going to marry her. Looking surprised and, worse, pained, he would explain that while he really and truly loved her, and the last thing in the world he wanted to do was hurt her, she—how could he put it without seeming like a total bastard?—she wasn't what he imagined when he thought of a wife. He would probably do better with . . . not a lawyer. You know, someone less challenging. More traditional. More—don't take this the wrong way—feminine. A teacher or something.

"I don't have any summer plans," Lee told Professor Poole. "I want to stay in New York." She was going to add something about wanting to be with her boyfriend but decided that might make Professor Poole think her frivolous, not the solemn sort who would work eighteen hours a day in mortal combat with Injustice.

"I cannot use you as a research assistant," Professor Poole announced. The awful thing was, every word was clear. Lee hugged the legal pad against her chest, close, like a teddy bear. What was she seeing in her mentor's eyes? Pity? "Not an academic, y'know." Not sorrow. Disdain?

"Oh," was all Lee could think to say. Not the rapid-fire response one might expect from a prospective litigator, but an understandable one, as she was concentrating on holding back a cascade of tears.

"Not that you haven't w . . . "

"I beg your pardon?"

"It's not that you have not worked hard this entire semester," Professor Poole said, pronouncing each word as if it were a separate sentence.

"Uh-huh," Lee replied.

"You're dedicated . . . to put in the hours." So? "But your talent . . . not in scholarship." What are you talking about? I have an A-minus average! I made *Law Review*. Where the fuck else does my talent lie? "It lies in being fast on your feet," Professor Poole went on. That means I'm shallow. Unoriginal. Unimaginative. "You were born to be a criminal lawyer."

"But not to argue before the Supreme Court?"

"You might. Never know. Solid student. If a case should bring you before the Court . . . Few lawyers could deny themselves . . . " Lee waited. "But you aren't . . . " Professor Poole's voice evaporated.

"A legal scholar."

" . . . good trial lawyer. Do you know how rare . . . ?"

"So this summer?" Lee was so ashamed. No, humiliated. No. She wanted to quit law school. She wished she could get married. "Do you have any suggestions, Professor Poole?" Lee inquired, her manner as casual as a customer asking a drugstore clerk for advice on choosing a lipstick. "I'd like something challenging." She wanted to add: you egomaniacal hag, letting me work nights, weekends. Sending me down to pick up your fucking bacon-mushroom-Swiss burgers because you think the delivery guy takes too long and they get cold.

"Yes." Something Lee could not hear, and then: " . . . Manhattan District Attorney's office."

"*What?*"

Professor Poole rose. "A good lawyer . . . argue both sides. Manhattan D.A. . . . best place . . . I'll . . . phone call."

Since Lee could not come up with another response, she said: "Thank you."

"That is, if you want . . . If you have other . . . "

"Your calling would be great," Lee answered. "I appreciate it." Oh, God, she thought, what the hell am I doing?

" . . . like it," Professor Poole said.

In fact, Lee loved it. By the end of her third week in the Rackets Bureau, she was working six days a week on the prosecution of one Howard "Howie the Hose" Fogelman for extortion: to wit, threatening seven kosher butchers on the Upper West Side of Manhattan with firebombing unless their stores carried the Gan Eden brand of knockwurst.

To Lee, the Manhattan D.A.'s Office resembled a late forties black-and-white crime buster—except it wasn't a movie. It was real and, miraculously, she was playing a supporting role. Forget being a star; she was thrilled to be welcomed, with an offhand "Hiya," as part of the cast. She belonged. No questions asked. Lee treasured every detail of the hard-boiled life: the endless cardboard cups of overperked coffee; the dented metal desks; the rough-talking cops from Hell's Kitchen and Harlem; the world-weary secretaries. She thrilled to the gruff, New York–accented banter of the assistant district attorneys out of St. John's and Brooklyn Law; the eager-beaver preppy enthusiasm of the A.D.A.'s out of Yale and Columbia as they mimicked the jargon and the hunchbacked slouch of the toughest of the cops. Most of all, she loved her colleagues' unspoken love for each other. She would gladly have worked seven days a week to see that Howie—whom, with the rest of the cops and A.D.A.'s, she referred to as "scumbag" or "that piece of shit"—got what was coming to him, but she knew it would upset Jazz.

They were living together for the summer in a sublet on University Place, a studio with a rain forest of plants and a narrow Murphy bed on which, after making passionate, athletic, and benevolent love, they slept, arms and legs entwined. But it was not the sex Lee marveled at. It was Jazz's sweetness. "Hi," he would say all of a sudden, at a moment in the act when all that the other boys with whom she had slept could manage was, at best, a grunt of encouragement best translated as: Hump harder. But as Lee and Jazz lay together, sweaty bodies sliding against each other in humid currents exhaled by an air conditioner not equipped to handle heated sex, Jazz would somehow find the tenderness to say "I love you so much." And he would gaze into her eyes as if he could see something breathtaking right behind them.

Lee felt beautiful that entire summer, even in dark, lawyerly skirts and businesslike white shirts. Her skin glowed a rosy gold; her hair—pulled back into compliance by a tortoiseshell barrette, looked as if it wanted to break free and fall, thick and wanton, over her shoulders. "I love the way you look," Jazz would tell her. And it wasn't only in bed that he admired her. That was the nicest part: his tributes offered beside the Saran Wrap and aluminum foil in Marty's Superette, or in front of the Abyssinian kittens in the window of Village Pets.

Lee noticed, too, that for the first time, strange men were eyeing her with admiration. Not because she was exhausting herself being charming, clever, amusing, but simply because living with Jazz had transformed her into a love goddess. The guy in the subway token booth gave her the once-over, then the twice-over. The cop who stood by the elevator in the D.A.'s actually winked. Construction men on a scaffolding across Centre Street discovered new adjectives, and an elderly man in a seersucker suit walking his Doberman down Tenth Street doffed his panama hat.

So while many in the D.A.'s Office gave up their Sundays to go in to work simply because they could not bear to be away from the pursuit of justice or the company of their colleagues, Lee kept her day of rest because she wanted to be with Jazz.

He needed her company. His summer job was less enthralling than hers. Through his father's connections at the U.S. Olympic Committee, he was working in the

office of the general counsel of the National Hockey
League. Sports law, Foster decreed. It's getting bigger
every day. Get yourself in on the ground floor, buddy-
boy. You'll thank me. But by the end of the first week
of July, Lee became aware that—as he was the previous summer, at the job his uncle had gotten for him at
Matthison, Appleby—Jazz was bored. She could see it
in his eyes, which lit up when she walked through the
door each night. Thrilled by the very fact of her, true,
but, even more, almost pathetically grateful for a friend
to play with.

"All you keep saying is that it's boring. What specifically don't you like about it?" she asked him the first
week in August. They stood on the platform at Penn
Station. Only nine in the morning, but the heat rising
from the tracks was already so wetly oppressive that
the few Sunday travelers had the glistening red faces of
foundry workers.

"I don't know. It's just boring."

"But you like hockey. I know a couple of people
who can name all the presidents, but you're the only
one I know who can name all the Stanley Cup winners
since 1704 or whenever."

"Since 1927."

"The fact is, you *love* hockey. So how can your job
be boring?"

He smiled, and for the hundredth or thousandth
time, she marveled at his sunny temperament, which
did not alter with adversity or foul weather or bad
news. And Jazz's optimism was contagious. With him
at her side, she could face the Black Plague or a
nuclear firestorm, knowing they would emerge
unscathed and smiling. "You're badgering the witness,
Miss White," he joshed.

"I'm not badgering. This is what's called probing.

And I'm probing because I care about you, you fool. I want to see you happy."

He crossed his arms tight over his chest, as he always did when he was reflective, a mannerism Lee found utterly charming. Despite the sapping heat, she moved closer to him and immediately felt better. "I guess it's boring because the job isn't about hockey," he explained. "It's about law."

"Is that it, Jazz?"

"Is what it?"

"Do you feel pressured? Because your father and all the Taylors back to Peking Man were lawyers: Does that mean you're doomed to be one? I mean, if you truly don't like it . . . "

"No. Law's okay. I mean, I don't wake up every morning all hot to discuss due process—"

"You're telling me!"

"—but I want to be a lawyer."

"Is it that you *want* to practice law or you can't think of anything else you'd rather do?"

"That's a big question for a Sunday morning."

"I know. You don't have to answer it if you don't want to."

She could tell Jazz did not want to give a glib response. He was considering her question, for both their benefits. "I honestly don't know the answer to that. I look at you, loving what you do at the D.A.'s. But if it weren't the D.A.'s, it would be the ACLU or the NAACP you'd be gung-ho about. You get wrapped up in stuff. I'm not like that. But maybe there's something out there for me. I think to myself: Maybe somewhere there's a job that'll make me jump out of bed every morning and say; 'Hey, I'm lucky! I get to go to work today!' Or lots of jobs. It's just that *this* job is boring."

Lee was very tired. In truth, standing on the platform

waiting for the train to Shorehaven, having this meaningful discussion, she wanted nothing more than to lean against Jazz's strong shoulder and close her eyes, save her strength for going home to Long Island. To Jazz's home, actually.

For the first time, he had suggested that they spend the day with his family. A milestone. Their relationship seemed to exist solely in Manhattan, as if he had come from a place like Bombay, she from, say, Montevideo, and there they were, alone together in New York. True, they appraised and analyzed their families often (Lee having taken Introduction to Psychology at Cornell and Jazz Introduction to Sociology at Colgate). But they spoke of their parents and siblings as if they were dead—or at least in a different hemisphere.

But the previous evening, Saturday night, Jazz confided that his old lady was bugging him: She never saw him anymore. Lee suggested he could visit his family alone, half hoping he would, but grateful when he demanded: Are you kidding? Miss my one day of the week with you? So she could not have said no, even if she had wanted to. And part of her wanted to, most desperately. Part of her dreaded that the Taylors would not approve. Within seconds after the introduction, with a mere frozen smile from Ginger or a too stiff handshake from Foster, her relationship with Jasper Taylor would come to an end. And that would be even before they learned she came from the family who lived in the modern house that lay beneath Hart's Hill. In Lee's secret heart, she regretted telling Jazz the truth about being White. True, he seemed to have found the Weissberg-Weiss connection both exotic and amusing. But what if it was secretly disturbing to him? What if, unable to admit to a touch of anti-Semitism in himself, he just happened to mention the fact of her Jewishness

to his parents, knowing that they would do the job—
getting rid of Lee—that he was not quite man enough
to handle?

But around three that afternoon, as Lee was passing
the kitchen on her way out to help Ginger feed the
basenjis, she overheard Fos, back from his golf game,
telling Jazz: "Nice girl you've got there, pal." And
since Jazz said "Thanks" and not "She's one of the
Jews from next-door," Lee felt somewhat reassured.

The Taylors's life, however, was less reassuring.
Take Hart's Hill. It was, to be sure, a great house, perhaps even a mansion. Its ceilings were impossibly
high, its rooms noble in dimension. Arthur Taylor, who
had built it in 1898, had given his architect an open
purse and his full confidence: Lay on the moldings, my
dear fellow! Panel those walls with the finest hard-
woods! Don't stint on the leaded glass, old chap! But
Hart's Hill looked as if it had fallen on hard times half
a century ago.

Lee glanced around the grounds as she hurried to
the doghouse. She staggered slightly under the new
twenty-five-pound bag of Blue Ribbon Champion
Chow. Ginger had forgotten to bring it from the garage.
The grass tennis court was in beautiful shape, Lee
noted, rolled every day. But the back lawn looked as if
it had not been mown all summer. It wasn't even a
lawn anymore. Weeds and stiff yellow reeds had
grown so high that the legs of the ornate wrought-iron
garden furniture were completely hidden; a bench and
four chairs appeared to be floating on amber waves of
grain.

The doghouse was not what Lee had imagined—a
mini-Tudor manor house designed by the original
architect of Hart's Hill. Instead it was scraps of nailed-
together lumber, a doggy-size Tobacco Road hovel.

"Over here!" Ginger called out to her. Ginger was hunched over the mother dog, searching its coat for something Lee knew she would not want to see. "They eat and poop out here," she explained. "Otherwise, they're with us all the time." Turning to the puppies, Ginger spoke in the squeaky baby voice the childless employ with small children. "You're really little piggies, aren't you? Making big, doody piles in the house!"

Kent, Jazz's younger brother, looked up from the dam's coat and smiled at Lee, a radiant smile. Had it been an illustration in an old-fashioned children's book, it would have been labeled: A Delightful Surprise. He had fine, tawny skin and golden-brown hair, along with the flattened features and epicanthic eye fold of Down's syndrome. "Hi," he said. "What's your name?"

"Lee."

"I'm Kent." He smiled, pleased that their interchange had gone so well. While Jazz, with his long, angular, well-chiseled features, was clearly his mother's son, Kent bore more of a resemblance to the middle-aged man Foster Taylor had become. However, Kent's rounded face, with its baggy double chin, was redeemed by blue eyes so bright they could indeed be called sparkling.

But his clothes! Okay, Lee told herself, even Sylvia White wouldn't expect a retarded fifteen-year-old to be a fashion plate, but it was not simply that Kent's red-and-blue-striped pullover did not match his brown plaid shorts. They were far too tight, the shirt's stripes making waves over his thick chest; they were clothes for a large boy rather than a good-size young man. The hem on one leg of the shorts had unraveled, and threads dangled down behind his knee. Kent kept slapping them away, but of course they continued to annoy him with their tickling.

Ginger seemed oblivious to her son's discomfort. And she appeared to be unaware of the ripped shoulder seam of his pullover, so the short sleeve hung down over his biceps like a striped armband. Yet she did not seem to be a cruel or an uncaring parent. She and Kent played what was evidently a familiar game: He picked up the pieces of kibble that had not made it into the dogs' bowls, as she counted. "Thirty-seven," Ginger pronounced, exhaling with only slightly weary finality. Kent appeared gratified by the total, although whether it was a high or a low number for them, or if he would be thrilled no matter what the tally, Lee could not determine.

Still, despite the counting game, Lee couldn't stop herself from scrutinizing mother and son as they headed back to the house: Ginger's tennis clothes could have been called grays rather than whites; the seat of Kent's shorts was black with what detergent commercials refer to, ominously, as ground-in dirt. Not just today's dirt, Lee perceived. She wished she could keep from knowing. She longed to think well of the Taylors. After all, she had expected them to be perfect. Okay, perhaps a little too casual about money, about each other, but essentially the best family in America. Yet here she was, dragging her feet through the high, scratchy weeds that were the back lawn, forestalling the disillusionment that she knew was inevitable once she got into the house again and—this time—allowed herself to really see.

It wasn't just the run-down condition of the house. Lee, who had been raised by Leonard to revere—if not worship—the upper-class god of genteel shabbiness, could not stop herself from noting that there was a profound difference between a threadbare Chippendale settee and a toilet dripping brown water onto a rust stain that had eaten through the tile floor. That single two-by-two-inch tile told Lee the story: The Taylors were either cheap or poor—poor meaning not rich enough to maintain an estate as grand as Hart's Hill. Her heart was heavy. She had wanted them to be inexhaustibly wealthy, to say nothing of benevolent and eccentric and effervescent—like characters in a thirties screwball comedy. However, what disturbed Lee most was not the lack of money.

It was the lack of care: breakfast dishes with bits of bacon stuck in gluey maple syrup never cleared from the table in the kitchen; moisture-beaded highball glasses exuding a stale liquor smell in the living room; the *Times* from the previous Sunday still spread out on the unvacuumed rug in the library. It was more than just mess, however. Taylor did not care about Taylor.

After saying "Nice girl you've got there, pal" Fos clomped up the grand staircase in his golf shoes. By the time Lee returned from the doghouse and passed the library, Fos was seated, barefoot, on a leather sofa. His toes, splayed out on the rug, were fat, shaped like a collection of tablespoons. He was scraping the cleats of his shoes with an ivory-handled letter opener. Scrape, scrape, and bits of grass and tiny clumps of dirt fell onto the rug. Later, when Jazz brought her into the library to show her his grandfather's maps of Shorehaven, Fos, hunched over the newspaper reading sports statistics, a smoldering cigarette held between his thumb and index finger, cupped in his hand, did not even look up.

"Looking for Granddad Toby's maps," Jazz muttered, and his father muttered back something like "Nnn" or "Mmm." Lee couldn't be certain because his head was twisted at an odd angle as he scrutinized a list of American League pitchers' earned-run averages.

Fos's conversation at dinner (pizza Jazz had volunteered to pick up, an offer for which Lee was pathetically grateful, sensing the alternative might be tuna-basenji-hair casserole) was not much more stimulating. The kitchen table around which they sat was an oblong of cherry wood more imposing than most people's dining room tables. Ginger, from the foot of the table, called out to her husband at the head: "Fos, Lee's working for the D.A. in Manhattan this summer."

Fos stopped flattening the fluting on the edges of his paper plate and squinted in Lee's direction. "Manhattan D.A.'s?" he said.

"Yes," Lee responded.

She must have looked pathetically eager for a response, because he sighed and came up with one further observation. "The senior litigating partner at my old law firm was there. Years ago. Cap Malcolm."

"Chester Malcolm," Ginger elaborated, sliding the pizza box across the wood to Jazz.

"Oh," replied Lee, a little too brightly, she realized. She wished she had heard something wonderful about good ole Cap Malcolm so she could have something to say to the Taylors. They seemed to have no need to say anything to one another, and hardly any to say anything to her. She wished Jazz's sisters were there. Maybe they would talk. But Hope, the eldest, was married to a golf pro and living in Palm Springs and Irene, a year older than Jazz, was on a commune in Oregon.

The Taylors ate slice after slice of the two large pizzas Jazz had brought home. Each chewed with intense concentration, as if he or she were dining alone in a tiny Neapolitan café and trying this dish for the first time. Jazz, usually full of bright observations or intelligent

questions, fell into a silence she wished was not so comfortable. In fact, engrossed as he was with the elasticity
of his mozzarella cheese, he seemed to have forgotten
she was his guest/girlfriend and that he was in love with
her. And they all ignored Kent, despite the fact that the
boy was having problems separating his slice of pizza
from the pie and, then, from the box.

Lee held back from helping, thinking that it was
some family decision, or possibly a principle of
Down's syndrome child psychology: Let the child fend
for himself. But as Fos was reaching for his third slice,
Lee could no longer bear the desperate, hungry look
on Kent's face. She disengaged a slice from the box
and handed it to the boy. Glancing around, fearful of
a rebuke, or at least a scathing look, she saw Jazz was
studying a cross-section of pepperoni and Ginger wiping off the olive oil that had dribbled down her arm.
Fos, head thrown back, chins quivering, drank from
his can of Coke with soft glugging sounds.

"Thank you!" Kent said to Lee, his gloriously blue
eyes shining brighter than ever. With a shudder of
anticipated pleasure, he stuffed the triangular tip of the
pizza in his mouth.

"You're welcome." Realizing that might be the end
of the dinner conversation, she asked him: "Do you
like pizza?"

"Yes," Kent replied, charmed by her question. "I
like pizza."

"I like pizza too."

"I like pizza," Kent said, his words filtered through
a jumble of crust and tomato sauce. "I *like* pizza." For
a frightened instant, she was afraid he would repeat the
sentence over and over, and Jazz—to say nothing of
his parents—would be irate with her for having set
Kent off: Doesn't the girl have the brains to know how

to behave with someone like that? But Jazz was now engrossed in the take-out menu taped to the cover of the pizza box, Ginger was breaking her crusts into tiny pieces and Fos was once again defluting his paper plate. "I like pizza." Suddenly Lee realized that Kent was making conversation, being hospitable, trying to put her at ease.

"I like pizza," she confided. "And Coke."

"*I* like Coke," Kent responded, amazed and gladdened by the coincidence. "I like . . . " He paused. No one noticed the hesitation; certainly no one jumped in to help him. "I like . . . " Abruptly he slapped his hand down on the table: I've got it! "I like chocolate milk!"

"Me too!" Lee answered. "And ice cream."

"Cake!"

"Hamburgers."

"Hot dogs!"

They might have gone from macaroni and cheese through Cocoa Puffs to Twinkies except Fos left the table. Then Ginger called in the basenjis and began flinging the bits of crust into their midst. Then Jazz told Lee it was getting late. They had work the next day. They really ought to get back to the city.

On the ride back, Lee read *Gideon's Trumpet*, while Jazz read a golf magazine he had fished out of his father's attaché case. As the train crept through Queens, he looked up and said: "What can I tell you? My old man isn't a laugh a minute." She felt she waited a second too long before responding: "Wait till you meet mine." The hesitation came because she had fully expected Jazz to add: "And my mother's not going to win the *Better Homes & Gardens* gracious hostess award either," as well as to offer an apology for the terrible condition of the house—or at least for the neglect of his kid brother. Kent had looked so bereft at her leaving that she'd wanted to grab him up in her arms, bring him back to their studio apartment. She would buy him new shorts and a T-shirt and a big box of Froot Loops, give him a bath and scrub his neck. Or if Jazz could not offer an apology, she mused, what about an explanation for his parents' behavior? But Jazz did not notice her concern, because he went back to reading an editorial about driving ranges in Maui.

Well, Lee had to concede, if he had been a visitor at her house, would she have spent the next thirty-six hours apologizing for her family's defects? True, her father had stopped trying to pass for what he thought the Taylors were. But now he had taken to acting as if he were Noël Coward's houseguest—kiss-kiss, dahling, a Beautiful People peck on each cheek. Would he kiss-kiss Jazz? Or would he shift back into High Wasp mode for the occasion and, in a voice pitched mortifyingly low, boom out: Glad to meetcha! What could she possibly say? Uh, my dad's a little affected. And gee, sorry that my mother just sat there picking on the nubs of her Chanel suit and not talking. And oh, yeah—my sister has a serious drug problem—and she's married to a junkie and a thief.

So they went back to their sublet apartment and, exhausted, went to sleep without making love. The next morning, they returned to work. Then, before they knew it, they were caught up in their third and final year of law school. So Jazz Taylor never got to meet Lee's family until . . . well, in fact, until the day after he married her.

Now, that might make it sound as though a long time passed, but it happened quite soon, sooner than either of them expected it would. And it was all because of Christmas.

A week before, Ginger called Jazz in his dorm room. As she had not phoned him since the beginning of law school, he thought (as he later explained to Lee) that something terrible had happened: The canine equivalent of Dutch elm disease wiping out all the basenjis. Or his sister Irene getting fatally mangled in some malevolent piece of farm machinery on her commune. What's wrong? Jazz had asked, and his mother responded: Your father had to fly down to St. Petersburg to play golf with Mr. Whosis from the Atlantic Citrus Council who is having a conniption about something your father forgot to do so please get yourself home in time to buy the tree and set it up— damn, I forgot to buy the ham—because I'm in charge of the entire dessert table at the Kennel Club's Yappy Yule party and Kent ate something funny and has the trotsies and I *cannot* get out of the house.

The next caller was Leonard White, who telephoned a mere hour and a half later. Jazz was still in Lee's room, expounding to her how profound his dread of Christmas was. Chaos. His father was always someplace else and always arrived late. His mother was perpetually overwhelmed. Two years earlier, she had given him a roll of gift paper and three stick-on bows along with the presents she had not had time to wrap.

Leonard sounded far less frazzled than had Ginger. In fact, Leonard sounded like a million bucks (which at that moment happened to be one-quarter of his net worth, part of the reason for his ebullience). But for the young couple, his call was even greater cause for apprehension than Ginger's had been.

"I've rented a house in St. Bart's for the holidays!" Leonard exulted. Lee got so irritated at his pronunciation, "holly-days"—an attempt to sound educated-at-Oxford? a non-sectarian Christmas euphemism among pro-Semitic jet-setters? a playful reference to the ever-green?—she did not at first understand what he was saying. "When are your finals over?" Leonard inquired.

"My last one's the twentieth."

"Then you'll have to meet us there."

"Where?"

"St. Bart's."

"*Where*?"

"St. Bart's. An island in the Caribbean. Everyone says it's very in. But not overrun, if you know what I mean."

Lee covered the mouthpiece of the phone and whispered: "St. Bart's?"

"A nickname for the church?" Jazz murmured back, knowing all about Leonard's Episcopaliphilia.

"An island," Lee whispered.

"Never heard of it."

"Lee?" her father demanded.

She turned away from Jazz so she could focus on her argument. "Why can't we stay home?"

"Because we have a magnificent villa right on the ocean, with a butler, a cook, and two housemaids, and I'd rather spend the holidays there with fun people than on Long Island with no one and Greta's greasy goose."

"But I made plans with my boyfriend—"

"Unmake them."

"Dad, I can't." Her parents knew there was some-one in her life. However, preoccupied as they were with their troubles, the continuing occupation of their house by Robin and Ira, Lee had never found the right moment for telling them just who the fellow was, much less bringing him home to introduce them. Sometimes she was afraid that her father, having for-sworn his Taylor fixation, would treat Jazz badly just to prove how little Protestants meant to him. At other times, she feared Leonard hadn't gotten over the Taylors at all, that he would grovel before Jazz in such a sickening, relentless manner—Can I get you a glass of Veuve Clicquot? A snifter of Rémy XO? A sable coat for your mother?—that even good-natured Jazz would recoil.

"Look, Lee," her father said, "I know people your age don't want to hang around with a bunch of old farts like us. But I've invited some terrific people. Bright. Movers and shakers. People who if you're going to be a lawyer you should meet."

"Dad—"

"Bob and Bobbie Prager. He's going to be Lindsay's next consumer affairs commissioner. *Very* well respected. And Bobbie's mother was part of the Frick family. From the museum. She's been a customer for years. And Polly and Lloyd Gilliam. The journalists. She's a contributing editor for *Vogue* and he—"

"Dad, please. I've been working like a madwoman—"

"And I haven't?"

"Dad, I know how hard you work, but I need time—"

"This is what St. Bart's is all about!" Leonard roared. "Relaxing!"

"Not for me!"

"Well, how about doing something for the family for a change? Or is it all right by you just to have me pay for your tuition, your room and board, your clothes, your whatever? You know damn well your mother is a little shaky."

"So why are you taking her down to the Caribbean and loading her up with houseguests?"

"Because the house comes with plenty of help. I'm

entitled to a little fun! Have you ever heard me say that before? No. You haven't. But *I am entitled*. I work like a dog, and I'm entitled to a little life in my life. I wanted to move to the city. No. Your mother's not up to it. Okay, fine. I want to go on a buying trip to Copenhagen, stop over in London, see some theater, and Greta—the maid!—comes crying to me that she's afraid to stay in the house alone with Ira. Don't worry, Greta. I won't go. But don't I *ever* get a turn?"

"Are Robin and Ira coming to St. Bart's?" Lee asked, imagining Ira's silhouette blackening the sun as the Fun Couples lunched on the terrace; Ira passing them on his way to sneak into their rooms and rip off their suitcases.

"I offered to send them to California, so they can visit with their friends. I really think . . . it looks like . . . I'm hoping they'll take me up on it."

"I can stay home with Greta."

"You can come with us. That's where you belong on the holidays. With your family."

Lee did not slam down the phone. She hung it up and turned to Jazz. "He wants me to be with them for Christmas. Translated, that means if he can't terrorize my mother into getting out of bed once they get down there, he'll do the old 'Sylvia has the flu' routine. She's pretty good at it. Once she coughs on cue, she's off the hook. Then he'll put his arm around me and say, 'Lee will fill in, won't you, dahling. Lee, have the girl bring the coffee out to the terrazzo.'" Jazz put an arm around Lee, she put an arm around him, and they stood beside her desk, rocking side to side, comforting each other.

A few days later, with final examinations behind her, Lee was back in her dorm room, getting ready for St. Bart's. More precisely, she was folding and refolding a blue cotton T-shirt as if expecting a grade in packing skills to be computed into her cumulative average. For the fourth time, she aligned the shoulder seams only to have a gigantic wrinkle pop up front and center. No matter what clothes she packed, she knew, her mother would be prepared with a fashion antidote. Lee would get to St. Bart's and there would be, God help her, a closet full of cruise wear in her room. Shocking-pink two-piece bathing suits with matching jackets or, worse, sarongs. Sun-yellow jumpsuits with palazzo pants legs. Lime-green shorts and halter tops, the sort of thing Robin could wear and look like an elf-queen, but that would make Lee look like a troll. Lee felt a lump midthroat. It's only for ten days, she soothed herself. At worst, I'll get a tan, and at best . . . Who knows? Maybe the fun people really will be fun.

She knew she was getting overemotional. It was not as if Jazz would meet some limpid-eyed beauty at the country club's New Year's Eve dance and immediately realize the error of his ways. Actually, Lee conceded, that *was* it. The lump in her throat grew so large it forced tears out of her eyes. A drop slipped from her cheek onto the T-shirt and made a sad little mark. All fumpfed up, that's what she was. Fumpfed—or something like it—was a Greta word. It seemed to mean something like filled with grief. It was a word she and Robin could never pronounce. But when one of them got upset, the other used to say, in a cruelly comic German accent: You are all fumpfed up.

Lee was so fumpfed up she did not notice that Jazz had come in. When he sat beside her on the bed—on top of her T-shirt, actually—she gave a too loud hoot of surprise.

"Sorry," he said. "I thought you heard me come in."

"No. I was so spaced out . . . " Her voice was excessively husky, she noticed, a combination of a constricted throat and a need to fight fire with fire and best the blonde hussy from Rolling Hills Country Club.

But such tactics were not necessary. When Jazz saw her tears, his eyes filled as well. They sat beside each other on the single, lumpy dormitory bed. Then they wept. "It's only for ten days," Lee managed to say. Not two seconds later, Jazz said the same thing back to her. "Why are we carrying on like this?" she demanded.

"Beats the hell out of me," he said, checking out the ceiling in the embarrassed way men do when they discover themselves crying. After a second, he added: "Maybe . . . "

"Maybe what?"

"Maybe we're all upset because our being apart is a crime against nature." Lee started to laugh, but her nose began dripping so fiercely she settled for a fast guffaw. "I'm serious," Jazz continued. "We were meant to be with each other. You and I . . . we're a given in natural law."

"Lee and Jazz. Axiomatic."

"Exactly," he agreed, without her irony. "And to be apart on Christmas is the worst. You know why?"

"Why?"

"Because the two of us, we're more family to each other than our own families are."

From there, it seemed only logical that the following afternoon, as soon as Jazz finished his Antitrust final, they visited Dr. Donald Humm, an internist known to the students around NYU for his fondness for writing prescriptions. He did the blood test. And a mere three telephone calls later, Judge Susan Margules Steinhardt, the august, cerebral New York State Supreme Court justice presiding in the Howie the Hose extortion proceedings, said that indeed she did remember Lee as the student intern from the previous summer—first-rate demeanor, so rare these days—and yes, she would be delighted to marry the couple Monday at noon in chambers and wasn't it, um, adventurous that the two of them were eloping and—no problem at all—she'd be pleased to read Shakespeare's one hundred sixteenth sonnet (her husband had in fact recited it to her while they were courting) and wasn't it romantic that they were going to spend their honeymoon in St. Bart's. Romantic and lovely. Just lovely.

It looked lovely: tropical twilight of Christmas Eve, coconut palms arching protectively over the pink villa with a red tile roof. An instant later, there was Sylvia meeting them at the front door, looking crisper than crisp in a white trouser suit with gold braiding—an officer in the world's most *au courant* navy. Her sleek champagne hair, now cut Cleopatra style, gleamed in the light of a chandelier consisting of six frosted-glass pineapples. Her flawlessly mascaraed lashes fluttered instinctively at the sight of Jazz, square-jawed and breathtakingly broad-shouldered in a well-worn blue blazer. Sylvia's lips, a juicy mango, pursed to kiss Lee, although she did not apply them to her daughter's cheek; instead she touched the side of her face lightly against Lee's and tweeted in the direction of the back of the house. Then, as if responding to some sharp command, she stepped back precisely eighteen inches: the perfect distance so her outfit could be observed in full, yet not a detail missed. Only then did she extend her hand to Jazz. "Jasper," she whispered tenderly.

"I hope you don't mind my horning in on your Christmas, Mrs. White." Lee looked up at him, at the sharp angles of his jaw, at his clear eyes and slightly-smaller-than-average nose, and knew, instantly, that had he had a Ph.D. in psychology and written his dissertation on the convolutions of the psyche of Sylvia Bernstein White, he could not have articulated a better sentence than the one he had just spoken. "Horning in" was something you could really get away with only after your tenth generation in America. "Christmas" of course was a word only his kind could pronounce perfectly, with that loving familiarity: their word. And the "Mrs. White" was masterful icing on the wedding cake: incredibly courteous, inviting immediate correction.

"Please! Call me Mom." Suddenly the woman Lee had known all her life disappeared. Snooty flared nostrils and puckered lips were replaced by soft diffidence. "Unless you'd rather call me Sylvia."

"I'd love to call you Mom," Jazz replied. Simultaneously, they moved in to kiss each other, then took a perfectly choreographed step back and smiled. In that same instant, Sylvia took her daughter's hand and stroked it. What amazed Lee was her mother's velvety warmth. She had expected a body temperature that was degrees cooler than normal human flesh.

Sylvia gave her daughter a benevolent smile and Lee found herself beaming back so broadly that for all she knew, her uvula was exposed. She could not help the peace that touched every part of her. Such utter peace that it made the transcendental meditative state she had managed to achieve twice in her junior year seem like a Led Zeppelin concert. Her every nerve felt soothed, her every muscle slack. For that moment, Lee no longer had to stand watch. She was protected.

Then, as the hand drew away, serenity vanished abruptly. Looking at her mother, Lee marveled that the bliss of seconds before could have come from that hand, that woman. There was her familiar mother, cheeks sucked in, stomach concave. "How was your flight, lovie?" Sylvia asked.

Lee realized that with Jazz by her side, she was now lovie, so she answered: "Not bad. But the little plane we had to change to . . . " She saw she had lost her mother's interest and rubbed her middle and little fingers against the solidity of her brand-new wedding band. Golden magic: She could face anything. But what was there to face? Sylvia was thrilled with her new son-in-law: For the Jew who prays for a Christmas gift, could there be any present better?

But, Lee conceded, her mother did not look well. True, Sylvia appeared normal standing in the foyer, regarding Jazz's scuffed loafers and, not unpredictably, gratified by them. Freshly polished shoes would have shown weakness, a pathetic need to please. Lee studied her mother as she stood, lightly brushing the outside corners of her mouth with the tips of her pinkies as if smoothing out some minuscule flaw in her lip liner. But her left eye had a staccato tic. Blink, blink, blink. It couldn't stay open. And she was swaying slightly, first left, then right, then back again. Was she dizzy from medication? Reeling from shock: How could you betray me like this? Elope! Deprive me of consultations with the caterer at the St. Regis and Jackie Onassis's calligrapher!

Blink, blink, blink. Left, right, left. But then the next sway to the right was greater than the one before. Sylvia would have crashed against the doorpost and cracked her head if Jazz had not been quick. In a single balletic motion, he was by her side, grabbing her elbow, rotating her one hundred eighty degrees, escorting her into the living room. "A piano!" he was saying, while he lowered her into a bamboo chair with giant pink hibiscuses printed on the white cushions. "If you want to get rid of your houseguests, I can play my famous Christmas carol medley. They'll swim home."

"Oh, God!" Sylvia suddenly cried, as if he had made whatever pain she was in ten times worse. Behind her, by the picture window facing an inner courtyard, a Christmas tree, brilliant with thousands of tiny lights, was hung with hibiscus and frangipani blossoms. Real flowers. They were dying, their petals drooping and brown-edged.

Jazz, stunned by the drama of her outburst, tried to make a joke of it. "All right, I swear. No Christmas carols."

"You have no idea," Sylvia said, staring up into his eyes. "This is a disaster."

Understandably, Lee thought she had retracted her initial welcome and was now referring to the marriage. Pressure built up on the sides of her head until it felt her skull was about to explode. So she could not make a quick comeback, or any comeback at all. It was Jazz who asked: "What's a disaster?" clearly secure that whatever the nature of the catastrophe, it had nothing to do with him.

In fact, it did not. "Bob and Bobbie Prager canceled at the last minute," Sylvia said. "They didn't even call. They just didn't show up at the airport. And the Gilliams were there with us, waiting at the gate. We were the only people who hadn't boarded. Leonard was trying not to show that he wasn't . . . " Sylvia lifted her hands. They were trembling. She could not find words to describe the depth of her husband's horror. "He called their apartment and the man—houseman, butler—said they were in Sun Valley. Skiing. And he had to come back and put on a good face to the Gilliams. 'Bob and Bobbie can't make it. Some last minute hitch.' I thought he was going to have a stroke. Two first-class tickets wasted."

"Daddy paid for their tickets?" Lee asked.

"That's how it's done," Sylvia explained, unwilling to meet Lee's eyes. "For a minute," she told the giant ceiling fan, "I swear to God, I thought the Gilliams were going to cancel."

"But they're here," Jazz said soothingly.

Sylvia kept her head tilted back. "In the dining room. With Daddy—and Ira. Ira! We tried to get them to go to California, but they wouldn't. And Ira is here. Oh God in heaven, Polly Gilliam writes about outerwear for *Vogue* and he has a goatee and is very important."

"Where's Robin?"

"Not feeling well."

Sylvia's face, made poreless and flawless by exorbitantly-priced foundation extracted from the placentas of white lambs, remained trained on the laconic revolving blades of the fan, although several times she did manage to turn her eyes back to Jazz. The point of her tongue slid out to moisten her lips, but it too was dry.

"Sylvia!" Leonard's voice called out. Even a stranger could hear the desperation behind the near-hysterical bonhomie. "Is that Lee-lee and Jasper?"

Sylvia nodded slowly and carefully, as though her head weighed several hundred pounds. Lee, who had not called herself Lee-lee since before her third birthday and who could recall no previous instance of either parent using that name, was so agitated she could not respond. How could she get herself and Jazz out of this nightmare? More to the point, the incipient prosecutor within her demanded, how could she have been so demented as to think Christmas week in St. Bart's with her family should be the place to begin a marriage?

"Lee-lee?"

Jazz answered for her. "We're here!" he called brightly.

And Leonard, as if blasted from a rocket launcher, shot into the living room. "Lee!" he called, flinging out his arms in a come-my-children flourish. "Jasper!" Jazz, watching what Lee did, the way a person faced with eating snails for the first time observes a table-mate, leaned in toward Leonard and allowed himself to be gathered into a desperate embrace. "Wonderful!"

"Hi," Jazz said. Because Jazz was significantly taller, his father-in-law was still saying "Wonderful!" into his neck. "I don't know exactly what to say," Jazz went on. "I mean, dropping in on you. It's not just like for a drink. It's like: Oh, hello and Merry Christmas and so nice of you to let us have our honeymoon here."

"Wonderful!" Leonard was still saying as Lee and Jazz managed to pull themselves out of his hug. "Couldn't be happier. So glad you came." With Jazz now a couple of feet away, Leonard was able to look up at him. Soak him in. His face began to flush with pleasure. And then he spotted his wife. His color ebbed. "Sylvia!"

"What?"

"They're waiting."

"I know." But her eyes darted left and right, searching for what they were waiting for.

"Well . . . ?"

"Um," she responded.

"Sylvia!"

"*What?*" she begged him, clearly at a loss.

"'*What?*'" Leonard repeated. "Oh, God, don't tell me. Oh, God!" His hands clutched at his fashionable thick sideburns. He might have actually pulled them out had he not caught sight of Jazz. "I'm so sorry you have to be here at a time—"

"It's okay," Jazz smiled. Could nothing affect his easygoing nature? Why wasn't he saying to himself: How the hell can I extricate myself from this lunatic family—Lee included? Can I get a fucking annulment in time to get home to Christmas dinner with people who have as their birthright the competence to decorate a tree properly? Je-sus! Dead flowers! Lee watched in wonder as Jazz rested his hand on her father's shoulder, the reassuring masculine touch a catcher would offer a rattled pitcher. Leonard stopped yanking on his hair and dropped his hands to his sides. Still, he remained agitated and looked from Jazz to Sylvia, his expression changing from longing to loathing.

"Dad?" Leonard glanced in Lee's direction, surprised, as if he had forgotten she had come to St. Bart's with Jazz.

"You have no idea," was all he could say.

"Robin?" Lee asked.

"The tip of the iceberg." Leonard rammed his hands deep into the pockets of his white linen trousers.

"Those people who didn't show up?"

Leonard's dark eyes narrowed into menacing slits at this reminder. "They're nothing," he said, trying to sound dismissive and, of course, not succeeding. His eyes narrowed even more, so that all light in them was cut off; he was furious at Lee for such a bitter reminder. "Social climbers," he mumbled to Jazz. "You know?"

Jazz nodded in weary commiseration, as if this were something he and his father-in-law were doomed to suffer every day. "What's going on?" he inquired. *Don't!*, Lee wanted to shout. Don't set him off! "Something wrong down here?"

But Leonard looked grateful for the query, as if he'd been waiting days for someone to ask it. "No servants," he managed to say. For an instant, he seemed so frail, so old, even, that Lee was afraid he would collapse into Jazz's arms. But then Leonard glimpsed Sylvia in the bamboo chair, wringing her exquisitely manicured hands. Immediately, he was filled with savage energy.

"Four in goddamn help were supposed to be here," he growled. "One—the driver, fellow who shops for groceries—was supposed to pick us up at the airport." He clenched his teeth so tight it seemed the enamel of the uppers and lowers had fused. Finally, he was able to pry them apart. "He never showed. Okay, I'm cool, calm, collected. I call the house. *No one is there!* Okay, I tell myself. It's the goddamn Caribbean. The phones aren't working. I get three cabs. No one speaks English for crissake." Suddenly, realizing "crissake," like Christmas, had Christ in it, he stopped his diatribe. "Sorry," he apologized to Jazz. "Anyway, finally I got Robin to look alive and tell the cabdrivers where to go in French, so we got here. And what happens? It's empty! An empty house! An empty refrigerator! I manage to grab one of the cabs before he takes off. I go to the local gendarmes. They call the guy who's the butler. He says he's off for Christmas! What? I say. *What?* I have a house full of people. Sorry, he says. Monsieur de Valois—that's the French bastard who owns this place—said they could have the week off. *Paid* them. Two weeks vacation pay."

"Did you—" Lee began.

"Please!" her father said, angrily, contemptuously. "I offered him twice that. Three times that. I told him: Name your price. He says: Sorry, we wish to be with our families for the holidays. So I called de Valois."

"And?" Lee asked.

"And he's off hunting something. Bear. Boar. I couldn't get what his wife was saying, with her stupid Frog accent and Robin was sleeping and I couldn't get her up to come to the phone. Won't be back till 'le tent of January,' she says. Sorry, a little misunderstanding. January tenth! When we'll be back in New York for four goddamn days!"

"I'll call her tomorrow," Lee said, waiting for her father to be grateful.

But he was glaring at her mother with an animus beyond hate. "I'm sorry," Sylvia cried, covering her face with her hands. "I just forgot!"

"Forgot what?" Lee asked.

"Dinner," Sylvia whispered.

The Whites' houseguests, Polly and Lloyd Gilliam, sat under a huge canvas umbrella, breathing in the sweet, soft Caribbean air, waves lapping near their feet. They sipped iced tea and looked put out. Actually, that is an understatement, for as Lee was slogging through the sand, bringing out a plate of cookies—which her father and the Gilliams insisted on calling biscuits— she overheard Polly grousing to her husband: "I am so supremely pissed I can't even discuss it." From the waist up, Polly was built the way she wanted to be, thin and breastless like Twiggy. From the waist down, however, she was heavy, bell-bottomed, like an accessory made for a boat, weighted not to tip over in rough weather. Thus shaped, she had wrapped a giant chiffon scarf around the waist of her bathing suit, but a random breeze had uncovered a hefty hip and a huge, dimpled thigh.

"Pissed?" Lloyd said. "Pissed? My dear, I am beyond pissed. I am in utter *extremis*. You, on the other hand, have no right to be pissed since it was *you*, love, who said, and I quote: 'No, not Mustique. We've been invited by Mr. Fur himself'—Mr. Fuh, as he

would pronounce it—'who's having all *sorts* of marvelous people to St. Bart's—'"

The Whites, Lee thought, did not think in terms of
family honor. Still, at this moment, she wished they
did, so she could avenge it. Punch that snotty prick in
the snoot he tanned at other people's second houses.
Jerk his well-stroked goatee. Pretentious asshole. At
dinner the night before, he pontificated on Whither
Henry Kissinger? as if he were James Reston. But it
hadn't taken much cross-examination to reveal that the
articles he wrote were celebrity profiles for magazines
like *New York* and *Esquire*—"Maria Schneider's Two-
Step: What the *Tango* Star Won't Say." Lloyd stopped
talking as Lee's shadow fell over them.

"Ah," Lloyd said, because he could not remember
her name, "the Bringer of Biscuits." He scrutinized the
proffered plate, then shook his head. Not good
enough, was the unsaid message. Polly, unable to
accept a cookie judged inferior by a cultural arbiter of
her husband's stature, would have had to refuse as
well. But before Lee could offer them, a hideous
scream—a woman's shriek merging with a man's
howl—burst forth from the pink villa, shattering a perfect Christmas peace.

"Stop it!" Lee shouted at her parents. "Be quiet, for
God's sake!" It was not that she wanted decorum. It
was that someone needed to think, and since her parents were standing in Robin and Ira's room, watching
their younger daughter convulsing on the bed—naked,
sweating, pale legs jerking, mouth foaming, eyes
rolling back—and wailing at the horror of such a sight,
Lee was going to be the one who had to think. Oh
God, why hadn't she taken the MCATs instead of the

LSATs? She could have gone to medical school; she'd know what to do now. When the shit really hit the fan, who the hell needed a lawyer?

Convulsion: Fever? She put her hands on Robin's forehead and neck. Drenched, but cool to the touch. "What is it?" Leonard cried out. Sylvia made terrible squeaking sounds, as if she were pretending to be a mouse: "Eeee. Eeee," over and over again. Could Robin be having some sort of allergic reaction? Lee turned to Ira. He was standing in a corner between the bed and the window, trying to fit his back into the right angle where the walls met. In black briefs: the bad boy, head hung. His arms and legs were as scrawny as a child's. Only the few hairs growing around his small, pale nipples showed he had passed puberty. "What did she have to eat today?" Lee snapped at him. "Ira!"

It took him what seemed forever to lift his head and say: "I don't know." But then Lee understood. Her sister was now on heroin. Too much? Too little? Oh, God, where was Jazz? Driving all over the damn island, looking for tonic for Polly's vodka. What? Polly had whined. No Schweppes? Don't they have Schweppes on St. Bart's? Isn't this civilization? I'll go on a search and destroy mission for tonic, Jazz told Polly, charming her. She'd actually smiled, and Leonard had been so grateful he'd walked Jazz to the rented jeep, saying, Thank you, thank you, thank you, practically sobbing with relief and gratitude. But now Jazz had been gone for over an hour. All right: Think. Okay, Robin was having either d.t.'s or convulsions, and that would suggest withdrawal. Didn't it? Jesus, what the hell did Lee know about heroin? She—all her friends—had ingested a pharmacopoeia of drugs, but not heroin. Who the hell would be so stupid as to take heroin? Robin.

"Out!" she barked at her parents. Paralyzed, they stood by the bed, her mother still making mouse sounds, but softer now. "Get out!" she said even louder, and to her amazement, they about-faced and double-timed out. A little too eagerly. Lee realized that now, if anything happened—if Robin died—she would be blamed. It was too silent. Then she heard the rumble of the jeep and then Jazz's voice: "Hey, I found this little store with gallons of tonic!"

"In here!" she called. "In Robin's room."

Ira shuffled his feet, probably meaning to move out as well, but he was too stoned to actually ambulate. "What the hell is going on with her?" Lee yelled at him. In slow motion, Ira raised his narrow shoulders into a shrug. She raced around the bed and stood right before him. He smelled musty, like a dank basement. "I know it's heroin. Is it an overdose or is it withdrawal?" Ira managed to hoist his head so he could look directly at Lee, but all he did was look; he had nothing to say. "Overdose or withdrawal?" she bellowed. Still nothing. She grabbed his throat in her hand and squeezed. His Adam's apple bobbed about in terror. He clutched her wrist and tried to pull it away, but he lacked the strength or the coordination. "Tell me, you son-of-a-bitch, or I'll squeeze tighter. I'll choke you to death and bury you in the sand, and no one except the fucking crabs will know about it. Overdose or withdrawal?"

Ira managed to get out a tiny sound: "Withdrawal."

"Why? Did she want to stop?" When he didn't respond, Lee slammed him against the wall. "Did she want to stop or did you just take too much?"

"Me," he said.

"How do the two of you take it? Intravenously?"

"Yeah." It was less a word than an exhalation.

"Do you have any more? Answer me."

"Not much."

Jazz came into the room, bouncing in his sneakers. Then he saw Robin and froze. "What . . . ?"

"Heroin," Lee said. She waited, expecting Jazz to do something, but he just stood there, hands at his sides, staring at Robin's naked, sweat-drenched body. Lee separated the sheet from the blanket that lay twisted on the floor and covered her sister.

"Listen to me," Lee said to Ira. "You're going to get the heroin right now and show me everything: the stuff itself, the needles, all the shit you use. So I'll know exactly what you have. Then you're going to put the smallest possible amount in the needle and give it to her so she comes out of this convulsion."

"Okay."

She looked over to Jazz, but he was looking down at the floor. "You're going to give it all to me," she told Ira. "I'll be first-vice-president in charge of heroin. If we can avoid going to a hospital here I'd like to, because I don't know if they're any good with drug problems. And I don't know anything about the island's drug laws. I don't want my sister winding up with a life sentence on St. Bart's. So if you can get her stabilized, we're going to hire a plane and get her to a hospital back in the States and get her detoxified properly." She took a deep breath. "If she needs another shot, you'll give it to her. How often does she"—Lee squeezed Ira's throat until his tongue bulged out— "shoot up?"

"Four, five times."

"A day?" He nodded. "Right before we land, we'll have to get rid of the drugs. We can't risk bringing them in. You're going to stay with us until she gets wheeled into the emergency room. Then you get a hundred bucks. You get your clothes. You get out of her life permanently. If you don't, I will personally take a knife and slit your throat. Do you understand me, Ira?"

"Yes."

"Do you think I mean what I say?"

Ira hesitated, but at last, wiping his nose on the back of his hand, he said: "Yeah."

"Then let's move it." She moved in front of Jazz, staying with Ira as he knelt down and pulled a leather shaving kit from under the bed. She watched as he prepared the drug and filled a syringe. His fingers seemed flaccid, and she winced as he fumbled with the drug paraphernalia. "Ira, if you give her too much, you're dead too. You understand that, don't you?"

"Yeah."

He took a length of rubber tubing, the sort that would be used in a hospital, and made a tourniquet around Robin's thin arm. Then, with a casualness more appropriate to handing someone a cup of coffee, he ran his finger over her skin until he found an accessible vein and injected her. Within seconds, the convulsion stopped. Robin's lashes fluttered as if she were a belle flirting with a new beau. She began to smile at Ira, but then she spotted her sister. "Hey," Robin said, the smile vanishing. She dabbed away at the dried white foam on her chin. "You don't belong in here. Out. I mean it, Lee. Haul ass!" Then she closed her eyes again.

It was only after Lee sent Jazz out to have her father hire a plane—now!—to fly to Miami that she came up on the side of the bed and smacked her sister across the face.

fifteen

My secretary, Sandi Zimmerman, was born with a happy face. Add to her button nose, round brown eyes, and congenitally upturned mouth a ponytail that curled up at the end into a cheery little smile-shape, and you had a person strangers wanted to meet.

People who knew her, however, avoided her whenever they could. It wasn't that Sandi was obnoxious or even mean; it was that beyond her two good qualities, honesty and diligence, she had no redeeming social value. Give her a friendly "Hi" and she'd act perplexed. "*Hi?*" she seemed to be wondering; how peculiar; how alienating. Finally, after a too long pause, Sandi would respond with an edgy "Oh. Uh ... hi." Invite her to join you for a cup of coffee, inquire if she'd watched the Oscars the night before, ask her what her vacation plans were—in short, treat her as you would any casual acquaintance—and Sandi would stiffen, jerking back her head as if you had suggested she join you and a quadruped in a bizarre sexual practice.

Then there was her nerves. From font changes on the office's word-processing program to the introduction of the four-digit suffix for zip codes—everything rattled her: There was nothing about which Sandi was not anxious. Every client walking into the office was a maniac about to pull out a machete and cut us down—or, if not slaughter us, at least set us up by means of a subtle and nefarious ruse so we'd be easy pickings for a malpractice suit. Although she had been working for me for fifteen years, I had no idea how she'd come to be so strange since questions about her family or her childhood made her even more apprehensive. All I really knew about Sandi was that she was my age, lived with a divorced sister and a bachelor brother in Huntington, was a terrific stenographer and typist, and had a fondness bordering on fixation for Celestial Seasonings Lemon Zinger tea.

Naturally, in the back of my mind, I sensed that a decade or two on the couch probably wouldn't hurt her. But in an office relationship, it's easier to assume the weird person you are dealing with is eccentric rather than a fellow human being in terrible pain. But Sandi kept getting stranger and stranger.

Being a forty-five myself, and a feminist, I was reluctant to blame her increasing oddness on menopause. But I overcame my reluctance. About three months before Norman became a client, she had started going nuts about dirty telephones: The only phone in the office she would use was the one at her desk; arriving in the morning or coming back from the ladies' room or lunch, she would spray the entire receiver—mouthpiece, handpiece, earpiece—with Lysol. A couple of weeks after that, she began to spend her lunch hour in the conference room, where, after glugging down one can of vanilla Ensure and one can of Diet Slice, she cut out elaborate doilies from old copies of the *Law Journal*. I was tempted to ask her what the doilies were for, but I was afraid my question might set her off on a psychotic voyage from which she'd never return and I would then become one of those lawyers who get ten years taken off their life by having to deal with temp agencies.

Still, it did come as a surprise to discover (as I was dictating a memo to files *in re* Torkelson) that Sandi had fallen madly in love with Mary Dean. "It is worth noting," I was saying, "that in a conversation with me on May ninth of this year—several days before Mary Dean admitted to having been in Bobette Frisch's house—Ms. Dean showed a familiarity with the layout and furnishings of the premises that indicated she had spent a considerable amount of time there." I swiveled around in my chair a few times as I constructed the next sentence and noted that the patent leather on my pumps was looking dull. Then I noted that Sandi was writing with her right hand—her usual practice, but toying with her bangs with her left. God knows why, but she must have curled her bangs; the rest of her hair was straight. It looked as if she had glued a piece of poodle to the top of her forehead. Nervously, over and over, she kept sticking her finger into the center of each curl. "The observations Mary Dean made—about a collection of purple perfume bottles on Ms. Frisch's dresser, the furnishings of a second bedroom next to Ms. Frisch's—suggest that far more than the hurried glimpse she has admitted to, she has a detailed knowledge of the house—"

"Because Norman *described* it to her!" Sandi broke in.

In all the years she had worked for me, she had never commented on anything I dictated. In fact, although her transcriptions were astoundingly accurate, I had always felt that while she got the words, she didn't hear the music. So I was stunned. My mouth may have dropped open in quintessential stupnagel fashion. Not that my reaction mattered to Sandi. Her face was flushed dark red. I could sense her outrage, although with her strange, upturned smiley mouth and round cheeks, she just looked happy.

"No, it was not something she heard," I responded slowly. "Mary said something like 'I couldn't believe my eyes.' She *saw* the place. She was in there."

"He's a con man!" Sandi insisted, a hysterical screech creeping into her voice. "He made it seem so real it became real to her."

"Boy, I'm glad you're not on my jury," I said. "Anyway, since when have you become a Mary Dean fan?"

Sandi set down her pen and steno pad. "My heart goes out to her. She's so good. You can see it!" Her lips parted. Her eyes shone. I sensed I was watching something that ought to have been private. "Oh, I know with those kind of clothes you think she's tawdry. Not a good person. *I* was put off by it at the beginning. But under all the makeup, she's so innocent." Sandi placed her palms together as if she were about to pray. "A saint, that's what she is! You can see it in her eyes." What I was seeing in Sandi's eyes was a moist, mad glow. "And she's been dragged down by that man, dragged into the gutter—"

"Before Mary Dean met that man she had twenty-seven arrests for prostitution, which might lead one to believe the gutter was not exactly terra incognita," I commented.

I was shaken by Sandi's outburst. Sure, there'd been plenty of emotion in the office, but it had come from my clients or their wives and girlfriends. Weeping, wailing, fainting, pounding on the desk—or on the client's head. Once, I billed the Perich brothers, two contractors I was representing for tax fraud, an extra two hundred bucks for a carpet cleaning to remove bloodstains after Frankie hit Billy in the gut and Billy socked Frankie in the face and Frankie had a nosebleed all over my rug. But it was easy to keep a distance from my clients' craziness. They were *supposed* to go off the wall.

Well, that makes it sound so easy: dealing with people who didn't feel obliged to keep a stiff upper lip. It wasn't. Even viewed from the objective distance I had trained myself to maintain, it often exhausted me. So what I needed to protect me from those client storms was tranquillity, peace in the workplace. That's why I found Sandi's explosion terribly jarring. Just as I depended on our receptionist to be obtuse, on our associate to try to act cool while walking up the courthouse steps, on Chuckie to be droll, I relied on Sandi to be reassuringly, perpetually dull.

"I'll tell you what," I announced. "Take a break. Then you can finish up the paperwork on that Eastern District case, that transportation of stolen property." I got up. "See you later." And I bolted.

For about half a minute I considered putting on the sneakers I keep in the trunk of my car and going for a five-mile walk to clear my head. But in the next half minute, I got into the car and headed toward Mary Dean's. Was she, as Sandi was maintaining, an innocent? Or was she guilty of murder and, perhaps, a con of her own?

"I don't want to talk to you," Mary announced. She stood in the doorway, blocking entrance to the apartment. Not inviting, but not belligerent either. She was wearing matching shorts and crop top in a peach so vivid it was almost a new color. Her hair, tossed on top of her head, was held in place with a banana clip. As I'd suspected, her complexion without makeup was without blemish. Her skin's only flaw was a patch of blue, a dried-up piece of facial mask, that was stuck between ear and jaw.

"I wish you would talk to me," I said. "I'd really like to see things from your point of view."

"Sorry." Inside the apartment, a TV was on, a talk show. One guest was shrieking at another, who kept hooting back: "I'm laughing in your face."

"I bought us cappuccino," I said, holding up the white paper bag. "One with cinnamon, one without. Which do you want?"

"Uh," she said.

"Either one's fine with me."

"Cinnamon," she said, standing back so I could walk into the house. "But I don't have any cookies or anything."

"I have a couple of biscotti. Those hard cookies."

"I was always scared I was going to break a tooth on one of those," Mary said, turning off the TV, clearing off a small round table on the far side of the living room. She had been clipping supermarket coupons. "Then I learned to dunk"—a coupon for Dove soap fell to the floor—"so it's better, except when you dunk for, like, one second too long. Then it gets all gooky and falls into the coffee."

We sat across from each other. The atmosphere was companionable, two hausfraus having a kaffeeklatsch. Mary, who was able to sit in shorts and a crop top without even a millimeter of flab showing anywhere, said she wished she and Norman could settle down in one place; there was a coupon-clippers newsletter she was dying to subscribe to, but since they were never in any town longer than three months, it didn't pay. Since we were getting on so well—she showed me the box in which she kept her coupons filed, a green metal thing decorated with rolling pins and egg beaters—I did not mention I was more than half hoping that her only long-term address would be in care of an upstate maximum-security facility.

"You know who I spoke to?" I asked, taking what I hoped was a casual sip of cappuccino. "Carolyn Knowles. The woman you had that altercation with in Annapolis."

"Oh," Mary said, a wispy sound. "Gee."

"She said you smashed her head against the sidewalk." Mary stretched out her hands in a gesture that said: I can't remember *what* happened. "Want to tell me about it?" I asked.

"How did you find out?"

"It wasn't hard."

"Do the police know?"

"I don't think so. If they knew the fingerprints at Bobette's were the same as those made in another instance of an attack on an older woman, they might have a few questions for you."

Mary toyed with a drip of coffee meandering its way down the Styrofoam cup. "Like what?"

"Like what happened? What set you off down there in Annapolis?"

"She said, 'Get out of here, you whore.' She didn't even know who I was! She kept looking at my dress like it was cheap. It wasn't!"

I tried to look shocked and distressed. "Tell me about it."

"I was just hanging around—"

"Her house?"

"Yes. I mean, just checking it out. Norman said it was gorgeous. You should see it, he said. It's called a landmark! She couldn't paint it a different color without permission because it was history."

"Were she and Norman there at the time?"

"No."

"Where were they?"

"They went for a drive. She had a convertible." She shook her head. "Why is it that when you *should* have a convertible you can't afford it, and every time you see a really great car, some old poop-head is driving it?" As I had just recently been wavering between a financially secure old age and buying a BMW 325i ragtop, I merely shrugged. "So I walked around her house. She had gardens. That's what you call it when rich people have, like, a place for roses and another place for vegetables and another place for tulips or whatever. Not a garden. Gardens, even if it's all in the same backyard."

"So you looked at her gardens."

"Yuck. Lots of little, low things. If you wanted to smell the flowers, you'd have to crawl around on your hands and knees."

"Did you go inside, Mary?"

She sat up straight, alert. "No."

"No? You didn't even try to get in?" She shook her head vehemently. "Mary," I said, giving her what I hoped looked like an indulgent look. "Come on."

She came back with a sheepish smile. "It was locked."

"Did you try the windows?" She chewed the inside of her cheek for a while. "Mary, I'm Norman's lawyer. You can tell me."

"I tried."

"Did you get in?" She nodded, not without a gleam of triumph in her eye. "And found some jewelry?"

"Yes. So great."

"What made you take the jewelry? Weren't you afraid you'd ruin Norman's chances of a score with her?"

"How would she know a robber had anything to do with Norman?"

"That's true," I conceded.

"She didn't even have, like, a safe or anything. It was in a jewelry box in her closet. A walk-in closet. With built-in shelves for everything. Baskets to pull out for sweaters, and a thing you hung scarves on."

"Where's the jewelry now?"

"I gave it to Norm. He said it was too hot to sell. He put it in a safety deposit box he has."

"Where is that?"

"In Atlanta."

"Why in Atlanta?"

"Beats me," Mary said.

"Didn't you keep any of it to wear?"

She screwed up her mouth and shook her head. "He wouldn't let me. I tried to hide the ruby pin. So gorgeous, I couldn't believe it. Like a fireworks: fat in the middle, with all those spray lines going out. I stuck it in the bottom of my Tampax box, but he found it. He said it was too . . . some word that means it would, you know, point the finger at me."

"Is that usual for you, Mary? Breaking in and taking jewelry. Something tells me . . . It doesn't sound like you."

She rested her chin in her hands. The blue dab of facial mask fell off. "It isn't like me," she said gratefully.

"So what made you do it?" I played a hunch. "Did something set you off to want to hurt her in some way?" She took our cups and napkins and stuffed them into the paper bag. "What was it?"

"Tickets."

I remembered her saying that she had gone into Bobette's house looking for airplane tickets for a honeymoon. It had been such a strong and specific image that it was jarring to me at the time. "You found plane tickets?" I asked.

"Yes."

"For Carolyn Knowles and . . . What name was Norman using then?"

"Arthur."

"Right. Arthur Berringer. Where were the tickets for?"

"Paris." She closed her eyes and took a deep breath. "I knew he could go with her. See, he had an Arthur passport. Usually he just has a driver's license and some credit cards, but for Arthur . . . for some reason, he got the works."

"And you thought he was going to marry her."

"He had a weak moment."

"Right. So you saved him, in a way. I mean, by beating her up, with him as a witness, he would have to make the choice right there: her or you. And he wouldn't choose her." Mary nodded, an agreement and a thank-you. But what I had meant was that Norman would not dare risk dealing with the police, even as a mere witness to a crime. He had too long a record; he would have known that a first-rate cop—like Terry Salazar had been—in two seconds flat could make him as a guy who had done time. "So you ran?"

"Yes. He was holding her and saying, 'Carolyn! Darling!' But he whispered to me, 'Get out. I'll meet you back at the apartment.' Except I was all, like, shook up. I went to the apartment, but it was such an awful place, in someone's basement, with no rug or anything. So I thought: Well, he'll be a couple of hours. So I left the jewelry there and went to a shopping center, just to pass the time."

"You had Carolyn Knowles's credit cards?" I asked casually.

"Yes. I only bought a camisole. Oh, and then I was walking over to a place where they had leather coats— just to look—and that's where the cops picked me up."

"You must have been scared."

"Was I ever! I thought: Oh, shit. I'll be thirty before I get out of jail, what with bopping her and taking her jewelry. I mean, thank goodness I had left all the stuff back at the apartment, but they'd know it was me."

"Did they charge you with robbery as well as assault?"

"Yes. Uh-oh, I thought. That's what my lawyer thought too. But the judge was such a sweetie. He said: 'I want your word that if I grant bail, you'll be back.' So I said: 'Oh, Your Honor, I swear I won't let you down.' "

"And then you were out of there."

Mary winked. "Straight to Baltimore. No bathroom stops, no frozen yogurt stops. Then the first plane out to anywhere. We wound up in Pittsburgh. Not bad."

"I've never been there."

"No, I mean, Norm made a forty-two-thousand score in less than three weeks. He said she was so easy, he hated to take the money."

"And all was well between the two of you?"

"Fine!" But she looked away, shamed by a memory, and tried to hide her chagrin by staring at a coupon for Joy.

"What was the problem?"

"He was so hurt that I hadn't trusted him."

When we first started seeing so much of each other, the man in my life and I recognized that such an alliance of two trial lawyers could be problematical. Unless we invited a judge along to hand down rulings on the almost daily basis we saw each other, our friendship could become one endless litigation, the first thing in the day one of us would say to the other being: Now, about the issue you raised on January fifteenth last. Let me enumerate the reasons why you were so pathetically misguided, to say nothing of lamentably wrong.

So we made a pact to listen to each other: really sit and hear, without structuring a response. We'd each get five minutes or whatever to state our case and after we'd both spoken, we'd work together to find a solution. This worked pretty well, except for occasional moments. Like when he threw a fit because I'd planned a vacation without consulting him. Without inviting him, to be perfectly honest, but it truly had not occurred to me that he would want to go to Disneyland. Or when I took one of the many, many jars of his mother's heinous corn relish that, like his mother, seemed threatening to take over my pantry, my dinner table, and my life, and threw it—at him.

Our other resolution was not to talk too much law, on the theory that, inevitably, my neighbors would report a strange smell and the medical examiner would rule that our deaths were simultaneous, due to acute boredom. So while we kept each other up to speed on our more interesting or troublesome cases, we usually spent our evenings doing normal-people things: watching TV, listening to music, reading, talking about life outside the law.

But that night, I was so upset about the Torkelson case I couldn't have talked about it even if I had wanted to. I made a lovely salmon tandoori style and basmati rice and couldn't eat a thing. Believe me, I had never been one to lose my appetite when under stress. With me, one small worry equals one thousand calories. And I was worried, big time. I couldn't distract myself. I picked up the novel I was reading and kept reading the same paragraph over and over; I tried crocheting but kept dropping stitches. I felt as if I had a tuning fork inside me, and its barely discernible, relentless hum was agitating every cell in my body.

"Lee? Where did you hide those oat bran pretzels?" my guy called out. He had just come in from the garage, where he was sanding an antique music stand he'd bought at a yard sale. Then I entered the kitchen. "What's wrong?"

"Nothing," I told him. I opened the pantry door and

handed him the pretzels, which, naturally, were right in the front, at eye level.

"Torkelson case?"

"Yes, but I'm so . . . I don't know. I can't talk about it." If he had tried to pull it out of me, I might have spilled everything, but he said he understood, and was off like a shot, back to his sandpaper. So I spent the evening leafing through old copies of *Gourmet* magazine from 1987, when I had a subscription, looking at recipes I would never try. Then he left to go back to his house, and I spent the night in bed, staring out into the dark.

Could Mary Dean have killed Bobette? She had a pattern of moving against women she perceived as rivals for Norman. There were strong parallels between her behavior at Carolyn Knowles's and Bobette Frisch's houses: breaking in, stealing. Were there others in this category? Or were these two so well-heeled and Norman so weary of the con that they presented a special danger that his other marks hadn't? If Terry's analysis was right, Norman, in Mary's eyes, was not merely the love of her life. He had taken her, a whore, and bestowed upon her coupon-clipping respectability. More, he gave her a home. He became her family. Wouldn't she do anything to preserve what she had with him?

The problem was, all the evidence—from fingerprints at the crime scene to marks on Bobette's neck to the probable time frame of the murder—pointed to Norman as much as it did to Mary. So which one of them had killed her? Was he covering up for her? Was her insistence on his innocence a cover-up for her knowledge of his guilt?

The next morning, first thing, I was knocking on Mary's door, sure I would have to pound away for a half hour before she would wake up and hear me. But she opened it on the third knock. "Hi," she said, and a moment later, reluctantly, she invited me in. Seeing that the goodwill I had established the day before had dissipated, I regretted not bringing more cappuccino.

The ironing board was set up in the middle of the living room and she was working on a pile of laundry: sheets and pillowcases, Norman's shirts, her clothes. She saw me staring at a pair of his undershorts that was on the board. For an instant, her manner eased, her mouth moved toward a smile as she picked up the iron. "He says not to bother, but ironing makes things so much softer. Doesn't it?" I nodded enthusiastic agreement. She ran the iron over the hems of the legs of the shorts, shooting small bursts of steam. It was an elaborate appliance, loaded with gauges and dials. Before her lips could part into a genuine smile, she remembered something. "How come you were asking me all those questions about Carolyn in Annapolis?"

Since I hadn't slept more than an hour, I couldn't come up with a decent answer. However, a lawyer has to appear—if not actually be—unbowed and uncowed at all times. I had learned to throw questions back on the questioner. "Why do *you* think I was asking them?"

"You think, like, because I beat up Carolyn maybe I"—she set down the iron but continued holding the hem of the shorts flat—"did, you know, the same thing to fatso Bobette."

"The thought crossed my mind."

"Except the report, the autopsy report . . . Didn't it say she wasn't beat up?"

"That's right."

"So I didn't! The report proves it."

"You didn't beat her up. I believe you." Mary, apparently feeling vindicated, took up her iron again. "Did you kill her?" I asked.

"*What?*" She stood there motionless, then slowly raised the iron off Norman's shorts and stared, stupidly, at its flat, shiny surface.

"Did you kill Bobette?" Drawn into the mirrored depths of the iron, she did not seem to have heard me. So I repeated the question once more, slower and louder.

"No! Of course not. Are you totally nuts?"

"Okay, I just wanted to know." Mary was either incensed or frightened. Whatever it was, she was so overcome by emotion that she could not do what she clearly wanted to do: throw the iron at me. "The reason I asked is that you seem so positive Norman didn't kill Bobette."

"I am positive!" Mary set down the iron and made a quick cross over her left breast. "I swear to God, my mother's life to die! Norman couldn't hurt anyone."

"Well, there are only two sets of fingerprints there, yours and his. And the marks on her throat . . . they were made by someone with big hands."

We both looked at the large, long-fingered hand holding down the hem of the shorts. "But I didn't touch her," Mary said. "I was never in the same room with her, ever. Do you think I could strangle somebody?"

"It's not what I think that matters. It's what the authorities think, and they think Norman strangled her. But you say Norman couldn't do it. I wish I could convince Holly Nuñez of that. She knows he has no history of violence, but she still won't believe me."

"It was someone else!" I made a motion halfway between a nod and a shrug and got up to go. "I didn't do it. Norman didn't do it."

"Even if that's true, it looks as if he's going to go to jail for the crime."

"For how long?"

"If we're lucky? Twenty years."

She braced both hands on the ironing board. "No," she whispered. "I hear people get out . . . much sooner than that."

"Not these days. Especially not with his record." Her

white face went from porcelain to sickly pale. "He didn't tell you how long?" She managed to shake her head once: No. "I'm sorry, Mary," I told her.

And I was.

Chuckie was the social butterfly of our firm, sitting on the secretaries' desks and passing the time of day, taking out our associate and paralegal for a Welcome to Phalen & White drink at TJ's, dropping into my office to talk about a case or simply to shoot the breeze if he got bored. So he knew something was up when I walked into his office and closed the door behind me. "What's the matter?"

"I just thought I'd say hi."

"Good!" he said. "Take a load off your feet."

"You're trying to sound hearty and it's not working."

"Well, missy, you're trying to sound jaunty but you're not Irish and you never will be and it's not working. What's up?"

"It's Torkelson. Torkelson's girlfriend, actually. Mary, the one I told you about."

He turned off his oxygen machine. "Hate that damn hum it makes. Can't hear myself think with it on. Talk to me. I'm your partner."

"I'm losing sleep. My stomach . . . Don't ask."

"You keep having doubts that Norman actually did it?" I think Chuckie may have been surprised that I was still in such a twit over Norman's possible innocence, but he's got the gift smart trial lawyers have. The unreadable face. Not quite a poker face. It's an expression somewhere between mild amusement and serenity—easy, pleasant, giving away nothing.

"I can't be at peace with myself if I have to go to trial on this one."

"Look, over the years you've tried—what?—two or

three cases where you were convinced one of your clients was innocent. I agree it's a big burden, but it's nothing you haven't been able to handle in the past."

"But this is different. What if Norman didn't do it but he *wants* to go to jail for it, to protect Mary? Sure, he'll go to trial, because what does he have to lose? I could conceivably get him off. But the more I look at the case against her, the more persuasive it is."

"Lay it out for me."

"Do you have time?"

"Lee, cut the gracious lady act. Give me your case against Mary."

So I went over all the Carolyn Knowles business, how Mary had robbed her, beat her up. "The details in Bobette's case appear to be the same. A robbery and attack on an older woman who was a real threat, someone she was convinced Norman was going to marry."

"Was he?"

"I'm not sure. On one hand, I'm convinced he is genuinely, madly in love with Mary. On the other hand, he wants out of what he's doing—the con. But it's not as if he could get some other job to support them. A confidence man doesn't suddenly become a shoe salesman, does he? He doesn't say: Gee, I think I'll go get a master's in social work and begin a whole new career. And my guess is, Mary is too scattered or dumb or something to hold a regular job. The only way she could support Norman would be if she started turning tricks again. But that's why she loves him and is so full of gratitude: He gave her Tupperware."

"Any physical evidence that she was inside the house—beyond her own admission to you?"

"Fingerprints. That's how we found out about her record." Chuckie's mouth turned down; his expression turned sour. He didn't like the "we." Like me, he used

Terry Salazar because he was a first-rate investigator, but he didn't approve of Terry's ways. "Fingerprints all over the house, including the site of the murder. And there's the stuff she bought with Bobette's credit cards. She showed us an expensive dress. She hadn't worn it yet; it may have still had the tag."

"Hmm," he said, and uncrossed his arms. "You're not there yet."

"Listen. In all his years of criminal activity, there was never one single instance of Norman Torkelson committing any act of violence. On the contrary: In all the witness reports I've read, the marks talk about what a gentleman he was, how sensitive. Now, Mary, on the other hand …"

"So she knocked somebody's head against the sidewalk a couple of times. That's not a pattern of violence. It's a single incident. Come on, Lee. You know the assistant in the case …"

"Holly Nuñez."

"Holly Nuñez isn't going to drop charges against Norman and haul this sweet, beautiful creature before the grand jury and say: 'She once hit a rich old lady. You can hand up the indictment, ladies and gentlemen.' Forget it, Lee."

"I can't. I keep thinking of him spending the rest of his life in jail—"

"For a crime he may have committed."

"But what if he didn't?"

"Then at least he'll spend the rest of his life feeling that he performed a single act that was fine and brave."

"But is that justice?" I demanded. "Is it?"

"You're in the justice business now?"

"I'm a lawyer!"

And for the first time in all the years I'd known him, my partner laughed at me. Not with me. At me.

Sixteen

✖

Students rarely live in luxury. Still, for a girl from a rich family, Lee had spent a considerable part of her adult life in wretched circumstances, beginning with the student-radical dump she shared with Flip Mullen. Her next year at Cornell, it was an apartment designated as off-campus housing but that, objectively, was a tenement so mouse-infested that when she and her roommates stopped talking or turned off their tape deck, they could hear a glee club of squeaks. She laughed about it, but in her heart the squalor frightened her and she wished someone would come and take care of her. No one did.

In her first year at law school, her dormitory room was clean enough; it even had a window overlooking Washington Square Park. But the woman next door had an illegal hot plate, and when she was not reading cases, she experimented with the cuisines of obscure ethnic groups, all of which had garlic as their principal ingredient. Complaining to the woman directly resulted in a raised middle finger and a fortnight of curried fish.

The dean of student life promised a remedy but in the end did nothing, perhaps fearing that all the ethnic groups represented on the hot plate would take offense and, armed to the teeth, hold a sit-in on law school property.

So Lee pleaded with Leonard to let her get an apartment. Nothing fancy: There were walk-ups in the East Village that were really cheap. However, at that particular time he was feeling put upon by women. Sylvia had just redecorated the house; Robin was shoplifting and on four different occasions he had had to buy the silence of merchants; Greta was threatening to retire unless he converted to gas and bought her a stove with a salamander; and Dolly Young, having hinted broadly, had been given a top-of-the-line Jaguar. So Leonard drew the line. Don't be ridiculous, he told Lee. The smell couldn't be *that* bad. Dad, you want to wish you didn't have a nose? she challenged him. Come on up, any hour, day or night. Leonard did not take her up on the invitation; instead he suggested that she learn to breathe through her mouth.

Ah, but she breathed easier as Mrs. Jasper Taylor. Upon their marriage, Leonard told them: Stay in the married students' dorm? How can I let my kids live in a dorm? On lower Fifth Avenue, he bought them a co-op in an upscale building, where the doormen called Lee "Madam." Although modest in size, the place had all the requisite luxuries New Yorkers ooh and ah over: parquet floors, twelve-foot ceilings, crown moldings. When Leonard and the real estate broker showed them inside for the first time and all but said "Voilà!" Lee waited for Jazz to protest: Sorry, very generous of you, but we can't accept this. What he said was: Hey, this is terrific! Thanks!

More than the fact of Hart's Hill, more than the way he pronounced "tomato," this was the moment she became cognizant of the class difference between herself and her husband. She was the daughter of *nouveau riche* parents who, now that she had married so well, were impatient to indulge her. But where she came from, the passing down of privilege was an option, not a governing principle.

In Jazz's world, it was the natural order of things. True, the Taylors were upset that they had eloped, upset that their son had married a girl whose forebears did not play golf, but not so upset that Ginger did not unload a mammoth chest of Victorian flatware monogrammed with a *T*, an embarrassment of old linens, and two Hepplewhite chairs. They themselves might have set up the young couple in an apartment, but they were, as Jazz revealed—with not a trace of shame or bitterness—dead broke. Fos's work for the U.S. Olympic Committee, although prestigious, paid just slightly more than nothing, and the cost of maintaining Hart's Hill, his accountant kept informing him, was eating away the capital he had inherited.

Still, as the firstborn son, Jazz was the beneficiary of his parents' connections. He had been admitted to prep school on the basis of a telephone call. When he decided that Colgate was the college for him, his father said a few words to one of his then law partners. The partner had a chat with President Barnett; the following week, the word came down that Jasper Taylor would be a member of Colgate's class of '71. Every summer job Jazz ever held was the result of someone lifting a phone on his behalf. So while the apartment Leonard bought was beyond the young man's expectations, the fact that his father-in-law was supporting him came as absolutely no surprise. It was the way things were supposed to be. That's what parents were for.

Accordingly, while Jazz was busy studying for the bar

examination, Foster Taylor made a couple of phone calls; the men whom he called did likewise. Not long after, Jasper Taylor, Attorney-at-Law, was obliged to get what he and Lee called his Establishment Pig haircut; he had his long, glossy hair clipped to a reactionary three-quarters of an inch. Then he donned a pin-striped suit and dark red tie and began working down on Wall Street at the eminent law firm of Johnson, Bonadies and Eagle.

When Leonard heard how Foster had gotten Jazz a job, he was galvanized and told Lee he was going to call his own lawyer, Seymour Breitbart, of Breitbart, Wasserman, Mishkin, Schwartz and Oshinsky, to see if there was a spot for her. They represent half of Seventh Avenue, Leonard ballyhooed. Two-thirds. The best designers. If you worked there, you could walk right into any of the showrooms—even the French places: Lapidus, Patou—and tell them, "I'm a lawyer at Breitbart, Wasserman," and get to-the-trade prices.

But she told him not to bother. She knew that she did not require a phone call. While not at the top of her law school class, Lee was close enough. True, in 1974, old-line law firms still subjected women to a remarkable array of insults and inequities. And the fact was, they rarely broke out the champagne upon the hiring of a Jew. Even so, she still could have gotten a job at Johnson, Bonadies and Eagle, or at Matthison, Appleby, or, for that matter, at the National Hockey League. Strictly on the merits. But Lee's first job as a lawyer was at the place where she had been happier than ever before in her life: the Manhattan District Attorney's Office.

Her first case as an assistant was a third-degree sexual abuse. She prepared for it as if she were lead prosecutor in the Rape of the Sabines trial.

"Look," Jazz said, during her second week of preparation. "There's such a thing as working too hard. I know you want to run with this thing, but it's not the crime of the century."

Lee laughed. "It's not?" Frankly, she did not feel like laughing about her trial, although objectively she realized that the case of *People* v. *Robert Steven McCarthy* was not a blot on the landscape of American civilization. It was merely a misdemeanor, to wit, the feeling up of one Joyce-Ann Goldenson on a northbound number 6 subway shortly after it pulled out of the Fifty-ninth Street station, a charge Robert Steven McCarthy vigorously denied. Not the crime of the century, but her crime. Nevertheless, Lee laughed along with Jazz, because here it was, one of the rare Saturday nights she didn't have to be a complaint assistant and spend from eight o'clock to midnight in court. But she was still working. She should have been playing—with her husband. A good-looking husband, lean, well-muscled, lying right there beside her on the bed, naked.

"Why don't you just let the poor sucker go?" Jazz asked with a grin. For at least the millionth time, Lee marveled at his natural happiness. He instinctively looked at the bright side. That, combined with his fine looks and inborn kindness, guaranteed that he would always be Most Popular Boy. "Seriously. Why not?"

"You're kidding."

"No. Come on, babe, be serious. It was a feel, not a homicide."

"If you give me 'She should have been grateful' …"

"No! You know I'm not some stupid Neanderthal."

"You're a smart Neanderthal."

"Right! Do you know what she should have done? Hauled off and smacked him. What was so terrible that she had to pull the emergency cord and call the cops?"

"Because he pressed up against her side and started humping her. And then he pretended to get jostled and—what do you know!—his hand happened to get pushed up onto her left breast."

"That's a crime?" Jazz asked, reaching up and letting his hand drift over both Lee's breasts.

She tried to relax, get back into the mood. She should be the one to initiate the next round of lovemaking. Hadn't the last one, an hour before, been truly fine? So why didn't she want more? But instead of tossing aside her yellow legal pad and stretching out along Jazz's length, Lee found herself quoting the law: "'A person is guilty of sexual abuse in the third degree when he subjects another person to sexual contact without the latter's consent.'" Even as she said it, she could hear how prissy she sounded.

"I know, I know," Jazz said, getting into an even more comfortable position on the linen sheets his mother had given them. The sheets were monogrammed *KVT*. Another Taylor bride, although when Lee had asked Fos and Ginger who she was, neither had a clue.

"I feel bad, being preoccupied like this," Lee said, trying to sound tender. To feel tender. But she couldn't. Jazz knew perfectly well she had to work late. Yet nearly every night for the past two weeks he had thrown some temptation her way: a movie, a Sly and the Family Stone concert, dim sum in Chinatown, a Rangers game. And each time she said no, sorry, the length of her apology grew. Jazz seemed surprised. He would say, in his usual sunny manner: Just thought I'd ask.

But what was he doing, asking? Where did he get so much free time? That was what Lee wanted to ask him. More than half their classmates from NYU were doing what Jazz was: working as first-year associates at big law firms. None of them were going to Rangers games. Not a single one had time to see a movie during the week—not when they were working until nine or nine-thirty every night, then dragging themselves home, praying they had clean underwear for the next day, and flopping, exhausted, into bed. How come only Jazz had time to play? Was there some secret footnote to the law firm work ethic that exempted prep school boys from the institutional nine-to-nine grind?

"Don't feel bad," Jazz said good-naturedly. "It's just that you never let up. Your father called the other day, worried. No, more concerned. Said you had circles under your eyes the last two times he saw you."

"I don't have circles!"

"That's what I told him. It's just that he doesn't get it."

"Get what?"

"Your . . . you know. Your ambition. In his world, a woman marries a professional and she quits her job— gladly—and devotes the rest of her life to picking out wallpaper."

"It's not that I'm ambitious. It's just that I love what I do."

"I know. Listen, stop apologizing. You're a perfect wife and a great fuck and I love you and you can go back to your work with a clear conscience. You knocked me out. I'd probably need a crane to get it up. This way, it's all your fault"—he grinned—"and I get to do exactly what I was dying to do, which is go to sleep." He blew her a kiss, slid under the covers, and turned over.

But what was he so tired from? Soon after the bar exam, when they both started working, she would call him at Johnson, Bonadies and Eagle in the early evening. Except he wasn't there. Uh, one of the other associates would say, I, uh, think he left already. Or (another might add, more charitably) maybe he's in the twenty-eighth-floor library. Not there at seven-thirty? She—making a third of what he was at her government job—was sitting in front of a mile-high pile of paper at her mud-green desk at seven-thirty, in the cubicle she shared with two other assistant D.A.'s, both of whom were also hard at work. Hesitantly those first few weeks, not wanting to embarrass him, she would call the apartment, and Jazz would answer: Hi! He was always in a bright mood, ready to chat. How's crime paying? he would ask.

Lee was so afraid for him. How could he just pick up and leave his office? Wasn't he terrified of being fired? But he didn't sound terrified: How did it go in court today, babe? Nice and easy. She'd chitchat for a minute or two, not wanting to seem as if she had something better to do than talk to her husband of eleven months. But the fact was, she had. Work. Or if work wasn't better than Jazz—and it wasn't, she assured herself—it was at least necessary. The first few years of being a lawyer were all about paying your dues.

Well, her first payment was *People* v. *Robert Steven McCarthy* and she was going to get the little son-of-a-bitch for groping Joyce-Ann on the IRT.

It wasn't going to be easy. Robert gave a great impression; he had the bantamweight charm of a Mickey Rooney combined with an endearing deep, dumb voice—a little like Smokey the Bear's. Joyce-Ann, on the other hand, came across like one of Freud's case studies in hysteria. She was so tense she did not speak so much as yelp, so tense that when being questioned about her allegations, she crossed her arms over her chest and rocked her breasts as if they were foundlings. I think she's going to make a lousy impression, Lee told the assistant supposedly supervising her trial, a man who had been a lawyer a year longer than she had. Do your best, he told her, not looking up from the lab analysis he was reading. Lee had a feeling that if he did look up, he would have no idea who she was.

But he did soon enough. Lee won *People* v. *Robert Steven McCarthy*, the case everyone who thought about it—and there were not many—thought was a real loser. She did so the way all good trial lawyers do, with thorough preparation and natural talent. Lee's gift was not for podium-pounding harangues or withering cross-examination, but for credibility. The very directness that had so often alienated her family worked in the courtroom. She did her best with what she had: intelligence, intuition, and common sense. If Joyce-Ann was tense, make her feel comfortable—or at least as close to comfortable as a Manhattan hysteric can feel. Lee spoke to her in a gentle voice and spent patient hours going over her testimony, until Joyce-Ann did not cringe at the word "erection." True, she did flinch a bit, but Lee decided rightly that the jury would find this understandable, even laudatory.

And if Robert sounded dopey like Smokey, it was just common sense to try and trip him up on some complicated question. So Lee probed: "You say you did not rub yourself against Ms. Goldenson that day. If you touched her at all, it was simply because you were jostled and fell against her. So then how can you explain your hand reaching around and squeezing her left breast?" I *didn't* squeeze it, he insisted, as Lee knew he would. "Well," she went on, "all right. You just touched it then." Right, the defendant agreed, and he agreed to her next question as well, that yes, he did in fact remember touching her left breast, but it was an accident, definitely not a squeeze. And then Lee (having rehearsed the scenario at least ten times with a crouching Jazz playing the much shorter Robert) asked him to come off the stand and demonstrate how it happened. Pretend I'm Joyce-Ann Goldenson, Lee suggested. Robert's lawyer objected. The judge overruled. Lee said: Okay, you grabbed for the subway pole in your right hand. That's right, make believe you're holding the pole. Now, if you were facing the direction both you and the complainant agreed you were facing . . . She positioned herself in front of him. Were you like this? she asked. Yes, he conceded. Then without actually touching me, show me how when you were jostled you came to rub up against Ms. Goldenson's side. And while you're at it, how your hand and Ms. Goldenson's breast came into contact.

The jury was out for just thirty-five minutes. When they returned with a guilty verdict, the first thing Lee did was race back to her desk and call Jazz. Fantastic! he'd exclaimed, and she could tell by his voice that he was truly thrilled for her. Brilliant! I mean it, Lee. All the courtroom stories are about great defense lawyers. Ever think of that? They're going to have to start a whole new category for you: Genius D.A.'s.

The truth was that Lee was good, quite good. But not a genius. There were two real geniuses in the District Attorney's Office. One was a bland-looking man five years older than she, who tried homicide cases. He was half-Polish, half-German, born in a cold-water flat on East Eighty-seventh Street, out of Brooklyn Law

School. His heart was so malleable it could assume the shape of any or all the jurors' hearts. He barely needed an opening statement: That great heart of his told them all they had to know. Whenever she had time, Lee sat in on his trials. At the beginning she had hoped to learn something: the way he related to the jury or handled cross or how he spoke to the judge. All she learned was that whatever it was he had, she did not.

But the following year, the other office genius, Melanie Tucker, the deputy chief of the Supreme Court bureau, had a great deal to teach her. "You ought to use your femininity more."

"*What?*" Lee asked, convinced she had not heard right. True, Melanie herself often seemed as if she had been sucked up by a cyclone from the tea party she had been hostessing and plunked down in the D.A.'s Office. A dainty perfumed handkerchief always peeked out of one of her modest long sleeves. Melanie was known as a genius strategist, the greatest teacher of advocacy ever. Lee, however, was appalled. This was 1975! The very idea of using feminine wiles to achieve a goal was disgraceful. "Use my *what?*"

"Your femininity," Melanie replied. She sounded so genteel that she should have been sitting before a silver tea service, offering clotted cream and marmalade, not at a desk with a stack of crime scene photos of a victim shot in the nose at close range. Her desk was a great and clumsy gray metal affair, but the photos were arrayed in a delicate fan shape, and all her papers were in folders on either side of a cream-colored blotter set in a tan leather holder. "The problem with women trial lawyers is this: They try to be men." She gestured to Lee to be seated, a gracious roll of the wrist.

"I'm not trying to be a man," Lee said, thinking back to the day before, her second trial in the Supreme Court unit. Simple. A one-witness robbery. Where could she have acted mannishly? A bodega owner in East Harlem claimed the defendant held a gun on him and then ran out with the three hundred dollars from the cash register and a carton of Camels. "Are you talking about the Suarez case?" she asked.

"I am." Melanie picked up a petal that had fallen from the single white rose she always kept in a bud vase on her desk and, with delicacy, sniffed it. She had gone to Radcliffe.

"But I won!" Lee exclaimed. "The jury came back about four-thirty."

"I know."

"So where was I mannish?"

Lee really didn't want to hear Melanie's answer. She dreaded it. It would be something humiliating— like telling her she should use lip wax because juror number eight seemed to be staring at the area directly under her nose. And indeed, he had, all during her summation. Or the answer could be something more profound—like she was acting so masculine that people would think her wedding ring was a phony.

Sometimes she actually felt like the man of the house, coming home late, neck stiff, muscles sore, bones aching, only to find that Jazz had prepared a big dinner. Why? They could have gotten a sandwich from the deli. He could have been working as late as she was. He should have been. Jazz said everything was fine. What was she worried about? And in truth, he had not been fired. But she had seen with her own eyes, at his law firm's outing the previous June, how the partners did not take him seriously. Hello! they would call to him, a little too heartily, without stopping to make conversation. Jazz didn't seem to care, though, or even notice. Boring, was all he could say about the partners. Workaholics, he remarked of his fellow associates. Not me. So he left the office while others still had three or four hours more work, while Lee herself still had three or four hours. He came back to the apartment, watched the news, listened to the radio, cleaned, did the laundry. And cooked. Then he showered to be fresh when she came home. Well, this was the wave of the future; that's what all the articles on the New Feminism told her. Forget sex roles. Be what you want to be. And if you have a husband willing to take on household responsibilities, then be grateful and give him a great big kiss as he hands you your pipe and slippers.

"I didn't say you were *mannish*," Melanie explained. "I said you are using tactics that are associated with men. Yelling, for instance."

"When was I yelling?"

"During most of your summation." She rubbed the rose petal between her thumb and forefinger.

"I wasn't yelling," Lee retorted. "I was trying to sound strong."

"But your talent is for being direct, down-to-earth. You're likable. I admit I was in and out of the courtroom, but I must have seen about an hour of the trial. You were very easy to take. You asked a question—a well-thought-out question—and you knew just what to do with the answer. You were polite to witnesses, to the judge, to Suarez's idiot lawyer. When you made an objection, your voice was firm but under control. Excellent."

"Thank you."

"But you almost blew it during summation."

"I wanted to be forceful."

"Be forceful for Lee White, then. You were forceful for some hairy-chested Italian guy out of St. John's. Sweeping gestures. Big voice. They could have heard you in Bronx Supreme. And that banging on the podium!" Melanie let the petal drift from her fingers. Then she crashed her fist on her desk. "Does that seem natural?"

"No, but I'm not like you," Lee explained, trying not to stare at the lace hem of Melanie's handkerchief.

"Granted. But you are not a stevedore either. You seem to be a bright, energetic young woman from . . . Where?"

"Long Island."

"Do they bang podia on Long Island?"

"It's not a local custom," Lee admitted

"And the women there: Do they speak forcefully and directly? Or do they shout?"

"They don't shout," Lee admitted.

"If you came from a long line of female shouters, it might be another story. I assume you do not?"

"I had one grandmother who was in the Yiddish theater. She had a healthy set of lungs, but no, I don't think she shouted."

"Nor do you."

"Right."

"You see, juries know that about you," Melanie said, looking at her short but perfectly buffed nails. "They watch you. During your opening. Walking up to the sidebar for conferences. Taking out a Life Saver during his lawyer's cross of the transit cop. You, the judge, the defense lawyers . . . All of you represent the law to them. Justice. For many of them, this trial will be one of the most memorable events of their lives. So they are riveted on you and everything you do."

"Sorry about the Life Saver."

"Perfectly all right. The jury understands reaching into a pocket or handbag surreptitiously and popping a Life Saver into a dry mouth. It also reinforces what they already know about you: a nice, normal person. A young woman from Long Island who was probably brought up *not* to shout."

"But this is a *trial*. I'm a prosecutor!"

"This is a trial, and more than anything, they have to believe you. During your summation, several jurors were sitting back and going: Huh? What's going on here? What's she yelling about? This isn't the assistant D.A. we've come to know and like. This is someone emoting. Being false. Can we trust her? Were we wrong about her being so nice?"

"But I won," Lee argued.

"Yes, but look what you had going for you. The bodega owner was a great witness. And the defendant looked like the punk he is; he didn't dare testify. The jury was out almost a full day. They shouldn't have taken longer than a couple of hours. That means you almost lost them."

"I didn't realize . . . I thought because they were out so long, I had done a great job."

"A good job. The summation . . . well, you made them doubt *you,* and therefore they doubted your case. But as you say, Lee, you did win it. Congratulations."

❁

The Whites and the Taylors got along amazingly well. That was because all four of them—Leonard, Sylvia, Foster, and Ginger—had good manners. If they hadn't, Lee and Jazz's third anniversary celebration at the Whites' might have ended with words, or even a "Well, I *never*!" followed by a slammed door. Each set of parents despised the other individually and collectively.

Sylvia stood by the Frank Lloyd Wright–style chrome and glass bar where Leonard was pouring drinks and whispered in a not very *sotto voce* about Ginger's outfit: "It's a slap in the face! Baggy cotton pants and an old sweater, like she was going out to mow her lawn . . . which would be nice for a change."

"She probably thought it was casual," Leonard replied. "Sunday afternoon, just to celebrate the kids' anniversary."

But Sylvia wasn't having any: "It's either a deliberate smack in the face or she's the dumbest of the dumb goys, which—believe you me—is pretty dumb."

At that same instant, Ginger was staring at the food on the dining room table—a turkey that looked as if it had been designed by Ralph Lauren, a glistening glazed ham, a jewel of a cranberry mold, a cornucopia of baby vegetables, a cheese platter that would cause the American Dairy Association to shout Hallelujah— and Sylvia's triumph, which she had ordered two months earlier: gingerbread models of the Whites' house and Hart's Hill. Ginger murmured to her husband in a voice accustomed to summoning dogs from several acres away: "Who does she think is coming for dinner? The whole Israel army?"

"Not with that ham," Fos countered. "Anyway, it's just us."

"I hate to say it, but it's true what they say about them: They know the price of everything and the value of nothing. They *wanted* us to figure how much it cost. Have you ever *seen* such a display?"

Since both mothers were talking at the same moment, they did not hear each other. The fathers kept their feelings to themselves, although Leonard, once enamored of Foster Taylor, then respectful, had been shaken to his core when Fos asked him for rye and ginger ale. Rye and ginger ale! A 1940s low-class woman's drink. Or was Fos kidding? Was it some Rolling Hills Country Club in-joke, where you ask for rye and ginger ale and everybody hoots with laughter and the bartender hands you an Absolut on the rocks with a wedge of lime. Leonard had tried an experimental chuckle when Fos asked for the drink, but there had been no corresponding laugh back.

Foster, in worn corduroys and a cotton turtleneck—which covered about a third of his sagging pelican chin—couldn't think of a thing to say to his in-law, this slim, platinum-at-the-temples man mixing drinks and wearing a double-breasted nipped-waist suit and one of those dime-thin gold watches . . . on a Sunday! Who the hell gets dressed up like that in his own house? Can you talk about the Giants with a guy like that? Politics? There was no doubt in Foster's mind that Leonard was a knee-jerk Democrat, and he'd wind up puking if he had to listen to him go on about liberal crap, like how Gerald Ford deserved to lose and how that liver-lipped cracker Carter was so great.

The elder Taylors were perched on the edge of one of Sylvia's decorating epiphanies, a leather and chrome daybed that sat, plunk, right in the middle of the Whites' living room. They were sipping their drinks, tiny bird sips, as if waiting for a moment when the Whites would turn away and they could bolt.

The Whites, standing by the bar, appeared almost paralyzed, their lips barely able to move. Lee assumed her mother was saying: Let's serve dinner now, and her father was replying angrily: It's only three o'clock. We can't serve until four-thirty—at the earliest. How the hell could you ask them to come at two for a four-thirty supper?

"I don't know," Jazz said to Lee, with that irreverent,

irresistible, and decidedly sexual half smile she loved. "Doesn't look promising, does it?"

"God knows why. Two Fun Couples like them, they should be whooping it up."

"What's so amusing, you two?" Ginger called out so cheerfully it was clear she was desperate.

"What's so amusing?" Kent echoed, sounding a sour note. His parents had stuck him with Lee's sister, who was trying too hard to find something interesting for him to do. He was tired of drawing pictures of his family for her and making Play-Doh out of flour and water and salt. It *wasn't* Play-Doh, and he'd told her he was too old for Play-Doh, and she hadn't listened to him. He wanted to be with Lee and Jazz. He wanted to eat. There it was, all set out on the table and they wouldn't let him even go near it.

"You two look happy!" said Robin, using her ebullient voice. After six months in rehabilitation, she had returned to Shorehaven for four-times-a-week therapy and a volunteer job at a day care center. She was trying very hard to show the Taylors a good time and, while she was at it, to show she was not a thieving junkie. She was aware that was her reputation around town, a reputation—she had learned to own up to in group—she had earned. But it was exhausting having to act so animated and to keep Kent amused.

Jazz and Lee waved her over. As Lee knew he would, Kent leaped up and came along. "Hi!" he said. He put his arm around her, laid his head on her shoulder, and heaved a satisfied sigh.

"Hi!" Lee smoothed his hair back from his forehead. Too shaggy again. Deciding not to ask herself why her mother-in-law could spend hours every day grooming her dogs but couldn't take the only child she had left at home for a haircut once every six months,

Lee made a mental note to take him to the barber the following weekend.

"Hi!" Kent said again.

"Hi!" She turned to Robin. "I know this isn't exactly scintillating for you. You're being wonderful."

"Stop it! Wonderful is having you guys here in the house. I mean, Mom and Dad have been great—especially considering how I made their lives a living hell. But they're so nervous with me. If I'm not constantly smiling, they're nervous wrecks."

Lee reached out and put her other arm around her sister. Physically, Robin appeared more fragile than ever. Her dark-blonde hair was swept straight back from her forehead and temples, accentuating the heart shape of her face with its pointed chin. She would have been beautiful or close to it—thin as a whisper, with whiter-than-white skin and eyes the color of an overcast sky—but the drugs she had taken for so many years had taken their toll. She had dreadful dental problems. To hide her unattractive teeth and bad gums, she puffed out her lips. While this made her mouth pretty and pouty in repose, when she spoke it looked as if she were imitating a fish.

Jazz stared at the sisters and, as people invariably did, marveled at their differences. Forget that they seemed to have come from separate families: They might have belonged to separate races. Although the same height, Lee was sturdy, with strong shoulders and hips verging on generosity. Her hair was thick and chestnut brown, her skin golden. In her walks through Greenwich Village, tourists would stop her and ask directions in French, Spanish, Italian, or Greek, believing she was one of their own. "The two of you . . ." he said, shaking his head in amazement.

"Night and day," Robin said.

"Rich and poor," Lee added.

"Black and white," Robin continued.

"Christian and Jew," Jazz chimed in. As if on cue, the sisters looked from Fos and Ginger to Leonard and Sylvia—and began to laugh. It was only then that Jazz could see the resemblance: heads leaning to the right at the precise same angle, cheeks red and shiny. They wiped tears of laughter from their eyes at the same instant with the exact same motion, an outward flick with their middle fingers.

"What's so funny?" Ginger asked too eagerly. She sounded beyond desperate now, so with Robin and Kent in tow, Lee hurried over to her in-laws to try and make them think they were having fun. This was no simple job. She became a jurisprudential Scheherazade, regaling them with one whimsical courtroom tale after another. Finally, after three-quarters of an hour, she succeeded. Sylvia had joined them in good-natured chuckling, and then Fos took the floor, telling horror stories of pushy parents of would-be Olympic competitors. It was only then that Lee looked around for Jazz and found him gone.

"In the den with Daddy," Robin informed her. Lee pictured Jazz and her father watching football, her father mimicking Jazz's "Yeah!" and "Asshole!" after various plays. Her father admired men who admired sports, and though he himself knew little and cared nothing about athletics, she was aware he was shamed by this defect in himself. Still, after another hour, Lee was astounded at her father's tenacity. True, she realized Leonard idolized everything about Jazz, from his Platonic ideal of a nose to the way he said thank you to busboys in restaurants when they refilled his water glass. Nevertheless, she wondered how Leonard could last through so much football. Of course, she admitted to herself, she could be wrong; there might be a documentary on Channel 13 on the history of the mink stole.

The two men came out moments later in high spirits, Leonard calling to Sylvia that he was *starved* and Jazz putting up his fists for a round of mock boxing with Kent. Sylvia whipped yards of Saran off the spread on the table. Leonard uncorked two bottles of wine Lee sensed were embarrassingly expensive, and the Whites and the Taylors dug into the buffet as if they had spent years in caloric deprivation.

"Mmm! Great turkey," Ginger said.

"Good vino, Len," Fos remarked.

Everyone, even Robin, had at least two portions of everything and at the end, they all applauded as Sylvia cut the gingerbread White house into slices.

"Yum!" said Fos.

"I can't believe something that looks so good can taste so delish!" Ginger remarked.

Sylvia insisted the Taylors take home the model of Hart's Hill. They made a brief, bogus protest, grabbed the cake, and, with an overenthusiastic chorus of "Thank you!" and ecumenical "Happy holidays!" they rushed out the door, forgetting Kent.

"Don't worry," Jazz assured Lee as she made for the door to call after them. "They know he's in good hands. I'll drop him off later. Sit down." He glanced over at Leonard who, as if by design, was sitting back expansively on one of Sylvia's newly acquired Corbusier love-seats, his arm resting on the back, legs crossed in leisurely *Gentleman's Quarterly* style. Jazz led Lee to the matching love seat, across from his father-in-law's. Leonard, meantime, patted the spot beside his own, inviting Sylvia to sit. When she took no notice, preoccupied as she was with watching

Greta clear the table, he called out: "Sylvia! Over here. Sit down. We have something to tell you."

Lee interpreted the "you" as meaning her mother, so she snuggled against Jazz, her cheek enjoying the incredible softness of the vicuña sweater Sylvia and Leonard had given him the previous Christmas. She half closed her eyes, the better to luxuriate in the blended scents of Woolite and Jazz's own virile odor. But then she opened them. He was not circling his arm around her in their customary marital embrace. No, he looked casual, legs stretched out before him, crossed at the ankles, but his torso remained erect, and the arm that always crooked so comfortably around her stayed on the back of the love seat. She sat straight up.

Her father cleared his throat, then Jazz his, even louder. Deep, manly sounds. But then Leonard met Jazz's eye, and the next sounds out of them were boyish chuckles. Lee couldn't be sure. Were they We've Got a Secret chuckles or Bad Boy sniggers? Had they planned something? A surprise New Year's Eve black-tie dinner at some four-star restaurant? God forbid, she thought, having to ring in the bicentennial year with her parents and Robin over mountains of shaved truffles and oversolicitous waiters instead of over a six-foot hero and Chianti with their friends. Or worse, had her father gotten Jazz involved in planning a lavish vacation the five of them could share in some exorbitant tropical paradise? She wished she could be certain that Jazz's increasing closeness with her father—the twice-weekly lunches, the frequent exchange of jokey notes accompanied with *Wall Street Journal* or *Forbes* clippings—arose out of Jazz's inability to hurt anyone's feelings and not from any commonality of interests.

"Lee," Jazz began. But then he stopped and looked to Leonard.

"Honey," her father said. Out of the corner of her eye, Lee saw Robin sitting Indian-style on the daybed with Kent, folding the *Times* into hat shapes, straining to hear what was being said. "Jazz and I have been talking," Leonard said. Jazz nodded, as if to quell any doubts that this was the truth. "We've come to a decision." For some reason, Lee suddenly remembered what Melanie Tucker had been saying when they had a drink a few weeks earlier, about never giving the other side any help in putting a knife in your back: I've seen too many women lawyers smiling supportively or murmuring comforting, maternal uh-huhs. Don't get caught in that trap. Just sit there with a neutral expression and let them get out the bad news as best they can. Sometimes they'll trip themselves up. "It affects all of us," her father was saying. This is crazy, Lee thought, my thinking like this. I'm not in court. I'm with my family. But her face could not move itself out of its frozen neutrality.

"What?" Sylvia demanded. "*What* is going on?" Her cajoling was so girlish it demanded a ruffled petticoat and a hair bow, not the sleek black velvet condom of an at-home dress she was wearing. "Come on. *Please*. I can't stand secrets."

Both men ignored her. Their eyes were on Lee. "Babe," Jazz said, "don't react. Just listen." An entirely unnecessary statement, since Lee was sitting as unyielding as a petrified tree. "This is going to be great for all of us."

"I can't take the tension!" Sylvia protested. "Pretty please!"

"This is the story, honey," Leonard said to Lee, ignoring his wife. "You know what's been happening with Le Fourreur. Can I say it? Can I brag? An unqualified success. A success beyond my wildest dreams."

When his satisfied smile did not elicit the same from Lee, he looked across the huge block of pink-veined marble that was the coffee table and winked at Jazz, bolstering and boyish. Lee did not have to look to know her husband was winking back.

"You men!" Sylvia declared. "Tell us!"

"Success brings rewards, enormous rewards, but it brings problems too. Dealing with top-of-the-line designers who have armies—I'm serious—of advisers. Dealing with suppliers, with foreign governments, for God's sake. Do I have to tell you who the number one importer of Russian golden sable into this country is? I mean, I should have my own embassy in Moscow."

Jazz let out a deep breath, reluctant to join the conversation, but he realized Leonard had stopped and was waiting for him. "You know how I've been trying to help," he told Lee. "Serving as a sounding board, really, so your dad can check out what his lawyers have been telling him. And in general, trying to be there for him." Lee was close enough to smell sweat-drenched vicuña. "But this is the thing: We talked. We went out to lunch. You know. Got to know each other."

"More than father-in-law and son-in-law," Leonard interjected.

"More like peers."

"Peers," Leonard echoed. "And friends, I hope."

"Friends," Jazz said, as if it could not be otherwise. "And besides that, I realized one thing. No. Two things. One, I was able to help your father."

"It was incredible!" Leonard said. "I had a whole law firm working for me. You wouldn't believe the fees they were charging. And what was I getting? A lot of 'On one hand, but on the other hand.' No one could make a decision. Until Jazz. He'd say: 'This is what I think you ought to do. Here are the pluses. And so you can reach a balanced decision, here are the minuses as well.'"

At that moment, Lee regretted being a lawyer, because she understood what was going on: What Jazz was telling her father was no different from what Breitbart, Wasserman, Mishkin, Schwartz and Oshinsky was telling him. But she kept stone-faced and stony silent. Because she thought she knew what was coming next—and she was right.

"It wasn't just that I liked helping your father," Jazz continued. "You know, being useful to him. I found out that all the times I was working with him, I was having fun. I mean, sometimes we'd have lunch uptown and then I'd go back to the salon with him and look at whatever needed looking at, and it was *fun*. Challenging. Interesting." (Naturally, Jazz did not mention, then or ever, that it had taken him about twenty minutes in Leonard's mahogany-paneled office to realize that his father-in-law and Dolly Young were longtime paramours, a state of affairs Leonard confessed to him anyway, at their next lunch.) "But then I found out something else. That when I was finished and had to go back to the office, I was . . . well, I felt really, really low."

"I sensed it," Leonard went on. Listening, Lee was somehow reminded of the oft-repeated stories married couples tell of how they met and fell in love. "And I thought about it. I mean, heavy thinking. I knew how much Jazz liked working with me, and it goes without saying that I was getting more and more . . . well, dependent is not too strong a word. Dependent on him. His advice was always great. And whoever I introduced him to at the place: my insurance man, the employees, the customers—my God, the customers!— they were crazy about him. So . . ."

"So . . . your father made me an offer, Lee."

They waited for her to ask what it was. When she didn't, Leonard finally said: "I offered him the presidency of Le Fourreur."

Sylvia clapped her hands together with joy, but then she bit her lip. "What about you?" she asked her husband.

"I'll be chairman of the board," he said proudly. "And founder. I'll do the buying of skins. I'll deal with the designers. Sell to customers who need special handling. Work on bringing in bigger names. But Jazz is going to take over running the show."

Lee sensed she should be angry, but she felt nothing. Nothing. No matter that the term "absolute zero" had a scientific meaning; that is what she felt. "You're going to leave Johnson, Bonadies?" she asked.

"Yes. Of course." Then Jazz added: "I already told them."

"You already told them?"

"You *know* I wasn't happy there."

"I asked you over and over again whether you were happy there, whether you would be better off someplace else, and you said—" She cut herself off because she realized there was no point in going on. Jazz was leaving the law. Unlike the five previous generations of Taylor men, he did not have the stuff. And there was another reason for her not going on. As any smart corporate wife knows, it is counterproductive to belittle one's husband in front of his boss.

The following year, the two hundredth anniversary of the birth of the nation, Lee successfully prosecuted an organized-crime figure on kidnapping and assault charges, shut down a major heroin wholesaler by going after him—nine times in four months—for building code violations, and convinced a notoriously lenient judge to sentence a pimp to the maximum seven years for the vehicular assault of a fifteen-year-old prostitute. As a reward for her achievements, she became part of the District Attorney's elite group, the lawyers who got to try homicide cases. The D.A. himself told her she not only was a natural in court; she had great judgment out of court.

True. Perhaps it had to do with growing up within Leonard and Sylvia's house. Whatever, Lee White had developed what the street-wise refer to as a built-in bullshit detector. Thus she was able to take the measure of her colleagues, judges, police, and others in the criminal justice system with a fair degree of accuracy. Her passionate soul—the part of her that could be captured at Dante's Pizza by Jasper Taylor, or that thrilled with anticipation and pride each morning as she walked through the hideously ugly D.A.'s Office at 100 Centre Street—did not get in her way at all. Rather, it helped. It kept her from becoming cynical; it kept her believing her efforts were, truly, on behalf of the People.

Her work was painful at times, all the more so because Jazz's was now so . . . well, the only word that came to her mind was "frivolous." Here was someone with the best education money could buy, and he was now spending his days taking department store executives out to long, extravagant lunches, cajoling them to carry Le Fourreur's exclusive sheared beaver ski jackets. Or poring over contracts with chinchilla ranchers. But she had to admit, he was happier than ever. His normal good cheer had given way to exuberance, now that he was liberated from what he thought was his life sentence at Johnson, Bonadies and Eagle. He loved his new job, loved his huge salary, loved being loved—adored, actually—by everyone from his father-in-law to the wealthy customers to the young man who swept fur scraps in the back room. He loved the leisure he now had. He took a wine appreciation course. He bought two seats at center court for Knicks games and a box for the Rangers. He arranged for their vacations, bought their theater and concert tickets, and began to keep up with art gallery openings. And he seemed to love Lee all the more for being the means by which he had secured everything he had ever dreamed of.

So with what little energy she had to spare, she took pains to hide her disapproval of his life. In fairness, if she did not love Jazz's choice, she still loved Jazz. It wasn't hard: In his custom-made suits, his gleaming brown hair growing fashionably long once more, he had gone from being good-looking to being devilishly handsome. Coming home from the D.A.'s, she was sometimes startled to discover the beauty of the man waiting for her. He remained an ardent and attentive lover. If he was not particularly inventive, at least he now had the time to read, and he bought books and videotapes and studied the arts and sciences of Eros so he might knock Lee's socks off. And when she was not in the mood—as she usually was not during the height of a homicide trial—he was the warmest and tenderest friend.

But her work was such a contrast to his. Unlike some of her male colleagues, Lee did not want a bubbly spouse to jolly her out of the black moods brought on by the horrors of the crimes she prosecuted. Rather than talk things out, and thus relive what she wanted to forget, she preferred to suffer in silence. There were nights, however, when she tiptoed out of bed, went into the bathroom, closed the door, and sobbed at the viciousness of what she had seen: tortured corpses, some of them women her age; photographs of children brutalized by the very people who were supposed to love them. Sometimes, though, she forced herself to remember. She would take a crime scene photo home with her to look at it last thing every night and first thing every morning while she was on trial—to remind her what she was fighting for. This isn't necessary, Jazz told her. It is, she said sadly. It is.

For the first half of 1976, his first six months with Le Fourreur, Jazz seemed content to live as they always had, albeit with better seats at sporting events. But by June, it was clear to Lee he wanted some changes made. Already drifting away from their classmates, he laid down the law on the matter of the Fourth of July: He absolutely did not want to go to a big, noisy keg party in someone's tiny apartment overlooking the Hudson River and watch fireworks. And he definitely did not want to trek to a mildewy house out in the Hamptons someone was renting for the month, to sleep in sleeping bags and get bagged on crappy Chablis. Okay, he was just twenty-six and maybe he was sounding like an old geezer but he was the president of a multimillion-dollar company. Not his, and—he was the first to admit it—he could never have done it on his own, and he didn't deserve it, but there it was. The fact: He was different from their old friends at law school and really didn't have that much in common with them anymore. At least, not enough to spend the Fourth of July of a lifetime with, the celebration he and Lee and the rest of America would always remember. Unless she really and truly *wanted* to go, and then of course he would, for her.

Lee did truly want to be with her law school pals, or with a group of assistant D.A.'s and cops who were planning a bash on Liberty Island, in the shadow of the Statue. But she knew Jazz now felt uncomfortable among lawyers. He saw himself through their eyes as a loser, a guy who couldn't cut it. Conspicuous by his comparative wealth. Made a target of gossip among their old classmates by his move out of the world of men and into the world of women—a move made more humiliating by his wife's success among the toughest of the tough guys.

They spent the Fourth with Leonard, Sylvia, Robin, the fur buyer from Lord & Taylor and a fashion writer from the *New York Times* and her whining husband and two sniveling children. Leonard hired a forty-foot sailboat and crew for the day at a stunning price, and they cruised along, watching the flotilla of tall ships and getting drunk on fresh salt air. That night, Greta made an all-American barbecue based on Sylvia's instructions for red and white food served on blue dishes. Lee did not have one moment of fun.

The following morning, Jazz drove her to the station for her train back into the city. She had a trial coming up, witnesses to prepare. Over and over she apologized for having to leave him, after she'd promised to take a few days off, stay out in Shorehaven, and play tennis at his folks' house.

"Don't apologize," Jazz told her as he pulled Leonard's Mercedes convertible into the parking lot. Even Lee thought he was being too tolerant. She had been the one who had made the big speech about having some balance in life, vowing she would take more time off. No more working on weekends, she had pledged. And if I don't get it done by eight or eight-thirty at night, it's not worth doing. Here she was, however, the only lawyer in America not on vacation, going back to Manhattan to interview a pickpocket, a chicken-hearted, mean-spirited liar who was her one eyewitness in what was going to be a miserable case to try.

"I can't *not* apologize," she said. "I feel terrible. But if I can't get this guy to tell a straight story, then there's no point bringing this to trial. So I'm sorry. And you're being absolutely wonderful about it."

"Thanks," Jazz said, a little absently.

"What's the matter?"

He glanced at his watch. "Your train is in two minutes. Better get going."

"Jazz ..."

"We'll talk tonight. I'll come back in around seven or eight. Maybe you can break away, and we can go out for dinner."

"Fine," Lee said. The door handle was in her grasp, but she let it go. "What's up?"

"Your train—"

"Forget it. I'll get the next one." Naturally, her stomach responded to her easygoing offer by immediately going into a spasm. The cop, the witness, everybody waiting for her, looking at their watches. "What's bothering you, Jazz?"

"I love it out here."

"I know." She smiled, indulgently. "Especially in the summer. But you love the city, too. Eight million stories, eight million movies, the theater, the Knicks—"

"Please, Lee." He took her hand between his and held it tight. "I want to *live* here."

"What?"

"I've made the best of the city, but I'm not a city guy."

"But, Jazz, I can't. Not now. I can't live here and be an A.D.A. in Manhattan. I have to reside in the jurisdiction. You know—"

But he wasn't listening. Or perhaps he knew so well what her objections would be that he didn't have to hear them. "I'm so miserable in New York. I want to be able to come home at night and breathe air that doesn't stink and see trees that aren't stunted. I need a break from the workaday grind. I know you think I've got it easy compared to you—"

"No, not at all."

"—but believe me, I feel I have to prove my worth every single day. And I'm good, really good. But it takes a toll. Why can't we come out here—"

"Don't you think commuting would take a toll?"

"Millions of people do it every day. You get to read the paper, do some work; it goes by like that." He snapped his fingers. It made a loud sound and she sat up straighter. "Your dad and I even talked a little about getting a driver, take the pressure off. So we wouldn't have to cope with sitting behind the wheel in traffic, and wouldn't have to be dependent on the Long Island Rail Road's whims. It would be the best thing in the world for me. And also, it would mean we could be near our families. I know, I know how much of your folks you can tolerate. The same with me and mine. But at least you'd be near Robin, now that she's a human being. And Kent. I know you worry about him a lot, and it kills me too, the way my parents ignore him. We could be there for him." He lifted her hand to his lips and kissed it. "I know it would mean a sacrifice to you. Your job. But you know you can't do the work you're doing and have a family. Isn't that something you want?"

"But we're only twenty-six!" ·

"So?"

"Do we have to do this now?"

"When, then?" He let go of her hand. His voice

took on a harsh, aggrieved edge she had never heard before. "Next year? Next decade? When will you have time for me?" She touched him on the shoulder, but he jerked away. "I've tried to support you in every way I can. But I need to know there's some mutuality at work, that I'm not the only one who gives and gives and gives."

"You think I'm crazy," Lee said to Melanie Tucker.

"Not at all," Melanie replied, rearranging her hand-kerchief in her cuff. "I think you're a fool."

"Oh," was all Lee could think to say.

They had deliberately chosen a deserted spot for dinner, a trendy place in TriBeCa where the chairs were made of rubber tubing. It was too expensive for cops and prosecutors. And at seven in the evening, it was far too early for the chic set who came for twenty-dollar variations on the sun-dried tomato.

"I don't see you rising to your own defense," Melanie observed.

"I'm too used to being the prosecutor. I'm cross-examining myself: How could you leave the best job in the world to be a furrier's wife on Long Island?"

"And your answer?"

"I have none." Lee moved an oily vegetable—on the menu it was called Sliced Sautéed Summer Squash in the Umbrian Manner—around her plate with a fork that resembled a hoe. "Well, maybe I'll find something in one of the law firms out there."

"That might be challenging," Melanie said in the upbeat manner of women who were girls in the fifties—with a rising lilt in a dead voice. A second later, she recovered; all she had learned since 1959 prevailed. "Personally, I don't think defending companies who corporately defecate in Long Island Sound will challenge you. But that isn't why I called you a fool."

Lee's fork pierced the squash. "All right? Why?"

"Because you are giving up everything you fought for and care about for a man."

"For a *marriage*."

"For a man who is eaten up by jealousy and for a marriage that—I'll understand if you never talk to me again—a marriage that will come to no good. Why move? You'll only want to come back. But then it will be too late."

Seventeen

❧

I had watched Norman Torkelson go from being the Cary Grant of the Nassau County Correctional Center to being just another dirty-nailed, unshaven con. Now he was at the third step: exactly where anyone in his right mind would be in similar circumstances: depressed. Not suburban depressed, with the standard loss of appetite or sleep troubles, the sort of malaise a little Prozac, a little therapy, or a new girlfriend can cure. No, this was the big-time despondency of a guy who was going to spend the next couple of decades in hell and emerge, somewhere around age fifty-five, an old man.

"Norman," I said, "we've got a trial date set."

"Okay." Just a wisp of the word came out; the rest lay heavy inside him. Sitting across the Formica barrier from me, slumped, round-shouldered, his head hanging down, you couldn't tell what a big man he was. Norman was fading, as prisoners do, out of the land of the living. No matter how long I practiced, I couldn't get used to seeing this kind of suffering. I guess it was the absolute loneliness of it that got to me. Sure, I knew many of my clients had inflicted much worse pain than this on their victims. Norman himself, even if he hadn't killed Bobette, had destroyed enough women's lives to deserve eternity in the worst jail there was. Nevertheless, part of me wished I could reach through the opening in the barrier and pat his cheek—just to let him feel human warmth.

But what I said was: "I think we should talk about whether or not you're going to take the stand." I waited for him to nod or give some indication he was hearing me. He just sat there, sagging, lifeless, as if he were the homicide victim. So I went on. "The reasons for you not to testify are obvious. You have a long record. And the sort of crimes you've been accused and convicted of aren't particularly sympathetic." That was putting it mildly. The twelve jurors would probably be shouting "Whoopee!" and giving each other high fives two minutes into deliberation—after their unanimous guilty vote. "Other than Mary—who I don't think would do well under cross-examination—is there anyone who could serve as a character witness for you?"

"No," he breathed. I waited for him to add something about moving too often to form close relationships, but he didn't seem to care anymore. He was beyond making excuses.

"I've been debating with myself whether we should risk trying to use your record to our advantage. I'd put you on the stand, have you admit to everything, tell them everything bad you've ever done. All to make one point: You never laid a hand on anybody. Of course," I added, thinking out loud, "what Holly Nuñez is going to say is that there's a first time for everything, that something went wrong with Bobette—"

"I didn't kill her," Norman said softly. Then he lifted his head and said it again. Tears were flooding down his face.

"I understand," I said, wishing he would wipe them away, or at least sniffle. "You've maintained your innocence all along. But if you didn't kill her, who did? Every time I bring up Mary's name you get furious. So I've stopped bringing it up. I'll do my best for you, but I can't hold out too much hope. I'm sorry."

"I know you're doing all that can be done, given these circumstances." He lifted a shoulder and used it to dry one of his cheeks, then did the same with the other side.

"I appreciate your confidence."

"I want to tell you what really happened."

I realized Norman was prepared to tell me something big, something new. I got that strange, anticipatory feeling I experience at moments of great drama. My senses grew sharper: I could eavesdrop on every lawyer-client conversation, all the guards' gossip, in the visitors room and not miss a word; read the entire "Visitors May Not Touch Inmates" sign, even the fine print; I could smell the menthol cough drop the lawyer three seats down was sucking. "I'm listening," I said.

"I know who killed Bobette," he said. I waited. I couldn't breathe. Then he whispered, "Mary," and began to cry again.

"Were you there when it happened?" I finally said. He shook his head slowly. Come on! I wanted to yell at him. Get a grip! *Talk* for God's sake! "No rush, Norman. Whenever you're ready."

"It was like I told you," he said at last. "I went out to buy the champagne. I told you that, didn't I? Like I always do. I leave and then come back. That calms their worst fear, that I am who I really am, that I'll take their money and leave town. So I went out, bought the champagne—"

"Do you remember where you bought it?"

"What? No, not the name of the store. But it was in a little shopping center about a mile away."

"You could tell me how to get there?" He nodded. "Do you think anyone there might remember you?"

"Maybe. Because of my height. And when I bought the champagne, it was expensive and the guy said something like 'This must be an important celebration.'" Norman started to cry again. No sobs this time, just a quiet dribble of tears. "I'm just telling you this because I . . . Who the hell knows? I can't stand having it inside me. But understand: you can't do anything about this. Even if you wanted to, what could be done? Even if I wanted to betray Mary—and I'm telling you, I don't—no one would believe me. Sure, her prints are there, but so are mine. And the marks on her neck. Even if I swore 'She did it,' they'd think I was full of it because of what I am." He swallowed. "I'm a con man. A professional liar. So what I'm saying is just for you."

"Go on," I said, trying to recall if the autopsy report mentioned anything about skin cells under Bobette's nails or any possible DNA evidence that would corroborate Norman's statement.

"Just for you," he repeated. "You're my lawyer. Anything I say to you is confidential." He wiped the tears away, this time with his hands. "Anyhow, I got back and went into the house."

"You had a key?"

"No. I'd pushed the little gizmo on the side of the door so it wouldn't lock. The door was open. I went in. I remember, I was calling out, 'Bunny'—that was my nickname for her. 'Bunny, if you have two glasses, I have a bottle of champagne.' Except I never finished the sentence." He rubbed his chin. I could hear the rough scratch of his beard.

"She was dead?"

"Yes. I knew right away."

"And Mary?"

"Standing there. Hysterical. Trying to talk."

"What was she trying to say?"

" 'I'm sorry! I'm sorry!' "

"To Bobette?"

"No, to me. I started saying, 'Why? Why?' But then I realized I had to get her out of there. I didn't know if she'd fought with Bobette and if there had been a ruckus someone could have heard. Even just her hysterics. She was getting louder and louder: If someone was passing by the house, or if for some reason the tenant came home . . . I *had* to move, so I grabbed her and pulled her out of the house."

"You didn't touch anything?"

He closed his eyes as if viewing the scene. "I bent over to see if there was a chance Bobette was still alive. Objectively, I knew she was dead. But I thought, well, maybe if the breathing was suppressed or something, I could call 911 and get out of there before they came. I may . . . I think I may have held her face in my hands." He shuddered. "Already, it was colder than a face should be. You know?"

"You didn't touch her neck?"

"I don't think so."

"Then what?"

"I took Mary by the arm and I pulled her toward the door."

"The front door?"

"Initially. But then—I couldn't believe this. She sticks her hand in her pocketbook, one of those shoulder bags, and takes out a tissue and starts wiping the doorknob and the thing where you turn on the lights."

"The switch plate?"

"Right. I knew the more we did, the longer we stayed there, the more chance there'd be for leaving some trace. So I grabbed the tissue. I was going to use it to open the door, but then I realized it would be stupid for us to be seen walking out the front together. Mary's—you know—noticeable. I was already thinking I didn't want anyone to think in terms of the, uh, crime committed by a man with a woman. I wanted Mary completely out of the picture. So I led her out the back door. I used the tissue to open and close it."

"Then what?"

"Then I went toward the front. I took a quick look around. No one was there. So I got her into my car and we drove home."

I waited. What was I expecting to hear? We lived happily ever after? Norman did look better for having opened up, that much I noticed. The crying had stopped, and some color had returned to his face. Still, he seemed feeble, as if trying to get back his strength after a terrible illness.

"When did you talk to Mary?"

"When we got home. She was too hysterical in the car."

"What did she say?"

"That Bobette had come down and surprised her. Started shouting at her: 'Get out!' That's the one thing that sets Mary off. Shouting."

"It makes her violent?"

"No. Not with me, anyway. We've had a couple of fights, and I've raised my voice, and all that happens is she"—he swallowed hard at some sad memory—"falls apart. But I think if someone else is yelling . . . I mean, that incident in Maryland."

"That incident where she beat up Carolyn Knowles," I elaborated. "Brain concussion, a couple of cracked ribs, facial contusions."

"Yes."

"Did Mary and Bobette argue? Did Bobette know her connection with you?"

"I don't know. I don't think so. All Mary told me was about the yelling, that all of a sudden she was on a different planet or something. She didn't know what she was doing until ..." His hand drifted up and softly touched his Adam's apple. "Until she looked down and saw the thing she was holding between her hands and shaking was Bobette's neck. I probably walked in a few minutes later."

"How long were you away when you went to get the champagne?" I asked.

"Fifteen, twenty minutes."

"You drove away. Mary probably went in right after you left. She surprised Bobette. Right? Strangled her. Bobette's strong, but so is Mary—taller, in much better shape. Did she have any bruises, by the way?"

"Bobette? I didn't notice any."

"No, Mary. Any signs of a struggle, of Bobette fighting back? Black-and-blue marks—"

"On her wrists," Norman admitted sorrowfully.

"So what happened next? You're back home. Is Mary still hysterical?"

"Close. I calmed her down a little. I kept saying: 'I know it's not your fault.'" I thought—as I often do when listening to accounts of my clients' lives—how pleasant it must be to receive such easy absolution. "Finally, she stopped crying," Norman continued. "I put her to bed, tried to give her a sleeping pill—"

"You have trouble sleeping? Or does she?"

Norman shook his head. "Neither of us. It's just sometimes . . . Sometimes I slip a pill—a capsule I open up—into whatever the lady I'm working on is drinking. I mean, if she's staying up late and being boring and I want to get home. I always carry a couple in my wallet. Anyway, Mary is very antidrug and said no. So I sat with her until she dozed off."

"Then what?"

"Then . . . nothing."

"You stayed home? Watched TV?"

"No. I went out and drove around. Tried to think."

"How long were you gone?"

"I don't know. Hours. It was pretty early—around six-thirty, seven, at night—when I found Mary at Bobette's. But by the time I got back home it was already getting light."

"Where did you drive?"

"I don't remember. I know I wound up on the New York Thruway. Finally, I got so exhausted, I pulled off into one of those service areas, where the Dunkin' Donuts and Burger Kings are all in one building, and had some coffee. Then I turned around and came home."

"And then?"

"Nothing. I told her we had to get out of town. Not that they could trace me, but why hang around Long Island longer than necessary. I wanted to leave then, but Mary was so shaken—she kept falling apart, crying hysterically. Then she got a bad period. So I made the mistake of letting her rest. We were going to leave first thing Tuesday morning, like at five-thirty, and go somewhere warm. San Diego, I was thinking. Once we got out of New York, we'd ditch the car I was driving and buy a new one."

"You had the cash Bobette drew out of the bank?"

"Yes."

"You opened the envelopes the cash was in?" He nodded. I was relieved to see he wasn't lying; his fingerprints had been on the tape that had sealed the bank envelopes. "Where did you open them?"

"At Bobette's."

"How come?"

"Just to make sure she gave me what she said she

would. I always do that. Hold up the envelope and make some little joke about can't wait to see the money that's going to change my life. Ninety-nine times out of a hundred, the lady will say: 'Open it.' Sometimes they're nervous about me. They go to the bank but only take out part of what they promised. But I always check. If I catch them, believe me, they're always ready to run back and get the rest."

I was feeling uneasy. Tales of masochistic women always make me uneasy, and unease makes me think of food. I had a little bag with a yogurt and a plastic spoon in my attaché case. Vanilla. I kept wishing I could open it up and gobble it down. "So, Norman," I said, trying very hard to forget the yogurt, "unless I can get you an acquittal or keep hanging juries until Holly Nuñez gets worn out, you're going to go to jail for a crime you didn't commit."

"Yes." His spine seemed to crumple, but he did not cry again.

I sat quietly for a minute and looked down at my hands, trying to assimilate everything Norman had told me and trying to forget I wanted to eat. My latest diet book said hunger pangs last only ten to twelve minutes. Think of something else: I noticed that I had chipped the nail on my right index finger, that I had what appeared to be a smudge of breakfast cottage cheese on my watchband, and that even under the harsh prison lights, I still did not have any brown age spots. By the time I looked back at him, I knew: "You're not telling me the whole story, Norman."

He didn't pretend to be stunned, and he didn't act as though I'd hurt him to the quick. "What do you think I didn't tell you?"

"Look, you and I seem to be playing poker now. So I'm not going to show you my hand. You tell me what you left out." It would be nice to say I knew precisely what he was holding back, but I didn't. I just had a strong sense that Bobette didn't simply surprise Mary, yell at her to get out, and then get strangled. It was too pointless. Yes, I know homicide often is pointless, to say nothing of stupid, but this story didn't quite add up to the usual senselessness.

"I think they must have had words."

"About what? You?" Norman nodded yes. "Somehow, Bobette found out that this intruder was connected to you?" When he didn't respond, I asked: "What were the words they had about?"

"Getting married," he muttered.

And then I was sure I knew. "You *were* going to marry Bobette, weren't you?"

"Yes," he said softly. "We got the license that day, before we went to the bank."

"If you were marrying her, why did you want the cash?"

"I just wanted it, free and clear. For all I knew, she could turn out to be a cheapskate. I mean, she kept saying she wanted me to take over everything for her so she could be—you know—a housewife. I'd oversee the bars, collect the rents and manage the properties. But I couldn't be sure. I figured if it turned out she wouldn't let me take over, I'd know in a couple of weeks. That way, I wouldn't have to hang around waiting for crumbs. I could leave and still have close to fifty thou."

"What were you planning on doing with Mary?"

"Nothing. I mean, we'd keep on like always. I'd be out all day, tell Bobette I was seeing to business. But I'd spend the whole day with Mary—and whatever nights I could. It wouldn't be ideal but ..." He wrapped his arms around himself. "I needed to rest for a year or two. To put my life on hold. I love Mary with all my heart, but I couldn't keep running around the country doing what I was doing, like I was still a kid. Being World's Greatest Lover to a bunch of ladies who . . . forgive me, but who I didn't give a shit about. Setting up the Love Nest over and over in every damn new town. Wading through the responses to my personals ads. I had been doing it so long. There was no fun left. Maybe because I really was in love. That's the kicker, isn't it? I'm in love with Mary, in love for the first time in my life. So what do I do? Get ready to marry someone else."

"Did Mary know?"

"I told her the night before." He looked away and mumbled to the floor: "I guess that was a mistake."

"I guess so."

"But listen, I swore to her nothing would change. All it would mean was that for a while she'd have to spend the nights without me. But in terms of real time, I'd be with her *more* than ever before. And then, in a year or two, I'd start making it so tough on Bobette that she'd pay me big bucks just to get out. Then Mary and I could go someplace, and I'd never have to work the ladies again." His eyes grew filmy. "We could have had a beautiful life."

"Except Mary didn't see it that way."

"No. She didn't believe me when I told her I would always be true to her." Norman looked me right in the eye. "But I will be."

"You could've knocked me over with a feather!" Terry Salazar said the next morning. Terry's life is a series of brief but passionate romances with clichés; he meets a new one, hangs around awhile, then moves on to the next. He'd been getting knocked over by feathers for the past couple of months, and it was starting to irritate me.

"There I was, in the county clerk's office, looking at this piece of paper that actually says that Bobette Frisch and Denton Wylie are okay to get married in New York State, and I'm thinking: Holy shit! Haul out the smelling salts! The guy told the truth for once in his life."

"All right," I said, swiveling back and forth in my desk chair. It's the sort of motion you see in the movies, big tycoons twirling from side to side, a phone in one hand, a cigar in the other. But it soothes me and helps me think when I'm feeling pressured. "This makes me so nervous. I hate it when I think a client is innocent. I mean, not guilty is different; that I can deal with. I *like* knowing someone has a real defense for the crime he's accused of, that I don't have to get overly creative. But actually innocent?" I shuddered. It was only part pretense.

"You think he's conning you, Lee?"

"How would I know? That's the whole point, isn't it?"

"Take me with you to see him. I'll let you know." Terry noticed I was looking on my desk for something to throw at him. "I'm not saying you're not smart. You are."

"Especially compared to present company."

Terry seemed to think I was engaging in banter, not truth telling, so he gave me his wink-grin combo. "But you're a *woman*," he insisted. "That's his specialty. Conning women."

"Stop it. I'm a criminal defense lawyer. I can't get through a day without someone trying to con me. Let's just dope this out." Terry looked agreeable. He loved long, meandering discussions—and why shouldn't he have, at his hourly rate? "Norman Torkelson used the name Denton Wylie with Bobette."

"Right," he said.

"Is there any possibility at all that there was a real Denton, that Norman is or was pulling some sort of scam involving a real person—or a dead person—that's beyond my ability to comprehend?"

"I can't see how. This Denton who applied for the marriage license gave his age as thirty-five, which is what Norman says he is. Now, objectively, Norman looks about thirty-five, doesn't he?"

"Somewhere around there," I agreed.

"And the lovely Bobette gave her real age: fifty-four. That is not your usual age difference: a dried-up old prune with a guy nineteen years younger, so already it sounds for real." Since by his standards I would be a dried-prune in nine years, I gave him a dirty look, which of course delighted him. "Also, there's the whole section of the marriage license application form that has to be filled in on former spouses. Bobette's is blank. Our pal Denton has one former." Terry consulted his little spiral notepad. "Lorinda Maddox Wylie in Westchester. Salem. It matches perfectly with his story about having a rich-bitch ex up in Westchester, except I checked. Lorinda—Maddox or Wylie or both—doesn't exist. The address he gave, White Horse Farm on Winding Way, doesn't exist. Winding Way doesn't even exist." Most investigators could have come up with this information, but it would take them two weeks. Terry had gotten it in a couple of hours, which was one of the reasons I put up with him. "You want me to bottom-line it, Lee?"

"Go ahead."

"Norman made Lorinda up. He made Denton Wylie up. So Denton Wylie does equal Norman Torkelson."

"Would you put money on that?" I asked him. "*Your* money?"

"Yeah." Terry took out his wallet. Instead of the five-dollar bill I expected, he counted out five twenties and slapped them on my desk. Then I was sure Norman Torkelson and Denton Wylie were one and the same.

* * *

I worked on some other cases the rest of the morning. Instead of going over to the Bar Association for lunch, I ordered in and went into Chuckie's office and watched my cooking shows on his TV. There was a French guy I was in love with—he got very passionate about using veal bones in chicken stock—but I had also taken a shine to an extroverted Chinese guy who was really cute with his cleaver. I was mulling over dinner, what to stew in a clay pot, when I realized I had one big fat ethical problem: What do you do if you believe a client is innocent but he is insisting on taking the rap for the guilty party and ordering you, his attorney, to keep quiet? Abide by lawyer-client confidentiality? Or figure that a larger principle is at stake—Justice—and that your first duty as an officer of the court is not to let an innocent man pay for a crime he didn't commit. Or try something sneaky. I called Holly Nuñez.

"Lee! Hi!" Now that a trial day was set and she was convinced she was going to nail Norman but good, her bubbliness knew no limits. "How *are* you? God, won't it be great to go out and have a drink together when all this is over?"

I admit I did stick my index finger into my mouth and make a gagging gesture, but I said: "I look forward to it. Speaking of the Torkelson case, I was wondering if you ever ran that other set of prints."

"We did!"

"Good!" I enthused back, thinking that if I actually did go to trial, I'd have to start hormone replacement therapy immediately. "What did you find?"

"They belong to a woman named"—I waited while she made noises with paper, pretending to look—"Marissa Shaw."

"The thing is, Holly, you're supposed to tell me about this."

"You beat me to the punch! I was going to call you this afternoon!" She read me all the stuff I already knew from Terry's investigation about the altercation in Maryland, with Mary as Marissa beating up Carolyn Knowles.

"Do you know who Marissa Shaw is?" I inquired.

"Do you have something to tell me?" Holly countered, with perky anticipation, as if I were about to impart some marvelous cheerleading secret.

So I told her that Mary/Marissa was a single dame. And what do you know, the man who bolted, the man whom Carolyn Knowles was set to marry, known as Arthur Berringer, was none other than six-foot-five Norman Torkelson. "Do you see a parallel, Holly?"

"Between what and what?" she asked.

I finished explaining twenty minutes later, and as I'd feared, it got me absolutely nowhere. She remained convinced Norman killed Bobette. The fact that he had a girlfriend who had once, as Holly put it, "blown her top" was of no interest to her. I urged her, then begged her, to at least interview Mary, but all she said was that she was "crazed, absolutely crazed" with work and couldn't find the time.

I put in a call to the chair of the Bar Association's Ethics Committee to sound him out about being able to tell Holly that Norman had admitted to me that Mary killed Bobette, but I had little hope on that score. He'd probably tell me to withdraw from the case and hint to Norman not to confide in his next lawyer. Even if he said to go ahead, you can talk, the chance that Holly would buy Norman's Mary-did-it confession was nil. And I knew the chance of my going over her head to the D.A., Woodleigh Huber, who not only was stupid, ambitious, and venal but couldn't stand me, was nil squared.

I left the office and picked up a cold bottle of Chardonnay and a corkscrew, then two cappuccinos. I figured one or the other would get me into Mary's apartment. Sure enough, the wine worked. "We don't have wineglasses. Just champagne glasses." She took out a couple of the old-style ones, the kind that are shaped like birdbaths. "I told Norman, we can't keep doing this forever, you know." She had just given herself a pedicure. The smell of polish permeated the room. A rolled-up sheet of paper towel, wound between her toes, was keeping them apart and the raspberry polish from smudging. "I want my own things. I want my own dishes. I want to pick out the pattern."

"It's nice to be settled in one place, with things you like, people you love."

"Silverware. And wineglasses, all the different kinds. You ever see when they show fancy tables in magazines? They have three or four different glasses. And a water goblet too." She was wearing a denim minidress with a lot of industrial zippers in what seemed to me to be useless places. Her hair was held back with a matching denim headband. "Do you want some honey-roasted peanuts?" I shook my head. "Pringles?"

"No thanks. How are you doing, Mary?"

"Fine," she said, but she was edgy. She couldn't seem to concentrate on anything, or to sit still. She showed me a project she was working on, a fabric-covered shoebox she was decorating with miniature fake seashells and a glue gun. She lost interest in it quickly and moved over to a laundry basket and began folding washcloths and towels, but that didn't last long. Then she searched the living room and the little galley kitchen for a bag of cheddar popcorn she was positive she'd bought. "I *know* I bought it," she told me. "It's a black, shiny bag. I didn't eat it, and I bought it after Norman . . . " All of a sudden, like a balloon losing air, she rushed around the room until finally, spent, she collapsed in an armchair.

"It's such a strain, isn't it, Mary . . . "

"Yes," she said, in a peculiar, high-pitched tone, as if she had something more to add to the sentence.

Then I realized it was because she didn't want to hear what I was going to say next: " . . . knowing Norman is going to be in prison for such a long, long time."

"Don't you think you can get him off?"

"It's possible. Not at all likely."

"I love him," she explained, as if letting me in on this for the first time.

"I know you do. I know it's breaking your heart to see him cooped up in that jail for a crime he may not have committed."

"He didn't!"

"I can't get anyone to believe that, Mary. I wish I could. But his record is working against him. And worse, all the facts are against him."

"What facts?" she demanded angrily. "There aren't any *facts*."

"There's an eyewitness who puts him at the scene very near the time of the murder. Now, I know you were there, too, but no one knows about it. And for all I know, there may have been other people there, but no one knows about them either. Only about Norman. And then there are his fingerprints."

"But mine are there too!"

"But no one thinks you did it, Mary. They all think Norman did it."

"But he'll get on the stand and swear—"

"He has a long record for fraud. As a con man. Even if I let him take the stand, there's very little hope anyone would believe him." I took a deep breath. "Of course, he has no history of ever hurting anyone."

"He wouldn't touch a fly!"

"But you . . . you have a history." For a moment, I thought she was going to spring out of her chair and go for me. Her eyes flashed: How dare you! I regretted all the adult-ed self-defense courses I never took. But the fire left her eyes, and she simply sat back in the big chair looking weary, somewhere between a tired child and an exhausted hooker. "You lost it with Carolyn Knowles." She bowed her head slightly: Yes. "And you lost it with Bobette." Her head came up. Her eyes widened. "Didn't you, Mary? Didn't you panic because you knew Norman was actually going to marry her? You waited till he left, and when you went in you lost it. You must have been overwhelmed with feeling, and you just fell apart."

"No!"

"I think it's 'yes.'" She turned her head away from me fast, and looked out past her shoulder. But she was staring at a blank wall. "It must have been an awful feeling."

Just when I thought I would be talking till I was blue in the face, she whispered, "Yes."

I forced myself not to move, not even to breathe. I kept my voice as soft as I could. "And it must be hell, every day. Thinking that Norman is getting blamed for something you did. Thinking how deeply he loves you, and how much he must be suffering for that love."

"Oh, Jesus God!" she cried out, and covered her face.

"I know you want to help him."

"I do!" she said, her voice muffled by her big hands.

I walked over and sat beside her on the arm of her chair. I wanted to pat her on the head, but I was afraid that she'd get upset if I messed up her hairdo. So rather awkwardly, I patted her shoulder. "There's only one way you can help the man who loves you so much."

It took her a moment, but she finally said: "By telling the truth."

"That's right. By telling the truth. That you killed Bobette Frisch." She nodded. Yes. I did. But I had to hear it. No, I had to make her say it. If I couldn't convince her to get it out at that moment, she would never do it in front of Holly. "It must be so awful for you, to have this burden. You're such a wonderful, sweet young woman."

"Thank you," she said in a little voice.

"Tell me what happened that evening."

"Like I told you. I was there that afternoon, watching them through a window. Not that I really saw anything much. Norman just opened up the envelopes from the bank. Those brown envelopes they give you." I waited. "He took out the money. It made a big wad. Then he kissed her." She shivered, as if recalling something hideous, unnatural.

"Was it more of a kiss than you expected?" I asked, keeping my tone as soothing as I could.

"Yes. And . . . I mean, it was like he was *enjoying* it. I know he's a good actor with them. He has to be. He told me: 'Sometimes they make me want to vomit, but they think I'm wild for them.' But I *know* him."

"And this time he didn't want to vomit?"

"No! He kept kissing her, and kissing her and finally *she* pushed him away. But he kept going after her. And then . . . " She couldn't speak.

"Did they have sex?" I recalled there was no evidence of intercourse on the autopsy report.

"No. She sat back on the couch, that cow, and *let* him kiss her for a while. Like she was doing him a favor. Then she pushed him off again and got up. He got up and followed her into the kitchen. Like he couldn't stand to let her out of his sight. I couldn't see them in the kitchen, because there's a big window there and they would have seen me out there. Anyway, the next thing I know, I heard him go out."

"That's when he went to get the champagne?"

"Yes."

"Did you go right in?"

"After his car left, I counted to two minutes. One-chimpanzee, two-chimpanzee . . . Then I went in."

"Which door?"

"The front. I told you, he doodled the button."

"I remember. Where was she?"

"I heard her clomping up the stairs to take a shower. So then, you know, I went through her things."

"Took her credit cards."

"Her whole wallet. She had over seven hundred dollars in cash, besides the cards! And then I heard her, so I ran downstairs."

"And she came down?"

"A little later. Wearing this ugly negligee. I mean, can you picture a cow in a lavender negligee? I mean, it got me so mad! How could he marry her? She's old enough to be his mother. How could he want to . . . I saw the way he kissed her. It was like it didn't bother him. Like he . . . liked it! Like he wanted more. And then I was standing in this little, like, vestibule, right by the front door, kind of peeking out but hiding and she's in the living room, and all of a sudden she says: 'Who's there?' In this big, scary voice. You wouldn't believe how scared I was! And then she comes running over and sees me and grabs me by the arm. She hurt me! She was screaming: 'Who the hell are you? What do you want in my house?'"

Mary started to shake violently, almost as though she was going through it all over again. "Take it easy," I soothed. "You're doing fine. What happened next?"

"I pushed her away, and she went, you know, like backwards into the living room. I felt better, because I'd been so scared she was going to beat me up. Or kill me."

I assumed this was Mary's way of testing to see if a

self-defense theory would fly. I just said: "It must have been terrible. What happened? Did you follow her into the living room?"

"I guess I must have. I mean, all of a sudden there I was, standing right in front of her. By the couch. She was screaming that she didn't have the money anymore, that someone had taken it. I guess she thought that's why I was there. That some way I found out that she took all the money out of the bank. Then she started screaming at me again to get out. And louder, because I was right next to her. And she had this pukey bad breath, and I was thinking: How could he kiss her? And then all of a sudden she stopped screaming and moved back. She was trying to run away. But I grabbed her." So much for a self-defense theory, I thought. "And she got all panicked. I mean, you could see it in her eyes. Like I was going to hurt her. And she started begging me: 'Please, please, I'll give you anything you want. I can get money—'" Mary started to shake again, and this time she gulped huge, terrified mouthfuls of air.

I knew I had to get her through, to the end. "She offered you money," I said, as though this was a terrible affront.

"I said, 'I don't want your fucky money, you fat old bitch.' Then she started acting real scared. And like, instead of that awful, scary voice, she sounded so pathetic. 'Please don't hurt me! Please!' I swear, I wasn't going to hurt her. But she kept begging me and begging me, and finally I just wanted to shut her up. So I grabbed her."

"Her neck?"

"And the next thing I knew, her tongue was out, and then I put her down on the floor 'cause she was so heavy and she was . . . "

"Say it, Mary."

"Dead."

Eighteen

✕

"How *nice*," said the real estate agent as he drove Lee and Jazz around the Estates section of Shorehaven. "That is what I call a *love* story." Mr. Chadman, for that was his name, then sang a few bars of "The Boy Next Door." He liked to think of himself as a late-twentieth-century incarnation of a Victorian eccentric, whimsical yet lovable.

When they passed the modern stone and glass house that Sylvia, Leonard and Robin White lived in, he nodded in its direction and decreed: "An important house." Its importance had to do not with the family that lived inside or the house's architectural distinction but with the fact that in that year, 1976, it would have brought at least half a million dollars had it been put up for sale.

"Important," of course, was too small a word for Hart's Hill. Mr. Chadman stopped his car in front of the driveway, gazed greedily through the trees that obscured the house, and remarked: "What *can* one say?" He twisted around to pay homage to Jazz, who was sitting in the back seat.

"One can say we're looking in the wrong neighborhood," Lee remarked. All right: Her temper was a little short. But there she was, stuck in the passenger seat beside the agent—a place she did not want to be. To be honest, Shorehaven was a place she did not want to be. But Jazz, of all people, had pronounced Connecticut too Wasp and Westchester too pretend-Wasp. New Jersey, he declared, was overrun with unassimilated members of obscure ethnic groups—none of whom could be trusted behind the wheel of a car. As for Long Island, all the towns other than Shorehaven were either glitzy or overly quaint or run-down. In the end, Lee had let him have his way. She knew she had lost the Battle of Manhattan and, as prisoner of war, her fate was in the hands of her captor. Nevertheless, she realized he was a captor who was generous in victory. Whatever you want, he kept telling her. Colonial. Tudor. Ranch. What she didn't want was a house within shouting distance of his and her parents—not that she could picture any of them shouting. "We really can't afford—" she tried to explain to Mr. Chadman, trying for honeyed tones to soothe whatever raw spot her last outburst had left.

"Trust me, my dear, if I may say 'my dear' without sounding like one of those male chauvinist pigs. 'Afford' is not the issue here." Lee and Jazz each suppressed a smile and took comfort in knowing that the other was doing likewise. "I have your dream house. Just on the market. Part of the old Howell estate. Finally subdivided now that old Mr. Howell passed on, may his soul find eternal rest. It was his estate manager's cottage." He made a quick right after Hart's Hill, then another, and bounced up a badly rutted road. "On the high end of your budget, maybe a tad over. But one must pay for charm."

"I don't think—" Jazz began as they drove under a canopy of elms.

"We don't want to live quite so close to where we grew up," Lee explained diplomatically as they passed a flame euonymus, so brilliant that its redness made her turn away. "We were thinking that some other area of Shorehaven—"

But they fell into silence as the car pulled up before their dream house. "Hey," Jazz said softly. "I never knew this existed."

"This place, it's . . . " Lee was going to say "perfect," but Mr. Chadman sat beside her, his chin raised in smug triumph, and she could not bear to give him the satisfaction. She turned back to the house. Not very big, built entirely of large, irregularly shaped stones held in place by gold-colored mortar. Nestled in a grassy glen, circled by ancient oaks and sycamores, it looked like an illustration for a fairy tale—a cheery, revisionist, non-Grimm tale, to be sure—with its quirky tilted chimney, windows like shining eyes, and a wide, welcoming red wood door. Rambling ruby roses climbed up the right side of the house. Nice, she decided to say to Mr. Chadman. No: Charming. Or maybe give the pompous ass Sweet. But before she could stop it, "Beautiful!" fell out of her mouth. Three months later, after the painters and floor sanders left and the carpenter screwed the final knob onto the last kitchen cabinet, they moved into the most wonderful house in the world.

Right before they moved, Lee made it clear to Jazz that she would not give up the law. Furthermore, she was not interested in some tame suburban lady-lawyer position—assisting a matrimonial specialist or pushing papers across a table at real-estate closings. No, she wanted to be in court. As a prosecutor. However, the district attorney of Nassau County was a Republican. So without even consulting Jazz, Lee went directly to her father-in-law and asked him to use his influence in securing her an appointment as token Democrat.

Fos told Ginger he was at least grateful someone connected with the Taylors was an attorney. What Jazz had done rankled him. He had not expected much from his daughters, and he had not gotten it: One did little but play tennis and golf and, at thirty-two, had skin like that on her brown alligator pumps. The other was becoming a hunchback, picking cucumbers on a commune. Kent was useless. But his Jasper! Fos was not merely anguished but infuriated by his son's new life: Leaving Wall Street! To take up with garment center types. He could not for the life of him understand it.

While ten generations of Long Island inbreeding may have diminished the once soaring Taylor IQ, Fos was no dummy. He was smart enough to realize that his favor-seeking daughter-in-law was not a party to Jazz's idiot decision. Further, Fos sensed that Lee might be an ally. Woo Jazz back to where he belonged. It would be such a relief, when the fellows on the Committee or at Rolling Hills inquired, How's that fine son of yours coming along?, not to have to go mumble mumble . . . fur coats . . . mumble, feeling he would die of humiliation. Accordingly, he was not only vaguely fond of Lee but also not unwilling to help her. In addition, while not a bighearted man, Fos was worldly enough to know that there are certain requests that cannot be denied. Since he could not dream of telling the future mother of his grandchildren to go stuff it, he picked up the phone and spent half a morning being jovial to a few of his fellow Republicans who, only recently, had been badgering him for myriad courtesies at the games in Montreal—and who owed him. He hated to waste his IOUs on a cause not his own, but that could not be helped. And so, two days later, Lee was face-to-face with the district attorney of Nassau County, Woodleigh Huber, in his office.

And what an office! Oak-paneled, with a desk so monumental it seemed that nothing less than a manned rocket to Mars or the D-day invasion should be launched from it. Behind it, three eight-foot flags, representing the county, the State of New York, and the United States of America, stood proudly against a blue-draped wall.

"*Homicide?*" Huber inquired.

"Homicide," Lee affirmed. That was what she wanted. And she had done her homework: The Nassau District Attorney's Office was considered middling to good—except for its Homicide unit. That was reported to be first-rate.

"Homicide," Huber sighed. If he was not incredulous, he was at least dismayed. "It isn't that I don't think you're up to it. I hear nothing but good things about you: smart, straightforward, no fancy footwork, but delivers the goods. What you've got to understand, though, is that this is not New York City." He nodded his agreement with himself, and his shock of white hair flapped in approval. Huber was a handsome fellow, high-colored and square-jawed. He looked like an actor hired to play the President of the United States for a television movie of the week. Seated as he was between his grand old flags and his important desk, his every action seemed calculated for a photo op. But if his moves appeared false and contrived that was not the entire Woodleigh Huber story. He did care that the District Attorney's Office was perceived as a fine one and, in fact, worked hard, if not entirely successfully, to achieve that goal. "Our jurors aren't so—shall we say—sophisticated as the ones you're used to."

Lee smiled. "I guess you haven't seen a Manhattan petit jury recently."

"I think what the Boss is getting at," Jerry McCloskey interpreted, "is that it might be too *upsetting* to a suburban-type jury to have a woman representing the People in a homicide trial." He was a squat pale mushroom of a man, who appeared to be the quintessential political gofer, existing solely to say or do anything his patron found unpleasant. "I don't have to tell you homicides can get pretty gory."

"So can rape. I hear you have a woman in your Sex Crimes unit."

"We do indeed!" Woodleigh Huber said, in the powerful voice he dreamed would be heard on a segment of *60 Minutes*. "Portrait of a Crime Fighter" he imagined it would be called. "Bonnie Brinkerhoff. Soft as a marshmallow outside but when she walks into that courtroom . . . hard as nails. A hell of a lawyer. I mean that." Lee nodded. She had heard Brinkerhoff was, on her occasional good days, mediocre and had inherited the job when the man who had previously held it was run over by his lawn mower. "Believe me, we welcome you women. We think you're a tremendous addition to the team. Tremendous."

"Except this is the thing," McCloskey explained. He smelled a little stale, as if he or his suit was overdue for a cleaning. "We're full up in our Homicide unit right now." Like Lee, McCloskey sat in a straight-backed chair before Huber's desk. Unlike Lee, McCloskey was perched on the edge of the hard seat, as if not high enough in rank to have the right to rest his entire backside. "Full up to the gills." Huber nodded.

Lee thought fast. If they were full up in Homicide,

that meant they were going to put her someplace else, some less plummy unit. But she was in, it seemed. Hired! A prosecutor again! Foster Taylor had come through for her! He'd had the clout. And if he had the clout to get her—a Democrat, a woman—the job, he must have been owed some big favors. So big, she suddenly realized, that the job had probably been hers before she set foot in the office. Before she could get cold feet, Lee turned from McCloskey to his master and blurted: "Give me a month's trial in Homicide."

"As Jerry mentioned—"

She cut him off. "I know how competitive it is, getting a spot in the unit." Huber's mouth compressed in annoyance until his near-lipless mouth was merely the width of a paper cut. "And because Homicide is so good, so public, that's all the more reason to give me a shot. If I can't cut it, I'll be glad to try cases elsewhere. But if I'm as capable as your background check suggests I am, then I can make the unit's statistics look even better."

"Well . . ." Huber mused.

Out of the corner of her eye, Lee saw McCloskey inch even closer to the edge of the seat. Had she gone too far? Had he gotten some signal and was he getting ready to show her the door? McCloskey didn't like her, she could tell. Why should he? She did not belong in his scheme of things, in which deserving people got what they deserved—and Woodleigh Huber received chits from them for future favors. True, Huber must have owed Foster Taylor or a Foster Taylor friend something major and had to pay up. But Lee understood that a two-bit pol like McCloskey would know in his bones that no further benefit would accrue from putting her in Homicide: Lee White would feel she owed the District Attorney her best efforts, nothing more. *Ipso facto*, a stinko deal. "Listen, Boss," McCloskey began.

But the Boss had already filled his lungs to declaim, and McCloskey lost his chance. "You've got one month, Lee," Huber said resonantly, imagining introducing her to Ed Bradley or Mike Wallace. A younger member of our Homicide unit. Nonpartisan. As you can see for yourself, it doesn't matter here if you're male or female, black or white or green. What matters is what you *do*. And this girl's won major cases. Toughies. He could hear Lee saying, I may be a Democrat, Ed, but this man is beyond politics. "Jer," Huber commanded, "bring her downstairs."

"Downstairs, Boss?" McCloskey asked, but without much hope.

"To Homicide. To Will Stewart."

William Hibbets Stewart was definitely not handsome, even though everyone would give you an argument that he was. He had a round face that lacked even a single arresting angle; small, undistinguished eyes; and a too awesome nose, big and down curving, a signal that one of his African ancestors had gotten quite friendly with an individual of Arab descent. But as she stood where she and McCloskey had run into him, right outside his office, Lee judged he was well over six feet tall. Imposingly built too, with shoulders so broad they were parallel to the floor. His skin was richly dark, somewhere between ebony and mahogany. His body, the ideal male V, was slim and muscular, and his carriage was so regal that even one of his most culturally illiterate colleagues had been heard to say: Will's like one of those, uh, African statues or somethin'.

What made Will Stewart a standout, however, was his elegance. It was the real thing. He was beautifully dressed, in a gray suit, white shirt, and burgundy tie, all so simple and yet somehow she knew: the best there was. Yet his bearing had nothing to do with money. Leonard's Savile Row suits and hand-stitched shoes made her father look like nothing more than a rich businessman. Even Jazz's new wardrobe showed him to be a good-looking guy with nice taste and a Hong Kong tailor. Will's elegance came from within.

"Hi," he said. "Good to meet you." He had a thrilling basso that could have been singing "Il lacerato spirito" at the Met, or moving huge congregations to leap into the aisles and shout "Praise the Lord!" To Lee, it was a huge, nineteenth-century orator's voice— a courtroom voice. "Good to meet you."

"Good to meet you."

"Will," McCloskey said. "Could I have a quick word with you, Will?"

With a sinking heart, Lee watched Will enter his office. McCloskey, clearly nervous, followed and closed the door. No one had prepared Will Stewart for her. He would be furious. Like hell I will! he would boom. McCloskey, terrified, would race back up to Huber, who would be forced to change his mind. Lee saw herself taking "Basic Puff Pastry" in the Shorehaven School District's adult ed program several decades sooner than she'd expected. No, it could even be worse. Will would view her as a party hack and treat her with contempt. It would take her years to gain his respect. If she ever could: Eager to prove herself, she'd screw up case after case so badly that not only would she get tossed out of Homicide; they wouldn't even let her try misdemeanor cases.

It was taking too long. She strained to hear shouts, but all was silent behind Will's door. Attorneys passed and glanced at her curiously. She should not have worn a beige suit. It was too late into the fall. She felt so wrong and wished that someone had mentioned the fact that Will Stewart was black and infinitely suave. The door opened. Will stuck his head out. "Who can I call about you?" he asked pleasantly, even warmly, as if he was so pleased with her that he couldn't wait to hear more good things. She realized that he was a smarter politician than Huber and McCloskey put together.

"You mean from the Manhattan D.A.'s?" she asked. What a moron she sounded like! What did she think he wanted? References from the eight million guys at Cornell she'd fucked?

"Right," he said.

"Well, the D.A. himself. Or the head of the Supreme Court bureau—"

"Melanie Tucker?" he asked congenially. At least, he seemed congenial. For all she knew, he loathed Melanie and any recommendation from her would mean automatic rejection. Yes, she nodded, her head bobbing like a fool's, Melanie Tucker. "Sorry to keep you waiting like this," he said.

"That's all right," Lee replied, but he had already closed the door. All right, she thought, as long as her tortured gut did not cause her to writhe and double up, groaning in agony. She held her handbag in front of her and pressed her forearms against her raging stomach. How much longer? She couldn't stand it. Maybe he would hate her because her last name was White. She could knock, say Excuse me, it's really Weissberg. Except maybe, despite all those rabbis on the March on Selma, he was an anti-Semite.

The door jerked open, and Jerry McCloskey flew out. "See ya," he muttered, and tore down the hall.

"Come in," Will called.

Although his name was on the door, Will Stewart's office had nothing to do with him. It was standard government issue, newer than its Manhattan equivalent and just as lifeless. But he had done nothing to make it his: no pictures, no mementos, no bound appellate briefs, no knickknacks. His pen was a twenty-nine-cent Bic. "Come *in*," he repeated. Lee took a deep breath and then, propelled by the exhalation, went into his office. He was standing behind his desk, but instead of the expected forefinger pointed toward the door, he was extending his hand. "Welcome," he said. She felt a little dizzy but noticed he had sat back down and seemed to be suggesting that she do the same. "Sorry to put you through all that."

"No problem," she said cheerfully.

"Lee," he said. With his voice, it sounded like a summons from God. He sat back comfortably in his chair, his hands clasped behind his head.

"What?"

"I'm your boss. Don't bullshit me: 'No problem.'"

"Okay. I had terrible stomach cramps, and I was afraid I'd embarrass myself in some particularly disgusting way. Or else I'd go into shock and convulse, and my head would bang rhythmically against your door and you'd think I was interrupting your discussion with Jerry McCloskey."

"I wasn't discussing with him. I was torturing him by not accepting you as a fait accompli. I sat here for a couple of minutes looking dubious. Then I called Melanie. She thinks the world of you, by the way."

"That's what I think of her."

"So do I. We testified together before a House committee." He did not smile, but his face softened. "She'd be my mother's dream girl, with those hankies up her sleeve. And pearls. The only way she could be more perfect would be if she were black." He continued to look faintly amused—either at his mother or at some recollection of

Melanie, but he did not smile. Then he leaned forward. "The stomach business. Do you get nervous in court?"

No, she was going to say, but heard herself saying: "Most of the time. Right before I open and when I sum up. But once I start talking, it disappears."

"Too bad they can't bottle that," he said.

"Do you ever get that way?" she asked. A second later, she shrank back, nearly crazed by her audacity.

"I used to. Not my stomach. I used to sweat, which is worse, I think, because everyone can see it. But it hasn't happened in years. I guess I've been doing it too long. You get numb to it, and that's not good. You lose your competitive edge." She nodded, suddenly exhilarated, realizing they were having a conversation. "I don't know, though. Maybe being numb is better than being scared shitless. Now, let's see: I've got to get someone to find you a desk. You want a chair too?"

"While they're at it." She smiled at him. Her infectious smile, Jazz called it. Or contagious. Whatever. You smile at someone and they light up, Lee. I'm telling you, it's true.

Will did not smile back. In fact, he looked away and opened a folder on his desk, passing a quick glance over the papers inside. "Okay, you get settled. Then you'll have to fill out all the forms. We Republicans say we don't want big government, but don't believe us. It will take you hours. Come back around . . . whenever. Five, six." He picked up what looked like a Justice Department newsletter and immediately became engrossed.

"Thanks!" Lee said. She waited a fraction of a second too long, hoping he would glance up and smile. Not a big smile, just something quick, spontaneous. Or at least say, You're welcome.

But she got nothing more from Will Stewart until

seven-fifteen that night, when he handed her five eight-by-ten photographs of Nicky "The Rooster" Gaudioso in the trunk of his Lincoln Continental—which had been found in the woods in Eisenhower Park. He was at least two weeks dead, his throat slit, his testicles stuffed into his mouth. "I think you'll have fun with this," Will said. Her parents, her sister, Jazz—any civilian—would have recoiled. But Lee nodded. She knew exactly what Will meant, and she knew he was right.

She took the photos home, and after dinner, while Jazz watched the Yankees getting creamed by Cincinnati in the Series, she spread them out on the kitchen table. With a flashlight in one hand and a magnifying glass in the other, she bent over them, studying Nicky and the trunk that had been his grave. Not much, she thought, although it might make a good ad for the Continental: Check out our roomy trunk! A few minutes later, she noticed: There was something pale and squiggly in the right-hand corner. What was it? More important, was it what she thought it was? She called the detective sergeant on the case, a guy named Brody. Yeah, he said, it's rubber gloves. You know it's after ten o'clock? Lee ignored his question and asked if he'd brought in the gloves to the lab to check for prints. Prints? Brody asked, as if it were a strange new concept. The perpetrator might have used the gloves to put Nicky in the car and simply forgotten them, Lee explained. Gotcha, Brody said wearily. I'm sure the gloves went in. It's automatic. Good, Lee said. Then let's not give the killer time to remember he forgot his gloves and skip town—unless you think it was Nicky who kept them there in case he had to perform emergency microsurgery. I'd like the answer by noon tomorrow.

When Eddie Marcantonio, whose fingerprints were

found inside and outside the gloves, was arrested for the murder of Nicky Gaudioso, he claimed that he was a salesman for Sunshine Garden Supplies. While he did collect a check from Sunshine, however, he would not have known a pile of manure from a hot rock. As Detective Sergeant Brody told Lee, his real profession was hit man for the Gambino family. His job required patience and not imagination or intelligence, so Eddie did quite well. He was not the sort who minded spending his working life sitting in a car, waiting hours for one of his subjects to emerge from a dinner of *cervelli fritti* at Vincente's restaurant or from a visit to his girlfriend's. He was patient, looking straight ahead, not listening to the radio, not reading a newspaper, with only his knife or his gun for company. Then he would do what he'd been sent to do: commit murder. Eddie knew, naturally, to try and avoid crowds, but if his business was ever observed, he did not worry. Should the terror of the moment not frighten an eyewitness, the notion of the cruel death that would follow a court appearance to identify Eddie as the killer worked wonders.

"Eddie didn't do it!" his lawyer, Chuckie Phalen, announced to Lee. "He uses rubber gloves all the time. In the garden supply business. Doesn't like dirt getting under his fingernails." Chuckie wheezed as he spoke. His pallor was almost as bad as Nicky Gaudioso's.

"This is your defense?" Lee asked. She neither liked nor disliked Phalen. He was one of the Old Boys, criminal lawyers who considered themselves archliberals in those rare instances when they managed to refrain from calling a female attorney "honey."

"Just because he has an Italian last name doesn't make him Mafia." Despite his breathing problems, Chuckie spoke with an energy that was rare for an Old Boy on a routine murder case.

"No," Lee agreed, already hearing his summation in her mind. She hated to admit it, she had told Jazz the night before, but it wasn't so terrible working out here—and don't say I told you so. He'd been thrilled, and his hug had been full of joy. Well, it wasn't *that* terrible. Lawyers waited until she finished her sentence before beginning theirs. The cops didn't pal around with the assistant D.A.'s the way they did in New York, but they were cordial enough. Brody had even shaken her hand when the fingerprints on the gloves proved to be Eddie Marcantonio's and then, for good measure, patted her on the back and announced: You're hot shit. "There happen to be three drops of Nicky's blood on Eddie's rubber glove," Lee informed Chuckie Phalen. "That doesn't exactly paint a picture of Mr. Sunshine Garden Supply planting petunias, does it?"

"I like your stuff," Chuckie said. It was, on the surface, a predictable compliment, the old pro patting the rookie on the back, hoping the rookie would feel enough of a personal tie to give his client a break. But Lee sensed it was sincere, and she wanted to smile and give him a warm thank-you, maybe even—after the trial—say something about her liking his stuff. But she could be wrong, he could be setting her up, so she just offered him a slight incline of the head that said: I heard you. "Aah, you think I'm buttering you up. I can tell. That's okay, I understand. Now listen, sis—"

"Lee."

"Lee, what I have here is a family man. Wife, two kids. A dog, even. So maybe we can talk."

"They don't allow dogs in Attica. The wife and kids can visit."

"You're a real softie."

"I keep trying."

"You want to check with Will on this?"

"No."

"Will is tough but fair."

"Good. That's how I want to be."

"So how's about five to seven?" Chuckie asked, the air creating a whistling sound every time he inhaled.

"That's what I'm hoping he'll get for illegally parking the Continental on county property." For the first week, she kept saying "city," and she was only now getting accustomed to glimpses of green outside and being greeted with actual hellos instead of grunts by the unit's secretaries. "The murder charge is extra. I can offer you something less if he's willing to discuss who asked him to kill Nicky and send a message."

"What message?"

"The message that this is what happens to guys who talk."

"You mean, the you-know-whats in Nicky's mouth?" Chuckie asked, with such false innocence that Lee couldn't help it. She threw back her head and laughed.

But she stopped laughing six months later, in court.

Chuckie was good, very good. The way he cut into the credibility of her expert witnesses: not with eye-rolling, give-me-a-break mockery or go-for-the-throat attack, but by respectful solicitation of their views, seeking ever more amplification until the experts were drowning in rolling seas of their own jargon. In addition, Chuckie had the New York–Irish equivalent of courtly Southern charm, calling prospective jurors "Ma'am" and "Sir" during voir dire, wheezing to the judge phrases like: "I respectfully submit to Your Honor" and "I would beg the Court's indulgence." There was not a hint of blarney. A gentleman, the jury was obviously thinking, and Chuckie's dignity subsumed the man

beside him at the defense table, Eddie Marcantonio—
who, after a Chuckie wardrobe consultation—was
looking like a deacon of an extremely sincere church.

But Chuckie's being good was only half the problem. It was that Lee was not. She could tell it by the
way the judge listened to her motions; no matter how
reasonable her arguments were, he reacted as if she
were being not merely frivolous but sneaky. And the
jury. For them, Chuckie was a good show and she was
the commercials. They kept tuning out.

"What's happening?" Lee demanded of Will. She
threw up her hands. Several shreds of coleslaw flew off
her plastic fork and landed on his office rug. She reached
over and picked them up. "You sat in yesterday. You
saw. They're not with me, and don't tell me they are."

He put down the huge, drippy corned beef and pas-
trami combo she had been coveting. "I won't tell you
they are, because they're not."

"You could at least be a little less eager to give me
the bad news."

"No. I'm giving it to you where it has to go: right
between the eyes. You're screwing up." But he said it
with affection.

In her half year in the D.A.'s Office, she had gone
from awe of Will Stewart to having a slight crush on
him, then a large crush, then to a realization that what
he was, above all else, was a great friend—although in
truth the crush never disappeared. Will had grown up
less than ten miles from her, in Glen Cove. His parents
had worked on one of the great Gold Coast estates, his
father as head groom in the stables, his mother as a
laundress. The owner of the estate had taken a shine to
him and paid for his education at Columbia. Will had
gone on to Columbia Law School on scholarship. She
found him a fascinating mix, a kid from a blue-collar

family who had grown up to be a down-to-earth working stiff—civil service division. Yet hand in hand with his lack of airs and his nose-to-the-grindstone work ethic, he comported himself with the polish of someone born to great wealth. It went far beyond his impeccable clothes and physical grace.

Time and again, Lee got annoyed with herself for comparing Jazz and Will, but she could not stop. She was dazzled at the differences between two men whose lives had been molded by old money. Jazz, at twenty-seven, was still the bright-eyed, high-spirited preppy who viewed the world as a fun place and Long Island as his own special playground. Will, at thirty-seven, was not the least bit bright-eyed. Lee could not imagine him that way, even as a child. He behaved as if he had seen it all and was faintly amused by it. But only faintly. He had a nice mouth, but it never smiled. She sensed there was sadness behind his elegant and wry facade, but since he played his personal cards so close to his exquisitely-fitting vest, she had no idea what the sadness was—or whether it was simply a romantic notion she had.

What she couldn't get over is that he seemed made for her. Not the way Jazz was. Taylor made, she called Jazz, the way he cheered her by his very nature, the way his own self-assurance gave her a confidence in herself she had never before had—because why would such a man pick her unless she was, in fact, as wonderful as he kept telling her she was? And of course, the way he made love: Taylor made. Still, once they finished the business of marriage, the routine recounting of their day, the gossip about their extended families, they had very little to talk about.

But based on their common interests, she and Will Stewart could have sprung from the same egg. They discovered they listened to the same radio shows driving to and from the office. They were passionate about music. Lee gave Will a tape of Fats Waller playing stride piano, which he loved, and he introduced her to one of his favorites, the late-Renaissance composer Frescobaldi, and after she heard it, she told him: I owe you for this. They both cooked and gardened; they enjoyed obscure off-off Broadway plays; they were intensely political, and while she was a Democrat and he a Republican, they were moderates, so their arguments over lunch were more about style than ideology. One weekend, shortly after she had once again taken up the crocheting she had learned from her Grandma Bella, she realized that making afghans was the sole interest she had that Will Stewart did not share, and that his abiding love of the New York Mets—he was at that moment at a game—was not going to be hers, ever.

Still, however close, theirs was an office friendship, and Will was her boss. Lee set down the plastic platter of tuna salad. "*How* am I screwing up?" she asked. Her answer was his glance, right at her stomach. She was barely six months pregnant but looked as though she was about to give birth to twin sumo wrestlers. "Being pregnant?"

"You don't want to hear it."

"Yes I do."

"You're not dealing with Manhattan juries anymore. Out here, they don't like to see women in court trying murder cases. Okay, Huber told you that, you didn't like it, and you fought him on it. Good. I'm glad you did. But they really don't want to see pregnant women in court trying a case where she has to talk about a guy's balls getting whacked off and shoved between his teeth."

"But I'm being feminine!" Lee made a sweeping gesture with her hand, indicating her soft silk blouse and small, antique locket. "I don't fucking shout!"

"You just did."

"I mean in court. I'm polite, nice. You saw how feminine I was yesterday, didn't you? What the hell else do they want from me?"

"They want you out of the courtroom and home taking care of your baby."

"I don't have a baby yet!" She rested her hand protectively on her mound of a stomach and felt a friendly kick of acknowledgment. "Look, Will, give it to me straight. Are you telling me I should stay out of court?"

"No."

"Good, because if you did, I'd fight you on it."

"I'm telling you that you have to adapt better. You're not just another lawyer. You're a pregnant woman in a traditional, middle-American community, and if you want them to approve of you, you need more than a little heart on a gold chain."

"What do I need? A gingham pinafore?" She felt weary. Pregnancy exhaustion, trial fatigue, as well as the cosmic weariness that comes with the fear that you have made the wrong choice in life. Maybe she was not good enough for the job, and the whole time in Manhattan she had been flying with Melanie Tucker's wings.

"You need to show the jury you're one of them. The judge too."

"I *am* one of them. There are seven women on the jury, and six of them have kids."

"And not one of them spends her days going after a ball-chopping mob guy. So you've got to show them what you have in common with them. Not your locket. Your values. You and I both know we have to be strong to stomach what we see in this job, and we help ourselves by keeping an emotional distance by being cynical. Nothing surprises us, nothing gets to us. But there's a difference between being strong and being tough. You're not tough. Deep down, you're shocked by what Eddie Marcantonio did to Nicky. Aren't you?"

She did not want to give him the easy answer he was looking for. But when she thought about it, letting him finish his sandwich in silence, she had to answer: "Yes. It's horrible."

"Then let the judge and jury see that. You don't have to go into a phony feminine swoon. Let them see the person who grew up around here and is appalled to find Mafiosi butchering each other and then—just as bad—*driving on the grass* in Eisenhower Park to leave the body. Your shock is real, and you've got to use everything you have. Use your shock. Use your normal, human response: Yuck! And I'd like to hear one reference during the trial to the fact that you were born and grew up here on the Island, and one more during your summation. More than that would be overkill. Trust me, Lee, I do it all the time. It calms their prejudices: Oh, local kid made good. Not some slick piece of work from the city. One of us. Makes them feel safe."

"Thank you," she said.

"Don't thank me. I'm here for more than lunch."

"You know," Lee said to her witness that afternoon in court, Detective-Sergeant Brody, "when I was growing up here"—she would have sworn the twelve jurors and two alternates sat up straighter—"we used to go to Eisenhower Park and run in the wooded area all the time. Wasn't it a terrible risk that some child would find Nicky Gaudioso's Lincoln Continental?" She wrapped her arms protectively on her pregnant belly. "And if they opened the trunk . . . " She closed her eyes, and thought of one particular close-up of Nicky's face, and a genuine shudder passed through her.

Use everything you have, Will Stewart had said. Chuckie Phalen lost *People* v. *Marcantonio*.

Lee was due to give birth on June 21, 1977, and since by the weekend following the trial she needed either Jazz or a derrick to pull her out of a chair, she began her maternity leave. In truth, her only regret in leaving the office was not being able to see Will every day. While she liked some of her colleagues and the cops she dealt with, the camaraderie she had felt in Manhattan, that elation that filled her at ten-thirty at night when some Homicide detective came in carrying a couple of six-packs and everyone gathered around to shoot the shit, did not come to pass in the Nassau County D.A.'s. No, this was the suburbs. Lawyers worked hard and went home to their wives to discuss whether to invest in an underground sprinkler system, while they waited for the charcoal to heat up so they could grill their marinated chicken thighs and vegetable kebabs.

Jazz called her almost hourly. Anything yet? Nothing, just Braxton Hicks contractions, she reported. They had been to natural childbirth classes and took comfort that by breathing properly and knowing what would happen, they would be in control. She did not feel in control. There was so much pressure on her bladder that if she sneezed or laughed she wet her pants. Not that she was laughing much. The start of the tenth month of pregnancy is not a good time to begin asking oneself: Have I made a mistake?

She never felt that way at night, when Jazz came flying through the door, all smiles and kisses, telling her to stop it, she did *not* look like a manatee; she was still a fantastic piece of ass. As they watched TV together, he would massage her feet and ankles on their brand-new cushy couch, and she would think: This is what love is.

But days were different. She had too much time to think. It bothered her a little that she, an ex-radical, had gotten co-opted into the system without even a peep from her conscience. Living in a rose-covered cottage and leafing through books of afghan patterns. Working for the government. If her conscience was not sticking it to her, then shouldn't her pride be giving her the business? Had her beliefs in her college years been that shallow? Or was she being too hard on herself? Was the lawyer who stood up and said "Lee White for the People, Your Honor" indeed the woman the Cornell revolutionary once dreamed of becoming?

What bothered her even more during those endless daylight hours was Jazz. When he was not with her, she wondered: Who is he? She had fallen in love first with a barefoot boy in a pizza parlor and, second, with a man utterly at ease with himself. How she had marveled at his simple acceptance of the fact that the world was his oyster and, then, at his invitation to come join him on the half-shell and spend her life with him. Come on, the invitation read. You don't have to prove yourself all the time. You don't have to push. You're with me. We're in like Flynn. More in, because Flynn is an arriviste and you and I, babe, belong.

"Don't you think," Lee asked Robin, "that Mom and Dad won?"

"Won what?"

"Won the war with us. We've become everything they wanted us to be."

Robin bit her rose petal of a lower lip. Her work at the day care center was voluntary, and she had stopped going in afternoons in order to be with Lee. When Robin announced her decision, Lee had been first appalled, then fearful of wounding her sister by explaining her need for privacy. After that she became angry, because she always had to tread softly where Robin was concerned; any serious obstacle to what sensitive Robin wanted might catapult her back into the darkness of drugs. But in the end, Lee found herself grateful for her sister's company. She was lonely, and frightened about going into labor alone. She had a recurring daydream of experiencing a fierce contraction and running for the phone to call Jazz and the obstetrician but stumbling, crashing to the floor, striking her head or breaking both legs, and lying, helpless, screaming out in pain for hours—and having the baby come out stillborn. So she felt safe with her sister in the house. Also, she found it fun to have a friend to talk to, especially a nonlawyer who was smart but who didn't always have a smart rejoinder.

"They didn't win with me," Robin said. "I'm not what they want me to be."

"Sure you are," Lee said.

"No. Only to the extent that I'm not a junkie now. I didn't finish college. I have a menial job—"

"It's a good job. You love being with kids."

"Not to wipe fifteen asses three times a day. That sounds terrible. I *do* like the job, and I know that if I went back to school, I'd major in education. But right now . . . I guess I'm doing the best I can."

"You're doing wonderfully."

Robin retied the ribbons of her cork-platform espadrilles. She had become her mother's shopping companion. Lee had observed to Jazz that her sister was the best-dressed day care worker in America.

Certainly the best-looking, Lee ruminated. Now that Robin was off drugs and had had her teeth capped, her fragile prettiness had bloomed into beauty. She had her mother's willowy figure and fair coloring, but with finer, sweeter features, as if a Pre-Raphaelite painter had given Sylvia a makeover. "I'm doing all right," Robin said. "*You're* doing wonderfully. You have it all."

"All by Mom and Dad's standards. A husband, a house in the suburbs. I mean, what was the point of all my rebellion? I married the man of their dreams, and I'm about to give them a grandchild who they're praying won't have a nose like Grandpa Nat, and I'm living in a rose-covered cottage two and a half minutes from their house. If they had given me a blueprint, I couldn't have met their specifications any better."

"You became a lawyer."

"I had to do *something* after college. No one was pounding on my door, shouting marriage proposals."

"Give me a break!" Robin said. "You could have gotten some normal kind of job." Having arranged the bows on her espadrilles to droop with the proper degree of casualness, Robin was now running her fingers up her shin, over and over, searching for a near-invisible blonde hair her razor might have missed. Lee could not get over how someone as intelligent as her sister could be so utterly serious about fluff. "Anyway, you're the one who chose this life, with Jazz, living here. You're just pissed off that it's what Mom and Daddy wanted for you. But you shouldn't be."

"Why not?"

"Because it's what everyone in the world wants. Love, marriage, a beautiful house. Ask yourself this: What would I rather have than love, marriage, and a beautiful house?"

"Nothing," Lee admitted. She glanced around the living room, with its comfortable overstuffed chairs and warm wood tables. The afternoon sun streamed through windows framed by ruby roses. "I can't believe we lucked into this place, can you?" Robin smiled, a fuller smile than in the past. Besides her teeth being fixed, she was also happier. "What's so amusing?"

"You're so sophisticated," Robin said.

"Sophisticated? Every time Mom looks at me, it's like she can't decide who to call first: a wardrobe consultant or a plastic surgeon. I mean, I'm one notch above dowdy."

"I mean intellectually sophisticated. You question everything. And whenever you talk about your job, you always wind up talking about how you didn't trust what some cop swore up and down to, or you didn't trust some lawyer, or even—before you started doing only murder cases—that you didn't believe what the victim of a crime was saying."

"So?"

"So you're funny." Robin lowered her head and chuckled. Then she looked back up at Lee. "Listen. This is just between us, okay? But do you think a gem like this house just *happens* to become available the day you decide Okay, fine, I'll move to the suburbs?"

Lee felt neither a shiver of foreboding nor an all-senses alert. All she experienced was the slightest shift in sensation, so that instead of feeling normal she felt nothing. "It was prearranged?" she asked offhandedly, as though she had suspected sly doings all along.

"I'm sorry. I probably shouldn't have said anything."

"It's okay. Tell me."

"Mom and Daddy went looking every weekend in the spring. Not this spring. Last. I don't know if it was even for you that much; it just gave them something to do. Anyway, the Howell estate had been up for sale forever, but no one was buying it, so it was being broken up."

Lee tried to fill in the blanks. "They negotiated for this house?" Robin nodded. "Without us ever seeing it?"

"Of course not! Daddy took Jazz over. He fell in love with it too. It *is* irresistible. But he knew you didn't want to move, so he said he'd have to convince you first, because otherwise showing you the house would be meaningless. But while all that was happening, Daddy was afraid it would get away. He wanted to make sure no one else got it. So he and Jazz did something financial, with money from the business—and they bought it."

Lee felt her belly growing rigid with a contraction. At first, it seemed like the ones she had been experiencing for weeks: awesome when you felt the strength of the muscle getting itself into shape, but certainly not painful or even uncomfortable. But this one! "My God!" She gasped at its violence. "I'm not sure if I can take this."

Valerie Belinda Taylor was named for two great-grandmothers, Valentine MacDougal and Bella Weissberg. Born on the fifth of July, she would tell her friends when she grew older: Even then I was slightly perverse. By the time she uttered that statement she was studying acting at Juilliard, and thus, hyperbole was not a stranger to her tongue. But the truth was, from day one, despite a tendency to make even the opening of a bag of potato chips an occasion of theater, Val was a good-natured, reasonable child.

A good thing too, because for the first few months of her life, her parents were feeling anything but good-natured. "How could you?" Lee demanded from her bed in the maternity wing at North Shore Hospital. She kept her voice down, because just beyond the drawn curtain, the woman in the next bed was having trouble nursing and a gynecologist and two nurses were standing around the bed, discussing nipples. "It's such a betrayal."

"What the hell are you talking about?" Jazz asked. Since the floor was made of hard tiles, and he could not dig his heels in and thus demonstrate his determination to fight this one to the finish, he simply crossed his arms tight across his chest. "You are blowing this way out of proportion. It was a business deal, for God's sake."

"You bought the house before I even agreed to leave the city!"

"Your father and I bought it because it happened to be an excellent investment opportunity."

"You're full of shit!" she said, obviously too loud, since the nipple committee beyond the curtain fell into quivering silence.

"Keep your voice down."

"How can I?" she demanded, although in a whisper. "You lied to me!"

"I did not! I went into a deal with your father, who happens to be my business partner. Okay, I admit this was—is—a great house for a young couple. A little gem."

"You know who you sound like? That oozing-charm jerk of a real estate agent. 'Little gem!' And don't tell me you didn't lie. We went to his office and you shook his hand as if it was the first time you'd ever met him. Then we drove to the house, and you looked around like Wow, gee, what a place, and you said you never even knew it existed." Lee could tell from the slump of Jazz's shoulders that she had scored. "If that's not a lie, what is it?"

"I did it for you."

"You did it for yourself. If you were doing something

for me, you would have let me stay in the job I loved."
He stood and walked to the foot of the bed, putting distance between them. "In the city I loved. What do you want? To grow up and become our parents?"

"We're not our parents," Jazz said, leaning toward her over the foot of the bed. Lee could hear him trying to remain calm, trying to get the anger out of his voice by substituting the tone of benign understanding that he knew from natural childbirth class one ought to use when dealing with a woman who is four hours postpartum. "And Valerie isn't going to grow up to be us."

Lee was about to demand: But what about your lying to me? It was too big a matter to let drop. But just then a nurse came in holding Val, and the tug at her heartstrings as well as the tug of the stitches in her episiotomy incision made her feel particularly vulnerable. So she reached up for her baby and put her to her breast and a moment later she was nursing for the first time and Jazz was back beside her on the bed, running his finger over his daughter's perfect pink cheek and smiling beatifically. They looked for all the world like a picture of paradise, so when Jazz whispered, "I'm sorry," Lee nodded and decided to let it be for the time being.

The time being moved very slowly when Lee came home from the hospital. Having spent all her adult life being overstimulated, she found that the peacefulness of maternity made her edgy. She held Val a great deal, unable to get over the wonder of all the tiny parts parents traditionally wonder at. She luxuriated in the serene lassitude breast-feeding induced and understood why cows were so content. She started to reread *Jane Eyre* but found it too rousing, so she put it down and picked up *Emma*. She wrote thank-you notes for all the little pink gifts friends of their parents had sent and for gender-neutral yellow and green gifts from their own friends.

Kent came over to check out his new niece and was so pleased by all the activity—the baby's diaper being changed, the interviews with prospective nannies, opening gifts, helping Lee make dinner and set the table, the new large-screen TV and videocassette player in their den—that he stayed. In her fourth week home, Lee sat across from Kent playing checkers—a game he did not quite comprehend but which he nevertheless enjoyed, trusting Lee to help him move his pieces and tell him who won. She realized he was now part of their household. What do you think? she asked Jazz, who replied, I don't know. What do *you* think? She thought it wasn't so bad having Kent around. He was really doing well. Not that she necessarily wanted the responsibility, but the thought of sending him home to her in-laws', where he would be, if not ill-housed, then surely ill-clothed, ill-fed, and ignored, disturbed her. So she said: Let him stay—if it's okay with your parents. They laughed, Jazz did a fine imitation of his parents celebrating, and they turned out the light; and since it was too soon after birth to have intercourse and since it didn't really pay to start fooling around on a Sunday night if nothing was going to happen, they went to sleep.

In Lee's fifth week home, Will Stewart came for lunch, bringing with him a silver cup with Val's initials and an autopsy report and crime scene photos of a double homicide in Hewlett Harbor—a banker and his girlfriend shot dead in the banker's sauna. "Beautiful," Lee said, holding up the cup to the sunlight.

"To go with the silver spoon she was born with," Will explained. "It's not quite an antique. It's from the 1880s or '90s. The dealer had a fit when I asked him to monogram it, but I told him this is for a very special young woman." He bent over Val's carriage and touched her nose and ran his finger lightly over her downy scalp, but he declined Lee's offer to pick her up. "Not for single guys," he said, sounding slightly nervous, as if by holding her he would then be held liable for anything that went wrong for the rest of her life.

They sat under an old linden in the backyard. Lee had spent the morning on a salmon mousse and was still edgy over the suspense of unmolding it. It looked beautiful, she had to admit, surrounded by translucent slices of cucumber and toothpick-thin curlicues of carrots scattered capriciously about. She had set the redwood picnic table with some of her Taylor linens, and although it was almost like falling on the point of a sword, she asked to borrow some of her mother's English china. Too showy, she had fretted, moments before Will arrived, rearranging an allegedly casual centerpiece. But there was something about him that made the gracious gesture seem all right—not ostentatious but a grand idea—and now she was glad she had fussed.

"This could have been your case," Will remarked, buttering his roll, watching Lee read through the medical examiner's notes. "Not that you have time to watch TV or read a paper, but it's all over the news."

"What should I have done? Stuck my uterus in a shopping bag and come to work right from the hospital?"

"If you were really dedicated."

"How's the office?" she inquired. For a quarter hour, they discussed the case he had brought to show her. Then he regaled her with amusing war stories of other cases Homicide was working on and added a few horror stories about Jerry McCloskey's increasing attempts to interfere with his running of the unit—and Woodleigh Huber's reluctance to put an end to McCloskey's political maneuvering. "Why are they doing this to you?" Lee asked.

"Because I fired one of their boys and refused to hire another."

"But you hired me. I was a political contract."

"You were different. You were good. The guys they sent me were consummate party hacks. Huber genuinely wants me to run the best Homicide unit in the state, but he also wants me to staff it with his imbeciles, so he sends McCloskey down to try and get me to comply."

Will looked wonderful, Lee thought. He sat relaxed in a lawn chair, the plate and napkin resting casually on his lap, his dark skin shining in the glimmers of sunlight that shot through the thick leaves of the linden. The only man on whom a seersucker suit was not baggy. Of course, Will Stewart could wear the salmon mousse on his head and look elegant.

"When are you coming back, Lee?"

"Soon."

"Define soon."

"Another six to eight weeks." They both turned to Val. She was fast asleep, but her tiny mouth was busy making nursing movements.

"She's a beaut," he observed. "Hard to leave." He set his plate and napkin on the table. "Are you thinking of not coming back?" Lee froze, thinking perhaps something had gone wrong and Will did not want her back. Or if not Will, maybe Woodleigh Huber had determined that her father-in-law did not deserve such a big plum as her job. "Now stop it," Will admonished. "I see you going off the deep end, and there's no reason for it. I want you back. So does everyone. Okay? But every time I call you about one of your cases and ask, Hey, when do you see yourself getting back here? you start obfuscating: I'm not sure. I have to speak to the doctor. I have to check a nanny's references. Can I call you back, I'm rolling out a pie crust."

"Well, I just told you," she said, wishing she had not made peach pie for dessert. "Six to eight weeks."

Will studied her. "Forget I'm your boss and you live and die by my whim," he said. "Talk to me. Is something wrong? I sense . . . I don't know. I sense something."

"I feel a certain pressure to stay home."

"From your husband?"

"From my whole family. I'm out of sync with them. Definitely with my mother and sister. My mother tries on shoes for a living, and my sister works as a volunteer in a day care center. You couldn't find two more traditional women's roles if you looked for them."

"Okay, so you feel pressure to be a housewife?"

"Yes. But there's a lot about being a housewife that I like. There's a part of me that would love to win a Pillsbury Bake-Off or learn to cut a dress pattern. But I want to be a lawyer too, more than I want immortality for my blueberry–ricotta cheese tartlets. Much more. Actually, the pressure isn't just from my mother and sister. It's more from the men. Here they are, Jazz and my father, going off to work. And what do they do there? Talk about sleeve lengths. Have coffee with rich ladies and butter them up—'Indulge me. Try on the lynx. I have a feeling it's right on the money with your coloring.' And what do I do? Hang out with a bunch of hairy-chested cops and criminal lawyers. Strategize how to demolish a witness on cross."

"So they're doing traditional women's work too?"

"Yes, in a sense, even though it's business. I think

they see what they do as not quite manly enough. Girl stuff. And I'm sure as hell doing the boy stuff."

"So you feel you don't fit in anymore?"

Lee nodded. Even though Val had not made a peep, she picked her up from the carriage and held the baby close against her. "It's not what I *do* at home that I don't like—the cooking, the crocheting, and all that. It's how I *am* that bothers me. I hear myself sometimes, and I'm talking half an octave higher than I do at the office. So girlish, so sweet, so un-ball-busting. I never talk about work anymore. Just 'Whew, had a hard day,' or something like that. Nothing of substance. Because nobody wants to hear it."

"Are you sure it's not just you feeling guilty about how much you love being a lawyer because your husband . . . couldn't cut it?"

"No, I don't think so. Does how much I love it show?"

"Sure, blatantly and flagrantly. For all your blueberry things, there's a part of you that loves a fight, *has* to contend. And isn't what we do a much more civilized way to deal with aggression than the way our defendants get rid of their hostilities? So if you're thinking of quitting . . . " Will reached out for Val. Lee draped a cloth diaper over his seersucker shoulder and handed him the baby. Although he did not smile, he looked extremely content with what he was doing. "Don't quit. You need a safe arena to fight in."

"I'm begging you," Jazz said, following Lee into the bathroom. "Please, just put it on hold for a year or two."

"We agreed—"

"Don't you want to spend time with Val?"

"Don't you? What kind of question is that?"

"You're the mother." She squeezed the toothpaste too hard, and a strand of aqua paste squiggled onto her hand. "I know it's not fair, but for thousands of years, mothers are the ones who stay home. I'm not saying give it up. I'm saying put it—"

"—on hold. Well, the answer is no. N-o. I know my being away all day is not a perfect solution, but I can't help it. I hired a great nanny. *You* said she was great." What Jazz actually had said was that the nanny, a woman from Iowa named Cherry Berkemeyer, was "a dream," and he had sounded so much like Leonard at his trendy worst that Lee had felt something fairly close to nausea.

"It's not just Val. We have responsibility for Kent now. You're the one who wanted to take him on."

"*We* were the ones who agreed to take him on, and if you'd like, I can quote back that conversation verbatim." She brushed her teeth with such force that her gums began to bleed. She wished she could put her hand right in the middle of his chest and shove Jazz out of the bathroom. Instead she rinsed her mouth as discreetly as she could. "And when I hired Cherry, it was with the clear understanding that Kent is part of the package, even though he's away all day. When he comes home, he's hers as much as Val is."

"What if Cherry leaves?"

"She was at her last job for seven years. We're paying her the national debt. Where is she going?" Jazz shrugged and turned to leave the bathroom. He was wearing pajamas that had his initials on the breast pocket. "Jazz," Lee said.

"What?" he said, exhaling slowly to show his patience.

"You're not the man I married." Before he could say that she was not the woman either, she continued.

"You've become a middle-aged Jewish furrier. What the hell has happened to you? Wanting me to stay home . . . where I belong! Where is the man I went to law school with, the man who was so proud of me—of what I did?"

"I was proud of you then. I admired your drive, your guts. But I think it would take a hundred times more courage to quit and not do the knee-jerk feminist thing and abandon your kids to someone else to raise."

She flung her toothbrush onto the counter. "Then let me make a suggestion. If you don't want your child abandoned to a perfectly competent and very nice woman, then you stay home. Quit the fur biz. I'll stay with the D.A.'s another year, then I'll go into private practice. Who knows, maybe we can even afford to keep the house. In any case, I'll make something we can live on, if not here, then someplace else that isn't a hellhole. Okay?"

"No," Jazz said very quietly. "It's not okay. But I see I have no say in the matter, do I?"

"In terms of my work, no. In terms of your own, yes."

"Then I'm sorry if I upset you." He turned and walked back into the bedroom.

"I'm sorry if I upset you," Lee replied to his retreating back.

"I guess we'll have to agree to disagree," Jazz called out as he kicked off his slippers and lifted the blanket.

"I guess so." Lee looked into the vanity mirror, feeling there was something more she had to do in the bathroom. But she could not think what.

The next day she returned to work.

Nineteen

Before Norman Torkelson and Mary Dean came into my life, I had tried fifty or sixty murder cases. So did I know what went on in killers' heads in the days and weeks following a murder? Not a clue. Elation? Maybe. Anguish? Could be. Or did they simply revert to regular life, thinking: Hmm, I've got to buy more oatmeal, or: Gosh, I'd better get to the bathroom, because *Seinfeld* will be on in two minutes? After more than twenty years as a prosecutor and a defender, all I knew was that killers keep their crimes to themselves. Except for the random teenage sociopath who brags to his friends, hardly anyone admits to murder.

An example: Take those times when the circumstantial evidence is overwhelming that X shot Y right between the eyes. Overwhelming means nothing: X will deny it. *What?* Me kill Y? Outrageous! If there are actual eyewitnesses—an entire order of nuns willing to testify that, yes, they saw X come over and whack out Y (who at the moment of his death was on his knees, saying his rosary)—then X will have to admit, Okay, I did it. But he will swear on a stack of Bibles that it was in self-defense.

So now that Mary Dean had actually offered me that uncommon gift, a confession—*I killed Bobette Frisch*—I wasn't about to throw it away. Forget about telling Norman. He would only fire me. And if he had half the brains I credited him with, he'd have his new lawyer start proceedings to keep me from talking about the case—if not to shut me up permanently, then at least to hassle me until Norman could get Mary out of harm's way. Or Norman would simply shove aside everyone in line at the jail pay phone, call Holly Nuñez, and claim that Mary was confessing to save him. Don't believe a word she says! I did it. And Holly would respond: Not to worry, Norman. I believe you.

So sitting there with Mary in the furnished apartment she and Norman had shared, I knew my only course of action was to keep her from talking to him. I sensed that with this case, considering all the webs a con artist could spin, any fancy footwork on my part would be counterproductive. Simple, direct action was best. So I invited Mary to come with me to talk to the assistant district attorney in charge of the case.

"You mean now?" Mary inquired, bending over to unplug a vacuum, one of those low, expensive chrome models fitted with tools for cleaning venetian blinds and upholstery. Too sleek to have come with the apartment. I wondered if she and Norman schlepped it from city to city on their travels or if they sprang for a new one in each place they stopped for a scam. "You really think I should?"

"You're the one who has to make that decision," I said, sounding like any proper, mealy-mouthed lawyer. Come *on*, I was thinking. Let's get this thing rolling! But my words came out as soft and sugary as cotton candy.

"If what you tell me is true, Mary, that you want to help Norman, then . . . "

"I'll go," she said quietly.

"I'm glad," I told her. Mary wheeled the vacuum into a utility closet crammed with an awesome array of mops, brooms, brushes, spray cans, bottles of scary-colored cleaning liquids and two pairs of rubber gloves. "Just get on a pair of shoes. I'll call a colleague of mine. A lawyer. I can't represent you, because I'm Norman's lawyer, but I'll stick by you and this woman will see you through it. We'll stop by her office, then go on to the D.A.'s. I'll drive you down there." I did not tell her to bring her toothbrush while she was at it; there was no point in putting her good intentions to the test.

Mary peered down at her denim minidress. "Is this okay to wear to the D.A.'s?" It was a mistake for me even to think about it, because in that microsecond, she was off to her bedroom closet, going through the rack, no easy task, since the clothes were packed in so tight, hangers were just an impediment. She eased out a black dress, only to reject it as "too evening-y, don't you think?" Then came three green dresses: olive, emerald, and bottle green. After a conversation longer than the ones I usually have to explain every single nuance of the plea bargaining process, we agreed the olive was best for such a serious occasion.

I was half expecting her to consult with me on her choice of shoes and bag. When she didn't and, instead, hopped into a pair of gold sandals, I found myself let down. Why? I suppose because I didn't want to face having to see Mary face the music. Yet that was precisely what I'd been working toward: fairness, justice, whatever you want to call it. The killer should be the one punished for the crime of murder. No matter what kind of louse Norman was, it was wrong for him to pay for what

Mary had done. Walking over to the telephone, though, I felt low, that logy premenstrual feeling. Just moving the three feet was almost beyond my capacity; I was slogging through a substance thicker than mere air.

While Mary put on makeup, I called Holly and announced I was bringing someone in to see her on urgent business. Before she could tell me she didn't have time for me, I hung up. I watched Mary at the bathroom sink, a magnifying mirror in one hand and a mascara wand in the other. Time trudged forward. It was taking so long, as if she were coating one lash at a time and letting it dry before starting the next. For all I knew, she was. When at last she picked up a blush brush I said: "It's better if you look a little pale, Mary."

I had met Barbara Duberstein in the Mommy Room— these days apparently called the Mommy-Daddy Room— on the first day of our children's nursery school. A five-foot-tall powerhouse—her husband called her The Little Engine That Could—she had just started at Hofstra Law School. We hit it off, getting into a fairly emotional discussion about the Eleventh Amendment and the limits on the jurisdiction of the Federal judiciary, while her son and my daughter watched the class guinea pig move its bowels—an apparently enthralling experience. She was now a single practitioner in Mineola with a solid general practice, doing everything from wills to matrimonials to an occasional criminal case. She was smart and savvy, one of the rising stars of the County's G.O.P., and I wanted her for Mary because I knew she had clout, in case clout would be called for.

But I knew, and so did Barbara, that clout couldn't do much for a client who wanted only one thing: to confess to murder. She tried getting Holly to agree to use immunity, in which we could go in for a single interview and nothing Mary would say could be used against her. But as we figured, Holly wasn't giving out anything, not to someone who is determined to confess to a homicide the D.A. already thinks has been solved. Are you *sure* this is what you want to do? Barbara asked Mary. Once we get there, you won't be able to take it back. And Mary replied: Let's get it over with.

Mary was staring at Holly's perfect oval pale-pink acrylic nails. Understandable. Nail-staring was definitely less distressing than looking into the lens of the video camera looking down at her, taping her confession. Earlier, she had tried to alleviate the awfulness of this brown, plastic-wood room by making goo-goo eyes at Sam Franklin, who was sitting on Holly's side of the table in the D.A.'s small conference room. But he had regarded Mary with such indifference that, wounded, she had turned away. It was strange sitting in that windowless, airless room: three women lawyers with shoulder pads, an about-to-confess killer in a halter-top dress, and a cop who kept looking from one of us to another, as if fearful of contracting estrogen poisoning.

Holly, unlike Mary, was not checking out nails. No, it only looked that way. For the last hour, she had been studying Mary's powerful-looking hands and long, strong fingers. "What happened when you choked her?" Holly was asking. "Did she die right away?"

"No," she said. "Not right away." At first, I had been furious with Mary. What a birdbrain, that she would be more interested in an assistant district attorney's manicure than in the fact the A.D.A. was going to send her for many years to a place where lack of emery boards would be the least of her problems. But then I saw how Mary was sitting: bolt upright, her hands clutching the brown metal arms of her chair, fingers curved rigidly, like claws, toes curled tight in the open sandals. All I could think of was that her posture was that of a condemned woman strapped into the electric chair, waiting for the juice.

"Tell me about it," Holly prompted. "The choking." Her usual cheerleader's perkiness was absent, but she couldn't fight her nature. Congenitally buoyant she was: chin up, shoulders back. Her hands, fingers loosely laced, rested on the edge of the table, but every once in a while they would flutter, as if seeking the crepe-paper pom-poms they were born to wave. From a professional point of view, I had to admit, she was handling the interview with the right balance of skepticism and encouragement. For Mary's sake, I was relieved Holly was prosecuting, and not one of Woodleigh Huber's other new assistants in the Homicide unit, two guys my partner, Chuckie, and I referred to as Venom and Spite. Holly, for once not looking as if she had something better to do, was making Mary go over her account again and again, each time seeking more detail. She got everything out of Mary that I had, and more: like the fact that Mary had been stalking Bobette and Norman for three days prior to the murder, peering into the windows of Bobette's house. Once, the day before, she had watched them as they made love on the couch in the living room.

"I'm waiting," Holly said. "I need you to tell me about it."

"You mean the neck thing?" Mary asked.

"You bet. The strangulation," Holly responded, a little too brightly for my taste.

"I don't know. I was, like, in this daze. But she kept trying to pull my hands off of her. Grabbing me here . . ." She lifted her right hand and brought it over, gingerly massaging her left wrist.

"She was grabbing you around your wrists," Holly said for the record. "Is that right?"

"Yes, she was trying to pull my hands away. She kept doing it, but I was stronger and she kept getting . . . you know." Mary looked away from Holly's nails, embarrassed.

"No, I don't know. Please tell me."

"She was getting weaker. So then she started making these noises." Mary croaked four times, brief, staccato froggy sounds. "I mean, it was awful, but not *really* like choking. More like she was trying to tell me something but couldn't."

"Were you saying anything to her?" Sam asked.

Mary turned to me and Barbara. We signaled it was all right to answer his question, so she turned back to him. Her expression eased: a man. The enemy, hostile, but still a man. "No," Mary told him, "I didn't say a thing." He and Holly sensed what I sensed, that this was a lie. He waited, fiddling with the clip of his photo ID on his breast pocket. "I *may* have said something about her getting out of Norman's life," Mary finally conceded.

"Be more specific," Holly ordered.

"That, like, Norman was in love with me and was going to marry me and the only reason he said he would marry her was for her money because she was . . . " She lowered her head and mumbled something.

"Talk a little louder," Barbara prompted her.

"She was a fat pig," Mary said defiantly, staring right into the glass eye of the video cam.

"Did she die right then?" Holly asked. Naturally, she knew from reading the autopsy report pretty much how death had occurred. She was trying to make sure that Mary's account concurred with the objective findings.

"Not that second. But the"—Mary made the choking sound again, but softer this time—"finally stopped. And her eyeballs got yucky. Then she shut her eyes and I let her down." She turned to Sam. "She was very heavy. I couldn't hold her."

Before he could make a nasty comment and rattle her, Barbara Duberstein asked: "Mary, remember when we started, how Ms. Nuñez asked you if you were making this statement of your own free will? You said yes, you were." Mary said yes, quietly and, for her, quite seriously, as if for once she truly comprehended the import of what she was saying. "Did anyone put undue pressure on you to make this statement?"

"No."

"Did you discuss making this statement with Norman Torkelson?" I asked.

Mary gave a loud, fast laugh. "Are you kidding?"

"Is that a no?"

"Of course it's a no. He'd kill me if he knew I was doing this!" She happened to glance at Sam as she said this, and shrank back. "I don't mean, like, really kill," she explained to him. Almost as if it were beyond Sam's control, his eyes changed from cold, dead cop eyes to sympathetic eyes, and almost instantly, into the misty eyes of soap opera close-ups. Holly glanced at me as Sam's face began an unfamiliar journey into softness. I shrugged, as in: What did you expect? Holly shrugged back, as in: Another one bites the dust. Barbara merely looked heavenward and exhaled. "But see," Mary continued, addressing only Sam Franklin now, "Norman said he should be the one to go to jail. Because he started the whole business and dragged me into it—which isn't true. I love him. It was my idea we should work together, not his. But he said it would be easier if he went, because he's been away before." Still looking at Sam, she explained: "To jail. Away to jail." He nodded his gratitude for her elucidation—passionate, all-out nodding that might never have stopped if Mary hadn't started talking again. "See, Norman knew the ropes about jails. But he said, like, it wouldn't be that long, with time off for good behavior. He told me: Just sit tight. But I can't! Not now. I didn't know they"—she turned from Sam to look at Holly—"were going to throw the book at him." Her beautiful green eyes filled with tears then, and in total disregard of her mascara, Mary began to weep.

"Well," Holly began when we were back in her office. She had called in a policewoman to baby-sit for Mary while she, Sam, Barbara, and I talked. But Sam had made some excuse about pressing business at a crime scene in Plainview. The last we saw of him, however, he was no closer to Plainview than Mary's chair. "I have to admit: You told me so, Lee."

"So now what?" I asked, crossing my legs, thinking about the inevitable call I would make to my guy to tell him I had no idea how late I'd be and would he be so good as to start thinking creatively about the defrosted chicken breasts in my refrigerator. This was going to be one long day.

"There's just one little problem," Holly said.

"What's that?" I asked.

"I don't believe her." Her voice was effervescent, like one of those bubblehead quiz show dames who think their co-host might be putting over a fast one on them.

"What are you talking about, Holly?"

"It doesn't play for me."

I hate hip new uses for old verbs. "It doesn't matter if it plays for you. It's not a record, it's not a movie; it's a confession in a homicide case."

"It's something they cooked up, some scam."

"Holly, they haven't connected on this. Norman doesn't know she's opened up to me. He sure in hell doesn't know she's here."

"I'll have to ask Jerry."

Terrific. Jerry McCloskey, the head of the Homicide Bureau, was so ineffectual that he'd probably want to commission a poll before deciding. "Go ahead," I told her. "There's really nothing much to discuss. You have a confession. You have physical evidence to corroborate the confession. Whether it plays to you or not is not a matter of law."

"I'll get back to you."

"No," I said. "I'm not leaving until you make a decision." So she went to speak to Jerry McCloskey.

While she was gone, Barbara and I discussed how it never fails to amaze us that even the most assertive people will knuckle under to outrageous behavior. How come it did not occur to Holly to say: "What do you mean you're not leaving? Get out of my office. I'll call you when I'm good and ready." Throughout my legal career, all I had to do was cross my arms and dig in my metaphoric heels. Okay, now and then a lawyer would tell me to take a hike, but if I'd sit there, unmoving, and maybe glance at my watch to let them know how much I resented their obstinence, they'd get up from their desk or pick up the phone and do whatever it was I wanted them to do.

The question neither Barbara nor I addressed was that if we were both such hotshot tough lawyers, how come we so often turned into wimpettes in our personal lives?

Holly returned in about fifteen minutes. "Jerry says okay."

"Good," I said, curbing a desire to leap up and shout with joy and do a jig.

"I want it clear that we're not disposed toward anything approaching leniency," Holly said to Barbara.

"Pray you get a female judge," Barbara replied. "Otherwise, you're going to get leniency up the wazoo."

"You're dead if it's a man, Holly," I concurred. "Did you check out Sam Franklin?"

"I know! Did you ever see such total mush?"

"Terry Salazar," I told her. "My investigator. Mr. Hard-Ass."

"He's kind of cute," Holly said.

"If you got to know him, you'd realize he's the most uncute man in America. Except when he met Mary: She turned him into marshmallow fluff. And the last judge she appeared before, the one in Maryland who granted bail after Mary smiled . . . "

"A man," Holly guessed. "Well, wouldn't you know it!" She laughed brightly. Too brightly.

For God's sake, I thought. It's one thing to be relieved that a matter is resolved. But she's just lost the chance at a big, fat, juicy trial that she was going to win. If this had been my case as an A.D.A., I'd be pretty depressed about that. Okay, she was doing what I wanted her to do, being decent, fair-minded, but Holly had gone for the easy out so damned fast. Barbara didn't seem troubled by Holly's cheery mood, but she really wasn't involved in the case. I had expected at least four or five hours of brawling, though, with Holly pounding her desk a couple of times, telling me that Norman wasn't off the hook yet, that he might have been an accomplice, or at least an accessory. Holly should have put up a fight, if only to save face, because her judgment had been wrong when I'd tried to get her to listen to my theory that Norman might have been innocent of Bobette's murder. But here she was, sitting back, yukking it up, having a high old time. Wasn't she in the least surprised at Mary's confession? Or at least thoughtful about the case: After all, she had almost sent the wrong person away for life.

She told Barbara she would do serious thinking about a sentence recommendation, which I doubted. Then

Barbara left, to allow me to talk about my own client. "When can you spring Norman?" I inquired.

"I don't know that he can get sprung. We may be holding him as an accessory."

"Holly, give me a damn break! There is nothing in Mary's confession that puts him there at the time of the murder, nothing that connects him in any way to the homicide. You know there isn't a judge around who's going to keep him in, so why do we have to go through all this?"

"I'll see," she said, making a little note to herself. She used a pen with aqua ink. "I would have to have his release approved upstairs."

"Huber will be thrilled."

"He'll be okay." Holly was chirping again. "Jerry's been putting tons o' pressure on us to push those cases through, so they're going to be *real* glad we can close the books on this one."

"It's not fair to Norman to have to stay on ice while you're waiting for your paperwork to go through. That could take weeks."

"It won't take weeks, Lee," Holly said, laughingly. I all but expected her to add: You old silly. "Days at most. I'll do my best to see to it that it gets moved through channels as fast as humanly possible." This last offer did not spring from Holly's usual chipperness. Having been caught prosecuting the wrong person for murder, she wanted to keep the case as quiet as possible. If she locked Norman in the cooler for too long, she knew perfectly well I would have to start making a loud and public fuss. "Okay?"

"Okay," I said. But I was reluctant to leave. I told myself that if Holly wasn't down about not going to trial, I was. Sure, I'd known *People* vs. *Torkelson* would be almost impossible to win. That didn't matter. I needed to try; I needed the fight.

"I can't believe I won't have to stay late tonight," she enthused. "I'm going to call up my boyfriend and say, 'Hey, let's have dinner.' I hope he doesn't die of shock that I'm actually free."

But this was a big deal, damn it! Didn't Holly have any emotion about it? Or was she some new breed of woman, so smart about the ways of the world that nothing got to her? Had she experienced everything—or seen so much on television—that she had no innocence left? No euphoria? No despair? Something important had just happened. Or was "important" just a word in her vocabulary, a tool in prioritizing? For Holly, life seemed to hold no surprises.

"Speak to you tomorrow!" she promised, trying to pry me out of my chair. Then she began leafing through her papers, searching for her next case.

Sam was the one watching over Mary. The policewoman, a cinder block in a blue uniform, was leaning against the wall opposite them, checking out the scaly skin on her elbows, now that it was Department-decreed short-sleeve season. Sam, leaning toward Mary, was saying God knows what into her ear. He was trying to soothe her. But all Mary seemed to hear was some tragic song in her own head. She did not even look Sam's way. She stared straight ahead, her eyes swollen, ringed black with dissolved eye makeup. But she was no longer crying.

"Mary," I said softly. I gave Sam a Get-away-I'm-a-lawyer look, but he wouldn't budge from her side. In fact, I was not her lawyer. And I was not on her side. I was the reason she was about to be fingerprinted, photographed from the front and in profile, and given the baggy blue female inmate's uniform. "Do you want me to get Barbara back here for you? Or do you want to discuss things with Norman?"

Suddenly Mary came back to life. She seemed to expand in her chair, a parched plant getting water. "I can see him?" she asked.

"I don't think so. But maybe I can talk them into finding a room for you up here, so you can have a private phone conversation." She slumped back down. "Barbara is quite good." I found myself wanting desperately to cheer her up. I gave her an encouraging smile that all but said: Help is right around the corner. Except it wasn't. What was wrong with me? I had done more than my duty. I had done the right thing. Except I felt like hell. God, how I hate ambivalence—and there's so damn much of it.

Mary looked down at her gold sandals, which would, in a matter of an hour or so, be replaced by a pair of often-worn, smelly, ill-fitting prison shoes. My heart went out to her. Not because she was a gorgeous-looking girl going into an ugly place. In the whole scheme of things, I told myself, why shouldn't she be going? She didn't deserve my pity. She had committed the ultimate crime. Taking away her gold sandals, her eyeliner, and her freedom would still not make up for the cut-off life of Bobette Frisch.

But what in God's name had brought Mary Dean to this place? What kind of home had she come from? What sort of family life turns a girl into a hooker at age sixteen? She was so beautiful. She had such a capacity for love. And, okay, she was dumb and coarse and selfish, but as even Sam Franklin had discovered, she was so sweet.

And any chance she might have had for a life was now lost forever.

Twenty

Naturally, Lee had heard stories around the office about Will Stewart's lady friend, Maria. So upper class that she was called Ma-rye-a, not Ma-ree-a. Maria Parkhurst. Half black, half white. Her father was either a rich Socialist or a surgeon, and her mother a dancer for someone—one person mentioned Martha Graham, another said no, Agnes de Mille, and a third was positive she had been the only black Ziegfeld Girl. Whoever her parents had been, Maria Parkhurst had inherited good looks. "Stunning" seemed to be the adjective favored by the lawyers, while one of the homicide detectives who had been invited to the previous year's Nassau County District Attorney's Office picnic preferred "like nothing I've ever seen before."

"You've never met her?" Jazz asked, surprised.

"No." Lee craned her head, looking over her colleagues spread out on blankets on the sand at a private club in Atlantic Beach, a low-key, relatively proletarian club the office had taken over for the day. She spotted someone tall and brown in a lime-green playsuit at the volleyball net, but when the woman turned around, Lee realized it was Wanda, the law librarian, who looked like Louis Armstrong with a wig. "Maria lives in the city, so she's not about to drop into the office. And Will is so close-mouthed about his life he'll only tell you something if you ask. Right around Easter, when he went to Greece, I asked him if he was going alone. He looked at me like I was asking him to see his privates, but he finally said no, he was going with Maria. 'My friend Maria.' Ha! Like they were going to take separate rooms."

"What does she do?"

"She's the assistant headmistress at a girls' school in the city. The Barton School. She teaches history there. It's supposed to be very exclusive, very—"

"It is," Jazz informed her as he returned Woodleigh Huber's wave and exhaled a small but patient sigh as Huber, his white hair rigid in its pompadour despite a brisk ocean breeze, jogged through the sand to greet him. "I guess my old man's party credentials are still okay."

Lee smiled at him. Why not? After the three months of discord following Valerie's birth, Jazz had gone out of his way to be a good and generous husband. Generous in gifts: a ruby ring for Christmas, a big Ford station wagon for her birthday. Part of her was mortified, feeling they were presents for a completely different kind of woman, someone decorative, useless. Certainly they were not presents people still in their twenties should be giving each other. Yet another part could not take her eyes off the sizzling red sparkle on her finger—and cried "Hot damn!" at the classic wood side panels of the wagon, grabbed the key, and went for a ride.

But forget largesse: Jazz had grown generous in understanding. He told Lee he was trying not to view each night she worked late as a personal affront. And as for having asked her to quit work, well, he'd done a lot of thinking about how his mother had stayed at home—and how thoroughly she'd neglected all four of her children. He had been wrong about pressuring her not to go back to the D.A.'s, and he was really snowed by the way she was handling it all. He hoped she would accept his apology.

Added to Jazz's reawakened good nature was the fact that he was now more attractive than ever. The sleek, self-satisfied sheen of young wealth that Lee found profoundly unappealing was being tempered by the loss of his boyish softness, the emergence of sharper, more manly features. To her and, evidently, to the female lawyers and the secretaries on the beach who trekked across the sand in Woodleigh Huber's wake in order to be introduced.

Of course, a woman's having a winner for a husband does not mean her heart freezes in the presence of other men. When Lee finally spotted Will and Maria on the wood steps that led to the beach, she was chagrined at the insistent *thump-thump-thump* in her chest. *Thump!* Will's here! In white shorts, no less— wow, does he have great legs!—and a yellow shirt, with a blue sweater tied with casual perfection around his broad shoulders. He looked as if he had stepped out of the pages of one of the debonair men's magazines Jazz read but had neither the guts nor the panache to emulate. *Thump,* too, because of the woman beside him.

An exasperated *thump,* because Maria really was as advertised. A knockout. No, more. She looked like someone wonderful to know. White pedal pushers, simple white shirt, a plain straw hat, holding Will's arm with practiced intimacy. A warm smile. Will waved. Lee waved back.

"That's got to be him," Jazz said.

"Who else?" she replied, smiling.

"And *her*," he added. "Holy shit!"

Lee behaved as if she were amused by her husband's reaction to Maria Parkhurst. But it is hard to be truly amused at the sight of one's husband googly-eyed over a six-foot-tall, amber-colored, hollow-cheeked beauty, especially when that beauty is on the arm of your great pal, your boss, the second man you think of as, somehow, yours.

Up close, however, Maria was not beautiful, merely fabulous, with almond-shaped hazel eyes and full lips that thrust forward slightly, as if in a kiss. Lee was nervous that Jazz, smitten by Maria, might act foolish, but his manner was perfect and his patter above reproach. She should have known better than to doubt Jazz's social skills, she later reprimanded herself. She did note, however, that he was aiming an inordinate number of four- and five-syllable words at the headmistress when shorter ones would have done fine. Their discussion was fairly straightforward and—so as not to affront Will's Republican sensibilities—innocuous about what the G.O.P. campaign strategy might be against Jimmy Carter. Such purposely inoffensive conversation did not require "eventuate" and "dissimilitude" on Jazz's part.

Fortunately, he calmed down later, reverting to short, friendly words, as the four of them made their way to tables set up on an awninged patio where an early dinner was being served. "How long have you two known each other?" he asked Will and Maria. Lee wanted to pat him on the back: Good work! Will, not surprisingly, remained mum.

Maria answered: "It seems forever, doesn't it?" Will managed to incline his head: Yes, it does. "Let me think. Twelve years, I believe." Her elocution was so perfect it made everyone else sound as if they were talking through huge globs of mashed potatoes. Upper class, but brisk, not with elongated, isn't-life-too-too-tedious vowels. Every word she uttered sounded perfect. And to make it worse, Lee thought—as she stood beside Maria, feeling excessively squat—the woman was nice. Maria disengaged her arm from Will's, turned away from the men, and focused on Lee. "I'm so glad to have the chance to meet you. Will is enormously fond of you."

Lee was about to say, The feeling is mutual, but felt that would be too corny, so she settled for: "Thank you," even though she knew she should have come up with a more graceful response, considering the company she was in.

Maria, meanwhile, was peering along the length of the buffet table. Lee assumed she would turn up her nose at the plebeian food—hot dogs, burgers and a vat of chili—but Maria grabbed a plate. "He used to feel terribly isolated." She plopped two hot dogs onto buns, added sauerkraut and mustard, then helped herself to a hamburger. Why did Will feel isolated? That's what Lee was dying to ask. Because beneath his savoir faire he was shy? "How do you think chili will look on my shirt?" Maria asked. "Oh, what the hell: I'll chance it." Isolated because he was a black working in a largely white world? "Could you pass me a spoonful of those chopped onions, please? Thanks. Oh, look! German potato salad! You know, you're his first friend in that office. I'm not talking about the usual collegial relationships. You're a real friend."

Lee was so thrilled to hear that her feelings about

Will were returned and so grateful that the formidable Maria had chosen to be cordial that it was only near midnight, leaving Val's room after watching her sleep for about fifteen minutes, then searching for an antacid to combat the effects of the chili, that she realized Maria and Will were perfectly matched. Together they dazzled. Together they were interesting, substantive, articulate. Both were decent and courteous well past the point of genuine kindness. And neither gave the slightest hint of what he or she was really feeling.

"Wait," Lee said as she climbed into bed. "Don't go to sleep yet. Tell me what you think about Will Stewart and Maria."

"I think she should buy a sable coat. She'd look magnificent."

"She looks magnificent without it." Lee did not even wait for the loyal, husbandly You look magnificent too. "Do you think they're in love?"

Jazz kept his teeth together, but she could tell by his flaring nostrils that he was stifling a yawn. "I can't tell."

"What do you *think*?" she insisted.

"I think she's awesome."

"But does he?"

Jazz turned over onto his side to face her, acknowledging that sleep was not to be his until the conversation was finished. "I can't tell. For two people who aren't all that demonstrative, they're very affectionate with each other. Holding hands, giving each other private looks when they think no one is watching. I guess they're in love."

"So why don't they get married?"

"I don't know. He works out here and she works in the city."

"Come on! That's twenty-five, thirty miles. And they spend a lot of time together. Weekends. She has a house somewhere up in Connecticut, and he's always going there. And vacations too." Then she added, in a voice she could hear was too emotional, "They're going on a photographic safari in Kenya in September!"

Jazz could not suppress his next yawn. "Can we talk about this tomorrow?"

Two days later, Lee took her five o'clock cup of yogurt into Will's office. He responded by getting a cup of coffee. "How's the *Yancy* appeal coming?" he asked.

"Fine." She stirred up the fruit on the bottom a little too vehemently. "I liked Maria."

"Good," Will said. Knowing something more of an intimate nature was required, he added: "She liked you and Jazz." He waited a fraction of a second and gave her: "I liked Jazz too."

The following week, they went out to a Chinese restaurant, ostensibly to discuss whether she had any thoughts on training the new assistant D.A.'s. But she and Will had been finding some excuse each Wednesday or Thursday for months. Just dinner: Lee could not acknowledge to herself that these evenings were the high points of her week. Their discussions covered a lot of ground: They bickered about politics and delved into legal issues. They discussed everything from how to marinate salmon to their personal lives, although "personal" was a relative term.

Will spoke with respect and affection and some degree of annoyance of his parents, of their ambition for him, and how he felt that no matter how much he accomplished, they were never quite satisfied. He went into some detail about the pain of growing up smart and black but isolated from any black community, a child of servants on the Giddings estate; and of being pressured by his parents to take whatever guff Mr. Giddings' twin sons, boys his age, dished out. To Lee, the twins sounded like everything Will was not: white, stupid, and incredibly mean-spirited. That was as revealing as he got. When he talked about Maria, it was more travelogue than disclosure: We went here; We ate in this restaurant; We heard this orchestra.

Lee, on the other hand, held nothing back, in part because for the first time, she had a friend who truly wanted to listen and had the time to do so and whom she trusted. She told Will about her early life, not just the outline of it but the texture, about her parents and sister and how she had always felt both her I.Q. and her weight were twenty points too high to allow her to be loved by her family. She confided in him all about her early obsession with Jazz, and they talked about what it meant in the marriage. Will was not just a polite listener; he was a rapt audience. He even relished all Lee's updates on Valerie: standing up by herself, sitting beside Lee and pretending to read *The New Yorker* aloud—in her baby gibberish—and the gleeful, devilish look in Val's eyes when she first tasted chocolate.

"Will," she said, so quietly he looked up from his hot and sour soup. "What about you and Maria?" The couple at the next table turned to stare, but whether it was because Lee and Will were white woman with black man or because they sensed an important turn in the conversation, Lee could not tell.

"What's there to talk about?" he asked.

"You know, we're friends. I don't hold back. Now maybe the average mature woman or the average shrewd lawyer wouldn't be so open. But I have absolute confidence in your friendship."

"Good," he said, and crumbled the crispy, greasy noodles he usually disdained into his soup.

"I wish you had the same confidence in mine."

"Lee, you're making a big deal over nothing. What you see is what you get with me. I don't have any secrets. There's no mystery."

"What about you and Maria?"

He took a slow sip of soup. "I love her."

"Does she love you?"

He thought about it for a moment. "Yes. But I don't think we've ever gotten to the point where we're *in* love with each other, at least not at the same time. That's why we never married. I guess deep down, we're a couple of romantic saps. We want it all. That's that."

"That's not that. That can't be."

"It is."

"I want to know how you *feel*?"

"About what?"

"I don't know. About anything. About not being married. About not having children. About being a Republican, for God's sake. How could you have retained your sanity during all those years of Silent Majority crap?"

"It's not that I don't think about things," he said cautiously.

"Are you the only person in the world who doesn't have an inner life?"

"What are you talking about?"

"I want to *know* you. Tell me something I don't know about you."

Will put down his soup spoon. "My biggest regret is that I've never had children. My secret ambition is to write a book about a case the NAACP brought in '38, where the Supreme Court ordered the admission of a black into the University of Missouri Law School because the state hadn't provided a law school for blacks. You want something else? I think tarragon is an overrated herb."

"You know all that isn't what I'm talking about."

"I had a brother who died when he was nine. I was six. Leukemia."

"I'm so sorry. Was it painful for you?"

"What kind of question is that? Of course it was. His name was Timothy. Timmy." He looked away.

So they talked about other things throughout the meal, especially about cooking, as they often did, and Will told her how much he liked shopping for food in Chinatown. After they paid the check, he mentioned that he was very serious about going to China for a couple of months to study cooking. Lee was amused. "When are you going to be free for a couple of months?"

"Soon."

"What do you mean? I can't believe you're actually going to take the time—"

"I'm leaving the office, Lee."

"What?" She didn't get it. "Leaving the D.A.'s?"

"Yes."

"*Why?*" He did not answer right away. Lee hugged herself as if she were cold, but it was summer. She felt frightened. I don't want to be left alone. Don't go! Ridiculous! Would any male lawyer feel like this? *Don't leave me! Don't leave me!* she wanted to plead. What's going to happen to the two of us? How could Will want to go someplace she wasn't?

Crazy, her reaction. She knew that. But she could not imagine a morning without Will opening the door of his office at nine-thirty on the dot and her strolling in with a bag with two cups of coffee and the one buttered sesame bagel they shared. Why, after spending his entire legal career at the D.A.'s, would he choose to quit? Especially now that she was there? "What made you decide to leave?" she managed to ask.

"There's a new chief of Homicide."

"What? Who?"

"Jerry McCloskey."

"I don't believe it!"

"I suggest you do believe it. Huber wants to run for governor in '82. I'm the one person getting in the way of his patronage plans. With Jerry in there—"

"The man's a nincompoop, for God's sake!"

"Well, Lee," Will said, and he reached out and took her hand, something he had never done before, "he's going to be your nincompoop."

The first six months after Will left the office were utter misery, and the next six months were so bad that Lee considered quitting the law altogether. However, she did not want to give Woodleigh Huber the pleasure of replacing her with one of his dum-dum cronies. Also, she sensed neither she nor Val would thrive if she became a full-time homemaker. Oh, it was tempting, but in her heart she knew she would come to loathe fresh-baked bread. She would never finish the complete works of Dickens. And a girl can crochet just so many afghans.

So she stuck to it, trying to compensate for her loss of spirit by throwing herself into her cases with increased vigor. Which is how she and Chuckie Phalen wound up screaming at each other. He was defending the owner of a cesspool service company, one Jimmy Durk, whom the grand jury had indicted for beating to death Marlon "Buck" Toomey, a service station owner who had refused to do any more work on Durk's truck until an outstanding bill had been paid. The beating had been witnessed by Durk's assistant, an eighteen-year-old with a history of drug use.

The fight had begun with Chuckie's outrage that Lee was charging his client with murder, not manslaughter. "There was no intent to cause death!" he shouted. It was not too loud a shout because his lungs were constricted with emphysema. It was, however, angry and antagonistic to the extreme.

"Of course there was. The kid saw Durk banging Buck's head against the car lift over and over and shouting at the top of his lungs—"

"'I'm gonna kill you' is just an expression, and you know it!"

"Murder in the second degree, Chuckie."

The fight had gotten worse when Chuckie discovered that Lee had taken the eighteen-year-old witness under her wing, getting him enrolled in a drug rehabilitation program, arranging with the minister of his mother's church to pay for tutoring so the young man could earn his high school equivalency diploma, getting him a part-time job as a janitor with a furrier in Cedarhurst, a man Jazz and her father knew from the Furriers Industry Council.

Chuckie stormed over to Lee's desk two days later. "You baked the kid cookies!"

"Brownies. So what?"

"'So what?' she says! '*So what?*' You're buying his testimony against my client. So what about that, Mzzzz. White?"

"I'll make you a batch when the case is over, Chuckie," she replied, not even bothering to look up. "Now stop it. You're not going to change my mind." If she had looked up, she would have seen that her opponent had gone from purple-faced to white with rage, and that his jaw was set in stone.

So it did not occur to her an hour later, when Woodleigh Huber's secretary called and said the Boss wanted to see her, that it had anything to do with Chuckie Phalen and *People* v. *Durk*. She only knew that she hated every sprayed-in-place white hair on Huber's head, hated his pale blue telegenic shirts, hated him for putting an incompetent, time-wasting, jurisprudential know-nothing bootlicker like Jerry McCloskey behind Will's desk.

"Come in!" Huber called out in his big, *60 Minutes* voice.

Lee opened the door and saw Huber positioned before his flags and, standing across the desk from him, Chuckie Phalen. She gave Chuckie the beginnings of a you've-got-to-be-kidding smile before turning her attention toward the man all the assistant D.A.'s except her called Boss. "You wanted to see me, Mr. Huber?"

"Are you out of your mind?" Huber roared. Shaken by his vehemence, Lee took a step backward. "Making all sorts of calls on a cooperating witness's behalf? Getting him a *job*?"

"What's wrong with getting him a job?" she inquired.

"What's *wrong*?" Huber cried out.

"It's like giving him money," Chuckie prompted.

"Shut up, Chuckie," Lee said. She was no longer mildly amused by his running to tattle. She was angry, so angry that for once her stomach did not hurt. She turned back to Huber. "What I did was entirely proper."

"Then you're even worse off than I imagined, if you don't get what was wrong! What you did was *outrageous*! You stepped over the bounds of proper prosecutorial conduct." He was booming, as if speaking to a great gathering without a microphone. Lee understood, then, that it was a performance. In part for Chuckie.

More, to show her he had no loyalty to her. She was not part of the team. He could not fire her for cause, but he could make her want to quit. "What you did is a discredit to law enforcement!"

She started to say: I'm sorry, but I don't see it that way, but all she got out was "I'm sorry—"

"Being sorry is not enough!" Huber must have moved, because the flag of the State of New York fluttered. "You're off this case!"

"Mr. Huber, this is—"

"One more word out of you . . . " He let the threat hover in the air, then turned to Chuckie. For Huber, Lee was no longer in the room. "Chuckie, Jerry will call you the minute he's reassigned the case. You have my profound apologies—"

Lee slammed out of his office.

The following day, Jerry McCloskey told her she was no longer in Homicide. If she wanted to, she could remain in the office, but because she had shown such lack of plain old common sense, they did not think she should be trying murder cases. Or even felony cases. The following day, she was assigned an unlawful-dealing-in-fireworks trial.

A week later, she walked out of the District Attorney's Office.

Chuckie Phalen must have heard Lee was packing up because he was waiting on the Courthouse steps, breathing hard. "I'm sorry this happened."

She knew the Old Boys liked lady lawyers to be ladies, so she said: "Fuck you. Fuck the horse you rode in on." Then she added "Ass-kissing snitch," and kept walking.

"What you posit is not without merit," Chuckie conceded. She turned. He fluttered a not-very-white handkerchief. "See? Now listen to me, Lee—and notice I didn't call you 'Sis.' I know you don't like that. I blew my cork and went up to Huber's to blow off a little more steam. I had no idea he'd lace into you like that, especially in front of me, that self-serving windbag. You know what that was all about last week, don't you?"

"Yes, I do," Lee replied coldly. "And he got what he wanted, didn't he? I quit. Maybe he's not such a moron after all." She walked away from Chuckie, but when she saw he was trying to catch up with her and the effort was too much for him, she slowed her pace.

"Buy you lunch?" he inquired, nodding in the direction of the silvery lunch truck parked around the corner.

"No, thank you."

Chuckie was gazing down at the framed photos poking out of her overstuffed tote bag. One that she herself had taken, Jazz and Kent at a Knicks game. Another of her and Jazz with the five pups of Ginger's latest litter. And a picture of Val, queen of the jungle, amid her stuffed animals. "Beautiful. How old is she?"

"Almost two." She could see him working very hard to hide his discomfort: a mother leaving a child that age to go to work.

"Wonderful age. Lovely child. Don't suppose you want to go over to TJ's, have a snort with me?" Lee knew the Old Boys meant by that a jigger of Scotch; cocaine was merely something their clients trafficked in.

"No, thanks. Too early for a snort. And even if it weren't, Chuckie, I don't want to drink with you right now."

"I understand," he said, and let her walk away. But he was waiting as she turned back to see if he was all right. "Lee!" he called out in his reedy voice. "Stick around. We'll open a bottle of glue." Weighed down by her attaché case, her tote bag, her shoulder bag, and a Saks Fifth Avenue shopping bag filled with copies of her appellate briefs and extra pairs of panty hose, she found herself returning to him. "Come in with me." At first, she thought he was suggesting TJ's Taproom again. "Come work for me, Lee. It'll be fun."

"I don't want to work for you, Chuckie. I don't want to work for anybody."

"Come on, Sis, wake up and smell the coffee. You know how many firms will hire a female to do trial work? You should jump up and down and clap your hands and say 'Goody-goody' that I'm making you an offer."

"I'll find something. Or I'll go out on my own." Her possessions felt very heavy, and she had to prevent herself from looking over at the courthouse, in the direction of the District Attorney's Office, wondering if there was a way she could talk her way back in, knowing there was not.

"And who's going to refer cases to you?"

"I hope you will, Chuckie. And I have a few pals." Lee knew Chuckie was aware that she was considered Will Stewart's protégée, and she had no doubt there were rumors of another sort of relationship between them as well. After a six-week trip to China, Will had returned to become a name partner at one of the biggest firms—and certainly the best—on Long Island.

"Will Stewart's doing civil stuff. Is that what you want to do? Rake in the money doing corporate litigation? Is that the kind of law you want to practice, each side trying to suffocate the other under reams of paper? Working ten years on a case, never getting into court? I don't see how your pal stands it. With me, you won't get rich, but you'll get the real McCoy."

"I can get the real McCoy without you."

"Bushwa!"

She knew she would never go to Will with her hat in her hands. She wanted him as a friend, not a patron. And Chuckie was right. How many lawyers would refer criminal cases to her? Corporate? The thought of doing corporate litigation made her want to take a nap. "Thanks, Chuckie. I appreciate your—"

"Aw, don't give me that hooey. Put down your things, would you, so's we can talk properly." She set down her shopping bag, tote bag and attaché case. This was nuts, she thought. Out of a job for five minutes and dickering over a new one on the courthouse steps. Take time to smell the roses. Get a subscription to *Foreign Affairs*. Go to the Frick and look at Dutch masters. "What do you want?" he inquired.

"A partnership."

"A partnership? You're talking through your hat! You're still a kid. You just got your walking papers from the D.A. You're not being realistic. Here I was thinking: This girl's got a head on her shoulders. I guess I was wrong. You're living in a dream world."

"We try it out for a year. You pay me fifty thousand dollars."

"*What*? That's crazy."

"That's a bargain. You've got a huge practice, Chuckie." She did not mention that he was ill and it was common knowledge that he desperately needed help with his caseload. She did not have to. "After a year, we're partners."

"What'll you be asking? Ninety percent of the take?"

"What do you think is fair?"

"Twenty," he muttered. "I'm the founder. I built it up."

She really was embarrassed about haggling with him. After all, she didn't need the money. Everyone knew she had a successful husband. Allow an Old Boy like Chuckie his male pride.

Not if she was going to be his partner. "Thirty percent, and fifty percent of any work I bring in."

"You've been smoking that funny stuff, Sis."

"Call me 'Sis' one more time and it's off."

"Lee," he sighed, and put out his hand.

She shook it and said, "Chuckie."

While Will celebrated her decision to join Chuckie
Phalen as if she had just been appointed attorney general,
sending not merely a case of champagne to Lee's new
office but a six-foot-tall flowering hibiscus tree, Jazz
reacted as if she'd told him she had bought new towels
for the guest bathroom. "Great," he said, bisecting his
baked potato and hiding it under a dollop of sour cream
only a person with a vigorous metabolism could consider.
"I look forward to meeting him." Lee ground some pepper
on her half potato and waited for questions about their
deal. Jazz wasn't just her husband; he was a smart businessman as well as a lawyer. But he had no questions.

Lee was furious at his reaction: I have to listen to a
two-hour diatribe about what the fur buyer at Bonwit
Teller said about the buttonholes on raccoon jackets and
then prove I'm listening by asking questions for another
hour, and he can't even ask: Hey, where's your new
office? But as she was doing with increasing frequency,
she quickly transformed her anger to hurt, and then
almost immediately transmuted her wounded feelings
into sympathy. I understand Jazz is having trouble dealing with my career because he was brought up in such a
hidebound, male-dominated world and because the
whole subject of lawyering is painful to him. He's trying
so hard to be supportive, and he's really thoughtful
about everything else.

This was true. When she was on trial, he took over

completely, coming home early from work, often giving their nanny a night off to be with her boyfriend, making dinner for two—him and Val. While Lee still fulfilled many of the usual female functions—buying birthday and Christmas gifts, keeping the social calendar and the family checkbook, gardening—Jazz took over the grocery shopping and stacked and emptied the dishwasher.

And he did it with such good nature. Lee could never get over his best quality, his innate cheer, and realized that it would have been wasted in the solemn halls of Johnson, Bonadies and Eagle. But in the retail business, his buoyancy, blue-blood manners, and brilliant smile brought him nothing but success. Where Leonard was insecure, Jazz was confident. The younger man was the one who decided to approach chichi department stores around the country and soon had them carrying Le Fourreur's line of fun furs—jackets and coats designed for everyday wear. Emboldened by his success in the upscale market, Jazz, subtly and diplomatically, convinced his father-in-law to overcome his snobbery and go out for the low-priced trade as well; there were now three Furhavens in New York and New Jersey, with a fourth and fifth on the drawing boards.

So before their thirtieth birthdays, Mr. and Mrs. Jasper Taylor—as the place cards at the Fashion Congress's annual Luxe Awards dinner had them—were already a well-to-do young couple.

"Turn around," Sylvia said to Lee, eyes narrowing as she assessed her daughter's outfit, a classic ivory strapless ball gown that gleamed, like the pearl choker she was wearing, against Lee's golden skin. "Nice. Whose is it?"

"Valentino."

"Impeccable. When did you get it?"

"Last month sometime." Then she added, because she knew it would annoy her mother. "I went one day during my lunch hour."

Sylvia sighed and shook her head at Robin, but fairly good naturedly. Now that her younger daughter was drug-free and dressed in a four-thousand-dollar blue-and-green Saint Laurent peasant gown, she was easier about granting her elder daughter the right to be eccentric. "And I'll bet you bought this because it didn't need any alterations," Sylvia said indulgently.

"Absolutely. My fashion philosophy is: If it zips up, I buy it."

"I knew it!" Sylvia crowed. "See? I know you, Lee!"

The Penthouse at the St. Regis was filled with men in their black and white tuxedos and with their women, gorgeous peacocks strutting their colors in silks and jewels. Even in the soft dimness meant to approximate candlelight, Lee was nearly overcome by the beauty of so much smooth, bare skin against lustrous fabric, by the sweet and spicy scents of extravagant perfumes, by these people's casual acceptance of their own incredible wealth. So different from her working world, from the savagery and sewer stench of the holding pens in criminal court to the wood-paneled, leather-chaired austerity of fine old law firms like Will's.

"Are you okay, Lee?" Robin asked.

"Fine," she said, as she watched Jazz dazzle a department store dowager agleam in emeralds and diamonds, the diamonds far whiter than the smile the woman was flashing back at Jazz. "I love to watch him work the room."

"He's not bad," Robin said, then flung back her head and burst out laughing at her own understatement. Her long blonde hair, held only by a velvet ribbon, shone in the pale light. Jazz glanced in their direction and waved at them. "He's a social genius is what he is. Can you imagine anyone feeling that at ease with themselves?"

Lee shook her head. She was glad Robin was there, because she certainly did not feel at ease. The cocktail hour was already stretched to nearly two, and no one except her seemed wiped out by the continuing parade of magnificence and the paucity of hors d'oeuvres. She needed her sister. Yet she wished Robin were elsewhere. It disturbed her that her sister's life had not changed. Twenty-seven years old and still a volunteer at a day care center, still a college dropout, still living at home and vacationing with her parents. But Robin herself had changed, Lee knew, from her old self-absorption to being the most loving and reliable sister, an adoring aunt, a fond sister-in-law. Lee and Jazz often included her in their plans not out of familial obligation but because Robin was good company.

Jazz came over and put an arm around each of them. "Bearing up?" he asked, just as the lights flickered, signaling dinner.

"We're fine!" Robin said happily.

"Fine," Lee assured him. He shepherded them into the perfectly proportioned ballroom to their table, keeping perfect pace with the rest of the graceful crowd. Not an elbow was jostled, not a hem stepped on. He held out a chair for each of them and Lee watched as Leonard mimicked his courtesy and did the same for Sylvia. Several men at other tables followed suit, until a contagion of chair-pulling overcame the ballroom. "See what you started?" she asked Jazz, delighted. She took his hand until the banquet was served, a menu chosen less for taste than for its lack of drippiness.

She ate and watched her husband pick at his food, too busy being the Golden Boy to eat. He waved, he stood to chat with table-hoppers. He shook hands, kissed cheeks, accepted compliments with sweet modesty, and laughed. It was only when Jazz sat back down that she caught a glimpse of him pressing his tired back against the rear of his chair, closing his eyes for an instant. When he opened them, there was not a sign of laughter. His eyes seemed as old as those of the ninety-year-old shoe mogul in a wheelchair at the next table. Older, because the shoe mogul was swiveling his head, taking everything in, tearing off bits of his roll and stuffing them into his mouth, greedy for now and for banquets to come. It was only then that she understood that Jazz was just as miserable in this splendiferous company as she was.

She kept busy with the cases Chuckie handed over to her: a criminal possession of stolen property here, a grand larceny there. But although Lee received a few referrals from the attorneys she had come up against as a prosecutor, they were relatively minor matters. She knew she had to prove herself as a defense lawyer. It was easy for the Old Boys, and the younger ones as well, to brush her off with the explanation that anyone can win when representing the People; the facts are on the People's side.

How do I get a big case? she asked Will during one of their daily phone calls. I want a showcase case, where they can see what I can do. Will said simply: Ask for it. What do you mean, *ask for it*? Start taking lawyers to lunch, he advised her. Tell them you're looking to build up your own practice, that you don't feel it's right to rely solely on Chuckie. Talk shop with them. Let them see you as a colleague, not as a girl lawyer. If someone has a big-mother case, ask if you can be second seat. *Ask?* she practically gasped. This is your professional livelihood—okay, Lee? It's not like asking a boy out on a date. It's permissible. It's also permissible, if you hear of a big, fat, juicy crime, to try to get there before anyone else does.

The eleven o'clock Sunday-night news is really a no-news broadcast. Politicians announce nothing new on Sundays. Not a single press release is issued, and no one marches to protest anything. So on that night, television journalists elaborate on sports and weather and offer horrific reports of fires, rapes, and murders. On a cold and sleety Sunday night in February, she heard that Eddie Urquhart of Locust Valley had been savagely beaten that morning as he slept late. He was in a coma, and although a spokesman would not comment, a source at Glen Cove Hospital said he was not expected to recover. Lee, who had spent the day making Valentine decorations with Val and Kent, organizing her scarves and sweaters by color, making love with Jazz during Val's nap, and going out to a new and mediocre Northern Italian restaurant with her parents and Robin, sat up in her bed. "Did you hear that?" she asked Jazz. "Beaten to death in his bed this morning. A million bucks it wasn't a burglar. What burglar sneaks into a house on a Sunday morning?"

He glanced over the top of the business section of the *New York Times.* "What?"

"Shhh," she said, as the barely postpubescent reporter, his face shiny with sleet, stood before a grand colonial house with white pillars and told her that Urquhart was the owner of Spectacle, a chain of eye-glass and contact lens stores located—"On Long Island!" Lee crowed. Nassau County police were said to be questioning Mrs. Urquhart for a description of the intruder. "She did it!" Lee announced.

"Who?"

"The wife." Her pulse was racing.

"How do you know?" Jazz asked. Not waiting for an answer, he went back to an article on regional customs unions.

"I feel it," she said, putting both hands over her heart.

At seven the following morning, she called and woke Chuckie, to find out who represented Spectacle. He didn't know. At eight, she called Will at home, who said it wasn't De Ruyter, Lefkowitz and Stewart, but he'd check when he got to the office, first thing, to see if anyone knew. At nine-twenty, she found out it was Keelan and Stern, Woodleigh Huber's former law firm. Damn! she said. Will said, You're going to worry if he bad-mouths you? His former partners probably don't trust his opinion any more than we do. Okay, Lee said. Let me give it a shot. Will wished her bon voyage and extracted a promise that she would call immediately if anything happened.

At ten-thirty, she was sitting in the office of one of Keelan and Stern's senior partners, Peter Pappas, a contemporary of Huber's, a man given to high Victorian-style collars that hid his entire neck. Thus his large, bald head was a giant bubble emerging from his shirt.

"You don't have to give me your curriculum vitae," he told Lee. "I've heard of you."

"From Woodleigh Huber?" she asked, prepared to defend herself.

"Nah!" he snapped, rather viciously, she thought. "Around. Grape-vine."

"Good," she said. "I appreciate your seeing me on such short notice. I don't want to waste your time."

Pappas nodded: good idea. "I understand you represent Eddie Urquhart. I'm sorry to hear about his troubles. But it's his wife I'm interested in."

"Why?"

"It sounds as if she might need a criminal lawyer. I'd like an introduction. For a woman of her background, I think I'd be the ideal choice."

"You do?"

"Let me tell you why."

At noon, Lee was in Locust Valley talking with Paula Urquhart, gathering information, finding out precisely how much the woman had already told the police. Two hours later, Paula Urquhart took Lee into the library, a low-ceilinged room filled with leather-bound unread books. It smelled like a crypt. Paula drew the dusty damask curtains and showed Lee the myriad lumps, concavities, and scars all over her body that were the result of the beatings Eddie inflicted during twenty-two years of married life. At a quarter to three, Paula signed a check for Lee's ten-thousand-dollar retainer. Then she made a pot of coffee, and they sat around until the police came to arrest Paula for assault with intent to kill.

"You're not giving me a hell of a lot to work with," Terry Salazar told Lee. He had just opened his own investigative agency. In a blue suit just slightly too bright to be called navy and crepe-soled brown suede shoes, he still looked more like a cop than a capitalist.

"I don't have a hell of a lot," Lee responded. "Paula told the precinct cops that she'd been downstairs, reading the paper. When she came back upstairs around eleven, to shower, the window was open and Eddie had his head bashed in. She thought he was dead."

"Except he wasn't."

"Right. Just comatose. The first cop on the scene noticed that the window was only open about nine inches. It would have to have been a pretty skinny burglar."

"Who, by the by," Chuckie added from the couch in Lee's office, "was so busy bashing Eddie's head in that he forgot to burgle anything."

"This Paula babe doesn't sound like a criminal genius," Terry observed.

"I think Eddie bopped her on the head one too many times," Lee said.

"Insanity defense?" Chuckie inquired politely.

"I'm not sure yet, but I don't think so. She doesn't seem at all nuts. Nice as nice can be. She put up a pot of coffee and defrosted a Mrs. Smith apple pie for the crime scene crew. Anyway, insanity is a real desperation defense. It hardly ever works."

"Almost never," Chuckie concurred.

Lee rubbed her face, trying to erase the fatigue. Now that she had the Urquhart case, she had no idea what she was going to do with it. Still, she finally had her own client, and a client who could afford to hire Terry. And Chuckie Phalen was sitting in her office, not she in his. It was all—she smiled to herself—exhilarating.

"What was the weapon?" Terry asked.

"One of her kids' old ice skates. The blade." Both men barely suppressed a shudder. "She says she was up in the attic going through the old sporting goods stuff, looking for a baseball bat, but then the bulb started to flicker, and she got scared so she grabbed the first thing she could. She knew it wasn't as good as a baseball bat, so she made sure that her first hit was a hard one, and right between the eyes."

"He's a vegetable?"

"Now and forever." She closed her eyes for an instant, trying to imagine Paula Urquhart as she made her first hit with the blade of the ice skate. Then she pictured the scarred, misshapen mess that was her client's body. "She was deathly afraid," Lee explained when she opened her eyes. "That's why she tried to kill him."

"Self-defense?" Terry asked with a chuckle.

"I hear it's worked in a couple of states," Chuckie said, squelching Terry's chuckle. Then he turned to Lee. "Wasn't Eddie sleeping at the time?"

"It's still self-defense," Lee told him. "He beat her, he terrorized her for years. She lived in that big house on the Sound. Alone. No housekeeper, no nothing. After the second kid went off to college, he took away her car. He said it was because she'd dented the fender twice and couldn't be trusted. He would not let her out of that damned house! The only time she left in the last year was for her two trips to the emergency room. He was holding her prisoner. She knew it was only a matter of time until he killed her. And she had to save her own life."

So this is the problem, Terry reported to Lee. I checked out all the hospitals she's been to over the years, all the doctors. And she never once said, Hey, my husband is beating the shit out of me, punching me in the stomach till I'm puking up blood. Paula tells them she was in a car accident, or she had her steam iron fall on her—she used that one a lot—or she was in the garden and got hit by a rake, or she was cleaning out a closet and all the stuff fell onto her. There's no record of her ever accusing Eddie of laying a hand on her. One doctor said he asked her: Is your old man beating you up? And you know what she said?: How dare you!

Go back, Lee told him. Find out if the doctors felt the injuries were more consistent with a beating than with an accident. And don't let your hospital contacts read her medical records to you. I want you to look at them yourself. Somewhere, someone must have made a little note about isn't it odd how her left wrist keeps breaking. Three times, as if someone twisted it and twisted it till it snapped. Ask if they're willing to testify. If they're not, tell them we'll subpoena them. Speak to all his employees at the Spectacle stores: Has he ever flown off the handle at work? Gotten into any fights?

She spoke with social workers, psychologists, psychiatrists and academic experts in the still burgeoning field of domestic violence and hired expert witnesses. She employed a photographer who specialized in medical malpractice cases to photograph Paula Urquhart's disfigured body. And she met daily with her client.

Paula Urquhart, unfortunately, looked perfectly capable of fending off whatever blows came her way. At forty-three, she was of slightly above average height and appeared solid, as if she was even larger but had been compacted. Her hair was light enough that the gray was not at first noticeable. She wore it off her face and seemed shaken when they took away her plastic tortoiseshell headband in the Nassau County Correctional Center. She was neither pretty nor homely, but totally forgettable. It was only when you stared at her, searching her bland face for the wielder of the ice skate, that you noticed one cheek was higher than the other, which had been flattened by repeated blows to the face.

"Paula, was there a telephone in the house?" Lee asked. They spoke in a small room in the women's section of the jail, an area referred to as the Waldorf, where inmates charged with highly publicized cases were held. The Waldorf had a common room for meals and TV, a few cells, and a small, square interrogation room, which was used for lawyers' conferences. It was furnished rather luxuriously for the center, with two chairs that were not nailed down and a couch covered in artificial blue leather. In her blue uniform, Paula seemed part of the furniture.

"A telephone?" Paula repeated, not seeing the point of the question. "Of course we had a telephone." She counted on her fingers. "Six extensions. No, wait, seven. There's one in the basement."

"And Eddie went to work . . . how often?"

"Six days a week." Her voice was strong yet sweet, like that of a teacher of early primary grades.

"If I put you on the stand, the prosecutor is going to ask why—in all those years—you didn't call for help."

"He said he'd kill me if I talked about our private matters. That's what he called it all the time: 'a private matter.' He'd come home and if he was feeling mean . . . it was hard to tell from looking at him, because he's got such a nice face. Friendly. With freckles. People always think freckles are friendly."

"'A private matter'?"

"Yes. He'd come in and put down his briefcase and hand me his coat and I'd hang it up. When I came back, if he'd say: 'Paula, I have a private matter to discuss with you,' then I knew I was in trouble."

"And then? He'd start hitting you?"

"No. He'd talk to me, tell me what I did wrong. Like he felt sorry for me and wanted to help me see where I was making a mistake. Then he'd get angry and say I wasn't paying attention or something. And then he'd yell, and pretty soon he'd start hitting."

"Did he hit you with his hands?" Lee observed Paula closely, looking for emotion, but could find none; she spoke as if what she was describing had happened to a woman she had never met. Lee knew her expert witnesses could explain this seemingly dispassionate account, this distancing of herself from the horror she had experienced, in order to survive. But come on, Lee thought. Cry a little, for God's sake. Help me out. Give me some tears for the jury.

"Usually he punched me, but if something was around, he'd use that."

"Like what?"

"Like anything. A wooden hanger. A pot. A Dustbuster."

"You have two children, twenty-one and nineteen. Right?" Paula nodded. Lee did not see the instinctive smile most mothers display when their children are mentioned. "Are you on good terms with them?"

"Oh yes. Very good."

"Did they ever see Eddie beat you?"

Paula's forehead creased. She touched her ring finger, probably to twirl her wedding ring around, but it was in an envelope in a safe in the correctional center's basement. "Not really."

"What do you mean?"

"They saw him get angry and shove me. Maybe smack me once or twice. But he was good about keeping his temper around them. He'd wait till after dinner and till I cleaned up. Then he'd say: 'Excuse me, kids. Mom and I have a private matter to discuss.'"

"But he beat you severely. Don't you think they heard anything?"

"I hope not. I tried very hard to keep quiet. I didn't want to frighten them."

"Ladies and gentlemen of the jury, good morning. My name is Lee White, and I am the lawyer for Paula Urquhart. Mrs. Urquhart is accused of a vicious crime: assault with intent to kill. As the prosecutor has told you, on Sunday morning, February tenth, someone entered the bedroom in the Urquharts' mansion in Locust Valley and beat Eddie Urquhart so badly that he is now in a coma and not expected to recover. That someone was not a homicidal maniac, not a burglar whom Eddie surprised, but his wife, Paula, whom you see there at the defense table in the pink shirtwaist. You may be asking yourselves: How come, if we admit to this crime, we're here pleading not guilty?"

The courtroom was packed. Chuckie, Will and a couple of his partners, Barbara Duberstein and a score of past and present assistant district attorneys sat comfortably, their arms draped on the backs of the wooden benches to display their proprietorship of the halls of justice. They were not there only to root for Lee or the prosecutor, however; this was one of the first invocations of the battered wife defense in the county, and they wanted to see it. Terry Salazar was right behind the defense table, wearing a new suit. He had been foul-mouthed and obnoxious but brilliant. Lee was amazed when he discovered how many people were aware of what Eddie was doing to Paula, and even more amazed at how many Terry had been able to convince to testify.

The press was there too, as were everybody's relatives, from the judge's incredibly fecund extended Italian family, which took up three rows, to Eddie and Paula Urquhart's—sitting on separate sides of the courtroom—to Lee's. Ginger and Fos fit right in, but Sylvia, Leonard, Robin, and Jazz were so glaringly attractive, so fashionably turned out, that they might have been VIP's in the first row for Thierry Mugler's latest collection. Lee made sure not to glance in their direction so as not to align herself with the overprivileged and, by doing so, alienate the jury. However, even without looking, she could feel, hanging heavily in the air, her mother's disapproval of her gray dress with white collar and cuffs. The few remaining seats were taken by courtroom buffs, including a retired mailman who watched all Lee's trials. When he took his seat, the mailman had pointed to his lapel: a white carnation. "White," he had called out, and winked.

"We're here because for twenty years of their twenty-two-year marriage, Eddie Urquhart beat this woman, sometimes once a week. Not shoved, not smacked, not even hit. Beat her with his fists, with broomsticks, with a lamp. The first time that he broke her nose and cheekbone, he did it by hitting her full force in the face with a telephone. Not just once, but over and over again." Lee stopped and took a deep breath. Oxygen, fuel so she could be propelled onward to talk about something so revolting she could hardly bear it. She, not Paula, would be the one to show the judge and jury the terrible toll of Eddie Urquhart's violence, since nothing—not even Lee's not very veiled suggestion that it was all right to show some emotion— could wipe the pleasant expression from Paula's face. She prayed that by the end of the trial, the jury would understand that this was one of the cruelest scars of all.

"The first question that came to my mind when I heard about this case was this: How come she didn't call the police if it was so bad? Eddie was a successful businessman, and he worked every day but Sunday. Paula had a phone. For a while, before he took it away, she even had a car. If she was too proud or too fearful to call the police, she could have taken her children, escaped. She could have told one of the emergency room doctors bandaging her fractured ribs: My husband did this to me. She could have called her brother or her sister and cried: Help me! Hide me! And if she was totally desperate, she could have armed herself, and the next time Eddie brutalized her, she could have shot him in self-defense. If she had done that, she would not be in this courtroom today. Well, in order to find her not guilty, you'll have to understand in your hearts just why Paula could not cry out for help, why she had to wait and strike at her husband the only time when he was not her personal terrorist, her very own torturer: when he was asleep."

Lee outlined for the jury the witnesses who would testify to Eddie's brutality: the frighteningly polite Urquhart children and an oil-burner serviceman. Paula was the perfect housewife, with a list of repairmen and a file of their bills. Every one of those people had been contacted by Terry. Only one had observed friendly-faced, freckled Eddie out of control, but the man could tell how Eddie had banged Paula's head against a wall near the thermostat six times. Then, moving the length of the jury box, Lee summarized the testimony her expert witnesses would give. "You will hear, ladies and gentlemen, that Paula was a prisoner of terror. The one reality in her life was that this all-powerful man would hurt her if he was displeased. It was not a fear: It was fact. He inflicted terrible pain on this woman two and three and four times a month. And he was displeased so easily. If a shirt button was loose, she got punched in the mouth so hard she lost three teeth. When she dared to serve him a steak that he said was over-cooked, he broke a bottle of wine over her head. It took two hours in the emergency room for them to get all the pieces of glass out of her scalp. She told the doctor she and Eddie had been having a drink in a bar and somehow she got hit when two men began to fight. If those were the punishments for the crimes of a loose shirt button and a well-done steak, can you imagine how she feared the punishment for telling the truth? The lawyer for the District Attorney's Office is going to try and make it sound easy. 'Dial 911. What was the big deal?' By the end of this trial, you will understand with terrible clarity what the big deal was."

After her opening, Jazz kissed her and said: "There are no words." Then he found one: "Amazing." Robin echoed "Amazing," and Sylvia and Leonard held back for a moment before embracing her, as if waiting for permission. They were not just proud, she sensed, but a little frightened of her.

"Good opening," Chuckie said, and pinched her cheek.

"A-plus, Whitey!" the mailman called out.

"I can't believe it," Barbara Duberstein said. "Me, buying this defense. But you got me."

Will waited for her by the water fountain. He seemed both amused and pleased by the fuss over her. She left the others and approached him. He had such grace, such stature, that he made everyone else in the hall outside the courtroom appear dim. "Well?"

"A great opening. Really. You're on your way."

"But not there yet. Did you see juror—"

"Number four?" Will asked. "With his mouth all screwed up, like he's saying 'Give me a break. Had to save her own life by cracking his head open with an ice skate while the poor guy was asleep. Ha!' Number four's a rough one, Lee. You're going to have to fight for his soul." But he said it with spirit, indicating it would be a good fight, one that would be worth something whether she won or lost.

"Any advice?" she asked.

He thought for a moment. "It's just a case. You've tried hundreds. Don't blow this up too much. Don't think this is going to make or break your career. If you lose, people will know you did a fine job, and you'll get some referrals. If you win, you'll get a lot of nice phone calls and a few more referrals but you won't make the cover of *Time*." She nodded, knowing objectively that he was right although not quite believing it. Then she began to go over the pros and cons of a particular line of questioning she was thinking of using with the government's expert on domestic violence—all the while wishing that instead of telling her it had been a great opening, Will had hugged her.

Nothing could have prepared her. She was so exhausted after the first week of trial that she wished she could have hired someone to brush her teeth for her. On Sunday morning, she sat at the kitchen table beside Kent, showing him how to hull strawberries. His hands and arms were covered with red juice. Val, in her high chair, was throwing slices of apple about in a spiteful manner, as if she had saved her entire quota of Terrible Twos egregious behavior for this hour.

Jazz had come in minutes before and was unpacking groceries, humming a sappy old song. He seemed so happy that she did not feel too guilty that she was not paying attention to him. She turned from Val—clutching the last apple slice in her hand, debating whether to fling it or eat it—to Kent. Now he had crushed strawberries in his hair. "How about a shower, kiddo?" she asked him.

"No."

"And a shampoo."

"No."

"New soap, new shampoo."

Kent considered her offer and decided to yield to temptation. Whenever they went on vacation, Lee saved the complimentary toiletries the hotels gave out, knowing that nothing made Kent happier than his own new cake of soap. She decided to go along with him to make sure he did not transfer strawberries to the wallpaper as he climbed the stairs. "You'll watch Val, Jazz? "

"Sure," he said. Lee glanced up at the clock. Nearly eleven. She was trying not to think about the trial. But it was at nearly that very hour, on another Sunday, that Paula Urquhart told herself that if she did not act soon, Eddie would be waking up.

Lee found a cake of soap—The Breakers, Palm Beach—where they had spent a week the previous winter watching rain on the ocean. But although there were four bottles of hair conditioner left in the box she kept in the linen closet, there was no shampoo. "Here," she said to Kent. "You start your shower and I'll go find shampoo."

"I'll wait," he said, clearly thinking she was trying to pull a fast one. She laughed at his suspicious expression and walked into the bedroom, to Jazz's closet. Stretching to reach the top shelf, she got down his travel kit. Beside the mini-can of Gillette Foamy and the smallest bottle of Tylenol was a miniature bottle of shampoo from a hotel. She sighed, relieved. Confrontation averted. She zipped up his case and returned it to the shelf. "See?" she said to Kent. "Would I kid you about new shampoo?" She glanced at the bottle. Hotel Carlyle. New York. New York? Why would Jazz have shampoo from a New York hotel?

"Give me it!" Kent was irate at her holding back. Lee checked it again, thinking she had misread it. Hotel Carlyle. New York. Kent grabbed it from her hand and went to shower.

All right, maybe the Carlyle was part of some chain and Jazz had really gotten the shampoo in Toronto, where he had gone for some big fur fashion show. Or it could have been from when they'd traveled out West and stayed in Portland for a long weekend to spend time with his sister Irene.

But in her heart she knew how the shampoo had got from the Hotel Carlyle into her husband's overnight kit.

The prosecutor waited until Jazz had been asleep for nearly an hour. Around midnight, she got out of bed. He did not stir. Methodically, she went through his closet. In a pocket in his camera bag, she found one of the miniature books sold at the counters of bookstores: Elizabeth Barrett Browning's *Sonnets from the Portuguese*. The tiny red ribbon bookmark was placed on what Lee knew to be the most over-quoted poem in the English language: "How do I love thee? Let me count the ways." She searched, heart pounding, but found no inscription, no "To JT with love from Whomever." Careful. They were being careful. She realized the sappy song he had been humming that morning was "Secret Love."

You've gone off the deep end, the defense lawyer in her declared. He bought the book in a sentimental moment on some business trip and forgot it in his camera bag. And the shampoo? An out-of-town department store buyer visiting New York could have given it to him. Do you honestly believe that? the prosecutor demanded. No, she did not.

She tiptoed downstairs. She knew Jazz would not be so stupid as to charge an extramarital affair on their joint American Express card, but she went through the receipts for the past twelve months: no evidence. At twelve-twenty, she woke Terry Salazar and told him she had a confidential matter she wanted handled. He understood that when she said "handled," she did not mean handled the following morning. When she called him back at one-thirty, he told her that a J. Taylor from a company called Le Fourreur had stayed at the Carlyle twenty-two times in the past year. She wrote down the dates. Thank you, she said to Terry. Please hand-deliver your bill. Don't send it to the firm. There's no bill, he said. And listen, Lee, I've already forgotten what I just found out. She thanked him and he told her he was sorry for her troubles and it sucked the big one, didn't it, learning shit like this when she was on trial.

She had forgotten she was in the middle of the Urquhart case. Absolutely forgotten. Twenty-two times. So he was seeing her twice a month. Was she from out of town? From New York and married? He traveled only about two or three nights a month. Except on buying trips to Scandinavia and the U.S.S.R. And for industry conferences. Or if a store executive needed special handling. Actually, he was away more than she had realized.

She took the list of dates she had written down and the little book of sonnets, and retrieved the bottle of shampoo from the floor of Kent's shower. She hid the evidence in the toe of her L. L. Bean Maine hunting shoe. Then she went back to bed, where the man who had betrayed her slept in perfect peace.

"Not now," Will told her.

"I have to," Lee insisted.

"Of course you have to. But you're on trial for two or three more weeks." At eight-fifteen the next morning, they were sitting in the empty courtroom. Lee realized that Will had simply assumed she wanted company, or was getting cold feet and needed bucking up; he arrived with a heartening greeting and a bag with two coffees and a sesame bagel. Still, when she told him of her discovery, he did not flinch or appear in any way surprised. She did not want to ask if there had been something about Jazz she had not seen, if Will had felt all along that he was a heel. For the time being, she took comfort in telling herself that Will was the worldliest man she knew and, therefore, nothing surprised him. "If you deal with your marriage now," he told her, "you won't have the energy to deal with Paula Urquhart."

"How can I not think about it?" she asked, staring into the tan depths of her coffee.

"I'm not saying not to think. I'm saying not to act— unless you feel there is some need for immediate action."

"Who could it be?" she asked. "*Why*? What did I do—"

"I'll take the day off right after your jury comes in. We'll sit down and talk about everything for the entire day. I'll even throw in lunch. Okay? Right now, tell me: What's your biggest problem in the case?"

"You're trying to get my mind off Jazz."

"Yes."

Lee was not sure if she had managed a smile or if her face had merely twisted. "My biggest problem?"

"That's right."

"It's that I am totally convinced of my self-defense theory when I'm in court. This woman was so terrified that she felt her husband was in sole control of her fate. She wasn't able to call for help because somehow Eddie would find out. He was her whole universe. He was God, and he was omnipotent."

"Why is that a problem?" Will asked.

"Because when I'm not in court, when I'm driving home or shaving my legs I start to think: This woman is full of shit."

"You do?"

"My own experts testify under oath that she could not have picked up the phone and called the cops or a priest or someone for help. They swear there was no way she could have told the truth about what hit her all those times she went to the doctors and the hospital. They say, sure, the kids heard what was going on, and yes, they're quite damaged, but she did the best she could, protecting them from seeing the worst of it by going upstairs. And you know what? I can't buy it. There's a voice inside me saying: No matter what, you have to take responsibility for yourself. It may take everything you've got, it may kill you, but ordinary people act with amazing courage every day. And even if she couldn't stop the abuse for herself, how could she not protect her children from living in that hell?"

"You don't think the killing was self-defense?"

"I think she did have to get rid of him. I think she could have done it two ways: with a call to a local cab company, saying come and get me—or with an ice skate. I think she hated him. With good reason. He did terrible things to her. He took away joy and he took away hope. She hated what she had become. I have no doubt that she was a victim of a terrible, continuing crime. And if I were on my jury, I'd tell myself: Self-defense? Bullshit! She murdered him in cold blood."

"How does the jury find the defendant Paula Urquhart on the count of assault in the first degree with intent to kill?"

"The jury finds the defendant not guilty, Your Honor."

The night after the jury came in, Lee slept for thirteen hours. The second night, she told the nanny to go out, visit her boyfriend, enjoy herself. She sent Kent for a visit with his parents. She sent Val to her parents' house with five stuffed animals. She knew Robin could be trusted to keep Val happy.

Jazz flew into the house at seven o'clock, a huge bouquet of white roses mixed with white lilies and a bottle of fine red wine to celebrate her victory. When he heard Kent and Val were spending the night away from home, he could not hang up his trench coat fast enough. He raced back into the kitchen, but Lee was not there. When he rushed into the living room and found her sitting at the end of the couch, feet primly on the floor, he said: "Hey, the flowers are still in the kitchen. You forgot to put them in water."

"I don't care about the flowers."

"What's wrong, honey?" He sat beside her, his brow creased with concern. She knew he was waiting to hear how exhausted she was, or that after all the adrenaline of the trial, she was let down. Lee could feel the warmth of his arm through the sleeve of his suit, so she got up and sat in a chair catercornered to his. "Something's the matter?" he asked.

"You are having an affair." He got out the "Wh—" of "What are you talking about" but she cut him off. "On nights that you were supposedly out of town on business, you stayed at the Carlyle. Thirty-five East Seventy-sixth, corner Madison." It is said that when people are shocked, they look as if they have been hit in the stomach. To Lee, Jazz looked as if he'd been hit in the face. His features went slack and so soft that the bones underneath could have been shattered into smithereens. "But then, I don't have to give you the address, do I? You found it twenty-two times." She watched as he tried to come back with something, but he could not find anything to say. He put his head in his hands. His wedding band looked dull in the lamplight, as if it had a film of soap scum over it.

Finally, he spoke through his fingers. "When did you find out?"

She wanted to tell him what a horrible blow it had been, seeing that little shampoo bottle. Twelve days I held it in! You know how they say in stories: She thought her heart would break? Well, my chest hurt on the left side for almost two weeks. A terrible, piercing pain sometimes. It would spread out and it would zing me, in the middle of the day as I was rising to object, in the middle of the night. But I'm too much the trial lawyer to give away my case, she told herself. And with that, she gave away her case. "Who is she?" she cried out, unable to stop herself from showing how little she really knew. He sat there, his head still in his hands, saying nothing. "Damn it, I have a right to know who she is!"

"No, you don't." He stood and walked across the room and poured himself a tumbler of vodka. He did not ask if she wanted anything.

"Do you love her?" she demanded of his back.

In his own good time he turned around. "I don't know," he said quietly. Then he added: "Yes."

It was worse than she had thought. In all her imaginings, he always started crying and begged for another chance, that the woman was nothing, stupid, not worth throwing away a beautiful marriage for. Please, Lee, forgive me. "What do you want to do?" she asked.

"I don't know."

"Do you want to end the marriage? Or do you want to give her up?"

"I wish I knew what I wanted. I wish I knew what would be the right thing."

"How could you sleep with me when you're sleeping with someone else?"

"Don't."

"Don't *what*?" she shouted. "Don't imagine you fucking your brains out at the Carlyle and stealing teeny bottles of shampoo, you cheap bastard!"

"Oh," he said. "Is that how you found out?"

She was not going to let him think he had been caught on that one false move. "One of many clues. You didn't cover your trail very well." She waited for him to hang his head, or put down his drink and run to her, kneel before her and cry how hurting her seared his soul. But he just sipped his vodka slowly and methodically, as if he were at a boring fraternity party at Colgate, trying to get drunk without getting sick. "I'll give you till tomorrow morning to make up your mind," she told him.

He whirled around the liquid in his glass. "I need more time than that, Lee."

"You don't have it. I've had all the pain I can tolerate. If you don't choose me by tomorrow, you've chosen her."

At seven-thirty the following morning, Jazz told Lee he wanted to stay with her.

Late that afternoon, when he had gone to pick up Val and Kent, it occurred to Lee that she had never even asked herself whether she wanted to stay with him.

Twenty-one

❧

There were gaps in my education. Take Spanish. For example, I can to this day have a conversation in Spanish, as long as no complex ideas intrude and it stays in the present tense. I can even quote several key lines of dialogue from *La casa de Bernarda Alba*. However, it took five years of visiting the Nassau County Correctional Center before I realized that a sign I'd thought was a rather menacing warning aimed discriminately at Latino inmates, EL VATO, was the result of someone's pinching the E and the R from the elevator sign in Building C.

Another gap? I had taken Psych 1, to say nothing of Criminal Law, but I hadn't the foggiest notion of how to deal with a client who refuses to get out of jail. So I just said: "Norman, you can't stay here anymore."

"Go to hell," he growled at me. He couldn't say much more because he was busy scuffling with two correction officers, who were trying to turn him over to me for the short walk through the door and out to the parking lot and freedom. Being six foot five, Norman was much taller than either of them, but as they were built along the lines of *corrida* bulls, his progress from the Return Uniforms Here window to the exit door, where I was waiting, was fairly swift. "You're making a terrible mistake!" he cried to his escorts, trying to pull his arms out of their powerful grips.

"Get your ass outta here," the beefier one of them grunted, displaying not the slightest intellectual curiosity about why an inmate would be so intent on remaining on the premises.

"Listen," Norman gasped at them, breathless from his struggle. He was not more than five feet from where I was standing, and getting closer, "I killed Bobette Frisch! Don't let me out." The smaller of the officers—but a guy who could lead the running of the bulls in Pamplona—seemed to hesitate.

"Check the paperwork," I advised the cop. "They want him out of here. Someone else confessed. They arrested her. He's trying to protect her."

"I choked Bobette to death!" Norman stretched out his fingers to demonstrate strangulation, but as his arms were so tightly held so far apart, he could not get his point across. "It was *me*. I did it."

"The one they arrested is his girlfriend," I explained. Unimpressed by Norman's gallantry, the guards heaved him in my direction.

The fluorescent lights in the jail are pretty strong, so I'm not sure that there is a physiological reason why every person who is released squeezes shut his eyes momentarily, as if to keep them from getting scorched by the sun's fierceness. Norman stood outside the closed door of the Center, using his hand as a visor. His red and white checked shirt and gray slacks—the clothes he'd been wearing at the time of his arrest—were now too big for him. Seamed with stiff creases from being folded into a plastic bag, the shirt and slacks looked shabby as well, as if they had contracted some nasty fabric infection that was out of control in the Clothing Storage Room.

I don't know what I expected for getting Norman out of jail and the murder charges against him dropped. Certainly not a thank you, as what I had done was explicitly against his wishes. Not a physical attack either, because the one thing I felt confident about was that Norman did not express his anger in a violent way. I figured I'd hear a big-time chewing out, really nasty, with bellowing and maybe some fist-banging on the trunk of someone's car, a diatribe that would end with one of the guards in the parking lot strolling over and threatening to arrest him for first-degree harassment.

What I did not expect was to be ignored. Once Norman got used to the sunlight, he stuck his hands in his pockets and walked away. "Norman." I tried to catch up with him, but with his long legs, he was taking two steps for my one. So it was not until he stopped, apparently confounded by the number and ugliness of the jail's pale, bloodless brick buildings, that I was able to apologize. "I'm sorry," I said. "This was not what you wanted—"

"Quite the opposite." Because he was so tall, it was easy for him to pretend I wasn't there. He kept his head high and moved it back and forth, trying to home in on some elusive target.

"Where do you want to go?" I asked.

He shot me a what-kind-of-stupid-question-is-that look. "To see Mary."

I realized he'd been in the Visitors Center as an insider, not an outsider, and hadn't a clue to where it was. "I'll take you over." When I had left my house, it had been a sweet suburban spring Friday, but the vast concrete parking lot in East Meadow seemed to draw down all the sun's heat. We made our way toward the entrance of the Visitors Center slowly, trudging like hikers lost in a malevolent desert. "Do you have any identification on you?" I asked.

"Leave me alone."

"Norman, they won't let you see her without your showing a driver's license or a birth certificate." He stopped beside an old car, dark green, filthy. In its grime, someone had drawn the opposite of a smiley face: a circle with two dots for eyes and an upside-down U for a mouth. "They're pretty strict about regulations here," I explained. "But then, you know that." He nodded, barely, a single shake of his head. "I'll be glad to drive you back to your place, although to be perfectly honest, I think the cops were probably over there with a search warrant after they arrested Mary, and if you had a pile of phony ID's, I can't guarantee they weren't seized."

He considered his options, pressing the top of his beaky little nose, right between his eyes, with his thumb and forefinger. "You can take me there. I'll change, then I can go get a birth certificate."

"If you have your choice of a name," I advised him, having seen in my years in criminal law a pretty fair selection of counterfeit documents from dealers in the area, "get something with Norman Torkelson on it. The guards at the Visitors Center know you by that name. It takes them about a week to forget an inmate your size, so you don't want to show up being Irving Schwartz—at least not today."

By the time I dropped him off, he was speaking to me, although not happily. I understand, he told me. You were faced with an ethical issue and you resolved it as best you could. However, he added, I must say that ethics or morality in the larger sense was *not* served by what you did.

On one hand, I thought he was beyond annoying. A con man spouting off on morality? On the other hand, I felt so sad for him. What a loss! Mary had allowed him to do something he had never been able to do before: love a woman. Everything about her had been perfect for him: her beauty, her sweet dopiness, her larcenous heart. Even her crime had worked for Norman, because it had enabled him to be noble, to offer himself up to save her. What a shock to his system those foreign two emotions—love and self-sacrifice—must have been to a rat like him. But after a while, I thought, he'd gotten used to feeling virtuous. It suited him. I considered it remarkable that this professional slimeball had not once tried to weasel out of taking the punishment that should have been hers.

Now, though, all his goodness had been for nothing. Sure, he was free. And justice had triumphed. But what did he care about justice? The one and only person who had given his life meaning—Mary Dean—was locked up in Building D, waiting to be processed so she could make the trip to Bedford Hills, where she'd stay for the next fifteen to twenty years.

I was not about to be an accessory to a felony and drive him to a date with criminal possession of a forged instrument, so I dropped him in front of the apartment he and Mary had been so happy in. On the spur of the moment, I told him I'd buy him dinner so if he had any questions about Mary's case I could answer them. He did not seem surprised—or seem anything else, to tell the truth. He was operating on automatic pilot, so in a monotone he said all right and asked what time he should be at my office. I was tempted to blare a trumpet and announce: Hey, I've never invited any client out to dinner, ever! But I just said seven-thirty—and make it casual.

* * *

Norman showed up in a tie and pin-striped suit, a little more Al Capone than Wall Street. But he seemed to feel Establishment, if not downright lawyerly, in it. With him so dolled up, I scratched plans for the glorified hamburger joint-salad bar I'd planned on and took him to a restaurant in the Garden City Hotel, a place with a great deal of soft light, pink marble, and waiters so terribly worried about your welfare that you fear for their blood pressure.

"I want the best lawyer for Mary," he told me.

"The one she has is fine."

"I'm talking about someone with a national reputation." I noticed that for a guy who would have to fill in a blank after "Occupation" with "Criminal," Norman had unusually genteel table manners. He had ordered snails and was managing the pincer with masterful dexterity. I wondered if he honestly liked snails or if ordering them was part of his routine, to display to his marks how cultivated he was. "I have the money," he said. "I can pay for it."

"Look," I told him, setting down my salad fork. "You can get anyone you want. And I'm sure with all the time Mary is facing, it's tempting to imagine a prince on a white steed coming in and, abracadabra, making everything all right. The problem is this: She won't be having a trial, so you don't need someone who has the reputation of mesmerizing juries. And there are no complicated issues, so you don't need a brilliant legal mind."

"But if someone can convince a judge—"

"Do you know someone who can do it better than Barbara Duberstein, the lawyer she has now? I don't. She's been practicing here for ten years. She's good and the judges like her, and even more, they trust her. You want my opinion? You're much better off with good local counsel than with some city slicker the sentencing judge knows has been brought in just to bamboozle him."

"How much will this cost?" Norman asked. Two middle-aged women at another table—considerably more middle-aged than I—were watching him. I thought I saw longing in their eyes. "Not that cost matters."

"I'm not sure. You can check with Ms. Duberstein."

"A rough estimate."

"A couple of thousand."

He seemed surprised. "That's like nothing." He looked around, and he caught the gaze of the two women on him. He seemed more saddened than pleased: He didn't want the game anymore. He only wanted Mary. "Isn't there some way, with, say, a six-figure number, that we can find a judge—"

"No."

"I know that's what you're supposed to tell me—"

"I have no doubt that you know all the fine points of what I'm supposed to tell you. So I'll save my breath. But it might be useful for you to know that from my experience practicing here—as a prosecutor and a defense lawyer—that your six-figure bribe will buy you a ticket back into the slammer. Now, I may be wrong. There may be a State Supreme Court justice sitting in Nassau County who can be or has been bought. I honestly don't know of any. And I don't know any lawyer here who would be willing to try and negotiate that kind of a purchase." While this was not strict truth—I had my suspicions about one or two of my fellow members of the bar—it was true enough to tell someone like Norman.

We were well into our entrée—prime rib for him, monkfish for me—when I started wondering why he had been asking how much Mary's lawyer would charge. "What happened to the forty-eight thousand you got from Bobette?" I asked, knowing that these days, the more intrusive a question, the more people seem willing to answer it.

"I sent most of it down to the place where I keep my money. That's why I needed to know what sort of expenses I'll be incurring with Mary's defense ... or representation, to be more accurate."

"Atlanta?" I inquired, vaguely remembering something Mary had said. Norman laughed too heartily. Then he seemed embarrassed. I couldn't tell if it was because I'd caught him in a phony laugh or if some memory was making him uncomfortable. "Do people in your business now have Atlanta accounts the way they used to have numbered Swiss accounts?"

"Atlanta is just something I made up for Mary," he admitted. "I have to go to Grand Cayman Island." The Caymans were in the Caribbean, not far from Jamaica, and had become a center for international funny money. I was surprised, because most con men I knew were spenders, not savers. Their lives were a never-ending cycle of scam and squander and scam again.

"Are you going to spend any time down there?" I asked. Not that I was curious, but even if we passed on dessert, we still had to finish our petits pois with mint and get the check. I was afraid of running out of conversation. "Don't you want to relax, get a little sun?"

"I can't afford that luxury. I want to see Mary again tomorrow. I'll see if I can get a flight out on Sunday and do business first thing Monday and get back here by midday to visit." He sighed and got lost in playing hockey with his fork and a pea. His goal seemed to be a curlicue of carrot, but before he got there he looked up. "Is there any chance of bail?"

"No, Norman. Try to understand: she isn't awaiting trial. She's confessed to a murder, and she'll be sentenced by the end of next week. Early the following week, she'll be off to Bedford Hills."

"I'm taking out a fair amount of money," he told me. "I'm buying a house."

"A house?"

"Yes. Up there, not far from the prison. I've already talked to a real estate broker in Katonah. She says she has a lot in my price range. A modest little house. That's all I need, because it will just be I. I'm viewing it as an investment. When Mary gets out, we can sell it and go to someplace warm."

"What are you going to do in Katonah?" I asked.

"Visit Mary in Bedford Hills every day I can." He patted his mouth with his napkin, a little too daintily for my taste. "I won't try to con you. At this stage of my life, what do you think I'm going to do? Get a nine-to-five job? Do you think I'm like all of you"—he swooped his hand around, indicating everyone else in the restaurant—"needing someplace to go to, something to do every single day? I've always enjoyed my leisure. Reading the financial pages, watching a little TV, working out. I like to read. I read an enormous amount of books. If I told anyone I talked to for more than five minutes that I didn't go to college, they wouldn't believe me." He was waiting for me to confirm this was true, so I nodded. "In any case, I have the wherewithal. I can live pretty nicely on what I've got socked away."

"You're a rarity," I told him.

He knew what I meant. "You mean most men working the con—I hope you'll pardon my language—piss it away."

"That's right."

"Not me. I have plenty for now, and I'll have a nice chunk left for Florida or wherever we wind up."

I signaled to the waiter for the check. "What about the con?" I asked.

"What about it?"

"You sound like you're thinking of retiring."

"Let me tell you something," Norman said, leaning forward, looking me straight in the eye. "I didn't do it just for money. You must know that. I used to love it. The travel, the setup, playing out the game. And the ladies: All you legal types and all the shrinks think it's just because I want to fuck them or, more to the point, fuck them over, if you'll excuse the vernacular. You're right in that the money *is* incidental, although I made a pretty penny. What you don't get is that every single time, it was a thrill. A *thrill*. I got to fall in love over and over again. You have no idea. What a rush!" He sat back. "But then I met Mary. And sure, we moved around, I did the con. She even assisted me. But from the second I saw her, I knew the game was over for me. I could never fall in love again with one of my marks. Because this time I was truly and forever in love." He folded his napkin and put it beside his plate. "I lost my gift. I was hardly able to go through the motions. I can't believe how I pulled it off with the last few ladies. Especially with a smart cookie like Bobette. She must have been so desperate." He shook his head. "Poor, pathetic thing."

Having gotten Norman off, I didn't shout "Whee!" and run around, giddy and gay. But I did feel relieved. Except just when I thought I was finished with the Torkelson case, I started getting calls from Mary Dean. I refused to accept them, telling Sandi, my secretary, to refer them to Barbara Duberstein. That should have been that, but Sandi was still unhinged on the subject. She would not let go of the idea that Mary was an innocent. Please, she begged me, *please* speak to her. I told her Mary might indeed be innocent of a great many things, but the crime of murder was not one of them. Mary called twice Wednesday morning and once Wednesday afternoon.

Tuesday and Wednesday, Norman called too. Mary was in a bad way, he reported. Very upset. Not depressed. Angry. She was being irrational, screaming. They had to haul her out of the visitors room and put her in Administrative Lock-in. She kept begging Norman to get her out. He knew he couldn't do that, he said to me, but was there anything—anything at all—he could do? Could he get her into some mental hospital? A private one would be fine. He had the money. I told him that Mary had already said she would plead guilty to murder. If she wanted to change her mind and plead not guilty by reason of mental disease or defect, he'd have to get in touch with Barbara. But I suggested that given Mary's videotaped confession, I didn't think it likely that kind of defense would succeed. It sounded, though, as if Norman was so deeply disturbed by Mary's behavior that he'd half conned himself into believing she might still wind up in a sanitarium with a rose garden.

By Mary's third phone call that afternoon, my secretary was in such a froth of distress over Mary and fury at me that I suggested she go home. She told me she didn't want to. I told her I wanted her to—and not to come back the following day if the pressures of the job were getting to her. Vacation time was due her, and what a beautiful time of year to get away.

Naturally, she was in the office before I was Thursday morning. But she left of her own accord before lunch. She had tears in her eyes: I can't take it, she said. If you could only hear that girl's voice. She's so sweet, so truly innocent, so . . .

The thought of getting away was beginning to appeal to me. My guy, the lawyer, was about to sum up in a trial in federal court, and was therefore unavailable, to say nothing of useless in terms of human companionship. I called my daughter, who is studying acting (and slinging hash in a restaurant in Tribeca) and asked if she was interested in a long, luxurious, and free weekend at a spa in the Berkshires. Usually she jumped at anything preceded by the word "free." But she actually had an acting job starting the following Monday, two scenes in a cable TV movie being shot on Staten Island, and she had to prepare. So I decided to settle for an evening in the city and called an old friend of mine at the Manhattan D.A.'s. We agreed on a restaurant in Little Italy.

As I was about to leave, around six, the phone rang. I picked it up, an act that I invariably discover is folly. "Lee?" It was Barbara Duberstein, and she sounded wiped out. Of course, I thought: It's the end of the workday, and she still has two adolescent children at home.

"How's it going?" I asked.

"Did you hear about it?"

"About what?"

"Mary."

In a theatrical gesture my daughter would have abhorred, I slapped my forehead. But I sensed this was drama. Maybe tragedy. "What happened?"

"She tried to hang herself." I couldn't find a thing to say. "They found her just in time."

"Did she say why she did it?"

"No." I could hear Barbara take a deep breath. "All she said is that she wanted you."

Twenty-two

❧

Take any group of associates—girlfriends, the National Conference of Catholic Bishops, professional bowlers—and set them to talking about treachery. A single truth emerges: Once someone betrays you, you can never trust him again. You can try to understand the reasons behind the double dealing, of course. Forgive it, even. (You really don't have much choice if you're a bishop.) But you can never forget, not entirely.

Hogwash. Maybe in those troubled, dark-souled nations where widows wear black the rest of their lives, they tend perfidy like a living flame. But Americans, those optimists who clothe themselves in bright team colors, are always ready for a do-over. Certainly, in the days and weeks following the discovery of defalcation or adultery, the torment seems unbearable; there is no hurt like being stabbed in the back by someone you trust. But then it is allowed to subside, so superficial relations can resume. In the months to follow, the absence of acute pain feels so good that you begin, now and then, like any good American, to let a smile be your umbrella. And your compatriots, seeing you happy, relieved that you are no longer a loser, pat you on the back and take you out to lunch, and pretty soon—providing the lying, cheating, unprincipled bastard doesn't act up—you are your old self again.

This is not to say that Lily Rose White would not have been wounded if someone had given her *The Collected Works of Elizabeth Barrett Browning* for her birthday. And Jazz had enough sense, when they spent the evening in Manhattan, not to drive up Madison Avenue; that would have brought them right past the Hotel Carlyle. However, by October of 1980, six months after her terrible discovery, Lee was a happy wife again. Sex, if not as frequent, was again becoming lively and satisfying. Jazz was, she had to admit, a devoted father, coming home early to take pictures of three-year-old Val dressed up for Halloween, in a garish pink costume Lee had tried to talk her out of. But Val had insisted on being Strawberry Shortcake, and so she was. Jazz joined Lee in taking the little girl around the neighborhood trick-or-treating. As they stayed back to allow Val to stand on tiptoes and try to ring each doorbell by herself, their shoulders touched and their hands sought each other out. After the neighbors stopped oohing and aahing over Strawberry, they beamed at her young and, obviously, very much in love parents.

By the beginning of November, Lee was thinking it was time to have another child. She even mentioned something to Chuckie Phalen: You know, at some point I'll probably have another kid. Chuckie said: I thought as much. A little concerned, Lee could tell, and when she told him she planned on taking no more than a three-month maternity leave, he seemed more comforted by the reassurance that everything would be hunky-dory with Phalen & White than dismayed that she was capable of leaving not just one but two little tykes.

A week later, on a Sunday night, sitting on their living room floor before a roaring fire, the first of the season, Lee kissed Jazz and whispered: Do you think it's time we had a burn-the-diaphragm party? He took her in his arms and said: "Wonderful!" Just like that. No hesitation, no catch in his voice to suggest reluctance. She heard what she wanted to hear, total agreement. "Wonderful!" offered with Jazz's typical exclamation point. Lee did not allow herself to think: Gee, he's being pretty casual about such a big decision. Or that "Wonderful!" was the same lyric, the same tune he used with department store buyers from Milwaukee when they upped their order (Wonderful! You'll see how they'll fly off the floor!) and with old customers who allowed him to charm them into fun fox for those occasions when their new mink was too serious (Wonderful! Call me in February and tell me how much you're enjoying it!).

Wonderful? So? She was right between periods. Ripe and ready. But the next night, Monday, was football, played on the West Coast. She understood that. Tuesday and Wednesday, Jazz had to go to Minneapolis and Detroit. They were big accounts, he told her proudly. Now they're bigger. And Thursday, Friday, Saturday, and now, Sunday, he was exhausted, enervated, fluish, finally just plain out of sorts. Not himself.

So by the time she got a good look at him the following Thursday across her parents' Thanksgiving table, handsome, broad-shouldered in a cashmered interpretation of a Harris Tweed sports jacket, beaming up at Greta as she served her pineapple–sweet potato casserole, Lee could see: Definitely not himself. "Wonderful!" he enthused to Greta. Yes, Jazz was being the movie star, putting on the shine for the plainest girl in his fan club, but as Greta moved on, Jazz's light went out. He was not a good enough actor to sustain his role.

Not himself? Then who was he?

Weary. Irritable, losing patience with Kent, insisting on getting rid of him for the holiday. His own brother, who made his home with them: Get rid of him for a few days, he commanded Lee. She had complied, but she felt sick at having double-crossed Kent, sticking him with his parents who did not want him.

Lee watched Jazz staring at his plate. Why wasn't he able to look into the eyes of her family? Leonard, stroking the sleeve of his double-breasted blazer, a new design by the latest *enfant terrible* of European menswear. Sylvia, holding her knife and fork daintily between the pads of her fingertips so as not to chip her nail polish: Pure Pomegranate, the latest tropical shade, so she could leave for Palm Beach the next morning and not be seen with northern nails. And Robin, pale and absolutely lovely in layer upon layer of intricate Italian knits, her exquisite little purple and blue and green vest alone costing more than the average day care aide's monthly salary, waving at Val across the table.

Jazz could not keep his eyes off the food mounded on his plate. He seemed defeated by a glob of cranberry-raspberry relish the size of a human heart. Not himself. This feast was a torment for him. It was only then that Lee permitted herself to understand: Jazz was indeed himself. And that self was a cheat and a liar. But a passionate one. The cause of his terrible pain was deep, deep emotion. Not an emotion like guilt over mere fornication: No, the biggest of all emotions. Her husband was in love. Not with her.

"You're sure?" Will Stewart inquired. He added more brandy to her snifter so discreetly that she did not notice until she took the next sip.

"Yes." She set down the brandy.

"Don't worry. I'll drive you home. I'll figure out how to get your car back tomorrow." She had left Jazz in front of the television, a dead man watching the Giants. When she told him she was running over to the office for an hour or two, his "Fine" was replete with relief.

"He wants out," Lee said. "That's what all his pain is about."

"Pain about getting divorced?"

She heard herself laugh—Ha!—the harsh, snorting noise lonely women make. "Are you kidding? No, he's in the fashion business. He's nothing if not *au courant*. Being divorced once or twice shows you're not a home-loving, uncool schmuck." She would have to watch herself. She was sounding so bitter. On the other side of his small living room, Will was observing her with concern. "Jazz has got a bigger problem," she went on. "Even if he'd made a fabulous impression at his old law firm—which he didn't—he hasn't practiced in almost five years. For a good reason; he hates the law. It would be very hard for him to get back to being a lawyer, even with his father's help."

"But he's doing so well in the fur business—" Will stopped and corrected himself. "Your father's fur business."

"It's not that he couldn't get another job. They're so thrilled to have someone like him in the industry, they all but raise the Episcopal flag every time he walks into a room."

Will got up from his chair and threw a couple more logs into his wood-burning stove and poked them in place. Not a plain black iron stove, of course, but a tall ceramic one, yellow and white, an antique he had bought in Sweden. His whole house, on an inlet of Middle Bay on the south shore of Long Island, was like that: modest, manly but simply beautiful, a home for one—but one with very good taste. She had been there only once before, for a Chinese banquet Will cooked for his old crew from the Homicide unit, but she had fallen in love with the place. "So Jazz can leave your father's company, but wherever else he goes, he's not going to be the son-in-law."

"I don't think it's only the money that made him hold back so long—although he is getting about three times what he could make elsewhere. It's the perks. The best restaurants, the best seats in town to whatever he wants to see, the car and driver: He goes in every day with my father, and before they get picked up, the driver buys two *New York Times*es, two *Wall Street Journal*s and two *Women's Wear Daily*s—so they don't have to lower themselves to read already fingered newsprint. It's a whole way of life he has to give up. He can charge anything he wants to the business...." She stopped and closed her eyes, listening to the never ceasing rush of water outside Will's back door.

"You mean his charging his entire affair?"

"Yes," she whispered, not trusting her voice. Lee was less afraid of crying than of making some hideous gargling sound that would repulse yet another man. Not that Will ever seemed unrepulsed. He was her friend. Her best friend. Not a day went by now that they did not speak at least twice. But not a glimmer, not the faintest undercurrent, at least not on Will's part. Maybe, Lee thought, sitting up straighter, trying to swirl her brandy in a sophisticated gesture, hoping it did not slop over the rim of the snifter, if I looked more like Maria—a bust of Nefertiti, not an Easter Island statue— he'd want to poke something white beside the damn stove.

She must be drunk, she realized. She did not feel drunk, yet she sensed that under normal circumstances, she would not be so aware that she had nostrils. Jazz loved someone else. She had loved him from the time she was fifteen years old and miraculously, he had married her. He loved someone else. Another woman would be getting dressed and she'd feel Jazz pressing against her back. She'd drop her panties and turn around and kiss him and then lower herself, her tongue trailing down his neck, his chest, his belly.

She might be drunk. She was sensing ears on the sides of her head. Lee fingered her earlobe. Soft, as soft as Valerie's sweet skin. Soft as a rose petal. Her middle name: Rose.

"Will?"

"What?"

"Do you know what my real name is, the one I was born with?"

He shrugged. She had to admit he was not exhibiting a pressing need to know. Fuck it, she'd tell him anyway. "Lily."

"Oh," he said politely. But then he must have said her name to himself: Lily White. He threw back his head, and for the first time since she'd known him, he laughed out loud. "Lily White." A deep and wonderful roar. "No shit!"

And she threw back her head to join him, but it didn't work, because she had already begun to weep.

Lee was not thinking clearly, but Will was. He drove her almost home but let her off a little more than halfway up the rutted hill to her house. Your car died, he coached her. Since you knew Jazz was watching the game, you called a cab. It's better if he doesn't see you get out of my car. When you open discussions about the possibility of splitting up, you don't want him to think: Hmm, she said she was going to her office Sunday. How come her close male friend drove her home? Don't give him an excuse to feel less guilty.

Okay, Lee said.

Obviously, Will went on, you only have to offer the whole broken-down-car–cab story if he notices you didn't get home under your own steam.

Obviously, she said. It wasn't obvious to her at all. She was relieved that Will was advising her. She wanted to be told exactly what to do and what to say, because otherwise she would be too afraid to go home.

You can handle this, Will assured her.

I know. She did not know.

Will made her promise—swear, insisting she actually raise her right hand—that she keep mum. You are Unfit to Think, he decreed. Wait till tomorrow. Then, when you're calmer—to say nothing of sober—you'll speak to my partner, Joe Clark. He handles our matrimonial work. Then Will waited while Lee trudged up to the house, his headlights illuminating her way, his Porsche purring like a protective mother cat.

Lee walked around the house so she could enter through the side entrance, as if coming from the garage. Evening was becoming night, and a cold wind was blowing in from the sound, but it was still crisp, perfect Thanksgiving weekend football weather. Twigs crackled under her feet. She inhaled the pungent rot of the leaves, smoke from the fire Jazz must have built. She hugged her blazer around her. Good smells. Before her mind could censor, her body reacted to the late-autumn air: Ah, how lovely. A night to cuddle up and keep warm. Then she shivered.

As she passed the den, she saw Jazz where she had left him, sitting on the couch staring at the television set. Concerned because Cherry, the nanny, had the day off, Lee was immediately relieved when she walked into the kitchen and found Robin sitting with Val, patiently watching the little girl interact with a bowl of the chicken noodle soup Lee had made that morning. A moment later, Val was in her arms. Lee went over to Robin and, as she usually did, touched her cheek to her sister's and chirped into the air, in their standard mockery of their mother's kisses.

"Jazz is in the den," Robin told her.

"Bad mood?" Lee asked, sidestepping so her sister would not sniff brandy breath.

Robin shrugged. "Not a good mood, I would have to say."

Too damn bad, Lee thought, setting Val back down so she could swish around the soup pot. She found a small piece of chicken and a carrot to cut up.

"No!" Val announced, shaking her head so ferociously at the carrot that her glossy pigtails whipped back and forth. In all honesty, Lee admitted to herself, repressing a smile, she loved that her nay-saying daughter was such an ornery pain in the ass. "Yucky peas!" To Val, every vegetable was a pea.

"Okay," Lee said, "I'll eat it," knowing her offer

would immediately stimulate Val's appetite. She picked up a circle of carrot. Val immediately stuck out her hand. "What do you say?" Lee demanded, depositing it in the child's tiny palm.

"T'anks."

"'T'anks,'" Lee repeated to Robin. "She sounds like Grandma Bella. Next thing you know, she'll say, 'You're velcome, dahlink.'"

"I really don't remember her too well." Robin had gone to the stove and was peering into the pot as if she had made the soup. "Listen, I'll keep an eye on Val. You ought to let Jazz know you're home. He keeps popping in, wanting to know if you're here yet."

Will was right, Lee mused as she walked toward the den. Unfit to think. She ought to be concentrating on keeping her face bland, unreadable, but her mind kept jumping: a cold-water washload with her burgundy sweater and black panty hose; that article on women playwrights she had torn out two Sundays ago, still on her night-stand; oh, and she had to add a protein conditioner to the drugstore list. The blue light of the television flickered inside the den. Lee stood beside the open door. She wished she had passed up Will's brandy because she really wanted a tranquilizer. No, general anesthesia: if only she could be put out until it was all over. She forced herself through the door.

"I'm home." Her weight rested on the balls of her feet. She was primed to pivot and get out.

"Come in," Jazz said, rising from the couch. He switched on a lamp and turned off the TV.

"I've got a ton of stuff to do."

"Please. I want to talk."

"Go ahead," Lee replied. Since she made no move to sit, Jazz remained standing. But he kept glancing back to the couch. Lee sensed he had rehearsed this scene in his mind, and this was not the way it had played. Her head hurt. Drunk. What was Will's theory about preventing hangovers? Water. Drink huge amounts of water. She wondered if it was too late.

"It's like this," Jazz began. Then he fell silent. She waited, but it seemed as if he was expecting her to speak. When she did not, he finally said: "I don't know how to say this."

"Say it," Lee snapped. She crossed her arms but felt awkward, unable to decide whether to rest them on top of her bust or beneath it. She glanced at Jazz to see if he had noticed her difficulty. No. He was looking past her. Lee turned. Robin was at the door, carrying Val as if she were an infant. "I'll be with you in a minute," Lee told her sister. But Robin merely stood there. Lee sighed. If she said: Excuse me, Robin, but Jazz and I need some privacy, Robin would say: Oh, sure, sorry. But for the next few days—just when Lee would need her sister most—Robin would sulk, answering all attempts to engage her in conversation with monosyllables.

"Come in," Jazz invited, making an arcing my-house-is-your-house gesture. Before Lee could think of a diplomatic way to bounce her, Robin, still holding Val, plopped into the biggest seat in the room, a high, fat-armed wing chair.

"When you found out," Jazz said to Lee, "I swore to you I would end it. And then I told you it was all over."

For a moment, Lee did not understand what he was talking about or, at least, could not believe he was speaking of it in front of her sister. And Val! She was too young to understand the words, but to have such a conversation in front of your own child? "Are you insane?" she hissed at him.

"It was *never* over."

"Would you be quiet, for God's sake." She could see Val struggling to climb off her aunt's lap and get closer to her parents.

"I'm in love," Jazz insisted. Lee shoved him away. The push said: Shut up! End this conversation now! Too hard a push. Jazz would have fallen backward if, in one swift movement, Robin had not set Val aside, vaulted from the big chair, and held him by his shoulders, steadying him. "I'm in love," he insisted.

"No," Robin corrected him. "*We're* in love."

Before Lee's mind could absorb the shock, her body did. It crumpled. Her legs turned from sturdy limbs into flesh without bones. She aimed herself toward the couch and, mercifully, fell into it.

"Mommy?"

"I'm okay. I just tripped."

A shudder passed through Lee's body, and immediately another. Oh my God, she thought, I'm having a convulsion. I've got to get Val out of here so she doesn't see me. She looked over at her child. Only three, but Val was no fool. Robin was attempting to distract her, offering the TV remote control, but Val knew there was a better show being broadcast. Emphatically, she shook her head: No.

In the ensuing silence, Jazz and Robin came together before Lee in such a fluid motion it might have been choreographed. Jazz and Robin, so close to each other that Lee's eyes were forced to see them as a couple. Beside him, Robin appeared so fine and fragile that she, not strapping, red-cheeked Valerie, might have been his little girl. Horrible: They looked so beautiful together. "We've been in love for a long time," Jazz began.

"Of course," Robin said, taking up the story, "we couldn't even admit it to ourselves for a while, much less each other." Lee was surprised to discover that she could stand. She went to Val and drew the child to her, putting her hands on the little girl's head, smoothing her silken hair. She mouthed: Stop! to her sister. "Lee," Robin sighed, exasperated, "a child that age does not have the language. She cannot comprehend. Okay?" Jazz flushed. A mustache of perspiration grew on his upper lip. Robin, though, was not in a sweat. She seemed to grow calmer. Lovelier, too, and stronger with each passing second, as though she were being transfused with magic nutrients. "You have to listen, Lee. Because if you walk out now, it will still be there when you get back. It is *not* going to go away."

Robin wore a white angora sweater and white wool slacks, and looked as though she had materialized from a cloud. Lee realized her sister had shopped for an outfit appropriate for the annunciation: I need something in an angelic fabric but that shows off my waist. Oh, and please, tight around the rear and the crotch. When did this begin? Lee cried, although not aloud. Still, her sister answered as if the question had been screamed out. "It happened the first time we saw each other." A quickly suppressed sound, something that might have been the start of a delicious giggle of reminiscence. "Well, not the first time, because I was at the worst of my drug problem, when I was in"— Robin took a big, brave breath and came out with it— "heroin withdrawal." That was in St. Bart's, Lee thought. What is she talking about? Why doesn't he interrupt her, correct her: No, no, St. Bart's was right after Lee and I got married. Except there was Jazz beside Robin, his head moving up and down: Yes, yes, that *was* the very moment I fell in love.

Lee was astounded at her own clarity, that a part of her—the lawyer, the wronged wife—was taking notes while the rest of her crumbled into pieces, like the dying leaves she had crushed just minutes earlier. She understood why Jazz had sent Kent back to the Taylors. This performance had been meticulously planned, and he and Robin wanted no unruly members in their audience. Robin, head high, hands on her hips, lips bright red against her white face, pressed on with raw-meat energy. "Jazz said that day he first saw me, he thought he was happy, that he knew where his life was going. Then there I was, on the bed. I'm sure I was pale as a ghost"—Jazz nodded his confirmation—"and naked. And he said his heart stood still."

"Too bad for all of us it started again," Lee said softly.

"Robin," Jazz said hesitantly. He spoke the name with a tenderness, a passionate doting that Lee had never even dreamed was part of his repertoire. "This probably isn't the time."

"No . . . Jazz," Robin said, faltering right before his name, so it was clear she had been about to call him Darling, or Love. "It has to come out."

"You're right," he agreed.

What kind of a lawyer is he, Lee thought, that he doesn't shut her up, blabbing on and on about the chronology of their adultery? "It was when we landed in New York," Robin continued, "and Jazz was carrying me out of the plane so the ambulance drivers who came to meet us could get me. I looked up"—Robin swallowed hard at the memory—"and there was this beautiful man I had never seen before. And I knew I would love him for the rest of my life."

"But we never said anything to each other," Jazz interjected. "Not for the longest time. I swear. And we didn't do anything until . . . " He gazed down at Val, who had taken a seat on the rug. "Until after . . . "

Lee knelt and hugged her daughter.

"I told you she'd use the baby as a weapon," Robin said to Jazz.

"Val," Lee said to the little girl, "I know you want to stay here, but this is grown-up talk. So I'll make you a deal. If you can get into your pj's all by yourself, no bath tonight"—she could see her daughter growing intrigued—"I'll give you two scoops of vanilla fudge." With less reluctance than Lee had imagined, Val hurried from the room, but then, two scoops were a bribe beyond Val's greediest imaginings.

With Valerie gone, the room's atmosphere altered. More danger here. Ominous silence until the wind rattled a window. Lee sensed Robin waiting for Jazz to take over, but when, looking expectant, Robin turned his way, he hunkered down and began to align the Sunday papers that had been scattered on the floor around an ottoman. Lee knelt beside him. "You didn't have the guts to face me alone," she whispered.

"What?" Robin demanded. "This isn't fair." Jazz stood. "What did she say?"

"Nothing," he replied.

Lee tried, and failed, to rise in a single fluid motion.

"Come on, Jazz," Robin said, a note of exasperation mixing with the sexual teasing. "Tell me what she said."

"Shut up, Robin," Lee barked.

"Don't tell me to shut up!"

Lee turned to the man she could not believe was still her husband, so thoroughly did he seem to belong to and with her sister. She noticed that he, also, was wearing a white sweater. "What do you want to do, Jazz?"

"I think it's clear that we have to end the marriage."

"Perfectly clear." Perfectly clear? she asked herself. She sounded crisp, like a character talking to Sir Alec Guinness in a not very serious English movie. How could she not be howling in pain? "I assume you already have a lawyer?" Unlike Robin, who started nodding, Jazz had enough breeding to look ashamed. But not too ashamed. Abashed only at having sought legal counsel so quickly. Not about adultery, not about the terrible betrayal of her, of his daughter. "I'll need a day or so to find proper representation," Lee told him.

"Take all the time—"

"Don't give me your gracious prep school manners. You're a cheap piece of work." Lee glanced at her sister, half expecting the old Robin—washed out, exhausted by the tension. But Robin looked radiant, so Lee turned back to Jazz. "Both of you: nice hair, great clothes, but cheap to the core. You were made for each other." She turned to go. "Even if there is no God, you'll get what you deserve."

It would have been a fine exit line, but as Lee passed through the threshold of the room, Robin called out: "We want custody of Valerie."

Lee did not freeze for more than a second. Then she whirled around and grabbed her sister by the front of her sweater, shaking Robin until Jazz grabbed Lee around the neck with a wrestling hold and pulled her back. "No!" Lee shouted. "Never! Over my dead body you'll get custody."

"I'm just as good a parent as you are!" Jazz shouted. "Better."

"Much better," Robin corrected him. "Much." She looked at her sister. "You're never home."

"What are you talking about?" Lee cried, sick at heart, knowing she had worked late two nights that week. "I love that child. I'm a wonderful mother."

"You consort with criminals," Jazz shot back.

"You're quoting your idiot girlfriend now," Lee snapped at him. "I don't 'consort,' you dipshit. I represent. You used to be a lawyer. A lousy one, but at least you used to know the difference." Tiny tufts of the white angora from Robin's sweater clung to her fingers. She tried to pull them off, but they stuck.

"I told you she'd bring up that you're not practicing law anymore," Robin practically sang to Jazz.

"I have spoken with my attorney," Jazz said to Lee, taking Robin's hand. "If we have to litigate, we'll litigate. Believe me, he won't shrink from it. It's his life's blood. But think about it. We have no intention of driving you out of Val's life. She just would do better living with us. With me. We have time for her."

"Sure. Because neither of you has a grown-up job. You don't have to work. Daddy takes care of you."

"I hope you don't think just because you're the mother you'll automatically get custody. Things are not what they were."

Lee wanted to curl into a ball on the couch and cry. No, howl. She was so frightened, thinking of some of the idiot judges she knew on the Family Court bench. How easy for them to rule for a smiling, handsome, rich, come-home-early father from a centuries-old Long Island family and against someone just like her. "You don't have a leg to stand on, you turkey."

"He *does* have a leg to stand on," Robin said, making it clear that she was tired of being understanding. "He has a damn good chance—"

Lee left them. As she rushed away, toward Valerie's room, she heard Jazz reassuring Robin with what she knew were his attorney's words. "She's going to find that custody rulings have changed since she went to . . ."

Valerie was not in her room. Oh, dear God, Lee

thought, they've arranged to have her . . . But she heard a high "Mommy?" and there was Val, in the kitchen, standing before the freezer. "Two scoops."

"Not here, Val," Lee said, and she grabbed her daughter and her handbag and was out so fast that Jazz still had not finished his discourse on matrimonial law when he and Robin heard his Mercedes pulling down the driveway and racing down the hill.

By the time Lee got to her parents' new house in Palm Beach late the following morning, she looked as bad as she felt. Her hair was unkempt in the manner peculiar to distraught people—sticking out in clumps from her head, each individual strand frizzled to a fare-thee-well. Her skin, if not blotchy, at least looked as if she were suffering from a vitamin deficiency and she was certain her eyes had grown smaller. Her clothes looked slept in.

They had been. She had been afraid Jazz would call the police and the cops would come pounding in the night at her office door. She dared not spend the night there. So she drove out of the county, into Queens, and checked into a motel near the airport, paying cash and giving her name as Lily Rose. The moment they entered the room, she gave Val the two pints of ice cream—chocolate and vanilla—she had bought at an all-night convenience store. She was so ashamed of herself, using food as a bribe. Nevertheless, to Val, the payoff wasn't good enough. Chocolate and vanilla did not equal her beloved vanilla fudge. The child began to wail. But she yawned mid-protest and two minutes later was sound asleep on the dubious sheets of the motel bed. Lee joined her, snuggling next to the warm little body, knowing that from now on, this was to be her only comfort. She knew, too, that she would not be able to sleep, yet she felt comforted by Val's nearness. Amazingly, her eyes next opened at precisely six-thirty the following morning, her usual wake-up time.

The trip to Florida was hellish, the entire plane jammed with people over sixty-five who did not try to hide their disapproval of a disheveled woman who would let her child out of the house in pajamas. As the plane emerged from the clouds, the first glimpse of palm trees buoyed her, until they reminded her of her honeymoon in St. Bart's. Why am I doing this, running home to Mommy and Daddy? To squeal on Robin? Mommy, guess what Robin did! To find solace? Maybe, but experience told Lee that Sylvia and Leonard were not likely to be listed in any Who's Who of great consolers.

The truth, she admitted to herself in the taxi, was that she needed someone to share more than her outrage. Will might have done that, but she had not been able to bring herself to call him. He could not share her shame.

"Little girl sick?" the taxi driver asked, looking at Val's pajamas in his rearview mirror.

"No. It's just more comfortable for traveling," Lee told him.

"Nice neighborhood you're going to. You live there?"

"No." He was waiting for something more. "My parents do."

Shame. They had indulged Robin for so long. All of them, Lee included. And instead of indulgence leading to mere sloth, it had bred viciousness. How could Robin have done this vile thing to the family, tearing herself off from them irreparably, taking her sister's husband and, not content with that theft alone, trying to grab her sister's child? Give me what Lee has. Give me! *Give me!*

But forget what Robin had done to Lee and Valerie: How could she have been so heartless about her parents, her father especially? Leonard had come to full life only in the sunshine spread by Jazz. Now that light would go out. And Kent. Robin wanted smart and pretty and bright-eyed Val, but Lee bet her sister and Jazz were planning to put a stamp on Kent's head and mail him back to his negligent parents.

"Once you get past the Palm Hacienda turnoff, do you know how to find the place?" the driver asked.

"Sorry, I don't remember." In truth, Lee had never been there. Her parents were only days in their new house. Old house. Not one of the major mansions, but still grand enough to have a name: La Luna. They had bought it from the social butterfly scion of a Pittsburgh corrugated box fortune, and while they laughingly said they had been merely looking for a nice place with a pool and a water view, it had been clear to Lee they were using the place to launch an incursion into Palm Beach society.

What would her father do now? More and more, he had been relying on Jazz. And Jazz had indeed proved himself reliable. At Thanksgiving dinner, Leonard had assuaged his guilt at leaving the salon for three months by chuckling: I'm just a phone call or a plane ride away. And, to give equal time, what would her mother do? Take to bed for months, as she had done so often in the pre-Jazz era? Would she sneak out for secret shopping trysts with Robin? Or would there now be inexorable pressure on Lee to become someone whose name, measurements, and style preferences were known to the salespeople in every boutique from East Fifty-ninth to East Seventy-ninth Streets?

"*Very* nice, ma'am," the driver said as they pulled up in front of La Luna, and Lee felt obliged to overtip him. As he was thanking her and as Val, barely toilet trained, was yelling "Pee!" the huge front door with its crescent moon knocker jerked open. Lee had expected a white-coated, brown-skinned butler. Indeed, one was hovering in the background. But in the foreground were her parents, looking almost as agitated as Lee herself.

"You're here!" Sylvia was crying, although on close inspection, Lee could see no actual moisture around her mother's eyes.

"Thank God!" Leonard bent down and took Val into his arms. "We were frantic!"

"Panicked!"

"Terrified!"

"Pee!"

"Lee, how could you have just taken the baby—" her mother demanded.

"Stop it, Sylvia," Leonard directed.

"—in the middle of the night—"

Lee grabbed Val and, with the help of the man in the white jacket, found a bathroom just feet away. Black marble with black fixtures. It looks like a toilet in hell, Lee thought. She squatted before her daughter, holding her up for lack of a potty seat. She could not believe that Jazz had actually called her parents. Could he be so stupid as to believe she would hurt Val? "What a big girl you are!" she told her daughter, pulling off a length of toilet paper. "I am so proud of you!"

As Lee and Val emerged from the bathroom, the white-coated butler was gone. So was Sylvia. "Where's Mom?"

"Sending the housekeeper out to buy clothes for Valerie."

"Thank you," Lee said, and allowed her father to take her arm and gently lead her, as he would someone suffering a terrible illness, to the back of the house. A huge porch overlooked a pool and, beyond it, a body of water that was not the ocean. "Beautiful," she said.

"Shwim?" Val asked.

"Later," Lee promised.

Her mother came out with the butler, who was bearing a tray of sandwiches, a pitcher of iced tea, and a smaller pitcher of milk for Val. To Lee, it was such an act of kindness that she felt herself choking up. That is, until she caught her mother eyeing her slacks and blazer. All that could be wrong with them was: wrinkled, a mismatched plaid on the seam of the sleeve—a red plaid, no less. "Why don't I bring you upstairs so you can take a shower?" Sylvia said. "I can lend you an outfit. I know I have a Vivienne Westwood that has a little give to it."

"Later," Lee said. "Thanks." She cut Val's sandwich into the finger-length shapes the child preferred. "What did Jazz tell you?" she asked her parents.

"It wasn't Jazz," Sylvia began. She stopped as Leonard cleared his throat.

"Robin called you?" Lee asked.

"She said there had been some disagreement," Leonard explained. "That you were very upset and you grabbed the baby and ran out in the middle of the night—"

"It was a little before seven o'clock in the evening."

"Oh. Well, you know your sister," he said. "High drama and all that." He paused. "You should have called, Lee."

"What would you have done at that hour on a Sunday night?" From a Fun! Sun! Florida! shopping bag, Lee pulled out a Weebles toy fire truck filled with little round Weebles firemen. She had bought it at the Palm Beach airport. She placed it on the grass below them, out of hearing distance.

"Well?" she asked Val. "Come here. It's all yours."

"T'anks, Ma!" Beside the truck, Lee set down a coloring book and a large box of crayons, more colors than Val had ever had. "Wow!"

"I mean," Sylvia was saying, "you should have called just so they weren't so worried—"

"*They*?" Lee inquired. Too loud, she realized. Her parents did not yet know what she did. "I have something to tell you," she said. "Something very painful." Leonard edged forward in his chair. Sylvia, though, just sat back and crossed her waxed legs. Her Pure Pomegranate toenails blended perfectly with her reddish-gold thongs. She did not look as though she wanted to hear anything painful. But whoever does want to, especially in a paradisiacal place like La Luna? And certainly not on this, Sylvia's second day as a probationary jet-setter. "Jazz and I are going to get a divorce," Lee said, trying to give them the good news first.

"Uh-huh," said her father.

"Oh," said her mother.

"He's been having an affair." To this they said nothing. "He wants to marry the woman." Her parents were more motionless than the palm trees in giant terra-cotta pots that ran the length of the great porch. Shock, Lee thought. What a blow. She looked to her father, knowing how Leonard adored Jazz. Driving to and from work with him every day. Popping in and out of each other's offices all the time. Chatting on the phone at night, on weekends. Shock. And he didn't even know about Robin yet. Just wait. The pain, the disgrace, the—

The butler appeared in the doorway. "Do you need anything more, Mrs. White?"

"No, thank you, Gibbons," Sylvia said sweetly.

Sweetly? Wait a second, Lee thought. It was one thing not to want to mess with a butler named Gibbons. Another for her mother to be able to keep up her gracious-lady act in the face of such awful news. Unless it was not news. "Dad?"

"Yes, sweetie?"

"Do me a favor and call my office, tell them I'm here. I don't want them to worry." She did not say that nothing short of reading in *Newsday* that the mutilated body of a thirty-year-old female had been found with a "Lee White, Attorney-at-Law," business card clamped between its teeth would cause anyone in her office to worry. Leonard, however, looked as if he was about to delegate such a potentially secretarial duty to Sylvia, so Lee added: "I'd like you to speak directly to Chuckie Phalen, Dad. He deals better with men. Don't give any details. Just that I had to come down on an important family matter."

"Sure, honey."

Leonard went off into the house. Lee waved at Val on the lawn, but the child was too busy with her fire truck to notice. Sylvia smiled at her daughter. "I know. One of those nonsexist toys. But why firemen? Ick. Oh, now's a good time. Want to try the Vivienne Westwood?"

"Sure!" Lee smiled back, then allowed her face to dissolve into sadness befitting the occasion. "In a minute. Mom, did Robin tell you the whole thing?" Sylvia's eyes darted around searching for Leonard, which answered Lee's question. "She told you about her and Jazz?"

"Yes. Lee, let's be honest: I know you feel it's the end of the world, but it isn't." Lee had been a criminal lawyer too long not to know the witness was not telling the complete truth. Check the demeanor. Brow drawn. Okay, was a drawn brow appropriate to the news that your younger daughter had been sleeping with your older daughter's husband? "You're still young, attractive—"

"I can't think about that now."

"I know. I can't tell you what this is doing to me."

A drawn brow. That was all. Was that a response to learning hours earlier from a phone call that your younger daughter was planning on marrying your older daughter's husband and had joined with him in demanding custody of your only grandchild? Lee did not want to know. And yet she did: That was precisely why she had sent her father to call Chuckie. "You've known about this for a while, Mom."

Since it came out as a statement and not a question, Sylvia was perplexed about how to respond. Lee looked at her mother: curious. So her mother said: "Not for *that* long."

"Dad kept it from you?"

"He didn't want me to get upset."

"I can understand that," Lee said. "It *is* upsetting."

"I know this must be such a shock for you, Lee. I'm so sorry."

"Thank you. It's been awful." Did she hear footsteps? "So Jazz will stay in the business?"

"Well, you know . . . "

"Dad's come to rely on him so much."

"Well, he has made a difference."

"And he'll still be married to a daughter, so it won't be that different than before." It was only then that Sylvia comprehended Lee had trapped her. And just as her mouth dropped open, her husband walked in, and her eyes filled with fear as well.

"What's wrong?" Leonard asked. "What is wrong?"

Before her mother could say anything, Lee said: "I'm here telling you my husband has left me, and you're asking what's wrong?"

"Sorry," Leonard breathed. "I spoke to Mr. Phalen. Some character! He says to tell you—"

"You knew goddamn well they were going to demand custody of Val, didn't you?" Lee snarled at him. Her father was literally taken aback. He retreated two steps toward the safety of the house. "Didn't you?" she demanded louder.

"Shhh!" Sylvia pleaded.

Lee ignored her mother and walked over to her father. "If you don't tell me what I want to know, I'm going to start screaming. Terrible things. The servants will hear." She paused. "The neighbors will hear. I will accuse you of the most vile crimes. I hear horror stories every damn day in my office, in the courts, and I'll accuse you of everything I've ever heard." She took her index finger and stabbed her father in the chest. "You knew they were going to demand custody?"

"Please, Lee, it's better for us all—"

At the top of her lungs, Lee boomed: "How would Gibbons like to know about the time you—"

"I knew," Leonard whispered. "I knew."

"How long?"

"That?" If there was a "that," Lee knew, there was also a "this." "A few weeks. Jazz told me after he spoke to a divorce lawyer."

She got to the "this" with another poke. "And how long have you known they've been lovers?"

"Just a few weeks more."

"You're lying!" Lee blared.

"Lee, *please*," her mother begged. "We love you. We're so sorry you have to go through all this terrible—"

Lee flipped her hand in her mother's direction:

You're dismissed. "How long have you known about Robin and Jazz? Don't think you can lie to me. I ferret out the truth for a living. I'll get it from you no matter how long it takes and how loud I have to yell."

"Don't threaten me, Lee," Leonard said, setting his jaw firm.

"What do you want to be accused of first? Embezzlement? Insurance fraud? No, that's boring. Why don't we jump right into a really interesting sex offense?"

"Let's stop the theatrics. They won't get you anywhere." He glanced toward the house and the unseen Gibbons. "I found out soon after it started."

"Which was . . . "

"When you were pregnant. The accountant was troubled by some charges Jazz had made to the business. So was I. I went and talked to him."

"And he said: 'It's okay, Dad. I was just fucking—'"

"Don't use that word!" Sylvia called out.

"'I was just having illicit sexual congress with your younger daughter while your older one was pregnant with your grandchild. Don't worry about the charges. It's all in the family.'"

"Do you think I was happy about it?"

"What did you do about it?"

"What do you think? I spoke to him. I spoke to Robin, heart to heart. I told her: It isn't right."

"Did you at any point threaten to throw him out of the business if he couldn't keep his pecker in his pocket?"

"Lee!" Sylvia called, getting up from her chair.

"Do you honestly think my threatening him like that would have stopped it?" Leonard inquired.

"Yes. If you had threatened to fire him. Or to kick that slut out of the house so she would have to earn her own living. Yes, indeed. But you couldn't, could you?" Leonard looked past her, as if waiting for a ship to come in. "Because you're afraid of Robin. But that's not the prime reason. It's not fear. It's love. You love Jazz more than any of us, more than all of us put together. If you had a third daughter and Jazz wanted her, you would condone that too. You would choose him over her. Protect him over her."

"You have your crazy theory," Leonard said quietly. "Nothing I say can stop you."

"That's right. So give your boy a message. He's not getting custody." She turned to her mother. "Call me a cab."

Sylvia looked to Leonard. "Go ahead," he told her.

"I don't know who to call," she replied.

"Tell Gibbons," Leonard said harshly. "He'll do it." She hurried into the house.

"'Tell Gibbons,'" Lee repeated, an unexpected smile forcing itself onto her face.

She hurried down to the lawn to pick up Val. "Shwim?" asked the little girl.

"Soon," Lee said, brushing off the grass from her pajamas.

"Shwim *please*?"

Lee looked down at Val, all thirty-seven inches of her poised to leap into her grandparents' pool and splash. Right on the spot, Lee determined she would not be on the next plane to New York. What was she rushing back to? All she had left was right there beside her. Chuckie could cover for her at the office. She could call the matrimonial lawyer at Will's firm and set him to work. And she could find a hotel with a pool—and allow herself and her daughter a day or two to shwim.

*　　*　　*

Joe Clark, Lee's divorce lawyer, was a tall, trim, broad-shouldered man in his forties, with a blond crewcut. He and Will, side by side in De Ruyter, Lefkowitz and Stewart's oak conference room, looked like photographic negatives of each other.

"Can he get custody?" Lee asked. Looking tanned and healthy, she felt embarrassed. She should be wan, frail, maybe trembling a little. That's how she felt. She had kept Val in Florida for a week, and every night after the child went to sleep in the middle of their king-size bed in the Miami Beach hotel room, Lee would stand over her and weep in silence, terrified that Jazz would win custody.

She finally forced herself back to New York, but there was no comfort there. Jazz's attorney was not what she had imagined—a sleek, shiny counselor to upper-class Manhattan husbands. No, much worse: Jazz had chosen Manny Plotkin, a short, bald, sputtering Long Island lawyer, a human torpedo who was fast making a reputation for himself demanding—and often winning—rights for men in child custody suits.

"Realistically?" Joe said. "It's the exception rather than the rule for fathers to get custody. Especially where the child is a little girl. It's just not done."

"They're going to say I'm an unfit mother."

"That's nuts!" Will said.

"You've got him on adultery charges," added Joe. "With your sister. Who's unfit?"

She could tell they were losing patience with her. "Look, I've read some of the case law," she explained. "There's a trend. Mothers don't automatically get custody anymore. And it's not as if he's bringing in some New York slicko to represent him. Everyone says this Manny has won a lot of cases out here and . . . " Fear overcame her, and she could not speak. She pictured all the nights she had worked late, how often Jazz had given the nanny, Cherry, the night off. He had said: I don't mind being home. I love puttering around the house, making dinner. Robin had been there every one of those nights. She fit in so well, as if she was one of the family. Which she was, someone whose presence Val would never question. The judge would bring Val into chambers, and Jazz and Robin would be sitting there, and before the judge could ask the little girl how she felt, she'd be racing over to climb onto Robin's lap.

And what could she offer? Jazz had taken Cherry away. Hired her to work for him and Robin. At first, Lee, although furious, was amused at his chutzpah, but then she realized how confident he was that he would win. Did he know something about the judge that she and Joe Clark and Will did not? Jazz was pushing this case with demented energy. He wanted it over. He wanted to win. Every day brought a new shower of paper from Manny's office, details—dates, times—of nights worked, meals missed, dinners Lee had had with Will.

"Do you think he had a detective following me the times I met Will for dinner?" she asked Joe quietly. Her hands were like ice.

"Sounds like it." With his close-cropped hair, rasping voice, and jutting jaw, he appeared to be the ex-marine he actually was.

"But that works for our side," Will added. "Nothing happened. I've been involved with Maria for years. He knows you and I are just friends."

They both looked at Joe. "In that case, nothing to worry about," Joe told them. "What can any picture show? A man eating a bowl of spaghetti talking to a woman eating a meatball?"

"How about a black man and a white woman

standing in front of the woman's car talking?" Lee answered.

"You *are* nuts," Joe told her, nodding apologetically to Will for having doubted him.

"Not totally nuts," Will responded after a moment. "What she's getting at is that it depends on what the judge feels in his gut when he's faced with an interracial relationship. Legally it's meaningless. Practically, if his gut goes into a knot at the sight of a white woman with a black man, it won't help." He rested his elbows on the conference table and gazed across at Lee. "But I can't believe that's going to be a deciding factor in this case. Look, this has been a nightmare for you. The man you loved betrayed your trust. That's a terrible thing, but you know what? It happens. Somewhere in the back of your mind, Lee, you know that in marriages, it is sometimes possible for a man to be unfaithful to his wife. It is even possible that he might want to leave her for another woman. So while this is a bad blow, it's something that you can deal with."

"I'm so damn tired of being strong," Lee said.

"I know. What I'm telling you is that nobody's strong enough for what you have to handle now. It's one thing for you to acknowledge that, okay, the marital contract might be violated. But there are certain social contracts that are assumed to be honored by everyone. The family: parent and child; brothers and sisters. Your husband can screw you forty ways till Sunday, but don't worry—there's always your family. They'll be there for you. So what I'm saying is that you've had the rug pulled out from under you in new and unexpected ways. The fact you're sitting here, brave enough to be able to talk about what happened—"

"What the hell choice do I have?" Lee cried out.

"Don't you think I'm up every night, sick with fear about Val and sick with thinking how I'd like to kill them? Some nights, I'm running over Robin with my car. Some nights, I'm taking one of those knives they use to cut fur and slashing my father's . . ."

"Understandable," Joe said with such placidity that she realized his practice was as permeated with threats of murder as hers was filled with the actual deeds.

"All that's keeping me sane is Valerie. And they want to take her away from me."

"We won't let them," Will said.

Lee pushed back her chair and stood. "Can you give me a guarantee?"

Will hesitated, then turned to his partner to speak. "No," Joe Clark said. "Wish I could, but I never give guarantees. Sorry. Especially not with a lawyer like Manny Plotkin on the other side."

"You're fucking crazy, Lee," Terry Salazar told her.

"I could take her anyplace. Ohio . . . Iowa . . ."

"Yeah? And how would you earn a living?"

"I don't have to be a lawyer."

She could say to Terry what she could not say to Will. That with the trial date set in the custody suit, she was growing sicker and sicker with fear. Joe Clark's rational "Highly unlikely" and "Not to worry, I can be as tough as it takes" did not bring her ease. Nor did Will's continual reassurance and his attempts to help her understand why she was so terribly scared: Was she frightened by the fury blazing up in herself? Racked with guilt about being a working mother—not just a mother who had to work, but a mother who loved her work almost as much as she loved her daughter? Did she feel that somehow, Robin—pretty,

clothes-buying, don't-want-to-work-for-money Robin—
deserved Jazz more than she did because Robin was
what a real woman should be and Lee was not? Or that
she owed Robin something because she was a success
and Robin a failure?

She was getting so tired of Will's constant company and loyalty and thoughtful analysis that she was
actually relieved when he went off to be with Maria.
Well, not so relieved. Lee told herself she did not
expect him to end a years-long love affair now that
she was free, that she was perfectly content with his
deep and devoted friendship, with his incredible
sweetness, now not only to Val, but to Kent also. But
in her heart, that was precisely what she had hoped
for: Will for herself.

"Listen, you want to be treated like an equal, but
you're talking like a real dumb broad," Terry told her.
"You got your head so high up your ass you can't see
daylight. You run with the kid, he'll find you. The bastard's got nothing but resources to squander on guys
like me, to say nothing of the cops and the Feebies
who would be looking for you if you went on the lam.
You know what this Jazz guy's worth?" He grabbed the
papers on his desk, looking for the figures he had gotten, with a hundred-dollar bribe and a great deal of
charm, from a secretary in Jazz's accountant's office.
"The mil he showed you and Uncle Sam and almost
two mil more."

Lee sat on the white couch in Terry's all-white
office, for once blending in. She was pale, almost col-
orless. When she looked at herself in the mirror that
morning in the house she was renting, she felt sure she
had faded, that she was already less. Jazz was winning.
She might even die. She was so tired she could barely
speak. "Then what should I do?"

"Do? You got a good lawyer. You got evidence up the ass. I got you that waiter who quit the Carlyle, who's willing to testify about him and her. What other detective could have come up with that, especially considering that I'm working for you on such a discount it's practically nothing? You've got his own admission, for Christ's sake. He's fucking living with your sister in your house. Jesus, you folded on that like a fucking wimp. All you had to say was 'Hey, get your cheating ass out of here and—'"

"It didn't matter. I couldn't stand the place anymore. He bought it under false pretenses, so right from the start . . . "

Lee stopped because Terry began playing an imaginary violin. She did not tell him to go to hell, because she knew he was expecting her to. "You know what gets me about you?" Terry demanded. "You're so tough. I'm not talking about butch. You're not. You're okay, if somebody likes ball-busting women. But look at you now: a fucking basket case. And over what? What are you scared of? A Wasp who was born to run the whole goddamn country and he winds up selling fur coats? What kind of a man do you think that is? For Christ's sake, Lee, you're a powerhouse. He's a pussy! What's with you?"

"What should I do?"

"'What should I do?'" he whimpered. His hands dangled from limp wrists. He pretended to cringe. "'Oh, what should I—'"

Rage propelled her across the office. It was only when Terry grabbed her arm and held it out to the side that she realized her fist was clenched tight and that she had been about to punch him. Not a stop-that-you-bully sock in the shoulder. A hard punch in the mouth. They stood there, facing each other, arms stretched out, perpendicular and stiff, as if in some travesty of a tango.

"Get rid of the fist and I'll let you go."

"Stop it, you jerk."

"I don't think so," Terry said. His voice was soft, velvet. Not the rest of him.

"Come on," she said lightly, as if this coming together were a mere annoyance, and that she could not feel his heat through his shirt.

He stretched out her arm even farther, bringer her closer to him. Her face pressed against his, damp with excitement at their dance. "Come on," he said, rocking his hips into hers. "Come on." He kissed her, not a gentle suitor's kiss. Inflamed, right away, with teeth and tongue working on her. She pulled her wrist out of his grip only to put her arms around him, to try to see if she could draw him in even closer.

Terry was good. Better than good. No finesse, no technique, no sweet words. Hot and hard and didn't stop: That was all she wanted.

That was all she got.

Jazz refused to meet without their lawyers present. Too emotional, for all of us. Sorry. That's what he said when she called to say she would like to come over, to speak to him and Robin. Too emotional? Terry laughed. That's not the reason. After another week on the case, tailing Jazz—just for practice, Terry told her—he had followed him and Robin to a doctor's office. A gynecologist. Oh, obstetricians too. A little charm, no bribe necessary this time for the cute little technician in the medical laboratory the doctor sent his work to. No, charm was all it took to discover that, indeed, an R. R. White, age twenty-eight, was pregnant. It's not "too emotional," Terry said. "The skinny bitch is probably showing."

Lee pushed her way past the two French-accented junior salesmen at Le Fourreur, past five astounded customers, past Dolly Young, past her father who pleaded, "I beg you, Lee, please don't—" into Jazz's office and slammed the door. "You've made my life a living hell!" she told him.

"Get out. This will count against you, you know, your not having the self-restraint—"

"I will make your life a living hell."

"You already did. For years. You can't anymore."

"Item one: My sister is pregnant. She can have an abortion—"

"Stop that!"

"—or she can be an unmarried mother, because I will drag on this litigation forever. Living hell. When I can no longer afford my own lawyer, I will appear *pro se,* and by that time I'll be such a genius at matrimonial law that I'll make mincemeat out of that shyster you've retained. It will drag on for *years.*"

"Stop it!"

"You'll be on your third illegitimate child by that time. And that's just the beginning. I'll bankrupt you. I'll kill you with paper. You won't have a dime left and Manny's wife will have five sable coats and you'll still owe him hundreds of thousands."

"Do you think you can scare me?" Jazz demanded.

"I hope so, because if you're not trembling in your Guccis now, you're a fool. I don't want alimony. This is what I want: I want you to speak to your parents. They don't want Kent. Do you?" Jazz said nothing. "Well, I do. I want them to agree to name me guardian. I want him to live with me. As far as Val goes, I want child support and a guarantee you'll split

her educational costs with me fifty-fifty. I get custody."
She paused. "I get what I want. Or you get a life that
won't be worth living."

On the first day of 1981, Lee and Will went to the
beach, a spot not too far from Will's house. The air
was cold—freezing, in fact—but there was hardly any
wind, so they hunkered down against the dunes,
looked across the powder sand to the churning gray
ocean, and ate their sausage and pepper sandwiches
with their gloves on.

"Brisk," Will said. "Good for the head, good for the
soul."

"Brisk? You call this brisk? I call this glacial." She
picked up her coffee. "My face is too numb to tell if it's
dribbling down my chin and giving me second-degree
burns, so let me know." She took a sip.

"You're fine so far." He lifted his Styrofoam cup and
touched it to hers. "Happy New Year, kid."

"Happy New Year," she said. "I'm not going to say
anything self-pitying and small-minded about this year
being better than last."

"I admire your restraint."

They set their cups in the sand and went back to
their sandwiches, huge, drippy, comforting things.
After a while, Lee felt warmer, heartier. She could be
one of those Polar Bears, those mad, jolly people who
dive into the Atlantic every winter at Coney Island, racing across the sand, rushing through the surf, and going
under, only to emerge with a cheer and a huge grin.
She turned to Will. "Did you have fun at the New
Year's Eve party last night with Maria?"

He set down his sandwich. "I wasn't with Maria."

"You told me . . . " He had mentioned in early

December that he and Maria went to the same party every year for New Year's Eve. Casual conversation, but meant, she knew, so she would not hold out false hopes.

"I know what I told you. It wasn't the truth."

"It wasn't the truth?" She knew it was an odd question for a criminal lawyer to ask. She was trained to doubt. Yet she had never doubted that every word Will uttered was the absolute truth. "Where were you?"

"That's a long story," he said quietly. "A long and difficult story."

Lee's heart began to beat faster. Perhaps Maria had only gone out of town or come down with the flu, but the "difficult story" was that they had finally decided to marry. Not now, she prayed. Please, plan a June wedding and tell me about it in May. "Are you going to tell me the story?" she asked him.

"Yes. That's why I thought we'd come here. No interruptions."

"Okay."

"You know how much you mean to me, Lee. Your friendship." Uh-oh, she thought. It's coming. She nodded, trying to seem pleased that Will valued her enough to really hurt her. "For me anyway, it's a life-long friendship."

"For me, too," she said.

"So let me tell you." She waited, but he did not say anything. Clearly, this was going to be painful for him. She could leave now, rush away, not have to listen, but he had driven his car to the beach, and he had the keys. And it was a stick shift. She wondered if it would be rude to take another bite of her sandwich. She laid her fingers on the warm, greasy, paper-wrapped mess and decided it would be. "I'm gay," Will said.

"Gay?"

"As in homosexual."

Gay, she thought. Oh. No wonder his sports clothes are always so perfect. Suits are one thing, but those slacks, those sweaters. Then a wave of grief crashed down upon her, the realization that she would never have what she now most wanted. What a man! She could love him. She already did.

Suddenly she became aware of what a horrible moment this must be for him, waiting to see how she would react. "I didn't know," she said brightly.

Too brightly. "Lee? Tell me what you're thinking."

"I'm very, very surprised."

"Surprised or shocked?"

"Shocked." Will looked out at the ocean. "Don't be sorry you told me. You're my friend and I love you. I understand how courageous it was for you to confide in me." She rubbed his sleeve with her glove: I'm with you, pal. She left a blotch that looked suspiciously like a mushed-up string of red pepper. "I assume this is absolutely confidential, that I'm not Step One in your plan to come out?"

"God, no!"

"Then I will keep it in absolute confidence for the rest of my life."

Again, Will's eyes searched the ocean. They looked watery to her, but it might have been the cold. "I started college in 1958. No one came out then, or at least, hardly anyone."

"Did you know you were gay then?"

"I knew I was gay by the time I was twelve. I didn't know what to call it. I didn't know it had a name, and to tell you the truth, I didn't know there was anybody else in the world who felt the way I did."

"It must have been a terrible burden."

"It was. But on the other hand, I was this bright,

healthy kid. Not a great athlete, not what they expected from a black kid in Glen Cove in those days. But good enough not to feel I stood out. And I was smart. Very smart, very reflective. When you're a teenager, that's a blessing and a curse, but at least I was able to begin to understand what I was and realize I wasn't the first boy in the world who didn't care what the girls were wearing underneath their outfits."

"But you checked out the outfits."

"Yes, I did."

"When did you first have sex?"

"I was fifteen."

"And? Was it okay? Traumatic?"

"It was fine. Very romantic. A lot of candles and massage oil. It was an affair that continued for four years. That's why I went to Columbia. So I could stay in New York, be near him."

"Who was he?"

"My parents' employer." Will came close to smiling as Lee's mouth widened into a huge O. "Clement Giddings. Clem. It sounds like a banjo player, but he was the most urbane man I ever met."

"I don't buy it!" she said angrily. "He was using his power and position to get a boy—"

"Grow up, Lily. He didn't seduce me. I seduced him. Not that he wasn't open to seduction."

"You were still a kid."

"I was. And he was very good to me. Not a great lover, but you're not looking for finesse at fifteen. And a decent man. Not a warm man, not a friendly man, but decent. He paid for college, even after I told him I'd found someone else."

"Who was that?"

"No one. A lot of different guys. I didn't want to be stuck with a forty-eight-year-old man who had never

worked for a living except to catalogue his wine collection and who had a wife and two really stinky,
obnoxious kids. He offered to pay for graduate school,
too, by the way."

"You must have been something."

"I was. His white dream come true."

"Your parents . . . ?"

"They didn't have a clue. They still don't."

"I didn't have a clue."

"I know. I'm good at what I do. I'm sorry I have to
do it. But by the time it was no longer necessary—in
terms of cultural acceptance of men living an openly
gay lifestyle—I was stuck in a suburban subculture
where if I came out . . . " He paused to collect his
thoughts. "Not completely stuck. I could have left,
gone to the city. It was my choice not to. I like it here."

"So do I."

"But there are drawbacks. You can understand,
being a woman who works in what is largely a man's
sphere: You have to be twice as good as any man to
get anything close to equal credit."

"That is a drawback."

"As a black man, twice as good isn't enough. I have
to be four times as good. I really believe that. I've *lived*
that. And I knew that, practicing law on Long Island,
being in the D.A.'s Office, dealing with the cops and
all, if I came out, four times as good wouldn't be
enough. I'd have to be eight times as good as any
white lawyer. And you know what? I'm just not that
good."

"Yes you are."

"Thank you. But not eight times. A flash of sheer
brilliance once or twice a year, yes, but nothing I
could sustain."

Lee glanced down at her sandwich. It was probably

cold. She took a bite. Cold but good. "What about Maria?" she asked.

"She's a professional educator in a private girls' school. She's a lesbian. She lives with a woman. We met at a gay Valentine's Day party in the city one of my friends threw. She's wonderfully intelligent, cultured, attractive, and black. The minute we looked at each other, we knew."

"The perfect couple."

"The perfect black couple. 'Aren't they stunning together? Aren't they nice? And *so* well-spoken!'"

"So you don't really love her?"

"No, but I like her enormously. She's an amazing person."

"And last night?"

"What? Oh, New Year's Eve. I was home. Alone. I stuffed a Cornish hen and opened a split of champagne and had a party."

"You don't have anyone in particular?"

"I have someone in particular. Unfortunately, he has someone in particular, someone he's been living with for ten years, so I suppose that makes me his little bonbon on the side. I have a studio in the city. We see each other one or two nights a week. Usually one."

"What does he do?"

"He's an architect. Very arty. Long, flowing hair, quivering nostrils. I can laugh about him when I'm not with him."

"Thank you for telling me, Will." He nodded and got busy putting their lunch in the plastic bag it had come in. She had not finished her sandwich but decided it would be churlish to stick her hand in the bag and grab it back. "I know you felt you had to say something because you sensed I had a crush on you and you didn't want it to ruin the friendship." He looked at her, almost boyishly embarrassed at being caught. "Well, I had—or have—a crush. I'll get over it. And thank you for valuing our friendship so much. I realize what a risk you took."

"Lee."

"What?"

"I know you. It was never a risk."

On February 29, 1981, the Honorable Anthony J. Paterno of Nassau County's Domestic Relations Court ruled, in the matter of *Taylor* v. *White*, that inasmuch as both parties agree that Ms. Lee White will be the custodial parent, all issues arising from the pending litigation are rendered moot and that custody of Valerie Belinda Taylor, an infant, will be with the child's mother. So Ordered. Submit Judgment.

Twenty-three

❧

Prisons are harrowing places. At night, amid the snores and sleep screams of fellow inmates, I don't know anyone who's so strong that she wouldn't think, even for a moment: I would be better off dead. And the days aren't a hell of a lot better. With no sharp objects, no pills, no tall buildings from which to jump, no car exhaust to inhale, the inevitable jailhouse means to the end is hanging. So Mary Dean was not exceptional. Suicide attempts are so common in jails that most places have a super-sharp blade called a 911 tool, which cuts through the bedsheets inmates use to hang themselves. The guards are so accustomed to these incidents they refer to them casually as "hang-ups." If there is no damage—I'm not talking emotional here, I'm talking if the inmate can breathe and walk—he or she is expected to be in line when the next meal rolls around.

There was no way I could be casual about it. That Thursday, right after Barbara Duberstein's call, I sat at my desk, shaking inside. What had gone wrong? Mary had not been pushed into confessing, had she? She had jumped. She had insisted, damn it! But had she insisted because I'd manipulated her into insisting? I tried to soothe myself by thinking she had to have known what she was getting into: Between the assault charge in Maryland and her various arrests for prostitution, she was no stranger to the inside of a cell. There were no surprises here for her. Were there? No, Norman had been innocent and she was guilty. Justice had been served. I had done what I had to do, period.

My serenity lasted about three seconds. Sooner or later, most criminal lawyers come across a client who tries to kill himself. And you have to be either stupid or a first-class putz if you don't ask yourself: Could I have done anything at all to stop it? Your heart is a stone if an incident like that doesn't summon up a time in your own life when you felt death might be preferable to the pain of living. But what made me tremble so was that of all the people who had sat in that armchair on the other side of my desk, Mary was the most likely to want to live. Sweet and stupid and blissfully amoral, delighted by her own beauty, by flamboyant dresses and ten-cents-off coupons for Niagara Spray Starch, madly in love with Norman, Mary was all loud colors and bright sunshine. Of course, I knew she wouldn't thrive in jail. No one would. But to try to hang herself?

My door opened. Chuckie Phalen, as he did every evening, stuck in his head to say goodbye before toddling off to TJ's Taproom. My face must have stopped him. He told me I looked like the wrath of God. When I didn't give him an argument, he knew something was wrong and came in. I told him what had happened. Both of us could hear the tremor in my voice. What are you going to do? he asked me. I'm meeting Barbara Duberstein. I'll play it by ear.

Mary looked as if her suicide attempt had been successful. Dead eyes, although still stunningly green and accentuated by thick black lashes. She did not walk toward us as much as allowed her body to be conveyed by a female corrections officer. The officer was either extraordinarily compassionate or in awe of Mary's beauty. She escorted her across the huge room not with the usual antagonistic impatience—Come on! Move it!—but with a degree of deference that might have been shown a queen on coronation day. Far from being pushed, Mary was being escorted by the officer: Turn here, good, that's right, and They're right over there. Mary was as unaware of the special treatment as she was of the officer herself, even when the woman supported her elbow and helped lower her into her chair.

"Mary," I said, "I had to ask Barbara to come along. I want to do everything I can for you, but because I was representing Norman, there are some things that need doing that I can't do."

"How are you doing, Mary?" Barbara asked.

"I'm sorry," she whispered to me.

I wasn't sure if she was apologizing for trying to hang herself or for asking me to visit her. "Don't be sorry. You must have been in a bad way to try what you did."

She covered her face with her big hands because she started to cry. Still, I could hear: "Norman."

"What about Norman?" Barbara asked, taking out her fountain pen and a small leather book she always carried. In all the years I'd known her, she had never run out of space in the thing. "I'll just make a note or two."

"Tell us about Norman," I suggested after a minute of watching her cry. Shoulders heaving, she sobbed wholeheartedly, gulping huge, noisy mouthfuls of air.

"He's gone," Mary finally said "Gone." She was hoarse, as would anyone be whose larynx had been compressed by a noose.

"Gone?" I said, relieved. I could ease her anxiety. Norman had called my office Tuesday and Wednesday, alarmed about her, trying to see if there was a way to get her out of jail, into some fancy mental hospital. He'd sounded very much *not* gone, very much involved. "He didn't come to see you today?" I was already kicking myself for having been so responsive to her suicide attempt. What a sucker I was! "Is that what got you so upset, Norman's not showing up today?"

"He didn't come to see me"—the tears started to flow again—"since last Friday."

I was stopped cold. "Last Friday?" Either she was lying or confused. Very confused. Or when Norman had called me, yesterday and the day before that . . . "Are you sure, Mary? Today is Thursday, right?"

"Don't you think I know what day it is?" she asked, her voice rising, echoing off the walls of the cavernous space. "Don't you think I've been counting every day since he left?"

"All right, then," I said, trying to soothe her. "Help me understand so I can try and help you. When did Norman leave?"

"Last Friday."

"And where did he go?" I asked, although I knew the answer.

"Atlanta, Georgia," Mary said. "He has his money there. He was going to go to where he hides the key to his safe-deposit box. Then, Monday, he'd go to the bank."

"Cayman Islands," I murmured to Barbara. "But the timetable's the same."

"What was the money for?" Barbara inquired. Mary did not answer right away. As far as I knew from Norman, he was going to get money for Barbara's retainer as well as for the house he was buying near the prison Mary was going to be transferred to. Nevertheless, Mary's silence spoke to me. It said that Norman had told her to keep quiet. She was torn between that obedience and five-foot-nothing Barbara Duberstein's natural authority. "Speak up. We have to know what the money was for."

"He said he needed it to pay a better lawyer."

"Better than me?" Barbara asked.

"Better than you and . . . "

"And what?" I prodded her. "Don't hold back, Mary. Do you mean a lawyer better than Barbara and better than I?"

" 'Better than I,' " she repeated. "Norman would like that."

"Norman thought he would find a better lawyer? More aggressive? More *what*?"

"More . . . better. I'm sorry."

"It's okay."

"He said he already called some famous lawyer in Texas and the lawyer was probably going to take my case."

"Do you know this lawyer's name?" Barbara asked, putting her pen to the paper. Mary shook her head. "All right, so Norman got the money—"

"That's what he was going to do!" Mary cried. "I haven't heard anything from him, not since Friday! That's what I've been telling you."

"Wait a second," I said. "He called me. Yesterday, and the day before. He said he'd been with you, that you were going through a bad time. He was looking for ways to help you."

"He wasn't with me," Mary said patiently, the teacher with a slow student.

"He wasn't here? With you?"

"No. Monday, I knew he'd be at the bank in Atlanta. Then Tuesday, I thought maybe there's some holiday down there on Monday, a Georgia thing or a South thing, so that's when he went to the bank. And then, after visiting hours in the morning on Wednesday, I thought: Oh, sweet Jesus, maybe he's hurt. Or dead. Maybe a bank robber could've been there and shot him. That's when I called you the first time. I was, like, starting to get hysterical. But then, today, I knew."

"Knew what?" I asked. Mary covered her mouth with her fingertips. A speak-no-evil gesture, and also, I sensed, a signal that said how humiliated she was to have come before us with no lipstick. It did not take much to distract her, and right then it was Barbara's rose-colored mouth. Mary had begun longing for makeup, and I took that as a sign of hope, that even if she did not know it, she did want to live. "What did you know, Mary?" I repeated.

"I knew that Norman wasn't coming back. And that's why I tried to . . . " Her fingers slid down to her throat. Her neck was striped with a red burn mark where the twisted bedsheet had throttled her.

"But then why would Norman call me?" I demanded, turning to Barbara. "Why would he say he'd seen her when he hadn't?"

"Well . . . " Barbara hesitated, but it was clear she knew and was simply reluctant to have to tell me.

"Don't hold back," I told her.

"Because he was conning you."

"Conning *me*?"

"He got you to think he was here, doing the right thing by her, so you would feel easy about him. He was buying a little extra insurance. Didn't want you thinking he might be disappearing into the night."

"But why?" I persisted. "What's his motive?"

It was Mary, not Barbara, who answered, with a calm

voice and dry eyes. "Because he didn't want anything to get in the way of my pleading guilty. I knew it today. I *knew* it."

"What did you know?" I demanded.

"Norman conned me too."

The visitors room seemed so frightening, now that all the dangerous inmates were safely in their cells. Just their odors lingered to prove that they had been there—and would be back. Not the raw smell of gyms or men's locker rooms: a meaner stink. And it was dangerously quiet. No movement except one officer patrolling the floor, her shoes making no sound. Another, cleaning his nails with his front teeth, monitored the closed-circuit TV. A prison movie without a sound track.

"How did Norman con you?" I managed to ask.

"He told me . . . " Mary closed her eyes, unable to bear reality any longer.

"Please, Mary. Tell us." I was sick. I already knew.

"Norman said you thought I did it. That gave him an idea."

No. It was worse than that: I didn't just give Norman an idea. He manipulated me. He made me think that here was a man who had killed, who had led a life without worth, who richly deserved whatever punishment he would get. A defense lawyer's nightmare, but also a defense lawyer's dream. The unwinnable case: To be able to turn that around! He must have started planning the moment he was arrested for Bobette's death.

"Oh, my God," I said. Barbara reached over and squeezed my hand. It did not reassure me. "Tell me about his idea."

"That I should say I killed Bobette."

"Did you kill her?" Barbara asked.

Mary turned to her, insulted, incredulous. "No. Of course not."

"Who did, then?"

Mary's liquid emerald eyes took us both in, pitying us for our lack of insight. "Norman killed her."

"But then why were you willing to say you did it?" I demanded. "Didn't you know it was a murder charge?"

"Why? 'Cause I love him."

"He asked you to do this?"

"No! Of course not." Mary ran her fingers through her hair. It lay oily and lifeless on her shoulders. She lifted a tress and stared at it, not believing it could be hers. "He told me what he was facing. All those years. He said: 'You can't wait for me, Mary. It would be like . . . '" Embarrassed at revealing such intimacy, she fell into uneasy silence and began to chew the inside of her cheek.

"What did he say?" Barbara asked. "Please, don't be shy with us. We came here because we care about your welfare."

Mary allowed herself to be persuaded. "He said if I waited, it would be like leaving a beautiful flower in the desert to die. He wouldn't let me. He didn't even want me to visit him in jail. He said: 'Let's end it now, because otherwise it'll be agony.' But I couldn't. How could I leave the one man in the world God meant for me? That's when I started to think about what he was telling me, about how people with long records get life, and how he was so sorry he had a record 'cause people who really haven't done anything much get off easy. I thought: Hey, it wouldn't be that bad for me, not like it would for him. And I knew he would wait for me. So I told him."

"Told him what?" Barbara asked.

"Told him I'd take the fall. And he said: 'Not on your

life!' But I begged him. I said, 'Please, let me do this for you, Norman. I mean, I don't really have a record. Not a bad one, anyway. Not like yours.' And finally he said let him think about it. He's a very deep thinker, so it took him a couple of days, but he figured it out. With all his money, he was going to get this very famous lawyer from Texas. He's never lost a case. He's always on TV, Norman says, on all the news shows. And even if he lost, you know, if the jury said I was guilty, if it's the first time you ever did anything, like a violent crime, you don't go to prison long. Like, your sentence can sound long, but you don't *stay* long."

"Did Norman tell you how much time you'd be away for?" I asked.

"He said the lawyer—the Texas lawyer—told him four years tops. But see, with this lawyer, even if he did lose, it wouldn't be more than two."

"Two years?" Barbara and I said together.

"And then, like, it might not even be *that* long, because the lawyer thought he could get me off on appeal." Mary made it sound so reasonable, so inevitable, that I could see she still had not stopped believing it entirely.

Barbara was staring at her. "And you believed him?"

"Norman loves me." She pressed against the barrier that separated us and asked me: "Didn't he? Tell her. Didn't he love me?" I was so sick at heart. Before I could think of something kind to say, Mary slumped backward. "So?" she asked us. "How many years is it going to be?"

"In this case?" Barbara said. "Actual time? I guess somewhere between eight and twenty years." She looked to me for confirmation.

"Mary," I said, "you can fight this. You can—"

She shook her head. "It doesn't matter," she said very calmly. "In jail, out of jail. He's gone. I'm going to die either way."

"No! Listen to me," I said, so harshly that she flinched and Barbara dropped her pen. "You want to die. You think you're going to die because there's no reason to live. When the only man you love suddenly whips around and sticks a knife into you—and then walks away because he's too sensitive to watch you bleed—you say: 'Okay. I'm giving up. Let me bleed to death, because I cannot stand the pain. And besides, it's what he wants. Maybe my dying will somehow make him love me again.' Screw that! I've been there. You *can* stand the pain. You and I are going to pull that goddamn knife out of your heart. Whatever happens—and I can't guarantee anything—you're going to live. You're going to have a big, ugly scar, but you're going to live."

Mary's eyes went from me to her lovely high-rise bosom. "You're just kidding about the ugly scar, aren't you?" she whispered.

I didn't know if it was the worst night of my life, but it was definitely one of my top two. Conned by my own personal con man. I, the one person under no delusions about Norman Torkelson, had been totally bamboozled by him. How he had picked up on what I had wanted! Not love: He knew he couldn't work that scam with me. I was far too wary of him. And where he was, in jail, what good would my going nuts for him do? No, he wanted me sane. At peak efficiency. Norman knew precisely what I was and what I yearned for: I was an ordinary criminal defense lawyer who desired, from the top of her head to the soles of her not too high suburban heels, to be special. To stand beside Justice as her sister. To save an innocent man.

And so he had set me up to save him. He knew that Mary had been in Bobette's house, knew her fingerprints were everywhere. He was probably outraged at the shoddy police work. How dare they not even mention a second set of prints! How dare they arrest him without investigating further! (And oh, how he must have hated Mary, blamed her for his arrest because she had stupidly registered his car in the name that led the police straight to his door!) So he set to work, dropping his poison into my ear drop by drop. And when it began to work, when I started to suspect Mary might have been at Bobette's, he grew so defensive, so protective, that my suspicions had to grow: not only had Mary been there, but *she* was the killer. Not my client. Not my client, whom I was going to get off!

And when I built such a brilliant case against her, he could deny it no more. All right, yes, Mary did it. But you can't do a thing about it. I'm going to take the rap. I, the con artist, the criminal, the moral leper, deserve this one chance to be redeemed. Allow me my humanity.

How poetic! How noble! How I fell for it! How much like all those piteous marks of his I turned out to be. Norman conned me and sent me out to con Holly Nuñez, and I did not disappoint him. I was so ready to believe him.

I took him out to dinner, and he ordered prime ribs of beef!

Forty-five years old: There had been a lot of water under my bridge. I was one street-smart dame, wasn't I? Who would have believed someone like me could be conned? A con man. Who else?

Forget my ego: What would this do to my career? Would my partner ever trust my judgment again? For that matter, could I trust Chuckie not to yuck it up with the boys at TJ's over how I'd been conned? ("Would a fella ever fall for a hoax like that? I ask you?") And what about Holly and her bosses at the D.A.'s? There wasn't much love for me in that office, but at least there was universal acceptance that I was a straight arrow. My credibility was my stock in trade. Now that it was shot, what did I have? And when word went around the Bar Association? Who would ever refer another case to me?

And Barbara? She had not yet been paid. I asked her—almost begged her—to let me split my retainer from Norman with her. Don't be ridiculous, she chided me. A right and graceful response. But a case that had looked like a few hours of easy work, watching over some killer desperate to confess, had turned into a misery that was eating up time from the rest of her practice.

And the worst of my nightmare: My guy. Not just a fine lawyer. There was nothing he did that he did not do well. What would he make of such a screwup? I had no doubt he would show me incredible compassion. He would say: It's understandable. Don't give yourself such a hard time. You're human. It could have happened to me, Lee.

In my heart I did not believe it could have happened to him. It had happened to *me*. Now he would know that I was not as good as he'd always sworn to me I was. What we had would never be the same again.

I had made a pretty good speech to Mary about pulling out the knife. Well, I couldn't get the thought of that knife out of my head. And I thought about twisting a bedsheet into a rope.

It was not a good night.

Holly Nuñez's young forehead was wrinkled. She squinted as if she was dying to be in a dark room. Basically, she looked like a dame with one hell of a headache, and when she looked at me, she acted as if I was the one who had given it to her. Well, basically that was right. And Barbara's forehead wasn't exactly smooth. If she wasn't acting as if I'd given her a headache, she could not hide the fact that she was under heavy-duty stress. After all, she was the lawyer in a case she never had control of—and never would have.

"So you're saying that once Norman allowed himself to be convinced to let you take the rap, he coached you on what to say to Ms. White and me?" Holly was asking.

"Yes," Mary said.

"All right," Holly said. "Tell me what he told you."

"Well, see, he told me what happened. Like, he described it. He said if I could see it through his eyes, it would be like seeing it for myself."

"So you're telling me he described the murder of Bobette Frisch to you?"

"Yes," said Mary, a little impatiently. Clearly, she did not think much of Holly's powers of comprehension. But Holly was comprehending, and she knew she had a terrible problem on her hands. She had tried, without any success, to trip Mary up in the hopes that Mary's story itself was a con, part of a labyrinthine scheme concocted by Norman with the aim of forcing the district attorney to let them both go. But in the end, Holly, Barbara, and I all understood: It was Norman Torkelson alone who had killed Bobette.

Holly was wearing a pink suit that looked like a major Easter mistake. Or perhaps it looked so awful, so Pepto-Bismolish, because its wearer was not her usual pink-cheeked, pink-lipped perky self. As she interrogated Mary, I could see her trying to figure out how she could manipulate this whole situation so she would not look bad. She couldn't seem to find a way. To her credit, she hung in there. She was of a new generation of women, one that admitted no obstacles to its upward march. It was not a matter of age so much as temperament: Holly Nuñez wanted to go to the head of the American Dream line. Well, why shouldn't she, now that the Establishment Wasps had become marginal and the Jews were fast becoming the new Wasps? Except in all her dreams, this was the one career move she hadn't planned on: humiliation.

"Tell me how Norman Torkelson described the murder," Holly ordered Mary.

"Like he was really tired. And crabby. She had been all over him before they went to the bank. He couldn't say: 'Hey, get off of me, Fatso.' Could he?"

"Did they have sex?" Holly asked.

"No, and that was part of the problem. 'Cause he couldn't, you know, get it up for her."

"You told me in your taped confession that you saw them having sexual relations," Holly said.

"Not that day, the day she got killed. The day before. I think. So do you want to hear about how she got killed or not?"

Considering that Mary's entire life hung on the slender thread of Holly's cooperation, I thought she was being a little imprudent. I considered a wink or a hint, but knowing Mary, I said: "Don't get angry with Holly. She's the only one who can help you, and if she walks out of here, you're going to be spending a lot of years in Bedford Hills."

"Sorry," Mary said, her voice still a little hoarse from her suicide attempt. Still she did not begin her account.

"What's the matter, Mary?" Barbara asked.

"Will this get Norman in trouble?" She had stopped her edgy cheek-chewing and was now openly nervous, biting her lower lip.

We three lawyers glanced at each other. She was still protecting him. "Let's put it this way," I suggested. "What kind of trouble can you get him in? What do you think the odds are that Norman is hanging around here, waiting for the police to come?"

"He's out of here," Mary said quietly.

"And do you think he's going to take risks that could lead to an arrest, knowing that with you facing twenty years in jail, the only sane thing for you to do would be to tell the truth? Do you think he's going to allow himself to get caught once he becomes a murder suspect again? His fingerprints are in the computer. If he got picked up, he'd be back here in a day or two. He's going to lie low for a long time. So you tell me, do you think you can get Norman in trouble, even if you wanted to?"

"No."

"Then please tell Holly everything he told you," Barbara told her.

"Where was I?" Mary asked.

"His not getting it up," I reminded her.

"Oh, right. He couldn't get it up, and all the way to the bank she kept saying things like: 'Maybe I'm making a mistake. Maybe I'm buying a pig in a poke.' On account of his not being able to."

"Did he ever have that trouble before?" Holly asked, a question I sensed was posed not for prosecutorial reasons but because she was dying to know.

"Not with me!"

"With Bobette?"

"I don't know. See, he didn't know that I knew about him doing it with her. I don't think there was any problem, because if it happened before, she wouldn't have gone to the bank at all, would she? Anyways, she was making these crummy remarks. And then she took a real long time at the bank, and he could see through the window this guy in a suit was talking to her. Norman was, like, pissed. Because of the pig in a poke thing and because marks *never* talk to anyone in their banks or anything. I'll tell you why. Norman says they don't want to be stopped. Deep down, they know, but they really don't want to, if you get my drift."

"Did he know what the man in the bank was saying to Bobette?" Holly inquired. I had never gotten to the point of reading the bank officer's account in the discovery material, but I was sure she already knew the answer.

"Not then, 'cause Norman was outside. But later. They got home and Bobette wanted to try again. Norman made some excuse about being real tired and also so excited that she was giving him this opportunity to start his life all over again. That's when she says the guy in the bank told her: Hey, this is an awful lot of money, and she told him it was an investment and he made some remark about being careful. About how there are con men all over the place! So Norman starts to laugh it off, and she just walks away."

"And then what?" Holly asked.

"She came back. She was stuffing her yap with a Snickers and saying: 'Maybe you are a con man,' with Snicker goo all over her mouth, and her teeth were, like, brown. Like teasing him, but he knew it wasn't only teasing. So he said that's where he made his mistake."

"Killing her?"

"No. Taking the bank envelopes with the money. He said if he'd left them there and walked out, insulted that she was saying he was a con man, she would have come running after him. But he took them. And she tried to grab them back."

"And?" Barbara said.

"And so they sort of started fighting, and she was pretty strong so he stopped her."

"How?" I asked.

"By choking her." All three of us looked at Mary's hands at the same moment. Big, yes. But not as big as

Norman's. With tapering, feminine fingers. Mary thought we were looking at her bitten nails and folded her arms so her hands were hidden.

"When you described the murder," Holly said, "you talked about Bobette's tongue sticking out, about how heavy she was. A lot of detail. It made it seem as though you'd gone through it."

"I did. Not in real life. But like when I played Norman's ex-wife, or Ms. McDonald from Pinnacle Collections. We rehearsed. A lot. Norman said I had to do it over and over until it didn't just sound good: It had to *feel* natural. And that's what we did with the Bobette business. Over and over. He gave me the story and he played Bobette. You know, like he pretended to be scared when he saw me, and he's so good, I really *believe* he's scared. And then we moved around our place like it was her place—going into her living room. It was so real. Like when Norman was saying, 'Please, please, I'll give you anything you want. I can get money,' I was so mad at her. But it was him! Except it felt like it was her." A nervous spasm made her head quiver. "A couple of times, like the night I tried . . . you know, with the sheet. I got this real oogy feeling. Like I had done it. Except it was worse, because I *remembered* I did it. Except I really didn't. Norman did."

"Well," I said, "do you think Norman feels oogy about it?"

"Norman?" Mary said. She almost smiled. Then she shook her head: No.

Before Holly was willing to sign off on the case, she had the police lab make prints of Mary's hand. It took two days, but they finally determined the hands were too small and the fingers too thin to have strangled Bobette

Frisch. By that time, I was a wreck, so exhausted from saying "I'm sorry," so ashamed of the whole Torkelson mess, that I was taking refuge in extralegal fantasies: Start a catering business featuring home-cooked meals harassed working women could pass off as their own: Gee, Mom, that was great meat loaf! Or open a little storefront wool-market-cum-crocheting school and blanket Long Island in afghans. I had fantasies of my daughter striking it so big in a television series that she'd say: You've worked long and hard enough, Ma. It's time for you to retire and enjoy life. But Barbara and I had a conference call with Holly, who finally conceded, albeit grudgingly, that we had a deal. Mary would go free. A warrant would be issued for Norman Torkelson, wanted for murder. And once again, for only the fiftieth time, I apologized.

Holly called me back an hour later. "I'm sorry, Lee," she began.

"What?"

"Woodleigh Huber won't let her go."

"*What?*"

"He says he doesn't believe her recantation. He thinks she's guilty."

"That's impossible. The hand prints! Did you—"

"He says it's a judgment call. He says the lab is wrong. It's his duty to stand firm."

I told her I would be down in her office in a few minutes. I hung up the phone, thinking: This case will never be over. And just moments before, I had been at the bank and withdrawn a thousand dollars to give to Mary so she could take some time and think about what to do with her life. I had a feeling that given the choice between hustling and dental hygienist school, she would go for hustling every time. Still, I had already called my across-the-street neighbor who owned a few franchise beauty parlors; he agreed that if she would go for her hairdresser's license, he'd hire her as a shampoo girl so she could have a foot in the door. In my mind, I was already assuring her that I'd pay for beauty school tuition.

"What the hell are you doing?" I asked Jerry McCloskey, who was head of the Homicide unit and Woodleigh Huber's chief toady. "We had a deal." I did not yell at him. He was wringing his hands, and I could see he was being pulled between Holly and Huber. What amazed me was that he was even considering Holly's position. And that Holly, legs crossed, arms crossed, and determined as hell, was still on my side. "We made a deal," I told Jerry.

"Calm down, Lee."

"You've known me for years, Jerry. This is calm for me. Now, off the record, what is this about?" McCloskey peered around his office as if he suspected I'd hidden a camera crew. "I said off the record."

"The Boss was fair with you, Lee. No partisan crap, no nothing. You got your guy off fair and square. But this time . . . No. She did it. And the Boss feels used. You have one success, and now—"

I cut him off. "Look, I apologized. I was conned. You were conned. But worst of all, Mary Dean was conned, and she's facing twenty years for murder. For the life of me, I don't understand why."

I thought this was between me and McCloskey, but Holly spoke up. "The 'why' is that Woodleigh Huber can't admit he was conned. He'd rather have her rot in jail than come out and say he made a mistake. There's an election coming up in less than a year."

"Holly!" McCloskey practically gasped.

"Oh, stop jerking us off, Jerry," she said. I truly did a double take. Her words, of course, were delivered with their usual happy gee-whizness, but she was standing tough—for me. "That woman was the victim of a clever and vicious criminal. You and the Boss should have some humanity, for heaven's sake!" She was making my argument, so I sat back and let her.

"This 'victim,'" he shot back, "besides being a hooker, has a record for assault."

"This victim has been used and abused by men for years," Holly retorted. I thought she might be stretching things a little. Maybe Mary was a victim, but she'd also been a pretty willing accomplice. Still, I was Mary Dean's advocate, not Woodleigh Huber's. Holly went on: "You and the Boss are sure flying the old male flag. 'A hooker!' She's twenty-two years old! Are you going to sacrifice her to the Boss's political ambitions?" Holly uncrossed her legs and leaned forward. "Come on, Jerry. This doesn't have to happen."

"You're overruled!" McCloskey barked. Then he flapped his hand to us: Out!

"If I have to," Holly told him, "I'll go to the press."

"You go to the press, Ms. Nuñez, and you're out of this office. As it is, you're skating on thin ice. Very, very thin." He jerked his head in the direction of the door: Get out! I waited to hear Holly's response. I didn't. I saw it: She left.

"Reconsider, Jerry," I pleaded.

"There's nothing to reconsider."

"To do this to someone for politics? How can you? It's not even good politics."

"Nothing the Boss does is good politics to you, and believe you me, he's well aware of it."

"Jerry, don't take it out on Mary Dean. Take it out on me."

He rose from his desk, strode more manfully than he ever had in his life and yanked open the door. "We are," he said, smiling.

Twenty-four

✣

They were only three: herself, Val, and Kent. Nevertheless, Lee bought a frame house in Port Washington so spacious that during the presidency of William Howard Taft, its first owners—a family by the name of Palmer—lived there with their five children; after a few years, they invited Mrs. Palmer's twin sister and her husband and their twin boys to move in, and then Mr. Palmer's bachelor twin as well. During the Depression, its second owner, Mrs. Schottland, a widow with three children, took in four boarders.

The first time Lee walked through the place with the real estate agent, she could almost hear the contemptuous questions people would ask: Lee, are you crazy? A white elephant like this? It's you and Kent and Valerie. However, she first saw the house on a late afternoon. Sun passed through a stained-glass window and broke into rich and melting colors on the wide-planked oak floor. She realized that although the objections were prudent, no one was making them. She was alone. And she wanted this house.

So she told the realtor the place was not for her. Sorry, I know I did say Victorian. But the size of this thing! Out of the question. It makes no sense for a divorcée. The following day, the sellers—Bill and Mopsy Tuccio, who were moving to Santa Fe in two weeks—came down another ten percent. The next day, they all shook hands and Lee bought their dining room table, which could seat twenty, and the five turn-of-the-century rocking chairs on the great wraparound porch. The Tuccios threw in their glider. We always sat in it after dinner in the summer, Bill told her. The whole family in that old thing. Back and forth, back and forth. Great being all together, the family. Mopsy gave him a subtle cut-it-out poke and Lee a too sunny smile. Family.

Americans are often uneasy about family. Occasionally unhinged. Give them a holiday gathering of their nearest and dearest, and a strong minority will renew their prescriptions for Xanax. Offer them more than a modicum of mother love, and thirty percent of them will move cross-country. Yet the moment Americans acquire their fifth freedom—from family—what do they do? Of course: seek out a family.

The aroma of turkey must be inhaled by a large group. A chorale of "Ooh"s is a necessary accompaniment to fireworks. And there is little to equal the comfort of being shoulder to shoulder to shoulder to shoulder around a bowl of eggnog. Cro-Magnons did not huddle around fires merely to form an alliance against saber-toothed tigers. They needed to feel they were a clan. For Americans, reared on Hallmark commercials, preferring as they do sentimentality to sentiment, to be simply one or two or three is not only to lack the crucial support of community. No: Painful as isolation itself feels, it is nearly as disturbing to be perceived as being alone. The question must arise: What have you done to make yourself unpopular?

So for her own sake and sanity as well as Val's and Kent's, Lee bought a house that demanded to be filled. For their first Thanksgiving, she invited Will, Chuckie Phalen, two of Chuckie's bachelor pals from TJ's, Melanie Tucker from the Manhattan D.A.'s Office, as well as Lee's new next-door neighbors, the Rothenbergs, and Lulu Martin, an emergency room nurse she met and with whom she became friendly when Kent, trying to help the movers, dropped a carton of books and broke his foot.

Hearing Lee was searching for a full-time housekeeper, a colleague who also did pro bono work for the county's coalition against domestic abuse introduced her to Puella Thorne, a former battered housewife. Puella, in addition to pressing criminal charges, had sued her husband so effectively that he had skipped town—leaving her with a seven-month-old son and a twenty-thousand-dollar debt. She and her baby, Harley, joined Lee's family at the table for Christmas dinner.

Lee might have been able to pull off a Chanukah party that year too, but she had by then pretty much forgotten that she had a religion. However, right after New Year's, she got to chatting with a couple ahead of her on line at the movie on Main Street. They had a son Val's age and mentioned he was enrolled in Sunday school at the local synagogue and actually looked forward to going. The following morning, Lee walked into a Jewish house of worship for the first time in her life. After a surprisingly lively discussion with the rabbi on medieval codifications of rabbinic law, she enrolled Valerie Weissberg-Weiss-White Taylor.

The Sunday school pleased not only the daughter but the mother, not least because Lee knew that not only would Jazz have to pick up Val at a synagogue—dressed, at Purim, as Queen Esther—but that the child, theatrical to the core of her almost-five-year-old soul, would perform Hebrew ditties for Grandpa Leonard and Grandma Sylvia, singing not just well but loud. Over and over. That Passover, Lee attended her first Seder: her own. Twenty-six people squeezed around the table for twenty. Later, she confided to Will that as she lit the candles, she thought about her grandmother. There was a grin on Bella's face. Not from pious pleasure—she hadn't been so pious—but because through her granddaughter Ms. White she had finally outfoxed her husband, Nat the Commie, who had hated God and wouldn't allow Him in the house.

There were too few feasts, though, and too many endless days, spent rushing from court to office and home to dinner, then racing out to a Bar Association program, a PTA emergency session on drinking fountains, or a support group for families of Down's syndrome adults. In the years after Jazz left her for Robin, what Lee missed most was not the conversation, not the sex, definitely not the fur, but the very fact of marriage: a union of two adults. Another body at whom to direct a casual comment while watching the evening news. Someone willing to take responsibility for choosing a new car or a plumber. Someone to share the burdens. True, Puella could drive car pools, offer milk and cookies after school, even prepare dinner when Lee was on trial—a luxury Lee was well aware most single mothers could not afford. True, Will became Val's confidant about her dreams of acting. And he spent so much time with her family that Kent took to calling him "Daddy." Yet Lee knew she was solely in charge of Val and Kent. No days off: Except for alternate weekends and two weeks vacation, she had to put in the time.

There was no: Hey, how about taking Val to the park for an hour so I can do the crossword puzzle? No: Why don't you take Kent with you when you're looking at snow-blowers so I can soak in the tub without someone banging at my door?

For an entire decade, Lee was always tired and usually exhausted. She took to wearing black panty hose because she often did not have the energy to shave her legs. She had time to read only half of the *Times*, so she relied on public radio to inform her about foreign affairs and Will Stewart to keep her informed of business and economic news, a proposition she knew was risky; even though he was a moderate, he was still a Republican. She lacked the concentration to read fiction. She went to museums only with Val and Kent, so she saw too many dinosaur bones, too much Matisse. She, the music lover, the Bach buff, the jazz aficionado, the rock and roller who could at one time quote every word of "Midnight Train to Georgia" and "Pride and Joy" and thum-thum the bass line to "Lucy in the Sky with Diamonds," did not even hear of Bob Marley's death until nine years after it had occurred.

Some nights, Lee was so weary she fell into bed without taking off her makeup or brushing her teeth or even getting into a nightgown. Yet once under the covers, she would turn from her left to her right, then back again, trying to recall which was her good side, unable to sleep for hours. She heard the wind, the scratching of a blue spruce against her window, the almost inaudible whir of her alarm clock, the snorts and deep sleep-breathing of her three dogs. Those nights, she thought of nothing, or everything. Her heart banged as if a momentous occasion were seconds away. Or if sleep was kind enough to take her before midnight, it never held her long. She would wake at four in the morning, her mind ragingly alert, racing from stir-frying parboiled carrots to the laws governing extradition from Canada to buying paper hats for Val's birthday party in school. Winter, summer, year after year, she played and replayed every scene in her marriage that featured a joint appearance by Robin and Jazz. Had those memories been a videotape, it would have disintegrated into shreds.

Every night, she thought about Will.

Now and then she thought about Terry Salazar. A little more than a year after their affair began, she read an article in a magazine in the dentist's office, yet another of those how-to-stop-humiliating-yourself-over-a-worthless-man advisories. Flushed with assertiveness, pumped with nitrous oxide and novocaine, Lee drove to Terry's office and gave him an ultimatum: No more sex on his white couch or white rug or white desk. If he wanted to see her, it would be at a nonsleazy motel. Naturally—being a feminist—she would pay half. Fine, Terry said, glancing at his watch. But shit, we only have an hour. Got a stakeout in Roslyn Harbor. Husband onto dyke wife and aerobics instructor. Hey, he added, inserting his hand between the buttons of her silk blouse, running his fingers along the edge of her bra, why don't we go to the Regal Motor Inn. About seven minutes from here. She realized from his very exactness what a patsy she had been, willing to abrade her knees, her ass, on his stiff, dry polyester rug. He had not dared been so cheap with his other women. He had probably used the Regal for so many other extramarital assignations they all but hung a plaque with his name on it over Room 204.

Terry was neither interesting nor nice. He was, however, a fine lover. Or—as Lee realized in the fourth year of their affair, not precisely a lover. A sex partner. He was always ready, usually raunchy, never not in the mood. And while not genuinely intelligent, Terry was shrewd enough to allow Lee to separate their work from their play. While he was working on one of her cases, he was all business. Or mostly business. He might stare at her thighs if her suit skirt was snug, or find an excuse to read a report over her shoulder, standing too close for propriety, but he never touched her unless she signaled that she was ready to begin. Nonetheless, after five years, he displayed a casualness with Lee, a comfortable slouch when sitting in her office, a lack of the hired hand's deference, that suggested a familiarity beyond the usual criminal lawyer–detective informality. Lee realized that Chuckie had guessed. So had Sandi. And although they said nothing, she knew that they did not approve.

In the sixth year of their affair, after three hours at the Regal that left them amazed at their prowess and barely able to stand, Terry finally offered to leave his wife. "Listen, the marriage stinks. It's stunk for years. We don't have to be doing it at a place like this. We could be together."

"You cheat on me now, when we're only having an affair."

"I do not!"

"You lie too. If you married me, you'd feel obligated to screw around twice as much. You'd be a lox. Totally useless. And I'd be stuck with your dirty laundry."

"This is what you'd be stuck with," he said, grabbing her hand, putting it on his penis, which once again, miraculously, was showing signs of life. "Think about it. We could have a lot of fun."

Driving home that evening, she was amused: Think about it. She could find only two pros about marriage to Terry: She could get regular sex and have an excuse to buy new pots. The cons? As if she would let him live under the same roof as Val and Kent. Puella would watch him swagger into the house and would quit five minutes later. The entire bar of the County of Nassau would laugh itself sick. Will . . . She couldn't even bring herself to contemplate Will's reaction. Think about it!

Indeed, she thought about it for more than a year. She had twice fallen asleep in Terry's arms, and he was surprisingly nice to wake up to. He kissed the top of her head and said "Hi!" as if he hadn't seen her in ages. She liked his easy, masculine competence: He could change a tire in three minutes, fix a sparking electrical outlet, pacify an armed opponent with easy words or a karate kick. It pleased her immensely that he was the sort of man who always carried a Swiss Army knife. But in the end it came down to this: She did not love him. She did not want him to sit at the head of her table, with all the people in the world she loved gathered round, and carve her Thanksgiving turkey. Telling Terry her decision was not a problem, because after that brief offer in the motel, he never again alluded to any marriage except his own dysfunctional one.

She tried to find a man. Really tried. She was certain that somewhere out there was someone just right for her. Well, in order to face grim-faced judges and glowering jurors, even the most cynical trial lawyer must, at heart, be an optimist. Lee was. She accepted every blind date arranged by friends, neighbors, and colleagues. You never know when it will happen, she told herself. She cut no corners on these occasions, always flossing first, always making up before a magnifying mirror in bright light, always opening the door with a welcoming smile. Thus she spent evenings with a drunken physicist, a cocaine-addicted journalist, an anti-Semitic swimming pool contractor, a forty-seven-year-old endodontist who referred to his mother as Mommy. She met men who became nasty when she refused to have sex with them after a three-hour acquaintance, men who told her she was too smart for her own good, men so busy fulminating over their former wives that they never asked her a single question about her life. True, she was introduced to a number of men who were decent and courteous, but few of them interested her. One of them, a veterinarian, admired her beagle and reminded her of John Lennon. But after three dates he stopped calling. When she screwed up the courage to phone him, he sheepishly explained he had, uh, um, gotten engaged. One of those love-at-first-sight things. His fiancée, Lee later found out, was twenty-six.

For a little more than a year, in the mid-eighties, Lee went out with Robert Mandelbaum, a pathologist from New Jersey whom she met when he was testifying for Chuckie as an expert witness in a murder case. For the first few months she was so grateful that, unlike many medical examiners, Robert did not expound on putrefying limbs over dinner that she was able to ignore the fact that she did not enjoy his company. He's perfect, she reported to Will. A widower, so there's no ex-wife he hates. I'm so tired of going out and hearing about some greedy, self-involved, manipulative, shitty mother-bitch-whore. Robert's a genuinely nice guy. We go hiking a lot. He's going to teach me and Val to cross-country ski. He loves music. He plays the cello in an amateur string quartet. He has a wonderful dog, a sweet, stupid Irish setter. A few weeks

later, Will observed: You talk more about the dog than
you do about the guy. Lee tried very hard to love
Robert, or even to like him. She could not. During sex,
she twice caught herself yawning and tried to hide it
by rolling her head and moaning, pretending she was
writhing in passion. She found herself faking ardor and
could not believe that a doctor trained to notice the
most minute evidence on the human body could not
pick up that he left her cold. Will told her: All he probably notices is you're not dead, which ipso facto
makes you hot stuff. After a year, she admitted to herself and then to Will that Robert's wife must have died
of boredom.

I have to face facts, she told Will shortly after she
stopped seeing Robert. I'm no bargain. She was grateful that Will immediately sprang to her defense, telling
her how intelligent, pretty, good-natured, and fun—
You're a good time, Lee!—she was. So she prosecuted.
Just imagine you're a man telling a friend about me:
She's a lawyer, so she can never let you have the best
of an argument. A real ball-breaker. She makes a
decent living, but that house! Crazy, huge old place
that sucks money out of her checking account. And
who lives there with her? Her kid. Pretty but, you
know, wants to be an actress and has a scene every fifteen minutes. Then there's her ex-husband's something
. . . brother I think. How she got stuck with him I don't
know. A re-tard. Big guy, too, but he can't stay home
alone. Needs a baby-sitter the times she goes out with
the daughter. Then she's got this maid, this scrawny,
white-trash woman who's always blasting Pentecostal
preachers on the radio. The maid lives there full-time
with her son, nine or ten years old, who's got Coke-
bottle glasses and keeps bumping into walls because
he's looking down at his accordion all the time. He's

not bad, but who the hell wants to hear an accordion eighteen hours a day? Oh, and she's got three dogs: One of them has only three legs. A stray she found, hit by a car. Ugly! You should see the way it hops around: freaky, disgusting.

Will, Lee said, name me one man who would want to marry all that.

"All that" isn't who they'd be marrying. It's you. And you're going to find someone, he assured her. Don't worry.

Do you think I stacked the deck against myself? I mean, subconsciously created a situation that no man in his right mind could possibly want?

I think you've created something for yourself. Something you had to have: a family. Look, happily ever after doesn't happen all the time. So what are you supposed to do when it doesn't? Keep looking at your watch until you're eighty, saying: Gee, he should be coming any second—I'll be glad when he does, because then my life can have meaning? Or do you make a life that has meaning for you?

But what has meaning for me could be a turnoff to some guy.

That's right, Will agreed. It could be. So what are you going to do? Create a life for yourself that's so man-pleasing that any guy in the world would fit in? Keep an electric drill and a jigsaw in the garage and a tape of NFL highlights on top of the VCR?

Meanwhile, she kept seeing Terry Salazar: sometimes once a month, sometimes four or five times a week.

And she saw Will. For his social events, he occasionally still escorted Maria. Lee went to weddings, bar mitzvahs, christenings, and lawyers' dinner dances alone. But he began coming to her house for dinner once a week, then four or five nights. They tried cooking together, but they had too many fights, so he often chased her out of the kitchen and cooked himself. They saw almost every movie that came to town. They bought a Philharmonic subscription together. They played tennis twice a week. He was the one who persuaded her to take Val's acting abilities seriously and did the research on acting classes in the city, and dramatics camp for the summers. They took Val to the theater and Kent to the petting zoo he loved. They spoke on the phone first thing in the morning, from their offices, and last thing at night, after Will got back to his house.

After ten years of friendship, he finally introduced her to his parents. His father had worked with horses all his life, and with Will's financial help, he and his wife had retired to a condominium near Virginia horse country. They were an imposing couple, dark brown, broad-shouldered, and big-nosed like their son. Jack Stewart looked as if he could tame a stallion with a withering glance, and Marjory, in her own way, was equally impressive; her palms were stained purple from the fruits and berries she was perpetually putting up. Except for the four hours a night she slept, she was never without something to pickle or preserve.

The elder Stewarts wore only plaid. Or, as they corrected Lee, tartan. The colors of the clan Stewart. Dress Stewart. A slightly larger variation of the pattern: Muted Dress Stewart. Then there was Gray Stewart. Black Stewart—which Will never failed to comment upon. Oh, I see we're in Black Stewart today, he'd say to his father. How apt. Quiet, William! his mother would command, coming between the two men. Will told Lee it was not until high school that he realized how odd it was for people to wear plaid every day of their lives. Plaid shirts, plaid skirts, plaid jackets. Plaid bathrobes. Plaid slippers. Plaid ties to church. Plaid seats on their dinette chairs. Only the Stewart tartan, of course, which made each sighting of a Gray Stewart raincoat or Black Stewart bathing trunks all the sweeter. In his sophomore year at Columbia, it hit him that the closest his parents had ever come to Scotland was the eighteenth-century farmer who had owned and perhaps sired Jack's ancestor. Again and again, Will asked his parents why, or more to the point, how could they. What were they trying to be? Why don't you wear a dashiki if you want to show what you are? Or all those ropes of beads, the way they do in Kenya? They became furious at his brass: We're Stewarts!

"Hey, Dad," Will said. His parents were visiting him from Virginia, and he had invited Lee, Val, and Kent to go with them to a Mets game. He and his father were fervid fans, transferring their Brooklyn Dodgers–Jackie Robinson fanaticism to the newer National League New York team. "Gray Stewart today!"

"Shut your fresh mouth!" his father barked.

Kent smiled in commiseration with either Will or Jack Stewart. Lee could not be certain. Or he might be happy simply because he was sitting in a box seat close to first, right over the Mets dugout. It was a sunny day, and he was devouring the two hot dogs Will had bought him and being allowed to sip Lee's beer. Valerie, at fourteen, was not eating or sipping anything. On a diet, she had brought along a bag of raw vegetables and was resting her carrot entirely too suggestively on her lips while making eyes at the first baseman, a fellow who looked like a descendant of the Jukes and the Kallikaks. Between batters, he seemed to be ogling her back. Marjory Stewart eyed the plastic bag of vegetables hungrily, as if she wanted to snatch it from Val's unappreciative grip and make a fast chutney.

Lee smiled in Will's direction but knew he would not notice her. He and his father rarely took their eyes off the field, as if they, and not Mets management, were responsible for any success the team might enjoy. To look at them, plaid-jacketed father and blue-blazered son—with mother in a plaid shirtwaist beaming on—was to think: Ah, *there* is the great American family.

In fact, they took no joy in each other. The Stewart men merely shared a love of the national pastime. And while both parents might enjoy a fine afternoon in box seats provided by one of their son's corporate clients, they were not happy with their son. Nor was he with them.

In Jack and Marjory's view, Will had let them down. He had not married and given them grandchildren. Bad enough, all those little plaid dresses and tiny plaid baseball caps going to waste. Worse, he was not the first black president of the United States. He had not even tried.

Will thought he had. He had bought them their condo and their Subaru station wagon, sent them on luxurious senior citizen bus tours all over the country, given them their dream, a first-class trip to the Kentucky Derby. He spoke to his father's cardiologist so often they were on a first-name basis. He donated such a hefty sum each year to their church that whenever Will visited Virginia, the minister came to the airport to greet him. He even tried to take his parents to Scotland: I'll *go* with you. But they declined, not approving of Europe. He told Lee that they might have accepted the trip if he could have flown them there on Air Force One. Back in 1980, his father had urged him to run, telling him it was a Republican year. Will, Jack counseled, the country is ready for a Negro president.

Nothing Will accomplished—*Law Review* at Columbia,

getting into the D.A.'s Office, heading the Homicide unit, becoming a name partner in the most prestigious law firm on Long Island—was enough for his parents. We expect the best from you, they had warned him when he went off to Columbia. He thought he had given it.

It's not that they want the best from you, Lee told him. It's that they want everything.

They're always disappointed, he'd replied.

As long as you're not. Will had nodded, but it was one of the few times his face turned sour. His expression was crabbed, angry.

But looking at those plaid people, Lee thought: better to want everything for your child than to want nothing, the way my parents did.

Well, when she thought about it, her mother at least had wanted something from her: better taste. Or maybe a more bubbly child, one who was fun to buy shoes for, one who could jolly her out of a clinical depression. In the years since her divorce, Lee often ruminated on the myth of the ever-loving, overprotective Jewish matriarch. How come she hadn't had one? Where were all those self-sacrificing mamas hiding? Was the Jewish mother a myth perpetuated by male writers and filmmakers—they being the boys, the chosen children who actually got the love and protection? Or in becoming White, did Sylvia make some final break with her heritage, taking on Anglo-Saxon Protestant restraint without the concomitant sense of duty, strength of will, and grace under pressure?

Still, every time Lee considered her mother's failings, she could not help but wonder what it was that formed the woman. A lifeless, unloving household? Lee had only a vague memory of her grandparents Bernstein, two pallid whisperers who, in their last years, when she

was a little girl, seemed to murmur only about the
Judge's gas. Was her mother a casualty of these two
people, dead decades before they died? Was there
something incomplete inside Sylvia, a spark that ought
to have caught fire but never did, so she never received
sufficient heat to make her truly human?

Yet could Sylvia truly be pronounced dead? Wasn't
she capable of passion? To be sure, it was passion for
furniture, passion for clothes, passion for appearances,
but still, she cared deeply about something. If mother
love did not come naturally, could she have worked at
caring deeply about her own child? And if she could
not have cared, what had kept her from behaving with
a little common decency all those years? Or like Paula
Urquhart, could Sylvia White mount a defense by
claiming to be a victim who could not help herself?

Maybe the jury had found her client not guilty, but
Lee did not believe she was innocent. And she did not
believe it of her mother either.

She could find no excuses for her father. He knew
his wife was more than defective; she was hurting Lee
by malign neglect. Why hadn't he fought for his daughter? What made him feel he had the right to now and
then shake his head over his wife's indifference—Too
bad—and then wrap himself up in his own furry world
in Manhattan? Would he have stuck around a little
more if it had been a son who was being damaged?

It was not as if Leonard was ignorant of what a
father was supposed to do. He had had two lively parents. True, Nat the Commie had not been the most
supportive father, but he was not an unfeeling louse.
He had wanted the best for his son and pulled all the
threadbare strings he could on Leonard's behalf. And
Bella, that loud, loving realist, would have done anything for him.

But as with so many children of immigrants, the world outside had meant more to Leonard than the world in his parents' one-bedroom railroad flat. To be part of that outside world, he needed to destroy everything of Bella and Nat that was inside him, for he lacked the imagination and the spirit to keep them with him as he refined himself. So Leonard grew whiter than white, so white he became invisible. But it was not only himself and his parents he obliterated. Lee came to believe that if you are willing to do away with your parents, you will then be willing to destroy anyone else in your family who gets in the way of how you want to be perceived.

So while Lee no longer saw her parents, she understood that for Valerie's sake and her own she could not kill them off. She had to let them live. She never spoke ill of them in front of the child. When Val came home from her weekends with Jazz and Robin and her two half-brothers/first cousins with reports on them and on her grandparents, Lee listened with interest and suppressed every hateful remark that came to mind. She never lied and told the child she loved Sylvia and Leonard, but she did tell her daughter: I know how much they love you. She did not add: Because you are Jasper Taylor's child.

She also searched her memory and found enough decent moments to use for show-and-tell with Val. Sylvia fussing over what Lee would wear to the prom. Leonard celebrating her acceptance to Cornell. Planting sunflowers. Going with Mom to buy new Mary Janes for the Young People's Concerts in the city. Going with Dad to buy our dog Woofer. Being allowed to buy all the paperbacks she could hold in her arms.

Lee looked at her companions basking in the gorgeous July sun in the box at Shea Stadium. The Stewarts, who were incapable of taking pride in their extraordinary son. Will, who could not give up trying to make them proud. Kent, whose parents had not inquired as to his welfare in seven years. Herself.

She turned to her daughter. "Hey, Val," Lee said softly.

"What?" The teenager's eyes remained on first base.

"I love you."

Val was wary. Fearful. But no, thank God, the first baseman had not heard her mother. Quickly, because she could not divert her attention for too long, she turned to Lee and removed the carrot from her lips. "I *know* you love me, Ma."

A half hour later, after the first baseman had struck out and the Mets shortstop slammed what looked like an in-the-park home run and the crowd stood up and roared, Val once again put down the carrot and murmured, just above the din: "Love you too, Ma."

Twenty-five

Despair. Remorse. Anguish. Misery. No one word in the language can express what I felt about Woodleigh Huber's decision to go ahead with the prosecution of Mary Dean. Sickened comes close, but that doesn't take into account the rage I felt at the injustice, or the shame I felt that I had allowed myself to be conned.

"The worst thing about it," I told Will Stewart as we sat rocking on my front porch, "is that I can't think of any way to put the scales of justice back into balance—short of running Huber over with my Jeep."

Will put his hand on my shoulder. "Stop trying to keep an ironic distance. You're a mess."

"Yes."

Will was a lawyer, and before Jerry McCloskey was sent in to degrade and dishonor the Homicide unit, Will had run it. Now he was a hotshot civil litigator, so his hand wasn't resting on my shoulder just because he was being Mr. Empathy. He knew precisely what I had done: come up with an alternate version of Bobette's murder that showed my client to be innocent. Okay, lawyers do that all the time. They tell a once-upon-a-time story that views the facts of the case in a soft pink light. If it's a really captivating fairy tale, some juries will buy it. Sometimes even the lawyer buys it.

But I just didn't think: Hmm, good argument. Better than what the government has. I bewitched myself—with Norman Torkelson's help. And then, because I believed in the story so completely—Love Triumphs over Wickedness! No-Good, Rotten Con Man Seeks Expiation Through Sacrifice!—my belief, my passion, gave me the power to enchant everyone else. Will Stewart knew: I hadn't been a lawyer; I'd tried to grab Justice's toga and wear it myself. Except it didn't fit. I was in large part responsible for a killer's taking a walk and an innocent person's paying for the crime. Earlier that day, a bus had rolled out of the Nassau County Correctional Center taking Mary Dean and twelve other female prisoners up to Bedford Hills.

"Don't run Huber over," Will advised. "You'd be the prime suspect. The minute the lab ran tests comparing the tread marks on his face with your Jeep tires, you'd . . . " His voice trailed off.

"Go ahead. Say it: I'd be sharing a cell with Mary."

"No. I'm not going to remind you she's in jail and Norman is probably sitting back, sipping a margarita in some Sun Belt state. I came over to cheer you up."

"Consider another line of work."

"No. And I'm not leaving until you're okay."

"Then you're in for a life sentence." I tried to keep my voice light, so Will wouldn't know how appealing his never leaving sounded to me. We rocked back and forth for a while in familiar silence, two old fogies on the front porch watching the twilight. Stars were coming out, and a gibbous moon. I caught the season's first hint of honeysuckle. "Will?"

"What?"

"Are there any other cute moves I could make to force Huber to let Mary go? Anything I haven't thought of? Because there are no more tricks left in my bag—not even ineffective tricks I could use just to piss him off."

"Nothing beyond what you're doing now—spinning your wheels with the habeas corpus petition."

"But we both know that's not going to work."

"Correct." Will leaned his head against the spindles of the rocker and closed his eyes, pretending to take in the honeysuckle. Except I knew him too well to be suckered by a deep sniff. He was thinking, so for a few minutes I got hopeful. He was such a fine lawyer. A clever strategist. A smooth negotiator: The other side never got up from the table feeling screwed, even if they had been, royally. But more than that, Will was creative. When he couldn't win by logic or law, he often won through sheer surprise. "Lee."

I rocked forward and stayed that way, ready, I suppose, to jump up and act. "What?"

"Lean on me for this."

"You have an idea?"

"For springing Mary Dean? No. Nothing comes to mind." I let the chair rock back. "Not right off the bat, anyway. But you're going off the deep end and you don't want anyone to stop you. That's crazy. You're not responsible for her being in jail. At worst, you made a mistake. Lawyers make mistakes every day."

"Not like this."

"Yes. Like this and worse."

"Everyone knows I was conned. Everyone knows that poor girl is spending the better part of her life in prison because I thought I was being such a hero."

"Everyone knows you misjudged Norman Torkelson. So did Holly Nuñez. Is she sitting in a rocking chair right now having a psychotic episode?"

"No. She's trying to figure out a way to put a hundred miles between her and me. So is everyone else, except you."

"You're always telling me how smart I am."

I looked at him, so dark he was almost a shadow in the nightfall. "You are. The smartest."

"So if it's my assessment that you made a mistake but not a fatal one, why can't you accept it? Or do you think my intellect has limits, in that the only thing I can't evaluate is how badly you fucked up?"

"I don't know."

"Trust me, Lee. What do you think is going to happen? You're going to walk into the Bar Association and all conversation will stop? And then—like in one of those old westerns—someone will spit on the floor? I hate to tell you this, kid, but you're a one-week wonder and your week is up tomorrow."

"You're wrong, Will." I was in a bad way. Sure, I would slog on and finish out my life, maybe chalk up a couple of big wins, maybe have a grandchild or two, but I felt a deep dullness, a sense that I would never again know pleasure.

"I don't know if it's because you're a woman or what, but you feel you've got to have the biggest balls in town. Everyone else can screw up: not Lee White. Or maybe because you got conned by that schmuck husband—"

"Ex."

"—ex-husband, you can't accept that it could happen again."

I got off my rocker and leaned against a post, looking out at the street, away from Will. "Give me truth or pretense, and what do I wind up going for every time?"

"Truth," he said.

"Like hell I do."

"You're a woman of the world. Why does it come as a shock to you that some men get away with murder?"

I turned back to face Will. "I let it happen."

"Come off it, Lee! You didn't *let* it happen. It happened. You see injustice every day of the week in your work. You think you're immune? Who the hell inoculated you?"

"I couldn't see past the surface. I thought I could. I thought I *knew*. That's what gets me. I believed I was different, that I had depth. If I gave my heart to a person, or to a cause, it would be someone or something worth fighting for. And what happened? I was duped."

"Yes, you were."

"So?"

"So why don't you go off and shoot yourself because you believed what appeared to be the truth twice in your life? Come on, Lee. What have you ever done that you feel obligated to give yourself such a bad time? Not even Woodleigh Huber, that shitheel, would dare to do to you what you're doing to yourself."

"So I should just forget it?"

He got up from his rocker and stood right beside me. "No. Not quite yet."

My daughter, Valerie, was a marvel to look at: cascades of auburn hair, peachy skin, and huge, intelligent hazel eyes that dominated her face—and any room she happened to be in. At two in the afternoon that Sunday, she happened to be dominating the kitchen and laundry room. She had invited a fellow actor—a tall girl from Chicago, who was trying to look like a born tragedian—to spend the weekend. It appeared that they had taken in laundry from the entire cast and crew of the cable TV movie they had bit parts in. Between wash loads, they watched the entire filmography of Maggie Smith. Val had said: Want to be a patron of the arts? So I'd paid for the video rentals as well as their foray into Ben & Jerry's—this a half hour after I had watched Val tearing a head of lettuce into tiny pieces, dicing a zucchini and slicing mushrooms and meticulously measuring out a quarter teaspoon of Parmesan cheese, agonizing over its fat content.

"Where are you going, Ma?" she asked, her spoon poised to dive into the ice cream again.

"No place special," I said, hoping she'd say: Hey, you paid for this stuff. Why not join us? Come on, dig in.

Chicago was working on Chunky Monkey while maintaining a sour expression that should have curdled the cream. Maybe she was involved in her process, as my daughter would say. Probably daydreaming about being Medea killing her children. I liked most of my daughter's friends, but this dame was a heavy piece of furniture. I wasn't in the mood for moods.

Val, I could see, had gone for her usual, a pint of New York Super Fudge Chunk. "If you're going to be passing the video store, we forgot *The V.I.P.'s.*"

"I'm not sure what I'm doing. I want to plant some nasturtiums, but if I do go out, I'll—"

Val smiled at me, a wide, incredibly friendly smile, so unexpected on a classic pretty face. Part of her charm, I thought for the millionth time. Surprise. That this lovely young woman was still entrancing with fudge chunk on her teeth and a chocolate ice cream coating on her chin— Suddenly I didn't fall into my usual isn't-she-a marvel reverie. Something wasn't wonderful. Something was wrong. My maternal instincts are pretty good. "Ma, you're looking at me funny."

"No I'm not."

"Yes you are." But no, it wasn't Val.

It was the chocolate.

I was rushing around, looking for my car keys. "It was the chocolate," I said. "I've got to go."

"What?" She knew my leaving would mean she was

going to have to fold her own laundry. She might be an actor, but she was not a lawyer's daughter for nothing. If she could not win one point, she'd try for another: "Do you want to take us out for sushi when you get back?"

"Very much. But now . . . Hate to rush out on you, but . . . " I was picturing Bobette's mouth and lips, thick with chocolate from the Snickers bar. "I've got to get to the women's prison in Bedford Hills before visiting hours are over."

On the drive up to Bedford Hills, I was thinking that I should have taken Chicago with me, to show her what a really tragic face looked like. Except even before Mary Dean spotted me and broke out into a big smile and a two-handed wave, she looked happy. All right, if not happy, then at least something between untroubled and carefree.

"Hi!" she enthused. "It was *so* sweet of you to come and see me. I was talking to one of the girls and saying, 'It's gonna be a bummer on visiting day 'cause I'm not from New York and I don't know anybody so how can anybody come and visit,' and the next thing, here you are!"

"You sound pretty cheerful," I said. "Considering the circumstances."

"Yeah, well, what can you do?" The blue uniforms of Nassau County were gone. New York State, for some reason, was pushing a deep green, a more flattering color for Mary because it matched the dark-green glints in her emerald eyes. "You know what? I'm going to finish high school. You can do that here. To tell you the truth, they kind of push you. I mean, you can't just go to work in the laundry or in the kitchen. No, before they even talk to you about a job, you gotta take all that English and history and—jeez, I hope not math. But that's New York for you. A very smart state."

I could see by the way Mary flashed little smiles at the other inmates, or made ooh-isn't-he-cute faces at their boyfriends or children, that she was knocking herself out being congenial. She was right to want to build up some credit. Beauty like hers was a liability in the slammer. If someone took a dislike to her and a fight broke out, they would go for her face. Bruise it the first time, disfigure it the second. In fact, her whole ebullient manner—upbeat smile, happy babbling—was a front. I was at least relieved to see the other inmates wave back with a reasonable degree of warmth, noting, I had no doubt, that Mary was obeying the unwritten law: scrupulously avoid eye contact with their men.

I handed her a bag of grapes I'd brought from home, red, purple, and green. "I wasn't sure what you needed."

"This is *so* nice," she said. "All they give you here is oranges. Sometimes bananas for breakfast, but they're . . . " She made a fairly hideous guttural sound in the back of her throat.

"Mushy brown spots?"

"Brown all over!" Her too cheery behavior was replaced by a sweeter, more genuine manner; she was getting into a real conversation. If I could stay on yucky bananas or a comparative analysis of eye makeup remover pads, we could have a fine visit. "I mean, if you really went like this"—she squinted—"you could find maybe one banana-color little teeny spot in all that brown ook."

"Mary." She saw something serious coming on, and her eyes darted left-right-left: Let me outta here. "I'm going to try and keep this conversation light, okay?" I assured her. "I know you're worried you'll start crying, and you probably don't want the other women to know how emotional it is for you right now." She nodded. "Okay," I said, offering her a big, phony grin. "If the discussion gets too rough on you, rub your nose. I'll go into a long song and dance about my boyfriend or something."

"Is he cute?"

"Who? Oh, my boyfriend?" She nodded. "Yes, pretty cute. And a really nice guy."

"Good, 'cause I was worried about you. I mean, your age, no wedding ring. I figured, Uh-oh, something must've happened. I remember I said to . . . " She looked toward the red Exit sign over the door.

"Now that you mention him, Mary: There were a couple of days between the time Bobette was killed and her body was discovered."

"Uh-huh."

"When the police came and arrested . . . "

"Go ahead. You can say his name. I don't care."

I smiled. "Thank you. When they arrested Norman, he wasn't wearing the same clothes as when he killed Bobette. Right?"

"Uh . . . No."

"It might be helpful if you could remember what he was wearing that Friday, the day he went to the bank, the day Bobette was killed." Mary screwed up her mouth and drew her lovely arched brows together in deep thought. Or maybe she was practicing looking cerebral for her high school equivalency diploma classes. But nothing was happening behind that beautiful forehead. I was such a New York knee-jerk liberal that I was always thinking: Hmm, this person must have had an emotionally deprived childhood to appear this dull-witted. Or, this person must have been dropped on her head. Maybe I was right. I certainly never thought: Holy shit, is she dumb! until that moment in Bedford Hills. "Did Norman say anything about ripping anything during the murder? Or about Bobette trying to fight him off, or just moving around and possibly getting something on his clothes?"

"Chocolate!"

"Chocolate," I repeated.

"On his sleeve. Like right on the top of the cuff. A teeny doodle of chocolate."

"From Bobette. From the Snickers bar she was eating."

"Right!"

"Did you notice the spot or did Norman?"

"Well, I *would* have, because I always check before I do a laundry or send stuff to the dry cleaner 'cause stains have to be specially treated. I have a Mary Ellen book, and it tells what to do for each one."

"But Norman saw it?"

"Did he ever! I mean, he came home and he was, like, crazy. It was right by the DW. The initials on his cuff. Denton Wylie. Well, I mean, I don't know whose initials they really were. Norman lifted this expensive suitcase in a little airport, Santa Barbara. He just picked it up and walked out with it. He said the guy was his size—and that didn't happen every day, a rich guy that tall, 'cause most rich guys are little teeny men with little teeny . . . Do I have to tell you? You're a lawyer. What happened was, the rich guy gave it to a skycap and the skycap put it down and when the skycap got busy doing something, Norman picked it up. And there were five shirts with initials and a whole bunch of ties in a leather case with a gold DW. A case just for ties! The shirts were silk, except they were so expensive they looked like cotton. Anyhow, that night, after Bobette. He tore off the shirt. I mean *tore*. A couple of buttons came off."

"And then?"

"And then? I forget. I guess he must have told me what happened. No, wait, he wanted a drink. Chivas over ice. You don't say 'on the rocks.' It's not classy. I made it for him, but he went right back to the bottle and poured, like, a cup more. Right up to the top of the glass."

"And the shirt?"

"Oh, he said: 'Get rid of it.'"

"Right then?"

She gave that a minute's thought. "Later. He drank so much, so fast. I mean, both of us like to have a drink, but you know . . . Sip. He was the one who taught me about sipping, but he wasn't sipping. He was glugging it down and telling me what happened."

"And he told you to get rid of the shirt?"

"Yes. He was pretty drunk, but Norman wouldn't ever get that drunk that he couldn't think. He said: 'Get rid of it,' and then he went to sleep. And when he got up, he said: 'Did you get rid of it?'"

"Did you?" I asked.

"You're asking too? Jeez! No one gives me credit for anything. I told him: Norman, relax. I told him I walked about half a mile to a used car lot—he knew which one—but naturally it wasn't open. It was spooky at night, I told him. And I used up a whole book of matches, but I finally burned it and stomped the gray stuff, ashes, into the ground." I supposed I must have looked as if my life was over, because Mary bent forward to look at me with a mixture of pity and curiosity. "I shouldn't have burned the shirt?"

"It doesn't matter." The guards were moving around. Inmates were starting to say goodbye to their families. It was easy to tell which were the troublemakers. For them the guards enforced the no-touching rule, but they bent it for the others. Mothers kissed their children, touched the cheeks of their parents. Women patted their hair, or moistened their lips, so their men would have someone pretty to remember after that last look. I stood to go. "Please don't worry about the shirt," I told her. "It might have been helpful if it was still around, but probably not. Don't give it another thought."

"Okay," she said, only too pleased to comply. Then she added: "Because I didn't."

"Didn't what?"

"Didn't burn it." I sat back down. "It was *silk*. White silk. Norman loved those shirts. You give it to the dry cleaner, you know what you get? A spot. They get the chocolate out, but leave a little drippy-looking raindrop thing. And he did say: 'Don't even think of giving it to the cleaners. Get *rid* of it.' Except I figured, what the hay: With some silk—not all, but some—you wash them on the cold, gentle cycle and then you pull it out. Don't let it go through the spin, just pull it out wet—"

"Mary, did you wash it?"

"I'm trying to think. I remember thinking: If it comes out nice, he won't know it's the Bobette shirt because they're all the same. White silk. But they were so expensive and beautiful and all with *DW* initials. We could've kept using them. There are lots of D names. Dennis and Dwayne and Dick—"

"Picture what you did with the shirt, Mary. Tell me what you see."

She closed her eyes. "I put it in a net bag like what you put your panties in. And then . . . " I waited. "I zipped it. It's one of the ones with a zipper."

"And then?"

"I put it in the washing machine."

I took a deep breath. "Did you turn on the machine? Do you remember taking out the wet silk shirt, letting it drip dry?"

"No. Oh, I know why. 'Cause Norman was home that whole weekend. Really bad. Drinking. Didn't want to have any fun. Kept sleeping and drinking and sleeping. So I wasn't going to do a wash, not with him there. I had to wait." She sighed. "That's not good to do with a stain. And now I'm up here for twenty years."

"You didn't wash the shirt once Norman went to jail?"

"No. Isn't that weird? Oh, I know why. I did some washes, but I took it out of the machine because, like, why not wait till I had a few more things for a cold water wash? I mean, if it was like her blood or something I would have done it separate. Or maybe I really would've burned it. But it was just Snickers."

"Where is the shirt?"

"In the net bag."

"And where is the net bag, Mary?"

"Let's see. I stuck in some panties and a teddy and . . . It should be right where I left it." She closed her eyes and lifted her left arm high, making a patting motion with her hand. "Right up there on that shelf, in the broom closet. Next to the Endust."

Next to the Endust! I tried to keep myself calm going home. I didn't go more than ten miles over the speed limit. Fifteen. When I got to the Throgs Neck Bridge, I called my investigator, Terry Salazar, and told him to meet me at Mary's apartment. It hadn't been a full week since she'd been arrested, and I prayed that even if Jerry McCloskey ordered a complete search of the premises, the cops would have overlooked a silk shirt stuffed under panties and a teddy on a shelf in a broom closet. Since Mary had confessed and pleaded guilty, they wouldn't have had to seize the contents of the apartment. Would they?

Except I didn't get a chance to find out, because when I pulled over to the curb, I saw Terry making a thumbs-down sign. "What's the matter?"

"Sealed," he said.

"Sealed?" I didn't want to believe him. I got out of the car and ran to the building. Sure enough, the cops had pasted their Sealed by the Order sign onto the door and jamb of the apartment.

"Want me to break in through one of the windows?" Terry asked.

"No!" I snapped.

"You on the rag?"

"What good will your breaking in do? I'd have gotten the shirt illegally. It's no use saying Mary authorized me to search the apartment now that it's sealed. Anyway, knowing Huber, he'd accuse me of faking evidence."

"If it has Bobette's saliva with her DNA—"

"What if it doesn't? What if it just has some Snickers juice and that's it? He'll say I got a silk shirt—"

"You're going off the wall, Lee. Calm down. I'm sure during the whole investigation with Norman they took samples from him. Didn't they?"

"Yes."

"So if we find some of his hairs with roots on the shirt, body hair, whatever, that shows it's Norman's. That you didn't plant it." I got back into my car and slammed the door. "Hey, now that you screwed up my Sunday, getting me over here," Terry said, "why don't we go for a drink or something?"

I turned the key in the ignition and left Terry behind. I went home to take Val and Chicago out for sushi. Home to figure out a way to get my hands on the shirt Norman was wearing when he choked Bobette Frisch to death.

I would have spent the whole night on the phone with Will, but at eleven-thirty, he said he wanted to get a good night's sleep. "You're going to ask me: 'How can you possibly sleep?'" he said. "So I'll tell you. I'm tired. But I can also tell you right now you're not going to change Huber's mind, because he's decided that letting

Mary go would show that he was conned, ergo a dupe, ergo not fit to hold public office. I've crossed him off my to-do list. As far as any other avenues leading to the shirt, the only one I can think of is Holly Nuñez. She did back down at the end, but she was on your side for a while. She went head to head with McCloskey."

"She lost."

"The point is, at least she had the guts to go stand up to that pathetic piece of white trash."

"Should I call her?"

"I think you should do nothing. Let me be your lawyer on this."

"You want a retainer?"

"No. I want a good night's sleep so my head can be clear. Is it a deal?"

"Deal," I acknowledged, and hung up the phone for the night.

De Ruyter, Lefkowitz and Stewart looked as if it had been designed by Thomas Jefferson on a bad day. It was a two-story red-brick building trimmed with white wood, with a Greek portico in front. It even had a Monticello-style Roman dome. But contrary to the usual Georgian symmetry, the building's right side had been overextended to accommodate the three senior partners' sudden, irresistible whim—after half the structure had been erected—to each have a private bathroom with a shower. The whim became a request, then a demand. The architect, a macho type with a chest-length beard and work boots, wept. The contractor all but swooned from joy at the cost overruns. What it came to was this: De Ruyter, Lefkowitz and Stewart, although not ugly, always looked unbalanced, as if it were about to slide down the hillock on which it stood.

I had been to the firm a few times for depositions or

meetings, and once as Will's date, to an impromptu champagne celebration after he'd won a big case for a defense contractor, a guy who had faced thirty years in jail and ten million in fines for selling gyroscopes used in fighter planes to Iraq. "Oh," said the receptionist when she saw me, glancing at the brass carriage clock on her desk. It wasn't even ten in the morning. Her "Oh" came out as "Ew," because she barely separated her lips when she spoke, De Ruyter, Lefkowitz and Stewart was such a tony firm. "Ms. White. Do you have a meeting today, or are you . . . ?"

"I'm here to see Mr. Stewart."

"Ew." I'm sure she was dying to know why, because she hesitated, as if expecting me to confide something fascinating about my relationship with Will. When I didn't, she punched a few numbers and murmured my name to his secretary in a refined but disappointed tone.

Instead of the secretary, Will came striding out. "Hi," he said, and led me to his office.

"You don't seem surprised that I dropped in on you."

"What surprises me is that you were able to hold off until ten o'clock."

Instead of sitting behind his desk, he took a seat on his couch and patted the cushion next to his. It was a very plain couch. His whole office was plain. Beautiful, simple, and austere, the sort of working space God would have. Will had perfect taste.

"Do you have any thoughts?" I asked. "Or thought? For what I'm paying you, I can't ask for too much."

"I got off the phone with Holly Nuñez about fifteen minutes ago."

"You spoke to her? About the Torkelson case? Do you know her? Have you ever met her?"

"Yes, yes, no, no. But she knew who I was." There was no false modesty and no genuine modesty in Will's remark: a simple statement of fact. "We spoke for nearly an hour."

"And?"

"And we're meeting for lunch today. At a little place near my house, where we won't be seen."

"What is this? A new chapter in your life?"

"I'm giving Holly Nuñez the chance to be a champion of justice and a defender of democracy."

"Are you nuts? She has acrylic nails and she wimped out to Jerry McCloskey."

"Lee, what do you say to your clients when they start to second-guess you?"

"Something like 'You hired me because you trust my judgment and know that all my years of experience count for something. You have to be willing to let me be the lawyer.'"

"Okay. You hired me because you trust my judgment and know that all my years of experience count for something. You have to be willing to let me be the lawyer."

I said: "So what time will you be back from lunch?"

Will did not seem surprised to find me waiting in his reception area when he strolled into his office a little before three. "What did you have?" I demanded. "A five-course meal?" He ushered me into his office. The receptionist looked so crazed with curiosity I thought she was going to leap over her desk, grab us, beg us: What is going on here? Which is what I wanted to know. The second he closed his office door, I said: "Everything. The tone of your voice when you said hello. Was her handshake warm or not so warm? From the first minute she walked into—"

"As we speak, she is taking Sam Franklin over to Mary's apartment. They're going to break the seal, look for the shirt, and if they find it, bring it to the lab. They should have preliminary findings by Wednesday or Thursday."

I sat there flummoxed. For the life of me, I could not

imagine how he had done it. "How did you convince her? What issue did you raise that would make her take such a huge risk? She's going to lose her job!"

Will said: "She won't be needing it. She's going to run for district attorney on the Democratic ticket."

I clapped my hands to my face. I must have looked like some Disney version of amazement. "*What*?"

"I pointed out that she knew what you had asked for was fair and just. Mary Dean did not kill Bobette Frisch. There is no reason for her to be paying for the crime. I also pointed out to Holly that all that was stopping her from following her instincts—her fine, commendable instincts—was Woodleigh Huber and his flunky, White Trash."

"And the only way to stop him is for Holly to run against him?" Will knocked me out; I couldn't believe the audacity of what he was doing.

"Right."

"But she's a Republican."

"That can easily be remedied. Huber runs every four years with no real challenge because everyone's convinced he's a shoo-in. Big voice, no controversy, all that white hair. Well, Holly wants to see to it that there is controversy. Mary Dean. She was the victim of one man, Norman. And now the victim of a second man."

"Huber?"

"Yes. He's pulling off Justice's blindfold and spitting in her eye."

"My God!" I said. "You gave Holly that line and she's going to use it."

"She probably will."

"I could use a hit of Chuckie's oxygen now. This whole thing . . . It leaves me breathless."

"It should leave Huber breathless. Holly wants to make the point that he's so stuck on image—on the old politics—that he can't admit he was conned. He's willing to let someone serve a fifteen-to-twenty sentence just to save his political ass. She knows he's going to fire her the minute he finds out that she authorized lifting the seal on the apartment. She *wants* to be fired."

"And the Democrats will want her?"

"Lee," Will said patiently.

"They'll be thrilled," I acknowledged.

"Exactly. And they'll be ecstatic when they find out I'm breaking with my party to fund-raise for her. I'm going to get her big bucks. She's going to give that slick piece of work a run for his money—and then some." He took my hand in his. "I'm doing this because I think Woodleigh Huber is profoundly fourth rate, and anyone below second rate is dangerous when he has prosecutorial powers. I'm doing it for Mary Dean, because I'm a sucker for the grand gesture. To sacrifice yourself in the name of love! At the very least, she deserves to get her life back. I'm doing it for myself too, because I have achieved everything I ever dreamed of achieving—and to tell you the truth, it's a little boring. I need a cheap thrill. Well, this campaign won't come that cheap. That's okay. But mainly, Lee, you know why I'm doing this."

"For me."

"Yes. For you."

It took quite a bit longer than Thursday, but the lab confirmed that the chocolate on Norman's cuff was like that of chocolate from a Snickers candy bar. Further, the saliva found on that same spot matched the DNA of Bobette Frances Frisch, deceased. Additionally, an almost microscopic smear of blood along the rim of the collar of the white silk shirt, consistent with a shaving nick beneath the jaw, matched the blood specimen taken from Inmate 1025567–95, Norman Torkelson.

*   *   *

I was planning on going to Holly Nuñez's press conference, but I had a sentencing. My client had been caught by the state police after his truck hydroplaned off the Long Island Expressway during a downpour and hit an embankment, causing many of the crates that contained the six-hundred-forty ducks he had stolen from a farm on the North Fork to break apart and set off a cataclysm of bloody feathers on the median, as well as drumsticks beating on the windshields of passing Range Rovers. It was his third duck-rustling offense. The assistant D.A., a new kid who had clearly read his animal rights literature, was annoyingly graphic on the subject of my client's genocidal proclivities when it came to poultry, and the judge refused to hear my argument for a suspended sentence with community service.

It wasn't until I got back and turned on the TV in Chuckie's office for the five o'clock news that I was able to see Holly announce her candidacy for district attorney of Nassau County. She had a new hairstyle, straight-cut with bangs, something between Cleopatra and Betty Boop— though instead of vampish, it made her look pure, a Madonna in a Puerto Rican church. She was wearing a navy suit and a crisp white blouse, so she appeared sufficiently lawyerly for the job. Whether she'd been coached to be low key or it was a natural television genius, I don't know, but instead of perky—her prosecutorial correlative of an *Entertainment Tonight* cohost— she merely looked bright and energetic. I kept waiting for the cameras to turn to her supporters so I could get a glimpse of Will, but the cameras liked her too much.

Naturally, I didn't get to hear everything she said, just a sound bite or two on the various local newscasts. She spoke about the Bobette Frisch case and how Bobette was the victim of one man, Norman Torkelson, but how

Mary Dean, the woman serving time for the murder, was the victim of two men: Norman—and Woodleigh Huber.

"It's easy to *look* tough," she told the cameras. Holly seemed so much the genuine article they all but nodded back. "We need someone who has the guts and the integrity to *be* tough, and that means standing up for justice no matter what the political cost." Her dark-brown eyes moved from lens to lens, giving each station its share. "It's *wrong* to run a D.A.'s Office by taking polls and holding press conferences and wearing hair spray. Nassau County deserves better than pretty-boy politics. That's why I'm running against Woodleigh Huber."

Will came for dinner and stayed for the ten o'clock news, and then the eleven. By that time, a couple of reporters had caught up with Woodleigh Huber as he was coming out of the Nassau County chapter of the B'nai B'rith Anti-Defamation League's annual black-tie fund-raiser, where he had no doubt been giving his usual Jews Are Good speech. He was looking spiffy, a blue silk handkerchief in his tuxedo pocket, his hair looking as if Michelangelo had carved it out of Carrara marble. "I have no comment at this present time," he commented. "All I can say is that Holly Nuñez"—he paused for effect—"was fired from the District Attorney's Office for *cause*." Not a particularly effective statement, or a terrible one. Or at least not until the same idea popped into every late-night news producer's head: a close shot of Huber's face, his luxuriant white hair frozen in the brilliant TV lights, followed by a clip of Holly declaring: "It's wrong to run a D.A.'s office by taking polls and holding press conferences and wearing hair spray."

I looked over at Will, sitting in a Papa Bear chair, his feet up on an ottoman. He was actually smiling. "She's better than I thought she'd be."

"Does she have a chance?" I asked.

"In this county, against one of the most proven Republican vote-getters? A guy with Conservative, Liberal, and Right-to-Life endorsements?" He thought for a moment. "When the press conference was over this afternoon, I told Holly how good she was. Know what she did? Took her hand and mussed up her hair a little. She said: 'No hair spray. In case any of the reporters asked.' Interesting: I was the one who suggested she run. But when I did, it didn't come as any surprise to her. None of that 'Who, me, run?' stuff. She said great, she'd use the Mary Dean business—woman-as-victim and all that—but she wanted to nail Huber on what she called the Politics of Fatigue: how he plays to the cameras but doesn't have the energy or the imagination to get to the root of crime."

"What does 'get to the root of crime' mean?" I asked.

"Damned if I know. She's big on the word 'proactive.' I told her to find a synonym. What was amazing is that she had the entire campaign against Huber already mapped out in her mind. True, she'd probably been thinking of a Republican primary challenge, not bolting and running as a Democrat. But I was just a catalyst, a guy who could raise money so she could do it four years earlier than she'd originally planned."

"If she wins, will she be any better than Huber?"

"Let's put it this way. She's smart. Smart enough. And she's a woman and a Hispanic, and she's enormously ambitious. Based on that alone, she's got to be at least two or three times as good as Huber."

"And now she's a Democrat, so she won't trample on people's Fifth and Sixth Amendment rights."

Will moved his feet from the ottoman to the floor. "Did anyone ever tell you that you're a political imbecile?" He stood and put on his jacket. "In my life, I've never heard such idiot stereotyping as comes out of your mouth every single election campaign."

"Fine," I said. "Be the Clarence Thomas of Long Island. That's your business. Just wait till your party pals learn you're supporting a Democrat."

"Please. They already know."

"So how many times this summer do you think you're going to be playing golf at their lily-white country clubs, big boy?"

"With any luck? Not a single goddamn one." He patted the top of my head. "Lily White," he said, and he went home.

Some men get away with murder. But some of their victims can come back to life. Not Bobette Frisch, of course. Mary Dean was a different story.

The day after Holly Nuñez's news conference, Woodleigh Huber held one of his own. He said he would not deign to address his opponent's hair spray remarks, except to say categorically that he did not use hair spray. That day he was telling the truth, but he made the mistake of speaking from the courthouse steps. Somber, pinstriped, every inch Mr. District Attorney. A breeze toyed with his hair, first lifting it up so it appeared electrified, then tossing it to the left, so it looked like the hair of a mad genius. Huber patted it back down once, then again. In the end, the only information most people watching him on television registered from his appearance was that the district attorney of the County of Nassau was horribly upset about his hair.

This is what he said that did not register: He welcomed the opportunity to debate the issues with Ms. Nuñez. He was proud of his record, darn proud, and was not afraid to run on it. And contrary to his opponent's blatantly false and spurious assertions, he was not keeping an innocent woman in prison because he was ashamed to admit he'd been conned. "The buck stops here," Huber announced. "I don't just take credit for all the successes of this office. I am willing to take full responsibility for my misjudgments. Now, there haven't been many, but in this case, like every single lawyer and public official involved, I believed Mary Dean's confession. However, subsequent information proved to me that she had been used by Norman Torkelson, a notorious con artist. The moment I heard the truth, I knew she had to be released. However, unlike my opponent, I do not shoot from the hip. I do not speak rashly or act rashly. There is a procedure to follow in these cases, and I had to follow it. *I am sworn to uphold the law.* I have devoted my life to upholding the law. And now that the procedure has been followed"—he patted down his hair and broke out his *60 Minutes* voice—"I am ordering Mary Dean to be released forthwith!"

I picked Mary up at Bedford Hills the next morning and drove her back to her apartment on Long Island. "Jeez," she said, opening the car window and letting the wind stream into her face. "A couple of weeks cooped up, you forget air. It feels so good."

When we turned off the Sprain Brook Parkway to the Bronx River, I asked: "Do you have any plans?"

"Like, for lunch?"

"I really meant plans for your life." The subject seemed to be of no particular interest to her, so I added: "But I was hoping you'd let me buy you lunch."

"You mean, you would buy?"

"Yes."

"I should be taking you out for a champagne dinner, getting me out of there. I swear to God, I thought I'd be stuck there till I was, you know, forty or something." Her eyes closed, and she turned her face to catch the sun.

When we got back, she told me she couldn't go to a restaurant looking the way she did. With her skin clean of the mask of makeup she usually wore and her hair deflated, she looked far more beautiful than anyone else on Long Island. But I understood her need to re-create the Mary she wanted to be, so I agreed to give her an hour before picking her up.

"We'll just have fun," I promised her. "No serious discussions about your future. No pressure."

"If I don't feel like going for my high school diploma, I don't have to?"

"Of course not. I told you: We'll just be two ladies out for a nice lunch."

I didn't mention that I had a few plans in place for her if she was interested. Beauty school, waitressing. I couldn't help find her a job in a bar, because the state liquor authority would run her prints and find out about her record. As far as that went, I had already spoken to a lawyer I'd once dealt with in Baltimore who had recommended someone in Annapolis; he was going to look into getting the assault and fugitive charges against her reduced. I'd spoken to a pal in the probation department who knew a social worker in Queens who had a grant to work with prostitutes, offering them alternatives to the life; I'd set that in motion too.

I was interested in Mary's past and her future. Ladies who lunch open up to each other. What had her family been like? What had turned her into a hooker? And was there any way to change her path so she wouldn't about-face and go right back to it?

And all right, I was not without hope that somewhere in an hour and a half of her ditsy chatter I'd find a glimmer, a hint that she herself hadn't picked up on, of where Norman Torkelson might have gone.

"What should I wear?" she asked as I pulled up to the

apartment building. She took in my gray linen suit, then looked into my eyes with something that might have been pity. "I don't have anything like that."

"Anything other than shorts or jeans," I told her. "It doesn't matter. You always look wonderful."

"Thanks," she said, pleased by the compliment but not thrilled: It had not come from a man. The second she climbed out of the car, she was rubbing a lock of hair between her fingers, checking what conditioning it would need. "Oh, and thanks a million for getting me out." She laughed. "I wish I could pay you a million."

"You wouldn't have to," I said. "I'd give you a discount."

Mary laughed. "A big fat one, I hope!"

"A big fat one."

I drove to my office to check my mail and returned to Mary's an hour later. She was gone. I never heard from her again.

When I think about the case and I'm in an upbeat mood, I imagine Mary on some Amtrak train out of New York, sitting next to a nice guy in a suit who knows she's not the kind of girl Mama wants him to bring home, but nonetheless, he's going to bring her home. I see her in a pretty house with a central vacuum system, pregnant, clipping coupons for Wisk and Just Right. When I'm feeling low, I see her punched in the face, kicked in the head by some drunken pig of a john who grabs back the fifty bucks he gave her.

And now and then, late at night, I think she knew all along where Norman was, and they are together again.

Twenty-six

✖

Of course, the Torkelson case wasn't even the half of it. To finish Lily White's story, it is necessary to backtrack a few years, before Lee met Norman in the visitors room at the Nassau County Correctional center, even before Mary Dean met Norman when she was working the bar at the Paloverde Cocktail Lounge in the Maricopa Motor Inn in Phoenix. We have to return to the early spring of 1991, shortly after Lee's forty-first birthday.

Sandi Zimmerman slid into Lee's office and closed the door. She kept her hands behind her on the knob and narrowed her eyes in the furtive manner of minor characters in Humphrey Bogart vehicles. "There's a man outside who says he's your father," she said. "His name is Leonard White." Blood rushed to Lee's head. She felt dizzy. She calmed herself: Great emotion—how could it not be? Or was this something beyond emotion? A stroke? "Is it?" she heard Sandi asking.

"Is it *what*?" Lee snapped. Her skull was expanding

against her scalp, desperate to escape the pressure inside her head. By the time Sandi brought her father in, she'd be aphasic, trying to make the *D* sound—Dad—but she wouldn't be able to move her paralyzed tongue up behind her teeth, and the only sound that would emerge would be a feral growl.

"Is it really your father?"

"Sandi, you're standing in front of a closed door. I can't see him." Lee realized then that Sandi was probably frightened the man was not her father at all, but a dissatisfied ex-client packing a semiautomatic rifle under his raincoat. She was irritated that everyone else got carte blanche to be crazy and she had to be the sane one. Reluctantly, she put her massive cerebral hemorrhage on hold. "If he's a spiffy-looking man in his mid-sixties, he's probably my father."

The man who came through the door was indeed her father. He did not look spiffy, however. Leonard had gone from slim to thin, but his trousers had not. They were held up by a pair of expensive suspenders—pearl-gray, with a black design. Plumes? No, bushy-tailed foxes. The suspenders held up his trousers, but he easily could have slipped both his arms inside the waistband. His hair had gone from distinguished silver at the temples to old man's white. His face was no color at all. In the middle of her cheerful blue and white office, Leonard looked diminished and passé, a scene on a tiny fifties black-and-white TV.

"Hello." Lee stood behind her desk, making no move to shake hands or come around to greet him. This was not a conscious, lawyerly ploy. Her body refused to let her move and her mind was in no condition to countermand the order.

"Sorry to drop in on you like this," he began. He sounded nervous, but she was relieved that his voice was still the same, a slightly raspy Brooklyn baritone, rather pleasing, but with an accent that made it sound as if there had been some game in his neighborhood in which all residents tried to speak with Oxbridge diction—and only Leonard had not gotten that it was a big joke. "I suppose I should have called first."

"Please sit down," she said.

Carefully, he lowered himself into one of the chairs that faced her desk. His thumb caressed the arm, reflexively checking out the fabric, as if considering it as a possible lining for one of his coats. "I don't know how much Valerie's told you," he said.

"About what? Look, I'm not being coy. She's fourteen and a half, and she tends to be a little self-involved."

"The actor. Did she tell you I called her an 'actress' and got a big lecture?"

"She doesn't talk much about what she does when she's with you or her father. Except if you take her to the theater, you and—" Lee realized her father was waiting to see what euphemism she would come up with for family members, so she came up with none. "—Mom or Jazz and Robin. What is it that Val might have told me about?"

Leonard shook his head: I can't find the words. Lee leaned forward. The swivel mechanism in her desk chair squealed. Maybe she wasn't having a stroke, but her head did not feel right. Healthy people do not feel pressure against their temporal bones. What could Val be keeping from her? Some relationship? Sexual? Could she be pregnant? She'd had her period for a year. But she had invited only two boys—old buddies from elementary school—to her bat mitzvah: two boys and twenty-three girls. Drugs? What else could it be? Had Val broken down and confessed to her grandfather that when Lee was working late, she sneaked bottles of wine spritzers up past Puella and was one of those secret teenage alcoholics? Had Lee been overestimating a child's ability to cope with a working mother, a retarded uncle, a Holy Roller housekeeper, a ten-year-old accordion prodigy, three dogs and two cats and a perpetually present black Republican?

"I don't know where to begin," Leonard said.

As this was what ninety percent of the clients sitting in that chair said, Lee at least knew what she had to do: ask something, anything, that would demand an answer. "How is Mom?"

"You do know!"

"No. What? Is something wrong?"

"Wrong? Metastasized stomach cancer."

Lee hugged herself, her arms enfolding her belly. "I'm so sorry."

"She's got two, three more months, the doctor says. Sloan-Kettering."

"She's in the hospital?"

"No. What can they do for her there? I have her home."

"Is she in pain?"

"No."

"Who's taking care of her?"

"I'm semiretired these days. I do what I can."

"Is there anything I can do?"

Leonard sat back and crossed his legs, too suave a gesture for talking about cancer. "Is there anything you can do?" he mused. "Let me give you a bit of background. I don't know if you read the financial pages, although you must. You're a lawyer."

"The financial pages?"

"Wait. Hear me out. The fur industry is, as they say, enjoying hard times." He gave a harsh laugh, the sort where no sound is emitted because the lips are too tightly clamped together. "*Our* business is not doing well. Don't worry. I didn't come here for a loan. I came because I felt you ought to know about your mother."

"I can't believe Val didn't say anything," Lee said.

"Well . . . "

"Have you actually told her that her grandmother has cancer?"

"No," he admitted. "Not in so many words. She knows Sylvia's been under the weather. But you don't say 'cancer' to a fourteen-year-old."

"Yes you do."

"Well, we don't. Anyway, this is the thing: about the business. What I was trying to tell you. All those anti-fur people were marching up and down in front of the salon." He uncrossed his legs and leaned toward her. "For three years! *Screaming* at anyone who came in. They picked four or five targets, and we were one of them. Because of our clientele. The best and the brightest: That's who we've had right from the beginning. We hired security men, but that just kept them from throwing red paint. It didn't make the customers come in. They were afraid. Those animal people are psychos. You know about them? They throw paint on the garments!"

"I've heard." About a year earlier. Will had been over. As they usually did before he left, they turned on the TV for the news and the Johnny Carson monologue. The screen filled with protesters in front of a department store, screaming, cursing, hooting at fur-wearing women. Spontaneously, Will and Lee broke into applause.

"And it's not just the psychos. The real problem is, it's not the eighties anymore."

"You were doing all right before the eighties."

"But all that was nothing compared to the eighties. We couldn't get to the bank fast enough. And now . . . dead." He rubbed his hands together. They made a sandpaper sound. The backs of his hands were protuberant blue veins, large brown blotches. "We had to close Le Fourreur. Valerie didn't tell you?"

"No. I'm sorry to hear it."

"Last year we did no business at all. Nothing. And this year is going to be worse. Less than nothing. All the Furhavens—the low-end stores: Our profit margins are shaved to almost nothing, and we're not even making our rent. We've already closed the two in Jersey. What can I tell you? Everything is nothing."

"What about all the money you made in the eighties?"

"It was tied up. Real estate. We both had co-ops in the city. Me and Jazz. Jasper."

She almost smiled. "I know who you mean. I didn't know you had places in the city. Val's not a very good gossip."

"I'm surprised she hadn't said anything. She'd been to both places. They were beautiful. I was on Fifth, near the museum. Jazz was Park in the Sixties, one of the most exclusive buildings in the city. And I had the house in Palm Beach." He looked to a wall lined with framed photographs Will had taken. "Not the house you were in," he said to the photographs. "Another one. On the ocean. And Jazz had one close by, and one in Vermont. They're all great skiers, the whole bunch—"

"I don't mean to be rude, but I'd like to know why you're here."

"We sold them all, but you wouldn't believe it. These days everybody's trying to unload everything they bought in the eighties, when prices were sky-high.

There's a glut on the market and everything, everything we sold we sold at a loss. Terrible. The art your mother bought. We practically gave it away. Robin's jewelry. Edwardian. It was auctioned at Sotheby's. They wouldn't have taken it if it wasn't quality stuff. Everything. We poured it into the business. We hired a new designer, someone very hot. I can't tell you what we spent on advertising and public relations. But in the end . . . nothing. It got so bad we had to let Greta go."

"I know she's not with you anymore."

"Val told you?"

"No. Greta comes to dinner every Thursday."

"She does? How is she?"

"She seems all right. She's been coming to dinner once a week for years—since Jazz switched sisters. It's the only way she could see me and Kent."

"For God's sake!" Lee could not tell if her father was angry at her remark about Jazz switching sisters or about his housekeeper's secret life. "Greta didn't tell you about closing the stores, or about us having to let her go?"

"No. We never talk about you. A few months ago, she told me she retired. She never was a big talker. And she's very proud. She wouldn't say she was fired."

"Believe me, I felt bad. But she had a nest egg. They're a very frugal people." He shook his head wearily. "In my life, I never could be frugal. It's not my nature. But it wasn't bad being the other way, generous, because I knew I had to make the kind of life I wanted. It was an incentive. The better I wanted to live, the more I made." He shook his head. "Not anymore. I had to put the house up for sale. The house you grew up in. Do you know why? Because we need money to live! It's come to that. Every night I pray for a buyer. Jazz and Robin had to put their place up too.

A showstopper. Right on the Sound. I wish you could see it."

Lee knew that when she repeated that line to Will she would laugh, but just then, she could not. "Why would you wish I could see it?"

"Sorry, I didn't mean to hurt you."

"Then or now?" Leonard pretended he had not heard her question. "You know, talking about then . . . Right after Jazz left me, I thought: It's understandable that he would want Robin. She's so helpless, so beautiful. She makes Jazz feel important. Useful. Manly. All I seemed to be able to do was diminish him. But now . . . I can see it more clearly. Once Jazz knew he had overreached, marrying me, there really was only one alternative: Robin."

"I don't understand," Leonard said warily.

"Sure you do. He couldn't make it as a lawyer and you gave him the perfect out: a thriving business. What a life he had with you! All he had to do was find some way to continue it without dragging me along. And he did. He found someone who hated what I had accomplished as much as he did, and together they were able to make their dreams come true: to bring me down and keep living high—off you. That's what happened."

"Then I guess this news is making you happy. You're probably thinking: This is justice. They got what they deserved. All of them." He waited, but Lee did not say: It doesn't make me happy, or You did not deserve to come to this. "I'll tell you why I'm here," Leonard said, just before the pause became unbearable. "Besides your mother. Do you want to hear?"

"Do you want to tell me?"

"Hart's Hill."

"What about it?"

"Fos and Ginger can't keep it up anymore."

"They couldn't keep it up twenty years ago."

"It's on the market now for next to nothing. Three mil. That's a *steal*."

"And?"

"We're hoping to keep it in the family." Lee studied the thin, gray man across from her. Had he lived with his own illusions so long that he now believed he and the Taylors were one? "I know this is a long shot, but hear me out. Hart's Hill means something. It has meaning for your daughter. It's her heritage. She's a Taylor."

"It may be part of her heritage. But the other part is a fourteen-year-old Jewish kid from Port Washington who gets ten bucks a week from me and baby-sits for the rest. Three million is a little steep for her."

"Lee," her father said, moving to the very edge of his chair, putting his dry hands on her desk. There was still a shadow of grace in his movement. For just an instant, she saw the man who could hold up a rat's skin and convince some rich matron it was better than mink. "Come on," he urged. "How about it?"

"How about what?"

"How about you? Who better? Think about it: You don't just have one Taylor, you have two living with you! Kent. He actually grew up there. And can you imagine how thrilled Valerie would be to move—"

"I don't have that kind of money."

"You don't need as much as you think. Jazz talked the whole thing over with Fos. He's willing to take back paper. He said he always liked you. Fos, I mean. And if it goes to a stranger . . . Don't you see? It would be out of the family."

"I don't care. It's not my family. My family lives with me in Port Washington."

Leonard pushed himself up using the edge of her desk, but he didn't get very far. Embarrassed, he pretended he had not tried to get up at all. "You're a lawyer. This is a good business proposition. The next real estate upswing, you could double your money."

"By the time the next upswing comes around, I'll be double my age." He braced his hands against the arms of the chair, but he did not try to stand. "Are you all right?" she asked. "Healthwise?"

"I'm fine." He pushed and, finally, with a grunt, managed to get up. "Don't close the door on this, Lee. For the sake of your child."

"For her sake and my sake, she's going to have to make her own way in the world." Leonard turned and moved to leave. Lee walked around her desk and held the door for him. "Does Mom need nurses?" He shrugged. "I'll be glad to help you with that."

"That you have the money for?"

"Yes, for that I do. My checkbook's at home. I'll have an envelope messengered to you tomorrow." Up close, just beside his mouth, she could see a small patch of white whiskers his razor had missed.

"You know what's interesting?" Leonard inquired.

"What?"

"From our room, lying in bed all day like she does: You look out the window and what's the only thing you can see? Hart's Hill."

The following day, Lee wrote a check. She took it herself to the house in which she grew up. When her father answered the door, she handed it to him, along with a list of nursing care agencies. It was four in the afternoon, and he had not yet shaved. The white whiskers near his mouth had grown, and they stuck out of his face like an on-off button. She told her father that her check would cover one week's worth of nursing care. After that, the agency could send the bills to her: simpler bookkeeping.

They both understood that Lee did not trust Leonard to spend thousands of dollars on a dying woman who was not in pain.

Lee told him she wanted to see her mother. He said he would go up and see if it was okay. She waited in the front hall and looked into the living room. She was not surprised that none of the furniture was familiar. Asian, she thought. Some country that had become stylish during the eighties. Sri Lanka, maybe, or Burma. Will would know. The fieldstone floors were bare. She wondered if that had been stylish or if they had sold the rugs. Leonard came down and said: You can go up. I guess I don't have to show you the way.

She was seven weeks away from dying, but Sylvia looked better than her husband did. Her frosted blonde and gray hair, pinned softly on top of her head, emphasized her fine-boned face and long, thin neck. She looked like Katharine Hepburn would have looked if Katharine Hepburn's forebears had come from a Galician shtetl. "Come in," she summoned Lee. Asia had been carried up to the second floor. The bed was a huge four-poster of white wood, every inch carved with flowers and—Lee looked closer—animal heads. It was the only piece of furniture in the room. For some reason Lee was not sure she comprehended, the bed stood at a forty-five-degree angle in the middle of the room. "Like it?" Sylvia asked.

"Yes. Beautiful." Lee stood at the foot. The bottom of each post tapered into the head of some big cat—panther, maybe, or jaguar, dangerously stupid, with a flat, broad skull and fashionably elongated snout.

"Turn-of-the-century. Ceylon." Lee realized her mother was watching her examine the room's bareness, its white-painted walls and white-stained wood floor. "You've heard the expression 'Less is more.'"

"Yes. Mies van der Rohe."

"I don't know anymore. I'm not sure he was right."

"I hear you're not well," Lee said. She had to force her eyes from the white-lacquered flowers onto her mother.

"You heard what it is?"

"Yes. I'm sorry."

Sylvia made a cynical sound, a sniff, a laugh. "How have you been?"

"Fine."

"I was positive you'd remarry."

"No." Lee knew that if her sister had been there in her shoes, she would have had the sense to perch on the edge of the bed and confide about each and every man she had dated, being fair about their assets—a firm chin, a thriving rheumatology practice, a powerful backstroke—laughing at their devastating liabilities. Why couldn't she do that? The woman was dying.

"Are you seeing anyone special?" Sylvia pushed herself higher up against a pile of white pillows. She looked interested, almost hopeful. The pillows were serious white: not a ribbon or a ruffle had been permitted. Her nightgown, too, was unadorned white, as if it had been made from one of the sheets, although Lee guessed it had been hand sewn by exploited child laborers. "I mean, seeing someone you're thinking of marrying?"

"No." She saw her mother expected at least something more, so she gave it to her. "I wish I could find someone. I tried not to be too exacting, but if a guy pees on the toilet seat—"

"Urinates."

"Or if he wears a gold ID bracelet there is no way I can marry him, much less love him."

Her mother smiled. "You can wipe off the seat, but the ID bracelet . . . Did you ever get over Jazz?" she asked quietly, as if afraid of being overheard.

"Yes. Do you want to know why?" Lee was surprised to find herself sitting on the edge of the bed, beside her mother. "Because there wasn't that much to get over. I missed his liveliness for a while. His energy. Jazz could make a party in a paper bag. And I missed the sex." Sylvia did not blanch, but she paled a bit. "I'll answer your unasked question," Lee went on. "Yes: He may have been carrying on with Robin for years, but right up to the end, he was getting two for the price of one."

"I always wondered," Sylvia said softly.

"Now you don't have to wonder. But getting back to the 'did-I-get-over-him' issue—"

"You really *are* a lawyer. Like my father. That's where you get it from. You can pick up right where you left off."

"Usually. I got over Jazz because my love for him was never that profound. He wasn't that profound. I guess that means I wasn't either. But beyond lack of depth, he wasn't interesting. He wasn't good."

"Good at what?"

"He wasn't a good person."

Sylvia studied her wedding ring. "Well . . . ," she said. It was a syllable pregnant with meaning. Pull it out of me, it seemed to say. It *wants* to come out. It may not surprise you. I might say: He's a good father. He had a good business head. Or: He's been a good husband to her. Not good. The best. Sensitive to her sensitivity like you would believe. But it may be precisely what you want to hear. He had a bad business head: If that fool had had any foresight, we would still be mink marketers to Manhattan's elite. Or: He's not good. He's cheating on Robin. Has been for years. Well, why shouldn't Lee be midwife to all the unfinished business of her life? It wasn't a hard job. She understood that all she had to say was: Come on, Mom. Please? Not in a pushy way. By being cute. A little tease in the voice. And out it would come. Such a small effort, and she would be the daughter this dying woman had always wanted her to be. And the dying woman had so much she could tell.

"It took two or three years to get over Jazz," Lee said. "What I have never gotten over is the betrayal of my mother and father and sister."

"Oh."

"I'm sorry, but that's the truth."

"If you want to know the truth," Sylvia said, "I thought the whole thing was terrible. Tacky."

"No. 'Tacky' is for tasteless clothes. This was treacherous."

"Whatever. I cried over it. I wanted to say something. I don't mean to Robin. I *did* say something to her. I said: 'Don't you have any feelings? Don't you care about what people are going to say? Your sister's husband!' And I even wanted to say something to you."

"What?"

"I can't remember. It was too long ago. But your father said: 'Keep your mouth shut, Sylvia.' Actually, he said 'yap,' not 'mouth.' 'Keep your yap shut. There's nothing we can do. We can't take sides. We have two daughters. And Jazz is my business partner.'"

"So you listened to him."

"He's my husband." Sylvia closed her eyes. Her

head wobbled until it found a place on a pillow. Her breathing was deep, untroubled. Lee thought she had fallen off to sleep. She got up from the bed. Sylvia opened her eyes. "What could I do?" she went on. "Go against my husband? Do you think he would have stood for that?"

"I don't know. We'll never know."

"I couldn't risk it. He could've walked out."

"I told Dad I'd take care of paying for nurses for you."

Sylvia perked up. This was clearly news to her. "Starting . . . ?"

"Starting now. For however long you need them."

"Thank you."

"You're welcome."

"They'll give me sponge baths."

"Yes. Whatever you want. They're going to be well paid, so let them treat you royally."

"Can you believe we've come to this? No money." Sylvia was not sad. She was offended, as if someone had pulled a cruel practical joke on her. "He canceled the gardeners. It's a good thing there hasn't been too much rain this spring."

"I'm glad I can help out."

"How come you're doing this? So you don't have a guilty conscience later?"

"I'm doing it"—Lee bent over and kissed her mother's cheek—"because it needs to be done. Okay?"

"Okay. I didn't mean that. About a guilty conscience. It just came out."

"Don't worry about it. If you need anything, call me. Or have Dad or your nurse call me."

"Lee."

"Yes?"

"I like your shoes."

Lee kissed her mother for the last time. What could she say? I hope it goes well? I love you? Good luck? Goodbye? Bon voyage? She said nothing. As she pulled back from Sylvia's cheek, she glanced past the foot of the bed, out the window. From her mother's eye level, she could see green lawn, the aqua pool, the trees, and just beyond, the poison-ivy-blanketed bluff at the end of the Whites' property, which rose toward the Taylors'. But her father had lied to her. You could not see Hart's Hill when you lay in that bed. It was much too high.

Lee White and Will Stewart did not stay long at the victory party in the catering hall on that first Tuesday in November. Being Holly Nuñez's first supporters and having made the most generous contributions the law would allow, they were now not only members of the inner circle but also on a hugging basis with her. So as "Happy Days Are Here Again" was played for the one hundred sixty-second time that night, they dutifully hugged Holly, congratulated her yet again, then allowed her to be swept away from them into a sea of red, white, and blue balloons by a wave of delirious Democrats.

Will walked Lee to her car in the parking lot of the Chateau Briand, a catering hall that featured linguine in clam sauce, shrimp teriyaki, fried wontons, and absolutely nothing that was remotely French. "Well?" he asked. "How does it feel to be a queenmaker?"

"She was wearing hair spray tonight. I smelled it when I hugged her."

"Not an impeachable offense." Lee searched through her handbag for her Jeep key. "Are you tired?" Will asked.

"I'm forty-five and premenopausal. How can I not be tired? The point is, I'm not overtired. What about you?"

"I'm not menopausal." She took out her key, but he leaned against the Jeep, right beside her, against the door.

"What's up?" she asked.

"What time is it?"

"A little before midnight. Is your watch broken? A hundred billion dollars for that fancy Swiss thing, and it's broken? You can't even call it a watch. 'Timepiece.'"

"It's not broken," Will said. "It's later than I thought."

Lee looked up at him. If the hard yellow light of the sodium-vapor lamp was unflattering to Will, she could only imagine how she looked at almost midnight. "Is this later than you thought business about the time? Or are you making a cosmic statement?"

"It's fairly cosmic."

"You're feeling old?"

"I'm ten years older than you, kid. Keep that in mind."

"But you don't show your age the way we do."

"Which 'you' is this?" Will asked. "Blacks or gays?"

"I was thinking of blacks, but now that you mention it . . . " He shifted his weight from one foot to another, then back again. "What's with you?" Lee asked. "Is something wrong? You're acting strange. Nervous."

"Will you marry me?" Lee's head whipped around as if looking for someone to ask: Can you *believe* this? But they were alone. All the gladsome Democrats were still inside. She turned back to him. "I'm serious," Will said.

"I'm sorry. I just can't believe it." She hesitated, then added: "It's one thing to switch parties for an election. But to switch your sexual orientation?"

"Please! Do you think I'm harboring an illusion of some elaborate conversion ceremony to heterosexuality? A notch on my foreskin and a Master Mechanic wrench set? Come on. I asked you a question: Will you marry me? I deserve an answer." There was no wind, but it was a chilly night. She looked to see if he was shivering. No. If his hands were in his pockets. No. "There are no better friends in the world than we are," he added.

"I know," she said.

"Neither of us is really the mushy sort, but we do love each other." She nodded. "Lee, you can say 'yes.' It's not binding."

"Yes, of course we love each other. I said it. Are you happy?"

He moved from the car and stood in front of her. "Not yet."

"I don't think you're going to be."

"We speak to each other first thing in the morning, last thing at night." Lee had watched him trying cases so many times. Will was a great planner. He believed in rehearsals. But in court he would stop, think, talk, then stop again. So he didn't trip up. So he didn't look slick. His performances always worked. Judges, juries, court reporters: They all believed Will Stewart was thinking as he talked, and talking right to them. From the heart. This time, though, there were no hesitations. Will being Will, she knew he had thought out everything he was saying. But he had not rehearsed. This time, there was not a single prearranged stumble, not one practiced pause. He was allowing his heart to be as articulate as it could be. "We're a unit. There are no decisions—other than about sex—that we don't make in consultation with each other."

"'Other than about sex'? That's one of the main reasons people get married, Will. For sex."

"What about the other reasons? For companionship. For fun. For love. For family. For a mutuality of interests. For security. For the social convenience. We have every single one of those reasons in our relationship. We've never had sex and we never will. But doesn't it mean something that every holiday we're together? Doesn't it mean something that when we win or lose a case, or we read about a new attachment for the KitchenAid, or we hear there's a new Sondheim show opening, we call each other? We're together five or six nights a week. I hold your wool when you wind it. You go to Mets games with me. Do you realize both of us got private lines in our office three or four years ago? How come? It wasn't to facilitate our sex lives. Those guys still have to go through our secretaries. It's because we both felt more natural making and getting—what is it?—seven, eight calls a day right to one another. 'Hi. It's me. I just got back from State Supreme in Suffolk County and I found wonderful bread-and-butter corn at a farm stand.'"

"So why can't we just continue the way we are?" she asked.

"Because it's later than either one of us thought. Because I don't want to be alone anymore. Because I hate it every time I have to leave. Every damn time. And so do you."

Will was facing her, so he did not see the doors open and a few celebrants emerge from the victory party and head toward their cars. "We would only hurt each other," Lee told him.

"How? I know all about Terry. You know I go to the city one or two nights a week. Would you be standing by the door with a rolling pin in your hand when I got home?"

Lee rested her head against the cold glass of the

car's window. "What if one of us met the man of our dreams?" she asked. "An *available* man of our dreams."

"I've thought of that. Quite a bit, because I've wanted to have this discussion since right after the whole Torkelson business. When it was over and you were thanking me, do you remember what you said?"

"I guess so." She remembered nattering on and on, but could not think of exactly what statement he was alluding to.

"You said the reason you loved me for what I did wasn't that I was brilliant and got Mary out of jail— although that hadn't hurt. It was that I knew my place was at your side, even when the shit hit the fan. *Especially* when the shit hit the fan. So my answer is this: I truly do not believe I could betray you or you could betray me. I love you. I would be your husband. That means for better for worse, for—"

"I'm acquainted with the language."

"Lee, you were conned by a couple of pros. You got hurt. Haven't you learned anything from that? Don't you know by now what's false and what's the real thing?"

"But it wouldn't be a true marriage."

"It wouldn't be a marriage with sex. And to the extent that it would provide a cover for me, that I could parade around as the Happy Hetero, it's pretense. But what's between you and me is real and true. And you know it." He held her face in his hands. "That doesn't mean I wouldn't have an affair with a dream man. That doesn't mean it wouldn't break my heart if he said goodbye. Not if. When. But this is the bottom line: I want to spend the rest of my life with you." He put down his hands. "I want a *home*. I've never had one. I was a black kid in a white world, a gay man in a straight world. When I'm in your house, with you, with all of them, I feel what I've never felt before. I belong here. This is my home. Now tell me your bottom line about me."

Her face still felt warm from his holding it. She wished he would put his hands back. "All right. My bottom line: I love being with you. There's nothing I do that isn't better with you along." She hesitated. "Except one thing." She waited for him to pat her head, amused. Or kiss her cheek. But he did not, so she stood on tiptoes and kissed his. "Don't take that as encouragement."

"I want you to ask: What's in it for me," Will told her. "Go ahead, ask."

"What's in it for me?"

"Family."

"I have a family. Do you feel you need one to pass or something all of a sudden?"

"*Need* one? No. People accept that I'm a bachelor. I don't have to say: 'This is my wife.' I'm not talking about the pretense of family. I'm talking about the real thing." He heard sounds and turned away from her. When he saw the people spilling out of the party, heard the car doors starting to slam, he turned back. "You know how important Val and Kent are in my life."

"And you in theirs."

"But they're adults. You're not the kind of woman who thrives on an empty nest. Everything I know about you—and I know a lot—tells me you would love to be a mother again." She knew he was waiting to see if she would deny his assertion. She could not. Will continued: "And all my life, I've wanted a child of my own."

"To have—"

"We could go to the lab together, hold each other's hands."

"While you're whacking off into a test tube? No way!"

"If you don't want to get pregnant, or if it's too late for it to be a healthy proposition, we could adopt."

"You could adopt as a single parent."

"But I want the child to have a mother. And more, I want you to be my wife."

Headlights came on. "You just want to go out and buy a Dress Stewart receiving blanket."

"You guessed it. And have it embroidered with the Weissberg family crest. Well, Lee? What do you say?"

She was not able to say anything, for at that moment, Holly Nuñez, trailed by her press secretary and two campaign aides, was upon them. "Hi!" Holly chirped. "God, you're still here! Hope I didn't interrupt anything. Did I thank you enough? The two of you! *So* great. I thought you left ages ago. How come you're still hanging around? It is *cold* out. You weren't standing here plotting my overthrow, were you?"

Will shook his head. "Not at all. We were planning your next campaign, Governor."

"Senator," Holly replied.

"I have no doubt we'll get to that," Lee told her. "But do you know what Will and I were planning just now?"

"What?"

"Our wedding."

As soon as they were finished with Holly's hugs and the press secretary's mazel tov and the campaign aides' Hey, fan-tastic! and waved goodbye, Lee put her hand into that of her future husband. "I have something to confess."

"What?"

"It never occurred to me that a black gay guy would turn out to be the love of my life."

"I always knew."

"You did?"

"Of course. Way back when, when I was this amazing stud with muscles on my muscles and the best Afro north of Niger, I always knew I was going to wind up with a middle-aged female lawyer."

"Go ahead. Tell me," Lee said. "It was written on the stars."

"It was. But most people can't read that kind of writing until they're old enough for bifocals. It's the fine print."

And as it turned out, the way it often does with choices made with wide-open eyes and wise hearts, it was fine. Not what they had dreamed of when they dreamed, mind you. But very, very fine.

Epilogue

Lily White had the first word but she cannot have the last.

There is only this to add about the Torkelson case. On a Thursday in March 1996, a night when Lee White and Will Stewart, husband and wife, were hearing *Un ballo in maschera* at the Metropolitan Opera with a group of friends, Carolee Eckhart of Portland, Oregon, went to the police to report that her fiancé, Douglas Wallace, had been missing for forty-eight hours. Ms. Eckhart was fearful he might be hurt. Or worse. His ex-wife was an unbalanced woman, hateful, wanted to see him ruined. No, she had never seen the ex-wife, but she'd overheard her once when she left a message on Doug's answering machine. Terrible, vile, crazy.

Ted Sato, the detective who took down the information, was new to Missing Persons and quite an eager beaver. He fired question after question. Following nearly an hour of polite interrogation, he discovered that in addition to Mr. Wallace, seventy-five thousand dollars in bearer bonds that had been left to Ms. Eckhart by her grandfather were also missing.

It took Detective Sato only seven minutes on his computer to discover that Douglas Wallace's modus operandi matched that of Norman Torkelson, and another fifteen seconds to learn that, like Norman, Douglas was six feet five with blue eyes, and knew all the words to "Bright College Years," the Yale alma mater. Subsequently, Sato had a chat with Detective Sergeant Sam Franklin on Long Island, who predicted, accurately, that the Portland police would never find the bonds, that Douglas Wallace was long gone—and that Carolee should be thankful she was still alive. Some people never learn.

Some people do.